Anson dreaded the coming scene between himself and Zarah. How could a loving husband coolly announce to a trusting wife that he proposed to disregard her deeply held views on whiskey? Zarah loathed alcohol. How could he explain his decision to become a whiskey-maker?

Subterfuge was beyond him. "I made a decision today, Zarah. It hurt me—but there was no other way out."

"I imagined that something was troubling you."

"The fact is . . . the fact is I'm going to get paid three thousand dollars for one hundred barrels of whiskey."

"Whiskey? *What* whiskey?"

"The whiskey I'm going to make."

Zarah quivered with conflicting emotions: Anger, compassion, self-pity, self-righteousness, understanding. The swirl of contending voices blew down the wind, clearing a path for her actual words. "You've changed, Anson. The first time I saw you, you were propping the bough of a fruit tree, your hands mending the broken place. It was a sign to me of the husband. I followed the sign, felt myself blessed among women." She gazed at him, eyes and voice asking: What has become of that love that capped your every act? Tell me, Anson, what has happened?

Fatigue, and the prospect of never quite persuading Zarah that he was taking the right course, prompted his question: "Can you think of any other way out?"

It was a mistake, and he tried to undo his clumsiness by the swift contrition of a caress. But neither then, nor when she lay in his arms afterward, did she soften under his lips and hands.

Water of Life

Henry Morton Robinson

ace books

A Division of Charter Communications Inc.
A GROSSET & DUNLAP COMPANY
1120 Avenue of the Americas
New York, New York 10036

An ACE Book by arrangement with
Simon & Schuster, Inc.

First Ace printing: March 1978
Published simultaneously in Canada

Printed in U.S.A.

For
ANTHONY ROBINSON
and
CHARLES ANTHONY ROBINSON, M.D.

"*Elixir and Opiate; Tonic and Pain-Killer; Running Riddle and Fluid Answer; Destroyer and Preserver; Universal Solvent and Mortal Stain; Setter-on of the Dream and Taker-Away of Performance; Joie de Vivre et Lachrymae Rerum; Winner by the Glass and Loser by the Bottle; Symbol of the Ferment in this Valley of Fog, Mist and Tears; Phoenix of the Maize; Spiritus Frumenti;* C_2H_5OH—*Carbon, Oxygen and Hydrogen blended together in Aqueous Matrimony; Leaning Tower; Anchor to Windward; Usquebaugh, Usquabeatha, Aqua Vitae,* Water of Life—WHISKEY!"

—From the Uncollected Lucubrations
of Johnno Normile

CONTENTS

PART THREE

Grand Right and Left

PART FOUR

The Rising Gale

FORESHOT: 1860

In the beginning *was the wort—and the wort was a gruel of coarsely-ground maize and malted barley fermenting in a huge tub beside Chance Woodhull's pot still. Before sundown, if all went well, the wort would become spirit. And the spirit, after a period of aging in an oaken cask, would be variously received among men as whiskey,* bourbon whiskey*—a reddish-amber distillate possessing the power to soothe, cheer, exhilarate, confuse, befuddle and stupefy.*

There was, of course, a knack to the making of good whiskey. Even a skillful man using the best of ingredients could produce a brutal liquor that made hog tracks all the way down your throat. Yet in the lustihood of his young powers Chance Woodhull had little reason to doubt that he could run off a batch of passable spirits. At thirty, this Indiana homesteader could do everything. Superlatively.

He could grow corn, cut millstones to grind it, then coax wayward water to turn the stones. He could break the wild mare and teach her to like the plow collar that he laid on her graceful neck. When her time came, he knew how to breed her; and when her time came again, he dared plunge his arm deep into her sheath to straighten the twisted foal. The secrets of the forge and tempering bath were known to him; his ax heads, chisels and drawshaves bore a stamp more personal than any trade-mark.

Other powers, bordering on the semi-occult, Chance possessed too. Needing honey, he could halt a swarm of wild bees in full flight and bring them home clinging to his massive shoulders and curly black beard. Because he knew the art of locating water, he was often called in by neighbors when their wells ran dry. Unarmed with the traditional dowsing rod, Chance would stride across a field, pause till he felt the underground water table trembling beneath his feet, then point to a certain spot and say, "Dig here!"

There was considerable interest, therefore, in Landmark County, Indiana, when Chance Woodhull let it be known that he intended to make a little whiskey for his own use. Such an undertaking along the banks of the Ohio River a century ago was neither illegal nor uncommon. To the farmers of Landmark County a barrel of home-made whiskey was a badge of prudent management—potable evidence that its maker was a paid-up member of the oldest lodge in the world: the Ancient, Honorable and Self-Reliant Order of Husbandmen.

True, one could buy any quantity of the stuff for twenty-five cents a gallon—the only hitch being that a thrifty man with a cash income of seventy dollars a year didn't like to part with that kind of money. The usual practice was to lend a hand to some whiskey-making neighbor, borrow his "receet," then go home and cook up a year's supply of whiskey at a cost of maybe two cents a gallon.

Tax-free, of course.

While a morning mist drifted in from the Ohio, Chance made a final inspection of his distilling apparatus assembled on a grassy bank beside his mill stream. The pot still that converts corn into alcohol has no moving parts. Distillation, like the seepage of glandular fluids into the blood stream, or the burning of oxygen in body cells, is as noiseless and mysterious as the chemistry of life itself. The belly (so to speak) of the still was a round-bottomed copper kettle supported trivet-wise by pylons of fieldstone. Past the kettle ran an inclined sluiceway of rough planks; cold water from nearby Paddle Creek raced down this trough, eddied around a coil of tubing—an ingenious twist of copper known as the "worm" —a device singing just below the wheel and lever in the choir of human inventions.

To work! A maple bucket in each hand, Chance began transferring the contents of his mash tub into the copper kettle. Then, like a shaman engaged in some primitive fire rite, he kindled the hickory faggots with a spark from his tinderbox. Breathing the spark into a brisk flame, he stepped onto a low platform that brought him waist-high against the kettle and began stirring its contents with a barrel stave.

Stirring, he sang, and his singing, which at first seemed merely an artesian uprush of well-being, gradually became a non-unmelodious mingling of the many rills and brooklets that fed Chance Woodhull's memory: whaling and tea-trade chanties learned on the Salem docks of his boyhood; snatches of revivalist hymns; wagon-train ballads and river-boat refrains sung by emigrants coming through the Allegheny passes into the Ohio Valley—all lifted in an exuberant canticle to the Maker of Days in general and this autumn day in particular.

It was turning out to be a handsome day, Indian cousin to summer, a golden gratuity to be spent on some pleasurable task midway between luxury and experiment. Such as whiskey-making.

While his cereal mixture simmered, Chance gazed at the tidy property he had hewn, single-handed, out of the wilderness: his house, a homesteader's cabin shaded by giant sycamores; his barn, high-peaked and cedar-shingled, with clapboards of weathered red; his grist mill perched on its millpond like a tiny side-wheeled boat about to tumble into the creaming waterfall below. Home, barn and mill—fixed, dependable legs of the economic tripod, sturdy enough (so ran the legend) to support an industrious man and his family.

From the contemplation of this pastoral scene, Chance was aroused by the tempest raging in his copper kettle. Under the sharp assault of fire, the mash had become a seething lava. Saffron-colored bubbles rising from the bottom of the caldron broke explosively, releasing vapors of dismaying foulness. To trap these vapors Chance clamped a curious goose-necked cover over the top of his kettle. Barely was the cover in place when a deluge of rank oils and half-digested solids gushed from the spout. This, the foreshot, was the corn's angriest bile and must be allowed to spend itself in purgative retchings. Attracted by the fumes of the foreshot, Effie, the black sow, came snouting toward the kettle. She slurped up the foul puddle and snuffled eagerly for more.

Cleaner vapors were now steaming from the goose-necked spout. Chance coupled it to the coil of copper tubing immersed in the wooden sluiceway. And now the miracle of distillation began. Alcohol-laden gases rising from the mash kettle passed along the cool inner surface of the worm. Here the disembodied essence of the corn was nebulized into a dew. And this dew, dribbling downward in tear-shaped drops, as hot and colorless as tears, was whiskey—liquid essence of the corn, tonic and pain-killer, opiate and elixir, elemental stain and universal solvent.

As the trickle swelled to a small torrent, a very practical problem presented itself. At what point should he cut off the flow of whiskey? Opinions differed. Many local distillers, eager for quantity, squeezed the last drop of liquor from their mash. Others, believing that the latter portion of the "run" contained undesirable elements, cut off the trickle too soon. The real test of a distiller's judgment lay in his ability to select only the "middle-run" for his whiskey.

At the optimum moment Chance removed the cover of his copper alembic and was almost asphyxiated by the fumes rising from its sourish slops. He ladled all but two gallons of these "tailings" onto the ground. Effie, snuffling up her perquisite, grunted for more.

"Sorry, Eff." Chance was apologetic. "Got to save part of the 'tailings' for the next batch."

It was true. The hot, unsavory slops were essential to the making of a sour-mash whiskey. Like the deer's muskbag which serves as the base of rare perfumes, these "tailings" would impart a bouquet to the next batch of whiskey.

By noon the barrel was about half full of corn liquor. Hands blackened by soot, kneecaps scorched, Chance shot a sextant glance at the sun. He had been working steadily for six hours. Time for a breather.

In these latitudes of plenty no man need feel hungry or thirsty long. Eulalia Woodhull, gauging the moment and degree of her husband's appetite, came toward him bearing a willow basket on one arm and a bouncing infant in the other. At seventeen, Laly had been the handsomest armful in Landmark County. Now, at twenty-five, she was a generously made creature, suggesting in color and contour the eternal Ceres, goddess of increase. On cheek and forehead, indeed wherever the sun touched her, Laly was sorrel gold. Her corn-silk hair, the basket in her hand and the leaping infant in her arms repeated the fertility motif—a contagious theme, to judge by Chance's kiss and Laly's full-lipped response.

Chance took the basket from his wife and linked his free arm around her. Together they walked toward a grassy tussock shaded by sycamore boughs—a once-private corner of Eden where they had lain during summer noons of early marriage. Still sweet with the remembered embraces of young love, the spot had become their favorite place for family picnics. From the basket Chance drew huge squares of buttered cornbread and thick slabs of cold roast pork, made relishable by draughts of jugaree, a marvelous thirst-quencher compounded of molasses, vinegar, ginger and water, cooled in a stone jug.

While Eulalia nursed the infant in her arms, Chance ate his lunch, then stretched out on the grass and gazed upward through a lattice of sycamore boughs at a china-blue haze. Save for a hawk with telescopic eyes scouring the fields in search of a rabbit or field mouse, sky and earth dozed. Scent of sweetfern rose from the warm earth, bearing an invitation to the man and woman resting in the dappled shade. On a tussock of grass Laly gently lowered the sleeping infant and, with the bosom of her dress still unfastened, nestled in Chance's arms. Briefly they found in each other the comfort that made life bearable to our first parents when the bright angel drove them from Paradise.

Then Chance dozed, a pastoral Adam reconciled to Eden's loss so long as Eve was at his side.

He was awakened by the war whoops of two Potawatomi braves in full war paint (rumcherry juice) thrashing up Paddle Creek on a log, straight into an enemy encampment. The attack was about to succeed when the younger Potawatomi fell off the log and had to be rescued—under a murderous hail of arrows—by Chief Anson Woodhull, age eight. The Chief pulled his brother brave, Platt Woodhull, six, into the safety of some willow trees lining the bank. Here, huddled around an imaginary fire, they held secret council and were off again on a foray deep in the forest. At any rate Chance saw no more of his sons until dinner time.

How different the boys were! Anson, grave, straightforward, chary with language, satisfied to let the accomplished deed speak for itself. Platt, mercurial, insecure, already adept at bridging with words or phantasies the gap between Anson and himself. Well, let them be different. No two leaves in the forest were identical. Nature had so planned things that everything she touched became a special act of creation.

So may it be with my whiskey.

While the September sun deepened from topaz to sepia, Chance toiled at his still. Morning's exuberance vanished as the work leveled off to a plateau of repetition. Twice he charged his kettle; twice the cereal mixture bubbled into saffron froth and gushed from the goose-necked spout. Foreshot, middle-run and tailings. When the sepia light darkened to umber, the mash tub was empty and the oak barrel brimmed full.

By a day's work, no longer or harder than any other, Chance Woodhull had transformed ten bushels of corn and small grains into forty gallons of new whiskey. He scooped up an ounce or two of the colorless liquor with a small dipper and lifted it testingly to his lips. Like all raw spirit, the stuff in his barrel tasted like hog-wallow filth laced with castor oil. No matter. Tomorrow he'd run it through his still a second time, plane off some of its "rough corners." Then, stored in an oak barrel, secret tinctures from charred staves would enter the whiskey and transform its pallor into a ruddy glow.

A trick of fading sunlight burnished the colorless liquid into a ruby mirror. Gazing into the mysterious glass, Chance foresaw the future of his whiskey. It would be generous-bodied in substance; hearty, but mellow, too; delicate, yet frank in its approach to the senses. He would use it in moderation to banish fatigue, ward off winter chill, deaden pain and celebrate festive occasions—christenings, husking bees, the raising of new barn timbers. His neighbors lifting a friendly glass would inhale its fragrant bouquet, then drink with confidence —admiration even—as deep spoke to deep.

Leaning over his barrel, Chance Woodhull made certain resolves. Every fall he would make some whiskey from his surplus corn; when his skills were perfected he would transmit them to his sons as part of their education in husbandry.

Chance Woodhull never broke the least of these resolves. It all came out as he envisioned it in the mirror of phophecy. His whiskey gained a certain local fame; he never used it to excess; and at least one of his sons became more skillful than himself in the art and practice of distillation. But what Chance Woodhull did not see was the effect of this day's work on the lives of his children and his children's children to the third generation.

How could he be expected to foretell the tale of brother against brother; of talents wasted and passions spent; of contracts kept and promises broken; of domestic trials and mortal temptations; of hopes never quite lost and faith never wholly *destroyed, but—like the corn in his mash tub—changed, only changed?*

A superstitious man might have interpreted unfavorably the squadron of crows that circled in from the left and settled over the pot still at twilight. The bravest of Roman augurs would certainly have hidden his face in terror at an omen so sinister. Not Chance Woodhull. He knew that crows always came in that way—against the wind.

At his well sweep he paused to hoist up a bucketful of clear, cold water; he drank nearly half of its contents and doused head and hands in the remainder. Senses cleansed, appetite honed, he welcomed the odor of frying pork chops wafting across the yard. He heard Laly singing: a hymn, of course—that was the only music she knew. It sounded like "Abide with me" but because she always sang off-key, you couldn't tell. Not until Chance opened the kitchen door at the final couplet did he recognize the hymn:

> Change and decay in all around I see,
> Oh, thou who changest not, abide with me.

PART ONE

The
Great
American
Confluence

1.

HUMANITY WITH A HARVARD ACCENT

A UNITARIAN DEITY had spun Professor Quincy Adams Osgood on a special wheel, baked him in kilns apart—Bonn, Heidelberg, Oxford—then finished off its handiwork with a not-to-be-duplicated Brattle Street glaze. Ceramically speaking, Quincy was the genuine Harvard faïence. The depth and luster of the Professor's thinking appeared in a thickish tome, *Die Grundwerke zu dem männlichen Fortschritt* (Bonn, 1869). The *Grundwerke* did not demand Leibnitz's best of all possible worlds: Quincy could say, "I accept the universe" with reasonable assurance that the universe would, in turn, accept the compliment. Diligent study of the *Grundwerke* disclosed, however, that what Quincy Osgood *really* accepted was a modified version of the universe—"a world steadily ascending" (as he said in his Preface) "through evolutionary cycles to an ever-higher phase of perfectibility and order." The ultimate goal was to be humanity with a Harvard accent. Admittedly, it would take a little time.

The Professor's wife, Louella, nee Allston (Allstons weren't born but *nee'd*), was, in Wordsworth's serviceable phrase, "A perfect woman nobly planned." Her nobility manifested itself in locutions as delicately porcelain as her husband's—only in French. For example: a woman with child was *enceinte;* the actual delivery of the child was an *accouchement*. And the organs responsible for all this procreative business were Latinized into *pudenda*—literally, "something to be ashamed of." Not that Louella was really ashamed. Being a busty, high-hipped creature, rather good looking in a pince-nez sort of way, she rejoiced when, after a perfectly normal *accouchement*, she presented her husband (right smack in the middle

3

of Commencement 1856) with a fine, healthy girl-child. Under the influence of a Byronic star, they christened her "Zarah."

In the nurture of their only child the Osgoods subscribed to Locke's theory that a young mind was a *tabula rasa*—that is, a clear, smooth surface, waxen, impressionable and eager for dainty tracings. From earliest childhood, Zarah's brain was systematically crosshatched by ten thousand lines of poetry selected from the Best that had been thought and said in the Western World. This process omitted the usual nursery rhymes, which, in Louella's opinion, were jingly and nonsensical. *Her* Little Miss Muffet would never sit on a tuffet eating vulgar curds and whey. She would be nourished, instead, at the high table set by Messrs. Longfellow, Whittier and Emerson. From a work entitled *New England Memory Gems*, Louella selected a suitable *bon bouche*—"I shot an arrow into the air"—and placed it word by word in Zarah's wet little mouth. Back came the echoes without a missed syllable, *Merveilleuse!* The child's repertory grew. At five, it included "The Chambered Nautilus," "To a Waterfowl" and "The Children's Hour"—a fat little portfolio that Zarah could open at a moment's notice for the benefit of Mama's teatime friends. Locke's *tabula rasa* theory went up thirty or forty points on Brattle Street and might have climbed still higher if certain inherent weaknesses hadn't appeared.

Zarah, not yet six, descended the back stairs one Monday morning in search of excitement, or maybe just someone to talk to, and there in the laundry she saw Delia O'Donnell, somewhat gone about the teeth and middle, who boiled, soaped and scrubbed the Osgood wash. A widow at thirty, Delia had no one but herself and three children to support—ever since Johnny her husband had been cremated in a snowbank after a night of wild goings-on with some young Harvard gentlemen who had tried to drive his sleigh—stove and all—up the steps of Holworthy Hall. Ah, well, the good die young and God takes care of His own. The Lord had taken care of Delia by giving her a washerwoman's job with Professor Osgood's family at seventy-five cents a day with a bite of lunch thrown in and some cold scraps to take home. Today she would be unable to eat the lunch because the last three of her upper teeth had been extracted.

Knuckles raw, her hair in stringy loops, Delia was bending over the steamy tub when she felt a tug at her skirts.

"Do you know any memory gems, Delia?"

Agonized by the pain of her missing teeth, Delia shifted her wad of spruce gum (healing properties well known) from one cheek to the other and asked what kind of gems they might be.

"The kind you recite when company comes." Zarah illustrated with the first three stanzas of "Excelsior."

The genre was unfamiliar to Delia; but because rhyme throbs naturally in the Celtic blood stream she *did* recall some memory-gemmery of her childhood. 'Twas but yesterday, it seemed, that she had stood barefooted on the earthen floor of her father's cottage in Connaught, lisping quaint verses, while the family pig rubbed his back against the door frame. Now she wiped her steamy face and rolled off the lines with diction spirited and gestures suitable.

Zarah clapped her hands. "Goody-goody. Say it again, Delia."

After a single encore, Zarah had the thing by heart. All she needed now was a piece of Delia's spruce gum. The request granted, a dutiful daughter, bent only on surprising Mama, was off in a cloud of happiness.

That afternoon, while Mother served tea to a group of academic neighbors, Zarah waited for the call. It came when Louella beckoned her prodigy to the center of the stage. "And now, my dear, will you climb onto the hassock and favor us with the very newest, sparklingest gem in your treasure chest?"

An angel in pinafores, Zarah mounted the hassock, spruce gum carefully pouched in her cheek. How elfin! How Botticelli! She adjusted her sash and took flight.

> *"Fire, fire," cried Maggie McGuire*
> *"Where, where?" asked Bridget O'Hare*
> *"Under the bed," said Mollie McNedd*
> *"Water, water," yelled Lizzie McWhorter*
> *"Heaven save us," cried Katie Davis . . .*

Heaven save us indeed! Louella whisked her angel prodigy off the hassock. "Where did you learn that outlandish rigmarole?"

"From Delia."

"What's that stuff in your mouth?"

"Spruce gum. You need it for the last line when 'Holy Jasus spits like blazes' and puts the fire out."

Incredulity and horror shook the pince-nez right off Louella's nose. She broke down sobbingly. "Ruined—ruined right under my own roof." The guests stood not on the order of their going but went at once. All except Mrs. Bancroft, who remained to console the stricken mother.

"The child's not ruined, Louella. She'll hear and say worse than that before she grows up." Then, being rather old-fashioned, she took a dig at Locke. "Remember, my dear, it's a poor theory that doesn't work as well in the laundry as in the parlor. . . . Why don't you send the child to Minerva Higginson?"

The upshot of it all was that Delia lost her job and Zarah became a student in the Grange, local day school for Select Young Ladies.

"We are at some pains here," explained Minerva Higginson during her first interview with Louella, "never to refer to our school as a 'Seminary.' The word is too suggestive of its Latin root—and you know how suggestive these roots can be." Louella nodded in agreement, and Minerva went on. "Although the Grange has no moat around it—nothing quite so medieval as that—our girls are spiritually protected, *sustained* is perhaps a better word, by a concept of personal purity nobly expressed in Milton's *Comus*. You know the line: 'Virtue may be assailed but never hurt.' In short, we buttress our girls from within."

The buttresses, Minerva went on to explain, were four in number: needlework, reading, penmanship and arithmetic. Then came the three "accomplishments": music, painting and elocution. Music meant the pianoforte, with side excursions into the dulcimer. *Très exotique.* Painting started with crayon sketches and found its highest phase in the decoration of china. Elocution embraced practically everything—literature, diction and gymnastics—woven together in a harmonious system devised by that eminent Frenchman François Alexandre Nicolas Delsarte.

All for $100 a year, payable quarterly, with 25 per cent reduction for the children of Harvard professors. French and German extra.

From the first day Zarah loved the Grange. It gave her a wonderful stage, a part to play, and agreeable companions to play with. As the school baby she was petted by everyone: the big girls curled her hair, the middle-sized girls gave her an extra shot at the croquet wicket (which Zarah didn't need), and the little girls fell into the natural pecking order found in schools as well as barnyards.

Zarah became a Grange showpiece. She tore through Dunkler's "Bouquet for Pianoforte" in six months; at the end of a year she was fingering the sonatinas of Clementi and Kuhlau, and could tinkle most exotically on the dulcimer. Her sole unorthodoxy appeared in a still-life sketch of three beets artistically arranged against a raffia curtain by Minerva herself. Zarah, seeing the beets as purple, so recorded them.

"My, my!" exclaimed Minerva. "This will never do. Everyone knows that beets are red. 'Red as a beet,' as the saying goes. Make your beets red, Zarah dear."

All right, beets were red. Between her eighth and eleventh years Zarah picked up other leading ideas as expounded by Minerva Higginson:

> Flowers had pistils and stamens.

> A single drop of nicotine placed on a dog's tongue would kill him instantly.

> Macassar oil was a greasy substance that men rubbed into their hair. Hence, women must labor untiringly at making antimacassars, pieces of linen pinned onto the backs of chairs, to prevent "soilure."

> All references to wine in the Bible were mistranslations of the Greek root which really meant "unfermented juice of the grape."

> Alcohol in any form was a rager and a mocker. See Paul, 20:6.

> Alfred, Lord Tennyson, was the greatest poet in the English language because whenever Queen Victoria heard "The Lady of Shalott" she broke down.

> Burne-Jones's picture of Sir Galahad was the

high-water mark in English painting because
John Ruskin said so.

By waving a piece of an herb called "moly"
at her would-be attackers, the heroine of
Milton's Comus got off scot-free. Every
girl carried a piece of this herb (figura-
tively) on her person. Again, let us
repeat in unison: "Virtue may be assailed
but never hurt."

Zarah found herself constantly at the edge of a mystery that kept receding as she advanced in knowledge. A dictionary might have helped, but under the Higginson Plan the Grange had no dictionary. So the big girls whispered to the middle-sized girls, and the middle-sized girls gave weirdly garbled accounts to the little girls.

Zarah's best "subject" was elocution. At the age of twelve she stopped a Grange Commencement dead in its tracks with her spirited rendition of Southey's tongue-twister "The Cataract of Lodore." It was a triumph of something called "onomatopoeia." Thus:

Gleaming and streaming and steaming and beaming,
And rushing and flushing and brushing and gushing,
And thumping and plumping and bumping and jumping,
And dashing and flashing and splashing and clashing,
And so never ending, but always descending,
Sounds and motions forever-and-ever are blending,
All at once and all o'er, with a mighty uproar,
And this way the water comes down at Lodore.

At fourteen, Zarah was a leggy, titian-haired anthology of the best that had been thought and said on both sides of the Atlantic. Her repertoire included the speeches of Portia, Ophelia and Juliet, all Bowdlerized, of course. She could tear Racine's *Phèdre* to tatters and portray a most tragic Andromache. To memorize these and some thousands of other lines laid no particular strain on Zarah's memory. The complications arose when you tried to deliver a poem in the manner prescribed by M. Delsarte. Under the Delsarte method you "clothed" each line with an appropriate gesture. But before you "clothed" the line, you had to *feel* it.

Most of the young ladies at the Grange, terrified at the prospect of feeling anything, fell into standard posturings. Grief knelt like Niobe. Ecstasy was registered by standing tiptoe, lips slightly parted, with an isinglass haze in your eyes. It was easier that way. Otherwise you were confronted by a bewildering choice of possibilities. How render, for example, the opening passage of "Kubla Khan"?

> *In Xanadu did Kubla Khan*
> *A stately pleasure-dome decree:*
> *Where Alph, the sacred river, ran*
> *Through caverns measureless to man*
> *Down to a sunless sea.*

The lines were mysterious; their meaning obscure. Zarah never found anyone who could explain the poem to her. Nevertheless, she won the Elocution Prize at her own graduation by delivering "Kubla Khan" with her diaphragm regally high, right arm upflung and eyes half closed at the dread wonder of its opening lines.

Despite this intensive culture, which sometimes weakens the stem and saps the bud, Zarah grew up to be a handsome creature brimming with juices that burst at eighteen into curves too jubilant perhaps for a Brattle Street vestal. The strictest corseting could not discipline the fore-and-aft rake of her figure; even the Tennysonian snood of the period failed to chasten the cedar flame of her hair. At a time when pallor betokened gentle breeding, Zarah's complexion was singularly fresh; and her eyes—set deep enough for inevitable woman tears—glowed with a far-from-defenseless green.

Bending over her embroidery tambour or playing croquet on various Brattle Street lawns, Zarah managed to give an almost convincing impression of repose. Or was it resignation —the standard adjustment that genteel wives and daughters were expected to make? While men crisscrossed the continent with rails of glistening steel, threw bridges across torrential rivers, and sank drills into anthracite mines, well-bred women were locked up in a nutshell prison of "accomplishments"— needlework, china-painting, and dulcimer-playing. Even though they were very beautiful in face and carriage (as Zarah was), they could not become actresses. Law and medicine were strictly masculine preserves. The era of the female secretary had not yet begun: male clerks took dictation in longhand. Seated on high stools, men balanced ledgers; behind ground-glass doors they loaned money to other men. While the imaginations of men seethed with wonder and surmise, the imaginations of women merely seethed.

Of course a woman could get married, But marriage, like everything else in the world, required the active co-operation of some man. Not any man. Not, for instance, Hugo von der Groot, exchange professor of law from Amsterdam, widower with three children. Not Major Griswold, Commandant of Governors Island, who reeked of whiskey and pawed you as though he were currying a horse. No, the problem was to find a man unafraid of your mind and unawed by your beauty (though not necessarily unimpressed by either) who could put you into that tender relationship of one-to-one which is the goal of human longing.

No such man existed in Zarah Osgood's world. All the eligible males were leaving Boston for somewhere else. Chicago, uncouth but expanding, magnetized many of them; Paris claimed the creative ones, and Vienna skimmed the cream off the medical contingent. Opportunities beckoned from Cincinnati and Cleveland, while the poor sticks who remained in Boston held strong views as to the desirability of bachelorhood.

Where, where, *where,* how, how, *how* (Zarah wondered) could a fully equipped woman, fastidious but yearning, come to grips with that seemingly impossible he—the unmarried, financially responsible male who combined masculine threat and romantic charm so plentiful in song and story?

There *had* been such a man in Zarah's life. At thirteen, troubled by a precocious hunger for maleness-at-prime, she had fallen desperately in love with Lyman Allston. *Cousin* Lyman, alas! (Everyone was cousin to everyone in the Boston-Cambridge circle.) Consanguinity seemed no great barrier to Zarah, but Lyman happened to be seven years her senior. How could a leggy adolescent hope to compete with grown-up girls who waltzed and went horseback-riding with this ruddy complexioned medical student, whose chestnut-brown eyes, curly hair and width of shoulder made him the observed of all the female observers? Zarah daydreamed, pined, languished, for two years, then finally watched Cousin Lyman marry Theodora Darke. Theodora was beautiful, and everyone said she was rich. But, *damn it,* thought Zarah, almost fifteen, she's twenty years old, that's what she is!

Cousin Lyman was now a Boston physician with a big house on Marlborough Street, medical degrees from Vienna, Paris, London, and a growing reputation as a neurologist. His patients were wealthy nervous women who responded marvelously to Dr. Allston's treatment. Well, who wouldn't? Handsome, magnetic, humorous, sensitive, kind, masculine—how often do such men appear in a woman's life, anyway?

They certainly were not present at the "parlor hour" held on Wednesday evenings in the Osgood home.

These "parlor hours" were conspicuous triumphs of culture attended chiefly by faculty members and their bombazined wives. At these feasts of reason, the editor of the *Atlantic Monthly* might favor the company with a preview of Anthony Trollope in *ms.* By special arrangement with the Transcendental deities, Ralph Waldo Emerson occasionally descended from Concord. At some point in the evening dear Uncle Waldo—a bit doddery, yet still able to swing a bag of duckshot—would bring down a few random pigeons. Afterward Zarah would play some *morceaux choisis* on the Hamburg Steinway; then cocoa very much *au lait*, an arrowroot biscuit perhaps, and the parlor hour would draw to a genteel ten-o'clock close.

Father would retire to his study to pick up his correspondence with Helmholtz or Mommsen (one simply had to render tribute to the Germans in those days) while Zarah climbed to her own bedroom with the casement windows and read Jane Austen. In her nineteenth year she began to suffer from insomnia, a not uncommon malady, complicated in Zarah's case by bothersome voices.

Long experience with these voices gave Zarah a certain insight into their nature and origins. They weren't accompanied by swoons or hallucinations. They were merely echoes of the countless verses that Zarah had learned at the Grange. At most times they lay passively awaiting memory's selective touch. But when Zarah was fatigued or overwrought, the voices took on a perverse will of their own; a random word or chance association—often quite commonplace—could set the wild echoes flying. Unbidden, a word or phrase would bubble up into conscious memory, arouse its dormant companions, and bring the whole pack yelping after her in relentless pursuit. Once in motion, nothing could stop the belling tongues, the hurrying feet. With many backtrackings, lost scents and irrelevant digressions, the chase would go on till the last lines closed in on their tossing, sleepless prey.

The amazing thing about these fugual voices was that they seemed to know exactly what they wanted to say. And their message, however disguised, revealed some aspect of the turmoil seething under Zarah's placid surface.

One winter night toward the end of 1875 the voices gave her a particularly bad time. The parlor hour that evening had been exasperating, though Zarah couldn't say exactly why. Of its kind, the conversation was excellent; yet as she pricked a gold thread into her tambour she wondered why no one on Brattle Street ever spoke of love. Any other theme—marine shells, Helmholtz's theory of light-waves, or the beautiful uses of leisure among tomorrow's wheels—these received ardent attention. Ideas, concave or convex, abstract or concrete, were accepted as legal tender and carted off in great bundles while the true gold of love lay unnoticed on the floor.

Zarah was glad when the mantelpiece clock struck nine-forty-five. At her father's request she sat down at the pianoforte and played two or three Chopin Preludes. The evening was over. Zarah pecked at her father's forehead; then, feigning the cheerfulness that he expected, she gathered the skirt of her silk dress and flew upstairs.

In her room she lighted a candle on her dressing table and stood gazing without pleasure at the image of a full-bosomed young woman reflected from the pier glass. So might the figurehead of a clipper ship, longing for the buck and drench of perilous seas, have gazed into the stagnant waters of a protected harbor. The need for crowding on emotional canvas quivered through Zarah's body. How long could a woman go on embroidering fantasy shallops when her deepest need was for freight, risk, *use?* Fretfully she unfastened her Burne-Jones snood, pulled out the amber pins anchoring the heavy chignon at the nape of her neck, and shook a billow of cedar hair this way and that, as if to ease the frustrating ache at its roots.

To cool her mounting fever Zarah flung open the casement window and saw the decorous snowscape of Brattle Street, its lawns as smooth as a counterpane, shining with cold purity under a winter moon. From every house a second-floor light gleamed in the study of some academic Galileo. How still, how sterile it was! In the midst of all this academic tranquility, a gust of sleet clashed against the windowpane and pricked Zarah's burning cheeks with needles deliciously chill.

Chill. That did it. As a snapping icicle may start an avalanche, the word set off reverberations in Zarah's mind.

Saint Agnes' Eve—Ah, bitter chill it was!
The owl, for all his feathers, was a-cold;
The hare limp'd trembling through the frozen grass,
And silent was the flock in woolly fold:

This was no ring-a-rosy rhyme. Rather, the announcement of a highly orchestrated work—a grand-scale fusion of wish and dream rising from the heart of the flawless poet who had died hungering for love.

"No, no," she whimpered. "Please . . . not tonight." Hastily she closed the window hoping to shut out the passional gale. Useless. The tempest was rising from within. The first quatrain beckoned to the next. On and on the stanzas came, loaded like galleons blown through defiles of lonely ice to crash at last against the nerves of an overwrought girl pacing a narrow room.

Dreading the penalty of long sleepless hours ahead, Zarah loosened her bodice before the full-length glass. As her silk dress fell rustling to her knees, she felt not at all like Madeline, the lovely dreamer who, trusting in heaven's mercy for all that she desired, had knelt in prayer, then, with poppied warmth of sleep oppressed, lay supine upon her chaste couch,

As though a rose should shut and be a bud again.

Pulling the coverlets about her, it seemed to Zarah that the throbbing rose would never shut. No Porphyro would steal into her chamber to set that wondrously symbolic table with "jellies smoother than the creamy curd." Fatigued but sleepless, she heard the sharp sleet pattering against the windowpane. Saint Agnes' moon waned and set while an overstimulated young woman, tormented by a fugue *appassionata,* lay sleepless on her narrow bed.

Zarah Osgood was a restless, shaken and unhappy girl when an event quite beyond her control changed the entire course of her life. That event was the Centennial Exposition held at Philadelphia in 1876.

2.

ZARAH GOES TO THE FAIR

With a flaming Liberty Torch as its emblem, the
Centennial Exposition was marking a century of America's political independence. Slow as a glacier, quick as a
dream, the first hundred years had passed; now, with fearful
hazards behind and much untransacted business ahead, the
American people were building a temple of Thanksgiving that
would be both pleasing in the sight of God and vastly annoying to His older children in other, less-favored parts of the
world.

The main building of the Exposition was a huge structure
of steel and glass crammed with the machines that had made
America great and were manifestly destined to keep her so.
Steam, then at its zenith, was the motif and motive power of
the exhibition. On a pedestal in the center of the main building stood the gigantic Corliss engine, capable of generating
100,000 horsepower with as little vibration as a fine watch.
President Grant himself came up to start the engine off,
and six million visitors—many of them from foreign countries
—gazed with openmouthed wonder at this latest proof of
American superiority in the field of applied power.

It was regrettable perhaps, with the eyes of the world
upon us, that a Sioux Chieftain named Crazy Horse should
have chosen this particular year of grace to massacre General
Custer at Big Horn. Indians! A boatload of frightened Dutch
tourists turned back to Amsterdam. Chancellor Bismarck sent
the German ambassador a cable asking (in code of course):
"This Crazy Horse affair, is it a *démarche* or the real thing?"
Quite the wittiest comment came from *Punch:* "Americans

defeat Indians: military triumph. Indians defeat Americans: massacre."

Viewed in its proper perspective, the Big Horn affair, along with a few other distressing incidents—a prostrate South, immigrant-crowded slums in the East, general unemployment, drought and crop blight—together with sundry oddments of malfeasance and nonfeasance—gave no cause for alarm. One need only stroll across the fairgrounds to realize how utterly America had outstripped the rest of the world in technology and invention.

To offset any hint of jingoism, the Exposition had generously opened its doors to European art, thought and commerce. Americans who cared about such matters might gaze at exhibits of French painting and Belgian lace. Tucked away in an obscure corner of the Fine Arts Building was a really impressive display of foreign philosophic publications—mostly English and German. Had anyone taken the trouble to browse through this section he would have been puzzled, shocked even, by America's cultural lag.

Here, for instance, was a copy of Sir Charles Lyell's *Geological Evidences of the Antiquity of Man*, a work that took a fearful slap at Genesis by pushing back man's appearance on earth by half a million years. Beside it stood Charles Darwin's *Origin of Species*, containing some really shocking ideas about *homo sapiens*. And this heavy tome was Karl Marx's *Das Kapital*, several hundred pages of pure rant predicting the ultimate collapse of the profit system. Here was a new edition of Laplace's *Calculations of Inter-Planetary Spaces* that made the distance between Cleveland and Dodge City rather puny by comparison. Of the fifty million people then living in the United States only a few hundred had read these books. Small loss. Let Europe worry about man's past. The big American push was into the future. Clear the track. And say, if you want a good laugh, just read Mark Twain's *Innocents Abroad*.

The task of arranging this display had fallen to Professor Quincy Adams Osgood, head of the Philosophy Department of Harvard College. Indeed, who else could handle the job? Long and intimate correspondence with Thomas Huxley, Herbert Spencer and Baron von Helmholtz had made Professor Osgood an intellectual carrier pigeon between the Old World and the New. His duties at the Exposition required that he give a weekly lecture and act as host to visiting scholars, an assignment that entailed so much running back and forth between Cambridge and the fairgrounds that Professor Osgood decided to establish himself and family in Philadelphia for the summer. He rented a comfortable house near the Exposition; then, in his best autocrat-of-the-breakfast-table manner, broke the news to his wife and daughter while breaking the shell of a soft-boiled egg.

He expected no objections; none were made. To Zarah, the prospect of exchanging draggy afternoons of croquet for the excitement of a World's Fair seemed quite supportable. By the law of percentages at least half of the Centennial visitors would be men. Louella put in a wifely demurrer: "Can we afford it, Quincy, dear?" After dear Quincy told her that the Exposition was "defraying all expenses," Louella geared herself nobly to the task of switching houses in the middle of a steamy summer.

The Philadelphia household resembled Cambridge in many ways; there were earnest evening *causeries* between Professor Osgood and visiting academicians; long, worried speculations about the impact of the Corliss Engine on the theories of Darwin, Huxley, *et al.* Could Herbert Spencer successfully integrate the concept of steam power into his all-inclusive theory of the Absolute? A parlous question, with Quincy Osgood maintaining the affirmative while Henry Adams predicted that the machine was leading men, manners and morals into the cul-de-sac of a new barbarism.

While Professor Osgood entertained the academic nobility, Zarah and her mother "did" the Exposition. They ranged through the art galleries viewing hundreds of landscapes, either frankly derivative or plain buckeye—nobly relieved, to be sure, by Thomas Eakins' masterpiece of realism, *The Clinic of Professor Agnew*. Thank God for Eakins. They attended concerts and were overwhelmed by the crashing brasses of a German innovator, Richard Wagner. "Very disturbing, that *Tristan* Prelude," observed Mrs. Osgood. Without quite analyzing the nature of the disturbance, Zarah agreed.

More fascinating than concerts or art galleries were the shops in the Continental Arcade—glittering booths that teemed with Parisian modes, heavy silk and deep velours in exciting fruity shades—puce, framboise, lime and nectarine; muslins, fine, superfine and virtually impalpable in their fineness; intoxicating perfumes—frangipani, bergamot and patchouli—

as different from lavender sachet as champagne from cocoa.
There were lacy parasols more daring than lingerie, reticules
of glazed kidskin and eye-catching Eugénie chapeaux with
creamy ostrich plumes. Not a stuffy draper's item in the lot.
Especially, thank God, no bombazines.

Who could resist such wares? Mrs. Osgood contented herself with a seal brown pelisse; Zarah, after a sharp struggle
between conscience and folly, spent her entire allowance on
a gorgeous ensemble, including a lace-scalloped parasol with
an ebony ferrule and a *mode des dames* corset that did
wonders for her growing-girl hips.

When, and for whose benefit, would she array herself in
this stunning outfit? Zarah was willing to bypass the problem.
Her time would come. It came when Mrs. Osgood's meta-
tarsals, weakened by Exhibition trotting, cried out for rest.
That day Zarah went to the fair alone.

Daring? Very! Girls of Zarah Osgood's station weren't permitted to risk the hazards of walking abroad without a responsible escort or elderly companion. Sustained by Minerva
Higginson's precept, "Virtue may be assailed but never hurt,"
Zarah decided to take her chances.

She began her toilette with three basic dabs of patchouli,
then laced herself into the sculpturesque French corset that
gave her a breathtaking eighteen-inch waist. Petticoats *du
jour* and camisole to match. On these foundations she laid a
bustled confection of olive silk that brought out the titian
glint in her hair. Violet gloves—demure with a difference—
and last of all the lace-flounced parasol, a provocative extra
that might have struck Brattle Street as not quite in keeping
with the character of a professor's daughter. Thus parasoled,
gloved, reticuled, corseted and unchaperoned, Zarah was off
to the fair.

Pointedly she snubbed the Corliss engine and entered the
Pomological Annex, a veritable hothouse filled with incense-
bearing fruit trees—peach, plum and pear. The place reeked
with fertility strangely undisturbing to the Cambridge vestal.
Pomona, the apple goddess, beckoned her willing victim
down a pathway ranged on either side by trees unlike any
that Zarah had ever seen. Boughs laden with redcheeked
apples sprouted from the trunks of pear trees; plums and
peaches hung from alternate branches. "Cross-fertilization,"
they called it.

Many of the boughs were so heavily freighted that they

had to be propped up by espaliers. One particular branch, overborne with luscious apples, seemed ready to break, when a tall young man with a curly black beard casually rearranged the prop under its bough.

An attendant rushed up: "Visitors must not touch the exhibits." A colloquy, officious on one side, rurally good-tempered on the other, ended with a victory for good temper. It seemed quite natural for Zarah to side with the dark young countryman who had saved the overborne branch from breaking. Quite natural, also, to join the little circle that listened to his remarks about the larger aspects of cross-fertilization with special reference to corn and hogs.

Quite a descent from espaliers and nectarines. Zarah pressed closer, not so much to hear what the young man said as to study him at close range. There he stood, barely a parasol's distance away, the central figure in a composition that cried out for Eakins' brush. He was long from knee to hip, and longer yet from hip to shoulder; maleness at prime radiated from his haycock-colored skin and burning-bush eyes as he gathered up the reins of attention.

"It isn't so much the freak varieties we're looking for. The important thing, as I see it, is to cross-breed selected strains in order to get a hardy seed corn that'll stand up against drought and blight." He pushed his Stetson back on a mane of black hair. "You corn farmers all know we've been pretty lucky up to now. But the safest bank we can draw on is some real scientific work stored up against the lean years."

His dark eyes traveled about the little circle and caught Zarah's gaze. Something warned her

> . . . beware, beware
> His flashing eyes, his floating hair . . .

But no thrice-woven circle of propriety could shield her now. Afterward, she found herself talking to him alone, not about apples, plums or peaches or corn or pigs—not even about the Corliss engine. What, then, did they speak about? Why, nothing except the two most interesting and important people in the world—themselves.

Strolling down alleys of fruit trees, they went through that first phase of mutual discovery and revelation that tests the fullness yet to come. Each question was a delicious probe.

Behind every answer lay an unspoken query. Commonplaces, loaded with intent.

"My name is Anson Woodhull." *(In all my life, I've never seen anyone so beautiful as you.)*

"I'm Zarah Osgood. My home is in Cambridge." *(You frighten me in a way that I don't understand.)* "Do you expect to spend the summer at the Exposition?"

"I'd like to, but my tour of duty ends in two weeks."

"Tour of duty? Are you in the Army?"

"No. I'm only a brevet captain of Indiana militia. Every state sends a troop of cavalry to the Exposition—a kind of honorary guard."

"Then I *did* see you riding behind President Grant's barouche! You were on a big black horse in front of the others." Zarah didn't add, You reminded me of a centaur. "Must you go back to Indiana with your company?"

"Does it make any difference whether I go or stay?"

The air around them became sweet with a special sweetness when Zarah said, "Yes!"

During the rest of the afternoon Zarah remembered nothing except a wild gaiety she had never felt before. When they parted before supper she agreed to meet Anson next day at the plum tree with the broken branch.

She almost didn't keep the appointment. The whole business was so sudden, unrealistic. Anson Woodhull was physically attractive, yes. But should she permit herself to become involved with a farmer, a man who had spent his mortal indenture among animals, in fields and barns? His hands showed the marks of that indenture—their tendons, bones and muscles all firmly articulated as in a textbook of anatomy. Very well, admit the hands. Concede the personal lightning that darted from Anson Woodhull's eyes. Acknowledge that his voice made her vibrate like a snare drum. What about the man's mind? He was convincing enough when discussing corn and hogs with tobacco-chewing yokels. But beyond that, what did she know about him? Zarah decided to spend a day investigating the matter. She would let the man stand near her, turning page after page in the album of himself. Then she could use her feminine prerogative by handing back the album and saying, "It's all very interesting, Mr. Woodhull . . . but, you see . . ."

To make things simpler for herself, Zarah wore her plainest dress and a sailor hat of black straw. At the appointed hour she slipped out of the back door of her house and met Anson near the plum tree.

"Where's your parasol?" he asked.

"I thought it wouldn't fit in with my costume."

"I like you better this way."

This proprietary male evidently had no idea that he was on trial. He seemed jubilant rather than otherwise as they started off together on a day of sight-seeing.

Seeing the Exposition through Anson's eyes was an adventure in vision. He avoided the mistake, prevalent among males, of explaining how a thing worked. Instead, he would offer some comment, not necessarily cheerful, that opened up fresh vistas of understanding. Pointing to the McCormick reaper, he said, "Goodbye, freeholders." When Zarah pressed for an explanation, he went on: "A machine that cuts and binds one hundred acres of wheat a day can't even get warmed up on a quarter-section farm. It needs more space. Speculators will move in and buy the land. The small farmer will have to sell or become a tenant."

There was nothing bitter in his remark. That was the way things were. He could be humorous, too. As they watched a flat-bed press turning out 50,000 newspapers an hour he asked, "Is it going to be harder or easier to fool some of the people all of the time?"

Before the day ended Zarah realized that her companion had a sure instinct for the reality beneath appearance, and that his knowledge stemmed from the intertwined roots of good and evil. His ranging interests dwarfed the academic minds she had known and made her own education seem narrowly specialized.

She did not hand back his album at the end of the day. She wanted to go on turning its pages forever.

After three days of sauntering about the fair with Anson Woodhull, she was desperately in love with him. Her heart was like a singing reed (no, that was Christina Rossetti's heart). Zarah Osgood's heart was a peach tree waiting to be shaken. At the first imperative brush of Anson's lips, the fruit came pelting down.

An enchanted twenty-four hours followed her quite untremulous "yes" to Anson's proposal of marriage. For a whole day she kept the secret to herself, scarcely daring to believe the choir of seraphic voices that greeted her at the most unexpected places with the announcement "*Hail, Zarah, full of grace, blessed art thou amongst women."* She went to sleep with that choir in her ears and when she awoke the next morning she decided to be a dutiful daughter and share her happiness with Mother and Father.

Such wonderful people they were! Father so brilliant, even though irritable at times. He was particularly irritable today; so cranky, in fact, that he had to take a double dose of Nervina after breakfast. Well, who wouldn't be cranky if, on top of everything else, he had been asked to write an essay for the *North American Review?* Zarah understood perfectly and postponed her announcement until the essay was finished.

It was late that evening, after a wonderful day with Anson, that she gathered up courage to tap on the door of Father's study. By the triumphant note in his "Come," she knew that the article was completed, or nearly so.

Seated at his desk, watch in one hand, pen in the other, Quincy Osgood was writing the final paragraph. He required of himself a minimum of fifteen words a minute, and in seventy-two seconds his paper would be done. Zarah browsed at a lower shelf of books and found a bottle of Nervina hidden behind Hegel's *Phenomenology of the Mind.* A whiff of father's medicine reminded her of Major Griswold's nauseating breath when he had attempted to kiss her. Was it possible (perish the thought!) that Nervina contained *alcohol,* the Bane? She replaced the bottle and waited patiently while Professor Osgood executed a compound-complex sentence, complete with parentheses, subordinate clauses, single quotes, double quotes, colons, semicolons, commas and finally—four seconds ahead of schedule—a period.

"Sit down, Zarah. Let me read my essay to you. I've entitled it 'The Great American Confluence.'"

Striding up and down the room with the exultant tread of a man who has driven Truth into a corner, Quincy Osgood read five thousand words proving that the Centennial Exposition had transcended the highest hopes of its organizers. It was, said Professor Osgood, "a cross-fertilization of modes, manners, even persons, from various parts of the nation; an American *convivio* at which the gruff vigor of the expanding West, the earthy accents of the honest husbandman, became more tunable to the politer eastern ear. Such cross-fertilization would be tremendously valuable in producing that indigenous hybrid, the American yet-to-be."

The essay was the mixture as before: three parts "Cham-

bered Nautilus," worked up with equal portions of Herbert
Spencer and Whitman's vistas of democracy—plus a startling
new contribution from Quincy Osgood himself (quite a departure from his *Grundwerke* position). Yes, the author of
"The Great American Confluence" was saying that our national culture, traditionally confined to the eastern seaboard,
would be immeasurably strengthened by intermarriage with
the energy, ideas—aye, the lifeblood—of Americans born west
of Brattle Street.

"Well, what do you think of it, my dear?"

Had Zarah's private case required a special pleader, none
more eloquent could have been found. Eyes wet with gratitude, heart glowing with love's surplus, she hugged her
father ecstatically.

"It's all true, Daddy—beautifully, wonderfully true. That
last part about intermarriage is just what Anson has been
saying all along."

Anson—who was Anson?

Anson, it turned out, was a western farmer who had asked
Zarah to marry him. More specifically, he was the tall,
bearded young man she had introduced to her father—was it
the day before yesterday, or eons ago?—at a tea given by the
Curator of Philosophic Publications. "Don't you remember
him, Daddy?"

Quincy Osgood remembered now; and what he remembered was altogether too unnerving for the author of "The
Great American Confluence." Truth spread elegantly upon
the pages of the *North American Review* was one thing. The
same Truth dressed in tubular trousers tucked into cavalry
boots was quite another matter. Professor Osgood stopped
being a five-dollar-a-page thinker and became the outraged
father. He began by putting some cool home questions to his
daughter.

"Where does this bearded young nobody come from?"

"Indiana."

"*That* savage place!" Salamanca or Göttingen seemed
nearer, less alien to the Professor. "Does this outlander hold
a degree?"

"No."

Shades of the Academy! A bewildered metaphysician gazed
at his obviously bespelled daughter. Gifted, multilingual,
handsome (Professor Osgood had never realized till now how
handsome Zarah was), there she sat drugged and inarticulate.

"Come, girl," he rapped out his challenge, "speak up. Defend yourself. *Say something.*"

Zarah found it impossible to say much. She murmured, not quite lucidly, that Anson Woodhull had a way with fruit trees, and an expectancy of someday inheriting a parcel of farm land. She mentioned his undramatic deposits of honesty and good sense. But what she couldn't explain was the ominous male ferocity that threatened her in a place that no Brattle Street girl dared mention to her father.

"You are incurably romantic," snapped Professor Osgood.

A year ago, a week ago, the charge would have rung true. Full sister to Elaine, the lily-maid of Astolat, Zarah had lived in a Tennysonian tambour land, embroidering her life away in delicate figures of romance. But now the embroidery hoop had been knocked from her hand and she was herself a tambour struck by the hard knuckle of love. The vibration shook her entire being. She liked it.

"No," she said, "I am incurably realistic."

Flat-voiced opposition (whether from students, colleagues, wife, daughter—in fact, from anyone except President Charles Eliot) infuriated the Professor. Long years of hurling thunderbolts from the infallible side of the desk had given him a Zeus complex, and Zarah's refusal to be shattered proved so shattering that Professor Osgood shook with agitation.

"You have painfully deceived me, Zarah."

"You have painfully *un*deceived me, Father."

"How, pray?"

"By your own words." Zarah picked up the manuscript of "The Great American Confluence" and riffled through its pages. "Here you say that 'the Exposition is a cross-fertilization of modes, manners, even persons from various parts of the nation.' Later you describe it as 'an American *convivio* at which the gruff vigor of the expanding West, the earthy accents of the honest husbandman, became more tunable to the politer eastern ear. . . . Our national culture, traditionally confined to the eastern seaboard, would be immeasurably strengthened by intermarriage with the energy, ideas—aye, the lifeblood—of pioneer stock.' And, finally, this pearl: 'Such cross-fertilization would be tremendously valuable in producing that indigenous hybrid, the American yet-to-be.'"

Zarah laid aside the manuscript. "The ink was barely dry on these pages, Father, when I told you that I wished to marry a man who was the living proof of your argument. Let me bring him to you." Zarah was pleading now. "Judge for yourself whether the union—or 'cross-fertilization,' as you call it—of Anson Woodhull and Zarah Osgood will be valuable in producing the American yet-to-be."

At the mention of cross-fertilization, Professor Osgood shuddered. It was no part of his system that Zarah should be cross-fertilized—or even fertilized. Hands trembling, he walked to the bookshelf where, in its customary place behind Hegel's *Phenomenology of the Mind,* stood a half-filled bottle of Nervina.

"My restorative," he explained, pouring a wineglassful of the sherry-colored tonic. Eyes closed, he sipped the fifth, or maybe the sixth, sedative draught since breakfast. *O excellent apothecary!* The dosage strengthened him for his ultimatum.

"You shall stop seeing this man as of today."

Disillusionment and anger struggled with Zarah's realization that her father had exposed himself on a weak and vulnerable flank. She would counterattack where it hurt most.

"Why, yes, Father, I will stop seeing Anson Woodhull . . . on one condition."

"What is the condition?"

"That you tear up this monstrous fiction called 'The Great American Confluence' and write another. Say that the Exposition is a triumph of vulgarity over taste; that the millions of Americans at the fair are an unwashed multitude. Will you do that, Father?"

The sixth glass of Nervina had steadied Quincy Osgood's resolve to quell insurrection in his own household. "I certainly will not."

"Then I will marry Anson Woodhull."

"You shall regret your decision."

"You shall never live to hear me say so."

"Why, then, I shall be obliged to live without hearing from you at all."

Cool as the lower eighth of an iceberg, Professor Osgood picked up his pen and began writing a note to the editor of the *North American Review:*

DEAR COUSIN ADAMS:

Enclosed you will find my article entitled: "The Great American Confluence," in which I have attempted to interpret certain hitherto unnoted aspects of the Centennial Exposition as the *Zeitgeist,* so to speak. . . .

Quincy Osgood did not see his daughter turn her head for a backward glance at the door of his study. He did not see her lips frame the imploring word *Father*. He did not hear the door close, softly, as one closes a door on the once-loved dead.

In fact, Quincy Osgood never saw his daughter's face or heard her voice again.

The Three Fates are traditionally represented as women engaged in weaving, measuring and snipping the threads of human life. But although the three women in the Osgood living room—Zarah, Louella and Theodora Allston, wife of Dr. Lyman Allston—were occupied with threads, needles and scissors, they could not pretend to be arbiters of anything so fateful as a wedding. Some male member of the family must bring in a decision; and because Professor Osgood had conspicuously defaulted (he was upstairs with a headache and a bottle of Nervina), Dr. Lyman Allston had volunteered to put the prop of masculine authority under the proceedings.

He had arisen that morning at the un-Christian hour of 6:00 A.M. in order to interview Anson Woodhull, and although the hallway clock that recorded the relative positions of sun, moon, Mars and Venus, as well as terrestrial time, had struck 7:00 P.M., Cousin Lyman hadn't yet returned. Ever since teatime the three women had been waiting for his report on Zarah's husband-to-be. Even without a report, Dr. Lyman Allston was someone to wait for. He represented the latest advance in medicine, a subject known as "neurology." In the dissecting rooms at La Salpêtrière and Guy's Hospital, he had pioneered in isolating the autonomic nerves of the human body. Dr. Charles Eliot had called him in to help reorganize the ill-governed, run-down Harvard Medical School. It was Cousin Lyman who had made an A.B. degree prerequisite to the study of medicine; he had established laboratories, wrung cash from the Board of Overseers for microscopes and other scientific paraphernalia. Having come to the Centennial Exposition for the purpose of reading a paper to his medical colleagues, Dr. Lyman Allston found himself acting as judge and jury on Anson Woodhull's qualifications to become Zarah's husband.

At 7:15 P.M. the female Fates scarcely knew whether they were snipping threads or their own nerves, when Dr. Lyman Allston entered the house. He was a huge mast of a man driven by some inner gale of controlled energy. The fresh wind of his personality blew away nine tenths of the enfolding gloom as he kissed the three women simultaneously, so close did they gather about him.

"Well," he announced, sitting down in the Professor's chair with no sense of *lèse majesté*. "Well, I've seen him. I've spent the day with him, I've talked with him, walked with him, messed with him, fenced with him, seen him naked, dressed, half-dressed, watched him break a horse, take orders from his superiors, give orders to his inferiors—and what do you suppose?"

Three "whats" chimed as one.

"This Anson Woodhull, brevet captain of Indiana militia, farmer by choice and temperament, suitor for our Zarah's hand—if that's the proper anatomical emphasis—this Anson Woodhull lacks two very important qualifications."

Zarah's heart performed a triple ruffle, then stood still.

"He lacks a Harvard degree and let's say, oh, a million dollars. If he possessed these two highly valuable assets, he'd be a demigod. As he stands now, he's merely the best, strongest, most sympathetic, resourceful, engaging and intelligent male specimen that I've ever met."

"Oh, Cousin Lyman!" Zarah was at him in a whirlwind of petticoats and kisses.

"Wait till you hear." Cousin Lyman began his recital. "I chose the most inopportune time to introduce myself. The hour was 6:30 A.M. Woodhull, naked from the waist up, was shaving. There I stood wearing a tophat, satin weskit, gold chain, polished boots, saying, 'I'm Dr. Lyman Allston, Zarah's cousin.' Did he stammer, make genuflections, pump oil from his personality glands to lubricate the situation? He did not. He dried his right hand on a towel, mopped some of the lather off his face and invited me to sit down on the edge of his bunk, until he had finished shaving. Lord Chesterfield couldn't have pulled it off half so well. Amazing, amazing! Now I'm not going into details, but the total effect of Woodhull's torso was that of an inverted pyramid fitted out with trapezious muscles, biceps and triceps fit to crush a Kodiak bear."

Dr. Allston poked the lower button of his sprigged satin weskit. "Poor puffy me."

"You aren't puffy at all," said Theodora. "You're as hard as . . . as Plymouth Rock."

"Thank you, darling. Remind me to have '1620' tattooed on my omentum next time I visit the Charlestown Navy Yard. But to get back to Captain Woodhull. Around 11 A.M. he inspected the horses, saddles, men and uniforms of his company. Now, mind you, this outfit doesn't belong to the regular Army. It's just a pickup team, so to speak. But if I were examining a blastopore through a microscope, I couldn't have picked out half the details he saw with his naked eye: saddle sores, loose buttons, fouled carbines and whatnot. I couldn't decide whether he cared more for the horses or the men—except that he never lifted his voice and no one even thought of giving him an argument. When the inspection broke up he dropped his authority like an old glove and went to work mending the very defects he had pointed out. Amazing. Amazing!"

Dr. Allston forced himself to be selective in his choice of incidents. Some western chunks—untamed draft horses—had been shipped in as artillery caisson pullers. One of them was a red-eyed brute. "I wouldn't have gone inside that breaking ring for . . . for the presidency of Harvard University. Everyone else leaped over the rails to safety. Woodhull just sat on the top stile and held out his hand; the horse came over and nuzzled him. Lord, what an exhibition!"

Lyman Allston paced up and down the Turkey carpet. "Next thing on the program was fencing with broadswords. Not the waggle-taggle foils you see in French exhibitions. These were cavalry sabers. Steel! As former champion of the Harvard fencing team, I requested permission to cross swords with our Indiana friend.

"Now this Woodhull either practices ten hours a day—which he doesn't—or his reactions are preternaturally *quick*, because he feinted me into the awkwardest, goddamnedest—"

"No profanity, darling." Theodora was being the wifely censor.

"Well, call them the most *gauche* positions I've ever fallen into. The remarkable part of it was that Woodhull allowed me to score when he felt that I needed a point. He knew that even a beagle has to catch a rabbit now and then. For that alone, I could love the man."

Dr. Allston meditated briefly on that rarest of virtues—understanding. "What else can I tell you? He uses a knife and fork like a gentleman, doesn't talk with his mouth full—

in fact, he doesn't say much at all, except when he has something to say. He apparently owns one suit of clothes other than his uniform, two white shirts and a black string tie. I gather that he has an active vocabulary of about thirty-five hundred words and a nice ear for the American vernacular. And by vernacular I do *not* mean that he twangs, drawls or mumbles."

Louella inserted a question between stitches. "In your opinion, Lyman, is Mr. Woodhull . . . a . . . God-fearing man?"

"God didn't enter our conversation. But we did discuss in some detail Mr. Woodhull's intentions toward one of God's luckiest daughters." Lyman Allston took a shrewd diagnostic look at Zarah, appraised her length of thigh, width of shoulder, and the thrusting power of her pelvic arch. One of God's luckiest daughters indeed!

"And what *are* Mr. Woodhull's intentions?" asked Louella.

"Quite briefly, he wishes to marry Zarah on Friday."

"Friday!" Mrs. Osgood dropped her embroidery tambour in horror. "But this is Tuesday. One simply can't marry a daughter off within three days. We must have bridesmaids, ushers, and a matron-of-honor." (The thought of Quincy, all unstrung, complicated matters. Why, it would take three days to restring Quincy.) "Besides, her father doesn't approve."

"Father and I have made our covenant," said Zarah.

"Who'll give you away?" quavered Louella.

"I will," said Lyman Allston. "And Theodora is just dying to be someone's matron-of-honor. We'll have a nice, cosy Episcopal wedding at exactly—" Lyman consulted his butter-gold watch—"nine A.M. on Friday."

It took a great deal of organizing, but in the end it all came about just as Cousin Lyman had planned it. In the presence of witnesses (Quincy Osgood's absence was conspicuous), Zarah and Anson were married at St. Ethelred's Church by the Suffragan Bishop of Philadelphia at 9:00 A.M. Friday, August 24, 1876.

Of the actual marriage ceremony Zarah remembered little —except that Cousin Lyman prevented it from being gloomy and tense-making. When the Bishop asked, "Who giveth this woman to be married to this man?" Dr. Allston said, "I." He squeezed Zarah's hand gently, then stepped backward and aside.

On the third finger of Zarah's left hand, Anson placed the circular golden link of the invisible chain that would henceforth bind them.

"With this ring, I thee wed—In the name of the Father, of the Son and of the Holy Ghost."

Nothing about bridesmaids, flower girls or ushers. No mention of kisses, fondling or laughter . . . of dancing, dishwashing and domestic drudgery. Only the sternest obligation that life can impose.

"I pronounce you husband and wife. Whom therefore God hath joined together, let no man put asunder."

Echoes of Sinai worn by long usage reverberated through the church. The words themselves carried no guarantee of happiness; rather, they expressed the fearful penalty—amounting virtually to a taboo—that would be visited on those who broke or disregarded the warning.

Was anyone listening? Does anyone *ever* listen? The echoes of Sinai were drowned out by a hymeneal chant from the organ loft. At the steps of the church, Anson, with Zarah on his arm, took a symbolic hail of rice and corn, then clambered into a barouche engaged by Cousin Lyman. And now this Dignified Ornament of the Harvard Medical School, this right-Bower to the Queen, Chief Intermediary between Lovers and Sworn Antagonist to Pomposity, stepped forward waving a piece of paper. He thrust it into the driver's hand.

"Take this message and ride like hell!"

To echoes of laughter, the barouche rattled away over cobblestones. They were fled, these lovers, and half the world a bridegroom was, the other half a bride.

3.

LA BELLE RIVIÈRE

ZARAH HAD SUPPOSED that they would travel by train,
but Anson said, "We'll sail down the Ohio on the *River
Queen*." Not since Adam suggested that first sight-seeing
tour with Eve through the Garden of Eden had any bridegroom come up with a lovelier idea.

The *River Queen*, newest and most luxurious of side-
wheelers, lay like a triple-decked swan alongside a flare-
lighted wharf bustling with freight handlers and last-minute
arrivals. The cindery, tedious ride from Philadelphia to Pittsburgh in an overcrowded railway carriage had pitched Zarah's
nerves to an almost unbearable tension. Swiftly down the
length of the mirrored saloon, feet barely touching its thick-
piled carpeting, she sped as in a dream, but with the dream
beside her, toward the haven of Stateroom No. 1, a wedding
gift from Cousin Lyman.

Once inside the stateroom, she sat down at the dressing
table and tried to remove, with a witch-hazel-soaked handkerchief, the grime of the day's journey. The handkerchief
produced a smudged, streaky effect—scarcely the complexion
of choice on one's bridal night. Peering into the mirror, she
caught the reflection of a bed, its counterpane turned down.
In a general way Zarah knew that brides, sooner or later,
took off their clothes, but exactly how did one go about it
for the first time in the presence of a man grown suddenly
enormous in the Liliputian perspective of the stateroom?

Anson was laying the key of the stateroom on the dressing
table. "You may want to be alone for a little while," he said.
"Think I'll take a couple turns on deck."

"No. No," she cried. "Don't leave me." Zarah heard the

panic in her own throat; felt it die away under Anson's consoling kiss.

"Never in life." He kept his voice promissory-tender lest she be frightened. "There's a lovely moon outside," he was saying. "Let's watch it rise and set. What difference does it make so long as we're together? Come."

Leaning against the after-rail of the hurricane deck (farthest away from the chuffing engines and barroom laughter) they saw a full moon rise like a fire balloon specially sent up to illuminate the dark Allegheny passes and its principal inland waterway. No buckeye painter, no painter of any school or period, could have caught the wild, demonic ruggedness of the scene. Night was having its way with Earth, and Earth was loving it; in every furrow, chasm and cranny she felt a velvet-heavy darkness covering her secrets, the better to penetrate them.

A midnight breeze springing up from the southwest rippled across the opal surface of the river. Anson took off his coat, caped Zarah protectively and added the supportive strength of his arm to the weary, apprehensive woman at his side.

Batts of mist enveloped the pair standing at the *River Queen's* rail. Earth, water, sky, breeze, clouds and moon turned on a noiseless axle. For the present Zarah was content to rest her head on Anson's shoulder while the vessel glided between sachem headlands or entered mother-of-pearl lakelets never invaded (or so it seemed to Zarah) until now. A midnight chill rose from the water.

The top hook and eye of Zarah's traveling suit presented no particular difficulty as they re-entered their cabin. Shoulder straps, buttons and the minor orders of ribbandry, carefully designed to discourage invaders, fell truant to the floor.

Shafts of moonlight slanting through the shuttered window revealed the upper half of Zarah's magnificent dowry; part river-nymph, all woman, no longer timorous, she closed her eyes and heard Anson murmuring, "My brave girl. . . . My brave and beautiful girl. . . . My wife."

The Great American Confluence, already taking place in other parts of the vessel and on the waters beneath her hull and in the windy pavilions above her smokestacks, began —so far as the occupants of Stateroom No. 1 were concerned —in a longitude immeasurably west of Brattle Street.

The geometric distance between Pittsburgh and Cincinnati

is three hundred and fifty-one miles; self-respecting locomotives usually made the trip in something under twelve hours. But the *River Queen,* enjoying a sovereign exemption conferred upon her by the river itself, took three leisurely days for the journey.

It wasn't true, as some said, that the *Queen* could "float on a heavy dew." She required a full six feet of water under her specially designed hull; to prevent her from running into unpredictable sandbars, a leadsman stationed in the bow constantly sang out the depth of water immediately ahead. His flat-voiced, monotonous announcements were calculated (during the summer months) not in fathoms but in feet. "By the deep eight" informed the helmsman that the *River Queen* had a luxurious two-foot margin of safety beneath her keel. At the ominous warning, "By the mark seven," the *Queen* slowed down. What with stopping in midstream, sending off skiffs to pick up passengers and freight from both banks, the royal procession advanced at a speed scarcely faster than a man and woman could walk.

La belle rivière gave Anson and Zarah an illusion of timelessness, imperative only in its demand that they spend it upon each other. There were so many things to do. They began by listening to the German band play *Volkslieder*—a kind of music composed for the special purpose of bringing tears to the eyes of homesick exiles doomed to grieve eternally for their lost Fatherland. Probably half the passengers on the *River Queen* were German immigrants—a sturdy, industrious, sentimental people—destined to prosper in *Amerika,* a land where "gold lay on the sidewalk."

So spracht das Märchen.

After the morning concert Zarah promenaded the decks of the *River Queen* with Anson. "I feel *flouncy*," she whispered. "Does it show?"

"Let it. Who cares?"

Freedom to feel flouncy; the authority to show it; knowledge that she, Mrs. Anson Woodhull, born Osgood, was the wife of the handsomest man ever devised—all these caused her to marvel not so much at the spacious blue skies arching overhead, nor the capricious, never-twice-the-same aspects of *La belle rivière.* Rather, she marveled at the depth, range and profundity of experience made possible by the Male Presence at her side. She neither felt nor acted like the timorous girl who barely two weeks ago had dared saunter down alleys

of fruit trees with a tall, bearded Captain of Militia. The
Male Menace was still there all right, and though it still retained the power of dilating her heart, she no longer feared
it.

What was there about this man who could stand, move,
speak or be silent, and by the mere act of being, take in,
absorb, envelop, use, decline to use, or elect not to be used
by, the people and events swirling about them on the deck
of the *River Queen?* Anson's ability to give himself (selectively
and in varying degrees) to his fellow passengers was natural,
easy; his authority over circumstance and other men was
beyond question. He could brush aside a proffered bottle or
"chaw" merely by saying, "Not just now, friend." When he
interposed his huge frame between Zarah and lurching drunks,
they simply evaporated. He could silence leerers, stave off the
most pugnacious challenge, merely by rubbing his chin bone
with a detachment that said. "Mister, take my advice. Don't
tangle with the ripsaw."

What would the ripsaw do, thought Zarah, if someone
tangled with it?

Slowly the river enveloped them in its mystery. On a
majestic tide, changing from burnished copper to jade green,
they floated around sweeping curves, willow-fringed, glided
between towering headlands and skirted the shores of islands
in midstream.

> *And here were forests ancient as the hills*
> *Enfolding sunny spots of greenery.*

Leaning against the rail of the hurricane deck, Anson
pointed out cities that had grown rich and populous on river
commerce; others that had fallen into decay when an unpredictable sandbar silted up its approaches.

After luncheon in the main dining room (very grand
with its parquet floors and mahogany paneling), they mounted
to the glass-enclosed wheelhouse (called the texas) where
Capt. Hubbell Jeffcoat held forth on the vagaries of the
Ohio's channel. Cap'n Jeffcoat took the traditional stance of
characterizing all rivers (except The Big One) as female.
"She twists, turns, broadens, narrers, deepens and shallers,
leanin' first toward one shore, then the other 'cordin' to the
way she feels."

Giving Zarah the benefit of his weather-cured profile, Jeffcoat sounded off in the manner of a fond husband grieving over the "onreasonability" of his wife. "Right now she's dawdlin' along like a girl betwixt and between. But take her, say, when she's full up with October rains, or worse yet, durin' a January thaw. Then she races along, petticoats tucked under her armpits, in a hull of a worry, disregardful of anything 'cept what's on her mind." He touched the visor of his gold-braided cap in deference to Zarah. "And how's any man to put his finger on the pree-cise nature of that 'whatness'?"

Was it Captain Jeffcoat's line of thought—especially that "petticoats-up-to-her-armpits" phrase—that caused Zarah to nuzzle her chin into Anson's shoulder, conveying the sweetest, most reasonable suggestion that ever entered a woman's mind on the second day of her honeymoon?

They barely made dinner that night.

Where had the hours fled? With a third of their river eternity lost, Zarah felt—quite definitely—that neither she nor Anson could afford the luxury of waiting for the moon to rise. So a West Virginia moon rose unwatched by a woman who had become an adept in getting out of her clothes in the presence of the man she loved.

The freedom of manners and easy communication between the passengers on the *River Queen* began to rub off on Zarah. Next morning when Anson and a company of men descended into the engine room (a nether region packed with fearful machinery), Zarah chose to sun herself on the hurricane deck. Five minutes later she was talking with a German girl, Gretel Bruckner, a Bavarian, to judge by her blue eyes and flaxen hair. Gretel, a seventeen-year-old counterpart of her namesake in *Grimm's Fairy Tales*, told of her new-world adventures as though they had never happened before.

She had crossed the Atlantic to marry her childhood sweetheart, Hansel. (Actually his name was Waldemar.) He had sent her a steamship ticket and then met her in New York with a pocketful of money. Such a beautiful wedding at the home of her *Schwägerin!* Combining business with romance, Waldemar had bought a *wunderbar* bottle-making machine. A glass blower by trade, he would open his own shop. The machine would transform glass into gold. In *Amerika* such things were possible, *nicht wahr?* A glaze of confectioner's sugar coated Gretel's eyes.

"Yes, everything is possible in America," said Zarah. She

herself was proof that fairy tales were poor wish-and-dream substitutes for the actual experience of waking up in Anson Woodhull's arms. What Sleeping Princess—including Keats's "lovely dreamer," Madeline—had been so blest? She saw her husband—no fairy princeling, but a Rafael become mortal—approaching with a company of men. The delectable difference between Anson and all other men—was it not self-evident?—triggered the pace-making mechanism of her heart. It slipped control as she rose to greet him.

"Anson."

"Waldemar," cried Gretel at the same time. Her voice was a brimming echo of Zarah's. She rose, eyes shining, to greet a plump little man carrying an alpenstock.

"Waldemar, *mein Mann.*"

Embracing first, followed by introductions all around. Waldemar removed his conical hat. "*Küss die Hand, Gnädige Frau,*" he murmured respectfully. Gretel made a pretty *Knicksel* to Anson. Zarah congratulated Waldemar.

And what did Anson do? He opened his great arms, lifted all three from the deck and whirled them around carousel-fashion until they were quite dizzy.

On the hurricane deck the *River Queen,* these four re-enacted the miracle-play that youth and love perform not only for each other's benefit but for reaffirmation of the faith and beauty that moves the world.

Fairy tales are but penny pieces in life's inexhaustible treasury of wonders. Or so it seems when love is young.

In their celebrated fantasy of Hansel and Gretel the Brothers Grimm omit any mention of whiskey. Departing from this classic script, Waldemar Bruckner, glass-blower, entered the bar of the *River Queen,* hooked his alpenstock over its brass rail, ordered a jigger of bourbon and lifted it in toast to his happiness as Gretel's *Bräutigam.* He shared his sense of well-being by telling the gentleman beside him all about the little house of cakes and cookies awaiting his bride in Zinzinnati. The gentleman responded by ordering up a second round of drinks. The heady double dose of bourbon caused Waldemar to accept the stranger's hospitable suggestion that they "break the bank" in the adjoining card-room. "*Heute, fühle ich sehr glücklich.*" Waving his alpenstock, Waldemar entered the gambling room where a quiet three-handed game of stud was in progress.

"*Ach, ja,* so this is schtud, the American card game. Already I have played it in Zinzinnati. *Wie hoch ist der Satz?*"

Mr. Damon Frye, presiding genius of the *River Queen's* cardroom, appraised the mountain climber as a two-hundred-dollar windfall. (His appraisal, based upon the "How much will it cost?" question, came well within the 10 per cent margin for error.) Privately Mr. Frye held that people who asked, "How much will this cost me?" shouldn't be encouraged. But since the pickings had been poor of late, he granted Waldemar admission to the game. Gently Waldemar was taken over the preliminary hurdle: the substitution of double eagles for dimes. On the first deal the *Bräutigam's* luck was phenomenal; his three queens topped Mr. Frye's wretched little pair of jacks.

"Your six tits win," said Frye.

"Tits? *Was bedeutet* tits?" asked Waldemar.

Such an explosion of laughter when the relationship between queens and tits was explained. So *gemütlich* this little group in the cardroom. Mr. Frye in particular. Sometimes dropping his cards with a "this-isn't-my-day" gesture, he would stand kibitzer fashion, behind Waldemar, restraining his eagerness to buck a possible pair of "bullets." "Bullets" meant aces. "*Ja. Ja. Ich verstehe.*"

Waldemar learned rapidly, his pile of gold pieces grew taller, he became a mountain goat leaping from precipice to precipice amazing everyone—including himself—by the agility of his bounds.

He was yodeling up a Matterhorn peak preparing to snatch a four-hundred-dollar bouquet of edelweiss with three aces—pardon me, I mean "bullets"—when Mr. Damon Frye buried him under the noiseless avalanche of a straight flush.

Pocketbook empty, Waldemar betook himself to the barroom to brood over his losses. How tell Gretel that he had lost the cash necessary to pay freight charges on the glass-blowing machine stowed in the *River Queen's* hold? He stoked up a full head of Dutch courage on straight bourbon, then compounded his original error by rushing at Mr. Frye as the latter emerged from the gaming room just before dinner.

From the hurricane deck Anson witnessed the semi-final act of an essay in futility: He saw a little German in a Tyrolean cap lifting a funny cane to strike Mr. Damon Frye, known from Pittsburgh to New Orleans as the King of River

Gamblers. Zarah, coming out of their stateroom, saw only the final act. And a cooler performance was never seen. Mr. Damon Frye casually cocked his derringer and drilled a hole through Waldemar's conical hat just above the hairline in much the same fashion as a man might flick a piece of lint from his sleeve.

"Down, *Schweinhund*," said Frye.

While Waldemar scrambled to safety, Frye whiffed the smoke from his pistol barrel, reloaded, shook his head at the folly of immigrants in general and continued his promenade.

His gait, a combination of contortionist glide and the languor affected by men of fashion, suggested brimstone menace deliberately underplayed lest public opinion deprive him of his double-dealing franchise.

"That man is evil," said Zarah, clinging to her husband's arm.

"Maybe." Anson refused to pass judgment. "I'll say this for him, though. Anyone who carries a single-shot pistol in this day of the six gun is either a conceited fool or a dead shot. If things could be arranged just right, I'd like to meet up with him sometime."

The meeting came about sooner than Anson expected. He was telling Zarah of the Serpent Mound built by a strange people who had given America its first culture, when their conversation was interrupted by a woman's sobbing. Eyes red with weeping, Gretel Bruckner approached Zarah.

"*Gnädige Frau*," she began, "my husband has been very foolish. All his money in the gaming room he has lost. Now he cannot pay the freight charges on the wonderful bottle-making machine that he bought in New York. It will go down the river—be sold at auction in New Orleans. Ah, if I could only speak English, I would kneel to this gambler, beg him to return Waldemar's money."

Confectioner's sugar no longer glazed Gretel's world as she pleaded. "Will you speak for me, *Gnädige Frau?*"

Her own eyes wet with sympathy, Zarah transmitted the plea to her husband.

Anson knew—better than Zarah or Gretel—the extent of Waldemar's foolishness. "This German, more or less drunk, made the mistake of attacking Frye with that pike staff he carries. Had Frye killed him, any jury would call it self-defense."

"Can't anything be done?" asked Zarah. "Couldn't you ask Frye—just this once—to give back the money?"

"It would be like asking the Ohio to run the other way."

"Surely Captain Jeffcoat would enforce the law."

Useless to tell Zarah that river law was a code apart, or that Jeffcoat himself was taking a juicy cut of Frye's winnings.

The realization that his wife's gentle spirit—a spirit that could be moved by the sight of an overborne fruit bough—was being troubled at the very entrance into her new life brought Anson's protective tenderness flooding to the surface.

"Do you really want to help Gretel get her money back?"

"Yes, oh, I do, *truly*, Anson. She—she's so bridelike."

"Are you willing to stack my nerve against Frye's? He's a killer, you know. I may have to show off a little."

"Darling, I'd *love* to see you show off."

"Then come to our cabin and listen to everything I tell you."

The encounter with Frye, Anson explained, would require three things: considerable stage management, a sympathetic audience and exquisite timing. The contest must come about with seeming naturalness, yet the trap could be sprung only after a careful process of planning and baiting.

As the first step, Anson donned the fatigue uniform of his regiment: a battered cavalry hat and a pair of down-at-the-heel boots completed his costume. Unshaved, he moved through the throng of passengers whittling, rural-fashion, with a staghorn case knife. His prowess at stick knife drew an admiring audience; the twelve standard throws, including Hop-o'-my-Thumb, Nosy-bluffs and Knucklesy-whacks, were executed with such ease and precision that Anson was obliged to explain.

"It's like this. I've had the knife ever since I was a kid, always honed it myself on a piece of soapstone. But here's the real secret. I poured melted lead into a little hole right here [indicating a spot on the lower edge of handle] so that the thing's *balanced*. No matter how high I throw it into the air, the blade always comes down point first."

He gave a sample exhibition by tossing the case knife in the air and letting it fall as it would. The blade quivered an inch deep into the deck planks. "Then sometimes I throw her up and catch her when she comes down." Once more Anson gave a free exhibition of dexterity with the marvelous knife.

To complete his preparations, Anson held a conference with some of his Indiana militia and a small group of German immigrants, sympathetic to their countryman, Bruckner.

"I haven't the money or skill to match Frye at the card table," he confessed. "But you've all seen what I can do with this knife. Now here's the plan. Tomorrow afternoon about five o'clock I'll begin jostling Frye. Nothing crude or heavy-handed, because my wife will be standing beside me. Frye will jostle back the same way—use every trick in the book to throw me off balance. All I need is the support of every honest man on board. Have I got it?"

"You've got it."

"Good. Pass the word."

The word was passed.

The final act of the unfolding drama took place next afternoon while Mr. Damon Frye was enjoying a cigarillo on the after-deck. The German band played *Heimatland* airs. A windless day was drawing toward suppertime as Anson and Zarah promenaded arm-in-arm past the gambler. Zarah was attired in the high-fashion gown of puce-colored silk and Eugénie hat that she had worn the day she met her husband. Anson in his broadcloth suit had cast himself as a substantial farmer. But it was Zarah who caught Frye's admiring glance. On the third turn of their promenade, Anson lifted his hat in acknowledgment of Frye's bow and paused for casual conversation.

"My wife and I admired your coolness in handling that funny little German, Mr. Frye."

"I thought you gave a remarkable exhibition of courage," added Zarah.

"Why, thank you." Frye doffed his gray tophat. "One seldom receives congratulations these days for acting in self-defense. Nerve, it would seem, is no longer *de rigueur*."

"*C'est vrai*," sighed Zarah. "You must at times feel a certain—how shall I call it?—*ennui*, in the practice of your profession."

Her sympathy, her knowledge of French and the relationship between this beautiful young woman and the tall provincial husbandman aroused Frye's curiosity. "That is true, Madame. The river is dying and although its scenic charm remains, I must confess that I sometimes suffer from boredom at the card table. I should enjoy nothing better than a . . . a . . . fresh sensation."

Anson came in on cue. "Then maybe you'd be interested in a test of skill and nerve that has nothing to do with cards?"

Frye accepted the gambit. "What kind of a test do you propose?"

From his pocket, Anson drew his staghorn knife. "This might be considered a deadly weapon in some quarters. Have I your permission to open the blade? You may cover me with your derringer, if you like."

Frye heard the hidden taunt. He glanced at the naked knife blade about four inches long.

"Quite a toy. Sharp, I daresay. What do you use it for?"

"Winning bets."

The German band stopped playing. The spectators, denser now, heard Frye's counter-question.

"What kind of bets?"

"Sometimes," Anson explained, "I toss the knife into the air and catch it." He flicked his wrist with an upward motion. His eyes followed the imaginary flight of the knife into the air. Frye looked up also, but instead of seeing the knife in mid-flight, he heard, *no*, he *felt* the zing of the steel blade quivering in the deck, scarcely an eighth of an inch from the edge of his polished boot.

"Sorry." Anson was apologetic. "Just another case of the hand being quicker than the eye."

Frye refused to acknowledge the jostle. "Know any other country games?"

"Back in Landmark County, we've invented a little variation. Two men stand facing each other, eighteen inches apart. One of them throws a knife into the air—as high as those smokestacks." Anson pointed to the twin stacks of the *River Queen*. "Sooner or later the knife comes down."

"Where does it land?"

"Between the players. The man who looks up or steps back loses."

"Sounds like fun."

"It is." Good-natured as sunshine, Anson asked, "Want to play?"

"What stakes do you play for?"

"Anything we happen to have in our pockets." Anson produced a dollar bill. "Care to cover it, Mr. Frye?"

Hooked! By a yokel who evidently had the support of his

audience. Taunts and jeers from the spectators, many of whom had lost to the gambler at the card table.

"*Put up or crawl, Frye.*"

"*Skeered?*"

"*We want the knife!*"

The situation, seemingly out of hand, was made to order for Mr. Damon Frye. He enjoyed resistance. Anson's challenge, seconded by the hostility of the crowd, gave the gambler an opportunity to display his own bag of tricks. Right thumb tucked negligently in the black silk sash around his waist, derringer half revealed, Frye went into his act. First, the exordium—flattering, stuffed with plums of cozenage; next, the appeal to logic and fair play. Then the punto-reverso crisscross with the red-herring counter-proposal.

"Friends and fellow chance-takers," he began, "we all want to see this wonderful knife trick, don't we?"

"Yes, yes."

"*Ja wohl!*"

"*By the mark, seven,*" came the leadsman's cry. Vessel and gambler were maneuvering at the minimum level of safety.

"Now I'm as confident as anyone," continued Frye, "that Mr. Newlywed here can pull it off. But it so happens that under our Constitution, a man has the right to place a proper valuation on his own life and I'm here to say that a dollar—one limp greenback—doesn't seem attractive enough to me." Candor couldn't speak fairer. "Of course, I could bluff our homespun hero right off the deck by raising the ante to a thousand dollars, two thousand, or even five thousand [Frye produced a sheaf of gold notes], *which* sum he wouldn't be able to cover." He turned to Anson. "Or would you?"

"Your money doesn't interest me, Frye. I'm testing your nerve, that's all."

Like a jet of spittle, Anson's taunt smeared Frye's vanity. The gambler, accustomed to controlling angry men, or frightening timid ones, found himself being outmaneuvered by a homespun tactician, willing, apparently, to risk his life for . . . for what? A dollar? Frye guessed that other motives were involved. No time to plumb them now. His professional reputation as a risk-taker had been publicly challenged in the presence of a hostile crowd. He must accept or back down.

He accepted.

That he was a treacherous, lecherous, sadistic whoremaster

with a streak of homosexuality in his nature; a murderer, a forger, a double-dealer—all this could be said about Damon Frye. But of fear he knew little. Steel, lead, broken bottles held daggerlike at his throat—Frye had seen, outgazed them all. Merely by breathing, by being, he had paralyzed or out-jockeyed every species of opposition.

"My 'nerve,' sir, has been tested by better men than you," he said to Anson. "I would rather let your clumsy knife split my skull than permit my courage to be questioned. I hereby cover your absurd bet. Where do you want me to stand?"

"Any place you feel comfortable. Upstairs, downstairs, or in my lady's chamber."

Anson's reply won a round of guffaws, broken by the leadsman's ominous cry *"By the deep eight."* Spectators and rivals knew that the keel of the *River Queen* was sliding along barely two feet above the river bottom. A silt bar, a piece of driftwood, or a slight shift in the wind would influence the outcome of the bizarre duel about to take place.

Anson moistened a forefinger and held it up to test the direction and velocity of the wind.

"Three miles, south by west." Frye smiled.

Anson corrected him. "Three and one *half* miles. South by *south*west." He spoke earnestly. "Look, mister, these things matter. I don't want to kill you; just be a good horse and stand still without hitching."

Eighteen inches apart now, the players stood face to face. Few rivals in the history of dueling were ever as equally matched. Frye assumed an attitude of seeming indifference halfway between jocularity and boredom. Actually, he had a slight edge on his opponent, who, under the terms of the wager, must toss the knife almost fifty feet into the air and cause it to fall point downward between the two men. Although Anson was testing Frye's nerve, the latter was testing Anson's skill.

Temperamentally unable to "stand without hitching," the gambler made a new proposition. "I feel lonely over here. Can't we stand a little closer together?"

"Suits me." Anson appeared to hesitate. "Only thing is, if we stand nearer, the knife might damage our clothes. Wouldn't want to spoil this good broadcloth coat."

"Oh, come now, I'll asume responsibility for damages—up to fifty dollars. Let's stand twelve inches apart. Agreed?"

"Agreed."

At point-blank range now, they scrutinized each other's faces for signals of weakness. A drop of perspiration? A twitching of lips? Nothing serviceable to either man. Anson saw the fine pores of Frye's olive-skinned cheeks; the silken texture of his mustache; the luminous oval eyes. Frye saw the crisp, Mosaic curl of Anson's beard, the haycock rubor of his face, the slate gray (or was it hazel, perhaps?) of eyes that told nothing, feared nothing. . . .

Result, *nullo*.

By sheer force of habit, Frye needled his opponent once more. "Perhaps a little music might help. How about *Ase's Tod?*" He hummed the opening bars of Grieg's Death March. Anson rejected the proposal. "A closed roll from the snare drummer might help."

Already coached in his part, the snare drummer went into his roll-off.

"Ready, Frye?"

"Ready."

In the military position of attention, Anson bent his right knee slightly for leverage; and, holding the knife blade between his thumb and forefinger, he flicked it into the air.

R-rrrrrrrrrrr—Close as an obbligato, the snare drum followed the knife like a steel bird in its upward flight.

R-rrrrrrrrrrrr-RRR

Cr-ack! The snare drummer caused one of his sticks to hit the wooden rim of the instrument. It told Anson that the knife, having described a tight parabolic curve, was coming down.

"You've got just about a second to step back," he warned.

Frye neither stepped back nor looked up.

Anson extended his left forearm slightly. The blade of the knife quivered shank-deep in the deck planking, squarely between the two men.

The band blared forth; Captain Jeffcoat gave a long tug at the steam whistle and the crowd went crazy in three languages.

"How does it feel to lose?" asked Anson.

"Have I lost?"

"Seems so. The knife nicked my coat sleeve. Quite a rip." He displayed the damaged garment. "That'll cost you fifty dollars, Frye."

"Well worth it," said the gambler, paying off in gold. "Never saw *that* trick done before."

"It never *was* done," replied Anson. He bent forward to drop a confidential word in the gambler's ear. "But in case you ever try it, Frye, here's the secret: *lean forward a little.*"

During the next two minutes, a couple of other secrets were revealed unto Mr. Damon Frye.

"Will Waldemar Bruckner step this way?" said Anson.

Sheepishly, the conical-hatted bridegroom pushed through the crowd. "Here's forty dollars; it'll pay the freight charges on your bottle-making machine." (Anson clinked two double eagles into Waldemar's trembling palm.)

"*Danke schön . . . veil' dank.*" The lights of Zinzinnatti, glimmering ahead, illuminated once more the pages of the American fairy tale.

"And you, Herr Trommler—thanks for that rim shot." Anson flipped a ten-dollar gold piece to the drummer.

Mr. Damon Frye had seen enough. "I wish that I might claim you as my disciple," he said to Anson. "With a little professional training, both of you—" he included Zarah in his patronizing gesture—"could go far."

Smiling, the varnish of his reputation not even scratched, Frye retired to his cabin.

Rounding the first of those graceful river curves that wind like a double S past Cincinnati, the *River Queen* nosed into her berth at the Public Landing—a quarter mile of cobble-stoned ramp sloping from Water Street to the edge of the Ohio. Boats stood three deep at anchorage; some were taking on southbound cargoes of pigs on the hoof, pyramids of whiskey barrels and huge sacks of corn; others, having ascended from New Orleans, were discharging hogsheads of blackstrap, bales of cotton and casks of cured tobacco that still entered the profitable northern markets through the port of Cincinnati despite the steely challenge of interlocking railway systems.

Anson and Zarah gazed down upon this vast wholesale emporium where buyers and sellers met in a frothy tide rip of commerce lighted only by smoky rock-oil flares. Zarah had never witnessed or even conceived a scene so utterly dominated by "trade"; freed of the anxieties that had distracted her at Pittsburgh, she could now observe almost intelligently the labyrinthine pattern of goods and persons entering or leaving the *River Queen*.

She picked out the Bruckners jubilant in the possession of

their *wunderbar* bottle-making machine on the thronging wharf below.

"There's Hansel and Gretel," she exclaimed. "Let's wave to them. *Weidersehn! Auf weidersehn*. I wonder shall we ever see them again."

"Probably," said Anson. "I'm more interested, at the moment, in watching our elegant friend, Mr. Frye, pick his way down the gangplank."

Evil is always more attractive than run-of-the-mill domesticity. "Where is he?" asked Zarah. "Point him out to me."

Anson pointed. Zarah saw Mr. Frye advancing toward a tall, handsome young man whose attire proclaimed him to be a fellow guildsman in the league of river gamblers. The younger man lifted his hat respectfully, as if to a master; then the two men embraced European fashion.

"They might almost be brothers," said Zarah, "except that the younger one has such beautiful golden hair."

"Yes," said Anson. "His hair *is* golden. Always was."

"You know him?"

"He's my young brother, Platt. Haven't seen him for nearly two years. Under Frye's professional direction he seems to have gone far."

Lying beside Anson on the last night of their voyage, Zarah wondered how long a woman could keep on discovering unsuspected depths in the man she loved. Every day he disclosed some fresh aspect of his character. Was there no bottom to Anson's tolerance, strength or—she struggled to find the right word—resourcefulness? In his contest with Frye, Anson had imposed his will upon a professional trickster, matched guile for guile, improvised stratagems, twisted every circumstance to his own advantage. Dear God, what a man!

By contrast, she thought of her poor father fumbling for his bottle of Nervina at every minor crisis. At Frye's "Boo" he would have fainted. Why, for that matter, three weeks ago Zarah herself might have fainted at the prospect of watching her husband stand under a pocketknife guillotine.

Would she be able to stand up with equal serenity under the burdens of everyday life on an Indiana farm? Anson described its hardships in a parable. Taking her embroidery scissors, he said, "It'll be like holding these against a grindstone."

Zarah smiled. "Well, as Minerva Higginson used to say, 'Rust doth corrupt more than Labor wears.'"

The plash of paddle wheels lulled her toward the feathery falls of sleep.

Then Anson was shaking her gently. "Wake up, darling. We're almost home."

A morning mist blanketed river and valley as the *River Queen's* paddle wheels churned in midstream.

"Stand by the dinghy," shouted Captain Jeffcoat.

Zarah stepped into a small rowboat swinging from the davits.

"Lower away."

When the dinghy struck water, *La belle rivière* was mothering an impenetrable fog. Zarah cupped its slow-moving flood in her hand—"Unless ye be born again of water . . ." She was being born again.

Two oarsmen, faceless in the mist, tugged at the long sweeps. "Which way, mister?" one of them asked.

"Let her drift a bit until we come to a cairn of stones," said Anson. "Now hard on the starboard oar for three strokes. So." The prow of the dinghy nuzzled into a tiny cove.

Like a bridegroom yet to enter his chamber, Anson lifted Zarah in his arms and ran up a grassy slope. He covered her face with kisses, then set her down gently at the edge of the cornfield.

"We're home," he said.

A shaft of morning sunlight pierced the fog as she followed him along the furrow toward rising ground.

4.

THE FRUITFUL EAR

To WELCOME his new daughter-in-law Chance Woodhull invited his neighbors to a husking bee.

The "bee" combined the best features of barbecue, barn dance and working party—a harvest ritual at which all hands stripped the garnered ears and had a good time doing it. A husking bee offered the older women an opportunity to exchange gossip and compare symptoms. For the menfolk, it provided a political forum and a wonderful excuse for uninhibited jug-hoisting. And for the young marriageable set, it was the rural equivalent of a cotillion with kissing privileges thrown in.

The bustle of preparation began at dawn with Anson digging a deep oblong pit in the middle of the barnyard. By noon the pit was an earthen brazier brimming with fiery embers. Hanging from a block and tackle beside the pit was Tusker, a three-hundred-pound boar gone ugly in his prime. When the embers cooled, Anson arranged a grid of iron bars across the pit and laid Tusker's beautifully butchered carcass over the ruby pyre.

Afternoon shadows were lengthening as neighbors drove up in farm wagons and carry-alls. The men tethered their animals to fence posts, slipped bags of fodder over their noses, then joined the circle around the fire, to pass the jug and talk politics—with special emphasis on the falling price of corn and the scarcity of good round minted gold pieces.

While matters of national concern were being settled, man-fashion, around the fire, the womenfolk swarmed into the kitchen to help Abigail (Anson's younger sister and charge-taker since her mother's death) in the mass production of eatables and—not too incidentally—gather firsthand impressions of Anson's bride.

Zarah had prepared herself for the ordeal by subduing every aspect of dress, manner and speech that might count against her. There she stood at the kitchen table washing radishes in a wooden bucket, hopefully awaiting any gesture of friendliness that might be offered. Might not such a woman, on the strength of her bridehood alone, count upon gentle treatment from those who had come to honor her?

Not if her gray woolen skirt revealed a pair of hips like Zarah's; not if the simplicity of her hair-do disclosed an unforgivable touch of elegance. Could any farm wife in that kitchen, seeing Zarah's head carriage, the upward-outward tilt of her breasts, be expected to welcome a creature whose existence they had never imagined?

Some of the older women were almost sympathetic in their foreknowledge of Zarah's fate as a farm wife and child-bearer. Younger wives who had already proved their endurance and fertility greeted the newcomer with a stand-offish "Time'll tell" attitude. Among the unmarried set, two or three good-looking girls displayed head-tossing disdain for this piece of eastern baggage who had snatched Anson while he was away from home.

At any period in her former life Zarah might have been crushed by such hostility. Now, supported by knowledge of Anson's love, she selected the only possible method of bringing this kitchenful of rude women to heel. Quietly she removed her apron and hung it behind the door. Dishes stopped clattering; corn muffins baked unnoticed; pickle relish took its proper place in the hierarchy of values while twenty pairs of feminine eyes watched an almost literal affirmation of the Psalmist's faith: Thou preparest a table before me in the presence of mine enemies.

They saw the miracle (which was no miracle to Zarah) of manners deciding to betake itself elsewhere. They saw a strange woman possessed of grace and courtesy not theirs move toward the kitchen door, open it, turn, smile pleasantly (with just a touch of "you asked for it" at the corners of her mouth) and say, "Excuse me, ladies. My husband is preparing a table for me."

The table that Anson had prepared was a typical harvest setup: wide boards supported by sawhorses in the center of his father's barn. Narrower boards, resting on nail kegs, served as benches. Lanterns with wicks new-trimmed hung from queen-trussed rafters overhead. Into this rustic banquet hall the sacrificial pig was borne on a palanquin of hickory poles and gently laid, legs upward, on a huge dripping-pan. Platters heaped with roasted ears, flanked by mounds of golden butter and slabs of cornbread hot and fluffy gave the table a sway-backed curve.

Anson, with Zarah at his side, sat halfway down the table. At one end of the board Old Chance occupied a proprietorial armchair. Senator Jubal Whissendyne (who later would make a speech) was given a position of special honor at the other end. At a signal from Chance—"You do the honors, Son—" Anson gave a masterful exhibition of carving. With a long knife he sliced off great segments of savory pork—chines, chops, juicy chunks from the haunch and thick slices from the shoulder. While Holly Dante scraped "Money Musk" on his cigarbox fiddle, loaded plates garnished with pickle relish and applesauce passed down the table.

And now, without grace of word or manner, the harvest supper began.

Half an hour later, Tusker was a picked skeleton; a brigade of barn mice crossing the table would be obliged to carry their own provisions.

The feast over, dishes removed, cries went up. "Speech, speech. Qui-*ert*. Silence for the Senator."

Jubal Whissendyne stepped onto a familiar stage. Here were fifty people, most of them voters and property owners. What they wanted was not so much a speech as a performance. They wanted laughter, gentle ribaldry mixed with "home points," something to talk about from now to election day. They expected the Senator to be humorous, learned, colloquial, statesmanlike, anecdotal, discursive, frank, elegant and patriotic.

A less courageous speaker might have quailed at the assignment. But Senator Whissendyne, fortified by a natural gift for "bloviation" and untroubled by fear or sensitivity, surveyed his audience. He hadn't the slightest idea of what he was going to say, and perhaps had underestimated the power of that stuff in Chance Woodhull's stone jug. Glancing down the table, he glimpsed Zarah's green-silk shirtwaist. Clue and keynote! He opened his large humorous mouth and let pleasant oils of flattery pour forth.

"Friends, neighbors. The formula for making good-looking women is one of nature's proprietary secrets. Yet though mystery veils the prescription, its ingredients are well known. Take an abundance of food such as we have enjoyed here tonight, add a lenient climate and a way of life that is neither too relaxed nor too crushingly hard, blend these tenderly at body temperature and what you get is a large number of girl-babies who will grow up—like Anson's bride here—to be beautiful, loving women. . . ."

Laughter and applause from the menfolk. Suspended judgment from the distaff part of the gathering.

"Anson's bride proves that in the sovereign state of Indiana beauty and wifeability amount to the same thing. In our rural Paradise every Adam wants a wife who'll be at once an Eve, a Helen and a patient Griselda. When knights were bold, men jousted for the favors of this not-impossible 'she,' or wrote roundelays to her . . . ah . . . eyebrows. [Titters.] But tonight the terms of beauty will be decided neither by the lance nor pen—nor yet by racing for the apple as in Atalanta's time.

No, in the husking bee about to begin, the genius of this time and place will declare judgment. *The cor—rr-rn-nn!* The maiden who plucks the red ear will be adjudged Queen of Beauty. And the young man she elects to kiss—or, in vestal shyness, permits herself to be kissed *by*—well, you know as well as I what the consequences of that embrace will be."

Prolonged laughter and cries of "Go to it, Senator!"

His exordium behind, Jubal modulated into his deepest chest tones. "Eager though we may be to dwell upon these consequences, I cannot let this occasion pass without directing your attention to several issues of local and national importance which affect our destinies." Whereupon the speaker proceeded to excoriate eastern bankers, condemn the greed of railroad builders and hymn the supremacy of the Ohio River as an inland waterway. In brief but extended remarks, he combined the vision of Thomas Jefferson, the pith of Poor Richard, the homespun democracy of Andrew Jackson and the jughandle rhetoric of Daniel Webster.

Ah, yes, the jughandle. (Aside to Chance: "Where's the jug?")

The jug being produced, Senator Whissendyne lifted it joyously.

"Friends, I give you our flag, symbolized here tonight by colors known and loved by all. The red ear, the white liquor and the blue sky of freedom arching over our Indiana fields. Fellow citizens, I drink too . . . too . . . If nominated, I will run; if elected, I will serve."

The speech was over. From the corner of the barn, young men pulled a heavy wagon loaded with corn and began dumping the ears onto the barn floor. The huskers took their place in a circle, men facing the women, and the bee was off in a gale of not-quite-delicate witticisms.

The act of husking corn sent a cerise tide up Zarah's throat and cheeks. It was warm work, of course; then, too, the hope of finding a red ear added an element of excitement. But deeper yet, she was aware of a significance never to be openly acknowledged. She picked up a solid ear, strangely gratifying to her fingers, slightly cooler than her hot palm. With tender violence, she stripped away the outer coverings. Then, passing her hands along the cob, twisted off its silken tassel.

The whole business had so many overtones of scent and touch. . . .

In a ton of corn there are never more than two or three

red ears. Ceres manages that. The bee was half an hour old and a hundred bushels of corn lay heaped on the floor when a scream from Alice Twentyman pierced the shadows overhead.

"Zarah's got a red ear!"

Sure enough, there was the token of fertility in Zarah's hand. She held it up proudly for the benefit of the kitchen jury.

Ordinarily every man in the barn would have tumbled over each other fighting for the privilege of kissing the Queen of Beauty. But no such tumbling took place. Zarah belonged to Anson Woodhull.

He stepped forward to claim his kiss. For the second time that night the exultation of the Psalmist was reaffirmed in Zarah's yielding response:

> *He maketh me to lie down in green pastures. He leadeth me beside the still waters. He restoreth my soul.*

Privacy, the most-prized possession of young lovers, was something that had to be grappled for, snatched at, in the Woodhull farmhouse. Actually, only during the precious hours before sleeping did Zarah have Anson to herself. Old Chance, sole arbiter of what was or was not to be, gave his new daughter-in-law her choice of the four rooms on the second floor. She selected a rough-plastered chamber at the end of the corridor; its diamond-shaped windowpanes faced the river and the rising sun. Here, on a four-poster rope bed, its mattress stuffed with corn sheaves, she discovered the joys—never twice the same—of being Anson's wife.

In amethyst-tinted dawns, she took tenderly regretful leave of him until the coming of twilight. Long, long the hours that he must spend plowing, sowing or reaping in a distant field. It was not considered good form to "bother" one's husband, to interrupt his labors with a plea for gratification. ("Now! Now!") Yet sometimes, bereft by his absence, Zarah stole secretly to the orchard, the hayloft, the barley field, where in a high-noon interlude, between furrows of brown corn, Anson requited her need with his own.

Consequences began to appear within two months of her marriage. The promise of the red ear was being fulfilled. Romantically girl-fashion, Zarah tried to place the hour and the circumstance of her conceiving. Had it been the rainy-twilight passion on the grass of Paddle Creek, the midday ambush behind the haystack or during that first nip of October frost, when the wild geese flew southward in night-long squadrons? Impossible to know. Try to isolate a four-leaf clover in a sea of waving timothy; trap the color of morning, or (as Donne advised) "Go and catch a falling star." But, never, never attempt to fix, amid so many comings-together, the particular spurt that had thrust life into her. She contented herself with the usual preliminaries of counting backward on her fingers and consulting the almanac on its nail over the kitchen stove. These elementary computations over, there was nothing else that she could do, or wished to do, except wait for Anson's discovery of her secret.

In November he became aware of a new richness in the curvature of her hips and breasts—a new fullness in the quality of her responses. He asked her a question, and her "yes" was prelude to a night of insatiable giving and taking. When Zarah awakened, the diamond-shaped panes were pink; she opened her eyes to find Anson gone. From the barnyard came the grunting of pigs, the cackling of hens. By what marvels of adaptability had she grown to love these animal sounds and odors? The answer was somehow bound up with the procreative fury teeming through every nerve and membrane of Zarah's body. Life had streamed into her; it lay there ripening, and in the fullness of time she would deliver it proudly.

Few periods in a woman's life are happier than the months of early marriage, when, discovering that she is already pregnant, she casts aside the fear of pregnancy, asserts the authority of bride-mistress-wife, and with all her female strength advances to subdue the would-be subduer. Anson had the power of probing the psychological needs of this passionate woman; of unloosening old cords that bound her, and of arousing Zarah to fight back with her gorgeous equipment of breasts, thighs, arms and voice.

In winter dusk came on more quickly; supper was served earlier, and it was possible for Zarah and Anson to retire sooner to their private refuge behind the bolted door.

Here, by the pleasantest system of education ever devised, Zarah introduced her husband to some of the books that had nourished her youth. While the mercury shriveled to the bottom of its bulb, and starving dog packs from Kentucky descended upon the comparative fat lands of Indiana, Zarah read (at the rate of a chapter every evening) *Pride and Prejudice* to a man who had never heard of Jane Austen's high place in literature. Anson listened without comment for the most part; smiled sympathetically at Mrs. Bennet's fear lest her daughters be contaminated by contact with young officers in the neighboring military establishment.

At one point he asked, "Did Jane Austen ever marry?"

"No. Why do you ask?"

"I get the feeling that she doesn't know what really goes on between men and women."

Anson's comment gave Zarah a fresh viewpoint on a novel she had always admired. Although *Pride and Prejudice* dealt with marriage and the natural machinations of sisters to secure husbands, it did seem a trifle *spinsterish*. Poor, dear, darling, gifted, world-famous Jane. Would I change places with her, thought Zarah, grappling with male reality in the trough of a corn-sheaf mattress?

There were other realities, too; the ordinary domestic chores of cooking, washing, ironing—drudgery without reward and without end. Grim, repetitive labors, unmentioned by spinster novelists or poets of the "hair and bosom" school, or anyone else, for that matter.

In the Woodhull family, these treadmill duties were performed by Anson's younger sister, Abigail. It was Abigail who rose before daybreak to send the menfolk, full-fed, into the fields. Abby (as she was called) had the stamina of a draft horse. To watch her soak, boil, scrub, rinse and hang out a Monday's washing before 11:00 A.M. "so's it could get the benefit of the noon sun," then gather it in before supper, damp it down in preparation for Tuesday's ironing—why, merely to observe these feats of cleanliness made Zarah bone-weary at first. Yet, under Abby's gradual conditioning, Zarah began to carry a portion of the burden that would inevitably descend upon her when Woolsey Hamer—a neighboring farmer—took Abby as his bride.

The understanding was that Abby would put off her marriage "until Zarah's baby came," or maybe a little after.

What will I do, Zarah wondered, when Abby gets married?

And the answer came: You will do everything that life and love demand of you. You will keep on doing it because,

God help you, there is nothing else in the world that Anson Woodhull's wife wants to do.

With a single exception Zarah's pregnancy was uneventful. She had been exempted from morning sickness or any queasiness. Then, on waking one May morning, her nostrils were assailed by a nauseating odor. The fumes seemed to be rising from the banks of Paddle Creek near the grist mill where Old Chance and Anson were engaged in some kind of fire ritual. On closer investigation Zarah discovered that they were cooking something in a round-bottomed copper kettle. As she approached the kettle, Chance cried triumphantly, "Thar she blows." Simultaneously an evil-smelling mixture belched from the gooseneck spout of the kettle.

Leaning against a sycamore, Zarah vomited. She tried to escape the odor by withdrawing to her room. Useless. The stench pursued her, took possession of the membranes of her nose and throat. At lunchtime she asked Anson what he was doing.

"Just cooking up a batch of whiskey," he told her. "We make two or three barrels every year. Never drink much of it. Chance likes to give it away. Why do you ask, darling?"

"I ask," said Zarah, "because the smell is unbearably offensive."

It was the first unpleasant remark she had ever made to her husband. Anson's reply, "All new whiskey smells that way," brought no balm to her heart or nostrils. Until the distilling process was over, she remained in her room.

Nature so plans matters that most babies are born without complications too difficult for a midwife to handle. In accordance with local custom, Mrs. Emma Fifield, midwife, appeared at the Woodhull place late in June, ousted Anson from his bedroom, and slept on a cot beside the expectant mother.

Emma's prognostications were favorable. "It'll be a boy," she predicted. "And you're going to have an easy time, dearie." But something in Emma Fifield's calculations went astray. Zarah's labor pains began at midnight of July 6 after a day of fierce heat and should have continued for the next twelve hours. The racking pains did continue with increasing severity until, around 6:00 A.M., the miraculous waters broke and Zarah's baby started to rush headlong down the birth canal into the world.

"Never saw a child in such a hurry," said Mrs. Fifield, holding back the infant's skull lest the mother be torn. "Now you just pant like a dog," she told Zarah, "while I get the shoulders clear." Emma, encountering serious difficulties, grew panicky. "Why, this ain't a baby, it's a cannon ball. Trouble is, I can't seem to get it aimed right. Guess I'll have to cut you a bit."

"There'll be no cutting." Anson stepped into the room, brushed the midwife aside. Expecting some such emergency, he had scrubbed his hands and forearms with castile soap, pared his nails, and now proceeded to do what he had done a thousand times—not to human babies, but to small animals: calves, colts, piglets.

Working wrist-deep in the secrets of the woman he loved, Anson rotated the child's shoulders until they were in line with her mother's mesial groove.

"Now, you little demon, come out. Easy does it. Don't be in a hurry." To Zarah he said, "One more spasm, darling. Just one more. Hold on till I tell you to let go."

Writhing like an enormous white whale on a sea of pain, Zarah gritted her teeth and held on.

"*Now*, darling." Something hypnotic in Anson's voice bade Zarah release the uterine muscles that expel a baby from its happy haven. *Inter feces et urinas,* covered with mucous slime, like all things born into this world alive, Zarah's baby came forth.

"Yowll!"

"Yell, you little beggar." Triumph and sympathy were in Anson's voice as he snipped the cord, knotted it close to the baby's belly button.

By the cleft, a girl.

He handed the child to Mrs. Fifield. "Swab out her eyes and mouth." Then, kneeling beside Zarah, he wiped the perspiration from her forehead and said tenderly, "My big, handsome brood mare. You were wonderful—just plain wonderful—just plain wonderful."

Zarah's mind must have been wandering because she said something rather odd.

"If Jane Austen only knew," she whispered to Anson. "Oh, if Janey had only known."

In deference to Old Chance's wishes, they baptized the infant "Eulalia." Zarah liked the name. "In Greek it means 'beautifully talkative,'" she explained to her husband—jiggling the child as though to shake a full-blown vocabulary (with a Harvard accent) from her wet little mouth.

Perhaps the jiggling worked, because when Eulalia—or Laly as they called her—was three months old she began speaking in root syllables comprehensible to no one but Zarah. Laly's first complete sentence, "Give me some more Indian pudding" (accompanied by an imperative banging of her spoon), was uttered on the 369th day of her life. After that, language welled out of her in a higgledy-piggledy uprush. At two she was a golden-haired, bounceable, affectionate daughter of Eve. All these, and smart too. Anson liked to lug her around tucked under his arm, perched on his shoulder or, when she was strong enough, pickaback style, as he went about his daily chores. Remembering the sparse communication between himself and his mother (*her* name had been Eulalia, too), Anson resolved that his first-born daughter should fulfill, to its uttermost limits, the promise of her given name. Yet under the rapidly deteriorating conditions of life on a small corn farm, how could this fulfillment be brought about?

Summer 1878: Not even the boldest prophet fingering the available omens would have dared predict that the United States was entering an era of prodigious expansion. Wherever one looked, wherever one listened, the jaws of farmers sank and the eyes of land speculators glistened. Budget balanced (a tax on whiskey represented half the Federal income), the Administration pursued a flinty anti-inflation program; little foxes gnawed at our vines; and fifty million Americans lay seemingly becalmed at the dead center of inertia.

While waiting for something to happen, jobless men drank —brutally, excessively and, thanks to the newly patented "continuous still," at reduced rates. (*The price of a drink? Five cents you say?*) The second whirlwind of Temperance gathered strength in the Middle West; its insigne was the White Rosette.

And the price of corn began to fall.

With an unmarketable surplus of three hundred bushels in his bins, Chance Woodhull took counsel with his second in command. "Anse," he said, "I hear there's quite a market for new whiskey in Cincinnati."

Anson, chopping ensilage, blew neither hot nor cold. "Where'd you hear that?"

"Judge Hardenburg. He says that rectifiers are paying ninety, ninety-five cents a gallon for all they can lay their hands on."

His father's need of ready money made one set of claims on Anson; Zarah's expressed distaste for whiskey-making checked his enthusiasm for the venture. Dual allegiance spoke. "How deep do you want to wade in?" he asked. "Remember, there's a Federal Excise Tax of seventy cents on every gallon. We'd have to lay out thirty-five dollars in taxes for every barrel of whiskey we made. Add the cost of the barrel itself—that's another dollar—freight charges, demurrage—they'll eat away the best part of another dollar. Then we'll need a special distiller's license—twenty-five dollars right there. Figure it out for yourself, Father."

With a carpenter's pencil Chance went through some simple arithmetical processes on a loose shingle. "S'pose we made twenty barrels—that'd be one thousand gallons—we'd come out a hundred and fifty dollars ahead of where we are now."

Because his father failed to mention the manual labor required to transform two hundred and fifty bushels of corn and small grains into a thousand gallons of whiskey, Anson could not, in good conscience, point out that this not-inconsiderable burden would fall on his shoulders. Old Chance, his joints prematurely gnarled by arthritis, might occasionally lend a hand. Most of the time, however, he'd be the rocking-chair superintendent—a crusty, pain-ridden piece of human machinery requiring special lubrication. Filial compassion for his father (and confidence that Zarah would understand the economic necessity motivating this brief foray into whiskey-making) ruled Anson's decision to go ahead with the job.

He went through the preliminaries of grinding up two hundred and fifty bushels of corn, neither too fine nor coarse and malting a sufficient quantity of barley. To Woolsey Hamer—Abigail's husband—he assigned the task of coopering a two-hundred-and-fifty-gallon mash tub and twenty new oaken barrels. Then, after setting up the classic sixty-gallon pot still (a little farther from the house this time) he submitted the over-all plan for Chance's approval.

"I'll begin by boiling sixty gallons of water in the pot still, then pour it over fifteen bushels of corn and small grains in the mash tub. When fermentation gets going I'll add another sixty, maybe seventy gallons of lukewarm water."

Chance sanctioned every detail. After all, Anse was his disciple.

"I'll work the still four or five times a day for three days," Anson continued. "Meanwhile the second tub will be fermenting."

"Second tub? We only got one."

"I ordered another from Wool Hamer. We need it to get the job done."

"Hm-m . . . Well, seeing as how you'll be doing most of the work, guess an extry mash tub's nuthin' to fuss about." He squinted affectionately at this tall son of his who knew what had to be done and how to go about doing it.

"You're a good boy, Ansy-Bub. Now let's get for'ards with the whiskey."

The first batch went through the still on September 25. The final batch brought Anson well into the middle of October and brought Zarah, already three months pregnant, into a lashing fury.

"How much longer will this sickening business take? I haven't had fifteen minutes alone with you for the past three weeks. You've been sleeping in the barn, working from dawn to midnight. Why, why—knowing that the smell of the stuff nauseates me, why do you—ah!"

Contempt and loathing brought Zarah to the verge of hysteria. Anson, freshly bathed in Paddle Creek to remove every vestige of the whiskey-maker's reek, folded her gently in his arms.

"It's all over, darling. The whiskey's been sold. Chance made a tidy profit on it. I've been sleeping in the barn because I didn't want to come near you while the 'reek' was on me."

That night, snuggling into Anson's shoulder, Zarah drew her first full breath for more than three weeks. "You smell like hay again. Like the man I love."

"Like the man who loves you."

Zarah went up like a hayrick and continued burning with a steady flame until the birth of her second child, another girl, utterly different from older, boisterous Laly.

They baptized the new baby Quincia. Like the fruit (and

the grandfather) from which she took her name, Quince was a strange puckery-faced infant. Silent, lonely, and liking to be left alone, she seemed a tiny Carmelite brooding upon the sins of the world.

Quince, almost two, had yet to speak her first word. Was she timid or tongue-tied? No one seemed to know until Chance picked her up one summer afternoon and patted her melancholy cheek as they sat in a rustic armchair on the veranda.

"You don't have to feel responsible, Quince, for everything that's wrong in the world. We both know that there's a lot goin' on as shouldn't be allowed. But you'n me, we can't do nothin' about it, Quince, 'cept turn the corners of our mouth up." With gnarled thumb and forefingers, he sculptured her lips into the semblance of a smile. "And pretend things aren't as bad as they seem."

The cords of Quincia's tongue were loosed. "Let me hear tick-tock, Grampy?"

Chance placed the silver timepiece against the child's ear. All she needs is bringin' out, thought Chance. "Any time you want to hear my watch tick, just come and tell me," he said to the little girl nestling quietly in his arms. She thanked him with the merest shadow of a smile, then drowsed, the battered watch against her ear.

Tick tock, tick tock.

No two leaves alike in the whole forest. What made sisters, sons, daughters, all different? No pair of days the same, and each hour of the day had its own color, shape. Quince's trusting quiescence, the midafternoon somnolence, age, fatigue, weariness at having seen so many hours come and go, caused old Chance's eyelids to droop late in the afternoon of life. He daydreamed a little of Eulalia under the sycamore tree, of Platt, who could learn, but would not, of Anson, of boyhood days on the Salem wharves, the smell of fresh tea and strong salt cod.

He fell asleep and dreamed that a great ship under full sail was bearing down on him. The ship had a figurehead with vermillion lips and cedar-shining hair. The figurehead stooped, lifted Quince from his arms and tiptoed into the house.

Tick tock, tick tock. . . .

Old Chance never lived to see the price of corn fall through the bottom of the basket. Dimly he realized that the small independent farmer was being threatened by forces beyond his control. Physical ills added their burdens; chalk and gravel (to give them their old-fashioned names) gnawed at his strength. Arthritic finger joints deprived him of the use of his hands. Sharp kidney stones cut at his will to live.

Occasionally, softened by a glass of his own mellow whiskey, Chance expanded a trifle. Brooding in the doorway of his barn, he would emerge from a chin-sunk reverie and sweep a feeble hand over the fields.

"By deserts, it's yours, Anse. Someday you'll get it all."

Precipitate haste did not, however, mark the conveyance of title from father to son. Chance Woodhull was no home-spun Lear eager to divest himself of lands and revenues held for half a century against blight, drought and panic. When cardiac asthma added its tortures, Chance only tightened his grip on purse and property. At night Anson would be awakened by the wheezing cry from his father's bedroom. "My powders . . . I'm choking." To a saucerful of stramonium and belladonna Anson touched a lighted match and held the fuming saucer under his father's nostrils while the old man struggled to expel the air from clamped bronchial tubes. Never a word about the transfer of property. Chance had the disconcerting faculty of looking death hard in the eye without a single mention of title, deeds or conveyances.

Death cannot be stared down forever. One night, with a jagged stone in his ureter and asthma's fist at his windpipe, Chance acknowledged that the end was near. "Listen, son. There's something I want to tell you. . . ."

Deathbed wisdom, though marked by epitaph sameness, has a certain validity. Chance, dying, tried to compress into a few words all that a good man can reasonably say about life. "It always had a meaning, Anse, even though I couldn't have told you on any particular day what the exact meaning was. The best can't be said, and the next best wouldn't be understood. So the things I tell you now are a kind of third best. Like when I say, 'You've been a good son,' or 'I never drew a happy breath since your mother died.' They're both true, but only a part of what I mean."

With a lift of his age-freckled hand, Chance combined counsel and prophecy. "Stick to the land, Anson. Things are changing. Struggle lies ahead. Money, power, machines—'business,' they call it—whether for better or worse, I don't know." His voice began to run down like a weary grindstone.

"Hold onto the land . . . keep your name off promissory notes. . . ." Then a mumble of incoherencies. "I take thee, Eulalia. . . . Going to build ourselves a wagon, boys. . . . Platt, come home . . . forgiven all . . . Zaccheus, he did climb a tree."

For a little while Chance drifted through mists of a coma, then sank like a heavy stone through deep waters.

The will, read on the day of Chance's burial, was a mixture of superb dignity and Mosaic unforgivingness.

In the name of God, Amen. I, Chauncey Woodhull, farmer of Landmark County, Indiana, being weak of body, but of sound mind, knowing that it is appointed for all men to die, do make and ordain this my last Will and Testament.

First, it is my wish that my earthly remains be given decent Christian burial beside those of my beloved wife, Eulalia Platt Woodhull, nothing doubting that our dust will be joined again in union glorious and immortal at the Resurrection of the World.

I direct my executors to distribute annually on September 17 one hundred bushels of corn and ten prime hogs to the poor of Landmark County, thus commemorating by substantial acts of charity that date on which my wife, Eulalia, died.

To my second son, Platt Woodhull, present whereabouts unknown, I give and bequeath the sum of $1.00 (one dollar) and a barrel of corn whiskey he helped me make in November 1873. May he have joy of both.

To my beloved daughter Abigail (Mrs. Woolsey Hamer), the best bread-maker in these parts, I give and bequeath the sum of $100.00 (one hundred dollars) in gold together with ten prime sows and a boar capable of keeping same in rotation.

To my patient and dutiful daughter-in-law, Zarah Osgood Woodhull, I give and bequeath the gold locket formerly belonging to my wife. She may remove the photograph and insert that of herself and my son Anson, to whom she has been a loyal and loving spouse.

The remainder of my estate, real and personal, I give to my son Anson, in recognition of his uncomplaining devotion and skill as manager of my property during the last years of my life. To him, his heirs and assigns forever, I give and bequeath my house, barns, out-buildings, livestock, together with the furniture, tools and gear of every description that may be found in my estate.

To the above-named Anson, I also give, devise and bequeath the lands described in Title Deed No. 105 surveyed by myself and bounded as follows:

On the south, seventy chains and three links along the Ohio River, thence inland N by NE ninety-two chains and seven links from a cairn of feldspar boulders to a clump of elms; thence eastward fifteen degrees and twenty minutes along a dry wall of fieldstone to a dirt road maintained by Landmark County; thence in a westerly direction to the center of a stream known as Paddle Creek, then southerly fourteen degrees, eighteen minutes, along the center of the Creek to the point where it flows into the Ohio River.

Full circle! At thirty, Anson Woodhull, son of Chauncey, entered into his inheritance—the Promised Land.

5.

THE PROMISED LAND

UNCHANGINGLY, WINTER OR SUMMER, this was the manner of Anson Woodhull's waking: like a tall spar he floated for a moment in the shallows of half-consciousness; then opened his hazel-gray eyes and woke up clear through, glad that the night was past and that the separate paths of sleep which even the tenderest lovers must take alone had led him back to Zarah, sleeping at his side.

Earlier in their marriage she had stirred drowsily at his touch, made unintelligible sounds of contentment as they exchanged—in the half hour between sleeping and waking—the gentlest gifts of domestic love.

Now in the amethyst haze seeping through the windowpane, Anson saw his wife lying in the posture of a woman exhausted by a love climb too steep for her strength. She had fallen asleep in the posture of fulfillment—right arm outflung, her left hand cupping the heart breast as if to cherish (or quell, perhaps) the turbulence beneath. To reawaken that turbulence now would be an act of pure selfishness. Anson arose, and by the very act of forbearance shifted the current away from Zarah toward the labors of the day ahead.

Crossing his farmyard in the morning mist, Anson saw much to content him: his house, a ramble of roofs and dormers shaded by sycamores ancient when he was young; his gristmill perched on the bank of Paddle Creek like a side-wheeler steamboat about to tumble into the foaming waterfall below; his barn, a high-pitched red structure, its roof supported by hand-hewn trusses. And the fields! All summer they had been an emerald flaunt; now, plucked of earage and windrowed with cornstalk tepees, and land lay russet exhaustion. The fertilizing union of spike and tassel was over; a thousand bushels of corn, husked and shelled, lay in Anson's barn; uncounted measures of golden meal overflowed the bins of his gristmill. The cornucopia school of art, so fond of tinting the walls of state capitols with allegories of "Ruralia Triumphant," might have found on the Woodhull farm an inexhaustible source of cereal fact.

Anson himself—had he been given to posing—might have stood for the portrait of homestead independence. At thirty-one, a dense black beard made his face seem ten years older than his body.

Any facile crayon or crisp lens could have recorded a dozen details of his appearance: the broad-rimmed straw hat worn with cavalry panache; the high-forked butternut jeans tucked into felt-topped farm boots. But where was the painter, poet or teller of tales capable of recognizing Anson Woodhull for the thing he was: the link between plow and ledger, tilth and trade, the transitional man who appeared so strikingly on the American scene in the final quarter of the last century?

Lifting the hasp of his barn door, Anson saw no portent of change in the flight of the barn swallows through the shadows overhead. The familiar gush of stable odors, warm and ammoniac, carried no hint that today would be different from ten thousand yesterdays. His horses greeted him with their customary banging of hoofs. "Steady, Hooker. Easy, Burnside." As he forked sweet timothy into their mangers, they fell to munching the forage that contained—for all they or Anson knew—the usual quota of four-leaf clovers. Above Anson's workbench, the spider waited for the blue-tailed fly; beneath the planked floor a giant bullsnake, harmless to man but death to rodents, lay in coiled ambush for the corn-thieving rat. Indeed, the auguries were so mixed and contradictory, so very nearly balanced between good and evil, that they resembled life itself. Who could *tell* what they meant?

A token less enigmatic appeared in the enormous farm wagon that occupied the center of the barn floor. Its coat of sparkling blue paint and jacked-up front wheels announced quite simply that preparations for an important journey were well forward. Tomorrow, Anson Woodhull was setting out on a venture that he knew to be hazardous and could only hope would be profitable. After loading his wagon with corn, he would drive forty-eight miles to Cincinnati on the chance that some maker of starch or sirup would offer him a fair price for his cereal cargo.

The chance was slight. With most Indiana farmers burning their corn for fuel, Anson Woodhull had no guarantee that any buyer would offer him the thirty cents a bushel that meant a cash profit on his crop. The profit, in any case, would be small. Loaded to its top boards, the blue wagon could carry only a hundred bushels of corn; with the luckiest management the whole transaction would gross not more than thirty dollars. Hardly a sum to excite avarice. Only a young farmer desperately pinched for cash could rub up enthusiasm for such a venture. Irrational, then, this journey to a dubious market? Say, rather, that certain corpuscles in the Woodhull blood stream battened on a diet of risk. Let neighboring farmers tamely accept the fifteen cents a bushel offered by speculators; Anson Woodhull proposed a chancier fate for himself and his wares. Tomorrow he would go forth to wrestle with the special destiny that dwells in the market place.

The trick was to get there. A wagon needed more than a new coat of paint to fetch it through the muddy sloughs and unbridged streams that lay between Anson's barn and the Queen City of the Ohio. The road would challenge the honesty of wagon pole and doubletree, of linchpin, wheels and axles. Especially the axles.

"Well-greased, load eased." Anson smiled as he found himself remembering his father's home-turned proverb. What a gift for the vernacular Chauncey Woodhull had possessed! He could turn a phrase or build a wagon—and both would be handsome, serviceable, *true*, a quarter of a century later.

With methodical strokes, Anson greased the forward axle, then—like a boy picking up a hoop—lifted the enormous wheel from the barn floor and coupled it snugly onto the spindle. Over the threaded end of the axle tree, he fitted a square nut, as big as a cupcake, and brought it home with the long-handled wrench. Then, facing the wheel, he gave it the counter-clockwise turn natural to a righthanded man. Not even the thrust of his powerful muscles could goad the circling wheel into anything faster than a jog.

The era of the Blue Wain was ending.

Anson slid back a panel of his corn bin; golden kernels cascaded to the floor and for the next two hours he swung a shovel rhythmically while loading the blue wain with corn.

Anson wiped his hands on a grease rag and paused to gaze out the barn door at his inheritance. Directly across the river he could see the low purpling hills of Kentucky—a dark, gloomy land. More cheerful was the barnyard scene directly under Anson's eye. Geese, gone to fat and feathers, waddled about in the phalanx formation of their flying betters, soon to be heard honking southward through chilly twilights. A parliament of fowls clucked obediently behind their presiding rooster. Roscoe, the black boar, wallowed in the ooze rimming the duck pond. The Bess mare, lean in the gaskin and knobby about the hocks, munched loose ensilage at the base of the silo. Rooting, scratching, cackling and procreating, the animals went about their private business of taking the abundant life pretty much as they found it in Anson Woodhull's barnyard.

He had never taken a census of his creatures, yet if a single pig, duck, or goose were missing, he would have felt its absence. Each animal had a sphere, a pecking order and a personality. He watched Ida, the brown hen, a pe-cu-liar fowl, sidling away from the flock. Like a circumspect spinster, she circled the hay-kicking machine, dodged under the strawberry cow and fluttered over the hog trough. Then, having thrown (as she thought) all observers off her trail, Ida darted furtively under the smokehouse.

The tip of Anson's beard wagged ever so slightly at Ida's duplicity. So that was where she laid her eggs. At supper tonight he would say to Laly, his small daughter, "Swap a secret. Tell me yours first." Eyes sparkling at the prospect of a whispered exchange, Laly would stand tiptoe to her father's ear and murmur something about beggar buttons growing in the sunflower patch. Then, quivering with expectation, she would turn her ear for his news. Ida's trickery would be the biggest surprise of the week.

Anson's puff of fantasy vanished as he saw the flaxen head of his six-year-old daughter, a blond Pocahontas, emerge from a heap of corn stalks. Laly's eyes were focused like a bird dog's at the precise spot where Ida had disappeared. Tell the beggar buttons to stop growing, bid the sunflowers be purple, but never, *never* try to keep a barnyard secret from Laly.

Back to work. From a wooden rack, Anson lifted a huge double harness and began inspecting the leathern gear. Mended at every point, the ancient harness was almost past saving; no quantity of saddle soap could conceal its worn tugstraps or strengthen the patched breeching. What he really needed was a new harness. He had priced one last spring. Thirty dollars. By now, thirty-five. Odd, he thought, that the cost of store goods kept rising while the price of corn fell steadily. Scythes and grindstones, combs, coffee and gingham went up and up, while corn—the prop and basis of the whole economy—had been falling steadily for the past five years.

Something was out of kilter. . . .

He was repairing the traces when Laly, sapphire excitement in her eyes, corn leaves in her flaxen hair, came skipping into the barn. Both hands were behind her back.

"Swap a secret with you Daddy."

Ritual of the game; private sharing of knowledge inaccessible to others. To prolong the shared moment, Anson asked, "A big one?"

Laly's bobbing chin assured him that this was the ultimate in secrets. "Tell me yours first," she bargained.

"Don't know's I've got anything special to swap."

The bubble of Laly's secret burst unbidden. She held out both hands, disclosing two large brown eggs. "Ida's!" she exclaimed. "One's still warm. Guess where I found them, Daddy."

Anson became a forty-niner questioning a fellow prospector about the source of some fabulous nuggets. "Where?"

"Under the smokehouse. Deep, *deep* under."

"H-mm. So that's where Ida's been laying her eggs. Was she setting on them?"

Laly volunteered some surprising information. "These aren't setting eggs, Daddy."

"How can you tell?"

Laly held the brown egg against her ear as if listening to a conch shell murmuring its secret.

"I just *know*."

Was it feminine intuition or did the child have actual knowledge of Ida's private arrangements? Anson decided not to inquire. To keep Laly near him a little longer, he coaxed, "How about a memory gem?"

Laly's memory gems were a marvel to her father. At three, while eating applesauce at supper, she had announced:

> *Water won't quench fire,*
> *Fire won't burn stick,*
> *Stick won't beat dog,*
> *Dog won't jump over the stile*
> *And the old woman won't get home tonight.*

Where had the child picked up this odd rigmarole?

"There's only one explanation," said Zarah. "She must have heard me saying it to Quincia when I put her to bed last night."

"It puzzles me, Zarah."

Delighted that the Brattle Street seed should flourish in Indiana loam, Zarah had sown diligently. Laly's repertory grew; at six it included "The Children's Hour," "The Chambered Nautilus" and "Sheridan's Ride"—complete with gestures from the Delsarte School.

"Which memory gem do you want, Daddy?"

"Let's see now. Run off a few samples."

Laly fell into a military stance. "Rifleman, shoot me a fancy ball/Straight at the heart of yon prowling vidette."

"Or—" her voice and lifted hand were elegiac—"I can give you: 'The breaking waves dashed high/On a stern and rockbound coast.'"

"Mighty fine pieces, both of them. Mention a few more."

Laly skimmed through her repertory. "Well, there's 'Between the Dark and the Daylight,' but that sounds better after supper. Then there's 'Lars Porsena of Clusium'—only it's got about eighty-eight stanzas, and there wouldn't be time for all those."

She wanted her father to say, "Go ahead, we've got all afternoon, Laly," but she knew that preparations for a journey were claiming him. Loneliness at the prospect of her father's absence saddened her for a moment; bubbling resilience brought her up on exactly the right note.

"I know just the one, Daddy, 'This Way the Water Comes Down at Lodore.' Mama gave it to me yesterday." Laly placed her eggs in a seam of the barn floor, straightened her little apron and was off in declamatory flight. She described the mountain source of Lodore's cataract; how it slept for a time in its own tiny lake; then, awakening, glided through meadow and glade, sparkling and darkling until it reached the place of its steep descent. Here Laly's voice really took hold:

> The cataract strong
> Then plunges along,
> Rising and leaping,
> Sinking and creeping
> Swelling and sweeping,
> Spouting and frisking,
> Turning and twisting,
> Around and around
> With endless rebound;
> Smiting and fighting,
> A sight to delight in;
> Confounding, astounding
> Dizzying and deafening the ear with its sound.

Awl suspended, Anson listened. He had never heard about this marvelous stream that somehow resembled the waters swirling toward the paddle wheel of his own gristmill. While barn swallows darted through the shadows overhead, and an autumnal haze filled the barn with golden notes, Anson was mysteriously transported as Laly continued:

> And dashing and flashing and splashing and clashing,
> And so never ending, but always descending,
> Sounds and motions forever-and-ever are blending,
> All at once and all o'er, with a mighty uproar,
> And this way the water comes down at Lodore.

Her memory gem delivered, Laly became a little girl again. Eager for her father's reward, she wrapped her arms in a catamount hug around his thigh. He kissed her flaxen hair, caramel-sweet with the odor of childhood. "My smart, wonderful Laly," he murmured.

Happy that she had pleased this best, most loved of audiences, she picked up her eggs and flew across the barnyard to the kitchen door.

One thing was sure—sure as the awl in Anson's fist: Laly was smart. She should be at school. But the nearest school was at Landmark, seven miles away. Whatever education the child received would have to come from Zarah.

And Zarah, heavens knew, already had her hands full.

A side slip of the awl gouged the horny flesh at the root of Anson's thumb. Always a bad sign when a tool slipped. "Pushing too hard," Chance would say.

Anson hung the refurbished harness in its rack and gazed at the two-o'clock aspect of the sky. Time for a pipe and a drink of water. He walked toward his well, fed by springs that even the longest drought couldn't discourage. Down went the bucket with a splash; the windlass hoist brought it up brimming. Anson drank nearly a quart, splashed some of the cooling lotion over his injured thumb. Refreshing, medicinal, cool. So *That's how the water came down at Lodore.* Maybe these poets dealt in something profounder than rhyme.

He was lighting his corncob when he saw Zarah rinsing a tubful of clothes on the back porch. Arms bare to the elbows, Zarah was performing the eternal female chore of scrubbing away the stains of the world. A compassion for all women, a feeling that they had gotten the thankless end of the stick, was mingled with wonder at the patience and durability that his wife brought to her tasks. Who would have thought that Zarah Osgood, daughter of a Harvard professor, could have put on the domestic yoke so willingly and borne it with so much grace?

Watching his wife pour the tub of sudsy water over the roots of a sunflower, Anson felt a sudden desire to summon her in the special voice that had brought her to his side so often during the first years of their marriage. Then she had come running toward him eager for secret renewal of the mystery that could take place anywhere. Lips wet, eyes closed, half distracted by her own need, she had strengthened him with the fresh lusciousness of love.

Seldom now in daylight did they even see each other. Well, it would keep. They both knew that. In token of shared certainty, he waved to his wife across the teeming yard. Busy at stringing diapers on the clothesline, Zarah failed to catch the signal. Anson had the slightly bewildered feeling of a boy whose pebble, tossed into a spring, makes no ripple.

He sucked at the gash on his thumb and felt a need to have Zarah tend it with arnica. Childish. A scratch wasn't that important. Amber-colored drops of lymph were already at work in the wound. It would be all right.

A truant mood induced by midafternoon heat tempted him into a little orchard between his house and the road. He sat on the grass under a gnarled winesap, resting his head against its shaggy bark. From the orchard floor he picked up a bruised windfall, bit absently into its one good cheek and let unexpected sweetness dissolve on his tongue. Semi-liquid honey oozing from its core resembled the colorless fluid forming at the root of his thumb; from buried springs of association rose memories of another hurt that had gone untended, too.

Long ago when this tree was young, his mother had called him from play. "Come along, Anse. Shake down some apples for me. Your father wants a pie." Eager at the prospect of helping, Anson had climbed to the topmost bough and brought down a hail of juicy winesaps. He had expected a rewarding word or smile, but his pie-minded mother merely gathered the fruit into her apron and marched off toward the kitchen without a single backward glance at her eight-year-old son.

Forsaken, Anson had consoled himself by pretending to be a lookout in the topmast of a whaler. The billowy cornfield was his ocean; imagination produced the necessary whale. "*Thar she breeches,*" he shouted, as leviathan flukes churned the green waves. "*She blows, she blows.*" (Those were the cries that put your shipmates on notice.) Then and there he decided to run away to sea and come back with gifts of jeweled combs for his mother. "*Lower away the whale boats.*" Standing in the bow of the first boat, Anson hurled the terrible harpoon. Doom-struck, the whale dived. Stepping aside to dodge the line that whizzed out of the bucket, Anson came tumbling down from the tree top, his hand scratched by

the rough bark. Surely this was worth a fingerful of maternal
salve. Yet when he showed his mother the hurt, she sniffed
impatiently.

"Don't plague me with trifles. You know where the arnica
is. *Your father wants a pie.*"

Not unloved. Worse. Not loved enough!

Jelly of remembrance, composed of many flavors—lymph,
apple core and lotion of love-denied—quivered within him.

Suddenly bereft, Anson longed for a glimpse of his mother's
face. From the fob pocket of his trousers he drew a silver
watch, the key-winder bequeathed him by Chauncey. He
opened the back cover and gazed at the faded daguerreotype
of a woman with severe cheekbones, tight-drawn hair and un-
compromising eyes (gray in the picture, deep blue in life).
It was Eulalia Woodhull, born Platt, his mother—a woman
worn out at forty by grindstone drudgery, childbearing, mis-
carriages, stillbirths, caused or complicated by the ceaseless
female disorders common to farm wives.

The seconds, each asking a bitter question, ticked past. . . .
Had Eulalia Woodhull ever responded joyously to love?
Yes.

When had rapture turned to staleness?

A bee droned past, legs heavy with golden dust.

Tell, bee. Say, flowers.

The faded photograph blurred; mother and wife merged
into a single image. At what moment of the future—gaunt,
dry-lipped, wearied by the act of love and fearful of its consequences—would Zarah begin to dread her husband's approach?

Troubled by the question, unwilling to hear the answer,
Anson snapped the watch case shut. Darkness imprisoned
the face of past and future as the seconds ticked on.

A squealing of pigs and barking dogs, commingled with
profanity grated from a voice box, human, male, aroused
Anson from his musings. A caravan was coming down the
road, kicking up a cloud of yellow dust. As the dust storm
approached, the din was subordinated to the overpowering
odor churned up by hogs in motion.

Leaning against his gate, Anson saw a hard-working collie
and a small boy worrying the swine to a halt. These were
merely outriders, guided by a central intelligence located
somewhere near the center of the herd. As dog and boy harried

the pigs to a grunting stop, a brown slat of a man extricated himself from the herd. The dust of many roads overlaid but could not fill the concavities of his cheeks and eye sockets. White eyelashes and red, sore eyes gave him the look of an albino. That such a parched, almost fleshless creature could still perspire was a marvel in nature, a marvel certified when the pig drover wiped his narrow forehead with the tail of a doughnut-colored shirt.

"One pig jes' standing still is ornery 'nough," he said to Anson. "But now you take a hundred pigs and try to *get* them some place—then, mister, you got trouble." With his whip he slashed at the swarm of green flies that followed him like miniature buzzards awaiting carrion.

"Name's Plaskett. Ludd Plaskett. Drivin' a few choice porkers up from Kentucky and thought I'd absquatulate past for a neighborly back and forth."

Anson had never laid eyes on Ludd Plaskett before, but the pig drover seemed to know exactly where he was. "Last time I came by here, we did a little business—me and a old party, that is." His emphasis on "old" was both a stress and query.

"That was my father," said Anson. "He died a couple of years ago."

The pig drover's condolences were interrupted by a russet boar making a wild scoot for freedom. He had traveled scarcely yards when the freckled youth pulled out a slingshot and brought the rogue down with a slug behind its ear.

Mr. Plaskett toyed proudly with the tassel of his whip. "My boy Reb," he volunteered. "Right name's Richmond, but I hold that Reb and Richmond are pretty well identicated by recent facts known to all."

Mr. Plaskett was about to fight the Civil War all over again when the swarm of horseflies stung him to the business at hand. "Got any sellable pigs?"

"Could be," said Anson. "Depends on the offer."

"*Which*, like the feller says, depends on the pigs."

The amenities over, Anson opened his gate and led the pig merchant toward a stout pen where seventy-five prime hogs were snouting at corncobs. Ludd Plaskett might have been watching a convocation of chipmunks. Willing to wound, yet commercially afraid to strike, he opened negotiations. "How many do you want to let go?"

"Fifty—if the price is right."

The pig drover decided to make things clear at once. "There's only one price, squire, and Ludd Plaskett don't have no say in fixin' it. I jus' perquestellate the pigs up to the slaughterhouse in Cincinnati and get my two cents a pound on the hoof, same's everyone else." He lounged, toadying-frank, a countryman lining up with one of his own kind against city practitioners. "Fact that a pig gets decarcerated into hams, smoked shoulders and chops, all fetchin' ten cents a pound *re*tail—not countin' the bristles, tripes and *lard*— why, the lard alone sells for a nickel a pound—as I say, leavin' out these various considerations of profit, Ludd Plaskett gets two cents a pound and no argle-bargle about it."

"You're crying on the wrong shoulder," said Anson.

Ludd Plaskett felt the master touch. He broke off his whining harangue and made a firm offer. "Give you a dollar a head."

Anson countered with a short, humorless laugh. "These aren't Kentucky shoats. They're prime Indiana porkers, corn-fed from the day they came off the buttons. Not a hog in this pen weighs less than two hundred pounds."

"Rate I travel at, they'll drop thirty pounds gettin' to Cincinnati."

"That'll still leave a lot of pig."

"If they all get there." Ludd Plaskett launched into a catalogue of the hazards connected with pig droving. "First off, the boars'll start fighting, and right away a couple of them kill theirselves. Then some of the sows get drowned crossing the ford at Squirrel Hash—not to mention the dozen or so that'll be so plumb tuckered they'll jes' lay down and die."

Balancing risk against profit, he revised his offer upward. "Fair's fair, though. Give you a dollar twenty-five apiece."

Anson had expected at least two dollars a head for his pigs. A compromise was in order. "Make it one seventy-five."

"Meet you halfway. Give you a dollar and half a piece."

Anson shook his head. "Guess we can't do business."

Ludd Plaskett called up his reserves. "Take eighty dollars and I'll throw in this whip."

"Never use a whip." It was true. Anson had never laid a lash on any of the creatures that helped him through the labor of the day. No use haggling further with this fellow. Like a wrestler breaking off an unproductive hold, Anson started to walk away.

Across his eye field, he saw Laly—pitcher in one hand, pie

plate in the other—dashing toward the pig drover's son. The feminine works of mercy. . . . Feed the hungry stranger. Send him on his way filled, rejoicing, even though your menfolks can't do business together.

The deadlock was broken by a new offer from Mr. Plaskett —an oblique, wheedling offer, with a smack of remembered relish about it. "Last time I came past here and traded hogs with that old feller—your father, I mean—we bound the bargain with a gallon of whiskey. Ain't never drunk nothin' so good." His parched membranes were delivering him up. "Got any left?"

"Barrels of it."

"Then you jes' fill me a gallon jug—providin' it's the same stuff I got last time—and we'll call it a deal at ninety dollars."

Fifty pigs—going for ninety dollars. The money (if Anson took it) would represent half of his cash income for the year. Absurd that so much care and toil, plus the tons of corn consumed by his pigs, should bring such a meager price. Payable not in good minted specie either but in greenback foxfire, illusive, receding in value when you tried to buy anything with it.

Going, going . . . No other bids? *None.*

Anson took the damp wad of greenbacks from the pig drover.

Gone! Ten thousand pounds of pork at less than a cent a pound.

"The whiskey," Ludd Plaskett was saying.

From beneath his workbench Anson selected a molasses-colored jug bearing the legend *1 Gal.* in low relief. "Sample this—it's eight years old."

Plaskett uncorked the jug, inhaled deeply. "A Blow for Freedom," he said, then closed his eyes and drank. Either the whiskey paralyzed his vocal cords or language failed him. Again he drank; this second tug broke the spell.

"Jee-*rusa*lem!" he gasped. " 'Milk of Paradise,' that's what I call it."

A wave of euphoria, the prime effect of good whiskey, began to rise in Mr. Plaskett. He had entered the yard a whining haggler, a dusty pendulum swinging between wheedle and bluff. After three drinks he became confidential, expansive, ducal in vista yet not above sharing his tipple with a worthy companion.

"Letsh both strike 'nuther blow for Freedom," he suggested and took no offense when Anson declined.

Mr. Plaskett culled fifty pigs from the pen, just as they came—no argle-bargle about it this time—and shooed them toward his roadside herd.

For that afternoon, at least, Ludd Plaskett need not fear the heat of the sun, the dust of the road or the hazards of the ford. Having consumed a scant pint of the amber-colored liquid from his jug, the pig drover was master of his fate, a conquistador of commerce and, withal, something of a jongleur. As he disappeared in a cloud of yellow dust he trolled a stave:

> *Come along, Jack, come along, Joe,*
> *We'll rove the banks of the O-hi-o.*

At the bend of the road, Reb turned to wave at Laly. Standing beside her father, the little girl answered with a lift of her hand.

"He's the nicest boy I ever met, Daddy," she confided. "See what he gave me." She showed Anson a Minié ball—a replica of the conical slug that had stopped the russet boar in its tracks.

Anson hefted the missile in the palm of his hand. "He must have thought you were a nice girl, Laly. A boy like Reb doesn't waste his ammunition."

The little girl started to ask, "Do you think he'll come back this way?" when she saw a red-wheeled gig pull at the gate. "It's the R.F.D. man, Daddy. He's putting a letter in our box."

"Fetch it, Laly. That's a good girl. I'll be in the barn."

The letter that Laly fetched bore the postmark *Cincinnati, O.* By the flourish of penmanship on its envelope, Anson recognized the handwriting of his brother Platt. With misgivings he slit the envelope and drew out a single sheet of note paper.

DEAR BRO ANSE [it ran]:

The bad penny again. This time plugged clear through the center till nothing's left but the rim and that's pretty well scratched up.

The reason I'm writing you is that I ran into Sen.

Whissendyne, the old wind bag, while standing at the bar at the Crescent House in Cincinnati. He told me Pa died a couple of years ago and remembered me in his will which sort of surprised me considering what I done. Old Whiskers didn't say what Pa left me or how much, but in my present circumstances anything, no matter how small, would come in handy because I'm flat broke. If it's land or gear I'll sell out to you cheap. Please let me know by return mail. Address me at 211 Gay St., Cincy. I've got a room here, not much of a place and behind in the rent at that. Regards at home.

Yrs,
PLATT

P.S. You and me always got along all right so I know you'll do the fair and square.

A typical Platt document. Tomblike silence for nine years, then a hair-on-fire cry for help. Vague rumors of Platt's escapades had drifted back to Landmark. Travelers had seen him dressed to the nines in the card saloon of some river boat or lounging about the paddock at Louisville. Faro, dice, roulette, horses. Poor Platt, always dependent on the fall of a card, the turn of a number. And now plugged "clear through the center."

The bad penny . . .

Still, Platt was within his legal rights in asking for information about his inheritance. Property with a certain value—to wit, one barrel of whiskey—was due him. Anson would only be fulfilling the word and spirit of Chauncey's will in rendering up an account of the property. Whatever Platt's knowledge of good and evil might be, Anson's deepest instinct was to bring aid and comfort to his young brother.

Purple dusk, grayed by falling mist, settled over the barn as he gave his animals their evening ration of corn and hay. After supper he would return to the barn and lash Platt's barrel of whiskey onto the tailpiece of the blue wain.

Hungry, tired, eager for the sight of Zarah's face, he crossed the farmyard to his house.

The kitchen was in a pre-supper hubbub not unpleasant to a hungry man who enjoys the odors of cooking and the clatter that life makes at close quarters. Laly was setting the table with blue-ringed crockery; Ozzie, a two-year-old Pantagruel, sucked his thumb and banged the tray of his highchair with a wooden spoon. On the built-in settle beside the sink, five-year-old Quincia was winding one of her eternal bandages around the tail of her newest patient, Frisk, a shepherd pup. And at the stove, Zarah Woodhull tested sizzling pork chops with a long iron fork.

To Anson, the central figure in this thronging kitchen was Zarah, the wife-mother on whom all action turned. At twenty-seven, she had taken on the ripe contours properly valued by sculptors and husbands. She wore a woolen dress of Shaker simplicity; the only ornament on her person was an amber comb, highbacked, adding the coronet touch that Zarah always managed to maintain through a long day of washing, cooking and serving. Now, as she patiently turned the chops, the comb was slightly askew.

At his touch the old throbbing began—but faintly, like the vibrations of a drumhead that has lost its original tautness. Anson sensed the muffled quality of his wife's response. He knew better than to ask, "What's the matter?" Many things could be the matter with a woman still in the third quarter of a long day's work; no important ground could be gained by discussing them at the wrong time.

At the copper-jacketed pump Anson washed his face and hands, then helped Zarah carry laden platters from stove to table: squares of hot cornbread, a platterful of fried pork chops, potatoes with their jackets on, all made the more relishable by pungent horseradish and mustard pickles.

Grace before meals was not a tradition in the Woodhull household. Sufficient praise, thought Anson, to enjoy food in the company of loved ones. As father and husband, it was his function to create an atmosphere of peace and good temper that children, particularly, look forward to and will always remember. He began by sympathizing humorously with Ozzie's spoon-thumping.

"Mother, Osgood's *hungry*. Don't know's I blame him. Works hard all day mopping up the kitchen floor and helping around generally. When suppertime comes, he wants his vittles." Anson laid a slab of butter between layers of hot cornbread. "Never mind, Oz, your own father will feed you."

He popped a morsel of crumbs and butter into the mouth of his infant son. The delicious mixture put an end to Ozzie's banging. Surfeit of oral bliss traveled along his digestive system and registered audibly at the farther end. Everyone laughed. Dizzied by applause, Ozzie tried for an encore. His eyes bulged while art vainly attempted to imitate nature. He drooled sheepishly.

"Close, but no cigar." Anson patted his son's head, then broke off another piece of cornbread and buttered it for Quincia. This timid second child of his needed bringing out. "What's my Pumpkinseed been doing all day?"

Quincia regarded the corncake wanly, as though it belonged to someone else. "Make bandages," she murmured.

The child was always making bandages from fabrics of every color, shape and material. A little Florence Nightingale.

"Fine, fine. How many did you make?"

"Eleven. A white one and a green one."

Laly's laughter was brassy-superior. "One and one ain't eleven."

Anson came to Quincia's defense. "Are you sure of that, Eulalia?" Gentle reproof lay in the use of her full name. He took a pencil stub from his pocket, fished out a piece of paper and drew the numeral 1. Beside it he placed a similar numeral, then held up the paper for Laly's inspection.

"There's one and one," he said. "Side by side, they make eleven, don't they?"

Laly was about to defend the common-sense proposition that one and one make two, when circling plates put an end to the discussion of higher mathematics. Zarah was having her own arithmetical difficulties serving the various members of her family. Anson got three pork chops and two boiled potatoes; Laly and Quincia one pork chop and a single potato. Ozzie's trencher consisted of a potato, mashed and doctored with brown pork gravy. Not Euclidian problems exactly, but something you had to keep your mind on.

She served Anson first, the others in turn, then began spooning gravied potatoes into Ozzie's mouth. Between gulps he sucked noisily at his thumb. Zarah pulled it out, each time wondering how long Ozzie's drooling and thumbsucking would continue. Privately she wondered if her third child were full-witted. Listless, withdrawn, Zarah picked at her own food; an unaccustomed scolding note edged her voice when Quincia spilled a glass of milk. What a treadmill she's on, thought Anson, this handsome girl with the coronet hair. How weary of kettles, tubs—and children! He wooed her obliquely in an effort to bring a nondomestic note into the conversation. Without laboring either humor or pathos, Anson succeeded in describing the drover, before and after the jug-handle incident.

"You should have seen his face when he took that second swallow." Anson mimicked Plaskett's exclamation: "Jee-*rusa*-lem . . . Milk of Paradise, I call it. . . ."

By a momentary lift of her green-gray eyes, Zarah rewarded her husband's try. She even smiled faintly at his portrayal of the tipsy pig herder. These coins of appreciation spent, she relapsed into an energy-hoarding silence.

Worried for Zarah's sake, Anson ate his dessert of Indian pudding. How happy the dinner would be if Zarah were at her responsive best! Yet how could any woman be expected to sparkle after twelve hours of domestic drudgery?

Laly, scraping her second dish of Indian pudding, was ready for after-supper fun. "Let's play 'Old Man's Soup,' Daddy," she suggested. "Me first."

Anson welcomed the opportunity for lightness. "Here we go: What do you put in the old man's soup?"

"Toenails," said Laly.

Anson turned a mock-horrified eye on his daughter. The object of the game was either to make her laugh or say something other than "toenails." He tried to come over her with his first question.

"Tadpoles, did you say?"

Laly's screwed-up face and determined mind were proof against such simplicities. "Toenails," she repeated.

"Who kisses you good night?"

"Toenails."

Anson probed for a weak spot. "What did you give Reb to eat this afternoon?"

Laly bubbled for a moment. "Toenails."

Suddenly Anson switched tactics. He stuck his forefinger between Ozzie's front teeth and was about to ask, "What are these?" Ozzie, pleased to find something really substantial in his mouth, bit down hard.

"Ouch, leggo, leggo," cried Anson. "Oww—oo—ow, help he's killing me." His exaggerated expression of pain pulled Laly into the tittering trap he had laid for her. She collapsed with laughter; even Zarah smiled.

Now it was Quincia's turn. When Anson put the question "What do *you* put in the old man's soup?" she looked up at him bravely and replied:

"Everlasting."

It was the name of a common field flower.

Curious to know how heavy an emotional burden Quincia could stand, Anson framed a tender question. "If you were going on a long journey far from home and could never come back—never, *ever*—even though you wanted to, who would you take with you?" Anson paused for emphasis. "Me, or Everlasting?"

The alternative was too much for Quincia's little soul. At the thought of leaving her home and father forever, or wandering through the world accompanied only by a wildflower, tears started from her eyes.

"I'd take *you*, Daddy," she sobbed, and ceased only when Anson comforted her in his arms. "Of course you'd take me, darling," he murmured, soothing her with caresses. And when he asked his strange second child to tie a bandage around his sore thumb, her tears were quite forgotten.

The supper was over. Ozzie slept face downward in his plate. Anson began carrying the dishes from table to sink. He would wash them while Zarah undressed the children and gave Laly a skimped reading lesson.

With a two-hour stint still before him in the barn, he lighted his lantern at the kitchen door. "Get the children to bed early so we can have a little time to ourselves," he said, bending to kiss Zarah's hair at the place where the amber coronet was still askew.

The dahlias on the china lampshade cast a coral glow over the marble-topped table, the Boston rocker, and the sewing basket on Zarah's lap. Chair, lamp and table made a three-piece sanctuary to which she turned for the pleasantest hour of the day—the "parlor hour" they had called it in Cambridge—a time for music, conversation and optional sewing. How distant, both in time and place, Cambridge seemed now! Yet its influence was visible in the sitting room that Zarah had created for Anson and herself. A hooked rug covered the center of the uneven floor; a spinet in one corner, book shelves in another, the drawn curtains of turkey red and gilt-framed daguerreotypes on the mantelpiece behind the Franklin stove all supported the parlor tradition of Zarah's past. In the early years of her marriage she had painted the china lampshade and woven the rag rug; she had dyed the curtains, snatched the spinet (for three dollars) from a farm auction, then arranged these poor props into a semblance of her Brattle Street background.

Usually the lamp-lighting ritual revived her, but tonight she was so exhausted that her pleasure died with the sulphur match between her fingers. Weary-eyed, she gazed about the sitting room, the Brattle Street islet she had tried to create in this sea of Indiana corn. Not that the corn was alien; no stalk or creature Anson loved was beyond her care. But somehow the thing had slipped out of control—the sheer drudgery of the place was wearing her down. How long could she go on being a childbearing, dishwashing slavery? A grindstone giving herself away in sparks?

Yet how, loving Anson as she did, could she escape being all of these? Every act and aspect of her life were part of the unbreakable contract between Anson and herself. The sewing box on her lap—Anson's gift on their first anniversary—was a token of that contract. On its lacquered cover were two mother-of-pearl initials: A to Z. Anson to Zarah. Alpha to Omega. First to last and everything in between. Till death do us part.

Dome

Unbidden, the phantom colloquy began. Of *many-colored glass?* No, that was Shelley's. Then it must be that other dome, the mysterious Coleridge thing. Yes, of course, *In Xanadu* . . .

> *In Xanadu did Kubla Khan*
> *A stately pleasure-dome decree:*

Seldom of late had the voices troubled Zarah. What had started them off tonight? The domed curve of the lampshade? The mother-of-pearl A on the cover of her sewing box? No matter. The pack was already in full cry; nothing could stop the remorseless baying now. Could Zarah have chosen her pursuer this evening, he would be someone soothing and manageable, like Longfellow, her old Brattle Street neighbor, whose songs gushed from his heart. But Coleridge! A mad, strange-making drug-swallower. And "Kubla Khan," the strangest poem of all. Zarah had never understood its meaning and would be no match for its dread imagery tonight.

To dull the insistent voices she opened her sewing box and hesitated between a spool of white cotton thread and a stouter grade of black. Should she patch the seat of Laly's drawers or anchor more firmly the suspender button on the pants that Anson would wear tomorrow? Wife tussled weakly with mother. Wife won.

The pants, like everything else in the Woodhull household, gave testimony to the relentless battle between stubborn material and hard wear. Use, scuffing away nap and pile, would reach the heart of the stuff at last—but, oh, the long dying. Zarah broke a length of thread, moistened the end with her tongue, then rolled the fiber strands with a point fine enough to enter the needle's eye. She doubled the thread for extra strength, knotted it and began sewing the bone button to the stout fabric. Wonderful stuff, thread—given enough of it, a good housewife could repair anything.

But what happens, Zarah wondered, when the threads of a woman's body begin to lose their stretch, when a night's rest no longer mends her for the new day? What happens when she realizes that love is exhausting her energy faster than life can replenish it? Shall she be sullen, resentful or resigned? Shall she make up the physical deficit out of untapped strength, or, mindful of self-preservation, cry "Enough, enough"?

Zarah Woodhull didn't know. She really could not decide. During the seven years of her married life, there had always been an emotional surplus, an artesian plenty. Now, signals of scant warned her that the sources of love were being overtaxed. Confirmed after weeks of anxious calendar-watching, the newest claim on her energy frightened her. Today and for many days past, she had felt herself being dragged toward a brink of desperation.

> *Where Alph, the sacred river, ran*
> *Through caverns measureless to man*
> *Down to a sunless sea.*

A slow suspicion began to form in Zarah's mind. Painful experience had taught her that these fugues were echoes rising from secret sources in her own life, that they were trying to disclose truths hidden below the surface of consciousness. What were they saying now? As the strange poem unfolded, Zarah listened more attentively. It was easy, she knew, to find parallels where none existed. And of course it was impossible to nail down, like a carpet, the fluid mystery of a poet's meaning. Still, if one had to, one could try to understand.

In lightning flashes the lines disclosed a landscape both familiar and demonic—sinuous rills, incense-bearing trees, and caverns slanting athwart cedarn covers. Peopling the scene were persons that defied too-exact identification. There was a damsel with a dulcimer, a woman waiting for her lover, and a man with flashing eyes and floating hair. Across this terrain Alph, the sacred river, meandered, gushed, flung up fountains. It was all quite mystifying, until the sacred river (on it third time around) flung up an unexpected image:

As if this earth in fast thick pants were breathing.

"Thick pants"? The absurdity of the figure phrase caused Zarah to smile. *There* was a Hibernianism for you—a comic tumble she had never noticed before. Had Coleridge realized it? And what would Monsieur Delsarte recommend as a gesture?

The fugal voices, encountering Zarah's funnybone, broke off with a humorous sputter.

Before they could begin again, she heard leviathan thrashings in the kitchen where Anson was giving himself a stand-up bath in preparation for his journey the next morning. Part of male cleanliness was the noise that went with it, a wonderful grampus noise, as though a creature half whale, half man were splashing about in the wash tub. Anson's off-key bass rose above the sloshes. It sounded like "Rock of Ages," but one couldn't ever tell.

The crockery doorknob turned. Anson, bare from the waist up, brown as a Lascar and smelling of tar soap, came in rubbing his hair with a huckabuck towel. The dahlia-painted lampshade cast a pinker glow; the fugal migraine stopped throbbing. This was the renewing hour, the trysting time, reached after a long day of waiting and postponement. Whether they spent it in silence or conversation mattered little to either of them. They would spend it together.

Anson shook himself like a retriever, sat on the hassock beside Zarah's chair, and handed her the towel. Head bent, he awaited her drying ministrations.

"Did you rinse out all the soap?" Not Thisbe to Pyramus, or Isolde to Tristan. Better.

"Tried to. Got some of it in my eyes."

"Some in your ears too." Zarah screwed up a corner of the towel and went in after the suds. Then, with fingers and towel, she fluffed up her husband's hair until it floated like a black thundercloud around his head.

"Now for the snarls," she said.

Anson handed her a gap-toothed thing used by every member of the family except herself. I must add "new comb" to my list, thought Zarah, raking the coarse teeth through her husband's hair. "Bend down so I can reach the back." Anson's forehead rested on her bosom while comb and fingers completed the grooming. "There." She gave the back of his head a finishing pat. As if expecting more, Anson waited. "And *there*." Zarah's kiss nuzzled at the nape of his neck.

Thin-walled, like a bubble, the moment of happiness expanded into a dome of many-colored glass. When it broke, Anson sat down in the horsehair rocker, selected a long-stemmed churchwarden from a pipe rack and hoisted his feet onto a shagreen-covered hassock. He was the householder at ease, the well-bathed husbandman, stocking-footed, content to puff at his home-grown tobacco, while Zarah busied herself scribbling notations on a slip of paper. This was her list—the little articles, mostly feminine, that Anson would pick up for her in Cincinnati.

Both were practicing a mild species of deception sprung of mutual solicitude: Anson hesitating to tell Zarah that he had lashed Platt's barrel of whiskey onto the tailboard of the blue wain; Zarah, not wishing to mar this shared hour of peace, had decided to let the calendar business go unmentioned for the present. They parried with commonplaces.

"Will you be starting early tomorrow?"

"First crack."

"How long do you think you'll be gone?"

"Five days, six maybe." The longest time they had ever spent away from each other. An eon. "Got your list ready?"

"Wait till I see if I've remembered everything." Zarah's eyes ran down the short column of needs that she had been compiling for the past week. To each item she added a private parenthesis of comment.

One bristle toothbrush (*was it true about a tooth for every child?*)

Three oz. lavender sachet (*frangipani, a long farewell*)

Two prs. fleece-lined stockings (*that draft along the kitchen floor*)

She completed the list, canceled one of the items with the scratch of her pencil, added, "New comb," then handed the list to her husband.

While Anson studied it, Zarah busied herself sorting buttons into a compartment of her sewing box.

At every item, Anson's churchwarden gave off an approving puff. A modest list indeed. Bare necessities, well within the means of a cash-pinched farmer. If the corn deal came off prosperously, Anson planned to add a few extras: a garnet brooch for Zarah; an opal ring for Laly; a doll that Quince could bandage to her heart's content. For Ozzie, an India-rubber ball.

His eyes encountered the canceled item. "What's this you've crossed out?"

Zarah dropped a mother-of-pearl button into her sewing box. "Birdseye," she said casually. "I won't be needing it for quite a while."

So many ways—joyous, sentimental, oblique—of announcing the same event.

Anson's eyes were searching, tender. "Do you mind?"

Silence while Zarah tested her heart for the truth. "No." Another silence while she tested his. "Do you?"

"For your sake, yes." Disturbed, Anson rose, strode stocking-footed up and down the parlor. "I wish there were some way . . ."

"There isn't." Zarah went on sorting her buttons. "There isn't any way."

Hearing the flatness of her own voice, Zarah's courage faltered. "I don't mind having babies, Anson. Or the work they bring with them. The worst part is, I get so tired that I neglect other things: Laly's reading, Quincia's shyness, Ozzie's [she hated to say the word] *drooling*. But most of all, I neglect you."

Self-accusation, bottomless regret, mingled with Zarah's tears. "I don't want to be a worn-out scold when you come in at the end of the day. I don't want to be a bleached bone when you need me for companionship and love."

No use to say, Darling, you're not a scold; you'll never be a bleached bone. Spoken endearments were valueless. What Zarah needed was a steady-going, helpful woman around the house. The standard wage for such a woman was twelve dollars a month. One hundred and forty-four dollars a year—almost the entire cash income on the Woodhull farm.

Anson felt the wind blowing from a hard quarter. The old remorseless wind of drudgery that had blown uncounted millions of women to death. For the lack of twelve dollars a month, the wind would destroy Zarah. . . .

Somewhere, somehow, he must get the money.

From the immediate surplus of his own strength, he consoled the tired body he loved. He knelt beside Zarah, fondling, sustaining her. For this moment she was the overborne branch and he the supporting prop. Gently he pulled the coronet comb from her cedar-colored hair. It was their signal for bed.

Behind the closet door, half closed in token service to modesty, Zarah took off one by one the weary garments of day. How good to get one's clothes off! She had once heard of a woman who slept in her corset to preserve her figure. Vain, deluded creature. What joy could equal the loosening of the stays? Zarah untied the drawstring of her camisole and stepped free, a naked, full-fleshed woman silhouetted by candlelight against the closet wall.

She rejoiced at the sight of her full bosom and the swelling curvature of her hips. The dome of pleasure expanding within her suggested a new meaning of the strange poem that had pursued her all evening. Its cunning sleights and devious twistings spoke only of one thing: the sacred river that seethed in procreative fury through the veins and organs of her body. Pluck any line, however lightly, and it proved! Who was the Abyssinian maid, if not Zarah Woodhull silhouetted darkly against the closet door? Her instrument? The dulcimer itself.

The old compulsion to clothe naked lines with Delsarte gestures possessed her for a moment. How render "Alph, the sacred river"? Too superficial, now, the ripple of fluttering fingers. The sacred river of life, whether Alph or Ohio, teeming Ganges or Irrawaddy, was both male and female—male in its swollen insistence, female because it bore on its flood the seeds of generations yet to come. The proper gesture therefore would be mysterious and ritualistic. It would begin with a priestess' lifting of the arms, then a slow descent in an hourglass curve, fingertips almost meeting at the navel, then falling away in a slow sift toward

. . . that deep romantic chasm which slanted
. . . athwart a cedarn cover!

Knowing what Zarah Woodhull knew about its insatiable claim on her life, could she deny that it was

A savage place?

From a chest, Zarah selected a freshly laundered nightgown and let it fall in cool folds over her shoulders. In through the open window came the unquenchable odor of cattle, the grunting of pigs. The upper cymbal of poetry clashed against the lower cymbal of reality, and the sound they gave off was the brass clang of life. Zarah blew out the candle and slipped under the blankets beside her husband.

With Anson's strong arms around her, Zarah closed her eyes, giving herself up to the unbreakable male enchantment that he always wove about her. She felt his rough male kiss travel along her throat, downward till it closed over the swollen tip nearest the heart.

Silent all, as fugal voices trailed off:

For he on honeydew hath fed
And drunk the milk of Paradise.

6.

DOUBLE EAGLE INN

IN THE LONG catalogue of river ports between Pittsburgh and Louisville, a forlorn settlement known as Peddler's Landing could make, in the year 1883, an unchallenged claim to last place. The town was not, as its name might suggest, a rendezvous of peddlers; for years the meanest pack merchants had shunned its tumbledown poverty. But originally a man named Tom Peddler had built a wharf there, hoping to attract some of the steamboat commerce bustling up and down the Ohio. For a time, boats of light draft had made scheduled stops at Peddler's Landing to pick up corn or passengers for Cincinnati. Then, by one of those fickle mutations common to the Ohio River, a sand bar began to form. The bar grew broader, higher, until even the shallowest boat avoided the silt barrier. Tom Peddler's dream evaporated until the only water traffic was a skiff ferry that linked Peddler's Landing with an equally forlorn settlement called Crupper on the Kentucky side of the river.

The rotting wharf at Peddler's Landing was flanked on the south by a blacksmith shop and a general store with a cast-iron front. On the north stood a rambling structure bearing the tabard *Double Eagle Inn*—a sign circular in shape and once yellow in color, purporting to represent that most patrician of coins, a twenty-dollar gold piece. All very realistic, except that the legend *E Pluribus Unum* now read *Liquor and Refreshments*, while the bunch of arrows traditionally clutched by eagles of the U.S. Mint had become *Jesse Rocamp, Prop.*

As twenty-dollar gold pieces grew scarcer in Peddler's Landing, the paint *pari passu* became more faded. Meanwhile, the hue of Mr. Rocamp's hopes (sanguine enough when he married Tom Peddler's daughter) was turning into a yellow sere. The last blistery flake of paint was about to blow off the Double Eagle's clapboards when a fresh source of golden hope swam, or fluttered rather, into Mr. Rocamp's ken.

Always a hand for "combinations," mercantile or biologic, Mr. Rocamp had tried just about everything. Then, in a moment of inspiration, he mated a yellow bantam rooster with a ginger-colored hen. The resultant issue of fighting cocks was really phenomenal. Noblest of this strain and champion of local champions, was a bird named The Hoosier Fancy that could—and would—for a side bet—strike down any feathered creature on the north bank of the Ohio. The Fancy's prowess had poured quite a trickle of side-bet cash into the pockets of Mr. Rocamp and his followers; tonight, the trickle would become a torrent when the gold-and-green Fancy ripped into the breast feathers of the visiting fowl that Tinney Figgatt and his Kentuckians were ferrying over from Crupper.

Idling in the doorway of his livery stable and annex to his tavern, Jesse Rocamp awaited the coming of darkness and Mr. Figgatt. While waiting, he took a small file from his pocket and began to sharpen two spurlike bits of steel technically known as "gaffs." When attached to the ankles of a fighting cock, these gaffs make a murderous whistling sound before they strike home. As Mr. Rocamp filed, he was joined by a little group of henchmen, cronies, handlers, trainers and just plain hangers-on. These were the "gentry," any one of whom would gladly miss a day's work or a night's sleep in order to witness a cock main.

After expertizing, gentry fashion, on the falchion sharpness of the gaffs and inspecting the Fancy himself (who stood on one leg the while in a willow crate), they came to the business at hand: the strategy of placing their bets.

"What kind of combination you goin' to spring on 'em tonight, Jess?" asked Judd Lougee.

Mr. Rocamp allowed that this question could be better answered if the meeting adjourned to his bar. Here, while serving jiggers of raw home-made whiskey at a nickel a slug, he outlined his strategy.

"Here's the combination, men. We'll start off the first main with Bob-tail. Bob couldn't lick a settin' hen. That'll lead Tinney Figgatt's crowd right down Confidence Alley. Then we'll feed 'em Shingle-Red—keep your bets low." Mr. Rocamp's policy held his audience bug-eyed. "Now, at this point, havin' tasted blood and drained off quite a bit of our cash, desperatelike we'll raise the ante, say, oh . . . to . . . mebbe a hundred dollars. Then we'll ease the Fancy into the pit. . . ."

The proprietor's lightning clap of strategy was greeted by a silence of pure admiration, not broken until Charlie Bowser popped his head into the bar and announced, "They're comin' across. Must be a dozen of them. Ferry's down to the rowlocks, she's that full."

Jesse Rocamp rose to generalissimo stature. "Now, men, just range yourselves behind me like you were a posse, and we'll go out to meet them hairy baboons. 'N' one thing more. Tinney Figgatt'll be full of wind and Kentucky corn. Let me do all the talkin'."

Thus instructed, the Indiana delegation gathered around the ferry slip to meet their opposite numbers from the Kentucky shore.

As the strangers disembarked, each bearing a willow crate, Jess Rocamp greeted them with conspiratorial signals; then, with an eye to business, beckoned the delegation through a side door and into his tavern. Once inside, the mutes fell from their vocal cords. Rebel yells mingled with the *Tr-rang* of Tinney Figgatt's zither and demands for strong liquor. By the preliminaries it was going to be a night that Peddler's Landing would long remember.

Into this highly carbureted atmosphere of dark policy, feathered partisanship and raw whiskey rode Anson Woodhull. The springs of his blue wain were flattened by a tremendous weight of corn. Since dawn he had been following the Ohio in a northeasterly direction across a bone-dry terrain that sent up a powdery dust irritating to the nostrils of horses and driver. After twelve hours of steady pulling, the animals were exhausted. The Bess mare's every other breath was a rasping cough. The sad fact was that somewhere five or six years ago Bess's lungs had lost their elasticity and she was now suffering from an aggravated case of heaves.

Driving his wagon into the deserted stableyard, Anson leaped from the seat and looked about for the proprietor. By the whoops coming out of the tavern he judged that everyone in Peddler's Landing must be celebrating some local feast day. Lodge night perhaps. Of more immediate concern was the Bess mare's heaving flanks; she must have attention. He drove his wagon into the stable, unhitched his animals and spent the next hour caring for his horses— the Bess mare first. Anson watered her slowly; then, after a good rubdown, he wedged open her jaws and dropped a black pill the size of a pullet's egg down her inflamed throat.

"That'll soften up your cough, old girl." Dampening some finely mixed grain, he tied a feed bag over her nose, then turned to Hooker and Burnside. It was dark when he finished grooming and bedding them down.

From Zarah's hamper, he drew a huge roast pork sandwich, sat on the whiffle tree of his wagon and began munching. Nothing quite so melancholy as a cold supper on the first night away from home. He was about to stretch out on top of his wagonload of corn when Jess Rocamp appeared, lantern in hand.

The presence of four horses, a large blue wagon and a bearded total stranger rather complicated the beautiful simplicity of Mr. Rocamp's program. Ordinarily he would have welcomed this unexpected source of revenue; tonight, however, with his barn "bespoke" as a cockfighting arena, he must somehow get rid of these unwanted guests.

"What the hell are you doing in my barn?"

Anson displayed a not unnatural surprise at this line of questioning. A soft answer, he saw, was indicated here. "My horses are plumb tuckered, so I just bedded them down for the night."

"Where you from?"

Anson wanted everything to be quite clear. "I'm from Landmark County, on my way to Cincinnati with a load of corn."

Walking around the wagon, Mr. Rocamp saw the barrel lashed to his tailpiece. "I suppose that's corn, too?"

Country innocence can be very disarming. "Ten-year-old corn."

At the mention of ten-year-old corn, fresh combinations began turning in Jess Rocamp's fertile mind. Solicitude thick as axle grease smeared his manner. "You must be pretty tuckered yourself. 'Stead of sleeping out here in the barn, why not enjoy a comfortable bed inside? No extra charge."

The prospect was inviting. Anson followed his host into the tavern and up a creaky flight of stairs to a room at the rear of the inn. He barely heard Jess Rocamp's murmur: "Make yourself comfortable." Pulling off his boots, he tumbled onto the moldy feather mattress and fell into the abyss of sleep.

Deep down, he struck a submerged roof of anxiety and grated across the sunken ledges of a dream. Zarah and the children were in the blue wain while the Bess mare struggled to pull them out of a quagmire. Anson awoke sweating. The Bess mare! He must see her. In the darkness he pulled on his boots and groped toward the door.

It was locked!

Whoever locked the door must be curiously naïve, thought Anson. The sort of person who would tie up a stallion with a piece of pack thread. He threw his one-hundred-and-ninety-pound frame against the door. The lock gave way. He heard the grunting of pigs and the twanging of a zither. What was going on here?

In the livery stable a circle of men were squatting around a bull's-eye lantern as they watched a miniature spectacle.

Anson climbed on top of his wagon and, peering downward, saw two bantam roosters settling some primitive grudge. Faster than Anson's eye could follow, the gaff hooks whizzed and sank into breast and neck. In a flurry of steel and feathers, the blue cock named Gasper nearly severed the green bantam's head.

Indiana, it seemed, was being badly beaten by Kentucky—and the Kentuckians gloated accordingly.

"Like I told you, Gasper warms up slow."

Tinney Figgatt, sole owner of the Gasper, stroked his bird affectionately. "You Indiana fellers got any more game roosters as wants their heads chopped off?"

Jess Rocamp produced a golden bird with purple wattles. "Fifty dollars says that this here Hoosier Fancy'll knock your rooster into next Thursday."

"Double your money, friend."

Jess Rocamp and his followers got their money up. In the first exchange the invincible Kentucky cock sliced the Hoosier Fancy's head half off his neck.

"*Ho-ho-ho* and *hee-haw-hee,* little brown jug, how I love thee." Tinney Figgatt led the gloating and drinking. "Another main," he cried. But now there were no more birds, no more Indiana money—and no more whiskey.

"Godamighty, we gotta have whiskey." Fiery-faced Mr. Figgatt turned to his host. "What kind o' hospitality's this? Ain't they no likker this side the Ohio?"

"I ain't got no *free* whiskey," said Rocamp, "but if you gen'lemen can pay the price, I've got some ten-year-old bourbon, jes' come in today."

"Who the hell's talkin' price?" roared Figgatt.

Lantern in one hand, jug in the other, Jess Rocamp walked to the tailpiece of Anson's wagon and threw back the tarpaulin. He lofted the lantern to reveal the date burned on the barrel head. "See what I mean. There's the year it was laid up—1873."

Amazement that whiskey could reach such age hushed Tinney Figgatt and his followers. "Can't spill none of that," one of them murmured.

"Don't intend to." Rocamp set his lantern on the tailpiece and drew a supple rubber hose from his pocket. "Tricks in every trade," he announced. "Now, after I work this bung loose, I'll siphon off some of the smoothest bourbon as ever trickled down your throats."

Rocamp's hand, reaching for the poplar bung, felt five hard fingers closing around his wrist. A voice equally hard descended from the shadows. "There'll be no siphoning off tonight, Rocamp."

Anson slipped down onto the tailboard. Standing on the narrow stage, footlighted by Figgatt's lantern, he towered in giant perspective above the cockfighters. The pitchfork in his right hand gave pronged emphasis to his words. "The first man that touches this barrel gets a pitchfork between his eyes."

"We could sort of . . . rush you," hinted Rocamp.

"And I could sort of kick over the lantern and you'd have a nice barn fire," said Anson.

Tinney Figgatt introduced a new idea. "We'll *buy* your whiskey, mister."

"I'm not selling."

"Now that's what I call a cowbuncle on the ass of progress." Tinney Figgatt measured his language seriously. "Becuz you see, we gotta have whiskey."

"Without burnin' down no barns," put in Rocamp.

"Course, course, we don't want no barn-burnin'." Mr. Figgatt struck a pugilistic pose as he addressed Anson. "But now with a game rooster like yourself, there might be another way. Kin you handle your dukes?"

"When I have to," said Anson.

Genuine chivalry, Kentucky style, inspired Mr. Figgatt's next remark. "Suppose the boys here make up a little purse. Say twenty-five dollars. Then you'n me could have a sparrin' match—trial of skill more'n anything else. Winner take all. Money, whiskey . . . 'n whatever honor there's in it."

A varnish of sportsmanship covered some of the uglier aspects of Figgatt's proposition. At least it offered Anson a one-to-one chance—a gamble much more favorable than the twelve-to-one odds he had been facing.

"What rules do we fight by?"

"Bare knuckles," said Figgatt. "A knockdown ends the round. Thirty seconds' rest and we fight till one of us don't come up for the next round." Mr. Figgatt added a touch worthy of Queensberry himself. "Your fellow citizen, Mr. Rocamp here, kin be referee and timekeeper."

Fair couldn't be fairer. Anson leaped down from the wagon tail, stripped off his shirt and took a hitch in his belt buckle. By the beam of the smoky lantern hanging from a rafter, he saw Tinney Figgatt squirt tobacco juice over his knuckles. With a chaw bulging in his cheek, the Kentuckian strode to the center of the ring and held up fists, in London ring fashion. All very sporting, except that he outweighed Anson by at least thirty-five pounds.

Disdaining instructions from the referee, Mr. Figgatt drew back an arm long as a wagon pole and fetched up with a reaping-hook punch that caught Anson behind the ear. "*Tr-a-a-nngg!*" Anson's head buzzed like a harp string. Figgatt spat and whaled again with his ham-fist right. This time Anson was inside the punch; at close quarters he sank his fist deep into Figgatt's tripes. Like hitting a pig. By the grunt, Anson knew it hurt.

While Figgatt clobbered him with lefts and rights, Anson kept working on the Kentuckian's suety guts. Figgy didn't like that and said so with an *ugh* and UGH! After stating his objections three times, Mr. Figgatt stepped back and belted his tormentor flush on the jaw. A whole octave of harp strings with jingle-bell accompaniments set Anson's skull twanging. Dazed, Anson took a second mouthful of knuckles and, still more dazed, found himself on the floor.

Above him, he heard Rocamp counting *four, five, six* . . . His opening eyes focused on Tinney Figgatt's bloated visage, all veneer of sportsmanship stripped away by the prospect of victory. And somewhere beyond Figgatt's huge head, in a dim region lighted only by a smoky lantern, Anson saw a boy's face—a pinched, freckly, far-off face—gazing down at him from the loft.

The face, though oddly familiar, had no business being up there. Yet, Anson was curiously glad to see it. Rocamp kept counting off the seconds, *six, seven, eight* . . .

As Anson's head cleared, he recognized the boy's face. It belonged to Reb Plaskett, the pig drover's son.

What was Reb doing up in the hayloft? What was he trying to say? Not that it mattered. The all-important thing was having a friend on your side—in your corner, so to speak. Even a scraggly ninety-pound kid, urging you onto your feet with jerking upward motions of his peaked chin.

At the count of nine, Anson managed to get off the floor. Sitting on a proffered knee during the thirty-second rest period, he revised his battle strategy. He must avoid Figgatt's hamlike fists, refuse to be drawn into any toe-to-toe slugging. Duck, dodge, parry—let Figgatt wear himself out. Then, while the Kentuckian's guard was down, Anson might reach his bristled chin.

During the next round, Anson's backtracking tactics enraged Mr. Figgatt and brought derisive hoots from his supporters.

"He's a barn-dancer, Figgy."

"Give him the ol' Gasper sashay, Fig."

Mr. Figgatt was eager enough to swing his barn-dancing partner into oblivion, but the Kentuckian's wind was giving out. With amazing economy of breath and movement, he worked his man backward into a corner of the barn. Too late, Anson saw the trap. Unable to retreat farther, he must again trade punches with his beefy opponent or have his brains splattered against the wall.

All or nothing now, thought Anson, hooking a terrific right into Figgatt's jaw. It was a good punch, the best he had thrown that night, but Anson knew that he had missed the button. Pinned into the corner by Figgatt's huge bulk, he no longer had room for another swing like that. Chin buried in his shoulder, he pummeled Mr. Figgatt's lardy guts and waited for a sledge-hammer fist to bang him senseless.

The sledge hammer never fell. Instead, Tinney Figgatt lurched forward, his head lolling helplessly on Anson's shoulder. The hinges of his knees buckled and he crumpled to the floor like a broken sack of grain.

Jess Rocamp, like the rest of the spectators, stood in boggling silence. He lifted neither voice nor hand to discharge his official function as referee.

"Start counting," said Anson.

Ruefully the referee began tolling off the seconds. At five, he paused for a sign from Figgatt's crowd. Not a sign. At eight, he waited for a miracle. No miracle.

Anson reached for his pitchfork. "Keep on counting," he said.

The referee tallied. "Nine, ten, and out."

He might have counted to a hundred and Mr. Figgatt would have still been out. His supporters lugged him to the center of the barn, propped him against a wheel of the blue wain, loosened his belt, fanned him, sloshed water over his face and shoulders. Still no sign of life from the inert champion. One of the Kentuckians turned to Anson and asked in a voice blended of meekness and wonder, "What did y' hit him with, Mister?"

Anson honestly didn't know. Perhaps that right to the jaw was a better punch than he had realized. He placed his ear to Figgatt's barrelly chest and was somewhat relieved when he heard the bass reverberations of a thumping heart somewhere under all that suet.

"This'll fix him." Anson siphoned off a small jug of whiskey, thrust its neck between Figgatt's lips, and poured. The high-proof liquor ignited a spark of consciousness and the spark leaped into flame as it reached the Kentuckian's blood stream. Figgatt opened his eyes. "What hit me?"

Rocamp soothed the fallen champion with apologies. "A lucky punch, Tinney. When you backed him in the corner, he must of reached your chin."

"Twarn't my *chin*," mumbled Figgatt, rubbing the back of his head, where a lump big as a hen's egg had risen. "He must have shoved his fist clear through my skull." Gaining his feet unsteadily, the Kentuckian shook hands with Anson. "Give him his purse, Jess. He won it fair and square."

Anson took the money. Then, in a sporting gesture, he handed the brown jug to Tinney Figgatt. "Guess I can spare this much," he said, grinning.

Somewhat heartened by the victor's contribution to good fellowship, the cockfighters led their wobbly hero from the barn.

Too late for any more sleep, Anson was measuring out corn for his horses when he heard a boy's voice in the loft above.

"You sure knocked him cold with that last punch, Mr. Woodhull."

It *was* Reb Plaskett; not an apparition seen through smoky lantern light, but the boy himself.

"How'd *you* get here?" Anson was trying to fit together certain unexplained elements in the night's adventure.

"Came past with a few pigs." Reb slid down the loft ladder, casually twanged his slingshot and began searching for something on the barn floor. In the very corner where Tinney Figgatt's knees had buckled so unexpectedly, the boy uttered a triumphant "Here 'tis."

The puzzle became clearer when Reb examined his find. "The durn thing's *dented*," he said ruefully.

"What's dented?"

Reb exhibited a Minie bullet, a leaden replica of the keepsake he had given Laly. Solemnly he rubbed the back of his head and mimicked Tinney Figgatt's "*Twarn't my chin.*"

Anson thrust out a long arm and hugged the boy close. "You little sharpshooter, Reb," he exclaimed. Then they both laughed. They laughed so loud and long that they woke up Mr. Plaskett in the loft overhead. Looking like a scarecrow with sore eyes and a post-alcoholic parch, the pig drover came down the ladder.

"Don't see no cause for laughin'," he said, gazing out the barn door at a gray, drizzling sky. "It's goin' to be a bad day for drivin' pigs."

It was a bad day for driving anything. The drizzle became a downpour; yesterday's choking dust gave place to sticky gray mud, treacherous to hoof and wheel. Twice in five miles Anson dismounted to pry his wagon out of wallow holes.

A bit early for autumn rain, he thought. But because no one had consulted him about the rain, Anson simply accepted it as something that would eventually stop.

Late in the afternoon, it did.

Evening found him striking camp at Toner's point, a hamlet fifteen miles south of Cincinnati. Here, in a grove of sycamores, an outdoor Grange Meeting was in progress. Around a fire disgruntled farmers were voicing deep but aimless protests against railroads, moneylenders, mortgageholders and all other enemies of agrarian prosperity. With cynical grimness Anson heard the oft-proposed remedies: co-operative marketing, political action and other Utopian schemes foredoomed to fail.

Wearied by his two-day journey, Anson was leaning against his blue wain when a high-wheeled gig drawn by a narrow horse entered the circle. Its driver, instead of dismounting and tethering his beast, drove to the very rim of the firelight, and pulled up with a baritone, attention-calling *"Whoa."*

Waiting till he had everyone's eye, the newcomer stepped onto the dashboard, balanced there a moment, then leaped into the air. His cape, opening like a parachute, enabled him to make a batlike glide that ended in a perfect landing close to the fire.

"Amazement is the mother of curiosity and the key to attention," said the stranger. "Therefore, we do all within our power to amaze. . . . No claim to the supernatural, you understand. Everything here works by the simple laws of mechanics." He opened his cape, revealing the ribbed umbrella structure of its wings. "Cause and effect, you might say.

Now, observe closely." From the depths of his cape he drew a small folding table and set it up before his amazed audience. He drew a wand from his sleeve and touched a spring which released a kind of oilcloth apron in front of the table. On the apron was printed:

Professor "Cartwheel" Jones
Author of "Hard Money or Hard Times."

"No ointments, salves or bulky literature. No obligation to buy—or even to listen. Just plain, unbuttered wisdom offered free of charge to Indiana farmers."

Cartwheel Jones made a magician's pass at the empty air and plucked a twenty-dollar gold piece out of the twilight. He feigned surprise; then, holding the coin in his palm like a lamp reflector, let it catch the red glint of the embers.

"In this hand," said Cartwheel Jones, descending to the vernacular, "you see a gold piece—the only one, far's I know, in this audience tonight. Gawp and goggle, my friends, 'twon't hurt the gold piece. Take a good look at the last double eagle you're likely to see in Landmark County for a lo—ng time. That is, unless you happen to own a bank— even in which case, it being only an Indiana bank, you'd be obliged by law to ship to New York on demand."

His canvass turned momentarily facetious. "Ever wonder why gold pieces are round? Answer used to be 'Money's made round, so it'll go round.' Well, folks, you know that's not true any more." Cartwheel Jones rolled the gold piece hoop-wise across his little table. "Gold pieces are made round so's they can roll right back east." He palmed the coin; at its sudden disappearance, he pretended to be as mystified as his audience.

"Well, our gold's gone. And what do Indiana farmers get in return? Presto chango." Cartwheel Jones made another pass and held up a handful of limp green paper. "Green-backs."

Amazement being the key to attention, the Professor had his audience where he wanted them. "Well, anyway, it's money. Suppose we count it." Elaborately he passed the bills from his left hand to his right. "One, two, three, four, five. In my right hand I have five dollars. But the longer we count the less we have." He reserved the counting process. "Five, four, three, two—danged if it don't melt away." He waved a solitary dollar bill at his audience, then tossed it into the fire. "Sort of reminds you farmers of what happens when you take your money to town."

He went on with his spiel. "Now we know where we're at. No gold; greenbacks fit only for kindling. What does Cartwheel Jones do now? Why, he does what any intelligent, right-thinking man would do. He asks for, he *de*mands, the free and unlimited coinage of silver. Let silver reign—or rain —any way you prefer." Into an agate basin on the table, he shook a clinking stream of silver dollars from his cuffs. Then, plunging his fingers into the basin, he held up dripping handfuls of silver, plentiful hard coin of the realm.

"Clean new mintage. Bites like gold, rings like gold. Equal to gold as a medium of exchange."

Cartwheel Jones entered his peroration. "You farmers have plenty of land and enough food—corn and pigs mostly—but what you *haven't* got, and can't get, is *cash!* And you won't get it while the gold crowd in New York writes the ticket. Farmers of Indiana, I urge you to end this shortage of currency by demanding the free and unlimited coinage of silver."

He began folding up his table. "Will the Republicans give it to you? No. Or the Democrats?" Cartwheel Jones shook his head gloomily. "Again, I say the only way you'll get cash is to vote Populist. *Friends, you've got to raise less corn and more hell!*"

There is an hour of day and season of year that compensates for all other hours and seasons—a time so mild, so clement, that most people wish it would never pass. It is the after-supper hour in mid-September. And at such an hour, on the third evening of his journey, Anson Woodhull drove his blue wain into the west end of Cincinnati.

Jolting across cobblestoned streets, he enjoyed the scene about him. Men in shirt sleeves were playing Stuss; their wives crocheted in rocking chairs or gossiped across picket fences. A lamplighter with his stick and ladder was making blue pools of gaslight at street corners. The sidewalks were marked with mystical diagrams drawn by children playing Hopscotch and Hoist-Your-Green-Sail. In front of a saloon, a three-piece German band—cornet, tuba and clarinet—puffed nostalgically at *Heimatland* airs. *Muss i' denn . . . Röslein auf der Heide.*

What could one say about such a scene? It was all very

human and tender—sad, too, with German overtones. In a word, Cincinnati.

At a street lamp, Anson asked some loungers, "How do I get to the Public Landing?"

They pointed. "Straight rechts; bear links bei Walnut."

"Will there be a stable there?"

"Ja, stables there will immer be."

Anson urged his weary horses forward. "Geet, McClellan, G'long, Hooker."

Down cobbled side streets came the cries of children at play: "Run, Sheepie, run . . . Lay, Sheepie, lay . . ."

When it got darker, older boys would play Jack, Jack, Show Your Light. And when the full darkness of evening came on, older boys and girls, now strolling in little parks, would kiss underneath a city tree to the sad sweet *umpah* of a German band:

> *Schön ist die Jugend*
> *Sie kommt nicht mehr.*

Cincinnati . . . Queen City of the Ohio . . . Porkopolis.

7.

QUEEN CITY

No ONE CAN TELL exactly when or why a city begins to falter in the race for size and importance. Everything appears to be marching on schedule: postal receipts and bank deposits are increasing; hotel lobbies and retail shopping places seem to be as crowded as ever. Municipal bonds are still prime, and steps are being taken to make the water supply adequate. Then one fine census morning the city wakes up to find itself occupying next-to-last place among the big ten.

"Someone has blundered!" cries the leading journal and demands a recount. The recount demonstrates that there has indeed been a blunder: Ward #3 has been counted twice! Civic indignation is accompanied by a grand marshaling of statistics. "Look, we are still first in production of soap, buttons, playing-cards and whiskey. Second only to Chicago in the numbers of hogs slaughtered. Shoulder to the wheel, chin up, once more unto the breach, dear friends."

Another decade passes; indignation turns to bewilderment as the city drops to last place. "Look, we are still first in the production of soap, buttons, playing-cards and whiskey. Our choral festival is unsurpassed. Visitors agree that we are a bastion of the fine arts, the Athens of America, an oasis in a cultural desert."

Maybe so, Cincinnati, but a blight is on your vine; the postpioneer rapture has faded; you will never get that first million population. Your dream of fluminal greatness has receded, leaving a sediment of moldering docks and vacant warehouses along your waterfront. Yet you still have Vieuxtemps, The Rhine Palast, Homer Addicks and 211 Gay Street.

Vieuxtemps, first.

VIEUXTEMPS

A HOUSE SET UPON A HILL has a double obligation: it must inspire pride in the valley dwellers below and create envy among the owners of other houses built on adjacent hills. Vieuxtemps, home of the late Enoch Battle, discharged both obligations with a monumental flourish; its crenelated towers were Norman Gothic; its bell tower was pure Alhambra; and its lightning rods came all the way from Troy (New York). This eclecticism paralleled the Battle fortune itself, impartially drawn during Enoch's lifetime from soap, beer, glue, whiskey, banking, real estate and pork. Especially pork. Starting with a single pig, Enoch's fortunes had grown with the city; and although there had been some slackening since Enoch's death, the money was still pouring in faster than his widow could spend it.

The mistress of Vieuxtemps, buoyed up on a flood of postmenopausal energy, regarded her fortune as a cultural trust. Stella Battle had her charities, of course—various orphanages and hospitals that received a benevolent tithe of her income. Her private pension list was extensive. Childless herself, Stella supported collateral tribes of nieces, nephews and nieces' nephews, including that prince of tomcats, Durkee Pyne, a weak son of Stella's weakest brother. Getting Durkee out of scrapes ran to five figures annually and might have soared higher if Stella hadn't kept him in residence at Vieuxtemps, the better to handle his problems with a vicariously maternal checkbook.

The problems that Stella enjoyed most, however, were cultural in nature. Was there an Aldine folio on sale at Sotheby's? A draft on Stella's London bankers would fetch it for the Cincinnati library. A guarantee for Bernhardt? "Bring on *Camille!*" Nor was Stella's bounty wholly institutional. She sponsored foreign portrait painters and imported her own artists. Pini Giambattista himself had done a huge mural in the Vieuxtemps reception hall illustrating (God knows why) the exploits of Orlando Furioso. And Sir Thomas Cockburne, R.A., had received a whopping fee for the portrait of Enoch that dominated the library. The fee must have been whopping, for as Stella liked to explain, Sir Thomas couldn't come personally so he copied it from a tintype.

Recently, to maintain her lead as benefactress of the arts, Stella had imported M. Feinture, the French sculptor, whose bust of Napoleon III was either in the Louvre, Versailles, or maybe the Eden Musée—Stella couldn't exactly remember where. One of those places. M. Feinture's arrival in Cincinnati was a tremendous coup, signalized by headlines in the *Enquirer:*

PARISIAN ARTIST CAPTURES QUEEN CITY.
FAMOUS SCULPTOR TO IMMORTALIZE
LOCAL SOCIETY LEADER

A project of this scope naturally required a few *pourparlers.* Stella spoke no French, and since M. Feinture had no earthly reason for speaking English, these delicate negotiations went forward with the aid of Solange Vincy, Stella's personal maid. Ah, Vincy—there was a girl for you! (Well, no longer a girl exactly; at twenty-eight, Solange, a violet-eyed brunette, reminded one of a concert piano that had been on too many tours.) Intelligent, discreet, very pretty, Solange was a genius with rouge, mascara and curling irons. She had a knack for selecting negligees that did something for those uninteresting places between Stella's chin and collarbones. A real confidante, too. She could listen listen listen, always with sympathy and understanding, without ever mentioning her own troubles or unbosoming her well-bosomed past. Having spent her youth in a New Orleans convent, Solange spoke a reasonably good brand of French and was at all points splendidly equipped to act as interpreter between Stella and the world-renowned sculptor.

First things first. When the question of price was broached to M. Feinture, he proved *très très* frank. Terms: a thousand dollars down and an equal amount when the masterpiece was finished. Done and done. Stella laid a thousand-dollar gold note on the barrel head; M. Feinture folded it reverently into a pocket of his lilac-sprigged weskit, and the discussion climbed to regions more *spirituelle*.

"How do you want me to pose?" asked Stella.

Before replying, M. Feinture rose and circled his patroness, making thumb-and-eye business in the round. Lest he appear to resemble a Nivernois peasant about to buy a cow, he accompanied himself with murmurs. "Mm . . . mmm, *la tête bien régale.*" He placed two fingers under Stella's chin. "*Permettez-moi, Madame.*" (Getting around those dewlaps would be quite an exploit.) "A little higher, please. *C'est extraordinaire . . . la cou de la Reine elle-même.*"

"He says," translated Vincy, "that your head reminds him of Empress Eugénie."

The delicious fear that this perceptive Frenchman would suggest a pose in the *ensemble* (partial or complete) prompted Stella's next question. "Does he want me on a couch perhaps?"

A lively exchange between Solange and M. Feinture ended with the sad announcement: "He says, 'We shall confine ourselves to the head.' "

Stella had expected more. She covered her disappointment with a this-better-be-good bluntness: "What will the statue be made of?"

Like a yardgoods man explaining the virtues of the fabrics on his shelf, M. Feinture ticked off the list of materials. "My thought turns immediately to marble—traditional choice of the masters. But I am obliged to tell Madame that marble goes very slowly. Chip, chip, chip. Tedious, *n'est-ce pas?* As for alabaster, it partakes of a certain *froideur*—a coldness—to which (if Madame will permit) I feel the opposite in her presence."

Stella put an abrupt end to this bush-beating. "How about gold?" she said.

M. Feinture's Gallic sense of reality nearly betrayed him. Tactfully, he suggested that in some unhappy hour of financial distress, the melting value of the statue might prove a temptation. "Would not this defeat the whole purpose of art? As Gautier himself has said, '*Le buste survit à la cité.*' We are dealing with eternities here, Madame. Long after Cincinnati crumbles, the poet's prophecy will be confirmed by the sculptor's triumph."

Solange had to reword this passage two or three times before Stella got the drift of the argument. Finally they compromised on bronze—"*aussi un matériel classique.*" There would, of course, be an extra charge for casting.

One last question from Stella. "May I have ringlets—like Eugénie?"

M. Feinture's bow subordinated art to gallantry. "This is a matter of taste that Madame alone can decide."

"He says you will be superb in ringlets," translated Solange.

With a kissing of hands, M. Feinture departed. There would be a brief interval while he assembled his materials. Stella welcomed the delay; she had some assembling to do herself. Even with Vincy's expert assistance, a full week of preparation would be required for that first sitting. To expedite these preparations, Vincy—instead of going home nights—would "stay in" at Vieuxtemps. She could have the Petunia Room.

With some regret, Solange announced that she couldn't occupy the Petunia Room.

"Why not?" demanded Stella.

"I have a husband, Madame."

"Everybody has a husband at some time or other," said Stella.

"But my husband is quite ill."

"An invalid?"

"Not exactly; but very weak. I must prepare his dinner in the evening."

"Nonsense. Here's a twenty-dollar gold piece. Let the man dine out a few evenings. You *must* stay, Vincy. It's a crisis; I need you, child."

So Vincy "stayed in" to help Stella through the crisis. And by staying, she precipitated a crisis of quite another kind.

Some men there are who interpret a demure management

of eyes (especially in a French-speaking lady's maid) as a veiled invitation to come closer. Such a man was Durkee Pyne. Durk had been wondering these many months just how deep the still waters ran beneath the violet fringes of Vincy's placid surface. He had made several fruitless efforts to wade into these depths, and now, with Vincy sleeping in the Petunia Room of Vieuxtemps, he decided to make a bold plunge.

A furtive plunge, rather. Arriving home early one morning, awash with much bourbon, he made a cautious try at Vincy's door. Locked. Just as he thought. All part of the come-hither technique. Well, he would try the terrace with the French doors. More romantic anyway. Rosy-fingered dawn was climbing over the jocund peak of Price Hill as Durk opened the glass doors very gently and found himself sitting on the edge of Vincy's bed. The sequence of events thereafter was blurred (as such sequences are apt to be), but the blurriness ended when Durkee was brought up sharp and short by a well-placed knee in his groin.

"Ugh!" (Where did a lady's maid learn *that* trick?)

Local agony prevented Durkee Pyne from going into the question. Instead, he set up a howl that woke his protective auntie, three doors down the hallway. Quite a scene was being enacted as Stella, crimped in curl papers, entered Vincy's room. Day, breaking over the crenelated battlements of Vieuxtemps, discovered Durkee rolling on the floor, while Solange tossed feminine oddments into her little valise. She paused long enough for an apology to her employer.

"I'm sorry, Ma'am. I knew it wouldn't be wise for me to stay." She snapped the lock on her valise, jabbed a long hatpin into her tricorne chapeau, then, with not even a contemptuous glance at the writhing Casanova on the floor, brushed past her becrimped mistress.

Stella followed her downstairs, pleading at every step. Yet even as she pleaded, Stella realized that Vieuxtemps wasn't the stage on which a perfect lady's maid and a favorite nephew could work out their destinies. If someone had to go, it had better be Solange.

"Where shall I send your pay, Vincy dear?"

"Two eleven Gay Street." Genuine affection for Stella's many kindnesses moved her to add, "I hope the sittings come off well, Madame."

The wound of Vincy's departure really began to ache when Stella took on a new lady's maid named Welch. As it soon appeared, Welch wasn't worthy to warm Vincy's curling irons. In three days she failed to produce a single satisfactory ringlet. Poor and kinky, Welch's curls were limp substitutes for the fat round clusters that Vincy knew how to make.

As the sitting with M. Feinture drew nearer, Stella became desperate. The cloisonné clock on her dressing table chimed twice; in exactly thirty minutes, the world-renowned sculptor would arrive for the first crucial sitting. Face still undone, nerves snapping with exasperation, Stella reverted to an earlier, pre-Vieuxtemps mode of expression. "Damn it, Welch," she screamed, "you've burned me again with that curling iron. Stop blubbering, girl. Here, let me do it myself."

An aging, desolate old woman whose bust—whether in bronze or living flesh—would survive no city sighed for Solange Vincy's deft fingers as she struggled to transform a few scanty wisps of dyed hair into foolish curls.

"Vincy, Vincy," she moaned. "Why did I ever let you go?"

RHINE PALAST

HELMUT ZIEGLER'S RHINE PALAST was the largest open-air beer garden in Cincinnati. On its dance floor of a Saturday night, two hundred couples whirled to the strains of waltz and polka; customers sitting at tables under real linden trees were entertained by Bavarian yodelers, bell-ringers and a Kasperle theater. To attract the Turnverein trade, Herr Ziegler had installed a complete set of gymnastic equipment—a trapeze, parallel bars, dumbbells—anything to increase a thirst. And because most Germans like to play cards, the Rhine Palast had a cozy back room where pinochle players could slap face cards with their peers. It was all very *gemütlich*—and quite profitable.

In the beginning, Herr Ziegler had been his own bartender, bouncer and cashier. Now, with his Rhine Palast spreading over a prosperous acre, he played host with a *Kontrolleur* accent. The natural blond curls that had formerly scalloped his forehead had been replaced by an expensive Siegfried hairpiece; his pomaded mustaches were, however, the genuine Bismarck article. The insignia of his *Kontrolleur* rank was an enormous bunch of keys that he swung at the end of a heavy

chain. Keys, keys, keys! Under the Ziegler system everything
was locked up. The beer vault in the cellar, the knobbed
iron safe in his office, the cigar humidor, the liquor cabinets,
even the sheet music played by his three-piece orchestra, were
under lock and key. A *Kontrolleur* controls, *nicht wahr?*

Everything was beautifully under control until Herr Ziegler,
taking his first holiday in twenty-five years, boarded the *River
Queen* southbound for New Orleans and its fabulous Mardi
Gras. For six wonderful days he fraternized with a set of
mysteriously elegant gentlemen in the card saloon of the *River
Queen.* What a breed they were! Suave and quietly flattering
when you won; inscrutably smiling when you lost. Win or
lose you could always learn something. Helmut Ziegler took
his most instructive and costliest lesson from a fascinating
character named Damon Frye. It was like hearing Liszt play
the piano when, at the showdown, Mr. Frye's meek little
pair of treys blossomed into a full house. An unforgettable
experience. In sheer gratitude Herr Ziegler gave his business
card to the gambler.

"Drop into my Rhine Palast when you're in Cincinnati," he
urged. "We play a little game that might—*ha-ha*—amuse you."

Returning to the little game in his own establishment, Herr
Ziegler suffered a terrific letdown. Where now was the
glamour of the nickel bet and the ten-cent raise? During many
an afternoon of dreary play, Herr Ziegler yearned for a
renewal of the excitement that his cautious card-thumbing
friends could not provide.

His yearnings were answered one afternoon in May 1883,
when a stranger, imperially slender (a trifle pallid perhaps),
sauntered into the Rhine Palast with news of chancelleries in
his walk. Bar rag in hand, Herr Ziegler stared at the casino
elegance of this newcomer who looked like Damon Frye's
younger brother. From top hat to suède shoes the stranger
was a rainbow in gray; his apparel murmured "gambler"—
a theme repeated *fortissimo* by the diamond horseshoe pin,
diagonally crossed by a whip of rubies, that glittered in his
gray Ascot tie.

"Rosemere, bartender," said the stranger.

The request skewered Herr Ziegler in his fat tripes. Rose-
mere happened to be the grail, so to speak, of eight-year-old
Kentucky bourbons. Herr Ziegler didn't deal in such rarities.
Sweating with embarrassment, he pushed a nameless brand

of bar whiskey toward his customer, who patted down his rising nausea with a pale hand and said, "I do beseech you . . . No."

A thoroughly disconcerting piece of business. But the stranger's next play utterly crumpled Herr Ziegler. From a rouleau of gold coins the man in gray tossed a double eagle onto the bar and said, "Lay in a case of ·Rosemere for me, *Gastwirt*, I may do a bit of drinking here this summer." His tone was ducal, patronizing—an aristocrat conversing with a cat's-meat man. Then he leaned toward Ziegler and whispered confidently, "My friend, Damon Frye, tells me you deal the straightest deck in Cincinnati."

Thus began Herr Ziegler's education in a new school of form. Platt Woodhull (that was the stranger's name) brought to the daily game a fresh repertory of usage—subtle, baffling, but packed with excitement. He introduced a whole set of professional conventions. You played with a fresh pack of cards every day and never shouted when making a bet. A bottle of Rosemere, flanked by a silver ice bucket and seltzer water, stood on a side table. Instead of bellowing, *"Gesundheit,"* you drank with a quiet meeting of the eyes across the top of your glass. In tone and tempo the play became more rapid. Draw poker was too slow; stud took its place. The stakes climbed, yet you pocketed your winnings or accepted a run of bad luck without comment.

Suffering from the fatal malady of trying to be a gentleman, Herr Ziegler bought a gray top hat and wore it cocked in the *River Queen* manner over his Siegfried hairpiece. He imitated his tutor's taste in cravats and cast a covetous eye on the diamond tie pin spangled with the whip of rubies. In fact, Herr Ziegler was kept so busy rubbing up a patina of surface gentility that at the end of a month he found himself five hundred dollars behind.

This was disagreeable enough, yet not nearly so annoying as the drum fire of small irritations that Woodhull kept up. He had a contemptuous way of inflecting the word *landlord*, but the trick that irritated Ziegler most was the gambler's habit of never looking at his hole card. This really baffled the proprietor of the Rhine Palast. How gauge your bet against a man who, whether through indifference or bravado, didn't know the strength of his own hand?

It was a bluff, of course, but how meet it?

Helmut Ziegler lost nearly one thousand dollars before he

discovered the answer to Woodhull's bluffing. Then he turned on his tormentor and found under the façade of Platt Woodhull's professionalism the meringue heart of a born loser.

HOMER ADDICKS

IN HIS PANTRY-SIZED OFFICE on Wharf Street, Mr. Homer Addicks nursed an after-breakfast cigar and beagled hopefully through the pages of the Cincinnati *Courier*. What did Mr. Addicks expect to find as he sniffed the columns of the Queen City's leading journal? Well, like many another American since and before, he was looking for "something with a future to it"—a quite unspecific something, large as to size and vague in nature, that had thus far eluded him.

In his time, Homer Addicks had promoted many schemes, most of them legal—the only clear exception being a magnetic belt that did *not* restore male vigor in thirty days (as claimed by its promoter). At present he was a commodity broker, which meant that he was in the market to buy or sell anything from bottle corks to buggy whips at a profit ranging between 5 and 5,000 per cent.

The *Courier's* coverage of world news, its lengthy reports on national affairs, were matters beyond the pale of Mr. Addicks' interest. The fact that Cincinnati was in the grip of a corrupt municipal ring depressed him not at all. He became melancholy, however, when, turning to the commodity page, he read that a distiller named Charles Moerlein was installing a new rectifying column to meet the increased demand for Old Settler. To make Old Settler Moerlein would require a thousand gallons of raw grain alcohol (think big, Addicks—a hundred thousand gallons) to mix with a few barrels of straight whiskey. He'd call it Old Settler, then sell it for seventy dollars a barrel. Mr. Addicks performed some arithmetical maneuvers on a pad of scratch paper. The basic ingredients of Old Settler cost, maybe, four cents a gallon. Packaging, shipping and Federal Excise amounted to less than a dollar a gallon. On fifty thousand barrels, Moerlein would net more than three million dollars. Neat. *There* was something with a future to it. Mr. Addicks placed his tabulations in the sweat band of his hat and continued reading.

By comparison with whiskey, everything else on the commodity page seemed sluggish. Cotton soft, groceries quiet, oats spotty, corn inactive, pork ditto. A man named Wurlitzer was offering Prussian tenor drums, sharp fine tone, six dollars and up. Who the hell wanted drums? Coke, clean and free from dust, five cents a bushel. *A pushcart business.* Petroleum for all lubricating purposes. A promising line, *if* you had a storage tank. Mr. Addicks had no such tank; only a few bins for corn. Hm-mm, let's see now. Tallow candles . . . washing soda . . . condiments. Overcrowded. Not big enough, anyway.

The broker's eye caught an item: *"Crisis in cooperage. A scarcity of white oak barrel staves has occasioned a price rise of one dollar per C in the Cincinnati market."*

Mr. Addicks tore the item out of the *Courier* and filed it inside the sweat band of his hat. *Keep eye peeled for oak staves.*

This peeling process was interrupted by a knock on the wicket beside Mr. Addicks' desk. He slid back the panel and saw a bearded face with a countryman complexion. "I've got some corn I'd like to sell," he said.

Mr. Addicks studied the Personal Column of the *Courier.* Fascinating!

Will Lady wearing green silk stockings communicate with top-hatted gentleman standing at corner of Vine and 4th, yesterday 5 P.M. Address with confidence Box XXX.

Ah, Romance!

"I s'pose you've got big ideas about the price your corn'll fetch," said Addicks.

"I've got ideas. I wouldn't say they were big."

"How the hell is the Queen City going to grow if everyone don't have big ideas?"

Anson Woodhull smiled. "I'm not worrying about the Queen City. It looks big enough to me. I just want to sell my corn."

Mr. Addicks slapped his desk irritably. "Corn, corn, corn! Why don't you farmers get into something with a future to it?"

"Such as?"

"Well—" Addicks consulted his sweat-band file—"barrel staves for one thing. My agents tell me there's quite a shortage in that line." The commodity broker turned sarcastic. "You wouldn't happen to have any oak staves on hand, I s'pose?"

"Only enough to go snug around a barrel," said Anson.

"Barrel?" Mr. Addicks feet were off his desk. A moment later he was scrutinizing the barrel lashed to the tailpiece of Anson's blue wagon. "Tight all round?" he asked.

"Hasn't leaked a drop in ten years."

At the key words *hasn't leaked a drop*, Mr. Addicks took another look. "Say, what's in that barrel?"

"Not codfish." Anson pointed to the markings burned into the barrel head.

C. Woodhull
Landmark Ind.
1873

Whiskey! This was something Mr. Addicks could use. Ten-year-old liquor had a high market value. Charles Moerlein was paying fancy prices for it right here in Cincinnati.

"How much you asking for your whiskey?" inquired Addicks.

"It's not rightly mine," explained Anson. "Belongs to my brother."

"I don't s'pose he'd object to getting . . . forty dollars for it?"

"I wouldn't know about that. The only thing I'm here to sell is corn."

Mr. Addicks seemed to know the whole story. "You've been every place in Cincinnati and they offered you twenty cents a bushel for it. Now you come to me and expect twenty-five."

"Thirty," corrected Anson.

"With the wagon thrown in?"

Anson let the gibe pass. Addicks wanted the whiskey—that was clear. If he wanted it badly enough, he'd buy the corn. A question of ethics arose. Did Anson have the right to sell his bother's inheritance? Yes. Platt's letter gave him that authority. *"If it's land or property I'll sell cheap."*

"Take my corn at thirty cents a bushel," said Anson, "and you can have the whiskey for forty-five dollars."

Mr. Addicks made some calculations on his scratch pad. "Give you twenty-eight cents a bushel for the corn."

"Thirty—or no whiskey."

"It's a deal." The commission merchant peeled eight ten-dollar bills off an anemic wad of greenbacks and pointed to a loading platform. "Set the barrel there—and shovel your corn into those bins."

Scooping his corn out of the blue wain was one of the sweetest triumphs in Anson Woodhull's life. He had risked the hazards of a three-day journey through dust and mire; he had steadfastly refused to accept offers of fifteen, twenty or even twenty-eight cents a bushel for his corn. The thirty dollars just received for his cereal cargo, plus the twenty-five he had won from Tinney Figgatt, gave Anson a total of fifty-five dollars—more than enough to make the purchases on Zarah's list and buy little presents for his children.

But first he must find Platt. From his pocket he drew Platt's letter and read the address 211 Gay Street. Anson chirruped to his horses: "Geet, Hooker; git along, Burnside."

The blue wagon, its springs eased, rolled out of Homer Addicks' yard and clattered over the cobblestones of the Queen City.

211 GAY STREET

WHEN ALL THE HOUSES on a mean street display the placard *Rooms to Rent*, melancholy has claimed the region for its own. There were many streets in Cincinnati, but by a twist of ironic nomemclature, none were more depressing than Gay Street. Among the houses in this beaten thoroughfare, Number 211 was the shabbiest of all. And of its ten rentable rooms, the third floor back was the dreariest. For three dollars a week, its transient occupants were allowed to dispose themselves on a stage set with standard lodging-house props: a sway-backed bed, a sag-bottomed armchair and a black walnut bureau with a leprous mirror. Alleyway lighting and a cold-water tap down the hall.

Still, it was a refuge, a place where you could take off your clothes. Solange Vincy, weary from job-hunting, unlaced her high shoes and eased the velour skirt down over curving hips. By old habit she studiously avoided looking at herself in the black walnut mirror; long ago Sister Paracleta, instructing Solange in First Communion, had advised, "In examining one's conscience before confession, always ask, 'Have I undressed immodestly?'" At the time, Solange's dark eyes had widened with surmise. How could one undress immodestly? Now, she knew the wisdom behind Sister Paracleta's injunction. To gaze at oneself, especially when fatigued or lonely, brought on yearnings scarcely helpful with the dreariest part of the afternoon still ahead. She slipped into

a violet silk negligee, thrust her tired feet into a pair of
slippers and started the coffee-making ritual.

The midafternoon use of coffee was part of the wisdom
that Solange had inherited from her Creole mother, Lutece.
No matter how badly things marched in that damp, overcrowded house on Cadeaux Street, a pot of coffee, New
Orleans style, with a little jug of warm milk to bring the dark
infusion to exactly the right shade of coffeeness, would buoy
Lutece Vincy over the shoals of a luckless marriage. After
the first cup, Lutece would start brushing her wonderful
hair. Two cups would bring songs bubbling from her neglected throat—chansons nostalgic of her girlhood in Provence
when Lutece could sing with truth:

> *On ne joue pas de nous*
> *Sans y être invite*

Humming the simple air, Solange lighted an alcohol lamp
in a curtained alcove, then started down the uncarpeted
hallway for the cold-water tap. Coming back, the heel of her
slipper broke off sharply in a crack of the bare floor. Bother!
Solange placed the coffeepot on the little flame and began
searching for a pair of mules buried somewhere in the cow-
hide trunk that had served her for years as hope chest and
garderobe. The trunk was plastered with hotel stickers and
baggage tags, scabby reminders of split weeks in Cosmopolis,
Louisiana, Vienna, Arkansas, Paris, Missouri. Never the world
city that young fancy had set out to capture. Always some
mud-banked river town. . . .

Kneeling, Solange lifted the cover and gazed down at the
faded finery in the trunk. How, she wondered, could any
reasonably intelligent woman collect so many mistakes, or
why, having cluttered her life with so much counterfeit,
should she continue to accept more? She rummaged through
layers of tinseled apparel, searching for a dream that the
battered trunk had never contained. In place of Juliet's
chaste cincture, she picked up the glass-studded belt of a
tent-show houri. *For Men Only! Hurry, hurry. This way,
Gents!* Under a bead-fringed leotard, she found not Titania's
scepter or Lady Bracegirdle's fan but a lizard-skin case containing a dagger. And not Lady Macbeth's. She dug deeper
and at last pulled out the slippers she was looking for. Soiled
violet satin, rhinestone-sprinkled, with maribou at the instep.

She closed the trunk, flexed her tired body on the black walnut bed and waited for the coffee to boil. Through the afternoon hush she heard footsteps coming up the stairs. Not the landlady's furtive padding or Platt's hopeless tread. Whose, then?

Firm knuckles, male, were knocking at the door. Should she answer or be still? Again the knock, followed by an indefinable silence of expectancy and a voice neither challenging nor fearful.

"Does Platt Woodhull live here?"

"He's not home."

"When do you expect him? I'm his brother, Anson."

"Ohh . . ." Solange rose from the bed. "Will you wait a moment, please?" No time to dress now. A swift glance at the mirror, two strokes with her hairbrush, a smoothing of her negligee, and Solange was at the door. There in the dimly lighted hallway she saw a tall, somber-visaged countryman, exuding an odor of hay and horses.

"I'm Platt's wife, Solange. Won't you come in?"

Her simplicity made it easy for Anson to follow her into the room. Unembarrassed, Solange sat on the edge of her trunk and motioned her visitor to the sag-bottomed armchair. Hat across his knees, Anson tried not to stare at the handsome creature who apparently thought nothing of receiving a man in negligee. His experience with women was meager; long contentment with Zarah had insulated him from any awareness that they existed. Yet now he felt himself making inevitable comparisons between Platt's wife and his own. The women were about the same age. Zarah was slightly taller, her curves less opulent, maybe. There were other differences, too. Anyone looking at Zarah Woodhull would have known that there had been only one man in her life. Solange, on the other hand, reminded Anson of a fine steeplechaser that, by some quirk of fortune, had never fallen into the right hands.

"You must be the 'good news' Platt mentioned in his letter." It was the boldest remark Anson had ever made to a woman.

"And you're the wonderful big brother Platt's always talking about."

Anson thought it prudent to check the current of mutual curiosity flowing between this woman and himself. "I gather Platt's been sick," he said.

"He never quite recovered from that New Orleans accident."

If wifely loyalty wished to hold back the nature of the accident, Anson decided to respect it. "Is he getting the medical attention he needs?"

From the curtained alcove Solange produced a bottle of cherry-colored fluid. "He takes a wineglassful of this after meals." Her manner of replacing the bottle was a comment on the medicine's inadequacy.

A silence fell between them. Anson had no desire to cross-examine Solange about her husband's activities or probe into their domestic relationship. Solange, on her side, felt that Anson wished to be of service to her husband, but the nature of that service must be discussed between the brothers themselves. The bubbling coffeepot gave her the opportunity to ask the question always permissible to a woman in her own home.

"Would you like a cup of coffee?"

"That would be very nice."

While she busied herself in the alcove, Anson gazed about the room. On the bureau he saw two pictures in a velvet case; he rose to examine them. One was a photograph of Platt, handsome as ever, quite the racing gentleman in his gray frock coat and top hat cocked over blond curls. Facing Platt in the photograph case was Solange wearing fringed tights and high-laced boots—a costume that Anson had seen only on cigarette cards and circus posters.

"Were you . . . an actress?" he asked.

"I never played Desdemona, if that's what you mean. But I had quite a reputation on the carnival circuit. When that picture was taken, I was Mme. Solange Vincy, willing victim in a buzz-saw act."

Anson had once witnessed such a performance at a county fair; he had wondered why any woman would degrade herself in such fashion. The puzzlement returned now, but he repressed it. If a woman wanted to live that kind of life—why, that was the kind of life she wanted to live.

On a spindly taboret, Solange set out her chipped crockery as though it were Sèvres. Pouring coffee, she created a chatelaine mirage, decorous, yet tinged with intimacy. Anson sipped his coffee and decided to enjoy the interview.

"Tell me about Platt as a boy," said Solange. "What was

he like? Did you get on together?" Bright, eager questions, deserving a happy answer.

"Platt was the best-looking, cleverest boy you ever saw," said Anson. "All gold and quicksilver. Everyone else seemed clumsy by comparison. He could do everything—especially with his fingers. Tie prettier trout flies, write a finer hand, outshoot, outbox anyone in the county—and all without ever seeming to try or even care."

"I suppose the girls were crazy about him?"

"Platt wasn't particularly interested in girls. He'd dance with them at husking bees and did his share of sparking, all right. He could have married any girl in the county, but that would have meant 'sticking to one furrow,' as Platt called it, and he wasn't a one-furrow man."

Anson channeled the mounting flood of reminiscence. "Our farm was on a bend of the Ohio, and when the big river boats went past our place, all blazing with lights, Platt used to say, 'That's the life for me.' So when he was old enough, he went piping after them, around the bend and far away. I wonder if he found the things he wanted."

Solange avoided the sententious counter-question "Who does?" She poured a second cup of coffee and said, "He wanted to be a professional gambler. Well, he is."

"Has he been successful at it? I mean, is he lucky?"

"You're asking two different questions." Solange spoke as one instructed in a special lore. "Luck isn't the most important thing in gambling. A man who plays cards ten hours every day knows that he will hold aces as often as treys. Any professional is expected to have a certain amount of judgment and coolness. Platt has plenty of both." Solange was trying to be objective. "But when the big money is on the table, he somehow manages to lose."

Anson looked puzzled. "If luck averages out, as you say, and he's skillful, why isn't he a success?"

"Why? Because his playing lacks threat. Platt knows all the tricks of irritating other players. He keeps them off balance with little mannerisms and gibes. But that's not enough." Womanlike, Solange sought to explain a general truth in terms of personality. "Have you ever heard of Damon Frye?"

"By reputation." Anson wanted to hear Solange's version of the Frye legend.

"Frye was—still is—probably the greatest of the river-boat

gamblers. He liked Platt, coached him—perhaps *trained* is a better word—because Frye was more than half animal trainer. When he sat down at a card table, you heard his whip cracking at your ear." She gave the figure a nightmarish turn. "He was like a stranger coming toward you in a bad dream, palms turned outward to show you there was nothing in his hands. He'd smile, let you look down his cuff to prove he had nothing up his sleeve. Frye didn't need anything in his hands or up his sleeve. He'd just chill your spine. It wasn't merely a trick you could learn by practice. It was Frye's *character*. And Platt for better or worse, hasn't that kind of a character."

She eased the tension by sugaring Anson's second cup of coffee. "Before his accident Platt did well enough. He was at his best when playing against well-heeled amateurs—cotton planters or whiskey salesmen who didn't mind losing a couple of hundred dollars to a charming professional." A note of quiet pride entered her voice. "Once on a trip between Louisville and New Orleans, he won twelve hundred dollars at stud."

"That's a lot of money."

"If the trip had lasted another day, he'd probably have lost it. Even amateurs catch on after a while."

Anson felt like a man peering into a series of obliquely placed mirrors that revealed secrets too intimate for gazing. No more probing now. He wanted some simple information. "Platt's accident—exactly how did it happen?"

Solange turned another page of her sibylline book. "The first rule of gambling is never to step out of your class. Platt broke that rule by getting into a dice game on a New Orleans dock. Instead of throwing the dice the usual way, he made the mistake of rolling them out of his hat. That's amusing enough when you do it with gentlemen. But one of the dock hands wasn't amused—and Platt ended up with the tip of a bailing hook in his lung."

Anson winced.

"It might have been worse," continued Solange. From the bureau she took the velvet photograph case and bent over Anson's shoulder. "See, the tip of the bailing hook got caught right here." She pointed to the base of the diamond tie pin. "No wonder Platt calls it his lucky piece."

A dubious amulet.

The recital of Platt's misadventures filled Anson with a protective urge. "Does he ever speak of Landmark?"

"Often." Solange was barely murmuring now. "And with great longing."

"Do you think he'd like to come home?"

A glance of wild beatitude burned up from the violet depths of her eyes. "Oh, it would be wonderful to get him out of all this."

Twilight was at the dusty windowpane. "Where would I be likely to find him?"

"He usually plays cards at the Rhine Palast on Vine Street." Solange hesitated. "The owner, a man named Ziegler, has been stripping him for the last two months." She burst into tears. "Ziegler isn't smart. He's just . . . *cruel*."

ROYAL FLUSH

IN THE BACK ROOM of the Rhine Palast five men were playing a final hand of stud poker for the biggest pot of the afternoon. Fifty-six dollars in coins and crumpled dollar bills lay heaped in the center of the table; four cards had already been dealt. Helmut Ziegler, with a pair of queens in full view, bet a dollar. Mr. Homer Addicks, hoping for the miracle that would transform his pair of jacks into three of a kind, did likewise. The other players dropped out. Whereupon Platt Woodhull, with a king, queen and jack of spades showing, casually flipped two silver dollars onto the table. He desperately wanted to win this pot. He *had* to win it. Yet his outward manner showed nothing of desperation as he said, "Up once more, *Gastwirt*. Don't let the royal family frighten you."

Unfrightened by the cards, Herr Ziegler was vastly irritated by the taunting inflection of *Gastwirt*. For some reason not quite understandable to Helmut Ziegler this threadbare faker with the trembling fingers and forced cough could still make him feel like a clumsy boor. Well, this was the boor's day for revenge.

"So you buck me, Woodhull. I buck you back. Up another dollar."

It was a small thumbscrew bet calculated to twist the last visible coin from Platt's white fingers. In eight weeks of daily play Ziegler had taken Platt Woodhull's measure and money, not to mention his gold studs and other oddments of personal jewelry. Now he was moving in for the gambler's diamond tie pin with its spangled whip of rubies.

To be casual about spending your last dollar on the turn of a card is either a free gift of nature or an acquired characteristic, depending upon what has happened to you a thousand times before and will keep on happening until you die. True to form, Platt tossed in his last dollar.

"Cards, dealer." In contrast to the fever spot on his cheek Platt's voice was cool—the coolness of an icicle about to snap.

Mr. Homer Addicks dealt. To Ziegler fell the ten of diamonds; to Platt, the ace of spades. Black and impressive, his ace buttressed one end of a possible royal flush.

According to house rules all limits were off on the last hand. Ziegler's pair of queens entitled him to bet first. He considered the situation carefully, then shrugged his suety shoulders. "So what are queens?" He gave the thumbscrew a punishing twist. "I check to Mr. Fourflush."

Negligence in full command, Platt smiled at the company. "With your permission, gentlemen, I will now scrutinize my hole card." Like a gourmet apologizing for the pinch of salt that he is about to sprinkle on a perfect dish, he turned up the corner of his bottom card.

The thing he saw drained the fever spot from his cheek. His hole card was the ten of spades! Of the 2,598,960 possible combinations in a deck of cards, Platt Woodhull held a royal straight flush—the highest hand in poker.

The single flaw in this otherwise perfect situation was an embarrassing lack of cash. A thousand dollars, ten thousand dollars, he would bet it in full confidence that the German (who probably held three queens or possibly a full house) would lock horns with him. His mind raced for a solution. How far would Ziegler hatred affect his judgment? A legitimate subject for inquiry.

"My credit is good here, I suppose?" He was a club member proffering an I.O.U. to an old friend.

The situation creamed Ziegler's appreciation of the jest. "Only the devil gives credit to a gambler, and I—*ha-ha*—am not that kind of a devil." The proprietor's Baltic-blue eyes focused covetously on Platt's stickpin. "Still, with the proper kind of security, I would advance you enough to bluff your way out."

Platt unclasped the horseshoe tie pin. It was his lucky piece and he hated to part with it, even temporarily. Yet there was nothing else he could do.

"You've had your eyes on this for a long time, Herr Landlord. How much do you offer me for it now?"

Ziegler carelessly appraised the stickpin. "Fifty dollars."

"Don't be ridiculous. Any jeweler in town would give me five hundred."

"We are not jewelers here. Only card players. Take this fifty dollars. Bet all or any part of it, and the bluff will be over."

Platt took the money and tossed it onto the pile at the center of the table. The German covered the bet. "I call you," he said.

In the approved *River Queen* manner Platt turned over his bottom card. "Can you beat a royal straight, Landlord?"

The bulge in Ziegler's eyes said that he could not.

"Your three little queens aren't any good, eh? Then, with your permission, *Gashwirt.*" Platt curved his arm exultantly around the hoard of bills and silver. This was the way to handle matters. He would take his cherry medicine regularly; pay his back rent, buy Solange a bangle, move to a better place perhaps. . . .

But first he must redeem his diamond horseshoe. He shoved a fifty-dollar bill toward Ziegler. "My pin, *Gastwirt.*"

"*Nicht so schnell.*" Ziegler took the pin from his pocket and examined it admiringly. "Now that I see it in better light, it is really a very pretty piece. I must have two hundred dollars for it."

Platt's lips went the color of zinc. "You're joking, Ziegler."

"The joke will get funnier yet. How much is in the pot?"

Platt counted his winnings. "One hundred sixty-five dollars and thirty-one cents."

"Then everything is easy. One hundred sixty-five dollars will make a substantial down payment on the pin."

A chill, aguelike in severity, racked Platt's body. The drawstrings of his lips quivered feebly as he realized that he was caught in Ziegler's trap. "But I need this money," he protested weakly.

"Who doesn't need money? Make up your mind, Woodhull. Which do you want most—the pot or the pin?"

Platt took refuge in a fit of coughing. The spasm helped him reach a decision. Without the diamond pin, his lucky piece, he could not go on. Whereas if he lost the money, he would be no worse off than before. Weakly, he shoved his winnings across the table to Ziegler. "Give me back my pin."

"Not yet." Ziegler counted the money carefully. "This is only the first installment. When you cough up, *ha-ha*, the balance—thirty-four dollars and sixty-nine cents—then I give you back your property."

Rebel murmurs rose from the other players.

"That's layin' it on pretty thick, Ziegler."

"It ain't right."

"He didn't *sell* you the pin," said Homer Addicks.

The proprietor's Bismarck mustaches stiffened. A *Kontrolleur* controls, doesn't he? Especially in his own place of business. "I'm not buying the pin," he explained. "Only holding it for our friend. To keep everything businesslike, I give him a receipt." He scribbled on a piece of paper, "Rec'd from P. Woodhull on acc. $165.31." Then he thrust the receipt at Platt. "In a day or two, with a change of luck, you can pay the remainder."

Herr Ziegler took on the magnanimity of a man who was at once custodian and host. "Come out to the bar. I buy everyone a drink."

Behind the mirrored bar he set out glasses and pushed an unlabeled bottle of whiskey toward his guests. Coarse witticisms greeted the nameless stuff.

"Old Panther Juice, or something else beginning with *P*."

"*This* panther must've died of diabetes," observed Addicks.

Clutching the bar rail for support, Platt lifted a glass of the harsh whiskey to his lips. The vile drench steadied the motor trembling of his hands but could not quiet the deeper agitation within. Through the fissures of his cracked vanity, one question rose: How could a professional gambler, holding the highest possible cards, mismanage his luck so fatally? He had been outwitted, overreached, not only by a Damon Frye, but by a stupid tavern-keeper.

As proof of his own futility, he held in his hand, dated and signed, the receipt for his own character.

"Another drink, Woodhull?" Ziegler was asking. "Sorry it ain't Rosemere."

Lifting the second glass of whiskey, Platt saw his own face in the mirror behind the bar. It was the face of a man haggard with disease, gouged by wasting years. The mouth was no longer beautiful. On thinning curls a soiled top hat sat askew; and from a greasy Ascot no diamond horseshoe flashed.

He could explain the loss of the pin to Solange with another lie. The habitual is easy. But life can't be perpetually cajoled by falsehoods. It had caught up with Platt Woodhull, cornered him at last. How endure the misery of luckless days ahead?

Was it an illusion that caused Platt to see another face in the bar mirror? No, it was not a fantasy. It was the face of his brother Anson.

The whiskey glass almost fell from Platt's nerveless fingers. Summoning up his last reserves of vanity, he greeted his older brother with a hand-pumping display of Virtue Abused, and Elegance Waylaid by Ill-bred Inferiors.

Anson listened to his brother's jumble of incoherencies regarding a certain tie pin.

"Here's the receipt to prove it," said Platt, handing Ziegler's chit to his brother. "And these gennelmen, well, thish gennelman, anyway, Misch Addicks here, meet flower of the Woodhull flock, good ol' Rock of *Jib-alter* himself. You tell him, Addicks, just wha' happened."

Anson put his arm protectively around Platt's waist. "Does it really matter, Platt? The blue wain's outside. I'm taking you and Solange home."

Platt turned childishly stubborn. "Can't go without my lucky piesch." He waggled his forefinger at the diamond horseshoe blazing in Ziegler's cravat.

The scene was rapidly falling apart. With Platt clinging to the bar rail and Ziegler sneering at his greasy, broken victim, there was little time for judicial weighing of testimony. Anson didn't pretend to be judicial. He merely leaned across the bar and whispered something into the landlord's ear.

Docility, terror and unseemly haste met head on as Zeigler unfastened the diamond horseshoe and dropped it into Anson's palm.

"Thanks," said Anson. "Now, Platt, here's your tie pin. Just a little misunderstanding all round. Hold him up, Addicks, while I pin his lucky piece back in place."

Darkness was caving in on Platt now. Weary and broken, he buried his lolling head in the hollow of Anson's shoulder; tears streamed down his sunken cheeks as the odor of hay and horses, the smell of his brother's body—warm family flesh in a world of cold uncaring—revived feelings of safety that Platt hadn't felt for years. The prodigal brother was going home. The luxury of surrender claimed him.

He was trying to say, "So long, *Gas'wirt*," when Anson picked him up bodily and carried him to the door.

THE PRODIGAL BROTHER

THE FLOOR OF A WAGON—even when padded by a double thickness of horse blankets—isn't the softest bed in the world. After two days of jolting over rutted roads, Platt Woodhull began to be fretful; on the third he became openly querulous. Yet, by Anson's order, he must lie flat on his back and conserve his little store of strength.

The first day on the road had been pleasant enough. Weak to exhaustion, Platt had been content to lie quietly on the wagon floor, gazing straight upward at the cloud-filled sky, while cool autumn airs sponged his hot face. By turning his head he could see Anson and Solange sitting on the high-backed seat; most of the time Platt had neither wish nor energy to move. Enough to hear the jingle of harness and the turning of wheels that were carrying him away from the quagmire of his past. Merely by unclenching his fingers, Platt let a series of humiliating yesterdays—shabby lodging houses, cheap beer halls, Ziegler's greasy patronage and Teutonic cruelty, all the dodges, pretenses and fumblings of defeat and illness—slip from his hands.

But what lay ahead? Bothersome questions began on the second day, when Platt ran out of fine-cut Virginia for his cigarettes. The crude home-grown tobacco from Anson's pouch burned the membranes of Platt's sensitive throat. Twice Anson stopped at crossroad hamlets to ask for fine-cut and rice paper. When Platt learned that country stores just didn't carry such articles, he began to feel like the prodigal brother whose homecoming wasn't being adequately celebrated.

And speaking of prodigal brothers, how should he approach the role? Repentantly, or with the bravado of a hunter home from the hills? Platt couldn't decide. As the sepia shadows of afternoon waned to violet, the jolting motion of the wagon churned up old sediments of fear. What were Anson's motives for bringing him back? Pity? Gloating revenge over a disinherited brother? On the subject of his disinheritance Platt became moody. For twenty years' service on his father's farm, he had received a single barrel of whiskey—market value $45.00. Four weeks' back rent had claimed more than half his legacy; Solange held the remainder in her pocketbook. He could hear her laughing on the front seat beside Anson. What was all the hilarity about? The laughter ceased; now Solange and Anson were talking in tones of subdued intimacy.

Platt permitted himself the luxury of a coughing fit, then peevishly asked Solange for his cherry-colored medicine. He took a double nip from the bottle and longed for something stiffer.

"Got anything to drink up there, Anse?" Mock heartiness masked his petulance.

"Sorry, the little brown jug's run dry. Plenty when we get home, though."

To amuse himself, Platt pulled out a pack of cards, riffled them accordion-style and played solitaire on the jolting wagon floor. In the course of the game he fingered the jack of diamonds, a card he had always identified with himself. His diamond-and-ruby tie pin strengthened the illusion. Then he remembered the ghastly half hour when his lucky piece had glittered in Ziegler's greasy Ascot. How had Anson retrieved the tie pin?

Now they were striking camp for the third night. Anson pulled up under a clump of sycamores and came around to the tail of the wagon.

"Feeling better?"

Platt rubbed his hipbone. "A little stiff from lying on these planks. Say, Anse, what did you whisper into that German's ear?"

"Just told him I'd tear out his windpipe unless he forked over."

"Suppose he hadn't?"

"But he *did*." Anson chose to underplay the affair. "Might do you good to move around. I'll help Solange rustle up some firewood while you catch a few catfish for supper."

"What'll he use for a pole?" asked Solange.

The two brothers looked at each other, then broke into laughter.

"Tell her, Anse."

"You won't believe it, Ma'am, but your husband—unless he's out of practice—is the only man in the Ohio Valley who knows how to catch catfish with his bare hands."

Whether Platt caught the fish barehanded or speared them with a pitchfork, Solange never knew. When he appeared half an hour later, salt pork was sizzling in a frying pan over the campfire. Supper that night was the happiest part of the journey. As they lounged around the fire, Platt displayed some of his old flashing charm.

"I've never seen your wife, Anse. Is she good looking?"

"Very."

"Better looking than Solange?"

Anson pointed to the sky, glowing with autumn constellations. "Well, like the Book says, 'Every star has a separate glory.'"

When the fire burned low, they bedded down for the night—Solange and Platt on the wagon floor while Anson stretched out on the seat. Night music came on: crickets sawing on two-toned fiddles, autumn winds choiring through the sycamore branches above them.

From his wagon seat Anson gazed up at the familiar Indiana sky. He was not an astronomer; he merely knew, in landsman fashion, the names and location of a few familiar constellations. There, in seven-starred splendor, glistened the Wain, wheeling on its great orbit around Polaris. Some called it the Dipper. Wain or Dipper, how comforting to know that men had named these distant bodies after homely objects of daily use, arranged them in families, giving each star a relationship to his companions.

On earth as it is in heaven.

The screech of a railroad whistle ripped the page of night music; a locomotive headlight outshone for a moment the cool brightness of the stars. A fast freight, symbol of the new age, swirled past, then an ageless silence settled down once more.

Drowsing on his wagon seat, Anson drifted toward sleep. On his trip to Cincinnati he had accomplished everything he had set out to do: sold his corn, made all the purchases on Zarah's list, bought gifts for each of his children. Best of all, he had found Platt. With a few weeks' rest, regular food and great doses of Indiana sunshine, Platt would be strong again, ready to pick up the heritage he had carelessly thrown aside.

"Anse?" It was Platt's voice. "Got another blanket? I feel chilly."

"Sure thing, Platt." He handed his own blanket across the wagon seat, curled up and smiled as he thought of the commotion in the barnyard when he reached home the next day. He could see Laly flying toward him, Zarah waving from the porch. He heard himself murmuring, "Zarah, this is Solange. Solange, this is Zarah, my wife."

8.

AUTUMN CONSTELLATION

WHAT HAPPENS WHEN two good-looking women, approximately the same age, one fruitful, the other childless, both saturated to their hair roots with feminine energy, find themselves living under the same roof? Will their rivalry stir up household strife, create disturbances at those deeper levels where women grapple for supremacy and love? It could happen that way; it usually does. But no such struggle took place between Zarah and Solange. At a glance each sensed the core of strangeness—and inviolability—in the other. To Solange, weary of wandering, Zarah seemed a fixed, unchallengeable star in the family constellation that she and Anson had created out of their own bodies. To become part of that system, to wheel through its seasons and aspects, even in a subordinate position, was happiness enough for Solange.

And Zarah? Where other women might have read danger in Solange's handsome figure, Zarah saw only a sister creature burdened with an ailing husband and eager for refuge. Exempt from jealousy, sure of her own place as wife, mother and chatelaine, Zarah could afford to extend a gracious hand and say—with only a vestige of Brattle Street reserve—"Welcome to this house."

Winning admittance through the central gate, Solange swarmed over the household. With Platt comfortably settled in an upper bedroom, she joyously took over a full half of Zarah's domestic burden. She scrubbed the children, made the beds, performed her stint at the wash tub, and rose at dawn to cook the heavy breakfast that sent Anson full-fed into the fields. An approach less generous, a manner even slightly servile, could easily have reduced Solange to the position of a household drudge. Again, too forward a disposition might have aroused in Zarah certain queen-bee resentments. But how could anyone resent this affectionate, eager-handed woman who marched daylong with the light tread of the volunteer, who needed no directives, never overstepped authority, and—in addition to her other virtues—spoke an excellent brand of French? Within a month Zarah accepted Solange as companion and confidante, kin and kind.

Solange had a flair for cutting cloth and sprigging out old clothes with ribbons or velvet drawn from her wonderful trunk. She made her first conquest of the children by edging Laly's best petticoat with lace.

"Will it make me rustle when I walk?" asked Laly.

"So you wish to rustle." Solange laughed. "For that, one needs taffeta." She pulled an emerald-green underskirt from a heap of faded finery in her trunk. "*Voici,* the very thing." An evening's work with scissors and needle supplied Laly with the genuine *frou-frou* article, particularly valuable when she mounted the living-room hassock to deliver her memory gems.

The wooing of Quincia took quite another tack. Watching the lonely child arranging a handful of timothy blossoms, Solange taught her the art of making clover chains. "It goes so. You tie a silky clover stem under the blossom of its sister. The knot is firm but not too tight. When you have a dozen yards of clover chain I'll show you how to make wreaths and necklaces." Quincia's gentle fingers readily caught the trick; soon she was trailing through the house bedecked like a little Ophelia who had decided not to drown herself that day.

Even lumpish Ozzie got his share of attention. When he sucked his thumb, Solange sympathized by saying, "The sweetest meat clings to our own joints—*n'est-ce pas,* Ozzee?" A gurgle indicated Ozzie's profound agreement. The gurgle became a noisy crowing when Solange poured gravy onto his suppertime mound of mashed potatoes, then stuffed him sausage-tight before putting him to bed.

As Zarah's pregnancy advanced, Solange kept her in bed till noon by bringing up wonderful breakfast trays tempting even to a morning-sick appetite. She had a delightful way of describing food, pointing out each item with a zestful forefinger. "See what we have today, Zarah. An omelette *baveuse* with green peppers. Cornbread toasted, coffee creole and some of your own strawberry jam. Remember, we are eating for two now."

After breakfast, while she brushed Zarah's hair into a cedar shine, they gossiped in the discreetly unguarded manner of women who have an inexhaustible curiosity about each other. Solange's account of her experiences as a carnival player gave Zarah an intimate glimpse of a woman who was somehow satisfied to accept less than she deserved of life. Like a fine Cremona that has never been played by a master, thought Zarah.

Solange, in turn, listening to descriptions of life in Cambridge, frankly marveled at Zarah's decision to escape from the cultural harbor of Brattle Street. The details of her nuptial flight with Anson revealed as nothing else could Zarah's need for crowding on emotional sail and maneuvering in waters alien, both in depth and hazard, to the conventional shallows in which she had been reared.

"You must have been strongly attracted to Anson."

"I was. I am. He is the only man who ever made me feel like being a woman." Self-disclosure merged with curiosity about how things went with others. "But is that so unusual between husband and wife? You and Platt are devoted, too."

"There is a deep attachment between us." Solange was plaiting Zarah's wonderful hair. "But loves differ."

"Love is never the same—even between the same people. How does yours differ from mine?"

"Platt and I cling to each other through weakness. You and Anson through strength."

"The need in either case is equally great."

"Weakness and weakness do not equal strength and strength."

A love theorem older than Euclid, and as true. Yet somehow its statement brought no comfort to Zarah. The novelty of childbearing had worn off. She lay back on her pillow. "There are times when my strength does not match Anson's."

"It is woman's fate to be overmatched."

A touch of bluestocking asperity rose in Zarah. Residues of woman's age-long resentment, buried beneath her passional need, broke to the surface. "Do you believe that, Solange? Must a woman prove her love by becoming a brood mare?"

"Love knows only one kind of maleness, Zarah."

"I know. I would not have it otherwise. Yet so much of me streams away year after year in bearing children."

For once Solange failed in her office of consolation, as her own private desperation disclosed itself. "Is it worse than streaming away month after month in barrenness? To watch a hundred love moons rise hopefully and to know that they will set without fulfillment—this is a sorrow you have been spared, Zarah. Ah—men and calendars—we can never free our thoughts from either. But come, this is not the mood for beauty. Today your hair shall have a turquoise ribbon." Solange's gaiety returned on a full tide. "Now a touch of color." With a rabbit's foot dipped in rouge, she lightly brushed Zarah's cheekbones, then handed her a mirror. "So beautiful . . . If you were not already pregnant, Anson would make you so tonight."

The pink flush on Zarah's cheekbones flooded her face and throat. "Solange, you are incurable."

"*C'est vrai*—love is a malady from which the heart does not wish ever, ever to be cured."

Only in Anson's presence did Solange mute her outgoingness. By an unspoken contract, they never remained alone in a room together or exchanged more than the necessary minimum of words. Still, ordinary household contacts were unavoidable. Anson could not help brushing past her as she carried a tray of food to Zarah or Platt, nor could he avert his eyes as she descended from the loft, her apron full of freshly gathered eggs. There was nothing of the flaunt about Solange. Only this: after-images of her movements, no matter how innocent or casual, returned to plague Anson's visual memory as he labored in the field or barn.

It seemed strange to him that he should always think of Solange in motion while Zarah appeared before him as the center of serene repose. Other contrasts and comparisons arose at every hour of the day. A laden bough in the orchard, the branch aching with fruit, hung close to the ground. That was Zarah. When he filled his basket, the unburdened bough sprang back to flick his cheek with a caress. That was Solange. Walking by the banks of Paddle Creek, he saw Zarah in the deep pool, tranquil and mysterious, while Solange rippled vivaciously over golden pebbles and polished stones. Of an evening as he watched the two women teaching the children, Zarah was the priestess transmitting wisdom and character; Solange's tongue darted deliciously between her teeth.

Beyond all comparisons, all contrasts, he realized that it

was neither Zarah's fruitfulness nor depth, neither her wisdom nor serenity, that made him love her above all other women. Solange was a grace note, Zarah the full chord. And in the quiet that came before sleeping, Anson listened, close to her heart, for variations, never twice the same, on that abiding theme.

While the fine weather lasted, Platt occasionally sauntered into the barn. Freshly shaved, his gray suit cleaned and pressed by Solange, he had regained a touch of his old casino elegance—strangely out of place against the workaday backdrop of a corn farm. Both his manner and attire indicated that he had no intention of helping with chores. Nor did Anson urge him to. If and when Platt wanted to pick up his share of labor, Anson would be delighted; meanwhile it was enough to see Platt on the mend.

Anson thoroughly enjoyed these hours of companionship with his younger brother. How good, after so much woman chatter, to let the rougher male idiom roll off one's tongue in the presence of a long-missed brother! There was so much to talk about—family and old times, sad, sweet, tender and comical. So much to find out, too, about the fifteen years since they had last seen each other.

In these conversations Anson uncovered no profundities in Platt's mind. Not that he was stupid—far from it. He had a lively narrative gift for describing his adventures, scrapes and close shaves. But of politics, agriculture—subjects dear to Anson's heart—he knew little and cared less. Even immediate surroundings failed to bother him. Once he picked up a set of blunted chisels and began sharpening them, but soon lost interest in his job.

Platt really never came to life until he pulled the inevitable pack of cards from his waistcoat pocket. The very sight and touch of the deck were medicinal to him. Like a pianist practicing velocity exercises, he frolicked with the cards, making them flutter like the spokes of a bright wheel kept in motion by his fingers. Sometimes the pack resembled a concertina opening and closing with a music of its own—a gravity-defying feat. What, Anson wondered, kept the cards from falling to the ground?

He watched his brother shoot out a long arm and let the cards ripple along his sleeve from wrist to shoulder, coil around his neck like a snake, then slither down the other arm

and slide into Platt's confident palm. These exercises over, he
would clear away a space on the work bench and become
engrossed in some form of solitaire, eagerly scrutinizing the
face of each card as a soothsayer might examine the entrails
of a sacrificial victim.

Curiosity tinged with good-natured skepticism caused Anson to ask: "What makes a deck of cards fascinate you so?"

Platt rolled a cigarette, thereby breaking the "No Smoking" rule that hangs invisibly in every barn.

"I'll show you." Platt laid four cards—a club, a spade, a
heart and a diamond—on the work bench. "Why do you
suppose the pack is divided into four suits?"

"Never thought about it before."

"Couldn't there be some connection between these cards
and the four seasons, the four points of the compass, the
four aspects of the moon, the four corners of the great
pyramid?" He continued earnestly. "Do you think it's an
accident that a full pack has fifty-two cards—one for every
week of the year?" Platt's excitement was rising. "And how
do you account for the fact that the total number of spots
in a full deck is three hundred and sixty-five?" He flung
down the joker. "With an extra card to account for the odd
day that sneaks into the calendar every four years?"

Platt gathered up the cards. "Sounds kind of mysterious,
doesn't it?"

"No more mysterious than a bed having four legs." Anson's
drawshave was putting a graceful curve on a home-made ax
handle. "It would be a nice subject to investigate in spare
time, but I don't see it as a life occupation."

"Life!" Contempt edged Platt's voice. "Getting up every
morning, repeating the same motions all day, then going
to bed so you can get up again tomorrow. Do you call that
life? With cards it's different. Every new hand is a fresh
combination, packed with new possibilities, never twice the
same. Anse, until you've played a game of stud for high
stakes, you don't know what life is."

Anson realized that Platt's cards were not only a protest
against the monotony of existence but a kind of life in themselves. And in this pasteboard sanctuary his brother had taken
refuge. For Anson, the only refuge was work. Without comment, he put a finer curve on his new ax handle.

"Still don't believe it, do you?" Platt was off on a fresh tack.
"Why do you suppose fortunetellers use cards? It isn't just

superstition, Anse. People fall into *types* that correspond with the face cards. Take yourself, for instance—what card do you think you are?"

"Me, a card?"

Platt offered a pack spread fanwise, face downward. "Pick a card, any card."

Anson pulled out the king of spades.

"See how it works?" Platt was laughing now. "There you are to the buttons—dark-bearded ruler of all you survey. And what do you survey? A quarter section of land that you dig up with a *spade!*"

"A nice parlor trick," conceded Anson. "Where'd you learn it?"

"From a pal, name of Damon Frye." Platt's voice, indefinably pathetic, took a reminiscent turn. "Frye was the top gambler of them all, a blend of perfections suspended in perfect balance. Cold as ice and hot as a woman's breath. A lightning calculator—not only with figures but with people. He was nervy, nerveless; charming most of the time; cruel as a wolf when cornered. Never saw anyone who could outmatch him."

"I clipped him for fifty dollars once."

"You? How? When?"

"On the deck of the *River Queen*. Broad daylight. Sucked him into that old jackknife game we used to play," Anson went on casually. "Must say that Frye stood up rather well under falling steel. Paid off like a gentleman, too. He never knew he was playing against a stacked deck."

Platt gazed at his brother with astonishment. "So you're the hayseed with the ripped coat sleeve. Well, I'll be damned." Unable to grasp the central fact of Anson's psychic supremacy over Frye, Ziegler or anyone else, Platt riffled his cards in silence.

Pity for his younger brother caused Anson to gloss over the matter. "You and this Damon Frye must have been pretty close friends?"

"We were." Sadness in the past tense. "Until we broke up."

"What caused the break-up?"

"A woman."

"Solange?"

Platt gazed at his brother in amazement. "How did you know?"

"Well, I've never heard you speak of any other woman."

Fatigue, regret, a wild desire to undo an old mistake, moved Platt to confession. "Yes, it was Solange. She was Frye's girl. He found her in some sort of carnival show—saw her one day, took her the next. They went together for a long time. Anse, you never saw a better-looking pair. He bought her clothes and jewelry, taught her how to wear them. Gave her everything, except the thing she really wanted—he wouldn't marry her."

"So you did," said Anson quietly. "You couldn't beat Frye's time at the card table, so you won his girl by marrying her."

"That's about the long and short of it."

"And now you're sorry."

Anson's simple statement of the truth, uttered without overtones of moral judgment, brought tears of yearning to his brother's eyes. Neither contrition nor shame, only a sense of something irretrievably lost and stupidly forfeited, moved Platt to reply.

" 'Sorry' doesn't say it, Anse. Frye gave me a confidence that I've never known since or before. With him in a game, everything always went right. But ever since I broke with him, my luck has never been the same."

"Luck!" Anson's wrath exploded. "Must luck be figured in terms of a tinhorn gambler's friendship? Does all luck turn on the fall of a card? This Damon Frye may be all you say he was. I don't know the details and it's none of my business. But hear this, Platt. When you met Solange, luck—if you want to call it that—dealt you the best hand you've ever held."

Dubiously, Platt fingered a card. The Queen of Hearts. "Maybe it did," he said. "Maybe it did."

Against the coming of winter Anson's barn and gristmill became workshops for the production of food. In the last weeks of September the racing torrents of Paddle Creek turned the massive stones that ground corn into golden meal. Later, skillfully slaughtered pigs hung from the rafters of the barn. Disjointed into hams and forequarters, they were smoked, salted, packed into barrels and rolled into the cellar. Before the year's last aster shriveled, Anson set out six acres of winter rye and three of barley. From daybreak till long after dark he toiled, singlehanded, at the endless routine of farm drudgery.

One cold November twilight just as Anson was closing his barn he heard a voice, croakingly familiar. "Need a helper, Mr. Woodhull?"

By his lantern beam Anson saw Richmond Plaskett, the pig drover's son. He had grown a couple of inches and his added height made him seem at least ten pounds underweight. The youth was wearing a coonskin hat and a buttonless jacket, anchored to his thin ribs by a horse-blanket pin.

"Reb! How'd you get here?"

"Shanks mare."

The original shanks mare went shod; Reb was barefooted. "Where's your father?"

The boy hung his head. "He got drunk and drownded hisself in the Cincinnati canal two months ago. They tried to put me into a orphingage but I broke away and then hit out cross country." Reb was pleading now. "Can't I do chores around your place? I'd work real hard for my keep, Mr. Woodhull."

Anson put his arm protectively around the boy. "I bet you'd be a regular six-handed centipede, Reb. We'll talk about it afterward. Come into the kitchen. You're just in time for supper."

Laly, setting the table with blue-ringed crockery, nearly dropped a plate when the pig drover's son entered the kitchen. Proprietary tenderness welled in her eyes at the sight of the scrawny boy. Then and there she took on personal responsibility for fattening him up—a task that began by making a place for him beside her at the table and heaping his plate with food. As pork chops and mashed potatoes disappeared in a rush of gaggingly bad manners, Laly's maternal instincts took a corrective form.

"Don't eat potatoes with a spoon," she whispered—the first of endless admonitions that gradually transformed Reb from a field animal into a fairly presentable specimen of an eleven-year-old boy.

At chores Reb turned to be a ten-handed centipede. He split firewood, curried the horses, fed pigs, killed rats with his slingshot; then, with Laly beside him, doubled as busboy and dish-wiper in the kitchen. His real trial came after supper during the period of study and games. Laly, competitive and bossy, easily outstripped him in reading and spelling; the advantage shifted somewhat when it came to arithmetic.

Reb knew his numbers; he was on the nines table while Laly struggled with her sevens. Checkers and ticktacktoe were a standoff, but Laly showed a clear supremacy when they played Authors. Reb would be left with a handful of jumbled cards while Laly triumphantly laid down complete sets of Whittier, Longfellow and William Cullen Bryant.

"Can't you remember *anything?*" she'd say, sorting out Reb's cards for him afterward. " 'The One Hoss Shay' never goes under Emerson. Now listen while I tell you for the last time." She fed him the syllables slowly. " 'One Hoss Shay' goes under Ol-iv-er Wen-dell Holmes."

"Wolliver Hendell Wolmes—yeah, sure, I'll remember next time."

Reb's greatest triumph was his skill at whittling; he could make a jackknife sing. From a stick of pine kindling he fashioned a set of dolls' clothespins for Quincia. He made a whistle of rum-cherry wood for Ozzie, and the whole family laughed at Reb's instructions: "Don't suck; blow!"—a trick that Ozzie mastered by sheer accident. To pacify Laly, Reb whipped up a dozen trout flies from varicolored rooster feathers. "I'll show you how to cast sometime," he promised in a voice that casually suggested the natural superiority of boys over girls at things that really mattered.

Sometimes when Uncle Platt felt strong enough, he came downstairs to instruct the children in penmanship. Such writing lessons he could give! It was a period of flourishes and arabesques, of ink-bottle doves and curlicues. Platt was master of them all. He could write with both hands at the same time, pen two different names on separate pieces of paper. He could write backward or upside down. And when it came to imitating a signature, why he'd merely glance at a greenback and write "Grover Cleveland" with one hand and "Ulysses S. Grant" with the other.

"How do you *do it*, Uncle Platt?" asked Laly.

"Simple," Platt explained. "You don't let your left hand know what your right hand is doing."

The parlor hour always ended with Zarah entertaining the lamplighted group with songs accompanied by her dulcimer. Listening to "Bendemer's Stream" or "In Old Madrid," Anson, puffing at his churchwarden, surveyed the little group with contentment. These were the rewards of life. This was what happened when a man was good, industrious and lucky. If

he could only add $200 a year to his cash income, he would
be the happiest man in Landmark County. But as December
came in, Anson was down to his last ten dollars, with no
prospect of additional cash until next fall.

9.

FIFER TANSEY

DIAMOND HARD and, like a diamond, testing all other
things with its hardness, winter set in. This was the
kind of weather that Anson liked, but under the relentless
scrutiny of cold everything on the farm began to fall apart.
The much-mended harness broke in three places; even the
ice saw snapped in Anson's hand as he hacked next summer's
supply from the mill pond. One of his horses came down
with a vicious attack of croup; all during a night of intense
cold Anson and Reb worked with hot pads to keep the animal
alive.

A leaden sun was twelve degrees off the horizon, and Anson
was patching the cracked ice saw when he heard across the
frozen fields a shrill medley of hoe-downs, hornpipes and
pigeon wings—airs traditionally frolicsome but now trans-
posed to a gloomy, even sinister music, as though the player
were breathing some uncapturable wildness into his instrument. The piping grew louder as a lanky figure in a stovepipe hat descended the crest of a knoll and strode toward
Anson's barn.

It was Fifer Tansey, field deputy for Apollo-Physician.

Anson knew a great deal about the man. Fifer Tansey had
prescribed the powders for Chauncey's asthma; he had held
the basin in which Anson's mother gave up the last green
ounce of death bile. The Fifer's circling orbit and lack of
fixed abode were certainly odd and his ethical standards were
matters of dispute. But no one could doubt the healing
motives that drove Fifer abroad in all weathers to heal the
ailing and infirm. Bone-setter, tooth-puller, farrier, obstetri-

cian, surgeon-at-large and internist extraordinary, he was, at any rate, the only physician in Landmark County.

Anson greeted him, country style, by pointing to the whiskey jug under the work bench. "Help yourself, Fifer."

"Don't mind if I do." The gaunt Esculapian unslung the huge black wallet from his shoulder and set it down with a metallic clank. The wallet contained, Anson knew, the standard equipment of a perambulating surgeon: a bonesaw, a half dozen lancets, huge shears and cruel probes. Fifer took a dollop from the whiskey jug; then, instead of sitting down, began pacing the barn floor in a kind of wolflike anxiety.

Legend said that this strange physician could smell certain kinds of illness—typhoid, for instance—halfway across a township. Well, what does he smell here? thought Anson. He waited patiently for the evidence to come in.

"Missus all right?" The Fifer made a trial sniff in the direction of the house.

"She's expecting a baby along toward May. Feels queasy before breakfast sometimes."

"Needs a touch of my Peristaltic Persuader." Opening his coat, Fifer Tansey brought into view a cincture not unlike a cartridge belt, containing phials of liquid, powders and ointments that he had compounded from roots and herbs. He selected a phial of green powder and shook a handful into a paper cone. "Have her brew up some of this every morning in a pint of hot water. Sort of keeps things in motion."

Anson accepted the cone. "Much obliged, Fifer."

"Varmints bothering you?" The Fifer was snatching at straws now. "Got a nice tasty exterminator here, harmless to man, death to rodents, skunks and coons."

"Wouldn't have any special call for it. Got things pretty well under control along that line."

Annoyance, puzzlement and balked vanity struggled for control of Fifer Tansey's voice. "You *sure* there ain't no sickness around here, Anse?"

The man's persistent probing found a tiny question in Anson's mind. Could Platt be called sick? Tired, yes; a bit thin and certainly not strong enough to pull his weight at field labor. Anson stated the case as he saw it.

"My brother Platt's been taking things easy for a while. Spends most of his time in bed."

A diabolical smile exposed the Fifer's canines. "Christ

Amighty, Anse, you *know* it ain't natural for a well man to lay abed. Let's have a look at him." He picked up his clanking wallet and strode toward the house with the air of a man whose worst suspicions were about to be justified.

As they entered Platt's room, Anson attempted to give the proceedings a routine turn. "Saw the Fifer passing and asked him to take a look at you."

Patient and physician recognized each other. Fifteen years had passed since Platt had last seen Fifer Tansey. The man had always terrified him. He knew, moreover, that the Fifer never came unless someone were gravely ill. What was he doing here now? In the act of rolling a cigarette, Platt spilled tobacco on the patchwork counterpane.

Fifer Tansey's hooded glance saw propped up on pillows a faded but still recognizable likeness of the golden youth he had known as a boy. He saw a man ailing and afraid, a weak, treacherous man who had broken his mother's heart. Not that Platt's foolishness or vanity made any difference. The man needed medical attention, and Fifer prepared to exercise his powers as a diagnostician and healer.

These powers were remarkable. Fifer Tansey had never seen a medical school or performed a scientific experiment. The uses of a stethoscope and clinical thermometer were unknown to him. He depended on his five naked senses for uncovering diseases hidden in the interior of the human body.

The truth about Fifer Tansey was this: he was gifted (or cursed perhaps) by a unique sensory equipment which, while working for the benefit of others, condemned him to a solitary existence. A staglike delicacy of nostril enabled him to scent typhoid and cholera infantum halfway across a county, yet so intensified domestic odors that he could neither sleep nor eat indoors. Hence, his wandering life under the open sky. But even here, he was defenseless. The Fifer's eardrums, which enabled him to hear and interpret the internal flow of blood, gastric juices and the passage of air through lung tubules, also exposed him to reports of the struggle which constantly went forward in fields, woods, in the upper air, and in caverns under the earth. What a frightening choir! The whirr of the plunging hawk, the scream of the fieldmouse borne aloft in captor talons; the lethal engagement of wasp and spider; the croaking frog in the gullet of the bull snake; the wind itself rushing overhead, and the waters gurgling through underground caverns—all these, every hiss, growl, lament, and despairing groan must be blunted, kept at bay, by constant blowing on a fife.

To the Fifer's tormented senses, the case before him presented no special difficulty. By Platt's rapid, shallow breathing, pallid complexion and the light sweat on his forehead, he knew that this was a lung involvement. A problem in differential diagnosis arose. Was it an early phase of consumption or a lung abscess? Like any explorer, Fifer Tansey wanted a full view of the terrain.

"Strip off your shirt." He placed an inquisitive forefinger on the scar under Platt's breastbone. "How long you had this?"

"About six months."

"Any coughing? Night sweats?"

"Some."

"Spit much? Rusty green stuff?"

"A little."

"A lot," corrected Solange. She had entered the room and was standing beside Anson at the foot of the bed.

The Fifer bent a deep-socketed eye in her direction. "Who's this?" he asked.

"My wife," said Platt.

The physician registered a quite unprofessional opinion of Solange's anatomical points. The eye that could detect treachery or fear was quite capable of appreciating beauty and a predisposition to be generous with it. Ordinarily the Fifer liked to see a buxom wife at the foot of the bed. Some of his choicest fees were collected from robust, grateful wives. Anson's presence ruled out any such possibility here.

Regretfully the Fifer turned from fantasy to auscultation, the art of divining through the eardrum secrets hidden in the interior of the body.

His only preparation for the practice of this was to remove his stovepipe hat. Until the present, Fifer Tansey had somewhat resembled a caricature of Abe Lincoln; now, hatless, his widow's peak of greasy hair made him look like a backwoods Mephistopheles about to cure a man's body in order to steal his soul. This impression was heightened when he crouched beside the bed, gripped his patient in a spiderish embrace and pressed a hairy ear against the extreme left side of Platt's chest. Eyes closed, he listened to the two-part voice of the heart, a ceaseless duet caused by the intake of blood through ventricular valves and its mighty expulsion through auricle and aorta. Without consulting a watch (he had none) he knew that the tempo of Platt's heart was a trifle fast. Eighty-four, eighty-five. He scrounged closer, listening for leaks, murmurs—none.

"Pump's all right." He shifted his ear to the base of Platt's bronchial tree. Here he picked up a coarse rasping gurgle as though the circling rivers of Platt's breath were being forced through a clogged bellows. "Enough pus to drown a beaver in," he murmured.

Laying two fingers of his left hand on Platt's rib cage, he began tapping them lightly with a gnarled forefinger. Tap, tap, tap—front and back, up and down the bony ladder, listening always to the resonance beneath. Like a violin-maker seeking a hidden flaw, the Fifer went on with his percussion until he struck a dull, flattish sound. Slowly he narrowed the area of his investigation until he brought the flaw into full focus.

"Well, sir," he announced with an air of relief, "you're lucky. It's not a lung abscess—just an inflammation about an inch below your chest wall. Trouble is . . . the thing ain't ripe for draining yet."

Fifer made some calculations involving time, distance and his own itinerary. Whatever his findings were, he kept the details to himself, put on his stovepipe hat and said to Anson, "I'll be back when he's ready. Meanwhile, in case his cough bothers, I'll leave the makings of my Golden Expectorant." From a phial in his belt he shook out a generous measure of colorless, transparent crystals into a paper cone.

"Here, ma'am—" he handed the medicine to Solange— "you've got some pure codeine. Mix it with a quart of honey, a pint of Anson's best whiskey, and give the patient a swollop three times a day before meals."

The compounder of Tansey's Golden Expectorant stored up a double eyeful of Solange's curves; then, slinging his black wallet across his shoulder, disappeared through the doorway. Anson followed him down the narrow stairs. No use to invite the Fifer to remain for supper. Like asking a hawk to perch on the back of a kitchen chair. Instead, Anson snatched up a joint of cold pork, a square of cornbread and pressed them into Fifer's hand.

Outside, hints of snow hung on the wind. The Fifer drew in great draughts of fresh air as if to cleanse his lungs from domestic contamination. He seemed calmer, all his earlier anxiety spent, as he munched at the joint of cold pork.

"Think he'll pull through, Fifer?"

Common honesty and a knowledge of what the human body can undergo met in Fifer Tansey's reply. "With a lung inflammation you can't promise a thing. His heart's in good shape, though." He gnawed at the pork joint and shifted his prognosis slightly. "A lot depends on the weather. The caterpillars had a big black band around them last summer. That means a hard winter, Anse. Even a well animal needs all his strength when the cold sets in."

"I know." Cold brought out hidden defects in men and creatures, houses, tools, trees—even rocks.

At the gate Anson pressed a half dollar into Fifer Tansey's unwilling palm. He wanted to ask, Where are you heading now? As well ask a wind-borne seed where it would land, a minor comet why it sped through dark spaces. The Fifer, responding to the mysterious law of his own being, would travel a road that he could not, at this moment, foretell.

At the gate, the perambulating healer unslung his fife, placed it to his lips; then, disdaining country roads, struck across an open field piping his own melancholy variation of "Over the Hills and Far Away."

Snowflakes were falling as Anson started back to his house. He lifted his face to catch their welcome sting. The flakes were hard and small; each crystal differed from the other and each traveled to a common destination by separate paths, alone.

All night the snow fell. Next morning Landmark County was covered by a seamless white counterpane masking familiar things with strangeness. Winter gripped sky and field. Under Anson's roof tree, the forces of life and death converged. While Zarah felt the flutter of new life within her, death struggled remorselessly for Platt. He burned and shivered by turns, coughed blood, and seemed at times to be drowning in a flood of inflammation; only Solange's heroic nursing kept him afloat.

Three weeks passed; then a great blizzard rode like a squadron of caped horsemen across the Ohio Valley. All living creatures took refuge—in farmhouses, barns, caves, in the half-frozen mud on the river bottom.

With roads blocked, Anson's house became a garrison

beset by freezing gales and flanked by the icy Ohio. Merely to exist was a triumph, as the column of mercury in the thermometer dropped to zero—ten, fifteen, eighteen below. This was Anson's kind of weather; it challenged him at the deepest level of his energy. Treading the narrow path between his house and barn, he fought off the challenge, protected his family and creatures by every device and stratagem at his command.

Inside his house, life centered around the kitchen stove, stoked with hard wood chunks. Drafts wide open, the eight-lidded furnace roared defiance at the invading cold. From its oven came great batches of cornbread, huge roasted joints of pork and apples bubbling in sugary juices. Solange did all the cooking and kept a gallon pot of coffee simmering on the back of the stove.

Downstairs all was vitality and commotion—children, dogs, cats and cookery all wheeling about Solange. Upstairs presented a less cheerful picture. In second-floor rooms lay Zarah and Platt, one heavy with expectant life, the other wasting with disease. Both rooms were heated by pipes from the kitchen; extensions of vital warmth generated by the great black stove.

As winter deepened, Platt's symptoms increased in severity; an odor of decay pervaded his room. After a night of plummeting cold, Solange met Anson with grim news. "Platt is dying. Will Fifer come in time?"

"No one can get through this blizzard, Solange. I guess I'll have to puncture the lung myself." Anson filed a piece of copper tubing into a sharp-pointed trocar and was about to plunge it home when, high above the shrieking wind, he heard a shrill piping.

It sounded like "The Campbells Are Coming" distorted by some vagary either of the piper's ear or the winds that tore at the melody in its passage. Anson brushed the frost off a windowpane. Could it be? Yes. Across the fields advancing through waist-deep drifts of snow, the scarecrow came nearer. Clearer now, but still twisted by demonic variations, Anson heard a wild flute playing.

It was—it *was* Fifer Tansey!

Bareheaded, Anson rushed out into the gale to greet this man who combined the healer's instinct with some curious time mechanism lodged within himself. The first instinct—

to reach his patient—was common to all doctors; the second lay deeper, in that mysterious region where the hour says, "Now."

Anson hugged Tansey, carried him bodily into the house. Soaked from the waist down, the physician stamped, shook a piece of the blizzard from his stovepipe hat and asked, "Got anything to drink, Anse?"

"How do you want it—hot or cold?"

"I want it *now*."

Fifer belted down three ounces neat, then asked, "How's the patient?"

"Come see for yourself."

Together they entered the bedroom where Platt lay dying.

Coolly, Fifer drew a hollow needle from his knapsack, dipped its pointed end into a phial of carbolic solution and turned to Solange. "Now, ma'am, this'll run to gallonage, so you better get a pail. Anse, prop your brother up so's gravity can get a better tug." Over the blunt end of his needle, Fifer slipped a length of rubber tubing. These simple arrangements completed, he turned cheerfully to his patient. "No worse'n tappin' a sugar maple."

Through his decayed teeth the Fifer was lying. To reach the pool of inflammation under his patient's chest wall, the needle must graze Platt's aorta—the huge vessel stemming from the heart. The slightest miscalculation meant that the gallon pail at the other end of the tube would be filled, not with greenish pus, but a man's life blood.

"Aren't you going to give me any chloroform?" quavered Platt.

"Chloroform's for wimmen. Just turn your head away. Steady now." Fifer Tansey thrust the trocar home. "Bulls-eye!"

The air became unbearably foul as a torrent of purulent liquid gushed into the pail. A pint, two pints, three pints. Then the torrent dwindled to a trickle.

"Now, ma'am, if you'll just empty this pail we can all breathe again. Your husband's going to be all right."

"Stay a while, Fifer. Rest yourself," begged Anson as they left the sickroom.

"Sorry, Anse, I got another patient eight miles away. She's dying of cancer, chewing on a stick to relieve the pain. Maybe I'll have to give her the Black Drop." He tapped significantly at a dark phial in the cartridge belt of medicine at his waist. Anson knew that the Black Drop was the ultimate spoonful of mercy that Fifer poured down the throat of hopeless cases. The scarecrow physician accepted a quart of whiskey from Anson and strode out into the storm.

PART TWO

The Education of a Distiller

1.

CHARLES MOERLEIN

SAVE FOR ITS SPUR TRACK and cobblestoned yard, the home of Hearthstone whiskey looked more like a small college than a distillery. Charles Moerlein had planned it that way; justifiable pride in his product had led him to create for Hearthstone an atmosphere of dignified repose traditionally associated with fine whiskey. The campus note, achieved by wrought-iron gates and a drape of ivy over the distilling towers, suggested that no barrel of Mr. Moerlein's whiskey left these quiet precincts without four years of baccalaureate ripening. Which in the case of Hearthstone—a patrician sour-mash bourbon comparable to the best of the Kentucky brands —was true. Yet because the making of a prestige whiskey was a slow, costly process, the bulk (and chief profit) of Charles Moerlein's business lay in the manufacture of Old Settler, a popular-priced blend that consistently outsold Hearthstone five to one.

Prestige sets a noble table, but, as everyone knows, sales spread the board.

Some people claim that the mystery attaching to the production of noble whiskey communicates itself to the men who make it. More likely the reverse is true, and that the character of a distiller affects every drop of liquor barreled in his name. However that may be, no one could stand in Charles Moerlein's presence without sensing his integrity, vigor and personal charm. At thirty-three, he was an undeniably handsome man: a warm physical glow, carefully muted by the sobriety of his attire, broke free in the rich chestnut tones of his brown eyes and curly hair. Bulk without heaviness —especially through the shoulders—made him slightly more impressive when seated behind a desk; yet in rising, walking, shaking hands or speaking with others, he generated a glowing energy best described by the term "animal magnetism."

Seated at his desk, which, after the fashion of the times, resembled an upright parlor organ, Charles Moerlein was opening his morning mail. It was his practice to answer important letters in longhand or make careful notations for the guidance of his chief clerk. The mail this morning was agreeably routine in nature. Orders from wholesalers were substantial; reports from Hearthstone salesmen were satisfactory, and the demand for Old Settler had taken a prodigious jump. The stuff was pouring out of his warehouses at the rate of three thousand barrels a month. A note written on crackling vellum reminded Mr. Moerlein that the Directors of the Atlas National Bank would hold their monthly meeting on October 3. From the treasurer of the National Protective Association (a liquor-trade organization) came a letter reminding Mr. Moerlein that his annual contribution must be doubled this year. Said the letter in part:

> To combat the increased activities of Temperance fanatics, our organization finds itself called upon to spend ever larger sums in presenting our side of the case to the drinking public—and, more importantly, to sympathetic legislators. Every distiller, brewer and licensed purveyor of malt and spirituous liquors must unite in a common front against those who would strike from the hand of American citizens the legitimate solace of whiskey, beer and wine.

Money down the drain, thought Charles Moerlein as he wrote a check in the amount of $500 payable to the National Protective Association.

The hands of the well-tempered clock on Mr. Moerlein's wall were scissoring toward 9:50 when he came to an oblong package, impressively sealed with lozenges of red wax. Slitting the seals, he removed an outer wrapper and uncovered a large book bound in white glazed kid and bearing on its cover the title (stamped in ornate gold Caxton): *Illustrious Cincinnatians*. The book's obvious intention to suggest *Burke's Peerage* failed to disguise its Chamber of Commerce origin. He scrutinized the volume with a skeptical eye. This was the lever that would turn the trick, eh? Bring new business to

Cincinnati, inform the world at large of Cincinnati's preeminence among the cities of the industrial plain. He thumbed through its glossy pages, gazing at static half-tones of public buildings. Of more interest were the short biographies written by that gentleman hack Alf Griscomb for an agreed-on fee of a penny a word. Since there is no sweeter meat than that which clings to our own joints, Mr. Moerlein was eager to discover how he had fared at Alf Griscomb's hand.

Mainwaring . . . Metcalf—ah, here it was—a full page devoted to the life and works of Charles G. Moerlein. Like any other man who had subscribed $100 for the pleasure of seeing his name and exploits in print, Mr. Moerlein read:

Active in many movements for the betterment of commercial and civic conditions in Cincinnati, Charles G. Moerlein is numbered among those whom the Queen City hails as a native son. He was born here on March 22, 1850, son of Andreas and Ludmilla (Lehrer) Moerlein, both of whom migrated from Oberndorf in the Black Forest region of Württemberg, Germany. Andreas Moerlein, a skilled woodturner, found ready employment in the country of his adoption until chronic illness obliged him to lay aside the tools of his craft. Charles, accepting his responsibilities as eldest of four children, discontinued his education in the public schools and secured employment in the establishment of the late Zachary Hildreth, rising rapidly to become head salesman and later general manager. Since the reorganization of the business, he has continued in the same field, so ably directing his efforts that he is now president and principal stockholder of the company bearing his name.

On September 11, 1875, Charles Moerlein was married to Ermengarde Fugelmann, daughter of Mr. and Mrs. Konrad Fugelmann of meatpacking fame. Mr. Moerlein was pleasantly situated in his home life until the death of Mrs. Moerlein after a long illness in December 1881.

Charles G. Moerlein's undaunted enterprise and unfaltering belief in Cincinnati have been salient forces in the development not only of his own company but of civic welfare generally. He is a director of the Atlas National Bank and the Cincinnati and Chattanooga Railway. Past president of the Ohio River Improvement Association, and a charter member of the Ramona Yacht Club, which he served as Commodore, 1881-1882. Until the death of his wife, he entertained graciously on his steam yacht *Charmian* and in his beautiful fourteen-room residence in the Avondale section of the city.

Not yet thirty-five, Charles Moerlein may be said to personify the spirit of progressivism which bids fair to achieve new mercantile laurels for Cincinnati and himself.

Well, there it was—pure aromatic puff—a blend of quarter-truth and outright evasion suitably tinctured with aromatic oils of hypocrisy. Mercantile laurels . . . undaunted enterprise . . . But not a word about whiskey. The hack who had written the sketch, the committee that published the volume and everyone who read it knew very well that Charles Moerlein wasn't manufacturing house paint or milk chocolate. The biography was factually correct, and flattering enough in its way. But concerning Hearthstone and Old Settler it was the equivalent of a long-sustained *shh—shh*.

Charles Moerlein closed the book with the helpless feeling of a surgeon placing a bandage over an incurable wound. Long ago he had accepted this verdict of silence as part of the social contract existing between those who drank whiskey and those who made it. Say what you would, there was a taint about the whole business. A whiskey-maker's forehead was branded with a scarlet A standing not for Adultery but for Alcohol. No one ever pointed at the brand or mentioned the taint. Your money drew the usual rate of interest at the bank and you were admitted to memberships in the best clubs. You were accepted—only you weren't.

Charles Moerlein rose and walked to the window overlooking the yard of his distillery. How much care and pride—not to mention capital—he had poured into his business! A dormitory silence hung over the four granite warehouses where half a million gallons of whiskey cradled in oak barrels matured without sound. Only the barred windows and padlocked doors of the warehouses suggested that the dreaming liquor was not utterly innocent. And the faintly acrid odor of fermenting mash told his accustomed nostril of the chemical change that was transforming guileless corn into a dangerous intoxicant.

Charles Moerlein knew that whiskey was part of the modern scene, a necessary buffer between the human nervous system and the abrasive burr of reality. Hearthstone, like any good whiskey, induced a sense of well-being, relieved anxieties, lubricated social gears and cast a warm glow over festive occasions. Yet the amber liquid had other, less desirable effects. Though it could lift men to the uplands of felicity, it could also send them tumbling into the trough of despair. At what point did the drinker descend from euphoria to folly? And who could draw the line between conversational brilliance and incoherent babbling?

No wonder that this mysterious, many-natured distillate should be socially feared, heavily taxed, abhorred by some, prized by others. No wonder that the penny-a-word scrivener had avoided all mention of whiskey in his meaningless sketch. What definitive statement could be made about Hearthstone or the man who made it? Who, including Charles Moerlein himself, knew the whole story?

No one.

Lifting his gaze to the S-shaped curve of the Ohio as it swept past the Cincinnati waterfront, Charles Moerlein remembered the beginning . . . the middle parts . . .

It had all begun when Charlie Moerlein, barely thirteen, dry-eyed with grieving for his father's death, fell into the one-armed clutch of Zack Hildreth's scrofulus charm. In search of a job, Charlie went down to the Cincinnati Public Landing—a quarter mile of cobblestoned ramp that sloped from Water Street to the edge of the Ohio; a vast wholesale emporium where buyers and sellers met in a commercial tide rip. The scene filled young Charles Moerlein with dreams of mercantile grandeur. Moving through the crowd of merchants, he was magnetically drawn toward the men who traded in whiskey. And of all such traders the most fascinating was Zachary Hildreth.

On a smaller stage, Zack might have sold snake oil to gaping yokels at a horse fair; given a bigger theater, he might have emerged as a manipulator of railroads or oil wells. Actually, the Landing suited this trader who bought cheap, processed quickly, then skimmed off his double profit as plunger and rectifier.

Zack's manner of doing business was summary, dramatic. He would drive through the crowd in his gig, pull up to a halt at the whiskey post and make his announcement. "This is double-eagle day for any as wants to sell corn whiskey. Here's my offer. I pay twenty dollars for fifty-gallon barrels delivered at my place of business, two Plum Street, before closing time. Here's the money [jingling a heavy bag of gold]; bring on your whiskey. One barrel, ten barrels, a hundred barrels. You all know honest Zack Hildreth, blender and rectifier."

Zack had earned the sobriquet *honest* by returning to its rightful owner a glass eye that he had found in a barrel of whiskey. The eye was blue and the whiskey so raw that Zack couldn't quite tell where it came from. He set the barrel aside and, sampling it three months later, decided that its contents must have come from Denton County. Whereupon he put an ad in the Denton *Chronicle:* "Found: one glass eye, in a hand-coopered barrel of whiskey. Owner may claim property by applying to Zack Hildreth, 2 Plum Street, Cincinnati."

Soon afterward a one-eyed farmer claimed and received the eye. "You sure are an honest man, Mr. Hildreth." Then, much puzzled, he added, "What I can't figure out is how you happened to put the ad in the Denton County paper."

Never the man to give away a trade secret, Zack explained his line of reasoning. "When I saw that eye wasn't bloodshot I knew right away there must be pretty good whiskey in that barrel. So I just ran down the list of counties that make good corn whiskey. When I got to Denton, the eye sort of winked at me."

To this pillar of rectitude Charles Moerlein offered himself as apprentice and disciple. "Mr. Hildreth, I want to learn the whiskey business. I'll work for low wages until I'm worth more, and I'll do everything you tell me."

At this frank avowal Zack Hildreth said, "Guess you're the boy I've been looking for. Come around tomorrow morning and I'll start you in the leaching pit."

The leaching pit was a five-hundred-gallon cistern sunk into the floor of Zachary Hildreth's cellar, a windowless cavern densely populated by rats. On either side of the cistern stood two wooden tubs; Charlie's first job was to fill these tubs with charcoal, finely powdered at the bottom, flaky toward the middle, with the largest chunks on top.

Into these tubs Zack then poured the anonymous bulk whiskies bought on the Public Landing for twenty dollars a barrel. It was brutal stuff—raw, colorless, fierce-tempered—a reeking affront to nostril and taste buds. No one knew exactly what took place when the whiskey (technically known as "low wines") seeped through the charcoal filter. In theory this leaching process absorbed certain objectionable flavors and odors without weakening the alcoholic content.

The job of crushing and packing charcoal made the young apprentice look like a chimneysweep. So nauseating was the stench from the leaching vats that no food would stay in his stomach. A horrible oily film, tasting like pigsty filth mixed with castor oil, clung to the membranes of his nose and throat, paralyzed all sense of taste and brought on terrible fits of projectile vomiting. During the summer of 1863, he dropped ten pounds from a frame already spare.

Watching her son push away his supper of tender sauerbraten and potato pancakes, Mrs. Moerlein (who had never learned to speak English) asked a natural question: *"Was für eine Gesellschaft ist das denn?"* By her choice of the word *Gesellschaft* she revealed her sense of bewilderment and alarm.. "What kind of an outfit is this, anyway?"

"Rege dich nicht auf, Mütterchen. It's a good outfit. Mr. Hildreth is teaching me the business."

There was indeed a great deal to learn. Zack Hildreth, noting the natural aptitude of his apprentice, opened the secret cabinets of his trade. The prime secret was "reducing to proof"—that is to say, cutting down the alcoholic content of the raw whiskey by diluting it with pump water—a simple process that gave Zack a quick thirty per cent increase in gallonage. To produce the amber color traditionally associated with whiskey, Zack dumped in a quantity of burned caramel, while Charlie stirred the mixture with a long paddle. "Flavor," usually peach juice, was stirred in ditto. The final step was the addition of beading oil, a glycerine compound that formed tiny bubbles at the rim of every convivial glass.

Thus leached, diluted, colored, flavored and beaded (all within twenty-four hours), Zack Hildreth's "goods" were pumped from the blending cistern into barrels, each bearing the stencil *Hildreth's Long Rifle.* Never was a beverage more aptly named. The first shot of Long Rifle jolted a man to the gristle of his metatarsal arch; the second glass numbed his central nervous system; the third (if taken) induced a condition of horizontal paralysis guaranteed to last from eight to twelve hours. Long Rifle retailing at five cents a drink was the favorite tipple of river-boat roustabouts and dollar-a-day laborers, who valued the high muzzle velocity of Zack Hildreth's whiskey. For those who preferred their liquor white, Zack produced a colorless, slightly cheaper equivalent of Long Rifle by leaving out the burned caramel and peach juice. Sold as Derringer, it was unequaled for accuracy at short range.

During the postwar blight that fell over Cincinnati, the air was loud with alcoholic musketry. Barrooms, grocery stores and apothecary shops sold Long Rifle and Derringer. Everyone drank. Tipsy teamsters beat their horses; befuddled men lurched out of barrel houses, fell asleep in alleys or collapsed in coma. Zack Hildreth grew rich and Charlie Moerlein, his first assistant, drew wages of ten dollars a week.

Someone is always rubbing the bloom off the rose. Early in the seventies, bands of female crusaders wearing the white badge of temperance began to crusade against a creature generically known as "Demon Rum." They knelt in front of saloons, prayed, sang hymns; the more militant members forced their way into dram shops, broke bottles and wielded axes. One day in 1871 a bevy of these females gathered in front of Zack Hildreth's rectifying plant. After the usual prayers and exhortations, they unsheathed their axes and smashed a pyramid of Long Rifle barrels piled on the sidewalk.

Sacrilege and desecration! From the door of his establishment, Zack bade the ax-wielders disperse.

"I'm a peaceable man engaged in a lawful business," he shouted. "Go home and take care of your children."

A bonneted leader of the Temperance platoon stepped forward. "Down with Demon Rum!" she cried.

This was the final insult. "Don't call it rum," shrieked Zack. "Rum's made from molasses. Every drop of my whiskey is a dewy distillate of corn."

"Corn or molasses, it's all *Poison*." The bonneted female sank her ax into another barrel head, while her companions chanted:

We gather, we gather—a strong little band,
On the right side of Temp'rance, we now take our stand

Zack Hildreth summoned his second-in-command. "Rig up the hose to the blending cistern," he whispered to Charlie. "Hand me the nozzle, and when I holler 'Shiloh' pump like hell."

At the battle cry, Charlie pumped. A deluge of evil-smelling liquid baptized the crusaders. Handkerchiefs to their noses, they stood courageously for a while; then, drenched and bedraggled, they broke ranks, crying, "Tremble, King Alcohol. We will return."

They did. The next year a reform ticket, swept into office by Temperance votes, closed seven hundred drinking places in Cincinnati. *That* hurt. Unsold barrels of Long Rifle clogged Zack's warehouse, overflowed into his yard. He was about to suspend operations when young Charlie Moerlein came up with a gilt-edged idea.

"Mr. Hildreth," he said, "why don't you let me try to sell some Long Rifle outside Cincinnati? We're in a backwash here, but other cities are booming. They'd be wonderful markets for a good reliable whiskey like ours."

"Like ours"—A junior-partner locution, brimming with confidence and pride. The old rectifier eyed his fresh-faced lieutenant hopefully. "Think we could crack them places, Charlie? We'd run into heavy competition from the bottle-goods people."

"We'll price them out of business," said Charles, laying some hard facts and figures before his employer. "We'll sell Long Rifle direct to barkeeps at forty dollars a barrel. That's two hundred and eighty quarts of whiskey, averaging, say, ninety proof. If he sells it at fifty cents a quart, he takes in a hundred and forty dollars and shows a clear profit of a hundred dollars per barrel. Peddling it by the glass, sixteen drinks to the quart, he grosses one sixty a barrel." Charlie clinched his argument with a question. "Now, honest, Mr. Hildreth, do you think any dealer's going to refuse a proposition like that?"

Zack Hildreth allowed that no right-minded dealer could. He had only one suggestion. "You better raise yourself a mustache, Charlie. You look awful young for a whiskey salesman."

So Charles Moerlein raised a mustache and went on the road at the fabulous salary of fifteen dollars a week, plus expenses and a 5 per cent commission on all sales. *Hallelujah!*

Carrying his shagreen sample case, Charlie walked into the

gilded saloon of Chicago's Palmer House and blithely asked for the manager. Mr. Otis Cubberley, morning-suited and florid, listened with a contemptuous half ear to the canvass of the gangling youth. Charlie played his ace. "Before making your decision, Mr. Cubberley, I want you to sample Long Rifle." He uncorked a bottle of Zack Hildreth's finest. Reluctantly, Mr. Cubberley held it under a connoisseur nostril, coughed (not from embarrassment) and quickly handed it back.

Not unkindly, he informed Charlie about the birds and bees of whiskey-selling. "Our customers expect, and are willing to pay for, an aged medium-proof straight whiskey. Tastes are divided between Pennsylvania rye and Kentucky bourbon, with a rather marked preference for bourbon. Now here's what I drink myself." From a bottle labeled Rosemere, he poured a glass of reddish liquor and offered it in evidence.

At the first sip, Charlie sensed the impassable gulf between Rosemere and Long Rifle. The difference between them was the difference between patrician and peasant, a hog wallow and a bower of roses. Then and there he received his first intimation that Zack Hildreth's whiskey was not a celestial dew.

"There are plenty of places where you can sell your line," said Mr. Cubberley.

A more sensitive plant would have faded and died right there, but Charles Moerlein, composed of the indestructible quartz that makes a salesman, hit the back streets and barrel houses of Chicago. He found other lines entrenched, but like any salesman who makes thirty calls a day, he made a few sales. A barrel at one place, two barrels, three barrels. The cadet wore out the soles of his parade shoes, had them cobbled for thirty-five cents and became a blooded veteran while wearing them out again. He shaved every morning, ate free lunches, and at night laid his blue serge trousers in a patented E-Z pants presser that worked while you slept. He made price concessions, placed the stuff on consignment, and at the end of a month had sold ninety-two barrels of Long Rifle and twelve of Derringer.

Total sales: $4,185. Charlie's commission: $209.26. Thereafter he wasted no time in Chicago. With the instinct of a herring skipper, he went where the fish were running. The best customers for Long Rifle, he discovered, were in the tank towns dotting the network of small railroads south and southwest of Cincinnati. In states with a predominantly colored population, he pushed Derringer—twelve hundred barrels of it the first year. In 1872, he sold nearly 4,000 barrels of Zack Hildreth's whiskey to new customers. Zack added another leaching vat to his establishment, and Charlie Moerlein had $3,200 in the bank.

He had himself measured for his first tailor-made suit, bought a dozen silk shirts, a pearl-gray derby and picked up a two-carat diamond ring for $300 from a fellow drummer in distress. Charles Moerlein and the United States were going places. Exactly where, no one knew.

It was an era of mushroom growth and toadstool stagnation; of bumper abundance and starveling scarcity. From the plush seat of his Pullman car, Charlie Moerlein saw it all: the prosperity and the squalor, the huge profits of the few and the low wages of the multitude. Farmers paid 12 per cent for crop loans; poverty, disease and child-labor gnawed at the growing bones of the nation. Looking at the record of panics, bank failures and evictions, seeing the drunkenness and corruption of cities, reading about the abortive strikes, one might wonder how it all would end.

Yet underneath the surface scum of political graft and human degradation Charles Moerlein felt the buoyant lift of an enterprising people and chose to put his faith in that buoyancy. It was hard for him to believe that the economic system was crumbling when a traveling salesman with a common school education could make $4,000 a year. And it was still harder to believe, with the white rosettes of Temperance blossoming everywhere, that the country was drinking itself to death. The taxes on whiskey grew higher; its manufacture was more strictly supervised by the Federal government. Many localities forbade the sale of distilled liquors. Yet the industry prospered.

Why anyone should like either of Zack Hildreth's brands, Long Rifle or Derringer, was something of a mystery to the young salesman. Dutifully he tried to acquire a fondness for Long Rifle; in vain. Every swallow reminded him of the leaching pit. When he drank from choice (which was seldom) he preferred Kentucky bourbon that had come of age in oak barrels. He particularly enjoyed a brand called Rosemere— a noble reddish liquor with an inimitable bouquet that suffused him with a sense of well-being.

"Sell much of this?" he asked the barkeeper in a Memphis hotel.

The barkeeper, cynical in the manner of his kind, countered with another question: "At a quarter a glass?" He pointed to a bottle of Long Rifle. "When a man can flatten himself with three drinks of *that* for the same price, he asks himself, 'Why pay more?'"

In the argument of pocketbook versus palate, pocketbook always won.

A good-looking young man with a flashy wardrobe and money in the bank has no difficulty finding a girl for himself. There were plenty of girls in Cincinnati who sat home waiting for Charlie Moerlein to ring their doorbell: buxom blondes with Teutonic blue eyes, teasing brunettes who knew the language of the fan and parasol—nice girls, the marrying kind—girls who liked Charlie to kiss them and would kiss him back with promises of more to come. But of all kisses, none were sweeter, more promiseful, than Josie Tucker's.

He had known Josie since childhood, had pulled her braids, chased her home, then stayed to play Hopscotch in her back yard. Together they went through the Post-Office and Spin-the-Bottle phase of adolescent discovery. Then for a long time while Charlie served his grimy apprenticeship with Zack Hildreth, they had lost track of each other, until they met again at a summer band concert on Price Hill. At twenty-two, Josie Tucker had a porcelain unfreckled skin and crinkly soft pink lips. A scissors artist cutting her silhouette would have encountered surprising curves and a pert upturned nose. Yet there was a suggestion of primness about her high-throated shirtwaist and severe hair-do. In short, Josie was that deadly combination of coryphee and lay nun.

"Why, Josie, you're grown up! Where've you been all these years?"

"At the State College."

Girls who went to college (so Charlie heard) were apt to be odd characters. "What were you doing there?"

"Studying to be a teacher." Note of fulfilled ambition in Josie's voice. "In September I'll start at the West Side School."

"West Side? Right here in Cincinnati? Then we can see each other again."

College hadn't dimmed the shine in Josie's eyes. "I'd love it, Charlie."

So they saw each other every night. They sat on benches in Mt. Adam Park, took Saturday excursions down the Ohio and drove out into the country in hired rigs to picnic on the grass. Riding along the northern bank of the Ohio, Josie learned the bitter-sweet difference between liking and loving: she discovered the special hazard of letting herself be kissed in a corn field (what was so intoxicating, she wondered, about standing corn?), and under August's climbing moon, while marrow and membrane, stalk and furrow cried, "Now, now," Josie traversed the enormous distance between a maiden's "no" and a woman's tremulous "Not yet, not yet."

Wonderful summers like this happen all the time to everyone, everywhere. And the people to whom they happen always talk about the same things. There are long discussions about the house they will live in—though actually anything with four walls and a roof will do. Regularly during these discussions, the question of children—how many, their arrangement as to sex—is bound to come up. Any logical train of thought on this theme soon collapses into such generalities as Josie's "I want my sons to have brown eyes and ears close to their heads like yours." Or Charlie's "All our girls will have lips that look as though they were stung by a bee"—which was a fair-enough description of Josie's lips. These conversations settle nothing and are chiefly valuable because they lead to much fondling of the very ears, eyes and lips that are to be perpetuated in dream-babies yet unborn.

In the summer of 1874 Charlie bought a buckboard—a light, smart rig, mostly yellow wheels and hickory slats. Price: one hundred dollars. He spent two hundred more on a graceful chestnut mare, a real stepper. Any young woman would be impressed by this dashing equipage; climbing into the wicker seat, Josie was breathless.

"Wherever in the world, Charlie Moerlein, did you hire this wonderful, wonderful rig?"

"Hire it?" Charlie tickled the filly's flanks with a glossy whip. "It's ours, Josie—yours and mine."

"Why, Charlie, you must be a millionaire."

"Oh, I wouldn't say that. Still, things are pretty good in my line." He became the expansive male. "With salary and commissions I'll net around four thousand this year."

To a young schoolteacher who would soon be earning seven dollars a week, it sounded fabulous. "What kind of business are you in, Charlie?"

"I've told you a dozen times, but you weren't listening. I'm a salesman for Zack Hildreth."

"I remember your telling me that. But what do you sell?"

"Mostly Long Rifle. That's popular all over. Then of course there's Derringer. That's popular, too, where people like their goods white."

A long silence from Josie. "What are Long Rifle and Derringer, Charlie?"

"Whiskey, goose." He added a proud coda. "Good reliable brands with a lot of fire power."

"Whiskey!" Josie's exclamation ended in a low moan. "Oh, Charlie! Don't you know it's wrong to make people drink that awful poison?"

"I don't make them drink it. They walk up and ask for it. Listen, Josie, Long Rifle isn't the smoothest drink in the world, but it's not the terrible stuff those white-rosette people make it out to be." It was Charlie's turn to do a bit of cross-questioning. "Sa-a-y, you're not one of those Psalm Singers that go around chopping up other people's property, are you?"

"We sang Temperance songs at college, if that's what you mean."

The ride—and the rest of the summer—was ruined. Josie withheld all courting privileges while Charlie vainly tried to break her down with appeals to common sense. Their evenings together turned into angry-sorrowful debates that always ended with Josie twisting off her engagement ring and Charlie refusing to take it back.

"Think it over, darling, while I'm on the road," he pleaded. "I'll be gone for a couple of months. Things may come clear to both of us while I'm away."

In mid-September, Charlie started out on the long tour of his southern territory—a succession of one-night stop-overs, in dingy hotels. Loneliness and desire for Josie caused him to begin a dozen letters promising to give up the whiskey business. But the heavy orders from his customers always prevented his mailing them. Finally, unable to bear his loneliness any longer, he wrote Josie from a little town in Mississippi.

My darling wife-to-be:

The road is so lonely without you, and I am miserable because something has come between us. Like today, for instance, I got into this town (Hamlin, Miss.) at 6 A.M. and signed into the Crescent Hotel, then had to wait three hours before I could go out to make calls on my customers. I guess I died twenty times in those three hours, Josie, trying to decide what to do about you and me. I love you so much I would give up my job in a minute if it was just an ordinary job, but what you don't seem to understand, Josie, is the wonderful chance I have handling Zack Hildreth's line. Today, I sold sixty barrels of Long Rifle and thirty barrels of Derringer, which means commissions of forty dollars, about twenty times as much as I'd make in any other line. And it's only the beginning Josie. I'm gaited to the whiskey business. This year I'll make five thousand dollars and we can buy a house and get married. But if I gave up my job with Zack Hildreth I'd have to work as a clerk for about nine dollars a week, and then where would we be?

You say you love me, but how can you say that, because even if you murdered somebody I'd love you anyway. But here I am in a perfectly legal business and you make me feel like a criminal. Oh, I know there's a seamy side to the whiskey business, I see it all the time. But is it *my fault* if people drink to forget the awful trouble they're in? Well, there's no use going on like this because one thing will lead to another and we'll be quarreling again. So write to me c/o Crescent Hotel (I'll be back here the end of the week) and tell me how we stand, only say that you love me and will marry me no matter what.

Now, my darling, I want to get this letter in the mail so I will close with the thousand xxxxx's I would give you if you were here.

Your loving sweetheart,
CHARLIE

Looping back on his homeward trip four days later, Charles Moerlein signed in at the Crescent Hotel. "Any mail for me, Luke?" The clerk handed him an envelope. Charlie walked around the hotel three times, then went up to his room, locked the door and opened the letter.

MY DEAREST CHARLES:
 I know it is uncharitable of me to blame you for some-

thing that isn't really your fault—I mean the business you have chosen for yourself and which you work so hard at. I know you are kind and loving, the best, most tender-hearted man I shall ever meet. If I could forget everything but your dear face and loving ways, everything would be all right between us and we could get married, and I would be the happiest woman in the world because I never loved anybody as I love you, Charlie, and I know that I will never love anyone again.

But it is useless to say these things because I could never marry a man who sells whiskey. No matter how much I loved him, I would always be thinking of the lives he helped wreck, without meaning to, or the homes that broke up on account of the poison he sold. (No matter what you say, alcohol poisons the body and destroys the soul.) So, if you cannot give up your business, then you must give up me, Charlie, and I must give up you and it's better that we do it now, instead of becoming bad friends and spoiling the wonderful memories we have about each other, the most wonderful memories a woman can have.

I will think of you always and pray for your happiness and maybe you will think of me sometimes and the plans we made together. Oh, my darling, I must stop now, I am crying so hard, so I will say goodbye, Charlie, and sign myself,

> Your heartbroken
> JOSIE

Sitting on the window sill of the dreary room, overlooking the railroad tracks, Charlie read the letter till its ink was a blur of tears. What difference now how many barrels of whiskey he sold, how many suits he owned, how much money he had in the bank? Without Josie Tucker life would be meaningless. He laid Josie's letter on a soot-grimed table near the window, then took a bottle of Long Rifle from his sample case. Privately, he had never liked the taste or smell of the stuff, but it undoubtedly possessed the wonderful power of making you forget your troubles by getting you good and drunk.

He was tilting the bottle for a swallow of forgetfulness when he heard a distant bellow coming down the track like a tornado equipped with bell and whistle. It was No. 16, the new Mainliner Express between Memphis and Cincinnati. Firebox gleaming, steam hissing from high-compression cylinders, it roared past like a black comet, trailing a cloud of smoke and cinders. The passage of No. 16 shook the Crescent Hotel, rattled the pitcher in the wash bowl and made the floor tremble under Charlie's feet. The draught of its passage caught Josie's letter, whirled it off the sooty table and down the cindery track.

The vibrations of No. 16 plucked at Charlie like an iron plectrum, and its after-hum said, "Mine is the mechanical power and the commercial glory. Follow me and my promises of sales unnumbered shall be fulfilled unto you."

Charles Moerlein did not get drunk that night. Instead he obeyed the first commandment of drummers by staying in his room and out of trouble. Next morning he got up early, called on six customers and sold seventy-five barrels of Long Rifle, more whiskey than any salesman had ever sold on a single day in Hamlin, Mississippi.

Ten months later he married Ermengarde Fugelmann, daughter of a small pork packer on Water Street. Ermengarde brought to the marriage a reasonable endowment of good looks, a placid temper and a *Hausfrau* knowledge of German cookery. None of these qualifications, or all of them raised to the tenth power, were enough to make the union a happy one. The fact that Ermengarde was unable to produce a child (in those days women took the blame for barrenness) caused Charles Moerlein's wife to fall into a melanchoy pit of self-reproach. She became a marshmallow bog clamoring for reassurances of love that Charles Moerlein could not give. Ermengarde's silly fetish—hanging a pair of baby's shoes over the bedpost—her midnight sobbings and litanies of self-accusation, became unbearable. She was a good girl, an excellent housewife, thrifty, home-staying and fastidiously neat about her person.

But the sad fact was that the thin, sharp silhouette of Josie Tucker fell like a guillotine across Moerlein's will to love.

Unhappy in his marriage, Charles Moerlein worked harder selling Long Rifle and Derringer. Then a shift in public taste struck at his sales. He got his first intimation of this shift when he tried to sell the usual hundred barrels of Long Rifle to Hoag Ramsey, a St. Louis wholesaler.

"Better make it thirty, Charlie," said Hoag. "The demand

for Long Rifle seems to be falling off. People want something lighter these days." Ramsey opened a bottle of Flintlock, a product of the recently formed Eastern Distillers Corp. "Taste the difference."

Rolling a half ounce of Flintlock around in his mouth, Charlie found it singularly lacking in character. It possessed neither the striking power of Long Rifle nor the bouquet of Rosemere. "It's lighter, sure," he agreed. "But so's pump water." He examined the label curiously. "Wonder what it's made of?"

It wasn't Hoag Ramsey's business to know the actual ingredients of any compound bearing the label *whiskey*. "Dunno,". he said. "But I hear Eastern's using a new process that'll cook the smell out of a turnip."

If Ramsey didn't know, who would? Why, Zack Hildreth, of course. Charlie brought a bottle of Flintlock to his boss. "Taste this, Zack, and tell me what's in it."

The rectifier's Adam's apple rose and fell as he took a prodigious gulp. "You mean what *ain't* in it," he bellowed. Zack gulped a second and a third time, then handed back the bottle in disgust. "It's like firing off a cap pistol," he said. "No *re*coil to it."

Recoil or none, Flintlock gripped the popular palate. In barrels, bottles and jiggers, it shoved Long Rifle off the bars. As Charlie's commissions dwindled, his curiosity climbed. What was the secret of Flintlock's appeal? Rumor said that Eastern Distillers were making whiskey by a new, altogether revolutionary method, involving a tall many-chambered still that gulped in mash at the top and transformed it into a torrent of clean odorless alcohol known to the trade as "neutral spirits." In the whole world of whiskey-makers, whiskey-sellers and whiskey-drinkers, no one could tell Charles Moerlein anything more about this new "continuous-still" process.

He was a baffled, almost commissionless salesman, when the Gulick murder case hit the papers.

The Gulick case began obscurely when a man was found dead in a hallway of the tenement in which he lived. According to the coroner, John Gulick, drunk, had fallen downstairs and broken his neck. Gulick's widow gave him a decent burial, then put in a claim for $1,000 life insurance. It was a modest claim, unusual only because the records of the Gibraltar Insurance Company showed that one of Annie

Gulick's previous husbands had met his death in a similar fashion, three years earlier.

On the grounds that fish are not habitually found in milk bottles, the Gibraltar people got a court order to exhume the body of the deceased. They then engaged Max Cellarius, Professor of Chemistry at the University of Cincinnati, to perform tests on the organs of the late John Gulick. Professor Cellarius made some ghoulish experiments, demonstrating that John Gulick had died, not from a broken neck, but because his stomach contained a quantity of oxalic acid, a substance commonly used in metal polish.

When the D.A. found a can of metal polish in Annie Gulick's kitchen, she was held for the murder of her husband. Max Cellarius was the chief witness for the state—and a very poor witness he turned out to be. How the oxalic acid got into the stomach of the deceased was a matter beyond his concern. "I only know," he said, "that people do not accept poison from strangers. Someone close to John Gulick, someone that customarily prepared his food and drink, offered him the lethal mixture."

"And who, in your opinion, might that person be?" asked the D.A.

"Objection," snapped Annie Gulick's lawyer.

"Sustained," droned the judge.

So nothing could be proved. Annie Gulick was acquitted, collected her insurance and moved away. Max Cellarius went back to his laboratory, where Charles Moerlein found him sitting on a high stool surrounded by an array of alembics and retorts, looking very much like Friar Bungay.

From his hip pocket, Charlie produced a pint of Flintlock. "Can you tell me what this bottle contains?"

"This is not another law case?"

"No, I'm a whiskey salesman. I've come in to learn."

Professor Cellarius took the flask in his large acid-stained hands, held it to the light and shook it gently. "I think we'll have no trouble determining the chemical nature of this compound." His white eyebrows moved ever so slightly upward. "The difficulty will begin when I try to explain my findings to you."

"Will it be as hard as that?"

"It depends on what you already know. Now then, a few questions. How would you define the term *whiskey?*"

Charles started off competently enough. "Whiskey is a

distillate of fermented cereals, mostly corn, rye and barley, containing approximately fifty per cent alcohol."

Max Cellarius seemed unimpressed. "What kind of alcohol?"

"Is there more than one kind?"

"Theoretically there is an infinite number of alcohols. Offhand, I can name fifty kinds, all differing in such important details as molecular structure, specific gravity and boiling point. Not to mention their effects on the human system. There is, for instance, amyl alcohol—with a formula $C_5H_{11}OH$. It excites the coughing centers and is . . . ah . . . a poison. Then there are methyl, butyl and propyl alcohols, all produced from the same innocent cereals, but scarcely desirable as beverages."

The Professor decided to simplify matters. "The kind of alcohol that you—and several million whiskey drinkers—are interested in is a marvelous combination of carbon, hydrogen and oxygen—three of the commonest elements in nature—called ethyl alcohol. Its formula is C_2H_5OH. Here, I will show you some in its pure state." Professor Callarius removed the stopper from a phial containing a white, colorless liquid. "This is alcohol absolutum—two hundred proof. It contains no impurities, adulterations or by-products—known as congeners. Yet, ironically enough, it is the *absence* of these by-products that makes absolute alcohol a dull, uninteresting beverage."

The Professor turned again to the flask of Flintlock, uncorked it and took an experimental whiff. "What we have in this bottle is a comparatively pure form of ethyl alcohol, a flavorless, tasteless product commercially known as neutral spirits. It has been reduced to potability by the addition of a large quantity of H_2O—that is to say, tap water." He smiled tolerantly. " 'Neutral' states the case exactly. It has no character of its own because certain elements that give true whiskey its taste and flavor have been systematically removed."

In his own way Max Cellarius was repeating what Zack Hildreth had already said. Both men agreed that Flintlock lacked some essential ingredient. Yet despite this lack—or perhaps because of it—the whiskey-drinking public preferred Flintlock to Long Rifle.

Charlie framed his thought carefully. "You say, Professor, that certain substances have been removed from Flintlock. Exactly what substances?"

"The young dunce asks a difficult question. To answer it, the old dunce must introduce a whole new set of difficulties. Are you familiar with the term *congeners?*"

"No," said Charlie. "But I suppose it's the vile stuff we try to get rid of by leaching whiskey through charcoal."

"Leaching, meaching." Only the teacher in Max Cellarius compelled him to go on explaining for the benefit of the bright-eyed young dunce. "Like original sin, these congeners come into existence during the process of fermentation. Their molecules, inseparably locked with those of ethyl alcohol, give young or inferior whiskey a horrible taste and odor. But—" he paused reflectively—"would it surprise you to know that these congeneric substances turn out to be the very ingredients that give matured whiskey its flavor and bouquet?"

"If congeners are valuable, why do we try to get rid of them?"

"You try to get rid of all but the tiniest fraction of these substances. One and five tenths per cent of congeners is already too much. But oddly enough *half* of this is *essential* to the making of a fine whiskey." He tapped the flask of Flintlock with a contemptuous knuckle. "In this poor stuff, even the irreducible minimum has been cooked to death. Its virtue, so to speak, has been destroyed."

"Why is it so popular then with drinkers?"

"Because the makers of this beverage have covered up their crime by adding five or ten per cent of genuine whiskey together with a modicum of prune juice and caramel to give the stuff flavor. I could tell you after laboratory procedure precisely *what* they have added. But why bother, when nature provides a simpler way?"

Max Cellarius moistened his lips with Flintlock, clucked his tongue and went on. "It is a mild, cheap and not unpleasing tipple."

"A lot of customers would agree with you there," said Charles despondently.

"Not everyone. A few of us still value quality." From a cupboard over the bluestone sink Cellarius produced a bottle of Rosemere. "There is a chemistry that time alone can teach, and this—" he poured the reddish liquor into a couple of jiggers—"and this is its noblest product. No tricks, no substitutes, no short-cuts, merely the incorruptible essence of the corn mellowed in oaken barrels for eight years."

They drank to that.

No amount of indoctrination could persuade Zack Hildreth to install one of the new fractionating stills. The cost, approximately five thousand dollars, was a not impossible sum. Zack's objection took a profanely moral turn. He'd stoke hell's boiler with brimstone, he announced, before he'd stoop to cook the re̶coil out of Long Rifle. A strong but unsatisfactory position. Sales plummeted; failing health and a general economic depression were driving Zack close to the shoals of bankruptcy, when one morning in 1877 he summoned his salesman and general manager.

"Sit down, Charlie," he said with unaccustomed gentleness. "I'm getting on—pushing seventy. Times are changing. New blood, new capital, are coming into the business. There's no place for an old-line rectifier like me."

"I wouldn't say that, Zack." A filial tenderness for the one-armed old rascal who had taught him the rudiments of the business caused Charles to add: "Tastes are changing, but drop for drop there'll never be a stouter tipple than Long Rifle."

"Mebbe, mebbe. The fact is, Charlie, I want to sell." He bent a wheedling eye on the younger man. "Think you could raise twenty-five thousand to buy me out?"

What is there to buy? thought Charles. A ramshackle warehouse full of unsalable whiskey, three leaching vats and a thousand-gallon blending cistern. Good will, zero.

Gently he made a counter-proposition to the old rectifier. "Make it ten thousand, Zack. Half cash, the remainder in thousand-dollar notes maturing annually for the next five years." Charlie pushed on. "That'll leave me just enough capital to swing the new operation I've got in mind."

"You ain't going to make neutral spirits?"

"No, it would be silly trying to compete with Eastern Distillers. That would take a million dollars, and I'll be lucky if I can raise the fifty thousand I need."

No regular banking house in Cincinnati would finance the operation Charles Moerlein had in mind. There was only one man in the Queen City with enough nerve, imagination and surplus capital to lend fifty thousand dollars to a fledgling whiskey-maker. Charles knew his man. Enoch Battle, last of the Porkopolis titans, retired, crotchety, a hard customer to shave.

Charlie found the old financier sitting drearily in the oak-paneled library of Vieuxtemps surrounded by folios of treas-

ures that he had never opened. A shawl around Enoch's toothpick legs warded off the climbing chill of age. The once terrible red mustache immortalized by Sir Thomas Cockburne,
R.A., had lost its bristle, and the fire in Enoch's black cur-
rant eyes was almost drowned by gathering rheum. Popular
estimates of the Battle fortune ran between twenty and
thirty million dollars—every penny of which was running its
legs off chasing eight, ten and twelve per cent interest for
its owner.

Prospective borrowers were no novelty to Enoch, and he
had his own short-question technique of handling them. He
listened to Charles Moerlein's request. Then he asked, "What
banks do you save in?"

"People's Dime and City Mutual."

"Got your passbooks with you?"

Charlie handed them over. This was the kind of reading
Enoch enjoyed. To hell with Aldine folios and first editions.
The brittle, purplish nail of his forefinger traveled up and
down the pages of the little books noting the steady, gradually
increasing entries over a ten-year period. Enoch's fingernail
came to a four thousand withdrawal.

"Bought a house, I see. Where?"

"Ten Elm."

"Children?"

"None."

"Debts?"

"Five notes of one thousand dollars each, payable annually
to Zachary Hildreth."

"That old pirate. Politics?"

"Republican."

Enoch's brittle fingernail scratched on, came to a last
withdrawal. *Five thousand dollars.* "Zack must've squealed
like a stuck pig."

"No," said Charlie. "I think he was glad to get out. Old-
line rectifying is dead, and Zack knows it."

Enoch Battle handed back the passbooks. "What kind of
whiskey are *you* going to make?"

"A good quality straight bourbon. I'll start small, buy my
own corn, run the mash through a triple-chambered still,
hold it in charred oak for a couple of years, give it an attractive name like Hearthstone, and sell it just below the
Louisville price."

The long-range strategy of this attractive young operator

appealed to Enoch Battle. "Fifty thousand dollars won't carry you for two years."

"I've got five thousand barrels of Long Rifle in my warehouse. As it stands there's no market for it, but if I run it through a doubler and get rid of the heaviest congeners, I can sell it for forty dollars a barrel."

Enoch Battle was busy casting up a trial balance. This prospective borrower was confident but not brash; steady as a rock yet a chance-taker too. Talked a good whiskey. But did he really know what he was talking about? The old inquisitor proposed to find out.

"You take a drink yourself now and then, I suppose, Mr. Moerlein?"

"In the course of business, yes."

Enoch yanked a brocaded bell pull. "What's your favorite brand?"

"Rosemere."

"Nothing finer. Drink it myself." To a butler who appeared in the doorway he said, "The usual, Hoops."

From a Florentine credenza by the great fireplace Hoops produced a squat cut-glass decanter, flanked by king-sized jiggers on a crested salver. Water. Then Hoops faded off-stage.

Enoch poured two generous drinks, then lifted his glass in the double ritual of inhalation and toast. "To the gold standard and Rosemere," he proposed.

Charles murmured appreciatively, swallowed and waited for the suffusing afterglow. A suffusion took place, and pleasantly too. But something was absent. What? It seemed to Charles that someone had clipped the stem off an American Beauty or pared a drachma of gold from a double eagle. Swallowing again, his membranes registered that this was an aged whiskey, 105 proof, beautifully cured, perfect in its way, but it wasn't Rosemere. Courtesy makes one set of claims, honesty another. The two virtues need not clash. As a guest and prospective borrower, Charlie felt no necessity of impugning his host's whiskey; but Enoch, having baited the hook, now pulled insistently on the line.

"What do you think of it?"

"It's excellent whiskey, Mr. Battle. Only, I'm sorry to say, sir, it's not Rosemere."

The old financier's wattles began to quiver, not with indignation but laughter. He brought a purple hand down slappingly against his lean thighs. "Well," he cackled, "you can't fool the horseflies. Young man, you're all right. You can have fifty thousand at seven per cent. It's going to be a long pull, but you'll make it."

It hadn't been such a long pull after all, and Charles Moerlein had certainly made it. A great part of his original capital had gone into remodeling Zack Hildreth's plant, setting up one of the new continuous stills, laying down the first batch of Hearthstone and storing it in the No. 2 warehouse. While waiting for this quality product to mature, Charles Moerlein had gone on the road with his Old Settler and sold ten thousand barrels the first year. In 1879 he doubled the sales of Old Settler, grossing two hundred thousand dollars, with a net profit of twenty-five thousand.

In 1880 Ermengarde died. "Heart failure," said Dr. Kleinert, the family physician, as he solemnly affixed his signature to a death certificate that should have read "Suicide."

Whatever the cause, Ermengarde's death made Moerlein a widower; the profits from Old Settler made him a millionaire. Taken together, these events exposed Moerlein to temptations that shook the pillars of his financial, moral and emotional life.

Even though a man is rich, good looking and free to marry —as Charles Moerlein was—he encounters after a certain age difficulties in his search for the right woman. Whether he is seeking a wife, a mistress or merely the companion of an hour, the difficulty persists. Cincinnati had a full complement of women: attractive widows with social position; warm-blooded maidens eager to exchange their single state for the fuller joys of matrimony; uncounted hundreds of discreet professionals willing to guarantee satisfaction—even fidelity— for prices ranging anywhere from fifty to five hundred dollars a month.

Far from naïve about such matters, untroubled by moral convictions, possessed of a normally masculine vigor, some three hundred thousand dollars in ready cash, and a rapidly expanding business, Charles Moerlein might easily have gone companioned through the first years of his widowerhood.

What prevented him from finding such companionship?

The question was canvassed by the mother of every eligible daughter in Cincinnati—indeed, by many of the daughters themselves. The subject of remarriage had been broached to Mr. Moerlein by his business associates and fellow club members. Parasoled ladies dropped handkerchiefs, gloves or purse in the lobbies of various hotels as Mr. Moerlein emerged from the bar, and were repaid for their advances by a courteous lifting of Mr. Moerlein's top hat as he returned the bait.

Nor did he rise to the lure of the half-hundred ads in the personal column of the *Enquirer:*

Will the driver of the barouche who gallantly swerved at the corner of Vine and 16th streets, to avoid splattering the Lady in the Green Silk Stockings, claim his reward from the lady herself? Reply in strictest confidence. Box X 14.

The well-intentioned friends, club members, conspiring mothers and the glove-droppers were wasting their time; as for the lady in the green silk stockings, she and her variously attired conspirators were pouring their money down the drain at the rate of two cents a word. As a result, there were evenings when Charles Moerlein, gazing over the city from his top-floor suite in the Thackeray Club, heartily wished that he could find, either in marriage or some other arrangement, a woman who could meet his specifications. Mature, she must be; Moerlein was definitely not interested in fledgling fluff. The woman of his choice must be full-plumaged, capable of flight beside a mate who could alternately tempt and be tempted by her, into a soaring relationship of one-to-one, followed by the quiet descent into ordinary domestic happiness. Physical beauty would certainly help. . . .

The specifications were met quite unexpectedly, when early in 1882, Moerlein's chief clerk, Moe Mogelson, announced a lady visitor.

"Who is she? What does she want?"

"Says it's private, sir; here's her card."

The visiting card of top-quality pasteboard bore the name *Miss Lucienne Bisguier.*

"Tell the lady to write me a note stating the nature of her business. Here. Return her card."

Back came blinkered Mogelson extending the card with the penciled notation *"I merely wish to return something you've lost."*

Watch, wallet, cufflinks, pearl tie pin, all present and accounted for. Curiosity or perhaps the faint musk of bergamot emanating from the card moved Moerlein. "Show the lady in."

Nothing quite so feminine had ever crossed the threshold of Moerlein's office. The lady was obviously—well, a lady. Deportment faultless. Nothing veiled or mysterious. Manner impersonal. Intonation coolly correct.

Charles Moerlein relaxed. "Please have a chair."

Miss Bisguier had evidently mastered one of the most difficult of social maneuvers: the act of sitting down. She composed her gloved hands over a small satin purse and gave Mr. Charles Moerlein the subdued fire power of her violet eyes.

"How may I serve you, Madame?"

The lady opened her purse, extracted a one-hundred-dollar bill, and laid it on Moerlein's desk. "This dropped from your wallet last evening while you were buying cigars at the Hotel Royale."

Mr. Moerlein *had* bought half a dozen Fuente Grandes at the Royale on the previous evening. The one-hundred-dollar bill might have slipped from his wallet. Still, certain questions had to be asked and answered.

"How did you know my name?"

"I was with a party of friends. One of the ladies knew you."

"I see." Charles Moerlein was seeing a great deal more than his visitor was telling—or showing—him. He saw the truth, and a more delectable, audacious, deceitful, bold, calculating and desirable piece of feminine truth had never confronted him.

Miss Lucienne Bisguier, or whatever the lady's name might be, was lying through her pearl-perfect teeth. Her tale was pure fiction, but the teller of the tale conveyed, from the roots of her strawberry hair to the tips of her glove-encased fingers, from her violet eyes and geranium-tinted mouth, from the *faux-maigre* concavity of her cream-white cheek to the undisguisable convexities of hip and bosom, from her short, pert nose to the only-to-be-guessed-at length of thigh —she conveyed to Moerlein information more desirable than truth.

I offer you an experience of life, she was saying in effect, and if you are not utterly dead, you will claim me.

He had claimed Lucienne's promise and she had fulfilled it in ways that Charles Moerlein had not hitherto imagined.

Marriage, even money (excepting those modest requisitions that women naturally make) were apparently not her objectives. She never drank excessively or complained about Moerlein's neglecting her. She was a wick saturated with erotic fuel, needing only a single kiss to spark the insatiable fire that burned in the marrow of her bones. She never spoke of love in the romantic sense; her substitute for the language of endearment was words held ordinarily to be obscene when uttered by a woman. Lucienne's passion burned away the obscenities of speech and made her commands a litany of exhortation. At such times Moerlein pitied her desperation, hushed her lips with his mouth and hands. At other times he would let the flood enter his ears unhushed.

Moerlein was extremely happy with Lucienne. He found in her an admixture of unleashed eroticism and a modesty almost virginal. Only in the dimmest of lights—a small, star-blue lamp on her side of the wide bed—would she permit Charles's eyes to gaze upon the still-budding opulence of a body made for love. Then, taking up the theme of pleasure, she improvised in sustained phrases, eyes closed, mouth open for the dissolving kiss. Rarely did she give him the feeling that he was being used solely for her private fulfillment; the geranium-pink lips never commanded "Now." Yet through his own half-closed eyes, Moerlein sometimes saw pearly incisors, part-cat, part-cobra, unwilling to toy longer with their victim.

Moerlein never learned her secret, never was able to resist her unspoken command. He would have prolonged the moment if possible and in those after-movements of love, while Lucienne lay passive, except for the triple tempo of her heart (which cannot be simulated), he covered her with caresses, searching out the neglected delicacies of underarm and navel, the inverted strawberry triangle and the long white column of her inner thigh, until he himself, exhausted, lay quietly on the pillow beside her.

Once, in an excessive passion, Charles had pleaded, "Darling, am I never to kiss the nape of your neck, your shoulders and . . . the dimples?"

At the word *dimples*, Lucienne's body stiffened. Then her laughing excuse. "Would you wear out your sweetheart in a single year? Let the dimples grow hungry."

"How shall I know?"

"I will tell you when."

She drew the covers about her, reached for the blue lamp and blew it out. "But tonight the nape of my neck waits with all its tendrils to be kissed." And so, consoled and consoling (one hand over her heart breast) Charles Moerlein fell asleep.

Fifty nights, a hundred nights, each began in a different way, took varying courses—with never a proprietary grasping of the reins by Lucienne—never a demand for company, or a complaint because there was company. Between Lucienne and Charles there existed a voluntary relationship maturely entered into and—except for one barrier—complete.

That single barrier grew higher, more mysterious. It lay somewhere between Lucienne's twenty-inch waistline and thirty-six-inch hips, as they made the backward sweep that lovers and sculptors agree is the beginning of everything. What could it be, Charles Moerlein wondered. A mole or birthmark, magnified by vanity into a disfigurement? His fingers told him little. These satiny twins dimpled by nature to guarantee elasticity and firmness that he never tired of caressing, these yet-to-be visioned curves of Lucienne's buttocks—when would his eyes behold them?

Once, in a warm June dawning, Charles awakened early and saw Lucienne sleeping face-buried in her pillow. Her shift had risen; the light sheet had slipped away, revealing the incredibly beautiful silhouette that his eyes had waited so long and patiently to see. As Lucienne slept, he leaned forward to kiss the nearest dimple, and there, just below it in the foreshortened perspective of his point-blank gaze, he saw the letter *D*, very small, tattooed in purple ink. On the other cheek, in exactly the same position, stood the letter *F*.

He covered the indelible initials with the sheet and lay back to assess the shock of finding a beloved body so intimately branded by initials not his own. Why, never in his most proprietarial fantasy could Charles Moerlein imagine imprinting his monogram on the flesh of Lucienne Bisguier or any woman. And the woman who had submitted to such branding—what of her? Would Josie Tucker have allowed her body to be emblazoned thus? For all her scraggle-baggle of bones and horsetail hairdo, Josie would have died first.

D.F.? D.F.? Who was D.F.? What diabolic sense of aestheticism could have prompted him to spare the white canvas of belly, breast, thigh, yet turn her over, take her from behind? Oh, merciful God, did it happen so? Charles Moerlein preferred to know nothing of the details. Fearsome enough to read the message aright. "Enslaved. In witness thereof, this seal: D.F."

Two angels were battling for possession of Moerlein's soul when Lucienne awoke.

"Such a queer dream I just had." She snuggled close to him. "I dreamed we were on board the *Ramona*. I was very young. A virgin, I think. We stopped and lay down in a field of wild strawberries. I was wearing a white dress, but you—you, Charles, were impetuous. When we got up, I saw that there were two spots on my dress. But they weren't pink, they were dark—more like blackberry juice. I was so frightened. Yet it was delicious being loved by you." She slid underneath him. "Oh, my darling, let me keep on dreaming."

Moerlein looked at his watch. "It's eight o'clock," he said. "I have an early appointment."

For three weeks Charles Moerlein debated the question "Shall I marry Lucienne?" Forget her past? Drink from the chalice without inspecting its hallmark? In healthy lives morality is concerned only with the future. Health, desire and propinquity conjoining, Moerlein decided to marry the woman who had trapped him with a variation of the dropped-handkerchief technique, then poured love philters into his blood stream.

As a formal token of his intention, Moerlein selected a flawless blue and white diamond, crown cut, from Messiers et Cie. Price $7,500. The gem was unset. Lucienne would choose the setting.

"Have you a jewel box, lined with absinthe-colored velvet?"

"Yes, Mr. Moerlein, I believe we have."

The salesman ransacked the stockroom and returned with the very article. He placed the gem into a box calculated to display its fire. In fantasy, Moerlein saw the diamond flashing in Lucienne's navel.

She allowed him to place it there that night. Hands beneath her strawberry hair, she smiled up at him, and her pearl-perfect teeth outshone the diamond. "Do you like the merchandise, Charles?"

"I love every bit of it. As of this moment I take it off the market. Will you marry me, Lucienne?"

"Do not ask me to decide tonight. It is so . . . so happy the way we are."

"It would be even better if I could proclaim our love to the world."

"Lovers need only proclaim their love to each other." Lucienne delicately plucked the gem from her navel and placed it on the night table. "Diamonds cut everything but themselves," she said.

Not precisely the way Charles Moerlein had planned it, but could he be blamed for failing to hear in Lucienne's imperious "Not now" the prelude to her ultimate "No"?

Not even when Lucienne let Charles slip the diamond onto the third finger of her left hand did she regard it as a pledge of marriage.

Moerlein shrank from exploring the reasons for her repeated delays and excuses for postponing the marriage ceremony. His previous experience with the dimples told him that Lucienne had reasons of her own and would announce them when she chose.

The announcement came, as most announcements do, in the form of a letter. Charles saw the envelope, among others, in the morning mail. He thought the handwriting rather too decorative. But the ink! Purple, and such a purple as could not be forgotten. A cloud of apprehension hovered over him all day. Lucienne had been waiting for something. Obviously, too tensely expectant for a long time. Was this letter the things she had been waiting for?

That evening Moerlein found Lucienne in traveling clothes. No need to ask, "Where are you going?" Her whole being conveyed the single idea of separation, immediate and forever. The only permissible questions—and Moerlein knew he was asking them at his peril—were: "Why? Who? What?"

All three were answered when Lucienne handed him a single sheet of notepaper. "It will not make you happy to read this, Charles. I would prefer that you did not. Even after you read it, you will not understand, nor can I explain."

Charles Moerlein picked up the piece of notepaper and read the few lines:

DEAR L.:

The dashing widow from Baton Rouge turned out to be mostly rouge. I've spent a painful year separating her from a miserable 25 M, in the course of which my derringer went off, unfortunately killing her brother. You can imagine.

The most I can say, L., is that you make all other women seem like tap water compared with the true, the Blushful Hippocrene.

Your technique of fading away into the "forest dim" is admirable. Commendations from Teacher.

This is neither a plea nor a summons. I merely state the facts. No guarantees given or required. Come empty-handed, or with eighty-one trunks full of fineries, or as naked as Godiva. When, as, and if you please.

Yrs., at the rendezvous,
D.F.

"Is this man your husband?" asked Moerlein.

"No."

"Does he offer you any security for the future?"

"No."

"Is the writer of this letter the reason you haven't married me?"

"Yes."

"You left him simply to be out of the way while he . . ."

"Why torment yourself further, Charles?" Lucienne twisted the diamond ring from her finger. "You are a good man; you have made me very happy. I wish it were beginning all over again. But I must go."

At the doorway she turned and saw tears of grief and bewilderment streaming down Moerlein's face.

Her voice was tender with hard wisdom: "In the future, Charles, never try to own anything that you can't afford to lose."

It was good advice. After a rugged six months of personal suffering, Moerlein emerged, not hardened in heart, but infinitely wiser, more sympathetic toward human error. His supply of Hearthstone was nearly exhausted; Moerlein's chief problem was to secure a sufficient quantity of new whiskey suitable for blending purposes. Scouring the country-side, he instructed small distillers in methods that would secure a clean, flavorful product of reasonable uniformity. Still there was an acute shortage of such suppliers, and as Charles Moerlein gazed out his office window on a snowy

March morning in 1884, he knew that fresh sources must be found.

His meditations were interrupted by a knock on the office door. Dick Semmes, yard foreman, stuck his head in the door.

"Excuse me, Mr. Moerlein. Thought you'd like to know about something's just happened." The foreman grinned sheepishly. "That is, it happened a couple of months ago, but I just found out about it today."

"What did you just find out today, Dick?"

"You know that shoestring commission broker named Addicks? Well, around the first of October he turned up with a barrel of whiskey. I was off duty, so McIver paid him the usual price for ten-year-old stuff—sixty dollars. This afternoon I came across the barrel, sampled it, and say, Mr. Moerlein, it's really something! I thought you'd like to come down and taste it yourself."

"Glad to, Dick." Bareheaded, he followed his foreman across the cobblestone yard to a loading platform. Dick Semmes produced a narrow dipperlike implement called a "thief," plunged it into the bunghole and drew out a brimming six ounces and handed it to his employer.

Charles Moerlein tasted the aromatic flavor. A wonderful glow filled the membranes of his nose and throat. "Hmm—premium stuff. What's the maker's name?"

Dick Semmes pointed to the name burned into the barrel head: "C. Woodhull, Landmark Ind., 1873."

"Whoever this C. Woodhull is, he knows how to make whiskey. Something tells me I'd better go out and see him."

2.

SHEAF OF GOLD

ANSON WAS CHOPPING ensilage when he saw the sleigh enter his yard; he recognized it as the best turnout from Tod Demming's livery stable in Landmark—a smart cutter drawn by a span of matched bays. The driver pulled up with a skilled rein, dismounted, and blanketed the hired horses as carefully as though they were his own—an action that placed him in the credit column of Anson's regard. Having made the animals thoroughly comfortable, the visitor walked toward Anson without too squeamish a regard for the mixture of barnyard slush and manure under his boots of polished calfskin.

In carriage and attire he was probably the most attractive man that Anson had ever seen. He wore a broadcloth greatcoat, collared with black seal, matched by a hat and gloves of the same glossy fur. Cleanshaven except for the full mustache of the period, his cheeks glowed with the rubor of health whipped to extra ruddiness by the tingling cold. The total impression was one of prosperity and physical vigor at prime. Long experience in dealing with farmers saved Moerlein from the mistake of offering a business card. Instead he drew off a fur glove, extended a hand and said, "My name is Charles Moerlein."

By nature, Anson was not a hand-shaker; he held the ancient view that the act of shaking hands was either a pledge—not readily given to strangers—or an embrace reserved for the warmer moments of friendship. Besides, a man had to keep his guard up: there were too many land speculators and loan agents riding around the country in hired rigs these days. Anson's usual practice was to acknowl-

edge their overtures with a cool nod. He was amazed, therefore, to find himself taking Charles Moerlein's hand. The
contact, indefinably pleasant, led to a further statement from
his visitor.

"I'm in the rectifying business; my plant is in Cincinnati."

"I've heard of you, Mr. Moerlein. You make Hearthstone."

Moerlein matched the countryman compliment. "You make
a good whiskey yourself, Mr. Woodhull. That 1873 barrel you
sold to Homer Addicks was as noble a liquor as ever came
into my place."

"Glad you liked it."

Advantage even. Moerlein's sense of pace, developed by
many years of salesmanship, warned him that this tall, deliberate farmer couldn't be hustled or patronized. While
Anson chopped at his ensilage, Moerlein gazed about the
yard and snowy fields, appraising the Woodhull barn, farmhouse and gristmill. Substantial, better kept than most, but
desperately patched, like the jacket of its owner.

"Whiskey-making is a sideline with you, I take it."

"Scarcely even that. My father liked to run off a couple of
barrels every fall."

"May I ask how many barrels you have on hand?"

"A dozen, fifteen maybe."

"If they're as good as that 1873 barrel, they should be
worth money." Moerlein smiled at his own candor. "Now
that I've tacked an extra ten dollars onto your asking price,
would you mind letting me see, and taste, your whiskey?"

"Since you've come all the way from Cincinnati, it wouldn't
seem fair to say no. Just follow me."

Anson led the way across the barnyard and lifted the heavy
bulkhead door of his cellar. A spicy aroma with an after-
bouquet of mold gushed up the short flight of wooden steps.
Lighting a lantern, he guided Moerlein through the cool,
dark labyrinth, past sway-backed shelves bending under
their freight of preserves, peaches, berries and plums. An
iron-hasped door barred the way; Anson lifted the hand-
hammered latch and warned, "Step down." From the rafters
of this cellar, deeper than the first, hung stalactites of meat,
smoked and salted—quarters of beef, chines and shoulders
of pork. Huge puncheons and hogsheads, their covers held
in place by heavy stones, contained pork swimming in salt
brine.

Another latched door, a brief descent, and now they were

in the deepest part of the cellar—an Aladdin's cave far below the surface of the earth. Three sides of the cave were lined by racks, supporting oak barrels; each barrel head bore the name *C. Woodhull*. Under the name, a date and four *X*'s had been burned into the wood with a hot iron.

Moerlein's brown eyes sparkled; solicitously he passed his hand under the belly of an 1874 barrel; it came away dry.

"Good cooperage. Do you lose much by evaporation?"

"The usual one per cent every year." With a mallet Anson tapped the poplar bung of a ten-year-old barrel. A rich perfume, the first test of a fine liquor, filled the cellar. To display the handsome color of his whiskey, he filled a Mason jar and offered it to his guest.

Like a lapidary appraising a rare gem, Moerlein held the jar about ten inches from the lantern wick and saw its clear carnelian liquor, finely beaded with bubbles. Color, perfect. He lifted the jar, inhaled gently, as if breathing a flower. A delicate bouquet dilated the membranes of his nose and throat. Almost fearfully, he hesitated before touching the edge of the jar to his lips. So many diseases could blight a promising liquor. Secret flaws in the grain, unnoticed by the distiller, often became noticeable when the liquor reached maturity. Chemic hostility between the whiskey and its oaken container sometimes embittered their marriage. And finally, as with other evolving organisms, whiskey (like men and women) went through phases of stale boredom and flavorless discontent.

Would this ruddy liquor live up to its noble advertisements of color and aroma?

To mask his hesitation, Moerlein offered a toast. "Friendship and good fortune," he said. Above the rim of the jar his eyes met Anson's. Both men smiled.

Moerlein tilted the jar. At his lips the once-separate attributes of scent and color merged into a liquid—ingratiating, rare. An expression of pure delight crossed the distiller's face. "Superb," he murmured, and sipped again.

This time he qualified his praise with a professional query. "A bit too ardent, maybe?" He passed the jar to Anson with a gesture that solicited the maker's opinion—plus the invitation "Won't you join me?"

Now there were two men performing the age-old ritual of libation. Anson sipped critically, then nodded agreement. "The proof does run a little high."

"About a hundred and thirty?" (Did this reticent farmer really know his whiskey?)

"Nearer one hundred and twenty-eight, I'd say. It certainly doesn't toy with your palate."

"Classic whiskeys never do." Moerlein pointed to an 1875 barrel. "May I taste some of that?"

"I'd rather you wouldn't. A bad stave spoiled it." No apology. Merely the simple statement of a hazard that all whiskeys must run.

Moerlein valued the quiet honesty of the statement. With horses, diamonds and whiskey, you had to depend on the integrity of the man you were dealing with. "Do you mind tapping this one?" he asked, pointing to a barrel bearing a date 1878.

"Glad to."

Again the ritual of tasting was performed. How pleasant, thought Anson, to go down the line with this charming visitor, sampling whiskey and exchanging connoisseur comments. Male companionship was now rare in his life, and after sampling three or four ounces of his own whiskey, Anson began to feel the wave of mild euphoria that is the sign of good liquor. Moerlein apparently felt it too. The barriers of reserve melted; tongue strings loosened; the earthen cave, lighted only by lantern rays, became a gentlemen's club whose membership consisted of two extraordinarily fine fellows.

In the midst of all this congeniality, Moerlein found it easy to broach the subject of his visit. He made an inclusive sweep of his hand and said, "I'll give you six hundred dollars for the lot—and pay the excise tax, of course." To support his offer, he drew a sheaf of gold notes from his wallet, counted out five twenties, two fifties, four mint-new hundred-dollar bills, and pressed them into Anson's hand.

Six hundred dollars was more cash than Anson Woodhull had ever seen at one time. The sheaf of gold notes, three times the amount of his annual income, would end his pressing financial difficulties, provide his family with necessities, comforts even. But a question rose in his mind. Wasn't six hundred dollars too much for twelve barrels of whiskey? He voiced the question: "Isn't a dollar a gallon a bit high?"

Moerlein's reply was an education in the economics of whiskey-making. "I'm not paying a dollar a gallon," he explained. "The first thing I'll do with your whiskey is reduce it to eighty proof by adding twenty-five gallons of water to each barrel. That brings the cost down to about sixty cents a gallon—a not unreasonable price for aged liquor."

He plunged deeper into his subject. "In the last five or six years there's been a complete change in American drinking habits. Old-fashioned straight whiskey is too heavy for the popular taste. More than two thirds of the whiskey consumed in the United States is a blend composed of neutral spirits flavored with straight whiskey, ranging from one to four years old. My Old Settler, for example, is a light, clean-tasting drink containing eighty per cent neutral spirits, fifteen per cent of year-old whiskey with just a touch—five per cent, to be exact—of the high-quality whiskey I've just bought from you."

Moerlein's discourse became fascinating, clearer, as he went on. "Your six hundred gallons of whiskey will add a distinctive bouquet to eighteen thousand gallons—seventy-two thousand quarts—of Old Settler. In case you're still worrying about it, let me tell you that my net profit after taxes, bottling and shipping, is about twenty cents a quart. So put the money in your pocket, my friend." Moerlein sipped appreciatively from his Mason jar. "I'll take every gallon of whiskey that you make."

"Thank you. But my wife wouldn't like the idea of my going into the whiskey business. She says there's a taint about it."

"Your wife isn't the only woman who thinks that way." Moerlein didn't add: There's a taint about poverty, too.

In silence they rethreaded their path along the narrow passageway to the door of the cellar. In the open air Charles Moerlein extended his hand. "I wouldn't dream of trying to change your wife's mind, Mr. Woodhull. But if you change yours, just let me know."

He unblanketed his horses, climbed into the sleigh, and with a farewell wave was off down the country road.

Anson's sheaf of gold notes, which at first seemed as endless as the pages of a great book, soon began to thin out. He spent two hundred dollars on desperately needed shoes, clothing and underwear for his wife, children and Solange; laid in a supply of staple groceries, a new set of table crockery. He deposited a hundred dollars in a bank for Reb Plaskett. Then he really plunged. To replace the crippled Burnside, he spent fifty dollars on a western two-year-old, Custer, another thirty dollars on a double harness.

Thrift, pale with apprehension, clamped on the brakes. Anson stowed the remaining cash in his money box and resolved to forget it.

Softened by March thaws, earth felt the lengthening shafts of the sun; in oak and sycamore, sap swelled from root to twig. It was rut-time for lowing farm animals. Reb's budding antlers were locked half playfully in a tangle of Laly's hair. Spring freshets, pouring into the Ohio, flooded the bank of that mysterious stream. Zarah was nearing the end of her term, and Platt was on the road to recovery.

While April sunshine flooded the fields, Platt sat on a nail keg in the barn. This is what Anson had hoped for—Platt, up and about, gaining strength, cheerful and seemingly contented. At certain skills—the use of a whetstone, for instance—Anson gladly conceded his younger brother's superiority. One day Platt picked up a scythe blade, nicked, worn and scarcely worth salvaging. He clamped it into a vise and bent over the blade, honing it with an oilstone (as one might hone a fine razor) to gleaming sharpness. Then, with good-natured rivalry, he showed the edged blade to Anson. "Still think you can sharpen a scythe better than me, Ansey-Bub?"

The almost forgotten nickname touched Anson strangely. "Never could, never will." He plucked a black hair from his head, flicked it across the sharpened blade and held up the severed strand as acknowledgment of Platt's wizardry. "Want to get busy on my chisels? They're dull as preaching."

Platt sailed into the job, masking with pretended cheerfulness his growing discontent with life on an isolated farm. A strategy of escape was forming in his mind: after lulling Anson into trustfulness, he would borrow his brother's buggy, wheedle a small loan (twenty-five dollars perhaps), then drive over to Peddler's Landing and lure Jesse Rocamp into a game of stud. With his winnings Platt would proceed to New Orleans and reunion with Damon Frye. Within a few months it would all work out. Meanwhile Platt dutifully bent over the chisels, like a man sharpening the edge of a secret purpose.

A light tattoo of spring rain was dampening down the

seed corn when the brothers heard the *clop-clop* of heavy hoofs in the barnyard.

"Looks like Woolsey Hamer," said Anson. "Hope nothing's wrong with Abby."

Wool Hamer, a stocky, chestnut-bearded man in his early thirties, was Anson's brother-in-law, a hard-working farmer, and a good husband. His place, some few miles distant, though not so picturesque or fertile as Anson's, was rated as a valuable parcel of property. Anson greeted him country-style. "Hello, Wool, you old bacon thief. Stopped robbing smokehouses yet?"

Wool made no attempt at heartiness. By his gait and down-cast manner, he was obviously in trouble. "I've come to ask a favor, Anse. A big one."

"Ask away, Wool."

Hamer glanced significantly at Platt as if to say, Can't we have a little privacy?

Anson's nod dispersed doubts. "It's all in the family."

Reassured, Wool Hamer tugged at a red-taped envelope in his coat pocket and drew out a sheaf of legal-looking documents. The very sight of the red-sealed papers filled Anson with foreboding. Had Wool got himself mixed up with promissory notes?

Wool had. And deeply. The details came out in his shame-faced confession.

"You know that hard spot I went through a couple of years ago, Anse? Poor crop and worse prices. Everything fell to pieces all at once. Gear, animals, barn, just wore out. The bank wouldn't give me a mortgage, so I had to borrow from one of those loan agents."

Anson knew the breed—a sharking gentry. Neither bankers nor capitalists themselves, they merely "arranged" a loan with some unspecified eastern "connection."

"How much did you borrow?"

"Five hundred dollars."

"I suppose you put up your title deed as security."

"No, just my signature."

At the word *signature* Platt bent closer to his chisels.

"What interest did they charge?" asked Anson.

"Fifteen per cent."

"Steepish."

"It sure is." Wool showed a stack of interest receipts totaling $225. "But that ain't the worst of it, Anse. The thing that's breaking my back is the agent's commission." Wool displayed a second document. With the stub of a forefinger cut off in a sawmill accident, he pointed to some fine print. "Just read that."

Studying the clause, Anson remembered his father's warning against loan agents. "Don't get your name on any of their paper, son. They've got sharp-print paragraphs that'll cut you down like a reaping hook." Fear rather than virtue had steeled Anson against the blandishments of satin-vested agents who had driven up to his door with offers of quick cash. Others, less fearful—Wool, for example—had accepted the cash, then felt the hook of Paragraph Four in their vitals.

Anson read the cruel paragraph:

> It is understood and agreed that the loan agent's commission of 15%, over and above the regular interest charges, shall be payable in quarterly installments. On failing to meet these installments the principal sum of the loan, together with the unpaid amount of the agent's commission, shall become due immediately.

"I got two payments coming May first," Wool said. "Ninety dollars interest, and fifty to the commission agent. I need a hundred and forty dollars, Anse, or they'll sell me out."

Could such things be? Yes, lacking the wretched sum of $140, a man could lose his acres, home, animals, farm gear —everything.

"How much cash have you got?" asked Anson.

Wool pulled out three silver dollars and six greenbacks. "Nine dollars."

The slow fuse of Anson's wrath crackled toward an explosion. What was wrong with a system that netted an industrious man nine dollars after a dozen years of back-breaking labor? Wool was neither a drunkard nor a wastrel—merely another victim of usurious moneylenders operating in the Ohio Valley. Thousands of farmers, dispossessed, were crowding into the cities to become factory workers, or remained on the land as tenant farmers, scrabbling out a meager existence.

Black anger burst from Anson. He purged himself in a torrent of profanity. Words that he had never used before sprang to his lips; his heavy fist struck the work bench as he gritted out his sympathy for Wool Hamer.

"May God damn their souls to eternal hell."

Calmer, he turned to his brother-in-law. "They won't get your farm, Wool—not while I've got money to hold them off. Come into the house."

When Wool Hamer drove off in his rig, only a single twenty-dollar bill—the last page in Anson's book of gold notes —lay in his strong box.

And in Platt's treacherous brain a grand design began to take form.

As April trended into May, Platt was no longer content to play solitaire on a nail keg in the barn. A born wanderer, he expressed his desire (natural enough, thought Anson) to get off the place for a day or two. He borrowed his older brother's horse and buggy, wheedled five dollars from Solange and drove off in glad raiment. Two days later he came back— haggard, unshaved and broke. A week later he repeated the performance; returning, he fell into bed exhausted.

Platt's profitless comings and goings were a source of anxiety to the entire household: Solange worried secretly; Anson needed the horse for farm work. It was Zarah who voiced the general concern. In the last stage of a joyless pregnancy, she snapped irritably at her husband, "Where does he go? What does he do?"

Anson replied in character. "Being one's brother's keeper doesn't warrant prying into his affairs."

Reb Plaskett, innocently enough, supplied the answer to Platt's mysterious activities. The lad was winding trout flies one day for a fishing expedition along Paddle Creek. Anson noticed that the blue and orange feathers on Reb's cunningly wrought flies came from no barnyard fowl.

"Where did you get these?" asked Anson.

"Found them sticking onto the buggy cushions."

The brilliant bits of plumage sent winged darts of association flying through Anson's mind. He remembered the Double Eagle Inn, the fighting cocks and Jesse Rocamp's low-grade trickery. Anson decided to warn his brother. "They're bad men, Platt," he would say.

Then, late in May, Zarah gave birth to her fourth child, a boy. Her labor pains were severe, protracted. Emma Fifield got stone drunk while waiting. "The most unpredicatable woman I ever seen" was Emma's last coherent statement. Solange took over the office of midwife; ordinarily her feminine instinct would have served. But Zarah's fourth baby was no case for an amateur. At the last moment Solange's agonized cry, "Anson, come quick," brought the begetter of this unwanted child into Zarah's room.

What a presentation! Buttocks first, with cord complications. Anson's skill brought the baby out alive; no mortal skill could have prevented the vaginal injury to Zarah. The laceration was slight . . . but, oh, to be wounded *there!* By . . . by whom?

Zarah's indictment of her husband, never spoken, took the form of an accusing passivity. Her milk dried up before it really began to flow. Solange fed the child with a bottle, bathed it, performed all the duties that normally fall upon a mother. The baby had never been baptized. Yet because he smiled early, because his first crop of hair was golden, because he was a bright, perfectly formed infant (and because Solange loved him) he somehow got the name "Sonny."

"He's going to look just like Platt," said Anson, gazing at the babe in Solange's arms. "Remember my telling you that Platt was the best-looking, cleverest boy I ever saw?"

"I remember."

Solange must have been living on memories because neither she nor Anson had seen or heard from Platt for the past two months.

In mid-August Anson received an oblong envelope, postmarked Buford, Indiana. Who do I know in Buford? thought Anson, slitting the envelope with his jackknife. On a sheet of paper, bearing the letterhead *Buford Loan Agency* was a single paragraph written in a clerkish hand:

> Sir:
>
> Your 90-day note in the amount of $500 (Five Hundred Dollars) dated May 10, 1884, is now three days overdue. Unless this office hears from you by return mail the title to your property, according to our agreement, will pass into our hands.
>
> Yours truly,
> Thaddeus P. Meakins, Agt.

Anson read the letter twice. The whole thing must be a clerical error. He had no personal knowledge of Thaddeus P. Meakins and hadn't been in Buford for years. He put the letter in his hip pocket but couldn't forget the ominous phrase *title to your property . . . will pass into our hands.* Well, there was one sure, quick way of settling the matter. He went to his strong box, found the title deed bound up with a copy of Chauncey's will. He felt reassured. How could title pass to other hands without physical possession of the deed? This gave rise to a whole new set of perplexities. The letter mentioned a note in the amount of $500. A note and a title deed were two separate documents. After a morning's worriment, Anson decided to hitch up his horse, ride over to Buford and have a face-to-face interview with Thaddeus P. Meakins.

Buford, ten miles northwest of Woodhull's farm, had originally been a canal settlement, a poor rival to Landmark, the county seat. Within the last decade, Buford had become a terminal spur of the Cincinnati Railroad and a growing community. Anson found the usual knot of low buildings huddled around the depot and without much trouble discovered Mr. Thaddeus P. Meakins seated in a barish office smoking a rank replica of a capitalist cigar.

The genus *carpetbagger* had flowered to full perfection in the person and philosophy of Thad Meakins. Scrupulously he observed Solomon's wisdom concerning the lilies; he neither toiled nor spun; enough for him to exact a modest 15 per cent from loans to those who did. Attire, rich but not gaudy; manner, false-benevolent; diction, colloquial with a varnish of legalisms. His sole defect as a first-class operator—the thing that kept him out of the really big money—was a massive tic that convulsed his trigeminal nerve at half-minute intervals. For twenty-nine seconds he would be in complete control of his facial muscles; then the tic would explode, exposing a wolflike set of teeth.

Mr. Meakins had just completed a complicated tic when Anson opened his door. With twenty-nine seconds of suavity at his disposal, Meakins boomed, "Mornin', friend. How may the Buford Loan Agency serve you this fine Indiana day?"

"You can serve me by clearing up this little puzzle." Anson placed the letter on the agent's desk. "Someone seems to have made a mistake."

With fifteen seconds to go, Meakins spent five gazing at the document, three puffing at his cigar, and three more appraising the burly countryman standing before him. "Sit down, friend, sit down."

While Anson turned to find a chair, Thad Meakins' tic went off. His left eye bulged, his cheek and lip bunched up, exposing a horribly decayed incisor; then the tremor passed down into his shoulder and out of sight.

"Everything seems to be reg'lar, far's this agency's concerned. Your note's overdue, that's all. Hope you can pay it. Otherwise . . . I trust we'll stay friendly while ironin' out the details."

"I don't know anything about a note, due or overdue," said Anson. "May I see the documents in the case?"

Mr. Meakins had a place for everything and that place was the top left drawer of his desk. From under a flask of whiskey and a much-thumbed volume of pornography, he lifted a miscellaneous bundle of papers and plunked them onto his desk. "Let's see . . . hmm . . . Tomlinson, Voorhees, Watkins—ah, yes, Woodhull." He produced a sheaf of forms held together by a common pin. "Here's the main instrument," he said, thrusting a slip of paper toward Anson. "The usual promissory note, dated, notarized, signed by the borrower. Everything seems to be in order."

Tic.

While Anson scrutinized the document, Thad Meakins inquired, "Recognize the hand?"

Anson did indeed recognize the hand. The name on the note was his own . . . but the hand that signed it was Platt's.

"Was this note signed in your presence?" asked Anson.

"Well, no—not exactly." Meakins examined another document on the pile before him. "This seems to be a little piece of business brought in by a sub-agent."

"Might that sub-agent be Jesse Rocamp?"

"Might be. But that don't make no difference. We investigated and found everything as represented."

"What kind of investigation did you make?"

"Why, we went over to the county court house, searched the title in the Office of Records and satisfied ourselves that the property in question actually existed. That's all we're interested in. Soon's we got the owner's signature on a note, we gave him the money."

"Who gave *who* the money?"

Cornered, Mr. Meakins assumed an offhand manner. "Like I said, the money-passin' was done by Jesse Rocamp. I presoom he gave it to the proper party." With a tic about to break, Meakins became aggressive. "You ain't sayin' the signature's a forgery, are you?"

"That's just what I'm saying. Rocamp is a cheap rascal and

someone, probably the Buford Loan Agency, is guilty of sharp practice."

"Hold your horses, Mister. What you just said would take a lot of provin' in court. All kinds of facts would come out. Now if you'll take a piece of friendly advice, just pay up. Either that—" Meakins' tic caught him in mid-sentence, face contorted, fangs bared—"or we'll commence eviction proceedin's."

Useless now to attempt unraveling the skein of conspiracy woven by Meakins and Rocamp. Platt had forged the note, and unless Anson paid its face value, his farm would be snatched from him.

"How much time will you give me to find the money?"

"Paragraph Four don't give you no time at all. This note's already three days overdue." Thad Meakins strained the quality of mercy. "But the Buford Loan Agency usually 'lows a mite of leeway. You can have another twenty-four hours."

Along the hot unpaved sidewalk, ankle-deep in August dust, Anson walked toward the hitching post where Custer lashed an exasperated tail at green flies. Similar torments, each a question mark, were stinging Anson's brain. The most tormenting question of all was: Where can I raise five hundred dollars?

He heard a shrill toot, saw a white plume of steam rising from the locomotive in the depot. That would be the noon train getting ready to pull out for Cincinnati. Anson moved quickly, untied Custer, and led him across the street to the livery stable. "Take care of my horse until tomorrow," he said to a lounging stableman. Then, by running toward the railroad station, he swung aboard the rear platform of the Cincinnati local.

Four hours later he was standing in the outer office of Mr. Charles Moerlein.

The rectifier greeted him with genuine sincerity. He was glad to see Anson; rising cordially, he said so. Under his visitor's homespun coat, rumpled and seedy in contrast with Moerlein's broadcloth, behind the tanned forehead, creased with anxiety, Moerlein saw the essential man. A good man. In trouble.

The nature of Anson's trouble came out in his second sentence. "I've decided to go into the whiskey business, Mr.

Moerlein. I hope the offer you made last spring still holds good."

The maker of Old Settler, remembering the time, place and conditions of the offer, was tempted to ask: Has Mrs. Woodhull changed her mind? He rejected the question as fringing on the impertinent. With a man like Woodhull, one didn't presume.

Still, certain practical aspects concerning the making, storing and shipping of Woodhull's whiskey must be ironed out.

"Will you be obliged to go into the market to buy corn?" asked Moerlein.

"No. My own fields will bring in a thousand bushels of corn and the necessary rye and barley."

"Good. How about barrels?"

"My brother-in-law is a part-time cooper. He'll make the barrels, char them too, for seventy-five cents apiece."

"Reasonable enough. How about storage facilities? I won't be needing your whiskey until next May."

"I'll convert part of my barn into a warehouse with open-end racks."

"There'll be a withdrawal tax of seventy cents per gallon," said Moerlein. "I suggest that you write to your local Federal gauger, inform him of your intention to make whiskey on a commercial scale. Tell him that he may look to me for payment of the excise."

Charles Moerlein arose to conclude the interview. "You've got three of the best whiskey-making months ahead. I warn you, though: it'll be quite a job to make a barrel a day. Well, good luck." He extended his hand—the equivalent of a signed contract. He felt in Anson's handclasp the pledge of responsibility. He felt more, and the thing he felt made him want to ask: What's really troubling you, Mr. Woodhull?

Instead, Moerlein kept the matter on a business level by saying, "You'll be faced by initial outlays of cash. Suppose I advance you a thousand dollars." Without waiting for Anson to comment on the proposal, Moerlein walked to his safe, opened a compartment and counted off ten one-hundred-dollar bills.

For the first time in his adult life Anson felt a thick wetness of his eyelashes.

At eleven o'clock next morning a quite dry-eyed farmer laid five one-hundred-dollar bills on the desk of Thaddeus P.

Meakins. An enormous tic agitated the loan agent's arm as he handed back the promissory note.

"Call on us any time, Mr. Woodhull," boomed Meakins. "That's what we're here for."

Riding homeward, Anson dreaded the coming scene between himself and Zarah. How could a loving husband coolly announce to a trusting wife that he proposed to disregard her deeply held views on the matter of whiskey? Zarah loathed alcohol as an evil in itself and as a shameful beguiler of man's nobler parts. Even the smell of the stuff made her ill. How could he explain his decision to become a whiskey-maker? Useless to plead that economic pressure had forced him to this expedient. And unthinkable (in terms of Anson's family pride) to admit Platt's treacherous part in the business.

"Geet, Custer, get on, boy." No need to prod the stable-bound horse. Twilight was settling over the countryside as Anson drove into his yard.

All during dinner Anson read the unasked question "Where have you been?" in Zarah's eyes. Nursing her wrath to keep it warm, she picked up her sewing basket with maddening serenity and began the nightly task of reinforcing with thread and needle, the worn, already patched fabric of her children's clothes.

Tired of pretending that his churchwarden pipe wouldn't draw properly, Anson laid it down. Subterfuge was beyond him, anyway. "I made a decision today, Zarah. It hurt me—but there was no other way out."

"I imagined that something was troubling you." Accustomed to seeing this resourceful man encounter and throw off challenges in the past, Zarah had no doubt that he would do it again. Could she best help him now by sewing calmly or by laying her needlework aside? A trace of perversity, an unwillingness to help, caused her to stitch on.

"I saw Moerlein in Cincinnati," said Anson.

Foreboding made Zarah's needle fly faster. "Did he ask you to come?"

"In a way, yes." Anson tried the softening influence of the past tense. "When he was here last spring he said he'd pay me a good price for all the whiskey I could make."

"I remember." Zarah's intonation suggested that the incident had been closed.

"Well, the fact is—" Anson tugged at his pipe as though

the smoldering tobacco could cast a glow over the difficult truth. "The fact is, he's promised to pay me three thousand dollars for one hundred barrels of whiskey."

"Whiskey? *What* whiskey?"

"The whiskey I'm going to make."

As if a hand customarily tender had roughly swept every string of her being, Zarah quivered with conflicting emotions. Anger counseled: Flare up, woman betrayed. Dash your sewing box to the floor. Scatter the tools and materials of your unrewarded calling. Break the cover stamped with the meaningless initials *A to Z*, first and last and everything between. Compassion, muted by truth, whispered: The box cannot be broken, its contents will never be scattered. The fabric you work in is indestructible. Self-pity murmured: You are like Ruth, condemned forever to stand in tears amid the alien corn. Came the antiphon: He shall be unto thee a restorer of thy life. Self-righteousness, prim as a Brattle Street zinnia, flowered for a moment: Zarah, born Osgood, is mated to a trafficker in whiskey. Understanding pruned at the roots of the patterned garden: He must have his reasons, even though he does not share them with me now.

The swirl of contending voices blew down the wind, clearing a path for Zarah's actual words. "You've changed, Anson. The first time I saw you, that day at the fair, you were propping the bough of a fruit tree. Your eyes found the broken place, your hands mended it. It was a sign to me of the husband and husbandman. I followed the sign, felt myself blessed among women for sharing you with the earth, crops and creatures that you loved." She gazed at him, eyes and voice asking: What has become of that love that caped your every act and thought with simple grandeur? Tell me, Anson, what has happened?

Zarah's plea, so just in presentation, free of small curiosity, so deserving of an honest answer, touched her husband at a depth that he himself had never fully explored. Until now Anson had hidden behind a common enough ideal of loyalty to a weaker brother. He believed that his reason for entering the whiskey business had been forced upon him by Platt's treachery. Now, in the light of Zarah's query, *Tell me, Anson, what has happened?* his true motive, hitherto hidden and unacknowledged, was clearly revealed.

This simple fact appeared. He no longer *wanted* to be a farmer. Circumstance had bred him to the soil; the iron contract of necessity had held him to its service. But the hard indenture was breaking now. After three generations at the ax and plow, the dormant mercantile strain in the Woodhull blood—a strain that had sent his ancestors scouring the seven seas in search of trade—was reasserting itself.

"You say I've changed, Zarah. No doubt I have. I began to feel it last spring at planting time. I remember looking at a handful of seed corn, just before flinging it into the furrow. As I looked at the kernels, I saw the hopeless fate of the independent farmer. Of myself, Wool Hamer, a hundred others in Landmark County alone, a half million of us in the Ohio Valley, going through the labor of planting a crop, the worry of watching it grow, of protecting it against blight, hail, drought. The terrible effort of harvest . . ." Anson's voice trailed off into futility. "And what happens then? We burn our corn for fuel, or sell it to speculators for fifteen cents a bushel. Our hogs bring in two cents a pound. Our total income for a year is two hundred dollars, or maybe less. Our gear and buildings wear out. To repair or replace them, we borrow money at fifteen per cent; accident, sickness, an unexpected flurry in the money market, and we're foreclosed, evicted.

"No, Zarah, a small self-sustaining farm is part of the American dream that has vanished. A new system is in the making—and I'm going to be part of that system. Do you want me to stand in a sterile furrow at the tail of a worn-out plow, or would you rather see me moving along the main current, bringing a salable product to the market place?"

Zarah brought the whole matter back into moral focus. "Even if that product is whiskey?"

Her question irritated him. "I've no other product that's wanted." Fatigue, distaste for his own cynicism and the prospect of never quite persuading Zarah that he was taking the right, the only course, prompted his counter-question: "Can you think of any other way out?"

It was a mistake, the first and clumsiest error that Anson had ever made in all the years of his marriage. He tried to undo his clumsiness by the swift contrition of a caress. Bending over Zarah, he kissed the cedar hair. He waited for the ripple of assent, prelude to the deeper responses that came before sleeping. But neither then, nor when she lay in his arms afterward, did she soften under his lips and hands.

3.

THE FEARFUL CONTRACT

To MAKE A SINGLE BARREL of whiskey is an autumn adventure, a pleasant break from farm routine. But to make a hundred barrels of whiskey that will be reasonably uniform in flavor and quality is no holiday affair. Such an operation requires foresight, rugged equipment and a variety of raw materials. During the last two weeks in August, Anson pressed all hands into his preparations.

He began by grinding seven hundred bushels of corn and four hundred bushels of winter rye. Anson himself set the stones of the gristmill so that the cereal would be ground neither too fine nor too coarse; slowly the undershot wheel of the mill began to turn, and on September 1, eleven hundred bushels of cereal lay heaped in the gristmill bins.

Under Anson's direction Solange took over the important chore of malting. She spread moistened barley pearls on flat wooden trays, exposed them to the sun till tiny green sprouts appeared, then halted the budding process by placing the trays in the oven of the kitchen stove.

"What does the barley do?" she asked curiously.

Anson explained that malted barley broke down the starch imprisoned within corn, changed it to a sugary substance which, after many chemical transformations, became alcohol. Solange's puzzlement amused him. "Just remember what old Chance used to say: 'The barley malt sort of kisses the sweetness out of corn.'"

"Ah, that is a science I understand."

With Reb's help Anson built a fireplace of boulders in the middle of the barnyard, heaped a dozen chunks of maple onto this crude hearth and said, "Keep the maple

197

burning steady till it's charred clear through. When the chunks cool, take a small sledge hammer and break them up into flaky pieces. Then wash yourself in the brook and begin all over again. In about two weeks you'll have a ton of charcoal. We'll need it for leaching the new whiskey." He tousled the boy's mop of ginger hair. "All clear, Reb?"

"There's only one thing, Mr. Woodhull. Can Laly . . . sort of . . . watch me?"

"Watch you? She'll probably boss the whole job."

Anson was right—for a time. The children danced around the roaring fire together for three days. Then Zarah, seeing her daughter's sooty face and hands, put an end to what she called "this whole barbarous business" by summoning Laly into the house. Thereafter, Reb worked alone until a heap of charcoal, flaked and powdered, stood like a black pyre beside the bouldered ring.

While these preparations went forward, Anson commissioned Woolsey Hamer to make three maple vats, each capable of holding five hundred gallons of mash. Glad to pay off his debt to his brother-in-law, Wool coopered up the huge mash tubs, then went on to make a hundred barrels of inch-thick sun-dried oak staves.

Anson had nearly completed preparations when James MacMonnies, the Federal gauger, rode up on a roan cob. By definition a gauger is an officer whose business it is to ascertain the content of casks and barrels. No mere curiosity animated him. His chief concern was to multiply any given gallonage by the Federal excise to be derived therefrom. He was, in short, that traditionally feared and hated individual, the tax collector.

Mr. James MacMonnies, being a Scotsman, brought to his office a wider-than-average vision. In the back of his head, a roundish poll covered by a crisp furze of hair, lay memories of a fellow exciseman, Bobbie Burns, a man who loved the thing he measured and celebrated that love in unforgettable songs. Not since James MacMonnies had left his native Glen of Spey had he seen a brighter, bonnier assemblage of gear—the new mash vats, the array of oaken barrels and such finely ground charcoal. His stubby fingers caressed the burnished copper cheeks of Anson's pot still; he noted with approval the inclined sluiceway of rough planks that brought water from the nearby stream; he peered into the box-flume arrangement that led the water past an ingenious coil of copper known as the *worm*.

"One of man's greatest inventions," said MacMonnies, pointing to the copper tube. " 'Tis here that the mystery of distillation takes place. Can you name me the man who figured it out?"

"Some Scotsman probably."

"Never doot it. And now I'll take a glance at your cereal bins. In Glen Spey they'd hold naught but barley. Changing times, changing customs." MacMonnies fingered the coarse-ground corn and rye, then asked an official question. "How many bushels of this will you be cooking?"

"Five hundred corn, two hundred rye, fifty barley."

"Figuring four gallons to the bushel, that means three thousand gallons." MacMonnies rubbed his plump hands. "One of these days, Mr. Woodhull, I'll come by on my little pony and pick up twenty-one hundred dollars in taxes."

Anson explained his arrangement with Charles Moerlein. "The consignee will pay the tax."

"So long as it is paid, I'd take it from the devil himself." He shook hands with Anson, settled himself into the comfortable saddle, clucked to his roan cob and galloped down the dirt road.

Every batch of whiskey—as Anson well knew—must take four hurdles: mashing, fermenting, distilling and barreling. Any of these might be a stumbling block, and no one could tell beforehand how a batch would turn out. If the whiskey was burned or diseased, its maker must have courage to dump the whole batch, scrub up his apparatus, and start over again. With considerable care, then, Anson began the mashing process on September 1, 1884.

While a predawn mist drifted in from the Ohio, he measured twenty bushels of corn, three bushels of rye, and a bushel of barley into one of his new mash tubs. He scalded it with fifty gallons of hot water, stirred in a cupful of yeast, then let the mixture stand for three days.

Bending over his tub on the morning of the third day, Anson gazed thoughtfully at the wort, a sourish gruel, quivering like a sea of yeasty foam. There must be, thought Anson, a secret fury in the corn, a stubborn unwillingness to let its nature be changed from patient starch to ardent spirit. He dipped up a handful of the mash and held it to his nose; inhaling the beery reek, he briefly mourned the corn's lost innocence.

No time for sentimentality now. Maple bucket in each hand, he began transferring the content of his mash tub into the copper kettle, supported trivet-wise by three pylons of fieldstone. Kindling the hickory faggots underneath the kettle with a sulphur match (Old Chance had used a tinder-box), Anson waited until the hickory was flaming briskly. Then he stepped onto a low platform that brought him waist-high against the copper kettle and began stirring its contents with a wooden paddle.

Tusker, the black boar, came snouting toward the kettle. He slurped up a foul puddle of tailings and snuffled eagerly for more. Again and again Anson filled his copper kettle from the mash tub; by noon, his barrel was about half full of colorless liquor. Hands blackened by soot, kneecaps scorched, he took a countryman glance at the sun. High noon.

Time for a breather.

Anson was disappointed when Zarah failed to bring him his luncheon. Solange appeared with a basket of sandwiches, made excuses, but Anson knew that Zarah's absence was a signal of her disapproval.

While the September sun traversed a sky that gradually deepened from topaz to sepia, Anson toiled at his still. Twice more he charged his kettle from the mash tub; twice the cereal mixture bubbled into saffron froth and gushed from the goose-necked spout in a flow of foreshot, middle run and tailings.

When the sepia light darkened to umber, the mash tub was empty and the oak barrel brimmed full. By a day's work, Anson Woodhull had transformed thirteen bushels of cereal into fifty gallons of new whiskey with a market value of $30.00.

If only Zarah would understand!

The breach between Zarah and Anson grew deeper as the whiskey-making continued. The once-tender moments before sleeping were no longer a solace. Zarah had never recovered from the birth injury inflicted upon her as her newest son breeched into the world. The lacerations did not mend as Fifer Tansey had predicted; nor did he regard it as a matter of grave consequence. His suggestion, "If you want to have a few stitches taken," sent shivers of revulsion through

Zarah. It would be like sending a fine watch to a blacksmith for repairs. Yet the prospect of going permanently untreated was an affront to her womanhood—an affront for which she secretly blamed Anson. Now, with the intolerable stench of whiskey filling her home, Zarah's nerves were frayed past endurance.

One night Anson wakened to find that Zarah was not sleeping beside him. Candlestick in hand, he searched the house and found her lying on a corn-husk mattress in an unused part of the attic. She was limp, unresponsive in his arms, her face averted, her eyes red with weeping.

"Zarah, dearest love, why do you leave our bed and sleep here?"

Convulsive sobbings shook her. How could she say to this man: I loathe the smell of whiskey that clings to your beard. You are an abomination to my nostrils. Unable to utter these words, Zarah's indictment turned inward. "I am a poor ripped thing, torn in childbirth. A good doctor could repair the hurt, but you take no steps to help me—even though your pleasure would be increased if I were mended."

Anson lay on the bare floor, attempting to sooth her. "Men are stupid about such things, darling. Tomorrow we will go to Cincinnati, find the best surgeon. My wife will be made whole again."

"And the whiskey-making?" asked Zarah, pressing her advantage.

There was only one reply that Anson could make. "I must fulfill my contract with Charles Moerlein. I intend to keep on making whiskey, Zarah. There is no other course open to me."

"Then why should I bother to visit a Cincinnati surgeon?" Disheveled, wretched, unwilling at that moment to fulfill a fearful contract entered into "before God and witnesses assembled," Zarah fell despairing onto the straw mattress. "Why should I bother about anything?" she sobbed.

"Because I love you. Because you are a great woman, a great, beautiful and brave woman. Because I need you. Because our children need you. And finally because—my darling, believe me—this fearful strain will pass."

Neither love nor logic could penetrate the cloud of desolation gathering in Zarah's soul.

Anson did the only thing that a patient and loving husband could do. With his enormous strength he lifted his wife

off the straw pallet and carried her like a baby back to their
room.

"Sleep here, Zarah," he said. "Forget me until the whiskey-
making is over."

Sorrowfully Anson labored onward to fulfill his contract
with Moerlein. He stopped coming into the house for lunch
and contented himself with the cold pork sandwiches that
Solange brought to him every noon. He slept in the barn and
doggedly continued the four-part rhythm of mashing, distilling, leaching and barreling.

Foreshot, middle run and tailings.

The mud-splashed group of horsemen that rode into Anson's farmyard on September 28 was neither a cavalcade nor
a posse. They were merely Indiana landsmen, some of them
mounted on spavined plow horses, others riding in buggies
and light wagons. All were armed with shotguns or muzzle-
loading rifles; around the pommel of the leader's saddle—
a man known to Anson as Jeff Swiggart—a thick rope lay
coiled.

Swiggart pulled up beside Anson. "Woodhull," he said
"we're looking for Fifer Tansey. Seen him lately?"

Anson paused in the act of stirring his mash. "Haven't
seen Fifer for two or three months. What's he done?"

"What *ain't* he done? He's been using that Black Drop of
his rather free lately—three cases we know about. But the
thing we want him for right now is rape. Yesterday he
clubbed Jeannie Deets over the head and was violatin' her
in the woodshed. We got witnesses." Swiggart turned to a
one-legged man seated in a buggy. "You tell him, Sime."

Simon Deets, husband of the wronged woman, gave a
circumstantial account of the affair. "Jeannie went out to get
a few chunks of wood when this medicatin' rascal leaped on
her and took her by main force. My boy Eph saw them and
yelled to me. I been laid up with an ampitated leg that
Tansey cut off month ago. But I jumped out of bed, hobbled
toward the woodshed just in time to see that black-hearted
villin lightin' out across the fields. Jeannie's got a lump the
size of an egg on her head where he hit her with a chunk
of stovewood."

Anson nodded with appropriate concern at Deets's recital.
He knew all about Fifer Tansey's weakness—and charm—
where farm wives were concerned. Unable to defend rape

and not choosing to range himself against the representatives of domestic virtue, he said, "Sorry to hear this, Deets. But I haven't laid eyes on Fifer since last winter."

Swiggart wheeled his heavy mount toward the road and gave orders to his armed band. "Trippet, you scour the country south to Peddler's Landing. The rest of us'll follow the river north to Racer Dam."

The whole incident took barely more than five minutes. Anson picked up his paddle and began stirring his mash once more. Whatever misgivings he had about Fifer's alleged act— or Jeannie Deets's integrity—were forgotten in the immediate business of clamping the goose-necked spout onto his copper kettle. The reeking foreshot gushed forth; his sixteenth barrel was completed by nightfall.

A full day's work awaited Anson in the barn. He fed and currycombed his horses, cleaned their stalls, then bedded them down with fresh straw. Old Chauncey's entry in the Rule-of-Thumb book had been explicit on this point. "An honest horse deserves a clean bed."

Another task—grim, laborious—faced Anson. He must build a cage of heavy planking for Tusker, the black boar who recently had shown signs of becoming a male rogue. Yesterday Tusker had eaten half a litter of young pigs. Until the animal could be slaughtered (and Anson had no time for such an operation) he must be confined in a strong, separate pen.

The making of Tusker's prison claimed two hours. Anson was about to drive the final spike home when he heard a low hissing sound from an empty stall.

"*Psst*—Anse, I'm in trouble." It was Fifer Tansey crouching under a heap of cast-off harness.

"So I heard this morning from Jeff Swiggart and Sime Deets."

"Hell, Anse, you only heard *their side* of the story. The fact is, Jeannie Deets has been puttin' out to me regular for a couple of years. We *like* each other. I take care of her family and she takes care of me. When her son caught us doin' it in the woodshed, I had to hit her over the head with a billet of firewood and make it look like rape. Couldn't let a nice girl like Jeannie lose her reputation for virtue, could I now?"

"What do you want me to do, Fifer?"

"Let me hide out underneath your barn for a couple of

days till the moon dies down," said Fifer. "Then I'll swim across the river into Kentucky. They need doctors there, I hear."

Compassion for this strange, hunted man was Anse's only emotion. The rights or wrongs of Fifer's deed were matters beyond his concern. He lifted a loose plank on the barn floor. "There's a bull snake down there, but he won't hurt you. Just lay quiet and make your getaway when you can. I'll bring you food every night."

Fifer Tansey squeezed his lank body into the darkness inhabited by snakes and rats. Heavyhearted, sad, but unjudging, Anson closed the barn door.

In his sadness he forgot to drive the last spike into Tusker's cage.

Another day, another barrel.

It was a beautiful day, a golden prelude to Indian summer. In midmorning, Anson walked toward his house for no better reason than to gaze at his infant son sleeping in a cradle on the back porch. The temptation to tweek the pink toes of his baby was strong, but Anson sat on the edge of the porch, content to marvel at the miniature perfection of the child's plump little legs. Bending over, he brushed Sonny's foot with his lips, then strode back to his still.

The middle run was in full flow when he heard Laly screaming: "Daddy . . . Mama . . . the pig . . . the pig . . ."

Racing across the barnyard, Anson saw the next-to-last act of a fearsome tragedy, with all the persons of the drama enacting their fated roles. Zarah, in a dead faint, lay prostrate near the porch. Laly was chasing Tusker with a hoop stick. And Tusker was making for the door of the pig-sty with the infant in his jaws.

Ghastly with fear and rage, Anson seized a mattock, overtook the gruesome beast and brained him with a single blow. He picked up Sonny's mutilated body. An arm had been chewed away: carnivorous jaws had gouged a gaping hole on the babe's right side. Like a man lifting a sacrifice to heedless heaven, Anson cried out in anguish, "Fifer . . . Fifer . . . for God's sake, help me."

A plank of the barn floor creaked and in the dark aperture appeared the head of a lank-haired apparition. Fifer Tansey was not a rapist now, not a fugitive from armed men. He strode into the clear sunlight, took the child from Anson and laid it on the tool-cluttered work bench.

Three armed horsemen rode into the barnyard as Anson pleaded, "Can you save him?"

What was there to save? The infant, in shock from loss of blood, had been hopelessly mutilated by the pig's teeth. One arm was gone at the shoulder joint. His rib cage, crushed and broken, was beyond Fifer Tansey's skill as a healer. He inspected the inert body scarcely larger than a doll's, then placed his hand on Anson's shoulder.

"Leave him with me. . . . I'll do what I can."

From the cartridge belt around his waist, Fifer Tansey selected a phial of white colorless liquid and doused the tail of his coat with its contents. Fifer had never taken the Hippocratic Oath; he was under no obligation to save a life past saving. With eyes closed, he pressed the chloroform-soaked tail of his coat against the babe's face.

The three armed men dismounted. Their guns were leveled at him as he covered the infant's body with a burlap sack.

"Be with you in a minute, boys," said Fifer. "I've got to take a look at Anson's wife."

"No tricks," warned Swiggart. "One false move and we'll plug you."

"Plug away," said Fifer. He walked into the barnyard, went down on one knee and examined Zarah briefly. Then, rising, he addressed his captors, who had ranged themselves in strategic positions around their man. Fifer's voice and manners were purely clinical as he began. "When this woman comes out of her faint, she's going to be hard to manage. For a while she'll be plumb crazy—probably try to kill herself. And who's to blame her? She'll need medicine, special care—and in all this God-forsaken county there's only one man as'll know what to do for her."

Fifer pulled a lank greasy hair from his head. "I wouldn't plead to save even this much of myself. Why should I? I'm only a raper of wives, the abortioner of young girls, raped— if you want to call it that—by others. I'm just a no-good murderer of babes and hopeless cases, set down in your midst to cut off gangrened legs, hold the basin while you and yours retch out the last ounce of cancer bile. Guess I'm not good for much of anything but curin' those as can be cured, savin' what can be saved, and to hell with the rest."

A low moan rose from Zarah's lips.

"Ha! You see." Prognosis and diabolism met in Fifer's exclamation. "In a minnit, she'll open her eyes. Now which'll it be, bully boys? Shall I close 'em again for a while? Mebbe you'd rather watch a woman writhe on the ground like a chopped worm."

"In Christ's name, Fifer, don't let her wake up," begged Anson.

"It ain't up to me, Anse. This committee'll have to decide." Tansey ran a long finger across the phials in his cartridge belt. "Here's opium, chloral hydrate—and Tansey's Sleepin' Water. All potent in different ways. You, Jeff Swiggart, name the medicine of choice. You, Sime Deets, tell me the proper dosage. What, no volunteers? Who'll risk pouring medicine down a human throat when the crows have picked out Fifer Tansey's eyes?"

Contempt for the shotgun-bearers modulated into pity as Fifer drew a phial from his belt. "Hush awhile, Zarah dear," he said, kneeling beside her. "This is my own Sleepin' Water —pre-scribed dose sixty drops, or one teaspoonful." Using his thumb as a drip-proof valve, he let some of the liquid flow from his phial into Zarah's open mouth.

Her head drooped against the physician's shoulder. The muzzles of the shotgun felt the hypnotic power of the draught; they drooped too.

Anson, lifting Zarah in his arms, tasted the bitter drug on her lips as he brushed them with his own. The odor reminded him of the foreshot from his still. As he carried his wife into the house, acrid fumes of smoke rising from the copper kettle billowed across the farmyard.

"The whiskey's burning!" cried Reb.

The cereal ferment in the cauldron, unattended during the excitement, had bubbled over; loaded with alcohol, the mash was prime fuel for a flash fire that threatened to destroy the sixteen barrels of whiskey standing nearby.

For the moment Anson was past caring. The whiskey, if lost, could be replaced; but the drugged woman in his arms claimed, above all else, his immediate attention. He carried Zarah upstairs, laid her tenderly on their marriage bed. Through the open window he heard Jeff Swiggart barking contradictory orders to the posse:

"Roll away them barrels 'afore they explode. Fetch water from the sluiceway. Look lively, lads! Get shovels, buckets . . ."

To shut out the acrid smoke and sounds of confusion in the farmyard below, Anson started to close the window of Zarah's bedroom. Fifer Tansey's voice brought him back to the realities. "You still here? Get down to the yard and help douse that fire, or the whole place'll go up like a haystack. I'll take care of Zarah."

"Thanks, Fifer." Anson dashed downstairs. A moment later his huge hands were tugging at the uprights that supported the mouth of the sluiceway. By a feat of strength impossible under ordinary conditions, he twisted the wooden trough toward his mash tub. The waters of Paddle Creek, thus diverted, fell directly upon the source of the blaze. There was a hissing sound, a column of dark acrid smoke, and the fire was extinguished.

Anson surveyed the damage to his distilling apparatus: one badly charred mash kettle; and a barrel of whiskey (standing directly beneath the still) consumed by fire. He thought of Laly's nursery rhyme. How did it go? Something like this: Water, water, quench fire/ Fire won't burn stick/ Stick won't beat dog/ Dog won't chase pig/ Pig won't jump over any more stiles. . . .

And Zarah . . . wouldn't get home that night.

Men, like metals, have separate vibrancies; struck, they respond in accents of their own. A dead baby, a wife prostrate with grief, a batch of burned whiskey and a posse surrounding his house brought no whimpering lament from Anson Woodhull. Prayerless, he surveyed the disasters that had struck his life; dry-eyed, he set about the task of righting them.

His first duty was to bury his son; closing the barn door, he fashioned a miniature coffin of pine boards, wrapped the babe in a linen sheet; then, spade in hand, coffin on his shoulder, he walked toward the family burying-ground, a half-acre knoll, fenced round with a dry-stone wall sloping toward the Ohio.

By civilized usage, every grave, even that of an infant, must be six feet deep; to dig such a grave requires a half day's expenditure of sweat and energy—sovereign substitutes for sentimental tears. Not until the last shovelful of earth lay mounded over his son's grave did Anson feel the onset of grief. While an afternoon wind grieved among the branches of fir trees, he resisted the temptation to throw himself sobbing on the fresh earth.

Weep not for me, but for your children. Whoever had said that must have possessed secret knowledge of the world's deepest sorrow.

Anson knelt momentarily on one knee and consigned Sonny's remains to all-mothering earth.

In the kitchen Anson washed his hands and face at the copper-jacketed pump, accepted the huckabuck towel silently held out to him by Solange.

"I've saved some supper for you," she said.

Wordlessly Anson ate a few mouthfuls of beef and kidney pie, the first food he had touched since daybreak. The savory dish with its delicate brown crust might have been raw bran, for all that Anson knew or cared. His chief concern now was for Zarah. Had the news been good, Solange would have told him; eyes averted, she merely said, "Fifer wants to see you."

Anson removed his earth-clogged boots, climbed stocking-footed to Zarah's bedroom and knocked at the closed door. A hoarse "Come" bade him enter.

The tableau before his eyes has been indelibly recorded on the racial memory, not by painters or writers but by numberless millions of anxious husbands, wives and parents entering a sickroom. There sat Fifer Tansey in the classic attitude of the physician searching his patient's face for an index of hope. By the dimmed lamp he seemed almost crouching; a long forefinger held against the root of Zarah's thumb was transmitting the ominously feeble message sent out by her drug-depressed heart. This was no bedside manner. This was the bedside *man*, with all the privileges, exemptions and responsibilities attached to the healer's office.

Without shifting his eyes from Zarah's face, Fifer spoke. "Gave her a fluidram about an hour ago. She's down deep now. Almost at bottom. I'd like to see her climb a little before her next dose at midnight."

"What would happen if you didn't give her another dose?" asked Anson.

"She might tear loose, jump out the window, kill herself."

Having listed these cheerful possibilities, Fifer raised a clinical eyebrow. "Her pulse ain't bad—sixty-five, as I make it. It's her breathin'—slow and shallow—that worries me." He placed his ear to Zarah's fully exposed bosom and let a full minute pass. "Between ten and eleven, 'bout half the normal rate." No Viennese specialist could have interpreted better the meaning of Zarah's blue lips and rolled-back eyeballs; she was approaching the point where coma touches hands with death.

Like many another physician, Fifer revealed only half of what he knew, yet that half was ominous enough. "Anse, you might as well get this clear in your mind. This kind of treatment can't go on forever. Settin' aside gastric complications, you just can't keep a woman doped up for more'n three or four days. Zarah ought to be treated by a first-class M.D.— which everyone knows I ain't, and never pretended to be. Why I never even *knew* a reg'lar doctor."

"I know one," said Anson. He was thinking of Lyman Allston, Zarah's cousin, who had flung a handful of symbolic rice at Anson and his bride after their marriage. Dr. Allston, holder of a dozen European diplomas, was one of the best-trained physicians in the United States. The only hitch was, he lived in Boston. Would he come a thousand miles to help Zarah?

"Send him a telegram and find out," suggested Fifer.

Anson had never sent or received a telegram in his life. With a broad-edged carpenter's pencil, he labored over the message. In its final form it ran: "Zarah desperately ill, needs skilled medical attention. Can you come personally? Signed: Anson Woodhull."

The nearest telegraph office would be in the Landmark railroad depot six miles away. Summoning Reb Plaskett, he gave the boy instructions. "Reb, I want you to run to the Landmark railroad station with this telegram. Take a day's supply of food with you and wait around the station until a reply comes in. Can I trust you to do this, Reb?"

"You can trust me, Mr. Woodhull." Reb stuffed the message into his pocket, seized a loaf of fresh bread and was off, a barefooted courier traversing the darkened fields that lay between his master's house and the county seat. He ran by starlight, he ran across corn stubble, leaped brooks, tore through blackberry briars and covered the distance (if anyone cares to know the exact time) in forty-eight minutes, thirteen seconds. He handed Anson's message to Chet Frisbie, the railroad dispatcher, heard Chet tick off the words in Morse code, then curled up on the only bench in Landmark station and fell asleep dreaming, not of Zarah, nor of Anson, but of their flaxen-haired daughter, Laly.

All the following day Reb waited within sound of the railroad-dispatcher's key. He munched the loaf of dry bread and drank water for exactly twenty-six hours before Chet said, "Here's your answer, Bub." He scrawled Dr. Allston's message on a yellow form, stamped its time of arrival, 9:22 P.M. In less than an hour the message was in Anson's hands. It read:

> YOUR TELEGRAM REACHED ME AT MEDICAL CONVENTION IN CLEVELAND. I CAN BE IN LANDMARK BY 3 P.M. TOMOR-ROW. PLEASE MEET ME AT RAILROAD STATION. WARMEST PERSONAL GREETINGS. LYMAN ALLSTON.

Through a blur of tears Anson saw Solange ladling out a bowl of thick stew for the freckled subaltern of Mercury. He clamped an affectionate headlock onto the skinny youth.

"He's coming, Reb. I'll meet him at Landmark on the three P.M. express. Zarah's going to be all right."

4.

THE TWO MAGICIANS

THE NECESSITY of fulfilling his contract with Charles Moerlein drove Anson to his still long before dawn next day. With seven precious hours ahead of him he might, by working his still five or six times, produce his day's quota of whiskey.

The barrel was one quarter filled when the first members of Jeff Swiggart's band rode up to take their accustomed stations. By ten o'clock a dozen wagons were tethered in the barnyard, while their owners lolled about in idleness, threw dice or played horseshoes. News of the Boston doctor's expected arrival had strengthened their wavering resolve to seize Fifer Tansey. Within a few hours, their patience (which had been wearing thin) would be rewarded. If everything went well, the desecrater of Jeannie Deets's virtue would be hanged from a sour-apple tree before nightfall.

At two o'clock, Anson took a quick plunge into Paddle Creek: a cake of tar soap removed the oily grime from his face and hands. He was pulling a comb through his drenched beard and hair when Fifer Tansey walked toward him, brushing aside Swiggart's posse like so many blueberry bushes.

"Got some bad news for you, Anse. I gave Zarah the last drop of medicine this mornin' and now she's heavin' around like a mountain lion. It's a question of tying her up or makin' a new batch of sleep-producer."

The thought of binding Zarah physically was repulsive to Anson. "What's the medicine made of?"

"Comes out of the foreshot of raw whiskey," said Tansey. "If the guardeens of justice here would kindly lower their shotguns, I could knock off a batch in less'n an hour."

Anson's watch told him that he should be on his way to meet Dr. Allston. He summoned Jeff Swiggart. "As a special favor, Jeff, will you let Fifer run off a batch of medicine that'll take care of my wife for the next three or four hours?"

"I ain't got no objections," said Swiggart.

And now began one of the most remarkable performances in the history of backwoods medicine.

The medicine that Fifer Tansey proposed to make sprang from no technical knowledge of chemistry. Fifer's lore went deeper; he knew that whiskey contained certain undesirable ingredients that every distiller tries to get rid of. Linked together in a carbon-hydrogen-oxygen chain, these elements bore the colloquial name "fusel oil." The trick was to break the chemical chain, isolate a certain noxious substance, treat this substance with acid and thus obtain a sleep-producing agent valuable in the treatment of persons emotionally disturbed. Intuition must pass into the realm of wizardry before this miracle could be accomplished, and the presiding wizard would need a little help from the gaping-mouthed crowd of men gathered at the base of the platform.

"Friends, former patients and defenders of female virtue," said Fifer. "Sorry to delay due process of law, but there's a small chore that comes first. Anson's wife needs some medicine to tide her over till a *real* doctor comes, and I'll need a little help." He ticked off the required apparatus for his experiment. "Get me a couple of wooden buckets, one of them empty, the other half full of clear cold water. Then I'll want a tubful of cracked ice and two glass jars. Now keep your eyes peeled for trickery 'cause there ain't no other name for what you're goin' to see."

Fifer stripped off his grasshopper coat and began stirring the mash in Anson's copper tub. Stirring, he gave directions. "Keep the fire low. The stuff I want comes out in the foreshot at about a hundred and twenty-six degrees. She's a'churnin' up already. Now in another minnit . . ."

He clamped the cover onto the mash kettle. "Hand me a bucket," he cried. "Thar she blows, thar she belches." His bucket was filled with malodorous liquid. "Here's the stuff that gives whiskey its bad name and worse smell." Like a magician assuring his audience that he had nothing up his sleeve, he passed the bucket around for inspection and slapped his thigh as the members of the posse held their noses.

From the cincture of colored phials around his waist, Fifer now selected a glass bottle jacketed with rubber. "Don't jiggle the platform, because if this stuff spills, it'll burn a hole straight down to hell. Show you what I mean." He uncorked the phial and poured a drop of its contents onto the rough plank flooring. There was a hissing sound as the acid ate through the wood.

"Liquid brimstone, some calls it. Only 'tain't *ordinary* brimstone. The devil saves this stuff to pour onto the cocks of fornicators. That's how I happened to come by it. Well, irregardless of details, I'll add a dollop of this acid to the contents of the wooden tub. Stand away from the froth, men, until it stops bubblin'."

The furious ferment in the wooden bucket died down. Fifer diluted it with an equal volume of clear water, then filled one of the Mason jars with a turgid brownish liquor.

"Where's that tubful of cracked ice, Jeff?"

"Here 'tis, Fifer." Jeff Swiggart himself was serving as apprentice-sorcerer.

The demon alchemist buried the jar in the tub of ice. "Boilin' purifies one way, freezin' purifies another. More rock salt, men. You ice-cream makers know what rock salt does."

While the freezing process went forward, Fifer lounged— a backwoods Prospero-at-ease—against the distilling platform. "I feel like puttin' in a chaw. Anyone got some good eatin' terbacker?"

From the half dozen plugs of tobacco offered him, Fifer

chose the one held out by Simon Deets. "Thanks, Sime. Small kindnesses appreciated. Now let's all chew in reverent silence till the stuff freezes."

Chewing and spitting, they marveled until Fifer removed the Mason jar from the tub of cracked ice. Holding it up for all to see, he pointed to the sediment at the bottom, topped by more than a pint of clear liquid. *"That's* what I'm looking for," he said, deftly pouring this colorless fluid into a second jar. "Now, if everything's gone accordin' to plan, the stuff in this here jar ought to be Tansey's Sleepy Water. 'Course, it has to be tested for strength and purity. Any of you bully-boys care to risk your lives with a swaller? You, Jeff? You, Sime?"

Fifer's invitation was greeted with open-jawed silence by every member of the posse. Here was a man who had commanded fire and water, cold and heat, to do his bidding. They had seen an act of magic and they were afraid.

The magician himself had no such fears. "Guess I'll have to test it on myself." Fifer placed the jar to his nose, inhaled deeply. *"Smells* like the genuine article," he announced. He ran his tongue around the rim of the jar. *"Tastes* like it." Swallowing, he gasped and rocked back on his heels for the benefit of his audience. "By the jumped-up Jesus, it is!"

A woman's hysterical shriek rose above the yokel laughter of Jeff Swiggart's band. An apparition in a white nightgown, hair disheveled, appeared at an upper window of Anson's house. It was Zarah, attempting to hurl herself through a broken windowpane.

"Let me out of this whiskey-reeking hell," she screamed.

Solange's restraining arm drew her back from the window ledge.

"Comin'," cried Fifer, "on the double." He hastened toward the room where Zarah lay moaning obscenities. Gentle as a father administering cough sirup to a sick child, he soothed her with a knockout draft of the medicine he had summoned up from the chemical deeps to serve him and his patient in a desperate crisis.

Charming, charming, thought Lyman Allston as he approached the Woodhull property in Anson's buggy. The ochre foliage of elms and sycamores, shot through with midafternoon light, might have been chosen by Constable to fill a corner of some pastoral canvas. And now, gleaming whitely in the near distance, appeared the gristmill. Pure Americana. Utterly bucolic. The heartland of the nation itself. How refreshing after thirty-six hours of soot and cinders to fill one's lungs with country scents. City born, city educated, Dr. Allston permitted himself the luxury of falling into the romantic illusion that Ruralia was a place where every prospect pleases, and only man is vile.

He was shaken into reality by the scenes and odors that assaulted him as he drove into Anson Woodhull's farmyard. His nasal membranes were assaulted by the overpowering smell—acrid, indefinable—of raw whiskey. No tyro when it came to odors (Dr. Allston could recognize foul drains or a Brighton glue factory at a hundred paces), he wondered what process of putrefaction was going on here. And what was the nature of the activity—or activities, rather—taking place in the yard? Here were a dozen men, most of them armed, lolling about in unseemly idleness, while others pitched horseshoes, squirting great quids of saliva at every toss.

News of Dr. Allston's arrival traveled like a fusee from mouth to mouth.

"The doctor from Boston's got here."

"Hooray for the Doc!"

"Now we can nut Fifer Tansey."

An uncoordinated salute of shotguns and Potawatomi war whoops, accompanied by the discharge of two horse pistols, ripped the air as Anson descended from the buggy. A man less sustained by natural dignity might have apologized for the disorder in his own farmyard; in fact, Dr. Lyman Allston expected some such apology. What he actually heard was a remembered voice—the voice of a brevet captain of Indiana militia issuing the Orders of the Day to his company.

"You, Swiggart, come here."

Jeff Swiggart slouched forward, a coil of rope hanging from his shoulder. He was taller than Anson, fifty pounds heavier and armed with a Colt revolver. *Mr. Lynch Law* in person.

"Swiggart, you're in charge of this crew. Pass the word to your men. The word is *Silence.* I'll hold you personally responsible for any violation of common decency. Hear?"

The brevet captain of militia vanished. A hush descended upon the farmyard as a solicitous husband offered country hospitality to the man who, next to himself, loved Zarah most.

"Won't you come into the kitchen and wash up?"

"Why, yes, I think I'll look more presentable after removing three or four layers of railroad grime."

A basin of cold water, a clean huckabuck towel and a cup of coffee—served up by Solange—refreshed Lyman Allston. The kitchen was cool, clean and uncluttered. The contrast between indoors and outdoors caused Dr. Allston to ask, "Who are those men in the yard?"

"A self-appointed band of moralists," said Anson. "They're waiting to hang Fifer Tansey."

"And who is Fifer Tansey?"

"A physician of sorts. A remarkable man. You'll discover his qualities when you meet him. Right now he's attending Zarah. . . . If you're ready, Doctor."

"I'm ready." Small black bag in hand, Lyman Allston followed Anson upstairs.

A light knock; Zarah's door swung half open. Dr. Lyman Allston saw a coatless apparition, suspenders hanging and a battered top hat askew, standing in the doorway. To the frock-coated Boston physician the figure in the doorway resembled a Daumier caricature of Ichabod Crane.

"Psss-st! She's sleepin'." Fifer's motion bade the visitors go elsewhere lest his patient be disturbed.

Anson made the introductions in the hallway. Though brief, they were marked by a ceremonial doffing of top hats in the best Viennese tradition.

"Fifer," said Anson, "this is Dr. Lyman Allston of the Harvard Medical School. He's come to consult with you about Zarah's condition."

The Harvard doctor lifted his top hat. "I am honored to meet you, Dr. Tansey."

Anson continued: "Dr. Allston, this is Fifer Tansey, physician-at-large to Landmark County."

It was Fifer's turn to acknowledge a fellow practitioner. He pulled up his galluses, lifted his battered stovepipe, and said, "Glad you made it, Doctor. Won't you come in?"

No layman could breathe in this ceremonial atmosphere. Anson, being only a husband, disappeared.

The consultation between Fifer Tansey and Dr. Lyman Allston followed the unwritten rules of medical protocol. Neither Dr. Allston's European diplomas nor his exalted position as Professor of Neurology in the Massachusetts General Hospital could override the fact that Fifer Tansey was the physician-in-attendance. His recital of the case history, his rationale of treatment, must be heard. And heard they were, attentively, even approvingly, by the Back Bay physician.

Emotional shock following the death of her child? Quite. But how had Dr. Tansey obtained paraldehyde, the somnifacient of choice—a drug isolated only last year by German scientists?

"Made it," said Fifer. "Don't know what's been holdin' those German fellers back. I bin makin' it for the past ten years."

"Your knowledge of chemistry must be profound." Lyman Allston lifted his top hat with genuine deference. "How did you go about extracting this polymer of aldehyde that unquestionably exists in raw whiskey?"

"Figgered it was there, and just went after it."

"Hmmm . . . I should like to have your procedural notes. Meanwhile, with your permission, Doctor, may I examine the patient?"

"Guess you're entitled to look her over. Mind if I watch you? Might be sort of instructive."

In his examination, Dr. Allston was aided by instruments that Fifer had never seen: a fat butter-gold watch with a minute-sweep hand, valuable in counting pulse beats; a stethoscope that magnified the sounds made by the patient's heart. Finally a small hammer with a wedge-shaped rubber head which Dr. Allston used to tap just below Zarah's knees.

"What's that for?" asked Fifer.

"The patella—the kneecap—is the only part of the body in which the nervous system lies—as one might say—exposed. Watch now." He tapped again with his rubber hammer. "See how the knee jerks. Her central nervous system is unimpaired."

It was Fifer's turn to doff his hat.

"Well, the evidence is in," said Lyman Allston. "What is your prognosis, Doctor? I mean, in your opinion, what are the patient's chances of recovery?"

At this point, Fifer Tansey relinquished his medical command. "I deal only with ailments of the body, Doctor. I know about bones, muscles, tendons, and most of the things that can happen to them. I can lance a felon, treat for dyspepsy and rheumatism, freshen up the blood, drain a bladder and physic the bowels. But Zarah's trouble lies too deep for me."

"You agree, however, that she must have competent observation, supportive treatment and the constant attendance of a trained nurse?"

"Yes, yes."

"Are there any nearby institutions that can provide such treatment?"

"There ain't *no* institutions, except the State Insane Asylum. I'd rather see Zarah dead than sign her into that place."

Protocol permitted Lyman Allston to ask, "Would you, as physician-in-charge, recommend that I take the patient to Boston with me? I have a small private hospital on the upper floors of my home. Zarah would receive the finest possible treatment there."

"I'd recommend it with a whoop and a holler—'ceptin' for one thing. How you goin' to get her there? When this drug wears off, she's goin' to claw around like a female mountain lion."

"*Why* will she claw?"

"'Cause she wants to get out of here."

"Exactly! And when I tell her I'm taking her out of here, ah—wait now, the paraldehyde is wearing off. Observe carefully, Dr. Tansey. You may find my technique, adapted from the experiments of Charcot and Breuer, helpful in your practice."

Lyman Allston removed his top hat and knelt beside Zarah's bed. Placing his mouth close to her ear, he began whispering her name. "Zarah, Zarah. This is Cousin Lyman . . . Zarah, can you hear me?"

"Yes, I can hear you."

"Tell me who I am."

"You are Cousin Lyman." Zarah's voice was muted, as in some secret exchange of confidences with a lover. Her opening eyes registered neither surprise nor terror. A single tear started down her cheek, Lyman Allston kissed it away.

"I have come to take you home, Zarah. Not to Cambridge, but to my own home in Boston. You remember the house on Marlborough Street?"

"I remember. There was a conservatory there, with flowers and a library lined to the ceiling with books."

"The flowers and books are still there, darling. Would you like to see them again, Zarah?"

"Very much, oh, very much, Cousin Lyman. Please take me away."

"We will start tomorrow. You must sleep now to be strong for the journey. Close your eyes, Zarah."

Like a docile child, Zarah obeyed.

"Never saw nuthin' like it," said Fifer as both doctors tip-toed from the room.

Each had performed a miracle that day. Guided by in-tuition, Fifer Tansey had extracted a powerful chemical from raw whiskey. By summoning up remembrance of childhood security, Dr. Lyman Allston had displaced fear with love. Granting that both effects were temporary, which was the more potent magic?

Neither physician debated the question, then or afterward. By the procotol that bound them together in mutual respect and admiration, each lifted his hat to the other when next day Zarah took the first step of her long journey home.

Dr. Allston had advised Anson: "Emotional upset can be avoided if you remain out of sight." Anson, his children gathered about him, watched Zarah drive out of the yard. With never a backward look, she stepped into the hired rig from Tod Demming's livery stable, laid her head on Cousin Lyman's shoulder and rode away.

Barely had the dust settled when Simon Deets's son, whip-ping a pair of wind-broken horses, careened into the yard.

"Pa . . . pa," he called from the seat of his buckboard, "come quick, and bring Fifer along with you. Ma's just spilt a spiderful of hot doughnut lard over her legs."

"How fur up?" asked Simon.

"Fur's the fur. She's screamin' somethin' awful!"

Fifer Tansey slung his bag of tools over his shoulder and stepped out into the barnyard. At his appearance the members of the posse edged forward like men who had forgotten their original purpose.

Jeff Swiggart slammed his coil rope onto a pile of chicken manure. "I give up," he exclaimed in disgust, and strode away.

"This calls for a little music," observed the physician-at-large to Landmark County. He clambered onto the buckboard, placed his fife to his lips, winked at Anson, and played an ironic variant of "Jeannie with the Light Brown Hair."

When a father (even the most loving father) leaves home, his absence is scarcely noted. But when a mother goes out the door, only a forlorn void remains in the hearts of her husband and children. No one else can fill the empty chair, soothe the little griefs, or hush the terrifying voice of loneliness that grows louder with every passing hour.

The house is both desolate and ghost-inhabited; every room becomes a desert, and the tiniest object—a thimble, a hairpin, an apron hanging on a kitchen peg—is a reminder of the departed spirit that once moved or used it.

Sometimes a mother's departure means summoning neighbors or relatives—loathsome invaders who take over the outward forms of household management, prepare food strange to the taste, scrub necks, grimy hands and comb out snarls with too much or too little energy, tuck children into bed and plant cheery good-night kisses, pitying or dutiful, on foreheads that yearn for the familiar love.

No such invasion took place in Anson Woodhull's home. Solange, already half mother to Anson's children, unloosed a flood of maternal love that almost (not quite) floated Laly, Quincia and Osgood off the reefs of motherless woe. In every detail the course of domestic life followed the pattern set by Zarah. They were fed, bathed, combed, read to, and, so far as possible, nourished by affection. Still, some odd things happened. One day Solange found Quincia hiding in the clothes closet of Zarah's bedroom.

"What are you doing here, Quince?"

Snuffles. Then the heartbreaking confession. "I'm smelling the sachet on Mama's dresses."

Solange inhaled the fragrance. "It *is* sweet," she said. "Perhaps you'd like to put a little bag of Mama's sachet in your bureau drawer."

"It won't be the same thing," sobbed Quincia.

Ozzie's loneliness took a still stranger, almost fatal form. He managed to climb into Zarah's trunk and pull the cover down as if to shut out the entire world. After frantically searching the house for her youngest charge, Solange discovered him limp and half suffocated under a heap of Zarah's nightgowns. Was refuge, or even death in the dark privacy of his mother's trunk, preferable to life in a motherless atmosphere? Remembering her own happy intimacy with Lutece Vincy in the otherwise wretched home on Ledoux Street, Solange wondered.

Thereafter, she locked all trunks, cabinets and closets that might prove tempting to heartsick fugitives from reality.

Of all the children, Laly grieved least, possibly because she was finding companionship and partial forgetfulness in the person of her twelve-year-old hero-victim, Reb Plaskett. Who was more devoted to whom? Solange couldn't tell. Reb submitted to Laly's bossiness indoors, stumbling awkwardly for weeks over a book that Laly gulped down in a few hours or days, yet he was more than her equal in the outdoor world of fields, forests and streams. Even here, Laly pressed him hard. One day, entering the barn, Solange looked up and saw Zarah's seven-year-old daughter teetering on one of the crossbeams over the hayloft. They were playing Stump the Leader, and Laly, as usual was the Stumper.

"You dassent jump into the hay," she challenged. (Grammar, grammar, thought Solange.)

"I dast so," Reb replied.

Not to be out-dast, Laly jumped first. As the girl took the not-too-perilous leap, her gingham dress ballooned like a parachute, and convent-bred Solange was mildly shocked to see that the child wasn't wearing drawers. Never one to interfere with good times in the hayloft, Solange came up with the perfect solution—drawers adorned with a narrow band of lace around each leg.

The next phase of this childish idyl disclosed Laly twirling on a barrel head, while Reb gawked upward, more in wonder at the exhibition than at the lace-edged drawers of the little exhibitionist..

At least she isn't lonely, thought Solange. And this, in a house of grieving, was something to be thankful for.

Bereft by Zarah's absence and driven to fulfill his contract with Moerlein, Anson had small interest in the amenities of life. From dawn till nightfall, he toiled at his still, working it twelve, fourteen, sixteen times a day, instead of the usual four or five. By mid-October, he had produced thirty barrels of whiskey; on two glorious Indian-summer days, he established a record by making five more barrels. Hugh Bailey, riding past on his roan cob, found Anson preparing his next day's mash by the light of a golden fireball high in the heavens.

"If I didn't ken this to be a legitimate operation, in truth I'd be calling you a moonshiner," said Hugh. "Why do you toil so late, mon?"

Anson paused for the only moment of rest he had enjoyed

since supper. "The rains are late this year. My water's running low."

"The rains will come," predicted Bailey.

And come they did—in a torrential downpour that caused Anson to build a roof over his pot still and mash tub. Soaked to the marrow, he distilled five more barrels during the third week of October. When the rains stopped, Paddle Creek was a foaming torrent, the sycamore branches were leafless and Reb Plaskett began to weaken.

The boy's spirit might be unquenchable but his physical strength was unequal to the heavy task of pouring mash buckets into the copper-mawed still. A flurry of snow brought on a chest cold in early November, and this in turn pulled the pins out of Reb's knees. His legs buckled with exhaustion. Anson picked the boy up, carried him into the house and gave Solange a four-word command. "Put him to bed."

"I don't want to go to bed, Mr. Woodhull. You need help makin' them last thirty barrels."

Anson laid his hand on the boy's feverish cheek. "Let Laly take care of you for a couple of days and you'll be with me at the finish."

The "couple of days" became a week, almost two weeks of mounting fever and racking cough. Laly prepared mustard plasters for Reb's narrow chest, heaped the blankets high and poured hot whiskey and sugar into her patient. While the mercury nestled into the bulb of the thermometer, Anson did the work of three men. Cold weather meant slower fermentation; the mash tubs of malted corn and yeast were set on sawhorses in the kitchen. To her other chores, Solange added the drudging labor of carrying mash-filled buckets from the house to the still. All amenities were swept away by the harsh gales of early November. Barely a word passed between the man toiling to fulfill his contract and the woman who voluntarily took upon herself the responsibility of helping him fulfill it.

Why does she do it? Anson wondered. Why should a beautiful woman wrap her feet in burlap sacks and silently put on the yoke of manual servitude? No word of explanation came from Solange. Grateful for her help, Anson asked no questions. Never a smile lighted his face. Solange, eyes averted, made up the deficit out of her own physical strength, until Reb, weary of female ministrations, tossed aside the blankets and took his place once more at Anson's side.

Those last ten barrels of whiskey were a race against the

seasonal drop in temperature that usually set in on or about December 1. Already Paddle Creek was frozen to a depth of three inches. Anson began every day's operation by cracking the surface ice with a mattock so that precious water would flow down the wooden sluiceway to the coil of copper tubing in which the miracle of distillation took place. The day would come, and soon, when two feet of ice would lock the valves of his machine. Against the day's coming, Anson and his young helper toiled without rest.

In snowstorm, in sleet, in cold drizzling rain, they advanced toward their goal.

On November 15, the hundredth barrel of whiskey was placed in its rack. On that night a white giant invaded the Ohio Valley and cracked the rocks by main force; it made earth and water ring under its icy tread.

But the fearful contract had been fulfilled.

Anson laughed as he saw the column of mercury register twenty below zero. With one hand he swung Reb in a carousel of exultation. "We made it!" he cried, then loosened his hold on Reb's wrist and watched him land spread-eagle fashion in a snowdrift. Anson jumped into the drift and frolicked like a bearded polar bear. Twenty years fell away from Anson's shoulders as he pelted the boy with snowballs and took Reb's bombardment full in the face.

Quincia, watching the scene from the kitchen window, lifted her gentle eyes to Solange. "Why is Daddy so happy?" she asked.

Trying to answer the child's question, Solange burst into tears. She had witnessed one of the greatest spectacles in the world: she had watched a man meet the challenge of personal grief, outface the bluster of sleet and wind, summon up his last reserve of energy to fulfill his contract with Moerlein. She wept for the courage that floats anonymous men over the ledges of despair; and she wept because she loved Anson Woodhull.

5.

ANOSMIA

IN THE "ETHER DOME" of the Massachusetts General
Hospital—the time being December 1884—Dr. Lyman
Allston arose to face an audience of his professional peers. In
this very room Dr. Oliver Wendell Holmes had read his epoch-
making paper on the cause and control of childbirth fever;
here Dr. Frederick Morton had demonstrated the use of ether
as a general anesthetic. Much that was new in American medicine and surgery had been tested in the laboratories and
wards of the M.G.H. (an abbreviation still in affectionate use
by men who served their interneship in the rambling structure situated on the water slope of Beacon Hill). Yet until
1884, no physician of repute had dared utter a word about
the nameless, not-to-be-diagnosed mental condition that swept
certain patients into the dark undertow of torpor and apathy.

Comparatively young—not yet forty—Lyman Allston was
perhaps better qualified than any doctor in the United States
to describe, on the symptomatic level at least, a malady that
had long baffled his fellow physicians. Recently returned from
a tour of European hospitals, he had seen with his own eyes—
particularly in Paris and Vienna—some of the pioneer work
being done by Charcot and Breuer, on the shadowy borders
of mental disease. To these professional advantages, which
he now proposed to share with his colleagues, Dr. Allston
could add the personal observation of his cousin, Zarah Woodhull, who for the past three months had been sinking into an
abyss of passive indifference to the world of reality.

Partly to disseminate his knowledge of this nameless disease, partly to encourage his colleagues to investigate it
further, Lyman Allston had prepared a paper entitled "With-

223

drawal from Reality Following Emotional Trauma." The subject was nebulous; Dr. Allston's information meager. He realized that there existed among his colleagues a disposition to classify all such mental states as "insanity." It required considerable courage to suggest that this blanket term was meaningless and still greater courage to demand that the general physician regard it as a manageable disease.

The first ten minutes of Dr. Allston's paper were devoted to the traditional description of the patient's age, color, sex, marital status and condition when first observed. Zarah's identity, though known to a few members of the audience, was professionally shielded in the opening paragraph.

> Z.W., white, married, multiparous, female, age 28, first came to my attention in September 1884. At that time she was in a condition of shock, induced by the tragic death of an infant son, approximately five months old. Lactation had been interrupted; the menstrual cycle has not yet recommenced.

Lifting his eyes from the written page, Dr. Allston made an off-the-record interpolation: "Frankly, gentlemen, I shall be obliged to grope for terminology in describing the condition of my patient. You must forgive me if I depart from the strict discipline in which we have been trained. The fact is, we lack even the simplest terms to describe adequately the mental condition I wish to convey. I beg you therefore to accept tentatively the phrase *Withdrawal from Reality* which appears in the title of my paper."

At a permissive nod from the Chair, Dr. Allston continued. " 'Withdrawal from Reality' creates a world of its own—a placeless, unboundaried refuge in which the fugitive may hide. This condition is not accompanied by delusions or violent actions on the part of the patient. Since apathy is the goal—the prize, so to speak, of the self-drowning soul—the patient wishes only to remain undisturbed."

Dr. Lyman Allston went on: "At present, gentlemen, we possess no medicine to halt or reverse the progress of this disorder. We are familiar with its gross symptoms and may, in exceptional cases, put a diagnostic finger on its cause. But since we know nothing about the nature of the disease, who among us can prescribe a cure?

"Beginnings—of what value I cannot say—in the investigation of this branch of medicine are being made at the present time in Europe. In his clinic at La Salpêtrière, M. Charcot has had some success with hypnotism. A personal study of Charcot's cases leads me to discount his technique—not on grounds of quackery, but on the simple evidence that the vast majority of his subjects have relapsed, after a period of seeming improvement, into their former state. Indeed, one of Charcot's disciples, a young Viennese physician named Sigmund Freud, has renounced hypnotism; and, as I understand, is probing an altogether unsuspected realm which he calls the 'Unconscious.' I shall not attempt to evaluate at this time Dr. Freud's techniques. From my colleagues in Vienna I learn that his experiments are regarded as highly controversial and that the man himself holds the dubious distinction of hailing cocaine as the panacea for all human ills. I refer you to his paper."

Dr. Lyman Allston glanced at the butter-colored Waltham watch on the lectern. Fifteen minutes already spent in preamble, with the main body of his argument yet to come. How compress into the next half hour the results of observations made at M. Charcot's clinic, or plumb the more profound depths of Joseph Breuer's work at Vienna? He decided to omit the next five pages of his paper, drawn largely from Breuer's *Studien über Hysterie;* the Ether Dome audience could read the monograph in cold print. Meanwhile, he must condense.

"I ask you now to enter that shadowy zone where neither medicine nor surgery can be of assistance to the patient. On this poorly illuminated terrain, both patient and physician wander in confusion. To add to our difficulties, even the symptoms disguise themselves, appearing masked, as it were, lest their real nature be disclosed. Such I believe to be a somewhat figurative description of the case of Z.W. Although she has lately emerged to a large extent from her earlier state of apathy, I discovered only the other day that she is still the prisoner of what I believe to be an hysterical case of anosmia.

"In non-technical terms anosmia is simply a loss of the sense of smell. It sometimes occurs temporarily during the course of a bad head cold. Medical literature reports cases of anosmia due to lesions of the fifth cranial nerve which in turn produce atrophy or thickening of the mucous membranes. Z.W. is not suffering from coryza or any noticeable disturbance of her nasal passages.

"My discovery that the patient had lost her sense of smell

occurred quite by accident about six weeks ago. I had just returned from the hothouses of Dr. Francis Parkman, a man who combines his pre-eminent gifts as historian with those of a pioneer horticulturist. Dr. Parkman presented me with an armful of roses; Z.W. commented upon their color and unusual length of stem, but when I held one to her nose, she remarked, 'It is quite without fragrance.'

"I immediately made tests of my patient's olfactory powers, employing the essential oils of verbena, peppermint, clove, bergamot, et cetera, and found that her sense of smell was utterly lacking."

Dr. Allston permitted a precious two seconds to elapse. During those two seconds he stood three decades in advance of his colleagues. Although no member of the Ether Dome audience fully grasped the significance of Allston's findings, they listened with varying degrees of professional courtesy to the curious three-part thesis that he now unfolded.

"Certain facts of Z.W.'s case history may pave the way for a better understanding of my conclusions. Let me tell you first, gentlemen, that my patient is the wife of a farmer who, from economic necessity, became a distiller of whiskey. Now if there is any smell in the world more repulsive than the odor of new whiskey, I have yet to discover it. Certain elements—ketones, the aldehydes—are an affront to the human nostril; they cling with oily persistence to the person of the distiller; the atmosphere reeks. There is no escape from its foulness. I learned from Z.W.'s husband, a man of intelligence and character, that his wife had no objection to the odor of hogs, animal manure or other smells common to the farm. She had a certain moral predisposition against whiskey; but she *loathed* the smell of it.

"Imagine, now, a sensitive, perhaps hyperesthetic woman of gentle breeding, inhaling at every breath the stench—and I assure you, gentlemen, that it *is* a stench—of raw whiskey. Imagine that woman, once passionately in love with her husband, disgusted by the odor clinging to his clothing, beard and skin; add pregnancy to her predicament; let the delivery of her infant result in a vaginal injury; permit that injury to go untended, and then, as climax to these, introduce a monstrous boar, half drunk on the slops of the mash kettle. The boar seizes her five-month-old baby from its crib and drags the infant toward a horrid lair to devour it."

Audience stiff-necked with attention, Allston proceeded.

"Under these stresses Z.W. fell naturally enough into prostration, followed by a long period of emotional apathy—culminating in the wishful atrophy of her sense of smell.

"I put it to you, gentlemen. Is it possible to mask under the relatively unimportant condition of anosmia, a deeper sense of sexual guilt? I need only point out to you the evidence from embryology. Here, we are on purely scientific ground. The tissues which form the sexual organs spring from the embryonic layer which gives rise to the nasal membranes. The resentment against her husband's trade, long repressed, has ended fortunately short of total immersion in the depths of apathy. What we have in the case of Z.W. is a partial withdrawal from reality—and to the best of my ability I have attempted to diagnose its causes in terms which will perhaps seem fanciful to you.

"A few words as to treatment. In Breuer's epochal *Studies in Hysteria,* he describes his technique of listening intently to words or phrases uttered by the patient. Such words and phrases are useful, Breuer believes, in revealing the hidden cause of the patient's illness. Sympathetic questioning as to the meaning of the words disclosed ever-widening areas of fancied guilt, very real anxiety, lying in pools (so to speak) beneath the level of consciousness.

"I shall not describe at length the gentle but persistent probing—aided at critical points by my use of autosuggestion—which led me at last to believe that Z.W. was reproaching herself for her infant's death. There exists some realistic basis for such reproach; at the time of the tragedy she was—to use her own words—'sulking in her room.' Frequently I ask myself, 'Do not her murmured lamentations seem to be saying, Had I been a dutiful mother, my child would be alive today'?

"The self-accusations were too much for Z.W. to bear. As a result she retreated into the world of apathy which I have previously described."

Amid skeptic silence from his colleagues, Dr. Allston continued. "Z.W.'s anosmia may be regarded, I think, as a protest against the odor of raw whiskey which hung so tragically over her home, marred her sexual relationship with her husband, and the farmyard stage on which the terrible denouement was enacted.

"A word now as to prognosis. In many diseases the physician is able to foretell with some degree of certainty what course the malady will take and whether a cure may or may not be effected. In the case of Z.W., I have noted slight but increasing indications of her desire to align herself with that mysterious life-force—a power without which the physician labors in vain. Her anosmia persists, however; and her menstrual cycle has not re-established itself. I can only say that the patient's recovery depends upon the eruption—if I may use so violent a term—of sealed-up emotions which at present block her return to normal life."

Discipline had made Lyman Allston a man of science; experience with afflicted human beings had given him understanding.

"Until and unless such an eruption occurs, Z.W. must be regarded as a sick woman deserving and in need of the same attention that the highest and lowest among us extend to a sufferer from tuberculosis, Bright's disease, diabetes or any other malady that afflicts the human body."

Dr. Lyman Allston wiped his forehead. "Thank you for your consideration, gentlemen," he said and sat down, quietly awaiting the inevitable challenge of discussion from the floor.

He had seen theories destroyed (he himself had destroyed a few) in the customary give-and-take of Ether Dome debate and was now prepared for the coolly incisive queries of his professional peers.

The first query came from Dr. Harlow Salton, Professor of Anatomy in the Harvard Medical School. "Salty," as he was known to his intimates, had hewn for thirty years to the Helmholtz theory that disease was simply a matter of disturbed mechanics. He wasted little time on amenities. A sentence or two of acknowledgment; then the probe sank home.

"I am somewhat disturbed by Dr. Allston's introduction of mysticism into his supposedly scientific discussion. I refer particularly to such locutions as 'self-drowning soul' and 'unconscious.' Admitting the uses of metaphor, I should like to ask Dr. Allston to give us, by page, author, and date of publication, the name of any reputable, scientific text in which these . . . ah . . . er . . . entities are to be found. Can they be seen under a microscope, isolated in a test tube, excised from the living body or exposed by post-mortem dissection?"

Dr. Salton huffed indignantly (maybe it was only his asthma) and sat down. A few more huffs like that, if left unanswered, would ruin a physician's reputation.

"I must point out," said Dr. Allston in rebuttal, "that since my patient is not yet a cadaver, I am unable to present evidence of pathology in the tissues of her brain. Projectile vomiting and staggering gait usually accompany brain tumors; no such symptoms have been noted in the case of Z.W. Nor would I know where to make the first incision on her living body to produce proof of pathologic change in her nervous system.

"I can reply to Dr. Salton only by saying that the foremost thought of Europe has progressed beyond the concepts of Helmholtz and now stands on the threshold of an unexplored realm to which Breuer has given the term *'Unbewissenfähigkeit.'* As for poetic license, I find myself in agreement with Walt Whitman's line: 'The body *is* the soul.' Shall living men and women be consigned to asylums because of emotional disturbances?"

The Chair intervened. "I pray you, gentlemen, let us cling to the subject. Has anyone else a question?"

Dr. Thorpe Richardson raised his hand. "I am much interested in the speaker's approach. Is this a diluted version of Mesmer's hypnotic technique?"

"I object to the word 'diluted,'" said Lyman Allston, "and most emphatically disassociate myself from Mesmer's practices. Experience has shown me, however, that it is possible—and notably so in the case of Z.W.—to calm disturbed states by the timely introduction of affectionate words and leading phrases. If evidence is needed, let me point to the fact that this highly agitated woman behaved in a docile, subdued manner during a thousand-mile journey in a public carriage, without sedation of any kind."

Dr. Cabot Cheever, Professor of Internal Medicine at Harvard, put a thoughtful edge on the final question. "You spoke of 'emotional catharsis,' Dr. Allston. Every physician realizes that catharsis—I speak of the colonic type—can be induced by certain drugs, or by irrigation with ordinary soap and water. Would you say that the emotional purge that must take place before your patient recovers can be physically induced? Or must it spring from some event in the emotional realm?"

Like any honest man who has been asked a question to which he does not know the answer, Lyman Allston admitted his ignorance. "I am sorry, Dr. Cheever, but neither I nor anyone else in Europe or America can enlighten you upon this critical point. Indeed, it is even possible that the emotional catharsis of which I speak may *never* occur. In which case, Z.W. will sink into an ever-deepening abyss of apathy."

He paused. "I am neither a faith-healer nor a prophet, and I should be guilty of quackery were I to predict Z.W.'s recovery. I will, however, say this much: the life-force, which is the physician's strongest ally in combating disease, has a way of asserting itself when supported by love. From my observation and knowledge of Z.W.'s emotional energy and marital background, I can dare express the hope that an emotional upsurge—induced by some occurrence impossible to foretell—will sweep my patient back into the realm of health and reality."

One hundred copies of the address were printed at Dr. Lyman Allston's expense; ninety were distributed among institutions and individuals who might conceivably be interested in matters lying on the periphery of mental hygiene. Dr. Allston reserved eight copies for himself. The other two were sent (with a covering explanatory note) to Anson Woodhull, Esq., Landmark County, Indiana.

Of the two copies received by Anson, one was inscribed in Lyman Allston's own hand as follows:

> *For*
> *Fifer Tansey, M.D.*
> *A colleague who labors in another part of the vineyard.*

6.

ORDEAL BY PROPINQUITY

Released from the fearful pressure of whiskey-making, Anson was thrown into daily, hourly contact with the woman who had taken Zarah's place in the snow-beleaguered farmhouse. Untapped springs of femaleness bubbled into Solange's voice and rippled from her common domestic motions. Merely to watch her standing tiptoe at the crockery cabinet, or hanging out clothes while a stiff wind whipped about her, was a visual pleasure. There was nothing of the flaunt about

Solange; she simply unwound like an endless spool of silk before the man she loved, entangling his senses in a skein of excitement that must of necessity be broken.

Anson found a hundred pretexts for staying out of the house during the day: he spent long hours in the unheated barn, caring for his animals and gear, neglected during the autumn; he tried his hand at coopering up barrels for next year's batch of whiskey and thereby discovered that a well-made barrel is both a container and a weight-bearing wheel. During these absences from the house, he felt the pressure of a double yearning: the ever-present anxiety about Zarah and a longing to see Solange—a longing that rose unbidden during the small hours of the afternoon and became almost a compulsion with the onset of snow-blue twilight.

Entering his house, Anson would see his children playing games in the kitchen—checkers, Gunboat (a variation of tick-tacktoe) and, of course, Authors. Had Longfellow heard Laly's bossy soprano contesting a point with Reb, the Bard of Brattle Street might have altered his famous line about "Voices soft and sweet." But to Anson it was home music— the sound that competitive children make and must be allowed to make, without interference from their elders.

The hubbub rose to a peak whenever Anson suggested a bout of Bear-Hug, a gentler variation of the game that Old Chance had played with his own children. Laly and Reb would give the bear a bad time the first five minutes, only to fall at last, together with Quincia and Ozzie, into the fearful trap of the bear's paws.

All passion spent, the breath squeezed from their lungs, they'd snuggle into Anson like motherless cubs until Solange announced, "Supper's ready!"

By tacit agreement the children were kept up long after their usual bedtime for instructions in arithmetic and reading. Solange read from the little shelf of books: Cooper's *Deerslayer, Robinson Crusoe*, the first book of *Gulliver's Travels*, a dog-eared volume of McGuffey's second reader and Noah Webster's blue-backed speller.

At 7:30, Quincia's head began to bob; often she fell asleep while Laly and Reb struggled on until eight o'clock. Maternal pity would prompt Solange to say, "Time for bed." Candlestick in hand, she lighted them up the stairs, folded them away in blankets, pressed a "sleep-tight" kiss onto drooping eyelids. Then, shielding the candle flame with her hand, Solange descended the stairs, took her accustomed place in the Boston rocker and picked up her ball of yarn.

Anson, puffing on his churchwarden, braced his feet against the Franklin stove; the living room, lighted by the dahlia lamp, became a closed field of intimacy, a winter-night's dream of contentment aching to be fulfilled.

Solange could make no overt move; by feminine tradition and loyalty to Zarah's invisible presence, she must wait for the man to take the initiative. The lead must come from Anson. How easily it could come about. Simply by taking the ball of yarn from Solange's hand, by laying it away in her sewing box, Anson might have announced that the struggle was over; that life was far more precious than the barriers set up by convention. But he gave no sign of his need. Evening after evening passed in consciously point-blank commonplaces:

"Ozzie's chest cold seems to be clearing up."

"Glad to hear it. Any news from Platt?"

"Not since the last letter three months ago. . . . And Zarah?"

"Unchanged, so Dr. Allston says."

Counterpoint of inconsequentialities—poor substitutes for the rhythmic exchanges of love! The unbearable pressure increased; the dahlia-lighted room became a torment chamber from which neither could escape.

Propinquity, unavoidable and constant, grew more painful as December deepened. The fearful contract of Anson's loyalty to Zarah was tested anew day after day, night after night, in the presence of a woman who equaled Zarah in beauty and emotional stature.

Virility at prime, unrequited, becomes a torment. At night, tossing on his lonely bed, Anson's need for the solace of woman-flesh took the form of remembrance and dream. But always of Zarah! In fantasy, he dreamed that she was walking beside him on the banks of Paddle Creek. The month was June, the triple-taken note of the bobolink announced the vespers of departing day. Sky and earth fused together in a heliotrope flame as they kissed, purely at first, then with mounting intensity. Zarah was on the grass now; he unfastened the bodice of her dress, took the heart nipple first. "You always neglect the other one," she said, her voice an invitation rather than a complaint.

Desolate, alone, he awakened. Overhead, uncaring winds

rode in caped squadrons. Down the hallway Solange lay sleepless in an anguish of deprivation, awaiting footsteps that never came.

One night as they sat together in the living room, Anson rose, broke the stem of his churchwarden pipe and faced her from the other side of the room.

"Solange!"

The choking desperation in Anson's voice conveyed everything that a woman wants to hear from the man she loves.

And how did Solange reply?

In kind. She who had uttered Anson's name longingly in her cold bed, spoken it a hundred times daily in the commerce of household, now compressed her own yearning and his unserved need into the whisper of his name.

"Anson."

What more could she say? That she would lie at the foot of his bed, or in his arms, or on the floor beside his bed; that she would do, be, anything that he wished; yield and surrender her lips, breasts and the warmth of her cradling body to his service—all this without hesitation or remorse, freely, unconditionally, for as long as he needed her; and, upon Zarah's return, would step aside, forget (yet still remembering) the least of his caresses, words and glances as the only encounters she had ever had with an emotional equal?

Unsayable.

Outside, a stallion wind galloped past. Its iron hoofs struck the house at all four corners. The chimney of the dahlia lamp rattled against its dome. The ball of knitting yarn fell from Solange's lap and rolled toward the man standing against the fieldstone mantelpiece.

He picked it up, advanced toward her winding the yarn as he came. Now he was standing above her, gazing down as he had so often gazed at Zarah, his eyes feeding on the cleft of a bosom that waited for the touch of his hands and lips. How many times he had knelt beside Zarah in surrender and discovery.

He knelt now. "Look at me, Solange."

From every tributary nerve of her body, from hair tendrils, fingertips, the roots of her toes, Solange felt currents of femaleness gathering at their central station of power. So charged she was that even the lifting of her dark, humid eyes might have ignited an inextinguishable blaze.

"Look at me Solange," he pleaded.

"I dare not."

"See my face and understand."

Like a woman looking upward through the ripples of an imprisoning tarn to a light high above her, she lifted her streaming eyes to gaze at the face of the man she loved. A spasm of exquisite joy began at the nape of her neck, quivered down her spine and broke in repeated waves at the center of her being.

She neither wept nor spoke. Grief and renunciation have their own language and it very much resembles the unsyllabled long-drawn-out moan of the orgasm.

The tension was unexpectedly broken a week before Christmas by a letter from Platt addressed to Anson. It contained two one-hundred-dollar bills and a characteristic message:

DEAR ANSE:

Lady Luck must of been smiling at me lately because I won $1200. So just to square things up with you I send the enclosed as a sort of down-payment on that note. I shouldn't of signed it, Anse, but I'll make every cent good to you in a few days. You can expect me home the day before Christmas with some presents from me for Solange, Zarah and the children.

Sincerely yours,

PLATT

P.S. The world is a pretty lonely place so that's why I'm heading home.

P.P.S. Love to Solange. Tell her I'll be a better husband from now on.

How like Platt! Anson saw in the letter a mixture of vanity, troubled conscience and a need to assuage the loneliness that makes Christmas a time for homecoming.

Without comment, he handed the letter to Solange. Wordlessly she read it, then covered her face with her hands. Secretly she dreaded Platt's arrival. It would mean the end of her parlor hours alone with Anson. More intolerable yet, she would be obliged to assume her wifely duties toward a man she no longer loved.

The shadow of Platt's coming fell between Anson and Solange. Christmas week was spent in dutiful preparations. But Christmas Eve came, and Christmas Day passed, without news of Platt.

The week between Christmas and New Year's was an eternity. "What do you suppose is keeping him?" asked Solange, as she and Anson shared their parlor hour on January 2.

"I can't imagine," said Anson. "The workings of Platt's mind are beyond my understanding."

7.

THE TRIPLE CROSS

PLATT WOODHULL ALMOST made it—almost. With a diamond horseshoe blazing from his ascot and a trunkful of new clothes in the back of his cutter, he left Cincinnati on the morning of December 23. By fast driving (his blooded mare Poppea could be depended on to clip off twelve miles an hour) Platt estimated that he could traverse the final forty-eight miles of his journey in a single day. It would be the final lap in his fruitless search for Damon Frye, a search that had led him successively to New Orleans, Louisville and Cincinnati. The quest for his long-lost friend had been unsuccessful because Mr. Frye—having murdered a passenger in the cardroom of the river boat *Great Republic*—was a fugitive from justice. No longer could he be found in his old haunts; the only information concerning him was to be found on the usual "Wanted for Murder" circulars posted *pro-forma* in post offices and railway stations by the not-too-diligent peace officers of the period.

Platt Woodhull had one of the circulars in his pocket, and very dreary reading it made, too.

Although the dream of rejoining Damon Frye had been shattered, fortune had proved to be not wholly unkind to Platt. A prodigious run of luck at Louisville had enabled him to parlay a minuscule stake into a fat sheaf of goldbacks. Trending southward along the Ohio, he was coming home with a chestnut mare, a red-lacquered sleigh, three complete sets of clothing, and, oh, yes, a few gifts for the home folks: toys for the children, an afghan for Zarah, a genuine meerschaum for Anson and a rather impressive brooch (its diamonds only slightly flawed) for Solange. The prodigal brother was doing it in style this time. He would pay off the remainder of his debt to Anson, accompanied by apologies, of course; tender the brooch as a peace offering to Solange; and enjoy for a time the domestic tranquility mentioned in the Preamble of the Constitution and celebrated in renditions of that oft-repeated barroom classic "There's No Place Like Home."

These attractive fantasies were interrupted midway in the afternoon by a noticeable limp in Poppea's right foreleg. Examination showed Platt that his mare had pulled a tendon. Her necessarily slower pace, the falling temperature and the imminent onset of darkness led to a recalculation of the homecomer's plans. A crippled horse and the danger of running into a dog pack forced Platt to make the Double Eagle Inn his goal that evening.

Here was the turnoff toward Peddler's Landing; half a mile onward, then both mare and driver would find accommodations, no matter how desolate, at the Double Eagle Inn.

Instead of the smoldering lantern that formerly hung by a nail over Rocamp's inn, Platt was amazed to see a pair of handsome wrought-iron carriage lamps illuminating the newly painted entrance. He was still further amazed when, opening the door, he heard the tinkle of a piano. Carriage lamps, piano, newly laid carpets, everything repainted and renovated! His amazement increased as he saw the throng of tipplers crowding around the bar. From upstairs came the delectable sound of women lightly laughing; somewhere nearby the click of billiard balls.

In a world of change, Platt barely recognized Jesse Rocamp, his moon-face ruddy with prosperity, standing behind the bar.

"What's going on here, Jess? Why, this is the liveliest spot north of Louisville! Who's behind it all?"

"Me, for one." Rocamp wasn't above taking his share of credit. "And a fellow named D'Arcy, for another. Say, that's a good-lookin' tie pin you're wearin'! Where'd you pick it up?"

"Ask me no questions and I'll tell you no lies."

The exchange of friendly insults might have continued but for the demands made by some dozen other customers at the bar. Platt sipped his drink, gazed into the mirror and was not at all displeased at his own reflection. His meditations were interrupted by Jesse Rocamp's hearty boom.

"Evenin', Mr. D'Arcy. The boys in the back room been waitin' for you."

Platt, turning, saw the patrician figure of Damon Frye!

Age had taken none of the eel-like glide from Frye's tread, nor lowered by a quarter inch the contemptuous jut of his clean-shaven jaw. Electricity of fear, generated by old guilt, sent tremors along Platt's spine as his former colleague acknowledged the bartender's greeting and continued toward the gaming room. Did no one else in the bar recognize the threat in Frye's glance and carriage? Apparently not. Insulated by a porkish layer of stupidity, Rocamp called out, "Like to interduce a gentleman friend of mine, quite a card-player. Mr. D'Arcy, meet Mr. Platt Woodhull."

D'Arcy's 180 degree eye-circuit had already included Platt. Immune therefore to surprise, he smoothed down an invisible hair on his left eyebrow (a signal which said, "We have never met before") and extended his falsely delicate right hand.

"Honored to make your acquaintance, sir."

The dream was coming true. Like all dreams, Frye's handclasp presented to the dreamer both wish and fear in exactly the desired proportions. The exchange of secret knowledge, the as yet unguessed conspiracy against the rest of the world —all these fell into the mold of barroom protocol.

"The honor's mine," said Platt. "I hear you've got a little game going in the back room."

"Do you play at cards?"

"Now and then . . . if the stakes are attractive."

Polite smile. Casual invitation. "Look in on us at your leisure."

Semi-military salute. Correct inclination of the head. Exit Mr. Frye.

What the hell's he up to? Platt wondered.

The determination to discover Frye's motives, the pleasure of taking part in his design—whatever it might be—caused Platt to forget temporarily the business of going home. All thoughts of home vanished permanently when he saw Lucienne Bisguier enter the bar.

Beauty is one thing; durable good looks are another. Poets have praised the first, and ordinary men are obliged to content themselves with some fractional part of the latter. Platt was neither a poet nor an ordinary man; as a gambler he valued aces above queens, and long intimacy with Solange had qualified him to judge the points, so to speak, of a well-favored woman. He appraised Lucienne as she circulated in the crowd: long legs, and the art of managing them in the not-so-simple act of walking; hips and bosom emphatically not to be wasted on the suckling of babes.

Her gown of lavender satin (though scruffed by too many cleanings) was basically right for her violet eyes and strawberry hair, parted down the middle and gathered into a Josephine chignon at the nape of her neck. In any setting, the total effect would have been demimonde—but demimonde with a difference. Nothing in Lucienne's background or present occupation could make it otherwise; although she typified a class, something unclassifiable, halfway between disdain and professional coquetry, rayed from her person.

She had entered the bar for the purpose of "counting the house" and saw the usual crowd of local tradesmen and transient drummers stupefying themselves to the point where a two-dollar outlay would be comparatively painless. With six girls in the second floor clamoring for action and the welts of D'Arcy's rawhide tongue ("Are you running a convent or a whorehouse?") stinging her cheek, Lucienne had hoped for something more promising both as to quality and number. (When would she ever see a ten-dollar customer again?) Descending to the realities she moved along the bar, tickled Charlie Gruber's nose with the plumes of her fan, and laughed at his exaggerated *kerchooo*. Symbol of masculinity. Her fan traveled downward to Charlie's fly.

"Sneezing won't cure *that*, Charlie."

Conveying some portion of herself with every solicitation, Lucienne straightened the tie of one "regular," accepted a cigarette from another, a light from a third. On a sawdust-strewn stage with brass cuspidors as her only props, Lucienne was creating the mirage of an intimacy that cannot be bought —but has caused men to climb shabbily carpeted stairs to embrace its two-dollar semblance.

In the midst of her routine Lucienne saw Platt drinking alone in a corner of the bar.

By every outward sign—gray top hat, winged collar, blossomy ascot and horseshoe tie pin—she recognized him, not by name or countenance, but as a member of the species she knew best: a gambler, a professional gambler; self-regarding, indifferent (though not immune) to women. He was gazing at her with a curious detachment, wondering no doubt why she, Lucienne Bisguier, would stoop to tickling a man's fly with a soiled fan. Was it a desire to explain herself, or perhaps merely the wish to *be* herself, that caused her to close the plumed fan and walk toward Platt?

"You're new here," she said simply.

Platt touched the rim of his hat. "Sorry to contradict you, Ma'am, but *you're* new. I live about twelve miles north."

"Why haven't we seen you before?"

"I travel a lot."

"New Orleans, for instance? Louisville, maybe?"

"How'd you guess?"

"By the hand-stitched seams on your lapels. My husband has a half-dozen coats that might have been made by your tailor."

"Your husband?"

"Ambrose D'Arcy."

Did the smoothed eyebrow-signal—"You and I are strangers"—extend to Mrs. D'Arcy-Frye? Lacking guidance, Platt was non-committal. "I've just had the pleasure of meeting your husband. I understand he's running a little game here."

"*Faute de mieux.*" For the benefit of Jesse Rocamp, some six feet distant, she toyed with the diamond horseshoe on Platt's ascot. "Such a pretty pin. It will cause a sensation among our girls, Mr. Woodhull."

Lucienne opened her fan. The interview was over. She retreated down the bar, coaxing with feminine allurements. Watching her from the back, Platt thought of another woman that he had married (how long ago?) for reasons that he could not now remember.

The cardroom drew Platt into Damon Frye's magnetic orbit. Here, Frye's coldly pure touch was evident. The place had been swept and garnished; its walls, once calcimined, were now a neutral gray. Since elegance could not be hoped for, Frye had obtained an effect of cool bareness found in monastic cells and surgical amphitheaters. A circular green baize table lighted by a hanging lamp was ringed by seven severely straight chairs. The sideboard bearing several whiskey bottles and an array of unchipped glasses completed the décor.

For what purpose had Frye created this severely classic

chamber? Surely not for fleecing the five pitiful victims now gathered around the table. Platt saw the meager stakes—barely twelve dollars in small coins and greenbacks—as the final card of this particular hand was dealt. He heard voices saying, "Open for a quarter, raise you a half. Raise *you* another half." Then the timid showdown as the pot, amounting to approximately $14.00, was raked in by Mr. Anonymous, a paunchy slob chewing a dead stogie.

Platt's blood seethed with indignation. That Damon Frye should descend to this, that his matchless talent should be wasted on bumpkins, filled Platt with pity for his exiled king. These clowns must be lessoned.

"May I sit in?" he asked, directing the question to Frye.

"According to house rules—" Mr. D'Arcy-Frye was coolly regretful—"strangers must be properly introduced." He sought confirmation in the eyes of his fellow players.

"Hell, Mr. D'Arcy—" Jesse Rocamp assumed a bluff proprietorial role—"Platt Woodhull ain't no stranger. I've known him since he was a colt, so to speak; glad to interduce him to the comp'ny."

"If you're willing to sponsor him, Jesse, I'll withdraw my objections." D'Arcy was a Senator yielding to the Chair on a point of order.

With Platt's legs under the green table, Frye facing him, the old duet began. Or trio, rather. The invisible member of the ensemble was neither luck nor chance but the secret communication that had always existed between Platt Woodhull and Damon Frye. Every gesture, rise or fall of voice, conveyed information, and the burden of this information ran: *Build up the betting—but don't win.*

During the game Platt introduced the novelty of a five-dollar gold piece as a respectable raise. Revolutionary—but at the end of the game Platt had lost sixty-five dollars. The big winner was Jake Barlow, a hay-and-grain dealer from Buford. At least twenty-five people standing around the table saw Barlow's three bullets beat the two pair—jacks over eights—held by the gentleman with the diamond horseshoe in his necktie. Simply by turning up his hole card (a jack), Platt could have converted his hand into a full house. But Frye's baton signaled: *Non troppo presto*—not too fast.

Flushed by his winnings, Jake Barlow shouted, "Set 'em up for everybody." Later, a delegation climbed the stairs to sample Lucienne's imported talent.

Jesse Rocamp beamed; everything was grist to his mill.

Platt, longing for Frye's signal—Let us speak privately—received only a stylized "I bid you good evening, sir" as the gambler rose from the card table.

Was that all? No. Mr. D'Arcy-Frye unobtrusively rolled a cigarette with his left hand, lighted it and blew a perfectly formed halo of smoke at the ceiling. No one except Platt noticed that the smoke ring moved in a clockwise direction. Dextral. A good omen. A second smaller ring ascended to the ceiling; it climbed counterclockwise and merged into the first. The sinistral wheel within a wheel told Platt all that he needed to know.

He turned to his host. "I think I'll stick around a while, Jess. Got a bed for me?"

"We're pretty crowded. Want to sleep with one of the girls?"

"Not tonight. How about the tack room behind the stable? There used to be a bunk there."

"It's still there." Marveling at the perversity of a man who rated tack room austerity higher than perfumed flesh on a full-sized bed, Rocamp asked, "How long do you expect to stay?"

"Just long enough to take D'Arcy's pile—unless you beat me to it."

A fool and his money are soon parted, thought Rocamp, as he accepted a twenty-dollar gold piece from his former conspirator and handed him the key to the tack room.

Feeling that he deserved a bit of relaxation, Mr. Rocamp hoisted his porky frame up the carpeted stairs and caught the last scene of a "Novelty Act" put on for the late-stayers. His optic nerves conveyed a message ardently addressed to Lucienne Bisquier but delivered to Miss Lola Alvarez. In the dark all cats are black. Midnight settled over the Double Eagle Inn.

Platt, sleepless, waited for the knock at his door. It came at 1:30. He lifted the hasp, and Damon Frye slipped into the small room lighted only by a dark lantern.

"Why don't you operate in a civilized part of the house?"

"Why don't you operate in a civilized part of the country?"

Neither question required an answer; both served admirably to chop off a past that seemed vastly unimportant as the two friends grasped hands and Frye unrolled the blueprint of his master plan. (Well, part of it, anyway.)

"I have established a most touching relationship with our porcine host, Jesse Rocamp, hereinafter to be known as Swino. Good heavens, what I haven't done to win that bastard's confidence." Frye ticked off the catalogue of favors and obligations. "Advanced him money to prop up this sagging hostelry; imported girls to attract bar trade. Why, I've even lost money to him!"

"What's the payoff?"

"Swino and his inn are a natural sink—may the patron saint of plumbers forgive me—into which, according to Newton's law of gravity and the much more ancient law of vice, cash flows from all points of Landmark County. We allow Rocamp to sell whiskey, overcharge the girls for board and room, share in their sweaty earnings while enjoying free of charge such little oddments of favor as Lola, Belle, Hilde—who cares what their names are—may grant. Like the fair god of the Aztecs, we allow him to enjoy a period of deification before trussing him up for the sacrifice. You follow me?"

"In a general way. But how long can he be fooled into thinking that he's a card player?"

"With a little tutoring I could teach your mare to play stud. Mr. Rocamp is not an *apt* pupil, but I take care of that by feeding him the right cards."

"So I noticed. How much do we drop to him?"

"What difference does it make? We get it all back when Mr. Platt Woodhull, professional gambler from New Orleans, starts off on an exceptional run of luck. Rocamp's loot is siphoned into the pockets of said Woodhull. Swino staggers about like a stuck pig. He is consoled by Benefactor D'Arcy, who furnishes him with several decks of cards, seemingly fresh but skillfully tampered with. Oh, the tragedy of that final scene! Despite the marked cards, Woodhull bleeds him dry in a single night of play."

"And after that?"

"Is it not crystal clear that Messrs. Woodhull and D'Arcy disappear in a one-horse sleigh?"

Platt recognized the admirable simplicity of Frye's plan.

"I must add," said Frye, "that you and I should pretend to be deadly enemies. We quarrel on any pretext. You cry, 'Misdeal,' question the honesty of the cards—anything at all to keep the wound open and well salted. Do you still play billiards?"

"I've managed to keep in practice."

"Good. Let our feud spread to the billiard room. While making a difficult massé shot, you sit on the edge of the table. I pound the floor with my cue and call your attention—"

"Rule forty-three. 'At all times the player must keep both feet on the floor.' "

"Excellent man! If the quarrel becomes heated, I display my equalizer—" Frye patted his derringer—"and in the interest of his own good repute, Swino acts as mediator." Frye indulged in a delicious mimicry of Rocamp's voice and manner. " 'Gentlemen, gentlemen, no gunplay, please. This is a respectable house.' "

There was a slapping of thighs. The sound of choked laughter in the tack room must have aroused envy in Poppea's equine heart. Her hoof banging against the box stall startled Frye.

"What's that?"

"A jealous female—my mare."

Frye thought it best not to say, You have a way with females. He slipped through the half-open door, felt his way across a labyrinth of darkened stables to the main part of the house.

In his room he read a scene or two from John Ford's morbid tragedy *'Tis Pity She's a Whore* before sleep claimed him.

The winter ruttime comes earlier than poets have led us to suspect. Springtime may be indeed the only pretty-ring time, but animals and men—including women—feel a peculiar thermal urge during mid-January. In the case of Mrs. Ambrose D'Arcy, better known to the New Orleans sporting trade as Lucienne Bisguier, this urge began to mount shortly after New Year's Day. She was twenty-six years old, and although she had a professional distaste for run-of-the-inn customers "serviced" by her girls, she was very much a woman—and a dissatisfied one.

As winter hardened, the catalogue of her dissatisfactions grew longer, more realistic. To D'Arcy's inattentiveness as a lover, Lucienne could add other traits that women find inexcusable. The man with whom she had linked her fate was— to put no fine point upon the matter—as stingy with money as with embraces. Lucienne's wardrobe, scanty to begin with, was becoming positively shabby, yet her requests for a new gown and much-needed lingerie were curtly refused. No bangles, no perfume, no endearments, from this man to whom she regularly turned over weekly amounts never less than a hundred dollars. Her complaints might have been uttered to the north wind, and her natural hunger for affection (she knew better than to ask for love) was poorly requited by a man who preferred the vagaries of chance to the certainties of sex.

The girls in Lucienne's charge could look forward, in the manner of prostitutes, to the visits of a favorite client who came bearing a box of sachet powder, a tinseled bijou, in addition to the professional fee. Nor did the givers of these trifles underestimate their effect. So cheaply can the hired performer be persuaded to imitate spontaneity, gratitude—or even to give an encore.

Both by her position as D'Arcy's wife and a natural fastidiousness, Lucienne was barred from giving or receiving anything. Spared from the dreariness of promiscuity, she found herself claimed by the equal dreariness of performing a madame's duties without prospect of pleasure or gain. The business of demanding two dollars in advance, of pulling up her dress to make change from her garter bank (a feature expected by Double Eagle customers), the necessity of maintaining a kind of Mother Superior discipline among her unwimpled, hard-drinking troupe, were not sufficient rewards for a girl of Lucienne's emotional caliber.

Desperate for a little stake of her own, Lucienne began holding out on D'Arcy. A dollar one night; two dollars the next; and on a particularly busy week end she retained eight dollars for herself. At Christmas Lucienne had almost one hundred dollars which she kept, not in a bureau drawer or under her mattress, but in the toe of an old high-buttoned shoe, which also contained certain medicaments, nozzles and rubber bulbs essential to feminine hygiene. Knowing Frye's aversion to these articles, she felt that the money was safe and added to it regularly.

Lucienne's pilferings grew bolder; to these she added, early in January, a fiery resolve to give, and take, any semblance of love that might be offered her. Her winter oestrum, now approaching its peak, demanded gratification. With her sapphire-blue eyes quite open to the risk involved,

she chose Platt Woodhull as the most attractive, eligible—
in fact the only conceivable—instrument of satisfaction.

The affair began innocently enough while Lucienne was
exploring the labyrinth of passageways that lay on the
farther side of the cardroom.

Restless, bored after her morning coffee, she noticed that
the icicles fringing her window were melting under the rays
of a forenoon sun. A January thaw, false predictor of spring,
gave a softness to air and snowscape. How long since she
had been outdoors? Weeks, months perhaps. Remembrance
of sledding as a young girl in Montreal tempted her to frolic
in the snow, fill her lungs with air unstaled by cigars and
whiskey. A scarf, a gored woolen skirt, a much-mended
cardigan jacket were costume enough. She glided downstairs,
passed the unattended desk, ran out the front door and
rolled in a snowbank. The melting white crystals cooled the
fever of her cheeks but left a residue of slush inside her shoes.
With a pair of rubber boots Lucienne might have gone
striding across the field, but her thin-soled slippers prevented
such an expedition. Instead, she skirted the front of the inn
and came to the livery stable annex.

There, with the barn door open, Platt Woodhull was currying his chestnut mare in the winter sunshine.

The graceful arch of Poppea's neck, the curve of her rump
—unbroken by hames and breeching—suggested a wild nude
beauty docile under her owner's hands. Silently Lucienne
watched as he brushed the animal's withers, then, with a
wider sweep of the currycomb, moved along her flanks under
her belly. (Skilled from boyhood in the care of horses, Platt
went about his work systematically and with a sure, gentle
touch.) The mare's quivering skin sent a corresponding tremor
through Lucienne. She envied Poppea's privilege of nuzzling
into Platt's body and nipping affectionately at his ear or
elbow.

"She likes you," said Lucienne.

Platt turned his head briefly. Strawberry hair and blue
eyes belonged to Mrs. D'Arcy; the voice and outdoor costume
made her seem younger, less tarnished by her trade. For
weeks he had been studiously avoiding Lucienne; the risk of
cutting athwart Frye's friendship prompted him to discourage her now.

"I take good care of her." Platt busied himself with putting
a sheen on Poppea's mane.

"That's one reason."

"Is there any other?"

"I can think of at least one. She's grateful for being used."

"Aren't you being used?"

"Not in the way I'd like."

Platt chose to break off this dangerous conversation. He had taken one woman away from Frye and had no intention of repeating the mistake.

"Your husband mightn't approve if he saw us talking together."

"I'm sure he wouldn't. But he's gone to Buford with Rocamp. They won't be back till late this afternoon."

Lucienne's statement checked with the facts as Platt knew them. The scarcity of well-heeled players at the stud table had made it imperative that fresh money be brought into the game. Rocamp had suggested Thaddeus Meakins as a likely prospect. "Thad's richer'n a manure pile" were Rocamp's exact words. To which D'Arcy had replied, "We'll go over and lay the finger on him tomorrow."

While the finger of fortune was beckoning to Meakins, ten other fingers, long and delicate, were searching out the flaw in Platt's character. Lucienne plucked a strand of Poppea's mane from Platt's corduroy jacket, then wound it about the staghorn button of his breast pocket. She was very close to him now; her fingers, like those of a harp player, were testing the strings of her instrument.

"Do you really care more about cards than women?" she asked, putting one hand in the pocket of his corduroy jacket.

Platt had almost forgotten that he cared about women at all. During his month's stay at the Double Eagle Inn, he had once climbed the stairs, accompanied by Frye, to pay his Christmas respects to Lucienne's girls. In his role of visiting prince he had given each of them a five-dollar gold piece.

Since then he had barely exchanged a word with Lucienne. Nevertheless there had been communications between them: covert droop of her eyelashes whenever she passed him in the cardroom, a semi-turn of her head as she lifted her dress preparatory to climbing the stairs. And now she was communicating a message that needed no words. Only fingers. And in the broad sunlight of a January thaw, they were speaking freely.

Searching both pockets of Platt's corduroy coat, Lucienne

discovered some lumps of sugar, a package of rice paper, and a sack of Latakia tobacco.

"I've always wondered what men carried in their pockets."

"Well, now you know."

"Women have no pockets. Men have so many." The articulate fingers began searching the side pockets of Platt's riding trousers. She pulled out a small pearl-handled penknife as her first trophy; after that she withdrew her hands no more.

She had found what she was searching for.

"For Christ's sake, make love to me," she begged.

The pride that goeth before destruction nearly burst the buttons off Mr. Jesse Rocamp's checkered vest as he figured his cash position on January 3, 1885. In five months he had amassed six thousand dollars in gold coins and bills of small denomination. The very stars seemed to conspire in their courses to pour new streams of wealth into his strongbox. Then, imperceptibly, the stars began to travel in a puzzling zigzag manner, comparable to the faint tremors that precede an earthquake.

The first tremor came when Sheriff Jonas T. Givens visited Mr. Rocamp's establishment for the purpose of collecting his monthly perquisite of twenty dollars—plus a free interview with one of Lucienne's girls. Jonas collected his money, enjoyed a satisfactory upstairs interview, then handed his host a handbill stating that law-enforcement agencies between Natchez and Louisville were interested in the present whereabouts of a man named Ambrose D'Arcy, alias Damon Frye, Daniel Freiberg, David Freyer, etc.

Rocamp's eyes boggled at the words:

$100.00 REWARD FOR INFORMATION LEADING TO DETECTION AND APPREHENSION OF THIS MAN

In heavy wooden furniture print the handbill set forth the various high crimes (including murder, forgery and counterfeiting) committed by the above-mentioned D'Arcy, Frye, Freiberg and Freyer. The wood-block cut of the wanted man had been pulled hastily.

"I don't see no resemblance between this feller and D'Arcy."

"Mebbe *you* don't," said Givens, "but there ain't no doubt

up here—" he tapped his forehead—"that I could c'llect one hundred dollars for turning him in."

He allowed Rocamp to digest the material, then added, "I don't mind a little gamblin', Jess. Personally, I take the position that a bit of female nonsense now and then is relished by the best of men. Yessir, professional entertainers *per-tect* decent wimminfolk, you might say. But murder's somethin' else, Jess. You'll have to give me your word of honor—or the equivalent thereof—that there'll be no gunplay round here."

The "equivalent thereof" was a hundred-dollar bill, plus the usual monthly perquisite. Not a high price for inside information about Mr. D'Arcy. In fact, a quite reasonable price, so long as the aforesaid Mr. D'Arcy continued to lose in nightly sessions at the stud table. Rereading the handbill privately, Rocamp was seized by a severe attack of shakes when he came to the sentence "D'Arcy is accompanied by a female companion posing as his wife, the former Lucienne Bisguier, who has a police record as a New Orleans prostitute and brothel keeper." It pleased him to know that the supposedly virtuous Mrs. D'Arcy might be levered, secretly of course, into a most desirable position. At the same time it frightened Swino to think of the vengeance that D'Arcy might wreak upon her seducer.

Tremblingly, Jesse placed the circular in the innermost compartment of his cast-iron safe and locked the door.

The next tremor began as an itch (with complications) contracted by Mr. Rocamp after a session of dalliance with Lola. Rocamp knew it must be Lola, because he had been faithful to her in his twice-a-week fashion. In a few days new symptoms—no worse than a bad cold—caused Mr. Rocamp to clip an advertisement for Mandrone from the Landmark *Cornet*. He mailed the advertisement, together with a dollar bill, to the makers of Mandrone and in due time received this nostrum of choice, recommended by leading physicians as the sovereign remedy for Male Weaknesses. Mandrone in hand, Mr. Rocamp retired to the privacy of the livery stable and proceeded to demonstrate the wisdom of the old adage "The patient who treats himself has a fool for a doctor."

Only the clothespin between his teeth prevented a yowl of anguish as Mr. Rocamp applied the liquid medicament to his parts. The brownish stuff smelled like creosote and burned like carbolic acid. He was hopping up and down in the darkness of an empty stall when he saw a female figure, her face hidden by a woolen scarf, emerge from Platt Woodhull's room and glide through the shadows into the passageway leading to the inn.

Which of the girls was visiting Platt privately? The proprietorial right to know what was going on in his own house caused the innkeeper to pick up an augur bit and bore an eye-sized hole into the planks dividing Platt's bedroom from the stable. Next afternoon, after taking his dose of Mandrone, Jesse Rocamp applied his eyes to the peephole and was rewarded by the sight of a man and woman performing a private ritual. The woman was displaying a remarkable erotic talent and a great deal of herself. The superb legs and educated torso were those, in short, of Lucienne D'Arcy.

The prongs of the dilemma hooking Mr. Rocamp were exceedingly sharp. Should he tell Ambrose D'Arcy of his wife's infidelity and thereby bring to a head the enmity already existing between D'Arcy and Woodhull? Na-nh! Swino remembered a fearful display of D'Arcy's pistol in the billiard room. If a man would kill for an infringement of billiard rules, what would he do had he the motive of jealousy? Moreover, Swino couldn't admit that he had beheld Caesar's wife naked, guilty and begging for more. The better strategy would be to drop the subject entirely. Meanwhile he continued to enjoy the vicarious pleasures of peepjackery as a kind of antidote to the burning power of Mandrone.

Ambrose D'Arcy needed no informer to tell him that his wife was being systematically unfaithful. By a dozen signs— some visible to the naked eye, others less tangible—he knew that his calculations were correct: that Lucienne, pining from neglect, had knocked at Platt's gate; and that the loose-hinged Platt had repeated the old pattern of lifting the latch and letting her in.

Proofs? One for every sense: the pungent odor of Latakia in Lucienne's hair; the purplish bruises left by passionate fingers and teeth on her peach-soft skin; the renewed interest in her evening toilette and a revival of that old habit of darting her pointed red tongue between flawless teeth when she laughed—all these were indications that someone was writing in an open book.

Was Mr. D'Arcy displeased? Not at all. He had planned it

that way. The next step in his grand design required only that he bring Rocamp abreast of developments.

He found Mr. Rocamp grimacing rather oddly in an empty stall. The innkeeper's breeches were half down and he was biting a clothespin.

"What's the trouble, Jess?"

"Gravel. Just passed a stone." Mr. Rocamp brought his clothing into some semblance of order, put the clothespin in his pocket and improvised briefly. "Agony . . . agony."

"Sorry for your trouble, Jess. But I'd rather have stones in my kidney than in my heart."

"What kind of stones d'ya mean?"

D'Arcy assumed a brooding attitude worthy of the Dane.

"Treachery, infidelity." The albatross of a nameless grief hung about the gambler's neck as he continued. "I have reason to suspect—delicacy prevents a rehearsal of the details —that the wife of my bosom—oh, Jesse, how can I say it?"

"Say what, Mr. D'Arcy?"

"Call me Ambrose," begged the gambler.

"Why sure, Mr. D'Ar——, Ambrose, I mean. What's up?"

"I don't quite know. Certain indications lead me to suspect that Platt Woodhull is having Biblical knowledge of my wife."

"Eh, what kind of knowledge is that?"

"Carnal, adulterous knowledge. You know what I mean, Jess."

Mr. Rocamp was in the unique position of knowing exactly what Ambrose D'Arcy meant. Had he chosen he might have given his friend a chapter and verse account, illustrated by eye-searing pictures. He thought it better to let the subject unfold itself.

"Have you noticed anything between them? Secret meetings, anything like that?"

"*Me?*" With Mr. D'Arcy's eyes boring into his skull and the peepholes aimed like a double-barreled shotgun at his buttocks, with Mandrone blazing a sovereign path along his urethra, Mr. Rocamp sought squirming refuge in an outburst of indignation.

"Why, for Chris' sake, Mr. D'Arcy—Ambrose, I mean—no such thing never even entered my mind. 'Twouldn't be fair to Mrs. D'Arcy."

"That's exactly the way Lucienne would want you to feel, Jesse. She's a good girl; been a splendid wife all these years.

We've had our ups and downs together, sure, but she's true as steel." To emphasize the steely note, Mr. D'Arcy whipped out his derringer.

Rocamp shook like a pudding.

"Didn't mean to frighten you, Jesse." D'Arcy replaced the pistol in his holster. "But if I had proof that anyone seduced Lucienne, I'd drill the bastard through his heart."

"Sure, sure, Ambrose. I understand. On'y thing is you ain't got no proof. A hair from a mare's tail—like you jest showed me—ain't enough evidence for killin'."

"You're right, Jesse. Let's put our heads together and figure out a way to establish Lucienne's . . . er . . . er virtue." Chin in hand, the gambler strode up and down the stable. "What we need is a combination of the strawberry handkerchief in *Othello*, and the paraffin on the soles of Ali Baba's boots." Inspiration struck like lightning. "Suppose you pound up a dozen squares of billiard chalk and scatter the blue dust on the floor of Woodhull's room."

"What'll that prove? Just standing on the floor ain't no crime."

"You'd have made a wonderful defense lawyer. Here's what you do—sprinkle the powder on Woodhull's sheets."

"Sposin' he asks me what I'm doing?"

"Just say you're sprinkling the place to keep down bugs."

Reluctantly Rocamp pounded up the billiard chalk and spread it as per directions. Somewhat less reluctantly he took his place at the peephole to watch the matinee. A terrific first act began when Lucienne kicked off her pink satin slippers with a touch of maribou at the instep. Crescendo action punctuated by fascinating dialogue. Exit Lucienne, leaving a trail of blue chalk.

Rummaging about in Lucienne's shoe closet that evening, D'Arcy found the fatally marked slippers.

His plot had come full circle. There was only one nick. In the tip of a high-buttoned shoe he found Lucienne's little cache, amounting to $106.00. D'Arcy grew livid with anger. Infidelity as planned was one thing. Holding out on cash was another. Of the two sins, the latter was far more serious. Should the outwitter be outwitted, the deceiver deceived? Wounded vanity kept D'Arcy's anger at white heat as he announced the shameful facts (well, part of them) to the innkeeper.

"I found the blue powder all over the soles of her pink slippers, Jesse."

"Find it any place else?"

A cascade of tears fell from D'Arcy's eyes. Sobs shook him as he confided the shameful facts. "She asked me to hook up her dress, dear innocent girl. I saw blue powder all over her beautiful back, neck, shoulder blades—everywhere. Why that black-hearted rascal must have used every ounce of strength to . . . to subjugate her."

The locution was new to Rocamp; the facts at variance with what he had seen. Still, if a husband wanted to believe in his wife's virtue, Swino wasn't the one to disillusion him. "What you ganna' do about Woodhull?"

Cold ferocity displaced domestic grief. "I'm going to kill him. Right now." Very deliberately Mr. D'Arcy examined the cartridge chamber of his pistol, drew the hammer back to half-cock and moved toward the tackroom.

"No, no," pleaded Rocamp. "It'll give my place a bad name. For God's sake, Ambrose, put away your gun."

The pleadings of friendship melted D'Arcy. He gripped Rocamp's pulpy hand and wrung it with the gratitude of a man who has been saved from the rash councils of passion. "Out of respect to your house, Jess, I won't kill him in his bed. Here's what we'll do." Magnetic clutch of eye and hand as he drew Rocamp into the deepest recesses of his plot. "We'll let the son-of-a-bitch win. We'll fatten him up till he's dead ripe. Then"—a conspiratorial whisper in Rocamp's ear, ending with "They'll find him in the snow."

Rocamp started to say, "It sounds sort of complicated."

His doubts were brushed aside by the gambler. "I'll leave Lucienne in your care. In a week or so, after everything's died down, join me at Granger's Hotel in Louisville."

The prospect of playing guardian to Lucienne for a whole uninterrupted week was the bait that hooked Rocamp.

"We'll play it your way," he said.

"Tonight," added D'Arcy.

Eight P.M., temperature 20 degrees below zero. No jingling sleighbells announced the arrival of customers. From the Kentucky side of the river, wild dog packs howled as hunger drove them toward the comparative fat lands of Indiana.

Bar and cardroom were empty as D'Arcy glided with contortionist tread down the passageways leading to the stable.

A lantern suspended from a wooden peg threw a smoky beam on Fifer Tansey applying a hot-water compress against a croupy colt. Why in God's name should this man care whether the colt lived or died? Simply one of those mysteries. D'Arcy crossed the stable and knocked at Platt's door.

"Come in!"

Buoyantly waving an envelope, D'Arcy entered. "Good news, Camarado. Just got a letter from my lawyer. He says the new D.A. in New Orleans will quash all charges for a thousand dollars. Just think of it! The two of us together again. Champagne, big stakes, the paddocks at Louisville." In his excitement D'Arcy dropped the envelope; picking it up he saw billiard chalk dust on the wide-seamed floor.

"We haven't got a thousand dollars." Platt displayed his flattened wallet.

"Oh, ye of little faith. Ever hear about the loaves and the fishes? Well, tonight, and I mean within the next three hours, Swino is going to walk the battlements." D'Arcy produced several packs of cards from various pockets. "The harvest will be great though the reapers are few. Get your clothes on. Pack your trunk. It's shearing time."

Without a bleat Rocamp lost seventy-two hundred dollars, most of it to Platt Woodhull, within the next three hours. When the game broke up, D'Arcy whispered to Swino, "Here's the key to my room. Guard Lucienne with your life, dear friend. Now get to bed. If you don't know or hear anything, you won't be an accessory to murder."

Meeting Platt in the stable, he said, "Hitch up Poppea. We're getting out fast."

"What about Lucienne?"

"I'm leaving her here temporarily with instructions to join us in Louisville. Say . . . that reminds me. I'll have to give her some money. Got a couple of century notes? Thanks, chum. I'll be back in two shakes."

In Room No. 12 Mr. Ambrose D'Arcy watched Lucienne brushing her teeth in a basin of cold water. "Such lovely teeth you have, darling! What a pity that you tried to bite me with them."

"Bite you?"

Frye went to the closet, found a certain high-buttoned shoe and produced it as Exhibit A. "Back-bite describes more accurately what you tried to do. In the toe of this shoe is a certain sum of money. Let's see how much. *Hmmm,* a hundred and six dollars in small, waddy bills moist with the damp heat of the harlot's hand. Did you forget the noncancelable clause in our contract whereby the Party of the Second Part (that's you) hands over all monies to the Party of the First Part—to wit, and to woo: Damon Frye, your protector, guide and erstwhile Bel Ami?"

"You remember almost everything, Damon sweet. In fact, you remember everything except the existence of a little boy, barely three, in a Montreal orphanage. When he grows to man's estate he'll refer gratefully and obliquely to you as his 'only begetter.' "

Lucienne performed a bit of cuticle clipping with a pair of Göttingen fingernail scissors, and continued. "The nuns agreed to take care of our little Lucien for the not unreasonable sum of eight dollars a month, which sum I have been unable to mention in your presence—let alone collect—for almost a year. The bills that you are now folding into your wallet were siphoned off, so to speak, from the sweat of my girls keeping time on their lumpy mattresses. A hundred and six dollars represents barely one year's board, room and religious instruction for a little bastard that I happen to love."

"Very touching. If I had tears to shed, I'd shed them now. Buss you perhaps. Call you 'Madonna of the Snows.' Beg for the privilege of claiming paternity to 'Baby (By-Blow) Lucien.' Let sentiment ring elsewhere." D'Arcy Frye tapped the region of his heart. "Not in this whoremaster's breast. And I am a whoremaster, you know."

Lucienne paused in the act of trimming a thumbnail. "Who should know better than I—I who was dazzled by the glitter of your talents—only slightly tarnished when I first saw you. What happened to the man who might have played the Royal Dane, or coached others in diction and carriage, as you coached me in the beginning? Damon Frye might have been the pleader of noble causes, a teacher, or the most accomplished high-wire performer that the world has ever seen. What happened to the man I loved at sight? Did he fall—or was he pushed?"

"Neither," said Frye. "He *chose.* After sufficient reflection and full consent of the will, he chose to leap into the void and is still falling." Frye glanced at his watch. " 'If there were world enough and time' I might explain the metaphysical reasons that led me to the brink. Stating the matter in terms of black and white, I saw Virtue so triumphantly rampant in the world that I decided to redress the balance and to become a spokesman for Evil."

"Dealing from a stacked deck, pimping for yokels, hiding in bayous, aren't Evil. They're just plain stupid."

"I agree. It is difficult to read from the book of Pure Evil. No light except a sulphurous glow enables the student to scan its page. The neophyte must pass through a long apprenticeship of Treachery and Low-Grade Cunning. The Decalogue isn't shattered at a blow." Frye drew his pistol. "At present I must content myself with an act of sheer, gratuitous Mischief."

"Such as?"

"Such as breaking your pretty teeth. Now, if the lady will be so kind as to say 'cheese,' thereby exposing her opalescent uppers, my pistol butt can emulate the Little Tailor by knocking off seven at one stroke."

"No, Damon, please don't break my teeth!" Terrified, Lucienne was pleading now. "I beseech you."

"No melodrama. It irks me. Just your teeth."

"One last kiss, Damon sweet. See, my eyelids faint; they are half closed with expectation. *Baise-moi.*"

"Dear weak girl. You deserve a better fate."

Holding his derringer by its barrel, butt uplifted for a downward chop, Frye walked into Lucienne's semi-swoon trap. Kissing her warm, half-open mouth he felt a steel lancet piercing his right eye. The lancet became a gouge as Lucienne twisted her fingernail scissors deep into the optic nerve. Her right knee clipped him in the groin.

"*Zavatt!* How you like heem, eh M'sieu?"

She booted Frye into the hallway, tossed his derringer after him, then slammed and bolted the door of Room No. 12.

Eyeball punctured, its irreplaceable sight-juice leaking away, Frye picked up his pistol. What a truly wonderful disciple Lucienne had proved to be. He had taught her every trick in the book, including the *Savate* knee-business, and here he stood, outpointed, half blinded, by a girl who, at his whim, had once yielded up her satiny buttocks to the tattooer's needle. Unquestionably she deserved a better fate than the long midwinter siege ahead: Swino beating at her door, and Lucienne, the once delectable, obliged by hunger to let him in.

With a snowy linen handkerchief pressed to his eye, D'Arcy

picked his way through labyrinthine mazes leading to the stable.

"Everything ready?" he asked.

"Ready and waiting," said Platt. "Hop in."

Fifer Tansey, watching from the hayloft above, saw D'Arcy tuck a buffalo robe around himself and companion. Merely by extending his long arm, Tansey might have seized either man by the collar. For what purpose? Healing, not law-enforcement, was Fifer's department. Suppose this pair of conspirators *had* robbed Rocamp and were making their getaway. What of it? The croupy colt in the chilly stall ranked higher in Fifer Tansey's scale of values.

He heard D'Arcy say, "One for the road," as he offered Platt a flask of whiskey.

While his victim drank, D'Arcy's snub-nosed pistol came out of its silken sash. He pressed the muzzle against Platt's heart and pulled the trigger.

"Dead? Quite dead, my love?" The line from *Midsummer Night's Dream* obtained precisely the desired ironic effect. "A tomb shall cover these cold eyes."

Mr. D'Arcy felt something very cold and sharp at his throat.

"This is a bistoury," a sepulchral voice explained. "Surgeons use it to reach the bone before cuttin' off a leg. It'll slice your jugular vein neater'n a meat ax, 'less you do what I say."

This was the kind of challenge that Frye really enjoyed. "What do you want me to do?"

"First hand up your derringer."

D'Arcy obeyed.

"Now the box of amminition." Fifer slid down from the loft. "Always fancied carryin' one of these things." He pressed the pistol barrel into the orifice of Mr. D'Arcy's ear and went into a bit of explanation.

"Now, Mister, I ain't an agent of the law and the fact that you just killed a no-good encumberer of the earth makes no partic'lar difference to me. So far's I'm concerned, you can drive off with the body and dump it anywhere's you like. But this man's got a wife and the least she's entitled to is the money and valuables on his person. So kindly hand over same to me and I'll see that she gets 'em. Wallet first. Throw it on the floor. Now his lucky piece, watch and cuff links. They'll be sentimental keepsakes."

"The keepsakes are hereby delivered." D'Arcy's tone was ironic. "Anything else?"

"Yes, now's you mention it, there is something else."

Fifer whetted the bistoury against his boot. "Think I'll slash your tug straps. Not all the way through. That wouldn't give you no pullin' power. But how 'bout leavin' you a half inch of good solid leather on each strap?"

Tansey sank the steel blade into each of the leathern traces that drew the sleigh, then stepped back. "Ought to last a couple miles, 'less you run into a drift—in which case somethin'll snap off short and there you'll be in the middle of nowhere with the dogs all over you."

"For God's sake," said D'Arcy, "give me a chance."

"I thought you was a professional chance-taker. 'Course, if you don't want to drive out of the barn, no one's forcin' you to. Just stay here 'till the sheriff comes."

Ambrose D'Arcy decided to take his chance with the slashed tug straps. "Geet," he said to Poppea and drove out into a night of iron cold.

It was simply a matter of figuring the odds. The village of Landmark lay only seven miles away: Poppea could cover that distance in half an hour. As for the dog pack, it might not be in the vicinity. A matter of odds. He brought the whip down on Poppea's glossy rump; as the mare surged forward, the runners of the sleigh hissed over the hard white snow. No danger of running off the road; a winter's moon illuminated the snowscape with lemon-silver light.

At Big Sycamore the road dipped, then swerved toward the left, and from this sinistral direction D'Arcy saw a moving shadow that would have caused the bravest of Aztec soothsayers to shield his face. Soundlessly the shadow moved in a tactical direction that would converge on the road five hundred yards ahead. This was to be no chase *à la Russe*: it was a flanking maneuver, executed with superb precision by the brute leader in command—a canine Hannibal who had planned it this way.

Frye laughed as he saw a low-hanging sycamore bough silhouetted against the opalescent sky. The bough offered him an avenue of escape. He tied the reins around the whipstock and stood up on the cushions of the sleigh. As he prepared to jump, a yellow-eyed mastiff leaped at the skirts of Frye's great coat and tore off a huge piece of cloth. By a singular feat of strength and agility, D'Arcy performed a giant swing and straddled the bough.

Unfortunately the torn coat skirt contained Mr. D'Arcy-Frye's wallet and, more's the pity, his gloves, too.

Safe in the tree, he watched Poppea race into the gambit. Her first whinny of dread was the signal that the dog pack had been instructed to wait for. The mare reared on her delicate hindquarters and trumpeted with fear. In bringing her forefeet down, she put an extra stress on the slashed tug straps. They broke. . . .

The gray shadow became an avalanche of bristle and fangs; it swarmed over Poppea and the dead man in the sleigh.

The river bend at Big Sycamore was a repetition of Cannae —with a couple of exceptions. Hannibal and his followers did not devour their victims. The dog pack did.

Under a waning moon, the pack trotted across the frozen river into Kentucky. It was the coldest night of the winter; and the really tragic aspect of the matter was that Damon Frye's ungloved hands were nakedly exposed to the Black Avenger—Frostbite—a delicate feeder who battens on unprotected fingers.

All night Frye clung to the sycamore bough feeling the Black Avenger gnaw at his priceless fingertips. From time to time he rearranged the handkerchief that covered his pierced eyeball. What becomes of a gambler, he wondered, when he loses ten dedicated fingers and a ninety-degree arc of vision. Simply this: So long as he doesn't lose his nerve (and Frye was in no danger here) he can rededicate his life to the complete service of Evil.

Clinging to the sycamore bough, Frye so dedicated himself.

In a periwinkle dawn, Frye was about to slip down from the tree, pick up the torn skirt of his coat containing his wallet and gloves when he saw a lanky, scarecrow figure coming toward him.

Fifer Tansey's sunken eyes were reading from the page of nature—a white record marked (until this point) only by Poppea's hoofs and the runners of the sleigh. The gaunt physician paused below the sycamore bough; then picked up the torn skirt of Frye's great coat.

"Your luck sure ran out," he remarked, examining the torn coat skirt. "Wallet full of money. No gloves. Well, well. Your fingers probably need emergency treatment as of this moment. C'mon down."

In the consulting room of a sub-zero dawn, Tansey examined the gambler's hands. "Worse'n I thought. Amputation to the second knuckle indicated here. Put on your gloves. I'm takin' you back to the inn."

"I couldn't stoop to accept a favor at your hands. Give me my wallet and I'll be off."

"Not so sudden, Mister. This here wallet is a treasure-trove. Finders keepers is the simplest way of saying it. I found it and I intend to keep it. If you want to claim ownership, we'll walk to the court house together."

"My derringer, then," begged Frye.

"Now that's plumb foolish. You might be picked up for carryin' a concealed weapon." Frye's handkerchief bandage fell from its place. "Good God, man," exclaimed Tansey, "What's happened to your eye?"

"You'll never find out from me."

"My admiration, sir, for playing your cards as they fall. Here's a hundred-dollar note. Cut across these fields." Tansey's bony forefinger was a weather vane pointing north by west. "Walk three miles and you'll strike the C.B. and O. railroad tracks. And one final note of warning, Mr. D'Arcy. Iffen you ever lay a hand on Lucienne Bisguier, or cause, or cause to *be the cause* of any trouble to that fine woman, I'll nut you raw. Godspeed and git! I see work ahead in the form of two skellingtons and one of them's human."

Ross Burridge, publisher, editor, advertising manager and reportorial staff of the Landmark *Cornet*, adjusted his green celluloid eyeshade, took a nip of Old Settler and proceeded to give an exhibition of the now-lost art of composing from an open font. In his left hand, he held the gunmetal case technically known as a stick; from the various compartments of the type case beside him, he selected letter by letter the opening paragraph of his story.

First, the headline:

DOG PACK KILLS LOCAL MAN

Without benefit of notes and utterly free from the malady known as "writer's block," Burridge put together his first paragraph.

The dog-pack raids on the livestock of Landmark County culminated in a gruesome tragedy early this

week with the death of Mr. Platt Woodhull while he
was riding in a sleigh sometime between Tuesday midnight and 6 A.M. the following day.

Having covered the five classic points of a good lead
paragraph—who, when, where, how and what—Burridge struck
into the developments of his story. They were many and
complex, but the printer-editor hewed cleanly to the chronolgi-
cal line.

The aftermath of what must have been a grisly encounter was discovered Wednesday morning by the well-
known medical practitioner, Dr. Fifer Tansey, who had
spent the preceding night poulticing a croupy colt at the
Double Eagle Inn. On foot as always, Tansey discovered
the overturned sleigh as he rounded the river bend at
Big Sycamore. The carnage, according to Tansey, was
indescribable. He immediately reported the event to
Sheriff J. T. Givens, who inspected the unrecognizable
body and the skeleton of a horse.

Burridge paused momentarily to get his bearings. Should
he describe the evidence collected by Givens or place it
where such evidence next appeared? In the interest of good
newspaper practice (getting as many names into the story as
possible), Burridge condensed the testimony of Sheriff J. T.
Givens. Unable to pad the story further, the editor-compositor
dashed off an editorial to the general effect that the dog pack
—inland equivalent of the man-eating shark—must go. Even
with this editorial flourish, two inches of space remained to
be filled. No problem here. Ross Burridge selected a wood-
block advertisement representing a weekly income of thirty-
five cents. The advertisement ran:

D R I N K
Moerlein's Old Settler
.75¢ per Quart

NEWS ITEMS FROM ALL OVER

BECAUSE ROSS BURRIDGE, editor, owner, publisher and make-
up man of the Landmark *Cornet,* had only one pair of legs,
he couldn't be expected to chase down every dark-o'-moon
rumor flying about the county. It was easier and more profit-

able to publish "Public Notices" announcing evictions, fore-
closures, the decisions of coroner's juries and Surrogate's
Court judges. Naturally he missed those hard-to-come-by
little items lying just outside the penumbra of good editorial
policy. His readers, therefore, had to content themselves during February 1885 by munching on "legal doings" and news
items from all over.

Among the "legal doings" for February 1885 was the
decision of the Surrogate's Court concerning the estate of
Platt Woodhull, deceased. Condensed and set forth in lay
language, the decision (based on Revised Statutes of 1852,
Chap. 27, para. 11, p. 248) held that Mrs. Solange Woodhull, widow, was entitled to all monies found in the wallet
of the dead man. The court further declared that a promissory note dated December 1884 in the amount of $500.00
bearing the signature of Platt Woodhull, payable to Anson
Woodhull, constituted a legal claim for said amount.

Thus the Law. Learned, just, supported by precedents
dating back to Coke on Littleton.

*But what precedents guided Anson and Solange as they
rode homeward from the Surrogate's Court through a dusk
of falling snow?*

*Half the distance was covered in silence broken only by
the jingle of bells on Hooker's martingale. Snuggling under
the warm buffalo robe, Solange kept her hands clenched inside her beaver muff and blessed every turn of the road that
caused Anson to sway toward her. Behind her widow's veil,
a slow mist began to form; tears, not sprung of grief, filled
her lower eyelids. To prolong the exquisite joy of being alone
with the man she loved, Solange murmured, "Anson, please
stop here. For a little while."*

*A curtain of dotted muslin fell slowly as Anson pulled up
his horse. Solange's human need of consolation, his wish to
gratify that need, prompted him to say, "Put your head on
my shoulder. So." He lifted her veil, saw the luminous eyes
gazing up at him. If I kiss her now, he thought, these snowflakes will become burning hailstones.*

*The falling crystals gemmed Solange's dark lashes as she
asked, "Why is it—with so much evil and weakness in the
world—why is it that you, all goodness, and I whose only
knowledge is to love—why is it that we can't help each other?"*

"We do help each other, Solange. I haven't any right to

*imagine what you feel about me. All I know is this: without
you, I would have died of loneliness and desperation. We'll
bring each other through, darling. I'll live on the memory of
this place, this moment. No one else has ever been here.
Nothing in the past or future will displace something that
is ours alone."*

*In silence, bound by a spell of sifting snow, they clung to
each other.*

JUDGE SENTENCES ROCAMP

In a double-barreled decision handed down by the Surrogate Court last week, Judge Wayne T. Feakins refused to entertain the plea of Jesse Rocamp that the money in Platt Woodhull's wallet was the result of deceit and trickery practiced upon aforesaid Rocamp by *two* persons: Platt Woodhull and Ambrose D'Arcy (alias Damon Frye, Daniel Freiberg, David Freyer, etc.).

Judge Feakins held Rocamp's story to be lacking both in merit and fact. The petitioner, Rocamp, was unable to produce a single witness to prove the existence of above-mentioned D'Arcy, Freiberg, Frye, Freyer, etc. Because no *corpus delicti* (so to speak) could be found, the court was about to hold that Rocamp's story was a figment of an overheated imagination, when the case took a strange turn by the sudden appearance of Sheriff J. T. Givens in the witness box.

Sheriff Givens testified that he had officially warned Rocamp of D'Arcy's existence in the neighborhood, and had tacked up a "Wanted for Murder" bulletin on Rocamp's premises. The Sheriff's testimony made it appear that Rocamp had, for some months, harbored and protected a known murderer, thus laying himself open to charges of felony.

Roswell Burbridge, appointed by the court as Rocamp's lawyer, pointed out that merely warning a man about the existence of a criminal was insufficient evidence on which to base a conviction. Judge Feakins agreed. His request for corroborative evidence was supplied by James MacMonnies, Federal Gauger for this district.

MacMonnies told the court that he had seen Rocamp and D'Arcy together on several occasions while they were operating an illicit whiskey still. MacMonnies also testified that he had reported his findings to his superior officers, who were preparing to take appropriate action against Rocamp.

At the end of one of the strangest judicial cases within memory, Judge Feakins sentenced Rocamp to five years' hard labor in the State Penitentiary for harboring a fugitive from justice.

LEGAL NOTICES

February 15, 1885. The bank of Landmark County, Gilbert Peaslee, Pres., hereby puts Jesse Rocamp, Prop. of the Double Eagle Inn, on notice that, being thirteen months in arrears both in payment of interest and principal on a mortgage of $1,000 held by the Landmark Bank, the aforesaid property shall be offered for public sale by the Sheriff of Landmark County on or before March 1, 1885.

February 27, 1885. Inn to Become County Hospital
The citizens of our county may congratulate themselves upon the generosity of Mr. Gilbert Peaslee, President of the Landmark Bank, in permitting the transfer of title on property formerly known as the Double Eagle Inn from Jesse Rocamp to Dr. Fifer Tansey. The details of the financial arrangements were not disclosed by Mr. Peaslee. It is understood, however, that Fifer Tansey has been extended a moderate line of credit for conversion of the Double Eagle Inn property into a Free Hospital, to be supported by voluntary contributions.

We believe that this is the first institution of its kind in southeastern Indiana and extend our wholehearted good wishes to the success of Dr. Tansey's venture.

Odd how facts get twisted around, dropped out, misconstrued in a clarion-call editorial. Could it be that the commendable generosity of Mr. Gilbert Peaslee might have sprung —well, partly, at least—from motives unmentioned and unmentionable? As a banker it was Mr. Peaslee's duty to liquidate when, as and if possible the interests of his depositors. In fact, the State Bank Examiner had urged Gilbert to convert some of his "old paper" (of which he held a great deal) into live assets. He was semi-disposed, therefore, to accept—and no questions asked—the four hundred dollars offered by Fifer Tansey in exchange for title to the Double Eagle Inn.

Before signing the transfer it occurred to Gilbert that his action might be better justified if he drove over and took a look at the place. Duty blended well with that type of curiosity—sometimes called prurience—which all too often festers in the back chambers of a naturally lewd but circumspect mind. Timid Peaslee! Afraid even to ride past Rocamp's place in daylight lest he be caught "peeking." How brave the banner that floats o'er the ramparts of a strictly business deal! Since Fifer Tansey was still traveling on shank's mare, Gilbert offered him a "lift over to the place."

The banker was favorably impressed by its excellent state of repair, its freshly painted outside and tight roof. A rather imposing portecochere excited Peaslee's avarice. Why, for $400.00 Tansey would be practically stealing a valuable piece of property. Conservatively speaking, the inn was a structure worth more than the face value of the mortgage. Peaslee was about to turn down Tansey's project for a community hospital when he saw Miss Lucienne Bisguier descending the stairs.

"Who's she?" asked the banker.

"What? You two don't know each other? Gil, I'm mighty proud to have this opportunity to present my assistant, Miss Lucienne, Practical Nurse. P'raps she's one of the most skillful handlers of aggravated cases as ever served sufferin' mankind." Fifer completed the introduction. "Miss Lucienne, this is Landmark's leadin' banker." A wink from Fifer's off-eye said the rest. "Gil wants to be one of our trustees. S'pose you show him our upstairs layout."

The rule that no lady ever precedes a gentleman while ascending a flight of stairs was broken to good effect by Lucienne's dainty lifting of her skirt and innocent exposure of a yellow garter just above the knee. Fascinated, Gilbert made the most of his worm's-eye view and followed Tansey's assistant upstairs.

"This is my private retreat." Lucienne opened the door of No. 12 and apologized for the presence of a large double bed with a silken counterpane. "Of course, when the infirmary begins its work, I shall be happy to surrender my cozy quarters. Shall we sit down while I outline the plans in more detail?"

The order of events thereafter simply weren't printable in a family newspaper. Mr. Peaslee accepted a glass of "medicinal sherry" offered him by Fifer's assistant and watched her attentively while she slipped "into something more comfortable," thereby encouraging Gil to slip into something even *more* comfortable and become—for the first time in oh, maybe twenty-five years—gloatingly, floatingly, bubblingly, untroublingly liquid.

Fifer got title to the inn for four hundred dollars with the understanding (verbal, of course) that so long as Gil Peaslee was a trustee, he'd be allowed to enjoy, gratis, the highly professional attentions of that very practical nurse, Miss Lucienne Bisguier.

8.

THE SUNWISE TURN

A RAW MARCH WIND, loaded with more than a possible hint of snow, had driven the children indoors; Solange, busy at the eight-lidded stove, was beginning preparations for dinner. She had just closed the oven door on a loin of pork and was laying out the ingredients for a batch of gingerbread when she heard a rap at the door. She glanced through the window; a stranger uncommonly well dressed was knocking the mud off his boots—an action which of itself would recommend him to any careful housekeeper. By feminine instinct, she rearranged an invisibly out-of-place wisp of dark hair, removed her apron and opened the door.

The stranger removed a glossy sealskin hat and without presuming to offer his hand—a well-kept masculine hand—already ungloved, introduced himself. "My name is Charles Moerlein. I have come to see Mr. Anson Woodhull. Is he at home?"

"He's planting corn in the lower field. If you care to step in, I'll send for him."

Charles Moerlein stepped into the warmest, coziest kitchen that he had ever seen. Against a backdrop of gleaming copper utensils, a huge stove and a brass-cylindered pump, heavenly odors of ginger, cinnamon and roasting meat floated like domestic incense borne ceilingward by warmth-bearing waves. In this atmosphere of contentment, four children, a large shepherd dog, a tortoise-shell cat—not to mention an extremely handsome woman—were engaged in various forms of activity or repose, individually satisfying and mutually satisfactory. It occurred to Moerlein that this peaceful intermingling of persons and things, ranging from the burnished kettles to the dozing child in the highchair, was no mere accident. Some common attachment to each other was evident here. Did the strength of this attachment proceed from Anson Woodhull or from the quiet woman in the form-fitting black merino dress? Possibly a union of the two!

The glowing woman at the stove was utterly at variance with Moerlein's preconceived image of Mrs. Woodhull. He had never met Anson's wife, but somehow he had gained the impression that she was an opinionated bluestocking, a New England transplant who preserved the mannerisms and cool fall of speech associated with Yankees. How wrong could a preconception be?

Solange, having dispatched Reb to bring back Anson, was now offering the visitor common hospitality in a voice that Moerlein associated with New Orleans rather than Boston.

"Would you prefer to wait in the parlor?" asked Solange.

"Thank you, no. I'd much rather meet these young people." He smiled at Laly. "Will you introduce me to this young lady with the corn-silk hair?"

The young lady in question needed no introducer. "I'm Laly," she announced, offering her hand.

"Laly? I don't believe I've ever heard that name before."

"It's short for Eulalia, which means 'beautifully spoken.' I know a great many memory-gems. Would you care to hear 'Sheridan's Ride'?"

Laly's mixture of confidence and poise was checked by Solange. "Let Mr. Moerlein meet the other children first. This is Quincia, a little Florence Nightingale. She likes to bandage her dolls."

"What's the matter with your dolls?" asked Moerlein.

"I don't know. She's my Mama-doll. I bandage her every day, but she doesn't get well."

Unable to grasp the child's fantasy, Moerlein appraised the full-figured woman mixing gingerbread batter. "Your Mama looks perfectly well to me."

"She's not my Mama." Quincia burst into tears.

Solange was comforting the child when Anson entered. "My wife has been in the hospital for several months, Mr. Moerlein," he explained. "This is Solange, my sister-in-law, who has taken upon herself the burdens of my household." It seemed superfluous to add that Solange was a widow. The master of the house continued the introductions. "This young fellow here—" he hooked his arm affectionately around Reb's neck—"is Richmond Plaskett. The best twelve-year-old whiskey maker in captivity. And here in the highchair we have Ozzie, a young gentleman who falls asleep very early."

"Would you like to hear 'Sheridan's Ride' now?" asked Laly, juicy-lipped at the prospect of having a new audience.

The new audience agreed that now, this very moment, was the best of all possible times for Sheridan to ride again. He handed his furlined coat to Anson, sat down on a kitchen chair, accepted a cup of coffee from Solange and gave the little performer the opening line.

"Up from the south at break of day."

"Author and title first," corrected Laly. She smoothed the folds of her dress, wiped her wet mouth on her sleeve, and began Mama's way. " 'Sheridan's Ride,' by Thomas Buchanan Read."

Twenty, fifteen, ten—Sheridan was gaining rapidly on Winchester. Laly put rowels into the steed of verse:

> *Under his spurning feet the road*
> *Like an arrowy Alpine river flowed,*
> *And the landscape sped away behind,*
> *Like an ocean flying before the wind,*
> *And the steed, like a barque fed with furnace ire,*
> *Swept on, with his wild eye full of fire,*
> *But lo! he is nearing his heart's desire;*
> *He is snuffing the smoke of the roaring fray,*
> *   With Sheridan only five miles away.*

When the foam-flecked General finally reached Winchester, Moerlein led the applause. "Bravo, *moltissimo* bravo." He caught the spirited little girl in his arms and kissed her caramel-sweet hair. Solange turned to the stove. This was Zarah's triumph, the fruit of Zarah's and Anson's love—a love in which Solange could have no part.

She heard Anson say, "We'll be in the parlor for the next few minutes." Turning her head, she watched the two men— each handsome, each virile—one wearing the broadcloth of a successful merchant, the other dressed in countryman wool, close the door behind them.

Anson offered his guest the Boston rocker; then, loading his churchwarden with rough-cut burley, waited country-fashion for Moerlein to open the conversation. Obviously the Cincinnati distiller had come to discuss terms of a new whiskey contract; good manners dictated that he be given time to compose his thoughts and familiarize himself with the rural parlor in which he was now sitting.

Moerlein, one of the truly great salesmen of his age, had the power of adapting himself to circumstances and persons as he met them. As some men loved horses, he loved to deal in bulk whiskey, especially when it reflected the character of its maker. His immediate object was to win Anson over to the idea of increasing his whiskey production without any sacrifice of quality. He began by expressing satisfaction with Anson's last batch of whiskey. He then proceeded to outline a method by which Anson could triple his production during the coming year.

"I realize it's hard work to make whiskey by the pot-still method, Mr. Woodhull," he said. "We rectifiers bypass much of the distiller's labor, skill and care by means of the patent still—sometimes called a fractionating column. Have you ever seen a fractionating column in action?"

"No. But I'm familiar with the general theory of the thing. As I understand it you pour the liquid mash in at the top, and allow it to filter down through a series of perforated baffle plates."

"That's correct," said Moerlein.

"Live steam, under pressure, is introduced at the bottom of the column, works its way upward until it meets the descending mash which is thereby converted—at very high temperatures—into almost pure ethyl alcohol." The faintest touch of disdain entered Anson's voice. "Commercially known as 'neutral spirits.'"

"I've never heard a better description of the process." Moerlein seemed surprised that a countryman should possess such intimate knowledge of the rectifying process. "I gather that you wouldn't call the resultant product whiskey?"

"Intending no offense, I'd say that a 'neutral spirit' produced in this manner should not be called whiskey."

"Why?" Moerlein asked.

"I'm not a chemist, Mr. Moerlein, but I know from experience that excessively high temperatures *kill* certain valuable ingredients that give genuine whiskey its flavor, body and character."

Moerlein pressed the point without seeming to press it. "In your opinion, Mr. Woodhull, what is the optimum temperature for insuring the existence of these valuable ingredients?"

"A hundred and thirty-five degrees Fahrenheit."

Charles Moerlein, having consciously maneuvered his man into a position of commitment, smiled. "A hundred and thirty-five degrees Fahrenheit is exactly right. By the exercise of extreme care, it is possible to keep the entire contents of a *sixty-gallon* pot still at that temperature. Now the question is—" invitation and challenge joined in Moerlein's voice— "could you undertake to keep a *two-hundred-and-fifty* gallon still at this optimum temperature?"

"Not over an open fire. The bottom part would scorch."

"Exactly. Every farm wife who has ever cooked a batch of cornmeal mush knows that starch coming into direct contact with heat tends to scorch. Hence the double-boiler. Now what I'm suggesting, Mr. Woodhull—" Moerlein drew out a pencil and sketched rapidly—"is that you weld a copper chamber onto the bottom of a two-hundred-and-fifty-gallon pot still. Into this copper chamber, steam is introduced under pressure. By this means you will be able to control, evenly and at all times, the temperature of your mash and triple your output without any sacrifice of quality."

Anson studied the sketch. "You certainly have a way of putting things. I feel like the fellow who sat next to Columbus after he broke the egg."

The two men were shaking hands when Laly popped her head into the room. "Supper's ready, Daddy. It's snowing cupcakes outside. I guess Mr. Moerlein will have to stay all night. He can sleep between me and Quincia if he likes. Only there's more room in Aunt Solange's bed."

Laly darted out of the room to announce the sleeping arrangements.

Charles Moerlein attempted the offhand thing. "Your brother is away, I take it."

"My brother is dead," said Anson.

The long table in the kitchen had seven place settings that night. Anson and Solange faced each other from opposite ends of the clothless board. Moerlein, at Solange's right, shared a side of the table with Laly. The other three children, scrubbed and shining, occupied the other side. The wonderful aroma of roast pork, pleasing to gods, men (and essayists) whetted Moerlein's appetite as he accepted the blue-ringed crockery plate politely handed to him by Laly. Applesauce *du jour,* but instead of the usual roast potatoes, he saw upon his plate two *Kartoffelpfannkuchen.* Moerlein waited until everyone had been served. At the lift of Solange's fork, he sampled them.

Kartoffelpfannkuchen as Ermengarde had cooked them were the greasiest, most leaden of all edibles. These delicately browned cakes swimming in pork gravy surpassed anything of their kind ever cooked by a German Hausfrau. As light as crêpes Suzettes, they had lost their Teutonic heaviness and assumed a Gallic accent.

"Your *Kartoffelpfannkuchen* speak French," he said to Solange. By a lift of her dark lashes, she acknowledged the compliment.

"It is the language my mother taught them." Solange took her eyes away, and Moerlein had the feeling that she was a moon voluntarily traveling an orbit of her own choice.

Gingerbread and whipped cream for dessert. Laly and Reb cleared away and washed the dishes as Anson, Solange and Moerlein adjourned to the parlor.

The classic triangle repeating itself. The stranger with a touch of chancelleries in his walk regaled his host and hostess by relating anecdotes drawn from Cincinnati life and personalities. If not precisely cosmopolitan, he represented the outside world of culture. Without pretense at name-dropping, Moerlein spoke of Bernhardt's "final" tour. Of music, of the great flood occasioned last year by the rising of the Ohio to record heights. Feminine modes, civic corruption, Cincinnati's struggle to hold its place on the commercial scene, were touched upon briefly.

Solange finally asked, "Do you happen to know a lady named Stella Battle?"

"I knew both Stella and her husband very well. Enoch Battle gave me my start in business—and Stella's benefactions are a matter of common knowledge. She will be missed by Cincinnatians in every walk of life."

"Will be missed? What has happened to her?"

"She died two weeks ago. I had the honor of being one of her pallbearers."

"Stella dead? Oh, *c'est dommage.*" Memories of the eccentric, vain, but essentially goodhearted old woman flooded into Solange's voice.

"Did you know Stella?" asked Moerlein.

"I was her . . . companion for more than a year. Vieux-temps was a refuge for me in a time of trouble."

"You may be interested to know, then, that Vieuxtemps is being sold by Mr. Durkee Pyne to settle the estate." Moerlein could have supplied further information regarding Durkee Pyne's intentions because that cash-hungry gentleman, the residuary heir, had found himself cut off with a mere $5,000 a year and title to Vieuxtemps. In his attempts to peddle the property, he had approached Charles Moerlein without success.

"Next week," said Moerlein, "the furnishings and art treasures of the late Stella Battle are being sold at public auction."

Solange thought of the bronze head done by the French sculptor, M. Feinture. How had the ringlets come out? Probably she would never know. *Ou sont les neiges d'antan?* And did it matter whether the bust survived the city?

"There was a portrait bust of Stella . . . If by any chance . . . No, it is too much to ask."

Charles Moerlein contemplating the full-figured woman resolved that "chance" would have little to do with the fulfillment of Solange's request. His fine brown eyes restored momentarily on the profile of this woman who would grace any home. His meditations were broken by a knock on the door. It was Laly hopping up and down with excitement.

"Aren't we going to play any games? My favorite game is Omnibus," she confided to Moerlein.

Omnibus turned out to be a home-made variation of Musical Chairs. "It goes this way," explained Laly. "I start telling a story and when I say, 'All Was Confusion,' everyone tries to sit in someone else's chair." With this explanation, the little mistress of ceremonies began her tale.

"Once upon a time, a stagecoach was crossing the dusty plains between Landmark and the, oh . . . oh, the Rocky Mountains." (Laly was giving herself a wide stage.) "The driver, a handsome, dark-bearded man—" she gazed at her father—"saw that the bridge just ahead of him was broken. Instead of stopping, he cried, 'Git along,' to his eight horses. He was a very kind man, and he raced across the bridge, almost reaching the further bank when the hind wheel fell off the stagecoach and—" demurely she smoothed down her pinafore—"all was . . . saved."

"She'll false-alarm you to death," whispered Anson to Moerlein.

"Again, the eight-horse vehicle raced across the prairies, inhabited by Indians, Sioux, Potawatomis, and forded rivers swollen by floods, until it came to the Grand Canyon. 'How beautiful!' exclaimed one of the passengers. Then, for no reason at all, the omnibus plunged over the rim of the abyss and All Was Confusion!"

Moerlein, fascinated by the child's dramatic narrative style, found himself caught in a swirl of migratory chair-seekers. They darted past, around and under him. Only one chair was vacant: he and Solange simultaneously started for it. Gallantry and the spirit of competition met head on. Moerlein slid into the empty seat and a second later felt the delicious heft of a full-grown woman sitting on his lap. The woman was all curves, laughter and gaiety. Who could blame Charles Moerlein if, in the spirit of play (play? what kind of play?), he momentarily hugged her?

Moerlein's first action on returning to Cincinnati was to make a firm offer of $35,000 for Vieuxtemps.

"That's fifteen thousand below my asking price," whined Durkee Pyne. "Why, the art objects alone will net me . . . a . . . ah at least . . ." Stella Battle's residuary heir found himself holding a pair of treys. "At least . . . well, a good round sum."

"The art objects, excepting the bronze bust of your late lamented aunt—which I want for personal reasons—will fetch exactly four hundred dollars."

"I'll settle for that," said Pyne.

Charles Moerlein counted out five one-thousand-dollar goldbacks. "Here's the down payment on the house. And here's four hundred dollars for the furnishings. When the title search is completed, you'll get the remainder."

The next item on Charles Moerlein's agenda was to send a large box containing gifts to every member of Anson Woodhull's family. Dolls of bisque and gingham, rubber balls, variously colored, jackstones, jackknives, jumping-jacks, the new game called Parchesi and a set of children's classics bound in buckram—these were some of the things in the box. To Anson, Moerlein sent a French briar pipe. And to Solange? Yards and yards and yards of dress stuff: velours, satin, plain and richly brocaded; silks in fruity shades—puce, framboise, nectarine; woolens black, gray, olive and a red halfway between poinsettia and flame color; together with spools of thread, papers of needles, a gold thimble and picot-edged shears. And when the box was opened—well, for at least a half-hour, "All was confusion."

Three weeks later at the closing of the Vieuxtemps deal (in the presence of three attorneys for both parties) Moerlein handed Durkee Pyne a powder-blue check for $30,000. Scratching of signatures, attestations, seals, handshaking all around.

"If you don't mind telling me," asked Durkee Pyne, "what are your intentions regarding Vieuxtemps? Plan to live there?"

Moerlein lowered his voice confidentially. "Bought it as a speculation, Durk. Pure speculation."

The common definition of speculation—"to make an investment involving risk, but with hope of gain"—was intelligible to Durkee Pyne. Lost upon him, however, were some dozen synonyms for pure: "absolute," "chaste," "clean," "clear," "continent," "genuine," "guileless," "incorrupt," "real," "spotless," "true," "unadulterated," "upright" and "honorable."

Focus these terms upon the image of a woman in a black merino dress; let the woman be emotionally mature, physically beautiful and eligible for marriage. Add an element of uncertainty as to where her heart secretly feeds and the male lodestone which may hold her in orbit (how could a woman live in the same house with Anson Woodhull without loving him?), balance these natural doubts and fears against the knowledge of one's own power to attract—and you arrive at Charles Moerlein's special use of the term "pure speculation."

As an honorable man must, Moerlein made a formal request to Anson while visiting Landmark a month later.

"May I have your permission to court Mrs. Solange Woodhull? My object is matrimony."

"Solange's heart is her own," said Anson.

NYMPH AND BASS

MAY 1885 WAS A MONTH of personal misery for Anson Woodhull. Zarah's prolonged absence had put his fidelity to a cruel test; more painful yet, Charles Moerlein, a rich, full-blooded male, was paying honorable suit to Solange. He was coming that very afternoon "to inspect the new still," as he said in his letter. Afterward, he'd take Solange for a drive, expose her to the radiance of his personality, wealth and undoubted affection until—drenched and softened—Solange would say "Yes" to a question that Anson could never ask.

To escape the torment of watching Solange step into Moerlein's carriage, Anson jointed together his bamboo fly rod and sought refuge along the banks of Paddle Creek. He would fish out his agony—alone.

Paddle Creek was an unusual stream for the Midwest—not a sluggish, brown-clouded haunt of catfish and mud turtles, but a clear, flowing body which drew its substance from the limestone caverns along its course—cool, mineral-free water that gave Anson's whiskey its special flavor. With his fly rod, he became one with the stream's clarity, its shaded pools dimpled by rising bass. He enjoyed the subtle rhythms of fly-casting and the incomparable thrill of playing a strong fish on a seemingly fragile wand of bamboo.

Anson plunged into the afternoon's fishing with the directness of fleeing men. He started casting instantly, whipping the long line back and forth as a rhythmical release for his mounting intensity. Legs in the mothering stream, he worked his way toward its source, a deep pool shaded by birch and sycamores about two miles from his home.

Anson creeled five bass. Content with his catch, he lay face downward on the grassy river bank and peered into the depth of the pool to watch the drama of life and death unfolding under his eyes. The afternoon was waning; it was the hour when small crustoid creatures known as "nymphs" made their bid for twenty-minute metamorphosis into May flies. How few lived to enjoy that ephemeral happiness. And there at the bottom of the pool, Anson saw the May fly's chief ememy: a huge bass, leviathan of its kind, keeping his place in the current by the merest fluttering of his tailfins. Small, inert organisms floated past: the bass ignored them. Facing upstream, with ceramic eyes, he gazed stolidly inward at the centuries.

In the quiet water close to the bank, Anson saw a small form struggling upward. The nymph! On gaining the surface, it would break out of the crustoid bondage where it had been confined for three years and emerge as a May fly. Gauze-winged, purified and totally absolved of the instinct to eat, the nymph would devote its brief lifespan to dancing above the stream; then, after a moment of procreative love, its destiny was to fall exhausted on the current.

The nymph struggled upward with spasmodic movements, its finlike tail propelling it with the urgency of a microid mermaid hungry for air. The nymph, impatient of gills, was eager to reach the rarer element where the promise of lungs and wings should be fulfilled. How else justify the years of cloistered life under stones and silt, waiting for the periodic moults from one shell into a larger, until, of a May evening, a giant urge would propel her upward? Through treacherous clearness, exposed to ravening fish and birds, her unopened wings quivered under the shell on her back. More than anything else in the world, it was important to gain the surface, emerge from her shell and flutter upward, her virgin eyes searching the trees and sky for her winged lover.

Anson allied himself with the fragile fly. Fervently he hoped that she might enjoy the precious moments of her maturity. He wished that somehow he could enclose the creature—give it sanctuary until its wings gave her the power of flight. Glancing cautiously toward mid-stream he saw the bass give an inward start. The creature appeared monstrous and unreal: motionless it waited, but there it was, natural enemy and finned Nemesis of the emerging May fly.

At the surface, the nymph, a perfect fly now, began to emerge from its cracked sarcophagus. Segment by segment, its perfect narrowing body followed by wisps of tail that tapered into spun air, the fly rested a moment upon the deserted shell, now merely a floating husk. Its wings expanded into a pair of minuscule sails, veined and translucent in their perfection.

Anson gave thanks for the beauty forming on the surface of the water. It would fly now. It must! The May fly gave a tentative flutter and stopped. Anson held his breath. He had forgotten that the creature must make a few trial efforts before gaining strength enough for sustained flight. Stronger this time. The wings began to vibrate; the fly rose in the air, fell, fluttered, rose and fell again.

Anson saw the bass closing the gap between life and death as the lovely creature struggled on the surface of the stream. Ready for flight, it started to climb, nearly straight up, its body arching and straining, head lifted toward the trees and sky.

The May fly's season of love had begun!

The surface of the stream bulged and broke; a mighty

bronze force leaped upward, gills gleaming. The bass struck, then fell back into the stream, the May fly in its jaws.

Something had to live, thought Anson. He rose from the mossy bank and took his way downstream; field and forest drowsed in the heat of an Indiana afternoon. Turning a bend, he saw his house in the distance, its green blinds drawn against the hazards of the sun. Moerlein would be arriving soon; Solange was probably dressing for him now, going through the feminine ritual of beautifying herself for another man's eyes. Honorable eyes, virile eyes, possessive eyes. Charles Moerlein was a good man, yes—but he was *another* man and his intention was to take Solange away. He had bought a big house for her in Cincinnati. In some room of that house, he would . . .

Against a green backdrop of sycamores, Anson saw a flash of white: ankle deep in pebbly shallows, a woman was wading toward him. It was Solange, nude; in one hand she held a cake of soap. With the other she pulled the pins from her hair. The pool began to deepen. When the water climbed to her mid-thighs, she paused, put the pins in her mouth, lifted her arms and started soaping her body. Another step and Anson heard the sharp intake of her breath as the water swirled with exquisite coolness around her secrets.

Until this moment, Anson had never seen Solange in the nude. Now he beheld, in unexpected detail, her high hips, slender waist, full pear-shaped breasts, nipples pointing up and sideways—the prime proofs of mature womanhood.

She turned slightly; Anson saw in profile that unbelievable curve beginning just below the shoulder blades, which forms the inverted question mark of the eternal feminine silhouette.

The responses that a normal man makes to a beautiful nude body are well known. Anson's eyes conveyed to his nervous system the traditional blood quickening. A desire not incomparable to that of the bass leaping for the May fly surged momentarily through him. Knowledge that the satisfaction of his hunger was impossible held him immobilized. Even the wish to prolong the joy of looking was, by the unspoken rule of chivalry, impossible.

Anson Woodhull was neither a bass nor a peepjack. The laws of love were not the laws of death. And Solange would soon be claimed in marriage by Charles Moerlein. . . .

Anson stored up the beautiful and unexpected vision in his memory and turned away.

9.

PORTRAIT OF A WOMAN

THE ELMS ALONG MARLBOROUGH STREET, putting forth the lemony-green foliage of early June, marked the re-awakening of Zarah's emotions. For months she had lain quiescently in a sunny bedroom, on the garden side of Cousin Lyman's home; she was neither violent nor disoriented. She knew, for example, that she had a husband named Anson, two daughters and an infant son who were living in a state called Indiana. But whether they lived or died—and this had been the saddest part of Zarah's ailment—concerned her not at all.

By some strange process, her emotions had been split off from the rest of her personality. She accepted food when it was given to her and retained control (thank God) of her eliminative sphincters. But Cousin Lyman's attempts to penetrate the shell that she had fashioned between herself and her past were unavailing.

Once (how long ago?) Cousin Lyman had gently lifted her chin and said, "Zarah, dear, tell me something about your feelings."

"There is nothing to tell."

"Do you remember Anson? Your children?"

"Yes."

"Wouldn't you like to see them again?"

Slow tears welled up into Zarah's green eyes. But no words accompanied them.

Gradually she began to emerge from the self-created retreat of her illness; she combed her hair and wandered into the small garden behind Cousin Lyman's house. The flagrant visual assault of peonies reminded her that earth was entering upon the cycle of its sunwise turn. Flowers had always been Zarah's special care; between her fingers she examined an unfolding iris and marveled at its procreative secrets symbolizing a mystery almost forgotten in her own life. She tried to recapture the memory of that secret by inhaling the fragrance of the bursting flower.

In vain. Forlorn to the point of melancholy, she returned to her room.

Next day she was out again with a trowel, transplanting a clump of dagger ferns, neglected, overshadowed by showier blossoms. On her knees she dug desperately among the fern roots, lifted a clump of earth to her nose, hoping to catch some echo of the familiar scent. Fortunate the woman who knows the pungency of fern roots! Nothing in the world so resembles the odor of semen. But the moist suggestive odor did not come. Frustrated, acutely aware of a deadness in herself, Zarah felt like a woman striking the keys of a harpsichord that evoked no sound.

"Wait, wait," advised Cousin Lyman.

His professional sense told him that the gathering thunderheads were about to burst. But when, how, and from what quarter the fury-charged spark would ignite Zarah's wish to live again—with all the senses, passions and functions of a woman—Dr. Lyman Allston could not tell.

That spring everyone was talking about Henry James.

Zarah had known the younger James boy as a visitor to her father's house, a restless, full-lipped young man who had just begun to make a reputation for himself by contributing articles and stories to the *North American Review*. Most of the young men had gone off to the war, but Zarah remembered that Henry James had been unable to pass the physical examination as a soldier (exactly why, she never knew). Now it would appear that this strange "James boy" had become a famous writer. His latest novel, *The Portrait of a Lady*, was fluttering the literary dovecotes not only on Brattle Street but wherever novels were read.

Turning his back on America as uncouth and lacking in culture and tradition, Henry James had spent the last fifteen years in Europe, and the fruits of his observations were contained, so everyone said, in his full-length study of an American girl taking on the challenge of a European marriage.

Zarah decided to read the novel, and Cousin Lyman fairly leaped to the bookseller's shop to get her a copy.

The most amazing thing about *The Portrait of a Lady* was the fact that an American could have written it at all. True, Hawthorne's *Marble Faun* had depicted Italian scenes; but poor Hawthorne seemed a mere journeyman-carpenter when compared with the fine cabinetry of James's rich style and his apparent intimacy with the continental mode of life.

The man must be a chameleon, thought Zarah, as James launched into his highly detailed description of the English landscapes and architecture, of the grand houses bordering the Upper Thames. Lawns, foliage, furniture—all these were handled with a fondness that the true artist either sincerely feels or else simulates by virtue of his genius. Although the material was not precisely new, Henry James had seen it from the fresh point of view of an American, an American who deliberately aspired to be, live and feel as one to Europe born.

As for the people encountered in *The Portrait of a Lady*, Zarah felt almost immediately that they came off less successfully. James was, to be sure, an exquisite draftsman, but his characters had the quality of flat drawings, composed of outline and indication, instead of flesh and blood. Isabel Archer, the generally admired heroine, represented a new departure in American fiction. That is, she had departed from her native city of Albany, and by a kind of fairy-godmother machinery was next discovered in the midst of British high society with a lord at her feet and a title within her grasp. It required considerable faith on Zarah's part to believe that Isabel Archer actually possessed the gifts ascribed to her by Mr. James. Nothing in Isabel's conversation or manner toward Lord Warburton seemed to warrant the nobleman's offer of marriage. You simply had to take Henry James's word for it—and most of the words weren't very convincing.

Every reader who has felt the searching power of love is inclined to be impatient with any literary expedition that merely cruises about the coast. While the vast continent of a woman's feelings lay waiting to be explored, Mr. James seemed content to sail from one port to another, avoiding even the shoreline of reality. Thus, although he transported Isabel first to Paris, later to Florence, Zarah found his heroine's travels about as exciting as a ship's log. Zarah decided that her own honeymoon on the *River Queen* was easily a thousand times more exciting than Isabel's various embarkations. In spite of Isabel's sexual timidity, it occurred to Zarah that certain areas of identification might be established between Isabel's voyaging and her own. Mr. James's heroine had crossed the Atlantic; Zarah had gone inland toward the heart of America. Both could claim to be pioneers; both were seeking the prize of marriage, and both had found it. But, oh, the difference in the men they had ultimately married!

Gilbert Osmond, dilettante, poseur, parasite, pretending to live only for aesthetic ideals, while in reality scheming for the advantages of wealth and social position, seemed to Zarah the last man in the world that any free-spirited American girl would choose to marry. Yet Isabel Archer had voluntarily stepped into the trap of this improbable union. Why she had done it was one of those unexplained mysteries that Mr. James felt obliged to perform behind a screen. With all his verbal dexterity he didn't dare to do it in public.

It mattered little to Zarah what devices the author had employed. She knew only that Gilbert Osmond was a monster and Isabel Archer a deluded simpleton. And how did she know these things? Simply by laying the stylishly false novel against the verities of her own life with Anson Woodhull. Where on the pages of Henry James did husband and wife embrace? Not that Zarah wanted peepjack details of the mating ritual. Yet, if *The Portrait of a Lady* was supposed to be a story concerned with marriage, what evidence existed that the marriage was ever consummated?

The evidence appeared casually in a single line: "Isabel had lost a child."

Mother of God! *Isabel had lost a child.* Just like that! How could any woman who had ever conceived a child, carried it, borne it, nursed it, be put off by such an outrageous dodge? And how had it come about that literary critics praised a novelist who dared palm off such a monstrous deception?

Memories of her own lost son, the miniature perfection of his fingers, toes, the roundness of his little arms, the eager suckling of his lips, swept over Zarah's defenseless nervous system. She hurled *The Portrait of a Lady* through the closed window and flung herself sobbingly on the bed. Tears, pressing hard against the gates of her emotions, forced open the locked reservoir of grief. And accompanying the tears, another flood broke, too.

Through the shattered windowpane poured a tidal wave of odors: lilac, freshly dug ferns, roses and honeysuckle. The waves struck the membranes of Zarah's nostrils, entered her blood stream and were carried instantaneously to the long-parched secrets of her being. A thousand, five thousand, associations with Anson triggered her feminine longing. The caramel sweet of Laly's hair, the faint personal smell of Quincia's clothes, the sourish quality of Ozzie's breath; and the rank, overpowering stench of hogs that had originally loosed a flood of sensuality during the early days of her marriage.

Inseparably linked with the odor of hogs was the reek of raw whiskey. The once-horrible odor now possessed the fragrance of the life stream itself; it clung to Zarah's fingers and hair roots. It recalled her first glimpse of Anson propping up the bough of an overburdened plum tree.

Rising from her bed, Zarah wrote a long letter to her husband. She was about to sign it when Cousin Lyman's gentle knuckles tapped her door. Seeing the overturned chair, the broken pane in the French window, an expression of alarm crossed the doctor's face.

"What has happened, Zarah?"

"Temper, temper! Forgive me, Cousin Lyman. I've just pitched *The Portrait of a Lady* through the window. Add 'One pane glass, twenty-five cents,' to the million dollars that you'll never get for leading me out of the valley of desolation. And please find a two-cent stamp so that this letter to Anson will get off in the evening mail."

"As your physician, and for purely clinical reasons, may I see what you've written?"

Had Henry James seen the tears flow down Dr. Lyman Allston's cheeks as he read Zarah's letter; had he witnessed the quite unprofessional kiss that sealed Zarah's certificate of discharge; had he watched the physician roll his cousin to and fro in his arms, murmuring, "Zarah, darling . . . my truest woman, dearest triumph of love over death"—had Mr. James observed all this, he might have remarked rather snappishly, "It's unfair. These people are *touching* each other!"

Anson received Zarah's letter on June 10; the sight of her handwriting on the blue-gray envelope traveled like a slow-burning fuse from eye to brain, from brain to the nerves controlling his hands. A tremor shook him as he placed the letter in the pocket of his butternut jeans and walked toward the barn. What would the letter say? He closed the barn door, sat down on a nail keg, and slit the flap of the envelope with a jackknife.

"God have mercy on me," he murmured, then, withdrawing the letter, he opened it and read:

ANSON, DEAREST HUSBAND,

Eight months have passed since I last saw the face of my beloved husband and dear children, or had the will to turn my thoughts toward the home we shared. I remember almost nothing of those eight months except the tragedy that caused me to seek refuge in a shadow-world from which I began to emerge—thanks to Cousin Lyman's care—about six weeks ago. I cannot say that I am wholly free even yet of the dark terrors that walked beside me, but as my fears dissolve, I begin to remember how it feels to love again. How it feels to be a woman, a wife, a mother.

To feel the first pulse of this quickening energy, to dare hope that it will flow at full tide once more, are only a part of my desire to return to you.

About a month ago Cousin Lyman showed me the many letters that you wrote me during my illness. They had lain unopened on my bureau, but nothing of their warm tenderness was lost when I finally found courage to read them. Oh, that desolate Christmas afternoon! You are a great and good man, dear husband, and I hope soon to entrust my re-awakening life to your care.

I say this with full knowledge of the consequences that may follow upon my return to our home. What are they that I should fear them? The bearing of new babies? The daily labors that are a woman's lot? I never feared or objected to these and now more than ever I realize that they are my choice and my fate; I embrace them in prospect.

It was my thought—when I began this letter—to lay down certain conditions that would protect me and our children from exposure to the trade that you are engaged in. But I cannot offer you a conditional love, Anson. You may find it possible to change the conditions under which we shall live in the future. If not, I shall do my best to accept the fact of whiskey-making as part of the prior, unbreakable and everlasting contract between us.

The date of my actual return must be decided by Cousin Lyman. How wonderful it would be if you could meet me in Pittsburgh on the ninth anniversary of our

*marriage (do you remember the exact date?). We could
sail down the Ohio, and from the depths of a needy
heart, I promise you that the gifts we exchange on our
second nuptial flight will be richer, more deserved, than
the first.*

*Until I feel the comfort and security of your strong
arms once more, I am,*

> *Your loving wife,*
> ZARAH

All tremors vanished. With the exultation of a bridegroom
about to enter his chamber, Anson strode up and down the
barn. He slapped his four horses jubilantly on their rumps.
"She's coming back, she's coming back," he cried to the barn
swallows. For a moment he had the illusion that he could
leap from the barn floor to the timbers overhead and perform
a giant swing. Instead, he threw his hat into the hayloft,
opened his throat to let an almost-hysterical burst of laughter
set the barn swallows flying in the queen-trussed shadows
overhead.

These paroxysms over, he leaned against the corn crib and
wept.

Calmer now, Anson sat down on the nail keg and reread his
wife's letter, eagerly scrutinizing every syllable for any want
of lucidity or sign of false resolution. He saw none. Zarah
was whole again. This established, Anson gave the written
pages a more sober examination. The final paragraph was
everything that a husband-lover could wish. A second honeymoon happier than the first! But the most touching words in
the letter were: "*I cannot offer you a conditional love, Anson.
. . . I shall do my best to accept the fact of whiskey-making as
part of the prior, unbreakable and everlasting contract between us.*"

To perpetuate that contract, Anson realized, his wife must
never again be subjected to the sight and odor of whiskey in
the making. Zarah and her children must live henceforth in
the county seat where schools and social opportunities were
available. Within the next month, he must find a suitable
home in Landmark. . . .

Already Anson knew the house he wanted: a huge brown
structure at the corner of Grove and Sycamore streets. There
was a For Sale sign on the wide unkept lawn; in smaller letters the sign advised interested parties to apply for further in-

formation to: Gilbert Peaslee, c|o Landmark National Bank.

That very afternoon, Anson drove into Landmark to see Mr. Gilbert Peaslee.

THE HOMING FLIGHT

SEATED IN A BUTTERY-SIZED OFFICE at the rear of his banking house, Mr. Gilbert Peaslee riffled through certain items of "old paper" (the financial term for overdue or stagnant promissory notes). Much of this "old paper" had been endorsed by friends, fellow directors, local businessmen and Mr. Peaslee himself.

Item: Personal note in the amount of twenty-five hundred dollars bearing the signature of Charles Towner. Well, you could say this about Charlie Towner. He was a fellow director, owned a nice apothecary shop right next door, did a fair business and paid his annual 7 per cent interest. Still no reduction of the principal. What would the United States Bank Examiner say about Towner's note when he next dropped in to plumb the depth of paper swirling around the Landmark National Bank?

Item: Mortgage in the amount of three thousand dollars on the private residence of one T. Herbert Ainsworth, formerly a prosperous ship chandler (now deceased these five years and by his own hand too, or shotgun rather, just after his chief creditors had put him through bankruptcy).

How in the name of common sense had Peaslee ever advanced three thousand dollars on this fourteen-room monstrosity at a time when the demand for ship chandlery was dwindling toward extinction? Well, he had paid for his lack of perspicacity by taking a five-year loss of interest on the "Brown Elephant," as he called it. Long ago, the bank examiner had stopped listing it as a "questionable asset." Ainsworth's creditors had wiped it from their tablet of memory as a dead loss, and there the house stood, or fell apart rather, waiting for someone to do a salvage job on its decaying grandeur.

Peering through the shutters of his window, Gilbert Peaslee saw Anson Woodhull drive up in a light single-seater, tie his rig to the nearest hitching post and enter the bank. This Anson Woodhull had made increasingly large deposits during the past twelve months. A strict moralist might quarrel with the source of these deposits; Anson, son of Chance Woodhull, had turned distiller. He made whiskey! Privately, Mr. Peaslee believed that the road to hell was paved with empty whiskey bottles; yet, even though he himself was a teetotaler and a Church Elder, he had no objection if a profitable section of that road passed through his banking house. Strong drink might be an invention of Beelzebub, but its distillation and sale were *business*. If one could equate godliness with business success (an equation not infrequently made in America), it was apparent that the Lord's finger—well, his little finger anyway—was in Anson Woodhull's latest venture.

Mr. Peaslee's clam-shell ears could scarcely believe his customer's opening statement.

"I'm interested in that brown house at the corner of Sycamore and Grove streets."

Recovery and forward motion by Peaslee. "H-m-m . . . I ain't surprised. Valuable piece of property. Heart of residential section."

"I know. But it's badly run down. Tell me, how large is the mortgage?"

"Three thousand dollars."

"Well, I'll take over the mortgage at six per cent, put the house and grounds in good repair and amortize in twenty years."

Ordinarily a country banker can outsmart three horse-traders. Gil Peaslee, misjudged Anson's character by some 20,000 furlongs, went into his trading routine. "Got to have five hundred cash down."

Anson countered: "I'll pay you two hundred fifty down. It'll cost me a thousand to repair the place."

Advantage even, Peaslee entered a fresh demurrer. "Where's the thousand coming from?"

Anson drew a document from his inner pocket. "This is a contract with Charles Moerlein, the Cincinnati distiller. It specifies that I shall make ten thousand gallons of whiskey at fifty cents a gallon on or before December first of this year."

"Quittin' the farm?"

"No, just changing it into a distillery. I want the Ainsworth place as a home for my family."

"Mind if I look at the contract?"

Mr. Peaslee became a horse-dealer inspecting the teeth of a blooded mare. Going over the "points" of the document, he saw that it was a perfectly sound instrument under which Anson Woodhull stood to make five thousand dollars. Five thousand dollars! Avarice diggeth strange pits. Gil Peaslee, sworn enemy to King Alcohol, found himself dickering for a piece of sour-mash profit.

"I'm 'fraid the directors of the bank will want a lien on this contract," he wheedled.

"The directors of your bank will be damned glad to get the property off their hands," replied Anson. "There'll be no lien on my contract with Moerlein. Just transfer two hundred and fifty from my account to the credit of your bank and give me the title deed."

Which is exactly what Gilbert Peaslee—in the interests of liquidity—did.

The repair detail started work on the Brown Elephant July 15, 1885. Anson's scythe cleared away the tall grass and underbrush—uncovering in the process a fine example of a cast-iron faun, some neglected lilac bushes and the ruins of a half-acre lawn. Afterwards he mixed a tubful of white lead, linseed oil and turpentine, then assigned Reb and Sid Hawkins—a local house painter—to their stations.

"Slosh the priming coat on any old way" was his first directive. The dry shingles soaked up the paint like a parched sponge. The second coat, applied more carefully, gave the Brown Elephant a disappointingly flat-white complexion.

"I want it to glisten, Sid," explained Anson.

"Let it dry a couple of days," advised Hawkins; "the third coat'll make it look like a wedding cake."

While Reb patched the roof with new shingles, sawed off the gingerbread scrollwork along the eaves and puttied in new panes of glass, Anson inspected the inside of the house. The best features of the interior were a really good staircase, a mammoth living room and a conservatory. On the second floor were six sunny bedrooms, square and high-ceilinged, and two bathrooms, both needing repairs.

Standing with Solange in the midst of the uncurtained, furnitureless living room, Anson rubbed his long chinbone in dismay. "Wish I had the cash to make this place habitable. I'll either have to ask Moerlein for a bigger advance on the new batch of whiskey or bring Zarah home to an unfinished ark."

"Let me take care of it," pleaded Solange. "Charles will do anything I ask of him." Then, as if confessing an infidelity, she told Anson of her marriage plans. She wept. "Oh, my darling, my darling, forgive me!"

Remembrance of the solace this woman had brought him during the terrible winter of Zarah's absence, memories of the priceless love-gift she had offered him and his children, knowledge that she was now betrothed to Moerlein, caused Anson to take her in his arms. He kissed her wet lashes and the throat formed for love.

"Charles is honorable, handsome, rich and lonely. He needs you as much as . . . I did. You have every right to be happy with him as his wife."

"Will you keep a place in your heart for me?"

"Always, Solange."

The future Mrs. Moerlein turned practical. "How long is it since you've bought yourself a suit of clothes, a new hat, new shoes! Ten years, twelve perhaps? Anson, take whatever ready money you have, make yourself—how does one say?—*resplendent*. Buy a bijou for Zarah. I promise you, dearest, that Charles and I will make this house a place worthy of you and your bride."

How often in life does a man hear the magnified echoes of a love like Solange's?

On August 19, Anson boarded a train for Cincinnati. There he spent three days and eighty dollars outfitting himself with fine raiment and a Gladstone bag for the rendezous at Pittsburgh. For Zarah he selected a small gold watch and *fleur-de-lis* pin. Brimming with joy, impatient as the wind, he arrived in Pittsburgh two days ahead of time.

Striding up and down a wharf while waiting for a river boat to come in ahead of schedule is scarcely a rational way of spending one's time. But who expects a lover to be rational?

One of the most difficult scenes that men and women are obliged to play is the face-to-face encounter after a long absence. Repetition of what has happened before under similar conditions; a natural tendency to overplay their parts; the possibility (always present) that either, or both, of the players has changed—all these tend to make a man and woman nervous, false-voiced, *afraid*.

How *does* one greet a life returned? With smiles, tears, kisses, as preludes to those deeper satisfactions which inevitably must follow? All reunions begin differently; but few mature persons can doubt what happens when a man closes the door of a six-by-ten cabin and faces the woman he has longed for during fearful months of absence.

Within twenty minutes after the meeting of Zarah and Anson, all preconceived notions of decorum, fear and reticence disappeared. Zarah became a swirling tumble of lace flounces and feminine gear in Stateroom 18 of the *Great Republic*.

"Isn't it strange," said Zarah afterward, "that a man and woman can't really *say* anything to each other until . . ."

"Talk, my love," said Anson, "tell me, tell me, tell me all."

Luxuriating in Anson's arms, Zarah told him of Lyman Allston's patience and kindness. She described the big house on Marlborough Street. "It has a conservatory, large square bedrooms and thick carpets on the floor."

"Fine things, all of them," said Anson. "Some time we'll have them, darling."

Zarah spoke of Professor Osgood's death, shielding the fact that he had been for years a secret alcoholic. "President Eliot himself delivered the eulogy. I have a copy of it somewhere in my luggage."

"Did you see your mother?" asked Anson.

"Yes. She has grown to be a very sweet woman. She sold the Brattle Street house at a fabulous profit, bought an annuity with it, and, oh, darling, she gave me five hundred dollars!"

"Everyone loves you, Zarah. But it's my turn now."

The sleep that follows love gives new strength to lovers.

The *Great Republic*, wearing her cracked-gilt finery like an ancient belle, bore Anson and Zarah downstream. The ship was practically empty; no brass band, no gamblers, no feature of their first honeymoon remained. But as *La belle rivière* enveloped them in its mystery Zarah fulfilled that paragraph in her letter which promised a second honeymoon, better than the first.

She was a calm, poised, humorous woman when the *Great Republic* nosed into a dock bearing the fingerpost "Landmark 6 miles." Reb Plaskett met them with the fringed surrey. He was holding a nosegay of jacqueminot roses—a trifle wilted because he had been clutching them in his hand for three hours.

"It's awful good to have you back again, Mrs. Woodhull. We had some lonesome times." Reb's spirit climbed as he presented the bouquet to Zarah. "Laly says these are the sweetest-smelling roses there are."

Zarah inhaled the perfume of the flowers. "They're sweeter than you know, Reb."

Afterward they drove along familiar roads until Reb took an unexpected turn. Now they were driving up the broad tree-shaded streets of the county seat. At the corner of Grove and Sycamore, Reb pulled up.

"Whoa."

The thing that Zarah saw was a vision fulfilled. A white house, mansarded, with an iron deer in the center of a green lawn and an American flag fluttering from a new flagpole. On the steps of the house her children stood for a moment in white dresses, then ran down the gravelly path crying, "Mama, Mama!" Hugs and kisses from Laly, Quincia and Ozzie.

Puzzled, Zarah turned to Anson. "What are the children doing here?"

"They're here because this house is theirs, yours, *ours.*"

Zarah's eyes dazzled. "It's like a wedding cake."

"Wait till you see the conservatory and the big square bedrooms. Come in, Zarah darling."

Solange and a handsome gentleman were standing on the verandah. Zarah and Solange exchanged embraces; then Solange introduced her companion.

"Zarah, I should like to present Mr. Charles Moerlein, my fiancé."

Too full for speech, Zarah murmured felicitations. The gentleman bowed and stepped aside as Zarah entered her new home.

Anson started to say, "It isn't furnished quite the way I want it yet. . . ."

"Why, everything is perfectly beautiful!" exclaimed Zarah. She gazed wonderingly at the fine carpets, richly upholstered furniture and Feuerbach grand piano that had been moved in from Vieuxtemps during Anson's absence.

Solange, finger to her lips, smiled a naughty-girl smile. And Charles Moerlein beamed at the handsome woman who would soon be his wife.

PART THREE

Grand
Right
and
Left

1.

SYCAMORE ACADEMY

PROBABLY NO PEOPLE in this world's troubled history
were on better terms with the *status quo ante* than the
fortunate few who lived in the big houses in small towns of
the Middle West between the years 1885 and 1900. Time
made a quiet sound as it strolled unhurriedly down maple-
shaded streets; a special sun shone on the big white houses
with wide lawns inhabited by cast-iron deer, Newfoundland
dogs and flagpoles topped with a gilt ball. Behind these
houses the lawns ran into tall grass or a fruit-bearing orchard
until you came to a white picket fence or perhaps a grape
arbor, the unmurmurous haunt of boyish pilferers on summer
eves. There was a great deal of space, vacant lots, even fields
of corn, potatoes and string beans between the houses. In
summer the unpaved roads were dusty and the fields simmered with north temperate heat; autumn meant tons of
deciduous leaves falling in motley reds and yellows. Boys
raked them into great heaps, struck a sulphur-tipped match,
and the air was filled with the lovely odor of burning leaves—
once inhaled, never to be forgotten.

Oh, it was a grand time to grow up in—if you lived in one
of the big houses or if your father owned a little business
which netted three or four thousand dollars a year. Yet, as
Zarah Woodhull soon discovered, mere residence didn't constitute a patent of nobility. Especially if your husband made
whiskey. Under the local option system, Landmark, like
many other towns in Indiana, had outlawed the barroom.
Although much good whiskey was made in the state, little
was consumed within its borders. The White Rosette, insignia
of the W.C.T.U., transcended even the cross as the symbol of

enlightened Christianity. The predominant tone of the town was Baptistical. Zarah, an Episcopalian with Unitarian tendencies, could not in good conscience expose her children to the brimstone oratory of the Reverend Leroy Ellsworth. At some point in his theological development, the Reverend Ellsworth had substituted the tobacco plant for the apple tree. Eve, it would appear, had led Adam astray after intoxicating him with a spirituous liquor distilled by the Serpent himself. As for card-playing, a man had better be cast into the ocean with a millstone around his neck than be caught playing whist.

In lesser matters, one was permitted a certain latitude. There was, for example, the matter of selecting a piano teacher. You could choose between Miss Pendleton or Miss Quimby. Zarah played the piano much better than either of these decayed virgins; she might have elected to coach her own daughters at the Feuerbach grand, yet in the interest of diplomacy, she interviewed Miss Quimby and started Laly and Quincia at the full fee of seventy-five cents an hour.

The dressmaker of choice in Landmark was Fessie Bonesteel, who had made bridal and mourning gowns for the Landmark elite ever since the Battle of Bull Run. At cutting taffeta, Miss Fessie's shears had never known or even suspected the existence of a rival. Moire, ditto. The fact that her gowns hung like sheet metal apparently made no difference to the women, perhaps thirty in number, whose fingers loosened the purse strings of Landmark. Solange, blindfolded, and with one hand tied behind her, could cut and drape cloth better than Fessie Bonesteel. But Solange, alas, was living a *grande dame* life of her own in Cincinnati. To Miss Fessie, then, Zarah turned as a prelude to social advancement.

The success or failure of her entire campaign depended upon the acceptance of the Woodhull children as day students at Sycamore Academy. Zarah made a frontal attack by sailing into the office of Headmaster Egbert Clavering and raking him broadside with the full fire-power of her Cambridge diction. In all his years as headmaster of Sycamore, Egbert Clavering had never heard anything resembling the elegance of Brattle Street English. He had never met the daughter of a Harvard professor. (Even in the lowest academic circles, these things count.)

The interview between Zarah and Dr. Clavering was a reprise of the interview between Louella Osgood and Minerva

Higginson, proprietress of the Grange. It was the paradigm of all interviews between a socially ambitious parent and the headmaster of one of the penny-pinching private schools that were springing up throughout the U.S. as a response to leisure-class demand.

Had anyone bothered to examine Egbert Clavering's academic credentials, he would have discovered that his title of "Doctor" was dubious, honorary, nonexistent or self-imposed. Actually, he had spent two years at a Biblical seminary preparing himself for missionary work among the unwashed paynims and might have gone on to fulfill his destiny as spokesman for the loincloth in lower Zambesi, Outer Mongolia, or Upper Nigeria, as the case might be, except that Fate had played a cruel trick on Egbert by making him share a hymnbook with Emmaline Bowser at a W.C.T.U. revival meeting in 1870. Unmelodiously, she carried the soprano part of "By Cool Siloam's Shady Rill" while Egbert put his puny diaphragm into the baritone. Thereafter, it was Brother Clavering and Sister Bowser, with never a kiss between, until Sister Bowser fell heir, at her father's death, to the only private school in Landmark County.

"Clearly God's hand is manifest here, Egbert. We can get married and bring the Word to the heathen right here at home."

"Let us reason together, Sister Bowser."

"Nay, let us pray together." She chose a text from the Bible, showed Egbert where to kneel—not to beat around Cock Robin's barn—and married him a week before the fall semester began.

In the course of fifteen years, the downy fluff on Emmaline Clavering's upper lip had become a frank mustache, and Egbert's receding hairline was covered by a roached toupee. Mysteriously, the hairpiece developed dandruff; at any rate, there was always a whitish powder on the narrow shoulders of Egbert's beetle-tailed coat. Acadamic defects were more than covered by the adroit use of a pince-nez with black cord attached, elastic clerical boots, a devotion to McGuffey and a knowledge of mathematics up to, but not including, quadratics. Egbert Clavering's only problems were how to keep the academy in repair, provide chalk, maps, heat and the lowest grade of yellow paper for his students.

The odd thing about Sycamore Academy was that it prospered. Mildly. It prospered because Egbert Clavering, *sans*

Latin, Greek, scholastic degrees or spinal fortitude, had somehow caught hold of an overriding truth that was beginning to take form in America. Without benefit of Thorstein Veblen, Egbert had worked out his own theory of the leisure class. Intuitively, he knew that a handful of Hamiltonian bourgeoisie (and a handful was all he needed) was getting ready to demand something better, finer and apart from Thomas Jefferson's unwashed mob. There was a good enough public school in Landmark, but a sprinkling of county families wanted conspicuous waste with a fence around it, a tradition behind it, and a gate in front of it. Egbert gave them a poor simulacrum of what they wanted, and they in turn gave him their children. Under the Clavering regime, Sycamore "attracted" a dozen boarding pupils from county families and some thirty day-students, who received a negotiable equivalent of nine years of grammar schooling.

Taking on the Woodhull children was one of those *quid pro quo* deals in which Dr. Clavering exhibited an unbelievable magnanimity in exchange for three hundred dollars. The girls were indeed charming, especially the older one, who offered to demonstrate with Portia's speech: "The quality of mercy is not strained," etc., etc.

Dr. Clavering interrupted Laly's "It is twice-blessed" with the remark "Yes, yes, I agree that Eulalia should enter with advanced standing. Let's say the third grade."

Quincia, enacting the part of a deaf-mute, must begin at scratch.

That evening Emma Clavering had words with her husband. "Do you mean to tell me that you've accepted three children belonging to a *whiskey-maker?*"

"For three hundred dollars," replied Egbert, "I'd accept six Hottentots, *without loincloths.*"

Attending school was no part of Reb Plaskett's plan. The freckled lad refused to take the academic bit between his teeth, until Anson had a man-to-man talk with him in the carriage house.

"School's all right for girls," said Reb. "You'll be needing me at the distillery."

"I know I'll be needing you, Reb. I'll need you more and more as time goes on. But if you can't read, write or figure, what use will you be when I need you most?" Anson went on. "There was a time in the United States when book learning didn't matter. A man's muscles and character were enough to pull him through the simple duties of running a farm. I don't say it is important to know who wrote 'Snowbound' or 'Lines to a Waterfowl.' But I do say this. Clean pronunciation, a knowledge of good grammar and neat handwriting will enable a man to take the station in life to which he's entitled. One of the saddest things, Reb, is to see a naturally bright boy like yourself dragging the ball-and-chain of manual service when he has a chance to break that chain. Someday I'll want to send you out on the road as my salesman. Yes, and there'll come a time when you'll manage the distillery, become my partner."

"I can't talk big words," said Reb.

"No one's asking you to talk big words. Just learn how to use the ordinary speech of ordinary men in the right way. Have you noticed how Mrs. Woodhull speaks?"

"Yes. I never heard no one else speak like that."

"Imitate her, Reb. Learn from her. Learn from Laly. Learn from Dr. Clavering—and you'll be able to walk into the presence of any living man—or woman—without fear."

"I'll do what you say, Mr. Woodhull. Only . . ." Reb became a shoe-regarding little boy.

"Only what?" asked Anson.

"Only this. No matter what I do, I'll never be good enough for Laly."

Anson put his arm around the scrawny youth. "It's too early to worry about that, Reb. Be as good as you can. If Laly doesn't think you're good enough for her, there'll be plenty of women who'll think you're wonderful."

"It won't be the same thing, Mr. Woodhull."

But for the next three years Reb fulfilled his promise to Anson. He learned from books.

Neither socially nor academically was the first day at Sycamore Academy a conspicuous success for any member of the Woodhull delegation.

It began badly when Quincia, unable to make the figure 2 on her slate, began to weep softly. Buck-toothed Miss Henshaw, having spent thirty years of her life teaching "numbers" to first-grade pupils, had forgotten how bewildering the reverse curl of a 2's tail can be. Nor was her annual wage of $187.00 any great incentive to patience.

"Girl, what are you crying about?" she snapped at Quincia.

"I can't make twos," said Quincia.

"Nonsense. Any Christian child can make twos. Here, it goes like this."

Quincia did everything perfectly, except that the tail of her 2 came out backward.

Was this Woodhull child stupid, willfully perverse, or mentally sodden by the fumes of whiskey? The last probably. No matter! A good boxing of her ears might slap the essence of 2-ness through the alcoholic fog. Miss Henshaw squared off for the corrective double slap. Too late. Quincia's quivering little bladder sphincter gave way. She wet herself. The evidence, a small puddle directly under her chair, began to spread.

"Stop it!" Miss Henshaw stamped her foot. "Stop it, I say."

"I can't," blubbered Quincia. "I can't." Ashamed, frightened, she buried her tear-stained face on the desk.

Titters from the other little girls and heartier masculine guffaws threatened to disrupt classroom discipline. Lest the foundations of Sycamore Academy be washed away by the spreading flood, Miss Henshaw lifted Quincia bodily from her seat and carried her to a dark closet labeled *Girls*.

"Next time hold up *one* finger like this." Miss Henshaw demonstrated. "If you want to go for the *other* reason, hold up two fingers."

"Yes'm," whimpered Quincia.

In the darkness of the water closet (that was what they called it at Sycamore), Quincia pondered the mystery of why she should hold up one finger while she was trying to make number 2.

Meanwhile, in another part of the academy, Laly, having covered fourteen laps in spelling and ninety-two in reading in Emmaline Clavering's grammar class, had earned the undying hatred of the headmaster's wife. Mrs. Clavering held that Janiculum (as employed by Macaulay in "Horatius at the Bridge") was a general. Laly maintained that Janiculum was a fort.

"Janiculum has fallen," quoted Emmaline. To buttress her argument, she recalled the pertinent case of General Stonewall Jackson, who had fallen at . . . er . . . ah—Shiloh, or was it at Chickamauga? Well, anyway, Janiculum was a general and Laly Woodhull was a brassy, self-assertive Jezebel up to no good. So ran the unwritten notations in Mrs. Clavering's little black book.

She took steps to separate Laly and that skinny Woodhull ward with the gingersnap freckles, Richmond Plaskett. They *communicated.* Not by whispering or passing notes. Exactly *how* Mrs. Clavering didn't know. Suspecting, however, that the communications flowed from the too-smart little girl to the older, ginger-haired youth, she placed Laly in the back seat of the back row in the farthest corner of the classroom and assigned Reb to first place in the "backward aisle," known as "Dunce's Row." The morning session drew to a close: Quincia was too wet, Laly too smart, Reb too dumb. The mingling of these elements with some twenty-five other personalities in the schoolyard at recess-time produced an explosion.

The first fusee went off when Gwendolyn Stires called Quincia "Pee-pee" and jerked one of her braids.

"Pee-pee" might have taken root as a permanent nickname if Laly hadn't heard the loathsome tease.

"Stop calling my sister that name, you hear?" Laly jerked the satin bow off Gwendolyn's hair and gave Gwendolyn the back of some quick knuckles. Gwendolyn's howl brought her big brother Wilmer lumping across the yard.

Wilmer Stires's addiction to penuche, fudge, jelly sandwiches and other saccharinous foods had developed his body (quite possibly at the expense of his brain) into an oafish 130 pounds. Almost fifteen, he was "repeating" the ninth grade in order to win the diploma that brought to all men these presents, etc.

"Whasha trouble, Gwen?" The syllables came out squshingly through a mouthful of penuche.

"She slapped my face." (Pointing to Laly.)

Out went Laly's chin. "She called my sister Pee-pee, and I'll slap her every time she does."

Under the chivalric code, even Wilmer Stires couldn't strike a little girl. He had in his possession, however, an alternative weapon. Quite willing to wound, he struck: "No wonder Pee-pee wets herself. It's the whiskey she drinks at breakfast. All you Woodhulls drink whiskey, I hear." Chorus of haw-haws.

"Where'd you hear that?" Reb Plaskett's freckles stood out like gingersnaps against a skin pallid with anger.

"All over," said Wilmer. From a cloud of Olympian fudge, he gazed down at the skinny youth. "Say, Bub, how tall are you?"

"Five foot, three."

"Didn't know they piled horse manure that high."

"Haw haw, ha-ha, ho-ho. Wilmer certainly is a card!"

Sixty seconds later he was a knocked down, much bloodied and pretty well beat-up card, with two front teeth missing. Of the four punches thrown by Reb Plaskett, two landed on Wilmer's face. A left hook doubled him up—not in laughter— and a right cross sent him down hard on his rump.

Reb wasn't even breathing hard when he asked, "Who's next as'll dare say the word *whiskey* around these parts?"

There were no takers. Neither Laly nor Quincia Woodhull ever heard the word *whiskey* mentioned again at Sycamore Academy. But there it lay just beneath the surface, a silent, unspoken, ever-present blight not only in the frog pond of Sycamore Academy but in the larger social stream of the town itself.

While Zarah played her role as mistress of the big house at the corner of Grove and Sycamore, Anson undertook the task of transforming his farm into a full-time distillery. Winter and summer he rose at six A.M. to make the seven-mile journey in a light buggy drawn by a gray gelding—a real stepper that could cover the distance in half an hour.

Soon the triple-chambered still would be under a full head of steam—and such a wonderful contrivance that still turned out to be! It pumped the beery mash from fermenting tubs directly into a 200-gallon copper kettle, thus eliminating the labor of hauling the mash by hand. As ethyl alcohol rose from the mash, it was redistilled (the technical term was "doubling"), and the impurity-cleansed liquor flowed into a large cistern packed to the brim with maple charcoal. Slowly it seeped through the charcoal at the rate of 200 gallons a day. In October and November 1885, Anson easily produced the 10,000 gallons called for by Moerlein's contract. Nor was the quality of the liquor inferior to the old pot-still product. Indeed, it had a greater uniformity and was remarkably clean and light. At Moerlein's request Anson made an additional 5,000 gallons in 1885. Total production: 15,000 gallons. Gross profit: $7,500.

Naturally, there were expenses. Anson had to buy corn from neighboring farmers at prices averaging twenty-five cents per bushel. Another item was the cost of new barrels. On the open market they cost a dollar, but Wool Hamer was glad to cooper up 300 barrels at seventy-five cents apiece. Anson foresaw the time when he must buy a barrel-making machine; for the present he was happy to give Wool the business.

The great queen-trussed barn, cleared of its agricultural past, became a storehouse in which the barrels of whiskey lay on specially constructed racks. No longer did Anson hold the key to his own barn. James MacMonnies, Federal gauger, padlocked the door and specified that iron bars be placed across its windows.

"Mind you," explained MacMonnies, "this new whiskey of yours isn't bonded. It must lay in the barrel two years before the proud green seal can be affixed to the barrel. Nor am I locking your barn because I distrust its owner." He winked a blue eye at Anson. "But 'it shall be the duty of the Federal gauger to padlock all premises wherein whiskey is stored, to protect such whiskeys from illicit withdrawal.'"

"I understand," said Anson.

It occurred to Anson that he might eventually make some whiskey on his own account, allow it to ripen until the coveted green strip stamp could be affixed. But not this year. There were too many other things demanding his attention.

The farmhouse must be remodeled; the kitchen would be an ideal malting shed; the living room where Zarah and he had spent so many happy parlor hours would become an office. To protect Zarah against any odor of whiskey that might cling to his clothing or person, Anson changed his clothing before commencing work and scrupulously bathed in Paddle Creek at the day's end, no matter what the temperature, to remove the odor that offended his wife.

"Tell me, darling," he once asked her in a tender moment, "does the smell of whiskey still cling about me?"

She pressed her lips into Anson's smooth-shaven cheek. "Not the slightest trace. But it wouldn't matter if it did."

Some two hundred and seventy days after Zarah had been tumbled on the narrow berth of the *Great Republic*, she gave birth to a male infant. It was a natural, easy delivery. Her milk gushed in streams from both breasts and the plenitude suffused Zarah with a feeling of triumphant femaleness —evident in the greedy little monster who bellowed every four hours for the life-sustaining nutriment of mother's milk.

Tug-tug-tug—that was the rhythm of it, the suckling instinct born into the human race, first for physical survival, later for psychic satisfaction, to be found (or grieved for) or placated with substitutes, but *tug-tug-tug.* That was it, until the little feeder lay glazey-eyed, full-fed, yet still unwilling to relinquish the source of his satisfaction.

Often while nursing her infant son, Zarah herself fell into a drowse, different somehow from the after-sleeping of love. Once she awoke from such a slumber to find the baby with her nipple still in his mouth and Anson kneeling beside her bed. Anson wasn't praying; he had knelt to observe at closest possible range this private arrangement under which Zarah had leased out, so to speak, an intimate part of herself to a stranger. For the time being Zarah's breasts were not Anson's property. Happiness enough that she was happy.

"If your contentment weren't so beautiful, it would be downright comical."

"You're jealous—isn't he an angel, Anse?"

"Wouldn't go so far as that. He just knows a good thing when he's got it."

"He" had no name as yet. "What shall we call him?" asked Zarah.

"I've always wanted a son named after my father."

And so, on June 1, 1886, the child was baptized Chauncey Adams Woodhull. Immediately after the ceremony everyone forgot his baptismal name and began calling him "Young Chance."

Viewed merely as volume in space, Young Chance was lucky. His cannon-ball head seemed to be screwed tightly onto a keglike torso; he had chubby limbs and a voice like a young Stentor. For the first three months he slept twenty hours a day; then, opening his eyes, he began to focus them on various objects in a world that was his for the clutching. Mother's breast; father's gold watch swinging like a pendulum above his nose; the rungs of his crib; a teething ring; an oilcloth rabbit—oh, a multitude of things made for the express purpose of being stuffed into one's mouth. Including that black rubber nipple. Roar till your lungs (or heart) burst, you ended up by taking it. That's the kind of decision They forced on you.

Chance was a year old now; he could stand on the palm of Anson's outstretched hand. Like Gulliver inspecting the Lilliputian Ambassador (or Joseph gazing at the Babe),

Anson held his infant son at arm's length. Feet planted on Anson's outstretched palm, Chance extended his arms like a tightrope walker and found his center of balance, smiling as if to say, "While your hand supports me, I cannot fall."

"Climb, son! Climb up my arm."

Leaving the safety of his father's hand, Chance ventured onto Anson's muscular wrist. Toes spreading to gain traction, up, up, he came, up across the palmar surface of Anson's forearm, then rested in the hollow of his father's elbow in preparation for the ascent of the mountainous biceps ahead.

A terrifying prospect! Should he quail, burst into tears? No. Magnetized by his father's confidence (and helped a little, too, by a guiding finger) the child came on until he stood exultantly at last on the wide plateau of Anson's shoulder. In this moment of triumph his head was higher than his father's.

"I think that's enough," said Zarah, snatching the child protectively. A few days later, catching them at it again, she realized that a boy child—*this* boy child, anyway—hungered for contact with masculine sinew as much as feminine softness.

Her breasts had served their purpose; they would be remembered (dreamed of, sought for elsewhere in manhood) but for the present the infant of her bosom must accept the challenge of becoming a boy. Like every other child, Chance would be obliged to find his place in the family, there to shine or be outshone—always with due consideration of the group to which he belonged—yet always contriving somehow, whether by stratagems, compromises or rebellion, to assert the separateness of himself.

As a latecomer, he encountered special problems best known to those who, gazing up the family ladder, find every rung occupied. It would have been easy to assume the baby role, to squeeze every ounce of advantage from Anson's favoritism and Zarah's maternal protectiveness. But there was nothing of the Benjamin about Chance. Scarcely larger than a doll, he renounced dollness; surrounded by petticoats, love (and rivalry also), he disentangled himself from the snares of passivity and met—without too much aggressiveness—circumstances as he found them. Of necessity he accepted Laly's brilliance and bossiness; Quincia's gentle pettings were part of the system too. Ozzie's advantage in size and weight were offset by Chance's greater agility—although he took his quota of fearful pummelings at first from Osgood's bullying fists.

His first teeth came in regularly and went out the same way—with the aid of a string yanked by Anson or Reb Plaskett. His mop of hair, wavy (not curly), was golden at first; then it darkened to a true auburn, thus escaping the less-attractive hues of cinnamon, carrot or brick. The early blueness of his wide-set eyes changed, at three, to luminous chestnut brown. He was neither stringy, pudgy, squat nor lank; a caricaturist would have found as little to work with as a valentine maker.

Young Chance was obedient but far from docile. Once, surrounded by Laly and her giggling playmates, he allowed his sister to put some "cute ringlets" in his hair. It was fun sitting on the verandah, the focus of big-girl attention, while they worked over him with combs and a curling iron.

"You look perfectly an*gel*ic," Laly assured him. All the other big girls agreed.

But Chance, gazing at himself in the mirror, didn't like the curls. With a pair of shears he marched into Zarah's presence and said, "Mother, cut these off."

"Why, Chance, they make you look very pretty."

"I don't want to be pretty. Either you cut them off or I will."

A command performance. Zarah obeyed.

Five minutes later she had a lapful of auburn ringlets. A little Samson, shorn, yet strengthened thereby, kissed her gratefully. "Thank you, Mama. Now I can start being a boy."

It was about this time, also, that Laly Woodhull, almost thirteen, began to suspect that she was an actress. If her suspicions were true, why shouldn't society enjoy—and applaud—her histrionic talents? For the past three years this question had been a very itchy hairshirt which became all the more itchy when Laly discovered a silky golden fuzz blossoming where none had blossomed before.

The appearance of this pretty *boscage* coincided with Laly's awareness that she had suffered an unforgivable suppression at the hands of Dr. Clavering and his wife, both of whom had said "No" (in assorted flats and sharps) whenever Laly offered to demonstrate her very real gift as an elocutionist. Dimly she realized that it was all part of a larger conspiracy by which the children of Anson and Zarah Woodhull

were regarded as second-class citizens by the teetotaling
aristocracy of Landmark County.

Late in the spring of her final year at Sycamore Academy,
Laly decided to break through this conspiracy. She put all
the pieces of her plan together, then went about the preliminaries of winning Dr. Clavering to her point of view.

Dr. Egbert Clavering was not a wicked man; he was merely
a forked carrot of a man who bore up with vegetable patience
under the strain of a nagging wife, a run-down school and
the problems—educational, disciplinary and just plain human
—of some thirty-five students, many of them girls. Little girls,
middle-sized girls, almost big girls. For fifteen-odd years
he had watched the little girls pass through various phases
leading to puberty; and when certain curvatures began to
appear, Dr. Clavering had to fight against a longing that
would be regarded by most mature persons as . . . well, as,
peculiar.

Impotent these many years, Dr. Clavering's "peculiarity"
sought gratification by means of a tape measure—an ordinary
yellow tape measure divided off into inches by big black
numbers beginning with one and ending with sixty. He carried the tape measure rolled up in the inside pocket of his
shiny frock coat, and took it out whenever his thoughts
turned to Azalea Larkin, Beulah Wiggins, Charlotte Tatspaugh, or any of a dozen girls who had contributed, in their
time, to the priceless data that Egbert Clavering was collecting, for a never-to-be-written paper entitled "The American
Adolescent Female: A study in Mensuration."

Phenomenal, that Tatspaugh girl! At fourteen, she had an
eighteen-inch waist, twenty-eight-inch hips, and a surprising
thirty-inch bustline. Dr. Clavering often re-created in fancy
that warm June afternoon when Charlotte, deficient in history,
geography, arithmetic and spelling, had lifted her pink
muslin dress for the most intimate measurement of all. No
deficiency there!

How grateful her parents had been when their red-haired
daughter had received a diploma!

On a particular afternoon in 1891, Egbert Clavering was
daydreaming of Charlotte's classic dimensions. Presbyopia
had thickened the lenses of his pince-nez but had whittled
nothing away from the headmaster's yearning to measure
a good stocky girl once more. As the hart panteth for the
doe, as the soul condemned to eternal flames longs for a

cooling draught, so did the headmaster of Sycamore Academy burn for an opportunity to wrap his tape measure around the thighs, bust and waistline of a nice big girl once more. Preferably Arlene Whipple.

Into this thicket of wish and dream walked not Arlene Whipple but Laly Woodhull, the second biggest (and by all odds the smartest) girl in Sycamore Academy.

No overwhelming desire to closet herself with Dr. Clavering had brought Laly into the headmaster's office. She was there for a Purpose. Peeping through the half-open door, she saw Dr. Clavering winding a tape measure around his bony forefinger. The shutters half drawn against the afternoon sun caused dust motes to lie in golden swathes. Silent all. Perfect timing. The school was empty. Mrs. Clavering was marketing in the village. Omens favorable—and the happiest omen of all was the yellow tape measure being drawn through the meditative fingers of the Great Mensurator himself.

Odd rumors clustered about Dr. Clavering's tape measure. Nothing specific. Mere whispers. The odd case of the Tatspaugh girl's diploma. Laly intended to find out why and for what purpose Dr. Clavering carried a tape measure. If her intuition were correct . . .

"May I come in?"

Startled, Egbert Clavering thrust the tape measure into his side pocket. The lust was on him.

"Why, yes, Laly." He indicated a swivel chair which had a demoniacal habit of tilting backward unless one were accustomed to it. Laly, sitting down, gave an unexpectedly generous exhibition of her underpinnings.

"I've come to talk to you about the program for the graduation exercises, Dr. Clavering."

"Ah, yes."

"There's barely three weeks left, you know—and it's such an *important* affair."

Laly's statement was incontestably true. The graduation exercises of Sycamore Academy were so important that they were held in the I.O.O.F. Hall—the only building in Landmark that contained anything remotely resembling a stage. By Baptistic tradition, dramatic presentations were taboo. Selected members of the graduating class said their pieces and tinkled on an upright piano to an audience composed of admiring parents, alumni and local celebrities.

Impressed by what he saw, Dr. Clavering said, "Yes, I've been making up a program."

While Clavering fished among the papers on his desk, Laly unbuttoned the three top buttons of her blouse. "It's so warm here." Leaning forward to examine the program, Laly exposed a cleft that certainly hadn't been there a year ago. "I've been working very hard on my Portia speech," continued Laly. "You know the one: 'The quality of mercy is not strained/ It droppeth as the gentle rain from . . .'"

"Yes, yes." Dr. Clavering temporized. For three years now he had held back the rising tide of Laly's elocutionary talents. Town sentiment (Dry) just wouldn't permit him to give this talented girl top billing on the graduation program. Roundhead hatred of play-acting raised the barrier still higher. And on top of everything else ran the spiked *chevaux de frise* of Emmaline Clavering's animosity. Her logic took the form of a sorites:

> Anson Woodhull makes whiskey.
> Laly Woodhull is Anson's daughter.
> Whiskey is amber-colored.
> There is an amber glint in Laly's eyes.
> Her hair is reddish yellow.
> Sorrel, they called it in a mare.
> Emma had once seen a sorrel mare being serviced.

Emmaline, adding up these facts, reached an overwhelming conclusion: "*You hear me, Egbert*—that Woodhull girl isn't *ever* going to take the lead in our graduation program."

Torn between Emmaline's ultimatum and a desire to test the docility of this sorrel-haired young minx, Egbert made a flank feint.

"I've put you down for the always popular 'Between the Dark and Daylight'—or maybe, 'I've Lost My Dear Kitty,'" said Dr. Clavering.

"But those are little-girl pieces." (Moue of disappointment.) "I've developed way past them. Haven't you noticed?"

"Well, now that you mention it, I do recognize certain signs of . . . er . . . growth. As to its extent and nature, they would have to be determined by scientific methods."

"I understand, Dr. Clavering."

"How long since your measurements were taken, Laly?"

"Ages and ages ago."

"Hm-m, well then. How old are you now?"

"Fourteen."

"Height?"

"Really, it sounds funny, but I don't know."

That did it! Out came the tape measure. "Stand against the wall, please. Eyes level. Heels together. Hm-m . . . five feet, two and three quarter inches!"

"Is that good, Doctor?"

"Quite within the norm. We must make comparative notations as we go."

Dr. Clavering opened the bottom drawer of his desk and drew out the diary of his delight—a combination of Pepys' journal and the Rosetta stone—a coded reminder of . . .

"Waist nineteen inches. An important finding. Lung capacity [meaning bust line] . . . Inhale. Deep. Hn-ah—a splendid thirty-two! From the waist up, you're a big girl, Laly. I trust the lower members won't prove disappointing."

"I hope not, Doctor. I'm so excited, I could . . . May I go to the Girls' Room for a moment?"

Dr. Clavering realized that every second was precious. Emmaline might return before the Great Mensurator completed his experiment.

"If you can possibly wait . . . we're coming to the most important measurement of all." Quivering of nostril, like a rabbit approaching a particularly toothsome bit of lettuce. "The patella to pelvic arch."

"What's a patella?" asked Laly.

"The knee. Stand on this chair, please, and co-operate by holding up your dress."

Shadows of blackmail-to-come lengthened in Laly's counterproposal. "Wouldn't it be better if you knelt down?"

"Angel girl!"

In assuming the posture of adoration, Egbert's pince-nez fell off the bridge of his nose. In a trice, Laly whipped off her lace-trimmed panties. Retrieving his glasses, Clavering implored, "Lift your dress again, Laly."

"*You* lift it, this time."

A fine ague, blent of fear and desire, shook Egbert Clavering. Lifting the double veil of muslin dress and cotton petticoat, he beheld at eye level the secret he had hungered so long, so desperately, to see. Tape measure forgotten in this moment of ecstasy, he gazed at the cloven mount covered with golden fuzz.

Tears for his own impotency—the life that might have been—fell from his oysterish eyes. Egbert was a pilgrim, yea, a mendicant, leaning forward to kiss a sacred relic.

"If you touch me, my father will strangle you," said Laly.

Terror at the knowledge of his own entrapment brought Clavering to his feet. He heard the wheels of Emmaline's carriage grinding up the gravel walk. As he turned to pick up the record book, Laly dropped her lace panties into the bottom drawer of his desk.

"May I go to the Girls' Room now, Dr. Clavering?"

"Yes, yes. Go, child, go."

With all the thumbscrews in her possession, Laly waited three days before re-entering the headmaster's office.

"Have you made up the program yet, Dr. Clavering?"

"Tentatively."

"Let me see it."

She studied the slip of paper, while Clavering bumbled, "You see, I've given you the Portia speech. 'The quality of mercy.'"

There was no mercy in Laly's voice. "It's not enough. I want to do Lady Macbeth, Juliet on the balcony, a translation from Racine and just a bit of Desdemona."

"But we have only ninety minutes," wailed Egbert.

"I can do them all in sixty-one minutes."

Clavering tried to bristle. "What gives you the authority to address me in this fashion?"

"Open the bottom drawer of your desk and you'll see."

A fumble of keys, and there under the cryptic ledger lay a pair of lace-fringed panties. Closer examination disclosed the name "Laly Woodhull" embroidered in silk thread along the waistband.

"How . . . how did these get here?" faltered the Great Mensurator.

"Perhaps Mrs. Clavering might know. Ask her in. She's right outside the door."

A change came over the headmaster of Sycamore Academy. Like Hans freed of his fabled grindstone, a weight fell from his shoulders. For the first time in forty-two years spent mostly in foot-swallowing, frustration and futility, he dared face the consequence of the foolish, but oh, so rewarding thing that he had done.

"Ask her in by all means. Expose me, Laly. But let me tell

you something first. You won't understand all of it and maybe you'll think that fear puts these words into my mouth. If you weren't the cleverest, schemingest, handsomest, most gifted girl I've ever seen, I'd feel guilty, ashamed. Well, I don't feel that way at all. The fact is, Laly, I'm grateful and glad about what happened the other day. Now call Mrs. Clavering if you want to."

"I don't want anyone else to know what happened, Dr. Clavering. All *I* want is sixty-one minutes on the Oddfellow's stage at graduation exercises. I've waited a long time. I *deserve* to be heard!"

The doorknob of the headmaster's office turned. Buck-toothed Emmaline Clavering had been listening.

"What *deserves* to be heard?" she asked.

Laly spun on the eavesdropper, declaiming:

Therefore hearken unto me, ye of little understanding:
Far be it from God that he should do wickedness,
And from the Almighty that he should commit iniquity.

"Come in, Emma," said the headmaster. "Laly is rehearsing a Biblical passage for the graduation exercises."

"Job, Chapter thirty-four, Verses ten to eleven," explained Laly parenthetically. "Then I skip to thirty-eight, sixteen to eighteen." She hurled a few questions at Emmaline Clavering.

Hast thou entered into the springs of the sea?
Or hast thou walked in the recesses of the deep?
Have the gates of death been revealed unto thee?
Or hast thou seen the gates of the shadow of death?
Hast thou comprehended the earth in its breadth?
Declare, if thou knowest it all.

Emmaline, having no knowledge of such matters, retreated.

Oddfellow's Hall was jammed to the eaves when Head-master Egbert Clavering, beetle-coated, toupee freshly roached, cleared his throat for the opening announcement. A two-ounce nip of Old Settler had given him a false jaunty feeling, best explained by the term *euphoria.*

"Friends, parents, fellow citizens," he began, "we mark on this occasion the twenty-sixth consecutive graduation exercises of Sycamore Academy. Mrs. Clavering, the teaching staff and myself are justly proud of the record established by the academy and its graduates—many of whom are in this audience tonight. To mention only a few, I see Congressman Lefferts and his charming wife. I see Judge Wayne T. Feakins, our eminent jurist, flanked by Mr. Gilbert Peaslee, our banker in time of need. The businessmen of our community are represented by Mr. Charles Towner, proprietor of our local pharmacy, Mr. Jasper Waldorp, the enterprising manufacturer of Waldorp's Saddle Polish. Yes, and among our business leaders, I see Mr. Anson Woodhull, accompained by Mrs. Woodhull."

There was a craning of necks, a virtual suspension of breathing. For the first time in Landmark history, distiller and business leader became synonymous.

"On previous occasions," continued Clavering, "our object has been to display a cross-section of the graduating class. Tonight, we shall depart from that tradition by devoting a full hour—sixty-one minutes to be exact—to the declamations of a single student who, by the display of her outstanding gifts, will renew in us those intimations of Truth and Beauty, lacking which er . . . er . . . um—" Egbert caught his wife's eye—"no nation can long endure."

"Ladies and gentlemen, I have the honor of presenting Miss Eulalia Woodhull."

Without footlights, props or any costume save the modest white muslin dress prescribed for sweet girl graduates, Laly took the center of the platform. Whatever effects she hoped to obtain must be wrought of pure histrionics. To shock her audience into submission, she threw her head forward and, with disheveled hair, became the most famous sleepwalker in literature. Imaginary taper in hand, she tottered across the stage, reciting the "Out, Damn'd Spot" scene.

"Rachel couldn't have done it better," murmured Solange to her husband.

Up from the hold of Laly's repertory, a swarm of characters came thronging. The mean platform of Oddfellow's Hall became Juliet's balcony. "Oh, Romeo, Romeo. Wherefore art thou, Romeo?"

Next the stage became the walls of Troy on which Helen tempted an outraged Menelaus to sink his dagger into her exposed bosom.

In turn, she was Titania, Pease-Blossom, Bottom. "I will roar you as gently as any suckling dove—I will play lion."

Finally as a sop to Headmistress Clavering, she belted out Jehovah's terrific rebuke to Job.

Time: 61 minutes, 4 seconds.

"More. Again." The audience loved it.

Charles Moerlein's *"Bravissimo,"* standing, brought them to their feet.

Laly Woodhull curtsied. Once more she became a little girl in a white dress and walked off into the wings.

After that Arlene Whipple's rendition of "The Happy Farmer" on an out-of-tune upright seemed somewhat less than soul-shattering. Nor did Gwendolyn Stires's handling of that ever-popular favorite "I've Lost My Dear Kitty" rattle the rafters of Oddfellow's Hall. As a matter of fact, everything after Laly's exit seemed anticlimactic. Which was just the way she had planned it.

Many questions were asked at the end of the performance.

"How did you persuade Dr. Clavering to give you so large a part of the graduation exercises?" asked Zarah.

"We talked it over, Mama."

Emmaline Clavering asked a question too. And for her pains, she got the flat side of a night jar smacked against her buck teeth.

The best families of Landmark didn't know what questions to ask. They stopped asking questions. The Woodhull family was accepted socially. Many mothers were glad, though, when Zarah, after taking counsel with Solange, decided that Rebecca Lansheer's Seminary for Young Ladies, in Cincinnati, would offer a wider stage, a larger horizon for Laly's talents.

Pledges were given, each and severally, by Solange Moerlein and Mrs. Lansheer, that they "would keep a special eye" on Laly's activities. In their time both women had seen dramatic talent in the bud; inferentially they agreed that they had never seen anything equal to Laly as an actress. Her superb physical equipment, her potentialities as a man-breaker, were not mentioned.

But everyone, including Zarah, felt that, yes, you *had* to "keep a special eye" on Laly Woodhull.

2.

RECTIFIER VS. DISTILLER

"Never try to own anything that you can't afford to lose."
Charles Moerlein was beginning to discover that Lucienne
Bisguier's farewell advice applied to whiskey as well as wom-
en. His desire to make, store and sell Hearthstone, a straight
four-year-old whiskey comparable to the best of Kentucky
bourbons, was—as his sales sheets demonstrated—being grati-
fied at a cost heavier than prudence, or even vanity, permitted.
For the past ten years, the public taste had been swinging
away from heavy-bodied, high-proof whiskeys toward the
lighter, neutral-spirit blend. In the spring of 1887, Mr. Moerlein had found himself with forty thousand gallons of Hearthstone in his warehouse, while unfilled orders for Old Settler
accumulated on his desk.

To discontinue the production and sale of Hearthstone was
painful to Charles Moerlein. It would rob him of his claim
to the noble title of distiller and write him down as an out-
and-out rectifier. If ever a term were more misleading than
rectifier, Moerlein had yet to discover it. In its purest dictionary form, *rectify* meant "to make or set right; to correct
from a wrong, erroneous or false state."

So much for the dictionary. In actual practice, a *rectifier*
(in the whiskey trade at least) was a despicable creature
who debased the original article with a cheaper product, mis-
labeled the mixture as "whiskey" and reaped an enormous
profit from the invincible ignorance of his customers. In
Cincinnati, center of the rectifying industry, scores of men
were doing the same thing—and were properly frowned
upon by proud, old-line distillers, centered chiefly in Ken-

tucky, Pennsylvania and Maryland, who obstinately refused to tamper with the contents of their patrician barrels.

Charles Moerlein had his pride too. It centered in Hearthstone, a prestige item, comparable to (and about as useful as) a coat-of-arms in a world of barbarous competition. The spiraling demand for Old Settler—600,000 gallons in 1885 and an estimated 750,000 gallons for the current year—had passed beyond his control. Should he go hat in hand to the Louisville bankers who dealt in warehouse receipts for straight whiskey—and charged accordingly? Unthinkable, if the price of Old Settler were to be maintained at a dollar a quart. There was an alternative. Charles Moerlein could ask his own suppliers of straight whiskey to increase their output.

Take Anson Woodhull as an example: for the past four years, Woodhull had been content to sell his entire output of new whiskey—and damn good whiskey it was—to Charles Moerlein. In turn, Moerlein had encouraged Woodhull to install new stills and employ a larger staff. Last year Woodhull had delivered 400 barrels (20,000 gallons) of prime 104-proof whiskey to his friend Charles Moerlein. By adding 5,000 gallons of distilled water, Moerlein had reduced Woodhull's whiskey to potable strength—and incidentally increased his own gallonage.

Moerlein made a scratch-pad calculation of his gross profits on the Woodhull transaction.

To Anson Woodhull	$12,000	(400 bls. @ $30)
To Neutral Spirits	$ 1,980	(17,820 gals. @ 9¢ per gal. made by Charles Moerlein)
	$13,980	
Plus Federal Tax	$18,000	(@ 90¢ per gallon)
Total Cost	$31,980	
Received from Sales of Old Settler	700,000 gal. @ 60¢ per gal.	$420,000
Deduct Total Cost		31,980
Profit on Woodhull Transaction		$388,020

Obviously the dictionary was wrong! A rectifier performed none of the actions prescribed therein: a rectifier simply made a great deal of money. Small wonder that distillers, pinched by decreasing sales and irritated by systematic mis-branding, should spit with loathing at the name *rectifier*.

From his office window overlooking the neat cobblestoned yard, Moerlein gazed down at the granite warehouses filled with barrels of unsold Hearthstone. He had urged his staff to push the sales of this honest, aged distillate. Yet last year the net profit from Hearthstone amounted to exactly $8,000. Why persist in pushing a product that somehow (despite its excellence) lacked the prestige traditionally attached even to inferior goods distilled in Kentucky? He gazed across the river to Covington. In the lexicon of straight whiskey, "Bottled in *Kentucky*" was a patent of nobility. But "Bottled in Cincinnati"! Humph! Cincinnati. A rendezvous of rectifiers.

While a half million gallons of neutral spirits lay in the mixing cisterns of his plant awaiting the advent of the true, the flavorful distillate, Charles Moerlein hung off. To mix Hearthstone with colorless, tasteless ethyl alcohol and send it forth as Old Settler was comparable to cutting the arteries of his own wrist and letting his heart's blood join with the muddy Ohio. Yet, if Charles Moerlein hoped to maintain his position in the personal $500,000 income bracket, it had to be done.

A new concept, struck from the hard flint of necessity, set a conflagration roaring in Moerlein's blood: Why, dammit, if I *must* be a rectifier (he thought), then Old Settler will be the best brand of rectified whiskey ever put on the market. I'll enrich it with the 40,000 gallons of Hearthstone, husband every ounce of it and keep the price at a dollar.

Charles Moerlein did exactly that for two years. During 1887 and 1888, Old Settler became the fastest-selling whiskey in America.

Probably not more than five hundred persons in the United States knew or cared what went into Mr. Moerlein's bottles. High on the list of persons who both knew and cared was a man who had prospered by supplying a considerable portion of the genuine whiskey used by Charles Moerlein.

The man's name was Woodhull. At thirty-six, Anson Woodhull found himself in a moral and economic fix, complicated by a fierce aspiration to be, in his own right, a distiller of four-year-old bourbon whiskey. A combination of many things—pride in the excellence of his product, a natural disinclination to see that excellence debased and become part of an anonymous flood of bulk whiskey—prompted Anson to straighten out—that is, to "rectify"—certain matters with his friend, Charles Moerlein.

The situation was complicated in April 1889 by a letter from Moerlein containing a new contract calling for the delivery of 25,000 gallons of one-year-old whiskey:

> *You see, Anson* [the letter ran], *for the past two years I have been bleeding, little by little, my stock of Hearthstone into the more popular brand, Old Settler. Now my supply of Hearthstone is exhausted and I am turning to you, dear friend, with a request which I hope will be mutually profitable.*

Here it comes, thought Anson.

> *It occurs to me* [Moerlein's letter continued] *that you might step up your production, let us say by five thousand gallons, making a total of twenty-five thousand gallons that will help me maintain the flavor and hence the popular demand for Old Settler.*
>
> *Should you need additional capital for wages or installation of new apparatus, do not hesitate to call upon me. Meanwhile I enclose a contract which you will notice gives you a ten-cent-per-gallon increase for your excellent one-year-old whiskey.*
>
> *Please do me the favor of replying at your earliest convenience to my request.*
>
> *With warmest personal wishes to you, Zarah and your dear children, I am*
>
>

Most cordially yours,
CHARLES MOERLEIN

How shall I answer him? Anson wondered.

How does one sever business relations with a man who has been a benefactor and become a friend; how does one express honest regret at the changed relationship; or forsake a net income of ten to twelve thousand dollars annually? How does one assert one's independence without sacrificing the friendship? These require courage when one is approaching forty and has a growing family. Anson Woodhull had the courage; he hoped that Charles Moerlein would understand the motives that were compelling one of his most trusted suppliers to "follow the gleam" and produce a four-year-old bourbon.

To fortify his resolution, Anson again tested the batch of '87 whiskey that lay mellowing in its oaken containers in Warehouse #7. With a wooden mallet he tapped at the bung of an '87 barrel, leaned over and inhaled the unmistakable aroma of a fine young whiskey.

"I can't let it go," he said to no one in particular. "I just can't."

That afternoon he wrote a note to Charles Moerlein suggesting that they meet for lunch at the Burnet House on the following Tuesday.

They lunched, rather too heavily, as was the fashion, at the Burnet House. It required no special insight on Moerlein's part to realize that some important decision had been, or was about to be, made. As to the nature of that decision, Moerlein could guess that too. But there they sat at table's breadth—dining, smiling, appraising and appreciating each other, remembering services rendered and value received, yet speaking of trivial matters: Solange's rock garden; Laly's histrionic triumphs at Rebecca Lansheer's Academy; anything and everything but the matter that must eventually be laid upon the table.

With the coffee, Charles offered his friend an English-market corona.

"Try this," he said, holding a match for Anson. "If you enjoy it, I'll send you a box."

The courteous thing was to puff appreciatively, nod, accept the offer. Anson went through all the motions, then placed the cigar in a bronze ashtray. "It's a bit rich for my taste," he said absently.

Voiceless jockeying for the rail. As they came down the home stretch, it was Moerlein who asked, "What's on your mind, Anse?" His tone of solicitude didn't make things easier for Anson.

"This is a hard thing to say, Charles. But I'd be guilty of double-dealing if I didn't say it."

Moerlein became interested in the ash at the tip of his cigar. "Say what?"

"It began about two years ago. Do you remember anything

special about that batch of eighty-seven whiskey I shipped you?"

"Yes. I thought it better than your usual best."

"So did I." Anson fingered his cigar. "It was as though everything that I knew about whiskey—the arts of mashing, distilling, barreling—came to a head all at once. Charles, will you believe me, I wanted to *keep* that batch? I wanted to brand every barrel with my name, let it ripen, come of age and see what would happen after it had lain in a bonded warehouse for four years."

"I know. I felt that way about Hearthstone once. You should have kept a few barrels."

"I did." Anson spoke retrospectively. "The weather was mild for December, so I went on and made an extra fifty barrels for myself."

"What happened to that fifty-barrel batch?"

"Last week I tasted some of it. Afterward I went out, walked around, looked at my plant, and thought, Woodhull, you're a whiskeymaker."

"From what you say, I gather that you repeated the performance last year on a slightly larger scale."

"Yes, I made a hundred barrels for myself."

"*Hmmm.* What's your program for this year?"

"That's what I'm coming to." Earnestly, Anson continued. "I want to make whiskey on my own. It won't be Rosemere, but I think it can make its own way in the four-year-old market."

Anson had laid his cards face upward on the table. That they were good cards, honestly dealt by a friend, failed to make them relishable to the rectifier who, having counted heavily on Anson's increased output, felt slightly embittered by the prospect of losing twenty-five thousand gallons of straight, flavorful whiskey. Something of that bitterness caused him to crumble a fresh unlighted corona in the palm of his well-kept hand. A flush of angry blood heightened the natural rubor of his cheeks. He clamped his teeth lest harsh words escape him. When words did come, they conveyed grating overtones of petulance and sarcasm.

"You've knocked my entire program off balance," he said peevishly. "Why didn't you tell me earlier of your decision to 'follow the gleam' or, in whiskey-making terms, 'go straight'?"

"Come off it, Charles. You have many other suppliers. How can you object to my striking out for myself?"

"Strike out if you want to." Moerlein applied the crusher. "But what makes you think your whiskey will succeed where my Hearthstone failed?"

"I know why it will succeed," said Anson, "and I know why your Hearthstone failed."

"As one old whiskey-maker to another—" Moerlein let the acid of understatement sizzle a moment—"I should be glad to hear your line of reasoning. Expound."

"No need to expound, Charles." It was Anson's turn to show where the real strength lay. "You know as well as I the reason for Hearthstone's failure."

"You're not answering my question." Moerlein was testy now. "I repeat: Why will your whiskey succeed when Hearthstone didn't? Is Woodhull's whiskey—whatever he decides to name it—superior in flavor, higher in proof, lower in price?"

"My whiskey may not, *need* not, have any of the qualities you've just mentioned. But Old Landmark—that's the name I intend to give it—will contain an ingredient that Hearthstone never knew. To state the matter simply, Charles, you didn't put your trust in Hearthstone. It was a good whiskey and deserved a better fate. But its maker—and I hope I don't sound pharisaical—elected to follow the triple gleam of bulk production, quick turnover and big profits. You sold Hearthstone down the river."

Anson's eyes sparked like gunflints. "Well, the maker of Old Landmark proposes to sell his whiskey *up*river—in bottles, not bulk; by cases, not in barrels. I'll stick with Old Landmark, believe in it, sink or swim with it. God knows what'll happen, but I'm willing to take the risk." Anson paused. "Do you understand what I'm saying, Charles?"

Moerlein's voice and manner were chastened, the man himself subdued as he said, "I think I understand, Anse. There are times when I wish I could retrieve the reputation that Hearthstone gave me. But, having taken the cash—and I've taken plenty of it—I've decided to let the credit go."

"If you had neither cash nor credit, no one could write you down—or up—in my book, Charles. You're a fixed star." Anson gave the figure a spin in the direction of cracker-barrel humor. "Strikes me that both our compasses need a bit of adjusting. Tell you what, Charles. I'll give you half my output for the next two years, if—"

Moerlein's countenance cleared. "If . . .?"

"If you'll undertake the job of distributing Old Landmark for me—at the regular commission, of course."

Moerlein couldn't help laughing. "Anson, do you know what you remind me of?"

"What?"

"A woman who wants to have a baby. She deserves to have a baby, and I'm going to help *deliver* it. Sure, I'll handle the distribution of Old Landmark when the time comes. Put it in the best hotels, fine eastern clubs, all the premium outlets. Otherwise, the wholesalers would cut you to pieces." The rectifier gathered momentum. "That idea of bottling your whiskey is revolutionary. Most of the stuff is handled in bulk, and Lord only knows what happens to it before it reaches a customer. But I know a bottle-maker named Bruckner who—"

Anson interrupted. "Waldemar Bruckner—a little gnome about up to my watch chain?"

"Yes. How'd you happen to know him?"

"Met him on my honeymoon voyage down the Ohio. Did him a little favor. I'd like to see Hansel again—that was Zarah's name for him."

"His plant is only three blocks away. Let's go down and look the place over."

The once conical-hatted mountain climber—the Hansel of Gretel's sugar-glazed dream—had become in thirteen years a prosperous Cincinnati *bürgermeister* doing a large share of the glass-blowing business in the Ohio Valley. His height hadn't increased, but he seemed considerably heavier to Anson as he and Moerlein entered Bruckner's substantially furnished office of the Bruckner Glass Works on Fourth Street.

Rising to greet his visitors, Waldemar sank back into his chair with wonderment and surprise. "You . . . *you.*" He pointed to Anson. "You are the Captain Woodhull who came to my rescue with your *wunderbares* knife. Is it true that I see you again?"

"Here's the knife to prove it," said Anson.

Waldemar Bruckner threw his short arms around the man

who had made his success possible. "Wait 'til Gretel hears of this."

"Wait 'til Zarah hears." Affectionately, Anson rumpled the German's close-cropped poll.

Moerlein introduced the business note. Could Mr. Bruckner make five thousand one-quart bottles of distinctive shape to be used as containers for Mr. Woodhull's whiskey?"

"*Aber Ja.* Five thousand, fifty thousand I can make."

"At what price?" asked Moerlein.

"For Mr. Woodhull, I will make bottles at a price fifty per cent below rock-bottom."

"I won't be needing the bottles for another year or so," said Anson.

"That will giff me all the more time to plan a distinctive shape and instruct you how to set up your own bottling plant. Labels also must be designed and printed. Everything must be ready before your whiskey comes to maturity."

So, while Old Landmark ripened in Anson's warehouse, Waldemar Bruckner set about designing a container worthy of the man who had saved the Hansel and Gretel fairy tale from being sold downstream.

Charles Moerlein received his twelve thousand gallons for the next two years. He and Anson might disagree concerning the nature of whiskey, but their friendship remained intact.

Secret roots, not stemming from the concept of commercial profit, bound these men together. The word *love* was never mentioned. Moerlein's services to the maker of Old Landmark; his pride in giving Anson's whiskey the stage on which it could perform most advantageously; his joy (shared by Solange) when Anson and Zarah dined with them on the terrace of Vieuxtemps were sufficiently rewarded when Anson laid his hand on Moerlein's shoulder and said, "Charles."

Gratitude, affection, trust—everything that one man can legitimately say to another, was uttered when the two met.

"Charles."

"Anson."

3.

COLUMBIAN EXPOSITION

THANKS TO MRS. O'LEARY'S COW, Chicago no longer deserved its Ojibway name: "a place of wild onions." Twelve years had passed since the great fire swept and purged its weedy riot of shacks, sprawling, plumbingless tenements and noisome slaughterhouses. With five continental railroad terminals within its city borders, Chicago was now hog-butcher to the world and proposed to let the world know about it with one gigantic yawp—the Columbian Exposition of 1893. Certain aspects of the exposition—Little Egypt, for example—were about to become part of the national panorama; a young poetess named Harriet Monroe wrote a commemorative ode; and medals of merit—gold, silver and bronze—were awarded to merchants whose wares seemed, in the opinion of competent judges, to rank above their competitors'.

In a small room of the exposition building, four gentlemen representing the Whiskey Division were gathered for the purpose of selecting a four-year-old bourbon-type liquor conforming to the highest standards of purity, flavor and excellence. One of the gentlemen wore a silver badge proclaiming his function as Official Chairman and Moderator. He belonged to that anonymous breed of faceless men who are constantly engaged in the threefold operation of listening to what is said, consulting their watches and gazing over their left shoulders, as though an invisible whip-master were chasing them down a narrow alley called *Agenda*. His name happened to be Quirk, F. X., Badge No. 331, which is all that anyone need remember about him.

Chairman Quirk (F. X.) stated the purpose of the meeting. "We are gathered for the purpose of selecting a four-year-old bourbon bonded whiskey which will conform to the highest standards of purity, flavor and excellence. Preliminary screening has reduced the number of exhibits to eight. Each whiskey is, as you see, contained in a clear glass bottle identifiable only by the initials *A* to *H*."

Mr. Quirk pulled out his silver Elgin as though it were the pistol of an Olympic Game starter. "The testing will now begin."

Of the three judges, none seemed to share the sense of urgency felt by the chairman. Apparently they regarded the tasting and testing of whiskey as something of a ritual. In other respects, little similarity could be found among them. The oldest in point of years and whiskey-making experience was Mark Chadbourne, dean of Kentucky distillers and sole proprietor of the fabulous Rosemere distillery. Because Chadbourne's whiskey had already won a gold medal in the eight-year-old class he could afford, temporarily at least, to mingle with the filesmen of the industry. Besides him sat Dr. George Washington Waley, former college professor, now a chemist and bureau chief of the Department of Agriculture. His face was the human equivalent of the field of Mars.

The third member of the tribunal, Mr. Charles Moerlein, president of Midwestern Distillers, carried a gold-topped cane as the insigne of mercantile nobility. His rich complexion, rubious lips, the elegance of the clothes he wore and his manner of wearing them proclaimed the man of Middle European descent fully ripened under the sun of American business success.

Slowly they began sampling the various whiskeys. After pouring an ounce or two into a crystal glass, they sniffed, inhaled and sniffed again. This olfactory portion of the test over, they exposed the pharyngeal membranes and taste buds to the effect of the separate whiskeys. After sipping the barest minim, they rolled it around in their mouths, then frankly spat it out into tall brass cuspidors.

More sniffing, more inhalations to judge the aftertaste. A swallow of clear, cold water and the process began again. In something less than two hours, the trial was over. The next voice was that of Chairman Quirk. "Consult your notes, gentlemen, or your memories; then mark a blank slip of paper with the initial on the bottle which, in your opinion, contains the best four-year-old whiskey."

The three ballots were duly marked. Matters so fell out that the committee was unanimous in awarding the Gold Medal of excellence to the contents in bottle H. Whereupon the clerk opened a sealed envelope bearing that initial and announced, "For your information, H was the letter assigned to the whiskey of Mr. Anson Woodhull of Landmark, Indiana."

Nothing is more stimulating to a man's *amour propre* than to find himself in agreement, total and complete, with his peers. Smiles, nods, handshaking all around.

"You can't fool the horseflies," said Mark Chadbourne.

The chairman, eager to keep a two-o'clock appointment at another trial for leaf lard, put the official question: "Will each of you gentlemen be kind enough to state the reason or reasons that prompted your decision regarding Old Landmark whiskey."

As befitted his age, rank and the sovereign state in which he conducted his distilling operations, Mark Chadbourne spoke first. "Maybe I was prejudiced. But this H whiskey, or as it now turns out, Old Landmark whiskey, has a kind of family resemblance to Rosemere." Reminiscence claimed him. "Plenty of reasons why it should. I gave Anson Woodhull's father the receet back there—let's see—before the Civil War. Yessir, seems only yesterday that Chauncey Woodhull came riding up on his chestnut mare, saddlebags full of swapping material—powder, flint, ax heads and the like. He found me sittin' with this here middle finger dipped in a saucepan of boilin' water and Epsom salts. I had a felon on my fingernail. Felt just like Job. 'Did you bring the sackcloth and ashes?' I asked him. He didn't answer. Just looked at the nail and said, 'Mark, this thing, meanin' the nail, has to come off. Now you jest turn your head; 'twon't hurt much.' Then he cut the nail out with the sharpest pocketknife I ever did see. Talk about gratitude. I'd have given him the whole plant; all he wanted was a good receet for makin' whiskey, so I told him, in a general sort of way, how to go about it."

Mark Chadbourne pondered the wisdom of those who have ears and use them. "Chaunce went home, follered my instructions, and eventchally taught his son how to ripen up a batch of proper whiskey. There's only one thing more I'd like to say: I've always figured that the crystal stream gushin' out of my hillside went *under* the Ohio River—don't ask me how—and came out on Anson Woodhull's property. Folks tend to neglect the importance of good water in whiskey-making. But after everything's been said about corn, yeast and low temperatures, barrelin', mashin', et cetera, whiskey turns out to be *half* water!"

His fellow judge, Mr. Charles Moerlein, might have added: "I'll raise you another fifteen per cent." Instead he patted his gloved hands in polite applause and waited his turn.

The chairman next called upon a shaggy individual, bald-domed and, barring a touch of myopia, in excellent repair. "Dr. George Washington Waley, will you fill in, for our bene-fit, the background of your decision regarding Old Land-mark?"

Though young in reputation, Dr. Waley was known as a fire-eater in the U.S. Department of Agriculture. As bureau chief, he had already cracked down on the makers of adulter-ated cattle feed and was now wheeling his caissons against the processors of food, drinks and drugs consumed by human beings.

"As a chemist," he began, "I was impressed by two features in Whiskey H: first, its reddish-amber color—usually produced by adding peach juice, caramel and commercial extracts to raw ethyl alcohol." Waley's bulbous eye rested on Moerlein with an "I-mean-you" emphasis. "Yet because all of these whiskeys—" his large hand swept the table with an inclusive gesture—"were drawn directly from bonded containers, no such adulteration could, in fact, have taken place."

Waley, former schoolteacher, was giving the committee the full classroom treatment. "Need I labor the point, gentlemen, that the term *bonded*, as applied to whiskey, is not of itself a guarantee of quality. It simply means that the whiskey hasn't been exposed to the tender mercies of the rectifier."

Mr. Moerlein nodded appreciatively. The doctor was in splendid form today.

"The second predisposing factor in Whiskey H," continued Waley, "was the discernible presence of certain elements known to chemists as *congeners*."

Mark Chadbourne shook his woolly poll in bewilderment. "Never heard onto them, Perfessor."

Undaunted by the invincible ignorance of a man who could make Rosemere for sixty years yet remain a stranger to the secret of its excellence, Waley advanced under cover of a simile worthy of Socrates himself. "I can understand your po-sition, Mr. Chadbourne. Few mothers know, care, or have ever heard about the science of embryology. Yet this minor gap in a woman's education doesn't prevent her from conceiving and carrying a healthy baby to term. The birth of a well-formed child, if I may extend my figure, neither depends upon, nor is negated by, scientific knowledge of gestation."

The skull of a practical distiller, especially a patrician Kentucky bourbon distiller, though crowned by thorny preconceptions, isn't necessarily impenetrable. Waley's augur-bit technique reamed open a passageway for the curiosity that must precede knowledge.

"Tell me more about these congeners," said Chadbourne.

"I shall be glad to send you a Department of Agriculture pamphlet in which I discuss the matter at some length. But because our moderator seems to be suffering from a severe case of Elginitis, or possibly pinworms [general laughter], I must be brief. When ethyl alcohol is produced at pot-still temperature, one hundred and thirty-five degrees Fahrenheit, it is closely interlocked—I speak chemically—with an excess of furfural, aldehyde and methane, to mention only a few. At the same time it suffers from a deficiency of acids, esters and volatile ethers which, with time—plus the tannin extracted from the oaken container—impart character, body—yes, life itself—to mature whiskey. I noticed in Old Landmark an aroma, mellowness and aftertaste which comes to a whiskey that has lain unadulterated and at peace in an oak barrel for a minimum period of four years."

Waley's broadside, delivered point-blank at Mark Chadbourne, ricocheted off the Kentuckian and grazed Moerlein's ruddy cheeks without inflicting perceptible damage.

Chairman Quirk heard time's chariot developing a hot box at his ear. "Mr. Moerlein, in the remaining three or four minutes will you state for the record what prompted you to vote for Whiskey H?"

Charles Moerlein leaned slightly forward on his gold-knobbed cane. "I have no set piece to deliver," he began. The irony was not lost on Waley. "At the moment, my chief feeling is gratitude that this committee should have remembered my long apprenticeship in the service of straight whiskey. The fact that I am now a rectifier is apparently overshadowed by the larger truth that I can agree with my distinguished colleagues in differentiating between excellence and run-of-the-mill goodness."

He paused to frame his next thought. "Possibly I should have disqualified myself as a judge of that excellence. While

I had no hand in the making of Whiskey H, my firm—Mid-western Distillers, Inc.—distributes it to the trade."

The chairman found himself faced with a technicality. "Are we to understand, Mr. Moerlein, that you were familiar with the flavor of Old Landmark before you took part in this trial?"

"No, I can honestly say that I had never tasted Woodhull's four-year-old product until a few moments ago."

"Why didn't you tell us that you are its distributor? Certainly this makes you an interested party."

"Only *after* the fact. I tasted all the other whiskeys, decided that H whiskey was the best of the lot. I had no knowledge that it came from the Old Landmark distillery." Moerlein rose, gathered his cane and gloves. "Feel free to discuss in my absence the financial or any other advantage that may accrue to me as distributor of Old Landmark. I only request, gentlemen, that my taste buds be spared from any suspicion of dishonesty."

Chadbourne saved the situation. "Even if you'd voted for another whiskey, we'd still have a two-thirds majority. The United States Senate don't ask for more'n that even to override a veto. What's good enough for the Senate is good enough for us."

"Be it so resolved," intoned the Chairman.

And thus it came about that Old Landmark whiskey was awarded the Gold Medal for excellence in the four-year-old class. Anson Woodhull received due notification accompanied by an impressive gold medallion. But the real impact was felt in sales. The national demand for Old Landmark increased steadily until Anson imposed a ceiling on its production.

"Ten thousand barrels a year is all that I care to make," he wrote Charles Moerlein in 1894. "Allowing two gallons per barrel for evaporation every year, this means that your sales department should be expected to market 400,000 gallons annually."

After deduction of taxes, costs of labor, material, plus Moerlein's commission of 10 per cent, Anson Woodhull found himself netting $25,000 a year—which made him the richest man in Landmark County. He became Gilbert Peaslee's largest depositor; paid the heaviest taxes in the county; brought his children up in a tradition nostalgically referred to as the "good life." He filled to perfection the role of "small independent businessman" depicted at the time as the bulwark and foundation stone of the American system of private enterprise.

Mighty fine thing, private enterprise. Had its faults, maybe; depressions, strikes, panics, lay-offs—in a phrase, "unequal opportunity for all." Nothing that couldn't be ironed out, though, despite the carpings of fellows like Marx, Veblen and that school of muckrakers. To offset these puny libels, just read what Ralph Waldo Emerson said about private enterprise in 1845 (he called it "Trade") and see how it jibed with the promise of American life some fifty years later.

> Trade is a plant which grows wherever there is peace, as soon as there is peace and as long as there is peace. Trade is a new agent in the world and one of great function; it is a very intellectual force. Trade displaces physical strength and installs combination, information, science in its room. Trade goes to make governments insignificant; instead of a huge army and navy and executive departments, it converts government into an Intelligence Office, where every man may find what he wishes to buy and expose what he has to sell, not only products and manufactures but arts, skills and intellectual and moral values. . . . The historian will see that Trade was the principle of Liberty; that Trade planted America and destroyed Feudalism; that it makes peace and keeps peace and it will abolish slavery.

Uncle Waldo wasn't talking through his mutton chops—or was he? The only clear exception to the foregoing verbiage was the whiskey trade. Obviously, whiskey was not an intellectual force. The whiskey trade, far from being the "principle of liberty," the maker and keeper of peace, was (according to some folks) a Very Present Evil and Ought to Be Done Away With. *Pronto.*

Hence the emergence of an egg-sucking, high-minded, knout-brandishing son-of-a-bitch who came to be variously known as the Dry Messiah (sometimes pronounced *Meshuggah*), the Locomotive in Trousers, the Sahara Sirocco, and Whirlwind of the Lord. His square name was Oliver C. Treadgood. You guessed it—the *C* stood for Cromwell.

4.

OLIVER C. TREADGOOD

FELLOW SCHNORRERS IN *the Great American dream bed!*
Dear steak-eating, vote-happy, short-memoried Manifest-
Destiny-Unconscious Camaradas! Écoutez! Horschen sie eine
Minute, Paesani, before the clock runs out and the goose eggs
are passed around again. Isn't it true, Amici (wasn't it always
true?), that you enjoy nothing better than a good, long-wear-
ing illusion—something you can cling to when the radiator
boils over and love flies out the window of your three-toned
hardtop right in the middle of the four-lane Turnpike o'
Dreams? Dites-moi, what specifically do you want? A cottage
small by a waterfall? A seat on "'Change"? An all-purpose
cruise to the Leeward Islands? Pick a number—any number
from One to Infinity. Drop it into this here little slot and don't
bother to watch the Birdie because, well—as you damn well
know—the wheel was rigged ever so long ago. Oh, ever so.

Let us be frank with one another. 'Fess up, fellows. Admit
that a really durable illusion is moughty hard to find. Take
that nonsinkable ship, for instance. Every wide-awake subscriber to Leslie's Weekly knew all about it back there in
1895. There were diagrams showing those watertight compartments built right into the hull, with doors that closed
automatically if (inconceivably) the keel were to be shorn off
by an iceberg.

Disconcerting, that Titanic business!

Yet how we still clung to the myth of "unsinkability." Remember the Normandie, that Lafayette-nous-sommes-arrivés
super-gangplank to Paris, das Zauberschiff with seven decks
and quadruple engines? She cannot sink, see, because, par-
bleu, waterproof bulkheads interpose between her outer and

329

inner skins in such cunning fashion that not even a drop of salt spray shall enter milady's bidet. C'est dommage, n'est-ce pas, to see the Queen herself, propellers indecently exposed, lying in the mud adjacent to Pier 65.

And those female hormones that were supposed to make menopause a gay marching thing. Whazzat? They turned out to be carcinogenetical. Quaere me reliquisti, Drs. Mayo? Almost as heartbreaking as the failure of them filter-tip cigs to absorb objectionable tars. And Jello Pud—the dessert with the extra tremble? Gone? Sorry, ma'am, they was took over by Frozen Fruities, a subsiderary of U.S. Rubberola. Yep. Gone with the snows of yesteryear, like the Villain says.

Fled is that vision; do I wake or sleep?

But stay, Amigos! Before you turn disconsolate to that crummy stucco dream house au Blanding, sinking slowly under its mortgage into the 40 x 70 plot formerly known as Mulligan's Dump, but now transformed by levity's wand into Landhurst Manor, try on this arch supporter just for size. Concave or convex, 'twill fit either sex, guaranteed to keep a stiff upper metatarsal and inflate the flat old mattress of reality chock-a-block with aerated gutta-percha.

Yense her! You'll get a lot of mileage out of it, gents.

Matthew, Mark, Luke and John, bless the dreams that I lie on and particularly bless a dream that Just Wasn't So, but for some reason or other came to be regarded as Holy Writ and discussed with equal ignorance around the family table, in the lobby of a Schenectady Hotel, up in Mabel's room, or wherever by chance you happened to be.

Here's the way it went:

While three million American males were qualifying to answer the question of some future hypothetical little toddler— "What were You doing in World War I, Daddy?"—a small group of professional Drys caught Congress with its pants down and rammed the Eighteenth Amendment right up the Arsenal of Democracy.

That's the legend, Libertados. Try'n change it. Carve 1619 onto Plymouth Rock. Disprove the equation $E=mc^2$. Make Priscilla say, "Sorry, John, there's Miles between us," or "Get with child a mandrake root and dodge that dread paternity suit"—but never, under any circumstances, peek into the keyhole of fact concerning Prohibition unless you're prepared to see an unwinding reel of phantasmagoria that would give Jean

Cocteau the hoogies and cause him to disavow his "Sang d'un Poète" as a piffling understatement.

Res ipsa loquitur? Does the Thing speak for Itself? It does not. It cannot. It will not. The Ding an Sich of Prohibition requires an Expositor, a chap afflicted so badly with cacoëthes scribendi that he'd write down his version of it on his own skin with ink made of sundry excrementals if non-drip ballpoints weren't available. This queer guy being obliged to invent characters, set a stage, spin a plot, and keep it spinning hereby asserts his inalienable right to imagine The Thing As It Must Have Been.

First, a flashback of the Protagonist.

Ollie of the watery eyes, puttyish features, bantam stature and brick-red mustache scarcely seemed to possess the physical equipment to coincide with the image of a man destined to fill a major niche in the Pantheon of American mythology. To offset these minor handicaps Ollie became one of the best constitutional lawyers and the slickest manipulator in all Lobbydom. Add a splash of paranoia and a passion of espionage to a weazened theologic background and what you've got is a portrait of Treadgood when he first emerged from the sawdust of anonymity (let's not be finicky about dates) sometime around 1890.

If you're ready we'll dolly up and take a peek at the man himself when he thought no one was looking.

Camera, camaradas. Dos passos fecit away.

Oliver C. Treadgood first appeared as a shop foreman in the woodworking establishment of E. K. Whittle & Sons, makers of doors and window sashes. Since the Civil War, the Whittles, father and son, had given employment to the deserving poor of Dansburg, Ohio, and so great was the demand for Whittle doors that even little girls and boys were pressed into service at the going rate of $2.08 for a seventy-hour week. If a circular saw broke loose and cut three or four children in half—well, that was just too bad.

"No law, no remedy," as good King Wiglaf used to say circa A.D. 691—and about twelve hundred years later, some of the Whittle employees, feeling rather cut up by the way things weren't going, staged a queersome performance called a "strike."

No? Yes! There was a fight at the factory gate, and in that fight Oliver C. Treadgood took his stand definitely on the side of Management. With a stave in his hands he beat back some of the strikers and received a nasty gash in the wrist from one of the knives that were flashing that day. He was proud of the scar and liked to exhibit it as an honorable wound.

"An eighth of an inch to the right, and it would have sunk into the pulse," he explained to his family as he pulled back his shirt sleeve. "But it didn't—" a note of righteous triumph entered his voice—"and the knife-pullers lost the strike, too. They wanted to start a *union*. Why, if we let them have a union they'd be running the mill. No, sir, we'll have no union while I can beat the swine back with a stick."

Shortly after the strike, Ollie was summoned into the presence of Cadmon F. Whittle, son of the founder and chief dispenser of wages in Dansburg. Square Masonic cap in hand, Oliver stood respectfully at attention.

"Treadgood, how long have you been with E. K. Whittle and Sons?"

"Fifteen years, sir. I came straight to the mill after graduating from grade school and asked your father for an opportunity to work my way to the top."

"My father seldom made a mistake." Cadmon Whittle examined the sheaf of papers before him. "You are now shop foreman, as I understand, at a wage of ten fifty per week."

"Yes, sir. I've been raised fifty cents a week—annually, that is—ever since I began."

"It's a steady-going record, Treadgood. But as of Saturday, week, we shall be obliged to dispense with your services as shop foreman."

"Wh . . . wh . . . what?" A runaway saw seemed to have clipped Treadgood's head from the rest of his body.

"Yes." Cadmon Whittle extended his hand. "The part you played in beating back the strikers, plus your triple-A record of Regularity, Sobriety and Church Attendance, has made it mandatory that E. K. Whittle and Sons give you the opportunity you have so faithfully earned. Beginning next Monday, your title will be that of Assistant Comptroller. Your duties will combine those of Paymaster and Timekeeper for the entire factory. Your salary—you're not a wage-earner any more, Oliver—will be twelve dollars a week."

Treadgood's promotion brought into prominence two aspects of his nature: a firm belief in the Calvinistic Doctrine of Heavenly Election and the tyrannical use of power over those unable to defend themselves. He became the straw-boss magnified. Sitting at the wicketed gate of the mill, he personally checked off every employee's time of entrance. If a worker was one minute late, he was fined a half day's pay. Five minutes' tardiness meant the loss of a full day's wages; and this offense, if repeated, led to peremptory firing. No tyrant can exist without espionage, and Treadgood honeycombed every department of the mill with spies. Did a male employee sneak into the lavatory for a quick puff at the Shrub of Evil, whether tamped into his corncob or rolled up in the more vicious form of a cigarette? Well, that employee received a warning in his next pay envelope: *Your attention is called to the "No Smoking" rule which exists throughout the factory. Failure on your part to comply with this rule will result in Immediate Dismissal.*

Did an adolescent female seek the seclusion of the girls' room to stanch a cyclic flow? In *her* envelope Ollie would place a red slip bearing this legend: *Employees are not permitted to leave their work bench between 7 A.M. and 12 N. or between 12:30 and 5 P.M.*

So the girls just had to stand and let the thing leak. Under the freedom-of-contract theory, they weren't obliged to take the job in the first place. Solid Manchester economics, eh?

When the five-o'clock whistle blew its releasing blast one winter day in 1893, Oliver Treadgood retraced his morning steps homeward, stopping only to buy a copy of the Youngstown *Cornet*. With this strongly Republican reading matter under his arm, he pushed open his kitchen door, silently hung up his hat and coat, and walked straight to the sink where a basin of warm water was awaiting him. He washed with yellow soap, baring his red-haired forearms to the elbows, wiped his face and hands on a clean roller towel, took a drink of God's own good water from the faucet, then came over to the kitchen table where his two children were standing behind chairs, waiting for him to sit down. At this point, Treadgood saw fit to break the domestic silence by addressing his wife and family.

"Have the children been helpful today?" he asked Elizabeth.

"Very helpful, very helpful indeed, Oliver."

"Did Clive sift the ashes?" (Never a glance at his nine-year-old son.)

"Yes, Father. I sifted them twice over and picked out all the clinkers."

"How many did you get?"

"Two coal-hods full, Father."

"There shouldn't be so many clinkers," said Oliver. "That furnace isn't burning as it should. Needs a new grate."

Elizabeth Treadgood didn't dare say that her shoddy winter coat was twice as old as the present grate. Oh, dear, she thought, $12.50 more on that furnace; now Luella's chance of getting a piano is further away than ever.

Treadgood bent a milder eye on his daughter; if he had any softness it was for Luella; yet he was utterly unable to show his daughter the single small candle of tenderness that he burned at her shrine. The only demonstration he could make was a moderate smoothing-out of his voice when he addressed her. "Did you help Mother with the ironing today, Luella?" he asked.

Eye-business between Luella and her mother.

"Yes, Father . . . I did."

"Glad to hear that you're getting to be some use around the house. You may say grace tonight, Luella."

The child bent her head over her plate and timidly murmured, "Bounteous and merciful Lord who watcheth over the granaries of His people, we humbly thank Thee for the food we are about to receive from Thy hand in peace and loving kindness. Amen."

For a moment the piano prospects seemed actually bright to Elizabeth. They were abruptly shattered when her husband thrust the carving fork into the cheap cut of beef and frowned at her.

"Elizabeth," he said with cold and nagging emphasis, "this roast is overcooked again. I want my beef rare! When it's overdone like this it doesn't set well with me. I've told you before—I've told you ten thousand times—my dyspepsia comes from your overcooked meat."

A dull and wordless oppression hung over the room. The worst was to come, and no one knew what form the worst would take.

After supper Luella helped her mother clear away, wash and dry the dishes.

"Shall I ask him for the piano tonight, Mama?"

"Not tonight, dear. He is not in a good humor."

That was the formula. The wrong one, if Elizabeth Treadgood had only realized it. Had Luella gone up to her father, put her hand on his cheek and said, "Father, if you get me a piano, I will be very happy and you will be happy, too," the unaccustomed wash of music might have salved Treadgood's cankered soul. But Luella hadn't yet received the first intimations of her womanhood, nor felt the first faint tremolo of her power over her father. And so the request was never made, the child's famine for loveliness went unappeased, and the bark grew stiffer around Oliver Treadgood's heart.

It was Treadgood's custom to read aloud from the Good Book for twenty minutes every evening, picking up the text where he had left off the day before. In this way he read straight through the Bible once a year and now had eighteen and a half complete readings to his credit somewhere. Like all confirmed Bible readers, he fancied his own exegetic powers and was forever on the lookout for hidden meanings, ambiguous renditions and obscure references. Tonight, he was reading from Matthew, Chapter XVII, 20:

If ye have faith as a grain of mustard seed, ye shall say unto this mountain, Remove hence to yonder place; and it shall remove; and nothing shall be impossible unto you.

"What does that mean, Clive?" he asked without warning.

These unexpected demands for interpretation came just infrequently enough to catch the boy off guard. Tonight, as usual, Clive was caught gaping in ignorance. He made a futile backward scratching with his mind to recall the last words he remembered. There was nothing to remember. . . .

"I didn't hear the verse, Father," he confessed.

"Didn't *hear* it?" Every word was an accusing gimlet. "You mean you weren't listening!"

Panic rose in Clive's narrow chest. "Yes, Father. I guess so."

"You *guess* so! I'll make you *know* it! Go upstairs and take your pants off! I'll handle you when I finish the Golden Text." Oliver brought some more troublesome gas off his stomach.

Tremblingly, Clive started for the door. He didn't want to cry in front of his mother, but the injustice of the beating that awaited him was too much for his anguished nerves. As he passed his mother's chair, the boy burst into tears and threw himself into her lap.

"Don't let him whip me, Mother," he sobbed. "Don't let

him whip me any more. I'll listen next time, honest and true I will."

Elizabeth put her hand protectingly on the boy's head. "You don't deserve a beating," she wanted to say, but checked herself, bit her lip futilely, and continued stroking the reddish hair of her son. There was a silence broken only by Clive's quiet sobbing.

When Treadgood spoke again, raw acid squirted from his lips. "I am waiting, Elizabeth."

Elizabeth bent over her son's head and said in a low, comfortless voice, "You must obey your father, Clive. He knows what is . . . what is best for you. Go upstairs now." She pushed him firmly away from her, and the boy stumbled snuffingly through the door.

The reading continued. In his best ministerial voice, Oliver intoned:

Verily I say unto you, Except ye be converted, and become as little children, ye shall not enter into the kingdom of heaven. Whosoever therefore shall humble himself as this little child, the same is greatest in the kingdom of heaven. And whoso shall receive one such little child in my name, receiveth me.

But whoso shall offend one of these little ones which believe in me, it were better for him that millstone were hanged about his neck, and that he were drowned in the depth of the sea.

There was a deadly hush throughout the neat and ugly house when Oliver laid down the Bible. It seemed as though a monitory presence filled the room, warning him that the thing he was about to do upon the body of his son could never be forgiven. Beads of perspiration glistened on his pale, bald forehead as he walked with exaggerated slowness into the kitchen, took down the razor strop, then strode upstairs.

For three minutes there was a muffled thud of blows and the imploring screams of a child as Oliver Cromwell Treadgood beat his nine-year-old son in the room above.

Downstairs a little girl clung to her mother, trying fruitlessly to comfort her heavy sobbing.

Later that evening after locking all the doors and windows in his house, Oliver C. Treadgood made his three-minute claim to the marital service of his wife Elizabeth. He didn't realize that Elizabeth was holding one of his straight-edged razors in her tightly clenched fist. Waiting . . . waiting . . . Soon Oliver's heavy breathing filled the musty room.

Now is my moment, thought Elizabeth. But the moment came, passed, came and passed again. . . . *I will wait till tomorrow.*

After her husband left for the mill the next morning, Elizabeth brought Clive and Luella into the parlor. She sat down in her sewing chair and spoke gently to the boy and girl kneeling at either side.

"Dear Clive—" she fondled his head—"dear Luella." Elizabeth stroked her daughter's hair. "I have decided to go away on a long, long journey, and I shall never return." From her sewing box she drew her husband's Sunday razor, opened the blade—a beautiful piece of Göttingen steel—and laid its edge experimentally on the thin blue vein of her wrist.

"I am not asking you to come with me, children. You may wish to stay here in this house with your father."

"No, no," they sobbed. "Mother, take us with you. Take us wherever you go."

That evening, returning home at 5:11, Oliver C. Treadgood found his parlor carpet utterly ruined by some ten or twelve quarts of blood. Three familiar bodies lay, not like the living, on the floor.

Elizabeth, Clive and Luella received decent Christian burial. The I.O.O.F. saw to that. And no one, including Oliver C. Treadgood, could understand how a tragedy like this could befall such a sober, industrious, *good* man.

Oliver Treadgood never slept in that ugly blood-soaked house again. He sold it at a slight profit, betook himself to Akron, hired a room in the Y.M.C.A. and for a full week felt kind of "lost-like." Naturally. He no longer had a roost to rule, little children to intimidate, or a wife to be ripsawed at will. It was a trying, soul-searching week. Basic thrift made it impossible for Ollie to part with a dollar for the personal service that he needed so badly. On still higher grounds he couldn't permit himself the solace that weaker men might have found, say, in a pint of whiskey.

On the highest ground of all—the Calvinistic credo of Predestined Election—fearful doubts assailed Treadgood. According to his most cherished belief, no living man could be certain of heavenly election; yet he received, while still on earth, definite indications that he stood among God's chosen ones. How possibly could Oliver interpret the destruction of his family as a mark of God's favor? *Every tree that bringeth not forth good fruit is hewn down and cast into the fire.* Thus Matthew 7:19. A suicidal wife and two murdered children could scarcely be construed as "good fruit." In very real agony lest his own soul (the begetting tree) be condemned to everlasting fire, Treadgood fell to his knees. Beads of perspiration dripped from his forehead as he pleaded with his Maker. "Withhold not Thy effectual grace from me, O Lord. Vouchsafe a sign unto Thy servant." Yet even as he prayed, Oliver Treadgood's theology told him that the iron door of Election had clanged tight before Time was. And how could mortal man appeal from God's decree? How escape the awful consequence of eternal perdition?

If Treadgood hadn't patterned himself in the image and likeness of an unforgiving Father! had he not received prior indications of Heavenly Election (the Assistant Comptrollership at the mill, for example), he might have examined his own conscience, prostrated himself in repentance, and promised nevermore to offend God. But Ollie, having a large amount of stretch in his make-up, managed to survive the ordeal by contrasting himself with the mass of mankind—corrupt, will-less, deserving the fate stored up for them. They *showed* it in their lives! They drank, chewed tobacco, swore, lay with whores (whether Babylonian or Akronian scarcely mattered). It came as a consolation to Oliver to inform God that he was not as one of these. Halfway through his argument, it occurred to Treadgood that God was merely testing him by saying, in effect, "Go forth, crush out those who disbelieve in Me." Yes, yes, that was it! Not merely by good works, but through an endless succession of *mighty* works— a dedicated Messiahship undertaken for the greater glory of God—only in that way could Oliver Treadgood hope to win new proofs of Heavenly Election.

After the first temblors of fear had shaken the temple of his theology without destroying the Image enshrined therein, Oliver took courage. He would become a preacher of the Gospel—a contemporary Job, an Ohio Milton justifying God's ways to man. There were plenty of empty or neglected pulpits right in the state. (Why shouldn't there be, when the average salary of an ordained Protestant clergyman was $5.00 a week, with perquisites from the "poor barrel" thrown in?) Chapter-and-Verse intimacy with the Bible, a Knoxian gift of disputation, and much Lodge experience of talking on his feet—all these drew Treadgood toward a life of apostolic service.

Must this service necessarily be confined to the pulpit?

Even the shabbiest Protestant divine was obliged to attend a seminary in preparation for his degree, and Treadgood's formal learning had ended in grade school. While browsing around a secondhand bookstore, Ollie came upon a tattered buckram-bound volume entitled *The Law of the Cadaver.* Odd title: fascinating. For a dime, Ollie bought the book, carried it to his dingy room and spent a breathless eighteen hours exploring that branch of law which deals with the dead.

Well, well! It would appear that a corpse possessed certain inalienable rights dating back to English common law and rather universally accepted among civilized peoples. Vesalius, father of anatomy; Harvey, who proved the circulation of the blood, had, by acts of grave-robbery, broken the ring of sanctity that hedged about a corpse. Autopsies were still forbidden without the written consent of next of kin. Or take that interesting case of the man who had walked into a jewelry store, asked permission to examine a tray of sapphires; then, selecting the largest, swallowed it. On being arrested, he gulped down a capsule of strychnine and sixty seconds later was beyond mortal authority. Members of his family claimed the body, performed a secret operation, recovered the jewel and were apprehended only when they attempted to sell it.

The book made Oliver wonder whether his call to the ministry was strong enough. A whole new *corpus* of law was then coming into existence; states, counties and municipalities were passing Dry legislation aimed at the abolition of the saloon. The law needed interpreters, defenders. Why not become the prosecutor of those who flouted such legislation—a latter-day Torquemada, a Grand Inquisitor, a gadfly of the Lord, a legalistic Jeremiah?

It was all very appealing. The only thing Treadgood needed now was the equivalent of the Voice that bade Augustine "Pick up and read." An inborn love of hocus-pocus led Oliver to test himself: he placed a Bible on one end of the bare table in his room; on the other end he placed *The Law of the Cadaver.* How choose between them? Blindfolding and picking at random wasn't the answer. The act of choice must be divinely inspired. Lover of law that he was, Oliver elected the number of chapters in Leviticus as his guide. Slowly, with equally measured steps, he walked around the table, eyes gazing straight ahead. And, lo, having taken the twenty-seventh step, he stretched out his hand and picked up *The Law of the Cadaver*.

Pretty conclusive. And speaking of conclusions, what was the last verse of Leviticus? *"These are the commandments which the Lord gave unto Moses on Mt. Sinai."*

You don't get good sound justification like that very often, would you say?

Treadgood might have dipped into his capital to support himself while "reading" law. He preferred, however, to find work—the right *kind* of work. Hn-nn. Was it instinct, chance, or a carrion delicacy of nostril that led him into the under-taking establishment of J. P. Coggins? No matter. Coggins needed a tough-stomached assistant to make night calls, learn the trade and serve as general handyman.

"You married?" asked Coggins. Silently, Treadgood produced his marriage license.

Res ipsa loquitur.

Nothing that follows herein shall be construed as prejudicial to the high ethical standards of American undertakers as of the nineties. They purveyed dignity, sincerity, etc., for sums ranging from fifty to five thousand dollars. Ollie, starting as an apprentice, gradually learned trade secrets which are, after all, scarcely secrets, being well known to the Aztecs, Baby-lonians, Carthaginians, Dyaks, Egyptians and Fescennines. He learned how to drain off a cadaver's blood, replace it with emblaming fluid—a wood-alcohol preparation containing ar-senic that acted both as preservative and as liquid insurance that the customer was actually dead. (Everyone's heard about people being buried alive, eh?) Coggins instructed him in the use of cosmetics suitable to the age and sex of the deceased and, oh, so comforting to the bereaved family. Ollie learned fast. He had to. Pretty soon old Coggins handed him the key and promoted him to night manager.

Jim Dandy! Treadgood now sat in the front office studying his law books, while in the windowless room behind him lay the newly dead, either in coffins or on wooden slabs supported by sawhorses. All decently draped, of course. Ollie might be described as custodian of Death's temporary waiting room.

Which indeed he was. But then again, because of a pitiful need, he sometimes betrayed his stewardship. . . .

For if it's passivity you crave, nothing quite equals a corpse.

On this mixed diet of law books and passivity, Ollie was doing rather well until one midnight the coroner's assistant came in with the report that a woman had died in a cheap whorehouse down by the tracks. Cause of death? Stoppage of the heart due to falling out of bed while under the influence. The madame of the house would fork over $50.00 for funeral expenses. Ollie hitched up the hearse and collected the corpse in person, which is to say, he carried her strapped to his back down three flights of dingy stairs and rolled her into the wagon. Arriving at the funeral home, he stretched the "remains" (that's the ethical term) on a marble slab in Coggins' back room and appraised his catch.

She was an emaciated strawberry blonde with long legs not yet stiffened by *rigor mortis* as Ollie discovered while swabbing her off with a carriage sponge. Her skin had an absinthe under-tinge that must have made her attractive to a certain type of customer. Did men find this necrotic hue stimulating to erotic ideas?

Could . . . such . . . things . . . be?

Indeed they could. In fact they were. Ollie was so eager to begin ripsawing this lathe-of-a-corpse that he forgot to inject the formalin into her arteries.

He was pumping his way toward a new endurance record of four minutes. Talk about artificial respiration! Well! There must be something to it because, when the cadaver felt new life spurting into her, she suddenly opened her eyes.

"Where am I?" she asked.

Some men have received Congressional medals for bringing the dead to life. Ollie would have received a penitentiary sentence. Cool in the presence of danger, he soothed, "Ma'am, you're in good hands. Just lay back now. This'll make you feel better."

Oliver thrust the needle of the hand pump into her iliac artery and pushed the handle down until she contained enough arsenic to kill a squadron of cavalry.

It was a close shave, but Ollie learned his lesson.

Thereafter, he always injected the embalming fluid first!

Few men have studied law under these trying conditions,

but after two years of study, Oliver C. Treadgood passed his bar examinations. Then, unlike other fledgling lawyers who serve an ignoble apprenticeship in the musty offices of Torts, Equity and Replevin, he went straight to the superintendent of the recently formed Anti-Saloon League.

"Give me your wettest cases and I'll dry them up free of charge the first year. Thereafter, if you like my work, we'll talk about fees."

Fair enough. Ollie went to work on the backlog of a hundred untried cases in the superintendent's files. He picked the ten most likely to bring in favorable verdicts and won them all. Was it a question of procuring a minor to swear that he had been "served" in Mike Flaherty's Saloon? Ollie could suborn a dozen such witnesses at the going rate of $2.00 apiece. The next step was to get a Dry-minded judge to issue a temporary injunction against the aforementioned Michael Flaherty—or a "show cause" order maybe. If the judge were not Dry-minded, Treadgood would dehydrate him by pointing out Section D, Article 22 of the recently enacted state law prohibiting the sale of liquor to persons under eighteen.

"We intend to enforce this law, Your Honor," announced Treadgood, "and things will look mighty bad for any judge who refuses to co-operate." So a writ would be issued. Flaherty might appeal, but in the end his place would be padlocked.

Fiat Justitia, ruat Gambrinus.

Variations of the "I represent the law and intend to enforce it" technique enabled Treadgood to win twenty straight cases. By the end of 1895 he had closed eighty-nine saloons in Ohio.

Thereafter, starting with an annual salary of $1,000, he took on all comers for the greater glory of the Anti-Saloon League.

5.

FAMILY PORTRAIT

LALY

"Soon" is a long time when you are almost eighteen and terribly in love. Soon you'll be a woman, free to accept the risks and enjoy the privileges of womanhood. Soon (meaning eventually) a gold-hatted, high-bouncing lover will carry you off to his silken pavilion—or at least something with a roof over it. Meanwhile, no matter how tedious the day or desolate the night, nothing can change "soon" into "now."

Letters help. Oh, most blessedly they do! Wherefore Laly Woodhull wrote daily to Arthur Coplestone during the summer of their star-crossed separation. She had met Arthur when he came in to assist Mr. Domily Muse, Cincinnati's bon-ton photographer, in taking a picture of the cast of *Lady Darlington's Dilemma*, a *pièce de théâtre* presented by Rebecca Lansheer's Seminary, which Laly had been attending since her graduation from Sycamore Academy. No one disputed her claim to the role of Lady Darlington. Indeed her portrayal of that noblewoman's dilemma (the discovery that her dearest friend, Lavinia, Marchioness of Wellbourne, had secretly pilfered some cuttings of the Darlington Delphiniums and was planning to exhibit them as her own at the Royal Horticultural Bazaar) had made the production seem almost credible.

Fate takes such casual forms. "Move the chair of Lady Darlington into closer composition," ordered Domily Muse. With a murmured "Permit me," Arthur Coplestone edged Laly's chair an inch nearer the camera.

A week later, on delivering the proofs, he contrived to slip a note into Laly's hand—a note pleading for a "rendezvous" (that was only one of Arthur's exciting words). *Mt. Adam's Park, Tuesday. Third Bench from the fountain, 2 P.M. Ayez pitié de moi.*

An unforgettable tryst. By stratagems best known to carefully guarded schoolgirls, April and May became a succession of secret wonderful meetings with Domily Muse's assistant. Although photography was the chief peak in Arthur's mountainous range of ideas and accomplishments, it was approached on all sides by foothills of curious knowledge. Arthur could read palms, cast horoscopes and was proficient in the Romance languages—"Romance" meaning the language of the fan, handkerchief and parasol. Laly quickly learned that a parasol twirled clockwise over her shoulder meant "You may address me." A counterclockwise turn warned "Dissimulate. We are under surveillance." Fan open, flutes quivering, said, "I am definitely interested." Fan closed, tapping knee *staccato* meant, "Ingrate! Never speak to me again."

As for the uses of a handkerchief, it had ten major functions, indicating—well, practically everything from *noli me tangere* to "You may fire when ready, Gridley."

Phrenology, too, was an open book to Arthur. "Your amatory prominence," he said, slipping his fingers with scientific detachment into the secrets of Laly's wheat-colored hair, "is very pronounced."

Other explorations, not nearly so detached, were interrupted by Laly's graduation in mid-June. Mother and Father, both looking *très distingué* (that was another of Arthur's locutions), sat on the seminary lawn, while Senator Regius Casseboom handed out diplomas tied with white silk ribbons. Afterward, during the dreary train ride between Cincinnati and Landmark, Laly read over and over the horoscope that Arthur had prepared for her.

Women born on your birthday (July 7) are very handsome, with regal figures and luminous eyes that are most attractive to the opposite sex. They have great powers of love, yet are not at all flirtatious. Though you are naturally aristocratic, you are also tender and domestically inclined.

How true, dear Arthur!
Laly read on:

You have an inner life which no one can ever reach until the right one comes along who will understand and appreciate everything about you. You can be a tremendous success as an actress if you will overcome certain obstacles in your environment. Believe in yourself; dare follow your star, and you will achieve the destiny that the future has in store for you.

Alighting from the train at Landmark, this regally molded daughter of destiny was met at the depot by Richmond (Reb) Plaskett, barbered to the nines. Reb hoisted six pieces of Woodhull luggage onto the top of a custard-colored surrey, then hopped into the front seat beside his employer while Laly and Zarah disposed themselves on the back cushions in fashionable attitudes of languor or maybe boredom.

For the past two days Laly and Mama had been in a state of mutual siege, sapping at each other with silences frigid, long drawn out, broken only by the coolest of amenities, or an occasional icepick thrust from Zarah. The hostilities had begun shortly after the graduation exercises. Laly, hot with triumph (she had received several prizes), had broken through a ring of admirers to greet her mother and father. Anson laughingly took the luscious smack she planted on his cheek and called her "my big clever girl."

Zarah's praise, muted by a headache, was on the tepid side. A headachey night at Vieuxtemps and breakfast in bed failed to improve Mama's disposition.

"Don't walk like that," she snapped as the sweet girl graduate swiveled toward a Vieuxtemps parapet.

"Don't walk like *what?*" flashed Laly.

"As though you wanted to give away everything you have. Try to exercise a minimum of control over your body movements—especially your hips."

Had Zarah taken a switch and struck her daughter across the bare nates, Laly couldn't have felt the sting more keenly. Was it possible that her handsome, full-grown mother was a creature of pique, of envy?

Laly sought advice from Solange. "Can I help the way I walk? And why should Mama be so disturbed about it?"

"Between mothers and daughters there sometimes springs up a passing rivalry." Solange offered a bit of autobiography by way of explanation. "When I was thirteen, my own dear mother—wise in her own fashion—sent me to a convent. It was her way of avoiding conflict. Trust me, Laly, when I tell you that Zarah is going through a difficult period; that you must exert every effort to avoid giving her additional pain. How does a daughter do this? By being dutiful, obedient and patient. You will bite your lips many times, *ma chérie*—but in the end, oh! the sweet victory of transforming one's mother into a friend."

Just now the friend-to-be was nipping at her smelling salts in an attempt to stave off one of her maddening attacks of migraine. As they drove down sycamore-shaded avenues, conversation of a kind went on between Reb and Anson. Judge Whitfield's house had been painted. Charles Towner had put one of those new-fangled soda fountains into his drugstore. (Did these people live on the same planet with Arthur Coplestone? thought Laly.) The factual litany continued until the surrey turned into a graveled drive and pulled up at the porte-cochere of the Woodhull home.

White, mansarded, bow-windowed and broad-lawned, the Woodhull place occupied a full acre at the corner of Grove and Sycamore. Its eighteen rooms were shaded by elms and sycamores of banyan proportions.

While Reb unloaded the luggage, Zarah went straight to the straw mail basket hanging from a hook on the front door. The basket was a symbol of upper-class "belongingness" as opposed to the rusty oblong tin boxes used by the lower classes. The prerogative of sorting the mail belonged to Zarah. In spite of her headache she gave a splendid exhibition of chatelaine power by fingering the envelopes as though they were her personal property. Coming to a mauve-colored envelope with a superscripture in emerald ink, she exclaimed, "It's scented!"

"It's mine," said Laly, extending her hand.

Showdown!

"You are quite welcome to it," said Zarah.

High in her chamber overlooking the apple orchard, Laly gazed at the mauve envelope, inhaled its delicious perfume (verbena) and marveled at Arthur's handwriting—"calligraphy," he called it. The Coplestone penmanship was a thing of art: each character uniform yet somehow individual; initials sprigged with tiny serifs, the lines coolly spaced. There was a decorative scroll at the top of every page and at the very end a winged dove bearing a missive in its beak.

The missive told Laly everything a woman wants to hear.

Cincinnati was a desert without her. The hours were interminably long. When shall we meet again? I miss you. What's this dull town to me? I love you. . . . Devotedly and eternally, etc., Arturo.

In her reply, strategically delayed for three ghastly days, Laly affected the gay tone of a woman caught in a crush of social events.

ARTHUR DEAREST:

Your letter has lain unanswered on the very top of my correspondence (such a heap of it) silently reproaching me for the seeming tardiness of my reply. But will you forgive me if I confess to the dizzying whirl that has engulfed me for the past week? I have had scarcely a moment to call my own, yet in the midst of balls, dances and social affairs, I have thought of you more than once, dear friend, and can no longer put off the pleasurable task of writing you.

First, let me tell you about the party my parents gave me on the day of my homecoming. . . .

So much for fiction. What were the facts? Sewing summer dresses under Zarah's supervision; walking down to Towner's drugstore for milk-of-cucumber lotion; stuffing her ears with cotton to deaden the brassy slides of Osgood's trombone; pretending an interest in the offspring of Chance's too-prolific rabbits. When these palled, she could always make penuche with Quincia.

To three cups of brown sugar, add one cup shelled walnuts. Stir constantly over slow fire until . . .

Until you almost screamed with vexation at the entire setup. Were brown sugar and chopped walnuts the ingredients that went into the making of a great actress? Decidedly not. How unerringly Arthur had divined the existence of certain obstacles that stood between her emergence as a theatrical star of the first magnitude. At eighteen Mrs. Siddons (nee Kemble), already married, had flashed across London, dazzled provincial audiences, and was playing Portia opposite Garrick himself. What would Sara Kemble Siddons do, had she the motive and cue for passion that I have? thought Laly. She would "drown the stage with tears, cleave the general air with horrid speech, make mad the guilty and appall the free, confound the ignorant, etc., etc.," while I stir fudge, tell Quincia to "stop sniffling" over those Temperance Tracts, put up with Mama's tantrums (what in heaven's name is happening to Mama anyway?) and waste my fragrance on the desert air.

Where, where, *where*, how, how, *how* could a fully equipped woman, fastidious but yearning, come to grips with that seemingly impossible *he*—the unmarried, financially responsible male who combined masculine threat and romantic charm so plentiful in song and story, but so conspicuously missing in the Landmark picture?

Unlike Portia languidly asking Nerissa to tell over the list of eligible suitors, Laly could tick off the local swains on two fingers: Wilmer Stires, addicted to pawing above and below the belt; and Reb Plaskett, her former playmate, who made the opposite mistake of deifying the object of his love. Reb was now a sparely built young man, a few inches below heroic height and several thousand leagues behind Arthur Coplestone as a conversationalist. Reb's chief topic was the distillery where he held the rank of lieutenant to Anson Woodhull himself. On matters pertaining to the distillation of whiskey, Reb spoke with enthusiasm, authority and alas, too great detail.

"We shipped eight hundred barrels to S. S. Pierce in Boston yesterday. Best firm in New England. They'd take more if we could send it." Pause. While rockers creaked and night breezes rustled through sycamore branches, Reb described the operation of the new fractionating column. When Laly asked what a fractionating column might be, Reb obliged in unintelligible detail. More rocking, then a nostalgic struggle on Reb's part to recapture some of their old intimacy.

"Remember the time you got stuck in the hay chute and I had to pull you down by your legs?"

At the very mention of Laly's legs, now covered to the ankles by three petticoats and a voile print, the "good times in the hayloft" note evaporated and Reb became what indeed he was, a gawky, fifteen-dollar-a-week workman trespassing via yesterday on forbidden grounds. One evening late in June, he rose awkwardly, murmured something about getting back to the plant, then clumped down the porch steps, heavy with the sense of his own futility.

That night Laly wrote to Arthur from an inkwell full of tears. "This evening I entertained a childhood admirer. Worlds separated us. Is it not strange that I feel alone even in the midst of my family and old friends? What is the matter with me, Arthur dearest? Do you feel the same way?"

By return mail, Arthur dearest acknowledged a similar state of mind. "Loneliness is the alembic in which the attars of love are distilled" (he wrote). Then, after drawing this metaphor out into a longish paragraph, he described a really amazing instance of thought-transference that he had recently experienced.

> *Last evening at the Astral Society, of which I am a member, Professor Alberto Morini demonstrated how powerful these transferences can be. The professor had a sheet of brass (called a Chladni plate) which he covered with a small heap of sand. Then he asked someone with a strong personality to come forward and be a "reactor." As I stepped toward the rostrum, he looked at me most searchingly, then said, "Smooth out the sand with your hand and concentrate on the person uppermost in your mind." (Of course you know whose name I have uppermost in my thoughts.) Then the professor tapped the edge of the plate with a small wand. The grains of sand arranged themselves into a pattern that looked like this: Λ. Professor Morini said that this was the Greek letter Lambda, which corresponds with the English L. So you see, my darling, you are so uppermost in my mind that even grains of sand on a brass plate catch the vibrations and spell out the initials of your name.*

The letter closed with an exciting P.S.

> *I have just bought a fine camera, secondhand, of course. It's an 8 x 10 E. A. Anthony box with a Goerz Dagor lens, as sharp as a steel etching. Why don't you suggest to your parents that I come to Landmark and take a picture of your family? In this way we can see each other. Please, my Queen Regnant, use all your powers of persuasion so that you can summon me into your presence once more.*

> *P.P.S. Domily Muse is closing the studio for a few days around July 4. Could you make it then?*

Laly fingered the mauve paper thoughtfully. Before Arthur could be invited to Landmark, Mama's consent must be won. By the code governing dutiful daughters in the matter of house guests, Mama alone could exercise the chatelaine prerogative of extending a written invitation. And if Mama's recent tantrums were any indication, the decision would be close.

The line between self-pity and clear-sighted recognition of one's fate—a line always difficult to draw—has a tendency to become blurred when certain biologic changes, euphemistically termed the *climacteric,* take place in a woman's life. Zarah Woodhull had already noticed the first signs of the thinning leaf-fall, melancholy precursor of autumn. Her physical ailments, ranging from hot flashes to migraine, were supportable. More difficult to bear was the ever-present sense of personal failure to become the Matriarch Enthroned in her own household.

In the earlier years of her marriage—even during that period of fearful poverty on the farm—Zarah had assumed that sooner or later she would emerge as the Queen Bee, the architect of her own destiny and the ultimate court of decision in matters affecting her husband and children. Now as she sat in her sewing room off the conservatory, Zarah asked herself, Wherein have I failed? With any other man but Anson, her feminine struggle for supremacy would almost certainly have succeeded. Tears of self-pity blurred but could not wash away the fact that after twenty years of marriage she had passed under Anson's yoke; she had been subjugated by him. This much-loved husband had quietly pried the scepter of command from her fingers; had outflanked and overreached her in the incessant maneuvering for position and power—whether masked or overt—that goes on in every marriage.

With a small lace handkerchief, Zarah dabbed at the tiny beads of perspiration on her forehead and upper lip, the visible after-tokens of the hot flashes that were tormenting her with increasing frequency. An interior monologue accompanied the staccato needle pricks that she was making in a pennon of green silk which would serve as a gusset—the second within two months—for one of Laly's shirtwaists. A false notion of economy plus a desire to humiliate her seam-bursting daughter, had prompted Zarah to undertake this delicate alteration. Gusset upon gusset! The black number 36 on Zarah's tape measure when passed around Laly's bosom seemed a personal affront to the mother whose own breasts were beginning to lose their firmness. After five children—one of them dead—had tugged at one's breasts, wasn't it natural that one's mammary equipment should show some signs of wear and tear? Natural, yes, but . . .

The pity of it was that Anson had escaped the physical consequences of bearing children and then feeding them. At forty-four he was handsomer, stronger than ever. Very much his own man, too, this husband of hers whose yea or nay could settle a dispute, quell doubt, cause other men to accept his judgment and cause Zarah Woodhull (nee Osgood) to lose her identity in his all-encompassing embrace.

In an attempt to reclaim some fragment of herself, Zarah had left the big double bed once joyously shared with this man, and for the past two or three years had occupied a room of her own. True, there was no bolt on its door. Anson might knock—as he always did—enter, appeal to her for that mutual consolation nominated in the bonds of matrimony. Indeed, he had so appealed. Neither as a suppliant nor proprietor but simply—and this was what killed Zarah—as one who had only to come, place his hand under her head, seal her eyes with the kiss that in some mysterious fashion threw back the locking tumblers of her innermost self, as often or as infrequently as he wished.

If, even once, Anson had displayed the slightest sign of clumsiness, haste, uncertainty or, worse yet, *certainty*, Zarah might have screamed, "In God's name, let me be. This is *my* body. I will not have it invaded. Used. Even for my own need and pleasure."

Anson had given her no opportunity for such protest. In fact, she had lain many a night wishing and waiting for the marital encounter that always ended—how? With a victory that was at the same time another defeat. Zarah could win, *had* won, every battle; yet somehow, somewhere, she had lost the war.

Time was running over her, around her, on this summer day in 1896 as she whip-stitched the gusset into shape. Had time used her? Passed her by? What was she hoping for? What was she remembering? The eternal note of sadness (heard from the Aegean to Landmark and all way stations between) began circling through Zarah's mind in the form of the Medea soliloquy. Men are troubled by other quite different soliloquies. Only a woman who had passed her fortieth birthday is eligible for the Medea sequence concerning the exotic queen, the strange woman led by love into a hostile land and somehow betrayed, forsaken or disappointed —after giving the best years of her life, mind you—to some Jason or other.

Riders on the Medea carousel should know that the ring is an alloy of gold and brass. Ideally they should recall their earlier joy in snatching for it and those wonderful voyages with Jason across the wine-dark sea of adventure and romance. Actual practice is quite different. Observing only their present condition (either real or fancied), they feel resentment taking root. From these resentments spring imputations of blame upon the married partner. And once the Medea machinery has been set in motion, how natural, how human, how *wifelike* to invoke the *lex talionis*—the law of retaliation.

Zarah's melancholy self-indictment, "I have failed," was neither fair nor literally true. In a thousand ways she had exerted a most civilizing influence in the lives of her husband and children. By her insistence on the well-set table; by her emphasis on indoor decorum; carefully brushed hair, scrubbed fingernails; rising when one's parents entered or left the room—these amenities, not native to Landmark, were wholly traceable to Zarah. Anson had always supported the exercise of her matron authority. He had never quarreled or even disagreed with her in the presence of others. Temperamentally he was not given to tyranny or the voicing of ultimatums.

Mutual affection and solicitude had remained steadfast. As before, they spent the parlor hour together. Anson's fidelity was beyond questioning. Possibly he was rather too preoccupied with the business of making and selling whiskey, a business that neither Zarah nor Landmark had ever been able to accept without reservations.

Long ago Zarah had become indifferent to the sterility of the social and intellectual aspects of Landmark. Did it really matter that she had never been "tapped" for membership in the Girl's Friendly Society, headwater of local gossip and fountain of social preferment? Her failure to accept the Second Baptist Salad Supper as the true equivalent of Christ's Body and Blood had opened an impassable rift between her and Landmark's theological elect. Apart from Solange, whom she occasionally visited in Cincinnati, Zarah's only woman friend was Alice Towner, whose mind—such as it was—had been formed east of the Alleghenies. Poughkeepsie, to be exact.

Zarah found herself longing for Cambridge ways, Cambridge manners, Cambridge diction. These midwestern yahoos. They were beginning to contaminate Chance's diction; Ozzie had already slumped into the pit of irretrievability when at fourteen he put in his first "chaw" and displayed a precocious skill at "drowndin" flies at ten paces.

Where would she ever see or hear again the inimitable New England thing? The Thing itself. Into Zarah's thoughts glided the boneless phantom of her father:

You shall regret this decision.

You shall never live to hear me say so.

Both speakers had been right. The difference between them was this: Quincy Adams Osgood had lain for the past eleven years in cool New England clay while his daughter Zarah was condemned to go on living in the dust of a midwestern county seat.

The competitive struggle, though cyclic in severity, was daily pressed into Zarah's consciousness by Quincia's impenetrable reserve, Ozzie's sour oafishness and, for the past six weeks, by Laly's seam-bursting nubility. That Laly! A scene-stealer, an eye-turner. Her very walk was a flaunt. Zarah remembered how the taffeta in Lady Darlington's costume had rustled much too audibly when Laly strode across the stage. She had played the part as though she were *a Restoration hussy.*

But, soft she comes! Winsomeness well forward, Laly entered the sewing room for the ordeal—tedious at best—of a "fitting." Wordlessly she slipped out of her cotton print; then, arms lifted, submitted first to Zarah's hostile scrutiny and, next, to the basting routine.

I might have spared myself this, thought Zarah. Whom am I punishing? As she slipped her hand over the gusset to smooth out its silken fabric, she felt the marmoreal contours of Laly's bosom. For a suspended tick of time Zarah saw in her daughter a fresh replica of womanhood, a volcano boiling toward eruption, an uncorseted cageful of leopardess talents, each talent rattling the bars and screaming vainly for expression. Into what socially acceptable channels could a girl of "gentle" breeding divert her teeming flood of energy? Answer, echo, answer! (Echo remained silent.) The same iron conventions that had bound Zarah, the taboo against a stage career, indeed any career except marriage, were now binding Laly.

Almost, but not quite, Zarah felt like dissolving into tears of sympathy and embracing her daughter. We gifted ones! Tell us, O Lord, what must we do! Instead she picked up a needle and started threading it from a spool of No. 70 green silk thread.

"Mama," she heard Laly saying.

"Yes." The "you-may-proceed" yes.

"Mr. Coplestone has suggested that he take a photograph of our family."

"How thoughtful of Mr. Coplestone! Who precisely is he? The gentleman that writes to you daily, in an outlandish combination of emerald ink and mauve paper? In Cambridge, young men wrote with black ink on gray paper. They avoided swirls that are better suited, I think, to illuminated manuscript than to a personal message. But go on, tell me more. What is Mr. Coplestone's background? Who are his antecedents?"

"Mama, Mama, stop this Brattle Street chatter. We live in Indiana. I'm your daughter. Remember? I don't know who Arthur Coplestone's antecedents are and I don't particularly care. He just happens to be the most interesting man I've ever met."

"I should like to hear some specific instances of Mr. Coplestone's . . . ah . . . charm."

"Well, for one thing he subscribes to *The Yellow Book*."

"I have heard of the publication. It is a journal devoted to decadence."

"If *The Yellow Book* is decadent what would you call the Landmark *Cornet?*" First blood for Laly. She continued. "Arthur has a wide range of intellectual interests and a thorough mastery of the Romance languages."

"Italian? French? Provençal?"

"Please, mother! By romance language, Arthur means the language of the glove, fan and parasol."

"Has he, by any chance, ever mentioned the dropped handkerchief?"

"Every servant girl knows about the dropped handkerchief."

"True." Zarah's detachment was maddening. "For a time I entertained something higher than servant-girl aspirations for my eldest daughter."

"Such as?"

"Your father and I discussed sending you to Radcliffe. It adjoins Harvard."

Laly sent her mother down for a nine-count, "Did *you* go to Radcliffe?"

"Women had no such opportunity in my day."

"Mother, I beg you. Let's not quarrel about Radcliffe or anything else. I'm merely suggesting we invite Arthur Coplestone to come here on July fourth to take a photograph of our family."

"Your feeling of urgency eludes me. What's so imperative about our being photographed?"

Borrowing selectively from Arthur's stock of arguments, Laly came up with a sparkler. "In the life of every family there is a moment of optimum felicity that cries out for perpetuation. In my opinion, Mama, that moment is at hand."

The moment of optimum felicity? The words had a knelling fall—part prophecy, part challenge to Zarah's private notion of what the future held for her family; part apprehension lest Laly be right.

With one of her hot flashes coming on, Zarah chose to postpone the decision by taking refuge in the very sanctuary that she most wished to avoid. Anson's judgment.

"I shall discuss the matter with your father," she said.

Laly had the whip handle now. "Do so, Mother. Urge it. Stop fumbling for something you've lost—or never had."

At the door of the sewing room Laly turned. "Be on the winning side for a change. It's more fun that way."

Two days later Zarah wrote a coldly correct note to Arthur Coplestone inviting him to Landmark. The note bade Mr. Coplestone make his appearance on the afternoon of July 3 with such photographic equipment as he deemed necessary.

SUPPER: JULY 3

IF NERVOUS ATTENTION to detail could guarantee success, Laly Woodhull's supper promised to be a triumph. In honor of Arthur Coplestone's visit, the best damask tablecloth and heaviest silver were on display. Laly had decided on creamed chicken and hot biscuits (which Mrs. Beebe did very well) together with corn on the cob and two kinds of relish—pickled watermelon and damson plum—for color and tang.

There was a centerpiece of pond lilies contributed by Quincia, and a glass pitcher of iced tea sprigged with mint. Zarah and Anson occupied their usual chairs at opposite ends of the table. Arthur, at Zarah's right, sat next to Ozzie, who had been kindly requested to wash up, brush up and shut up for the occasion.

The guest had arrived that afternoon with a staggering load of photographic equipment. After changing from his traveling clothes to a suit of tan pongee, a black silk tie and chamois-topped button shoes, Arthur descended to the porch for introductions and was now asperging charm over the supper-table audience. Laly's tide of tension could ebb a little. She dared glance at Arthur as if to say, See how easily I can make things go? She hoped with all the intensity of a young woman in love that her family would like Arthur. So much depended on first impressions. She passed damson plums to everyone with almost hysteric eagerness, while her father opened the conversation with a bit of man-to-man talk.

"You must meet a lot of interesting people in your line," said Anson.

Laly winced at her father's unfortunate locution. Photography wasn't a "line." As Arthur had explained a dozen times, it was a specially sensitized way of life, a marriage of art, science, vision and design. Under cover of pickled-watermelon business, she waited for Arthur's reply and was amazed by his tactful handling of the matter.

"That's just about the truest thing you ever said, Mr. Woodhull." Arthur registered surprise that the lay mind could arrive at such a novel conclusion. "Meeting distinguished people is the photographer's chief reward. Scarcely a day passes that some bigwig doesn't drop into the studio. Financiers, social and religious leaders, theater folks—sooner or later everyone sits for the little box with the long memory."

Laly liked that last phrase. She liked Arthur's firm emphasis on "studio." Not office, not shop. *Studio.* She hoped he would underscore the point and bring a spark of approval into Mama's eyes by an offhand reference to atelier.

Arthur didn't disappoint her. "Take last week, for example. Our atelier was a madhouse. On Monday, the Divine Sarah *swam* in on ten minutes' notice for several portrait studies—Imperial Size. Next day it was Philip Sousa and three society weddings. Wednesday was normal—the usual run of *carte de visite* sittings and babies on bearskin rugs. No pun intended.

Then the deluge! Alfredo the Cloud King, balloon and all, had to be sandwiched in between Senator Casseboom and the Cincinnati baseball team."

Arthur's shot-making policy—a ball for every pocket—was scoring heavily. At the mention of Sousa's name, Ozzie missed a beat in his load-and-fill technique of eating. Young Chance stopped nibbling corn to stare at the man who, in a single day, had taken pictures of a big-league ball club and the world's foremost balloonist. Laly, by a process of identification, was *in* the balloon—not with Alfredo but with Arthur. They were soaring above the clouds, taking pictures as they climbed.

Anson brought down the balloon with a well-ballasted question. "Do I understand, Mr. Coplestone, that you take these pictures on your own?"

Arthur chose to interpret the question as favorable. Here was a fond father, substantial to wealthy, sounding out the status of a prospective son-in-law. Everything must be made clear. Arthur's manner was frank, his voice tinged with half-humorous regret.

"I'm sorry if I gave that impression, Mr. Woodhull. Put it down to my enthusiasm for photography—present and future. To answer your question, Mr. Domily Muse *owns* the studio and reaps the harvest. I'm his chief assistant. I do all the retouching, developing and handle a growing clientele of my own. One of these days, not too far distant, I plan to open my own studio."

It all sounded reasonable enough to Anson. In that era of unlimited opportunity, any alert young man could set up shop for himself and—barring serious defects of judgment or character—would prosper. Anson himself had shown that it could be done. Like an interested but impartial juror, he decided to wait until more evidence came in.

Zarah alone refused to be blandished by the Coplestone charm. Under his pongee veneer she saw a pushing, conceited young man with more than a hint of the charlatan in his conversation and attire. She wondered why Arthur's affectations—the snake ring on his little finger and his odious habit of name-dropping—should arouse so much hostility on her part. It was absurd—like a piano-tuner competing with a pupil of Liszt's. Zarah decided to observe the bare amenity of listening while the piano-tuner held forth.

Her bleakness puzzled Arthur. Accustomed to the simpering attentions of Cincinnati dowagers, he was unable to interpret Zarah's "we are not amused" expression. To soothe his vanity, Arthur was obliged to assign reasons for Zarah's disdain and shrewdly enough proceeded to do so. His professional knowledge of women gained under the harsh lights of the photographic studio told him many things about the disdainful Mrs. Woodhull. It was apparent that she felt discontented, cheated even, about something. Arthur saw the defeated matriarch who would have snatched the baton of family command from the hands of a weaker husband. Then, too, she was worried about her age. Arthur placed her at about forty—a remarkably handsome forty—still firm-fleshed and proud-walking. Yet there were critical places—shadowy eye sockets and a certain lack of resiliency under the chin— that would require the services of a retoucher's pencil. But not even the most skillful retoucher could obliterate the evidence of a blooming eighteen-year-old daughter, who was at this moment exercising her hostess prerogative by tinkling a hand bell for hot biscuits.

What a triumph, thought Arthur, to slip through the fine-meshed veil of Zarah's defenses, engage her mature intelligence and enlist her feminine sympathy. Knowing the power of his eyes, Arthur brought them oftener and more boldly into the private contest between Laly's mother and himself.

Zarah found his close-range scrutiny objectionable. She had the feeling that he had inserted a peepjack lens somewhere behind his eyeball and was now recording naked images on his too-perceptive retina. She was unused to such appraisal and waited her opportunity to chastise this liberty-taking young man who had apparently bewitched everyone else in the room. Anson, usually so judicial, seemed fascinated; Laly, her lips slightly parted, was nodding an uncritical yes to everything that Arthur said. Zarah fumed inwardly. Her finer nostril, having inhaled the true scent of an older culture, detected the cheap drench that Arthur was spraying about the table. With photography as his theme, he was sprinkling his conversation with such terms as "chiaroscuro," "visual counterpoint" and "dynamics of composition." Did the fellow think he was an *artist?* Was he claiming that photography had displaced painting?

Apparently he was. Listen to him now.

"The oil portrait, as we all know, was a product of an earlier, more aristocratic age. It flourished at a time when only the nobility—the very rich—could afford to have its picture painted. Commoners certainly couldn't pay Gainsborough's fee of five hundred pounds. But the growth of a merchant class created a demand for likenesses—a demand that oil painters couldn't possibly fill. The camera was invented to satisfy that demand.

"Manet, I think it was—one of those *plein air* fellows anyway—said that light is the most important thing in a picture. Personally I wouldn't go that far. It's the mysterious counterpoint of light *and* dark—half-tones, *shadows*—that gives a picture excitement, drama, threat." He leaned toward Zarah with a mixture of deference and familiarity. "Don't you agree, Mrs. Woodhull?"

The question caught Zarah on an exposed flank. Manet was a new name to her. She had never heard of the *plein air* school. What, she wondered, had become of Burne-Jones, Millet, Alma-Tadema and Rosa Bonheur? No matter. From dusty shelves she gathered up a double handful of Brattle Street crockery and came in firing.

"Shadows aren't exactly a modern invention, Mr. Coplestone. Rembrandt regarded them highly. Titian's favorite color was umber, which, as I recall, stems from the Latin *umbra,* meaning shadow." For good measure Zarah heaved a loose brick from Ruskin's *Stones of Venice.* "And certain medieval architects, who for some odd reason preferred to remain nameless, practically *built* Chartres and Notre Dame with half-lights, quarter-darks and a choirful of hemi-semi-demi shadows."

Snub. Check. Your play, Mr. Coplestone.

Zarah's momentary triumph was marred by the instant realization that she had tumbled headlong into Arthur's trap. What this scheming young man really wanted was her attention. Failing to win it on the level of social acceptance, he had lured her into controversy. And having won her attention, he was quite willing to lose the argument.

"You crush me, Mrs. Woodhull. I'll be climbing out of the ruins for weeks." Arthur's humility was almost convincing. "I suppose our trouble—the trouble with photographers generally—is . . . well, we're so dazzled by our own technical advances that we sometimes forget to acknowledge our debt to the old masters."

Arthur's persistent linking of photography with art goaded Zarah beyond the bounds of courtesy. "My knowledge of your profession is slight, Mr. Coplestone." (As slight, her voice suggested, as my knowledge of counterfeiting.) "Until now, I had always supposed that photographers contented themselves with obtaining a good likeness of people. But from your remarks I gather that such a likeness is merely incidental to your . . . ah . . . larger aesthetic interests."

Pennons of restlessness began to flutter at various stations. Laly thought it naughty of Mama to monopolize Arthur's attention; she reached for the bell but dared not ring for dessert. Anson, hearing the shrillness in his wife's voice, gave her a worried glance. The whole argument was beyond Ozzie's comprehension. This guy Coplestone was full of bunny-water—no substitute for the lemon-meringue pie that Ozzie now craved.

"You may ring for dessert, Laly," said Zarah. Having reestablished the domestic pecking order, she proceeded to demolish Mr. Coplestone. She must work rapidly now: from interior depths she felt a tidal wave of heat signaling the onset of the dreaded hot flash. In a few seconds the wave would suffuse her cheeks and forehead, bring on accompanying symptoms of dizziness, a ringing in her ears and a light fringe of perspiration on her lip and forehead. Suddenly Zarah lost her sharp appetite to continue the attack. The ground was unfamiliar; the subject not hers. She did not *care* as she repeated her question.

"In taking a picture do you confine yourself to obtaining a mere likeness, or does your chief interest lie in expressing your own personality?"

Zarah's intent to wound was apparent enough. But what piqued Arthur most was the weary, beneath-notice tone of her attack. He longed more than ever to capture the regard of this woman who, if she cared to, might understand him. Humility, salesmanship, glibness (and he had tried each in turn) had failed to penetrate her unassailable guard. He stripped himself of vanity, laid aside affectation and, for the first time perhaps in his life, addressed honest words to an emotional equal.

"In every creative process—and I should certainly include photography among them, Mrs. Woodhull—a trial of strength takes place between the artist and his material. Each attempts to impose its will on the other. The colors on Titian's canvas, the stones of those cathedrals you spoke of, didn't fall into place *willingly*. No, the raw material of art is stubborn, perverse, like a puzzle that doesn't want to be put together, and never *will* be put together until the artist comes along and imposes meaning on it. Only when the artist is stronger than his material does its concealed truth become clear."

The hot flash swirling through Zarah's body climbed to the roots of her hair. Dizziness blurred her vision, blocked out the other faces at the table. For a moment she had the strange feeling that she and Arthur Coplestone were alone and that her matron virtue was dissolving under the acid insolence of his gaze. She heard a conchlike roaring in her ears and Arthur's voice was saying, "The lady is not unassailable. . . . She is not too old. Will she kindly signify her interest by dropping her handkerchief at the proper time?"

The whole episode was fantastically unreal and its unreality became apparent to Zarah as the hot tide receded. There she sat at her own table. Anson was nipping the end of an after-dinner cigar. Laly was pouring coffee. And Chance—his blue eyes fixed on Arthur—was asking a question.

"When you took that picture of the Cincinnati ball team, Mr. Coplestone—" awe and curiosity caused the boy to gulp —"what kind of a bird did you use?"

"Bird?"

"Yeh. Like when the man comes out from behind the black cloth and says, 'Watch the birdie.' "

A wave of laughter swept the table, cleansing the last remnant of tension. Anson roared. Ozzie guffawed and Zarah herself smiled at Chance's innocent expression of surprise. Arthur waited for Ozzie's last *haw* before answering.

"We don't use birds any more, Chance. They've disappeared, along with such other relics as the head clamp and the fringed chair. Nowadays we gain the attention of our sitters by other methods." Arthur illustrated his point with a homely anecdote. "A couple of weeks ago an elderly couple came in for a sitting. They wanted to celebrate their fortieth wedding anniversary, but somehow I couldn't get them into the 'picture mood.' They were as grim as a couple of epitaphs until I noticed an old-fashioned tourmaline—evidently an engagement ring—on the third finger of the lady's left hand. 'Now, Ma'am,' I said, 'I want you to think of the time when your husband slipped that ring onto your finger.' Then I turned to the husband. 'And you, sir, I want you to gaze at your wife as if you were saying, "Emma, this isn't much of a stone, but no diamond will ever be as bright as the tears of happiness in your eyes right now." ' "

Arthur drew the entire company into the circle of his narrative. "Well, do you know, that woman burst into a torrent of tears and said, 'Young man, you must be a fortuneteller because that's exactly what my husband *did* say.' " Arthur sipped his coffee and brought his tale to an offhand close. "After that I had no trouble in getting a natural, affectionate pose."

The anecdote had various effects on the Coplestone audience. Laly's eyes were blurry with pride and gratitude. Arthur's magic had saved her supper party. Anson was offering the visitor a cigar, and a match to light it with. Zarah dabbed her cambric handkerchief at invisible beads of perspiration on her upper lip and wondered what conjurer element gave this cheap young man his indefinable strangeness and power.

After-supper silence, as soft as an unspoken grace, hovered over the table. For a fleeting moment, Time rested on a peaceful plateau as if content with the prize that only family life at its best can offer. The moment swelled for a slow second of ripeness, then was broken by a conspiratorial *sol-mi-do* whistle coming in through the open window.

At this secret signal, Chance rose from the table. A force stronger than pie, mightier than domestic tranquillity, gripped him. Hastily he folded his napkin into its bone ring and said, "Excuse me, everyone. That's Wayland Towner; we're going to play catch behind the carriage house."

Not even his haste to join Wayland Towner caused Chance to forget a regular part of the Woodhull family routine. It was his custom on leaving the room always to kiss his mother. He planted his lips on her cheek, then stopped to pick up something from the floor.

"Your handkerchief, Mama. You must've dropped it."

"Kissing never solves anything *really*"—a canard set in motion by come-lately members of the psuedo-Rochefoucauld School—overlooks the demonstrable fact that countless millions of orally oriented Occidentals regard the kiss not as an accidental aspect of, or solution to, anything else, but rather (especially during the middle-late-teens) as the be-all, end-all and *sine qua non* of love. Hence the cry "kiss, kiss, kiss" arising from adolescent throats and taken up by the adult population as the basis for the sheet-music conception of love later to be puréed by women's magazines and gelatinized by movies yet unborn.

Standing or sitting, Laly Woodhull's kiss potentiality—if properly wired up—could have burned out all the arc lights in Akron, Ohio, or any city of comparable size. Since she had never been kissed in the horizontal position, she longed for a maiden spin over the supine course. By eight-thirty P.M. she was aching, fainting, dying for that privacy which precedes any wholehearted yielding up of dewy lips, pearly teeth, darting tongue and adjacent membrana to the oh-so-wonderful, make-it-last-forever treatment of her highly accomplished guest, Arthur Coplestone. If Arthur could perform such tongue and cheek miracles on a park bench, what might be expected of him in a gazebo?

More to the point: how could she get him there? For the past half hour, Arthur had been scrupulous in the performance of his rocking-chair duty, verandah division. Governed by the ancient rule of protocol which decrees that no guest shall address royalty until expressly invited to do so, Arthur waited for Zarah or Anson to break the silence. *Creak. Creak. Creak. Creak.* Rocking chairs to the right of her, rocking chairs to the left of her, Laly suggested music of another sort. Would Mama play the piano? Mama would not. She didn't feel quite up to acting the part of a Liszt pupil for the benefit of a piano-tuner.

Would Arthur have a lemonade? Thank God, Arthur said yes. Resisting an impulse to scream, Laly started Operation Lemonade in the kitchen. When she returned with a tray bearing four tinkling glasses, Anson had drawn Mr. Coplestone into a conversation.

"No," Arthur was saying, "I have never had the pleasure of visiting your famous distillery, Mr. Woodhull. I must confess, however, that on those rare occasions when, say, a friend was celebrating the birth of an heir, or the members of our Camera Club were taking a night cap, my expressed preference has always been for Old Landmark."

"Nice to hear a thing like that."

Laly offered lemonade to all hands while her father continued. "Have you ever asked for Old Landmark and been served something else?"

It was no part of Coplestone's plan to pose as a toper when more important dice were in the cup. On the other hand, he must avoid milksop attitudes.

Arthur considered the implications of the question. Then, striking a nice intermediate balance, he gave off in frank man-to-man chest tones. "My experience is not extensive, sir. There was, however, an incident." Reluctantly Arthur proceeded to describe a Roland at Roncesvalles brush with a fictitious barkeep.

"You must respect my wish to preserve the man's anonymity—after all, he merely worked there."

"I quite understand."

"Well, on one occasion he attempted to pass off some spurious whiskey as Old Landmark. When I ragged him for this monstrous piece of deception, he pointed to the label on the bottle and shrugged. 'The label says Old Landmark.' 'I'm not drinking *labels*,' I said. 'No, sir. I called for Old Landmark. I'm perfectly willing to pay the price differential if, in return, I receive the genuine article.'"

At this virile display of connoisseurship, Zarah rose, gave a brief impression of being seasick, and wombled toward the living-room door.

"Are you quite all right, Mama?" Laly, all solicitude, accompanied Mama to the foot of the grand staircase where, after expressing herself in terms never heard on Brattle Street, she faded from the scene.

The gazebo prospects were brightening. If only Arthur would cut short his play-by-play description of Old Landmark's effect upon his senses.

"First, there's the bouquet. Inimitable, sir. Then the slow ascent via taste buds and nasal membranes to a center somewhere up here." Arthur indicated the frontal sinus region. "Finally that afterglow so typical of your *Aurum Potabile*. I translate freely, 'Liquid Gold.'"

No man objects to hearing his horse, wife or whiskey flattered. "Liquid gold." Anson savored the description. "That's good."

"I dare say, Mr. Woodhull, that other cheaper whiskeys have been poured into and out of your Gold Medal bottle."

"Many a time. A ring of swindlers in Cincinnati is in the business of printing up Old Landmark labels. They buy up empty bottles—heaven knows where—fill them up with raw, inferior whiskey, paste a counterfeit label on the bottle and peddle the stuff around as Old Landmark."

Laly broke the rubric which holds that "horses sweat, men perspire and women glow." The corn starch under her armpits was turning into a damp paste. Would these men never stop talking about "liquid gold" and false labels while the genuine chalice itself, clearly marked and filled with aromatic spirits of yieldingness, nervously plucked at its humeral veil in preparation for the gazebo ritual?

Like a clergyman with one eye on the sacrament and the other on the contribution plate, Arthur figured the long-range take. "Couldn't you halt the activity of these criminals by increasing your own production?"

"I've given the matter some thought—a great deal of thought—Mr. Coplestone, and the answer always comes out the same. The simple fact is that my distillery, like your studio, is geared to a certain rate of production. Ten thousand barrels a year seems to be the figure. For the present I am content to let it stand."

The noiseless whirl of multiplicand and multiplier, subtrahend, divisor and dividend produced the figures Arthur was looking for. Gross income nigh onto a million annually. Allow a decent net of 10 per cent and what you got was . . . plenty.

Feeling the heat waves emanating from Laly's banked furnace, Arthur wound up with a diplomatic question, "May I convey to Mr. Domily Muse, my employer, the flattering comparison you made between your distillery and his studio?"

"If you think it's worth mentioning, why not?" Anson rose. "Well, you two young people probably want to enjoy the beauties of our Indiana moon." He extended a hostly hand to Arthur. "Feel free. Looking forward to watching you in action tomorrow. Good night, Laly dear."

Daughterly kiss. Regret half expressed. *Que sera sera.*

Laly felt the oncoming holiday in her blood. She waited a decent interval of one hundred and twenty heart throbs. Then: "Come. Take my hand, Arthur. Don't be afraid. I'll lead the way to the summer house."

A light Indiana breeze carried midsummer scents into the latticed gazebo, an octagonal summer house built in the farthest corner of the Woodhull property. A wainscot of tongue-and-groove fir, highly varnished, rose to a height of four feet above the floor, just high enough to protect a rattan couch from weather and observation. Illumination, such as it was, began with a string of Japanese lanterns leading from the big house and ended at the smooth lower limb of a first-growth copper beech.

An oblate spheroid (the moon), about 35 degrees off the horizon, cast rosy-orange beams through the Jacqueminot latticework of the summer house. Laly need not have been so outrageously beautiful in such an aura. On sofa cushions carefully prearranged, she now disposed herself in a semi-reclining position, Récamier fashion, and awaited the moment of optimum felicity. The only power capable of keeping a man's hands off a predisposed girl at such a moment was Arthur's acute sense of future profit as opposed to present enjoyment. Attentive, but not precipitate, he seated himself in a wicker rocking chair, gazed at the object of his controlled passion and seemed content to let this impetuous one float, run or dawdle as she pleased, toward an inevitable and quite overwhelming question.

He opened his silver cigarette case, appealed for permission to smoke one of his flat-oval, cork-tipped Narghiles.

"Please do." Laly loved the special attar, unknown to her by name, of Arthur's cigarettes. History was made then. By thirty years she anticipated the first American cigarette ad in which a lovely girl breathed ecstatically, "Blow some my way." The requested incense previously dipped in tincture of cantharides, known to coarser lips as "Spanish fly," was a well-known stimulant to the genito-urinary mucous membranes.

Rational conversation seemed unlikely. But Arthur succeeded in advancing, under cover of his concealed ledger, to a fiscal-exploratory probe tipped with flattery. "Your father is one of the most charming and strongest male characters I have ever met. I can easily understand how you come by your independence of spirit." Arthur puffed twice, lazily. Let the moon of an Indiana midsummer night get its work in. "What I can't understand is why a man in *his* business didn't offer his guest an *apéritif* or an after-dinner liqueur."

"Mother disapproves." Laly's gesture was suitably vague.

"That's a mother's prerogative." All gallantry. "I only hope that her disapproval doesn't extend to me."

"How possibly could she disapprove of you, Arthur? It's merely that—well, the idea of the photographer-as-artist has never been brought to her attention. I must say that you made a superb statement of the photographer's case at supper this evening."

"Thank you, Queen Regnant. Ah, that moidore moon!" exclaimed Arthur.

Laly thought it not at all odd that her companion should describe the moon in terms of a gold coin. In fancy, Arthur was handling bushel baskets of such coins. Two streams of coins, one emanating from the Old Landmark Distillery, the other from the atelier of Arthur Coplestone, were converging (or could be made to converge) by the very pleasant act of melting into Laly's lagoon o' dreams.

This sweetest of all solutions to Arthur Coplestone's problem—which was, in brief, to obtain a dowry of not less than ten thousand dollars from Anson Woodhull (and this, mind you, despite the disapproval of the bride-to-be's mother, herself a festering marsh of female dissatisfaction and dormant lust) must be temporarily postponed. At the proper time the thing could be carried off. Meanwhile Arthur contented himself with playing the classic role of *feignant,* the suppliant, not-yet-accepted, docile and oh, ever-so-devoted suitor, grateful for such teensy-weensy bits of *merci* as milady might choose to grant, strew or bestow.

The lady was in a bestowing mood. Her mouth, when Arthur got around to covering it with his own, was a rose that never could be a bud again. . . .

"Darling, darling," he murmured, "we really must get back to the house."

"Not just yet."

"Parents, you know, expect a certain punctilio from a first-time visitor. And because my regard for you and your mother is something quite sacred, we must tear ourselves apart."

He slipped off the sofa and drew Laly to her feet.

"Rearrange your bodice, Pretz. No one must suspect that I have been rifling the twin Jacqueminots that lie concealed from other mortals."

ENSEMBLE: JULY 4

WITH PROFESSIONAL TACT Arthur Coplestone was outlining his plans to Zarah. "Your conservatory appears to be the ideal setting for the composition I have in mind, Mrs. Woodhull. The light is more than adequate. Your palms and drapes will form a perfect background. Now here is a sketch—subject to your approval, naturally—that will give you a clearer idea of the seating arrangements. As you will note, I have chosen the classic triangular design. You and Mr. Woodhull will occupy the center chairs, with Laly directly behind, flanked by Osgood and Quincia on either side. Chance, as you see, sits cross-legged on the floor, resting his head gracefully against his mother's knee."

Zarah studied the sketch. In its carefully executed detail she saw the preliminary trial of strength between Arthur and his material. Already he had begun to impose his vision and design on the Woodhull family. Since Zarah had no specific suggestions, she approved the sketch with a complimentary nod. Arthur spent the morning assembling his equipment and arranging a suitable backdrop for the family picture. The big Anthony box with its folding bellows was wheeled into position, and at 12:30 the sitters were asked to take their places.

Zarah and Anson first. At Arthur's suggestion they faced each other in three quarters profile, Zarah's summery dress of white Battenberg forming a perfect contrast to her husband's sober broadcloth. Laly, graceful as a young birch queen, took her assigned position behind Anson; from a surplus of affection, she kissed the top of her father's head, then laid her hand on his shoulder.

"Excellent," cried Arthur. The picture mood was building. . . .

It collapsed into rubble when Ozzie entered with his trombone. Taking his place in the back row, he lifted the instrument to his lips and extended the brass slide to its full length.

"You can't bring *that* into the picture," snapped Laly.

"Why not? The circus poster down at the railroad station shows a trombone player riding on top of an elephant."

"Well, this isn't a circus poster and we aren't elephants."

Arthur saved the situation with a touch of humor. "If this were to be a picture of the Six Musical Woodhulls, with each member of the family playing some instrument, your trombone would be quite in order, Osgood. Let's see if we can't compromise. How about letting your instrument stand beside you on the floor?"

Ozzie was planting his feet for a balk when Anson settled the matter quietly. "Do as Mr. Coplestone says, son."

"Ah, that's much *much* better." By a slight adjustment of his camera Arthur managed to lose the instrument entirely. "Now, Quincia, will you please stand beside Laly? A bit closer, please."

The slim, unbending girl obeyed, but still seemed isolated from the group. Like an architect sketching the façade of a temple, Arthur temporarily abandoned this unsatisfactory column and moved to another part of his design.

"Where's Chance?" he asked.

"He'll be right down," volunteered Quincia. "I saw him combing his hair."

Definitely the picture mood was slipping away. Ozzie sulking, Laly taut with anxiety, Quincia refusing to be pulled into the composition, and Chance, the missing ingredient, nowhere in sight. Arthur felt like a water-colorist who had been asked to produce a nocturne with a pailful of hardening cement.

The cement loosened somewhat when Chance entered the conservatory. In his white starched blouse and Eton collar, his thick chestnut cowlick partly subdued by hasty brushing, he resembled a choirboy late for practice. Somewhat too eagerly Arthur snatched him by the elbow. Chance allowed himself to be molded into place at his mother's knee.

Arthur stepped back a few paces to view the over-all contours of his design; then, covering his head with a black photographer's cloth, he gazed at the ground glass of his camera. There, in an upside-down image, he saw an approximation of the effect he had planned. A slight want of clarity blurred the base and tip of the triangle; to produce a uniform depth of focus, Arthur gave his lens screw a quarter turn. The responsive glass performed a miracle of refraction by merging three dimensions into a single plane.

Still shrouded by the black cloth, Arthur studied the group under his eye. He saw six people bound together by blood resemblances, shared tradition and domestic habit—a group so typical that it might have served as a family tableau of American life at a moment of expanding promise. Beneath these resemblances, he saw dramatic variations of countenance and character so strongly marked as to be disturbing. How reconcile Ozzie's sour clay with Laly's bursting loveliness, or account for the contrast between Chance's competitive fire and Quincia's timidity? Arthur possessed neither the power nor interest to alter the personality traits of his sitters. Yet if his picture were to be successful, he must harmonize—momentarily at least—the invisible tensions that stretched, thinner than cobweb filaments, among the members of the group.

He emerged from the folds of black cloth and stood before his audience like a magician about to perform a difficult trick. He proposed to select a felicitous moment and, by squeezing the bulb secreted in his hand, imprison it forever on the plate of his camera. But first he must create the atmosphere of felicity! Exhortation could not persuade Chance to stop grinding his teeth; finger-snapping commands would never relax the flares of Laly's nostrils or induce Zarah, the defeated matriarch, to accept her more becoming role of loved wife and handsome mother.

From a secret phial of his conjurer personality, Arthur began silvering the mirror of illusion into which his sitters, each and severally, must gaze. He flashed the mirror from face to face, murmuring in a lulling monotone, sometimes unintelligible, sometimes not.

"*Lambda, lambda.*" A sedative aroma of association relaxed the membranes of Laly's lips and nostrils.

"Mr. Woodhull, will you please hook your thumb negligently under your watch chain?" Anson's too-patriarchal stiffness dissolved into the flexibility of the gold links between his thumb and forefinger.

"Watch the birdie, Chance." Instead of a bird Chance saw the ruby eyes of Arthur's snake ring glittering at the camera lens. He was fascinated.

"Excellent, rare, oh, rare!" Quincia's slender stem became part of the family bouquet. Zarah, last to surrender, felt a compulsion to yield herself up and become part of the illusion that this strange young man was creating.

The colors of Arthur's picture were flowing together now. The moment of felicity drew near. As if applying a fixative to the canvas before him, Arthur murmured, "Chladni once, Chladni twice . . ."

Click.

A beam of light emanating from a star ninety-three million miles distant penetrated the triangular aperture of the shutter. The moment of felicity was committed forever to the sensitized plate in the Anthony box.

"Now another one for insurance," said Arthur.

A specimen proof of the picture, delivered ten days later by Arthur Coplestone, was a triumph of half-tone photography. A less-expected visitation would be difficult to conceive. Zarah, suffering from migraine, was dozing on a chaise longue in the small room adjoining the conservatory when she heard a light tapping on the triptych screen that enabled a current of air to circulate through the lower floor of the empty house. Who could it be? It was Mrs. Beebe's afternoon off; all the children had gone picnicking; Anson wouldn't be home for another three hours.

"Yes?" Her voice, drowsy, unsuspecting, gave Arthur the permission that accompanies summer-afternoon malaise. He peered tentatively around one of the panels of the screen and saw Zarah reclining. She was wearing the lightest peignoir permissible for a downstairs interview—a violet *mousseline de soie* that matched the throbbing veins visible at her temples, inner arm and unsandaled instep.

"Please forgive this intrusion, Mrs. Woodhull." Arthur made no pretense of withdrawing. "I knocked at the front door and, receiving no answer, thought that I might take the liberty of leaving these proofs on the conservatory table."

Zarah's impulse to say, "Leave them on the table then and go away" was offset by her Pandora curiosity to see what had come out of Arthur's magical black box. She sat up and was rearranging her hair with fingers and hand mirror when Arthur took the liberty of drawing a wrought-iron chair close to her sofa.

Professional pride and personal vanity emanated in equal portions from the young man attired in a loose-hanging blazer, English flannel trousers, white shoes and a loosely knotted mauve silk tie.

He laid aside a Malacca stick and produced a beautifully mounted photograph taken only a few days before. Studying it, Zarah marveled at the professional skill that had enabled this bizarre creature to portray in the most flattering light the individual characteristics of her family in precisely the right order: there sat Anson, the archetype of all that was desirable, the unshakable male, the loving husband and father, the prosperous businessman, gazing eternally at an unbelievably handsome woman of forty, proud, even haughty, who returned his gaze with a glance tender, loyal and submissive by choice. Around them stood their children. And here Arthur had indeed achieved a miracle. No great task to make Laly appear beautiful. But how had he overcome Quincia's shyness, made Ozzie intelligent (well, almost), and pinned that cherubic half smile on Chance's lips?

Zarah reached for her vinaigrette to allay the racking pain in her forehead. "I congratulate you, Mr. Coplestone."

The chilly reserve of the bourgeois chatelaine piqued the young photographer who had recently finished reading the *Memoirs of Casanova.* How gratifying, he thought, to make a double conquest of mother and daughter, both in their own home—and on the same day. Patiently, he stalked his unsuspecting prey. He would follow where she led. Experience and self-esteem not unfounded had taught him that the fowler's net shouldn't be brought into play until preliminary risks had been tested.

"How did you achieve this effect of . . . unity?" asked Zarah.

"By vision and design. As you will observe—" Arthur bent over the picture, caught the warm musk of ripe fruit, gave in exchange the scent of a handkerchief doused with Jockey Club—"as you will observe, I employed the classic pattern. A line from apex to base passes directly through—" he indicated the center of focus—Zarah herself. "But it is cruel to discuss such details with a woman suffering as you are from the torments of migraine."

Arthur's manner became clinical. "May I sample the nature of your smelling salts? Hmm, as I suspected. Oil of lavender. Scarcely the attar of choice. From my own sainted mother, a martyr to this malady, I inherited a tendency to migraine." From his waistcoat pocket, he produced a crystal phial. "This mixture of ammoniated verbena is infinitely more effective." He removed the glass stopper. "Of course I am not a physician and have no authority to prescribe it in your case, but may I suggest . . ."

He passed the phial under Zarah's nostrils. "How perfectly this heliotrope crystal matches the veins of your closed eyelids."

Zarah thought it strange that the afternoon sunlight took on the quality of violet dusk. Evening so soon? A languor displaced the tightness at the nape of her neck. Where were the children? Anson?

The last sound that she heard was the buzzing of a thousand golden bumblebees.

Zarah was awakened by a gentle tapping of knuckles on the triptych screen. Who in the world could it be? She felt dizzy after her long midsummer afternoon nap. She said, "Yes."

It was Laly. "Mama, Mama, guess what? Arthur's here with the picture. It's wonderful!"

"Arthur? How long has he been here?"

"We found him sitting on the verandah when we returned from the picnic. May I ask him to stay for supper?"

"Of course."

In a daze Zarah mounted the stairs to her bedroom. The nauseating odor of Arthur's perfume, mixed with the after-scent of chloroform and, oh, the terrifying smell of spent maleness clung to the secrets of her body. What had happened, Zarah wondered, in the interval between the buzzing of the golden bumblebees and Laly's knock on the triptych screen?

She bathed, threw her negligee into the hamper, put on a fresh summer dress. No matter what had happened she had been victimized by Arthur Coplestone. Gathering up all her courage, Zarah descended the stairs to take her place at the supper Laly had prepared.

Scarcely had she seated herself when Laly handed her the proof of the family portrait. "Father thinks it's a triumph of half-tone photography."

Zarah gazed at the picture she had seen three hours before. "I'd call it a triumph of vision and design."

"Thank you, Mrs. Woodhull." Arthur smiled. "I've been eagerly awaiting your opinion. Your husband has asked me the price per dozen. I told him there is no price. I have been amply repaid by contact with your charming family."

Staying overnight, Arthur made still closer contacts with Zarah's eldest daughter, Laly. The contact took place on a cushioned bench in the octagonal-shaped summer house, half hidden by sycamores. Jacqueminot roses covered the latticework. It was all very romantic, quite natural and, considering the circumstances, inevitable.

Inevitable, too, the cyclic consequences.

Laly missed her August period; she waited without too much alarm for its appearance in September, then quite casually announced its non-arrival to Zarah.

"Have you been swimming?" asked Zarah hopefully.

"No, Mother. I'm pregnant." Her voice was flatly triumphant.

"Pregnant? By whom? When did it happen?"

"The evening that Arthur delivered the picture."

Crimson humiliation stung Zarah's cheekbones. "Misery, misery, what have I done to deserve this?"

"You didn't do anything, Mama. I did it. Arthur did it. We both did it. What else is there to do in this backwash river village?" She laid violent hands on the green silk shirt-waist that already needed another gusset. She ripped its fabric, tore at the underlying camisole and exposed her breasts like a county Helen. "Should I let Wilmer Stires fumble with these? Should I play with dolls? With myself? Tell me—what did *you* do?"

Face downward on her pillow, Zarah wept. Not because Arthur Coplestone was a cheap mountebank unworthy of her daughter; not because her love for Anson had been defiled (though this was part of her grief). Zarah wept because she too had reason to believe that she was pregnant—and not by her husband.

Normally a young woman of Laly Woodhull's station is married in her home town by the family minister. Since no such personage existed in Landmark, Laly was married to Arthur Coplestone at Vieuxtemps by the Episcopalian bishop on October 10, 1896.

Anson gave the bride away; Solange was Matron of Honor and Prof. Alberto Morini, President of the Cincinnati Astrological Society, acted as Arthur's best man.

The ceremony took place in the presence of God and a few friends; Mr. and Mrs. Charles Moerlein tendered the happy pair and assembled guests a champagne luncheon; the principal gifts took the form of two rather substantial checks instead of the usual silver bric-a-brac. The larger check, in the amount of $5,000, payable to the bride, bore the signature of Anson Woodhull. A powder-blue check from Charles Moerlein for $2,500, payable to Eulalia Woodhull, went half-way toward salving Arthur's disappointment at the size of Laly's parental *dot*. He had hoped for something really munificent but concealed his chagrin when, during a man-to-man talk with Anson directly after the ceremony, Arthur announced a change in his original plan to establish a pho-tographic atelier in Cincinnati.

"Mr. Domily Muse, my recent employer, has, so to speak, pre-empted the field here. I have decided to open shop in St.

Louis, pick up a small but select clientele in that city and spend most of my spare time in perfecting the invention of a camera shutter that represents a great advance over the present method of taking motion pictures."

Arthur Coplestone happened to be telling the truth. At a critical time in the development of the motion picture, he thought he had hit upon a new and practicable method of halting the film for that necessary fraction of a second which enables the camera to record seriatim, but independently, the component parts of a fluid movement.

"Given enough time and money, I am certain that success will crown my work."

How broad can a hint be?

"I'm sure you'll succeed, Arthur." It was characteristic of Anson that he should not promise more than he could deliver. He committed himself to nothing but a father's sincere hope that the man who was taking his daughter away should be successful in whatever he attempted.

Charles Moerlein's best coach-and-four stood ready at the porte-cochere of Vieuxtemps. Everyone knew that Laly and Arthur would spend their honeymoon at French Lick, a fashionable resort, but by that species of innocent deception, practiced at all times and places among civilized people, no one mentioned the fact. A kind of mental health bred into the race also prevented the wedding guests from imagining what would happen when this young, handsome pair locked the door of their honeymoon suite behind them.

Only Zarah was bothered by phantasies. Bitter, cruel pictures flashed across the retina of inner knowledge of what would take place a thousand times. Moreover she had a very real problem of her own—a problem that required immediate attention.

Instead of returning to Landmark, Zarah pleaded fatigue—natural enough after marrying off her daughter at an *haut monde* wedding.

"I need a rest, Anson. Oh, so desperately!"

Anson felt her desire to be alone. "Of course, darling. Why not stay here with Solange for a few days?"

The mistress of Vieuxtemps fairly bubbled. "You shall have the Louis XIV wing all to yourself. Go 'way, you men." She shooed them off. "This is to be a private performance of *Lysistrata*. No males needed. *Va!*"

Alone with her guest, Solange lowered her voice. "What is the trouble, Zarah?"

"I think—" Zarah made a faint attempt at humor—"that I'm just the tiniest bit pregnant."

"*Ma chérie. Un enfant!* How I envy you! A baby will fill your life."

"With guilt and shame. Solange, you must believe me, it wasn't entirely my fault. Partly perhaps. Yes, in some way I must have exposed myself." Anger flared in Zarah's nostrils. "How else would he have dared?"

"Who . . . who? No. No. . . . I prefer not to know."

On her knees she attempted to console her distracted friend. "These things are quite understandable, Zarah. Once doesn't count. Do not torment yourself. Tomorrow I shall begin making inquiries of my own. There are ways of handling such problems."

"Charles must know nothing," said Zarah.

"*C'est entendu.* As my mother used to say, 'Everyone should have a little money and a little secret of one's own.' Meanwhile there are home remedies."

"I've tried them all. This particular little treasure seems to be *bien emplanté.*"

"We will rout him out. Dr. Portnauer shall help us."

Dr. Portnauer, all respectability, vetoed the assignment. "I intend to perform one such operation in my life," he said half humorously, "and my fee will be ten million dollars. However, there is no cause for desperation. I understand that some very competent persons handle this business in Cincinnati." He gave them a list of six names; then added: "Let me warn you that some of them are notoriously unclean. Many of their patients die of generalized septicemia. The mortality is high. Moreover, there is danger of blackmail."

"No lectures, please, Doctor. Give me the name of *the best man* in the business."

"I can give you only his address. Here, write it down. Number Two Wharf Road. Ring the bell three times. That's the signal for the particular kind of treatment indicated here. A woman attendant will open the door (so I am told)."

Native discretion (feminine gender) served Solange ably in conducting the actual business of transporting Zarah to the address. As guardian of Moerlein's reputation and Zarah's identity, Solange resorted to the common enough wile of letting her own coachman drive them to the Hotel Sinton. Alighting, she dismissed him.

"You may take the afternoon off, Roswell. Mrs. Blessington or one of the other ladies will see us home safely."

In the Ladies' Parlor of the hotel, they removed their silk net veils (then fashionable and most provocative, too) and draped their faces with the heaviest, most impenetrable black mourning article. Emerging, they might have been a pair of recently bereaved sisters.

At the public cab rank on the corner of Fourth and Vine streets, Solange thrust Zarah into a narrow-bodied, high-wheeled herdic, slammed its door, drew the curtains, and commanded the driver, "Number Two Wharf Road."

"Sure *that's* the address, M'um?" The man on the box, bulbous nosed and no more soiled as to neck cloth and conscience than any other jehu of that time and place, almost swallowed his quid of tobacco.

"Number Two Wharf Road. Drive on."

Across the cobblestone pavements into the sink of Cincinnati the cab rolled south by west, past the Public Landing and into precincts seldom entered, even at midday, by persons of quality.

Along the waterfront, down Wharf Road. The houses were becoming more squalid. The open spaces between tar-papered shacks were filled with noisome garbage and unlicensed drinking places frequented by watermen and their sodden doxies. Integration? Drunkenness? Moral debauchery? No problems here.

At No. 2, Wharf Road dipped toward the river. Of necessity the cab man pulled up his nag. "Whoa." World's End.

"Shall I wait, Mum?"

Unwilling to be trapped in a *cul-de-sac*, Solange instinctively said, "Turn around and await further orders."

Carefully pulling aside the carriage curtain, Solange peeped out and saw the establishment at No. 2 Wharf Road—a gaunt three-story brick building; its sinister façade was pockmarked by grimy windowpanes in which roller curtains of faded scrim were drawn day and night. Solange glimpsed a sign in one of the second-floor windows: *I Cure Diseases of Men.*

Rusty iron balustrades flanked its dirty marble stoop on which a man, hands encased in black silk gloves and a black patch over his right eye, alternately harangued his wretched audience and tapped a flip chart depicting the various designs and compositions so beloved by tattooers: anchors, hearts intertwined, roses, serpents, clipper ships and, for those who could pay the fee of Dreadnaught Dan, a Crucifixion *à la Titian*.

Solange heard the spieler's voice; saw his ferule pointed at a towboat Lascar. "Now there's a river man's chest if I ever saw one. Been pressed, I warrant, against the bosom of many a wench, lecherous or treacherous as the case may be. Own up, Jack. Damn their eyes, who can remember their names? Dolores, Florrie, Rosa, Lulu, Kitty, Katey, Lucienne or Solange. Imagine a world without those solacing cushions of delight. Hah! And figure to yourselves how any girl would respond to the supreme compliment of her name woven amid a nosegay of roses, serpents or thorns in living color on her lover's chest. Step up. Step up. Men only, and I mean *men*. Let Dreadnaught Dan the Tattoo Man exercise his unique art at a dollar a letter—on any part of your anatomy. Buttocks and ballocks included—*ha! ha! ha!*—yessiree, privacy respected here."

The speaker broke off his harangue.

"Pardon me a moment, gentlemen, I see a carriage at the curb. Prince Charming, incognito, doubtless wishes to engage our Regent Suite, second floor, back—linen changed after every interview. Something always doing at Dreadnaught Dan's. . . ."

Like a high-wire aerialist, the spieler seemed to float across the unpaved sidewalk toward the curtained cab. Now, with dancing-master exaggeration, he was lifting his top hat. . . .

Solange managed to gasp, "Whip up the horse, driver. This is the wrong address. *Vitement, cochon.*" Then she collapsed against her companion.

Zarah's preoccupation with her own problem—a problem that nestled deeper every day—prevented her from cross-examining Solange when they reached home. She accepted Solange's explanation: "The place looked unsuitable. Really, I had no idea. We must start all over again."

A week, two weeks passed while Solange canvassed a dozen possibilities. There was the herb-pack woman, for instance, a former midwife, cheerful, seemingly discreet, who most indiscreetly gave the name of a certain Mrs. Ballinger as reference. It so happened that Mrs. David Ballinger belonged to the intimate circle of Solange's friends. Would the name of Mrs. Anson Woodhull or (for that matter) Mrs. Charles Moerlein be bandied about in similar fashion? Risk to reputation, danger to health, even to life, were the choices offered.

At the end of two weeks Zarah received a note from Anson. "Has my dearest wife deserted me for another? Shall I step aside gracefully or come to bring you home? Please advise your anxious and loving husband, Anson."

Then and there Zarah decided to take the matter into her own hands. "I know a man who'll do it for me," she told Solange.

"What's his name?"

"His name is Fifer Tansey and he runs a small hospital at Peddler's Landing."

An old man was scrubbing up carefully in the manner prescribed by Dr. Lyman Allston in a paper entitled *Asepsis in General Surgery*. Fifteen minutes with castile soap and surgical brush. Tincture of green soap. Rinse. Plunge hands and forearms elbow-deep into potassium permanganate. Rinse again, holding hands vertical the while. Remove surgical gloves from sterilized cabinet.

From the same cabinet, Fifer Tansey selected a small surgical instrument and approached the patient lying veiled on the operating table. He had performed this particular operation some three hundred times, and in forty years of practice had never lost a patient. Well, hardly ever. He most certainly did not intend to lose this one.

Fifer's voice carried sedative assurance. "It'll be all over in less'n twenty minutes. The pain is no more than a woman can bear. So relax now. Do like I say. Put your feet into these stirrups. Yes, your friend can hold your hand. Nurse, drape the patient."

Following a technique older than Dr. Lyman Allston's, Fifer went in and came out safe.

"Would you like to stay overnight?"

"No, thank you," said Zarah. "My friend is taking me home."

Solange handed him an envelope containing a hundred-dollar bill. The fiction of anonymity was maintained. You see, never having taken the Hippocratic oath, this old rascal, Tansey, didn't have to be bothered about such matters as professional ethics.

As for Zarah Woodhull, she went home with humility and gratitude to an acceptance of her lot. For better or for worse, living with Anson Woodhull was not, after all, such a terrible fate.

6.

THE BAMBOOZLERS

OF THE SEVENTY MILLION GALLONS of spirituous liquor distilled in 1897, thirty-three million gallons poured from rectifying plants of the so-called Whiskey Trust. In that year Mr. Charles Moerlein of Midwestern Distillers, Inc., could inform his stockholders that their corporation had made, sold and paid taxes (ninety cents a gallon) on eighteen million gallons of Old Settler and Champion whiskeys—the latter being a "white" whiskey much in demand in the southern parts of the country. Old Settler, having a well-established name in the industry, sold all over.

"During the past fiscal year" (so ran the president's report), "the directors of your company engaged the services of a prominent artist to redesign the label for Old Settler. Using a wood-cut technique, the label depicts a homesteader, flintlock at the ready, protecting the humble cabin that he has hewn from the virgin forest. . . . The expression 'aged in the wood' remains unchanged on the label. Credit for the tremendous leap in the sales of Old Settler should be divided, of course, among our growing sales staff, the new label and the undeviating quality of the whiskey itself."

Mr. Charles Moerlein knew (who should know better?) that Old Settler bore as much resemblance to "aged in the wood" whiskey as a square-dance fiddle bears to a Stradivarius. No drop of Old Settler, despite its claim to antiquity, had ever slept more than two weeks in a wooden barrel. Much of it passed directly from the filling cisterns into glass bottles retailing at eighty-five cents a quart. Because the total cost of producing, bottling and merchandising Old Settler lay somewhere between twelve and fifteen cents a gallon, an attractive profit remained, even after the excise tax was paid.

All the arts that Charles Moerlein had learned under the tutelage of Zack Hildreth—the art of doubling gallonage by the discreet use of distilled water; of adding a groat's worth of bourbon flavor to raw ethyl alcohol (sometimes called "neutral" or "silent" spirits), mixing these with a proper amount of beading oil and prune juice—all these were revived on a vast scale by the maker of Old Settler. The formula enjoyed such wide popularity that Charles Moerlein never dreamed of changing it.

Few living Americans knew that a gross fraud was perpetrated whenever a customer asked for a bottle of whiskey and received instead a bottle of Old Settler, Champion, Charter Oak, Old Monongahela, Pebble Brook or a hundred other names suggesting age, nobility or pioneer virtue. Charles Moerlein knew it; Anson Woodhull knew it; and their knowledge was shared by some four or five hundred distillers of straight whiskey. But since there was no Federal law to compel a rectifier to acquaint his customers with the true nature of the concoction he was selling as whiskey, nothing could be done about the matter.

As good King Wenceslaus said in 867 A.D., "No Law, No Remedy."

The rectifiers waxed fat until . . .

Until in 1897 Anson Woodhull noted the perilous drop-off in sales of Old Landmark. Ever since his whiskey had won the Gold Medal Award at the Columbian Exposition, sales of Old Landmark had averaged around five thousand barrels a year. Anson deliberately chose to keep his product in short supply. His share of the straight-whiskey market had seldom exceeded 500,000 gallons—that is to say, ten thousand barrels annually. Now with the 1897 figures at hand, it appeared that Old Landmark, which ordinarily sold to distributors at ninety dollars a barrel, must undergo surgical price-cutting. To make room for his 1897 production, Anson sold five hundred barrels of Old Landmark at the distress price of sixty dollars a barrel.

Attending a Whiskey-Makers Convention late in 1897, he discovered that all makers of straight whiskey were being pinched. Anson presented the following resolution:

Whereas, rectifiers are cutting us to pieces with their

cheaper product which doesn't deserve the traditional name of whiskey,

And whereas, rectifiers have performed an unblushing act of expropriation by taking over the name *whiskey* while their unsuspecting customers get a mixture of neutral spirits and flavoring in return for their money,

BE IT RESOLVED, THEREFORE, that legislative relief be sought to protect the name *whiskey*.

Copies of the resolution were duly sent to members of Congress. Naturally, nothing happened. Anson Woodhull took it upon himself to follow up the resolution with a personal appearance in Washington, D.C., where he told his story to Congressman Alpheus Hinckley, Representative of the Seventh Indiana District.

Congressman Hinckley agreed in principle that some form of legislative relief was indicated. "It seems unfair," he said, "that a man in your position, a man who lays out capital in storing whiskey for four years, should find his product undercut by an article that's made overnight. But look at these figures, Mr. Woodhull." Hinckley picked up a copy of the Treasury Report for the preceding year. "The excise taxes paid by these rectifiers amount to seventy-five million dollars. As things stand now, nearly one third of our national income is paid by rectifiers."

"I'm familiar with the figures," said Anson. "What I'd like to know, Mr. Hinckley, is this: Does the payment of a large tax justify fraud, counterfeiting, piracy?"

"That's harsh language, Mr. Woodhull. Narrowly construed it might come under the head of libel."

"Broadly construed it falls into the category of truth."

Alpheus Hinckley wasn't the kind of man to win an argument and lose a vote. As a Congressman, his overriding concern lay, or must appear to lie, with the interest of his constituents. Yet as a member of the House Finance Committee, Alph Hinckley didn't propose to tamper with the source of revenue paid by the rectifiers. Like any politician who expects to survive, Representative Hinckley went through the classic motions of passing the buck.

"Tell you what, Mr. Woodhull. There's a fellow in the Department of Agriculture—'Old Borax,' they call him—and he's mighty active in the field of adulterated foods and drugs. I don't know that he's ever looked into the whiskey business, but he'd be a good man to have on your side. I'll give you a letter of introduction. . . ."

Hinckley's note, addressed to Dr. George Washington Waley, Chief of the Bureau of Chemistry in the Department of Agriculture, was not, of itself, an important state document. It merely served to bring Anson Woodhull into the presence of the only man in the United States who had a complete knowledge of, and violent antipathy toward, the complex, deep-rooted and seemingly ineradicable frauds that were perpetrated on the bodies of American citizenry whenever they opened their mouths to eat a piece of bread, swallow a glass of milk, a teaspoonful of patent medicine or a jigger of whiskey.

For twenty years Dr. Waley had been the outstanding figure in the crusade for a pure food law. By training, temperament and sheer physical resiliency, he was equipped to take on all comers. A massive neck and chest formed a pedestal for his bisonlike skull, which contained one of the best medico-legal minds in the country. After winning his M.D. at the Indiana Medical College in 1871, he had taken a B.S. at Harvard, teaching Latin and Greek as a means of support. When Purdue University was founded in 1874, George Washington Waley was its first professor of chemistry. Nine years later, the year being 1883, he became Chief Chemist of the Department of Agriculture. From this obscure post, he watched with the eye of an expert the evils and abuses accompanying the mass production and merchandising of food and drugs. Endowed by nature with a capacity for passionate indignation, Waley dedicated himself to waging war on "bamboozlers" who adulterated or misbranded anything that went into the human gullet.

At fifty-three, standing amid his test tubes, Waley glanced at Anson's letter of introduction. "I've heard of you, Mr. Woodhull."

"In what connection, Doctor?"

"You're the maker of Old Landmark whiskey. It won a gold medal at the Columbian Exposition." Not ordinarily humorous, Waley gave a fair demonstration of a man recalling a private joke. "I sat on the board that made the awards. Let me see now . . ." Invisible fingers raced down the multimillion cabinets of the doctor's memory and, like Puck, was back instantly with the precise document. "Your whiskey contained fifty and five tenths per cent alcohol by volume. Expressed in grams per liter, it also contained eighty-nine one thousandths of total congeners."

The old Latin teacher quizzed his visitor. "Can you give me the derivation of *congeners*, Mr. Woodhull?" Waley's hand was a broad semaphore beckoning. *Yes you can; come on now.* "I'll give you a free clue. *Con* means 'with.' Now what words begin with g-e-n-e-r?"

"Generate?"

"Excellent. A congener is something that is generated with, and at the same time as, whiskey." He went on with his Socratic questioning. "How many people understand the origin, nature and necessity of these congeners, Mr. Woodhull?"

"About five hundred—that being the number of straight-whiskey distillers in the United States."

"Good. Now what percentage of the so-called whiskey produced annually in the U.S. deserves the name *whiskey*?"

"Probably five or six million proof gallons."

"And what would you call the rest of the stuff that is sold as whiskey?"

"I'd call it Imitation Whiskey, Fake Whiskey, Counterfeit Whiskey. I've been calling it all these things for years."

"But it hasn't done anyone any good. And it won't do you any good, Mr. Woodhull, until you and your fellow distillers agree to co-operate with this department in establishing standards of purity—standards that can be translated into law."

"I'd be very glad to assist you in any such undertaking. That's why I came," said Anson.

"Good man. Now here's the procedure. Acting under special Treasury permits, my department will purchase from you and other bonded distilleries a barrel of whiskey every year during a four-year period. I, together with my assistants, will make monthly chemical analyses of the whiskey so purchased. I am empowered by law to do this. The interim procedures will be secret but not stealthy. Meanwhile, we must expect the enemy—the bamboozlers—to continue their counter-operations in Congress in powerful lobbies, in the public prints and, what concerns me most, upon the bodies of our uninformed and all-too-gullible fellow countrymen."

The term *bamboozler* was always a vulgarism. Yet because it carried a fairly explicit freight of meaning, *bamboozler* was a favorite locution with George Washington Waley in his uphill struggle for pure food law. Waley could plaster the epithet *those bamboozlers* against the back seats of the gallery and make it reverberate (sometimes) into the local papers.

At the invitation of Anson Woodhull, Waley addressed a convocation of state chemists in Lexington, Kentucky, in October 1898. It suited Dr. Waley to suggest the Preamble to the Constitution of the United States should include "the right to be bamboozled" as part of the basic social contract.

"In the light of my researches for the past twenty years on adulterated, misbranded foods and drugs," said Waley, "I have come to the melancholy conclusion that the American people *want* to be bamboozled. They *want* to have formaldehyde pumped into rancid butter. They *like* their fresh milk better if it is preserved with borax. It seems to me that they *prefer* coffee adulterated with charcoal, red slate, bark of trees, date stones and roasted chick-peas. This quaint preference for the adulterated article is, of course, encouraged by large proprietary interests who find that profits can be reaped from the sale of drugs and medicines under false, misleading or incomplete labels. I hold in my hand a list of twenty-five patent medicines that base their cruel and nonexistent curative powers on the opium, morphine, cocaine and alcoholic content not mentioned on the label. Among them is a well-known Soothing Sirup for quieting the 'fret of teething babies.' In England—" Waley pressed the double-forte pedal hard—"this Soothing Sirup would be labeled POISON."

He growled at his audience. "Not until a nation-wide pure food bill compels manufacturers to print on their package or bottle the ingredients it actually contains can we hope to reverse the present tendency toward adulteration and misbranding. One of the steps toward the passage of such a law must be the establishment of standards of purity. Without such standards, both manufacturer and buyer are in the position of a dry-goods merchant who lacks a yardstick. As Chief of the Federal Bureau of Chemistry, I have already begun to collect samples of straight whiskey from distillers with well-recognized names in the industry. Thus far twenty-two distillers in Kentucky, Indiana and Maryland have sold to my department, under special permission of the Treasury Department, thirty-one different barrels of their product just as it came from the still. These samples are analyzed monthly to determine the chemical changes that take place when whiskey ripens in the barrel.

"To my knowledge, no such experiment has ever been undertaken. Years must elapse before final conclusions can be reached. I am able, however, to give you at this time an interim report covering some of the chemical changes as they occur month by month. You have in your possession mimeographed sheets especially prepared by members of my staff. You will note that much of the work is necessarily technical and requires special training in chemistry."

Waley the fire-eating crusader became Waley the patient teacher. "I believe, however, that we have already demonstrated that purity in whiskey can be ascertained by means of four characteristics: (1) Total Acidity, (2) Esters, (3) Aldehydes and (4) Solids extracted from the wooden container. Scientific methods employed for measuring these factors and cross-checking out results will eventually lead to an indisputable standard of purity for whiskey."

Waley became a mountain lion. "And when we have established these standards, gentlemen, I promise you on my sacred honor as a scientist that any distilled liquor not conforming to these standards will bear the label *Imitation Whiskey*. I predict that the bamboozlers will wrench heaven and earth—strike out *heaven*—they will wrench *all hell* in their efforts to strangle my findings."

George Washington Waley loosened his size 19 collar.

"Bamboozlers," he challenged, "here is my neck: just you try to strangle me!"

7.

THE KINDS OF LOVE

OZZIE (1898)

ALONG TOWARD the middle of Sousa's "High School Cadets," there's a passage where the composer really shows what a trombone can do. The cornets are advancing in a column of squads; there is a preparatory flam of snare drums—ta-*rump*, ta-*rump*, ta-rumpety *bump*—then the trombone breaks loose. For eight bars it snarls and glitters on a highwire trapeze, biting off notes that never were written until John Philip Sousa set them down just before the Spanish-American War.

To a professional trombonist the passage presents no insuperable problem. But Ozzie Woodhull, practicing with the Volunteer Fire Company band on a hot June evening in 1898, was having trouble with his slide horn. In fact, the entire band—a motley group of amateurs—found itself bogging down for the fifth time. Kapellmeister Milt Bierweiler tapped his music stand with the shagreen spectacle case that he used as a baton and gave off with patient counsel. In matters musical the Kapellmeister was competent to advise. He had given his first trumpet solo in Düsseldorf at the age of eleven; and had played for forty years with the best bands in Europe and America. Now, with most of his front teeth gone, Milt Bierweiler, a grain-sorter in Anse Woodhull's distillery, was still the best musician in Landmark County.

Like a Dutch uncle, he spoke to his charges. "We play badly because we forget what the composer is saying. What is the name of this piece? Grieg's Funeral March? A medley from *Martha?* No. It is the 'High School Cadets'—not a great composition when compared with Beethoven's Fifth Symphony, but a sincere expression of the American *nationalismus*, full of noise and excitement, a something that will be yet heard in the world."

The Kapellmeister wiped runnels of sweat from his neck and went on. "The young men in this composition are not conscripts or professional soldiers. They are students, wheeling on the parade ground in front of their academy. Their step is light, hopeful; their maneuvers are brilliant. Young ladies are watching, each with her eyes fixed on some handsome youth in a white shako, who will afterward waltz with her, kiss her; God knows what she hopes he will do." Laughter, coarse to knowing, was broken by Bierweiler's next remark. "When you play this on July Fourth, whom do you suppose these young ladies will be looking at? Congressman Kniepfeld, with a long speech rolled up in his hind pocket? No, they will be looking at you. Show off for them a little, as the composer intended. Here, I will show you."

With Bavarian gentleness, Bierweiler took the trombone from Ozzie's thick fingers. It occurred to him that there was an element of *lèse majesté* in his action. Back in Bavaria, you didn't risk offending the son of your employer by correcting him in public. But at this moment Milt was not a distillery worker. He was a musician, and he was about to show a slobbery, untalented youth how a passage should go.

"Take it like this—*maestoso.*" As a prelude to his demonstration, Bierweiler assumed the personality of a brass band in full career. He flammed like a drum, *um-pahed* with the basses, set off a crackling fusee of cornets, then placed Ozzie Woodhull's trombone to his lips, and blew eight measures of sheer wonderful virtuosity into the Indiana night.

"See how it goes, Ozzie? . . . Together now, we will take it once more from the top."

Somehow they struggled through the piece. The big clock on the firehouse wall struck nine. Rehearsal was over, but Ozzie Woodhull's program of pleasure had yet to begin. Hastily stuffing his trombone in its cheap leatherette case, he sought the seclusion of the shed where his horse was tethered, took a nip from a square-jawed bottle of Landmark, followed Napoleon's advice to his marshals (never miss an opportunity to take a leak), jumped into his light two-seater, and was off to see the last performance of Dunleavy's circus.

Romanticists bred on Barnum's tradition of the three-ringed circus, with lions, n' tigers n' everything, have no apparatus for picturing the function and nature of Solomon Dunleavy's show, which, for the past three days had been entertaining the venery-loving blades of Landmark County. To begin with, the Dunleavy troupe had no itinerary. It merely started out from Biloxi with three red caravans early in March, crossed the Ohio at Squirrel Hash and reached its northernmost point, Indianapolis, in mid-July. Then it turned around and went whence it came, minus a caravan, a few performers and any semblance of profit.

Catering as he did to an all-male audience, Solomon Dunleavy's troupers dealt with fundamentals: Mandrone, the sovereign remedy for gleet, falling hair, piles and other maladies (no worse than a bad cold); a tattooed lady who doubled as snake-charmer and ticket-taker, a four-piece brass band and Irish Jack McGinty, a heavyweight boxer who guaranteed to lay any local boy stiff within three rounds (with the help of a mallet skillfully applied to the local boy's skull as the Champ worked him against the canvas backdrop). But the stellar attraction was Princess Sultana, the Persian belly dancer, formerly a member of His Majesty's harem, but now temporarily at liberty and transported at great expense to initiate all red-blooded men, at a nickel a head, into the mysteries of the O-rient. "Step up, step up, step up. See Princess Sultana, daughter of Persian royalty, perform her ed-u-cational dance. Men only, men only, men only. Last show of the evening about to begin. Tickets five cents, six for a quarter."

Thus the spieler, Solomon Dunleavy in person, having seen Little Egypt at the Chicago Exposition in 1893, knew what an all-male public wanted.

Barely in time, Ozzie Woodhull plunked down his twenty-five-cent piece, got a good seat in the front row and watched the Princess reposing on her carpet puffing at a Narghile in a corner of the hootchy pit. At a signal from the master of ceremonies, she rose, placed her hands on her hips and began her first gyrations to the *um-pah* of the bass drum. She gathered momentum as the beat accelerated; gradually her red mouth widened in a smile of brassy insolence and her elastic torso quivered under an Oriental veil. With professional cunning, she built up her stuff in cumulative waves, coaxing the yokels in the audience along with her until they were ready for the tidal finish. Then, with a series of deep, no-feeling thrusts, she landed them high, dry and gasping for more as the ticket-taker came around for repeat orders.

Ozzie's six tickets vanished in an hour. He brushed a hand across parched lips and nipped at his pint. He had seen enough. In a wavering daze he started to leave the tent, but as he neared the exit he was overtaken by a desire to have one more look at the girl who could smile such a cool smile right in the middle of such scorching business.

It was easy to get another look at her. Bending over the low rail of the pit, he could see her stretched out on her strip of faded carpet. She was resting on one elbow; bright drops of sweat beaded her forehead and her diaphragm was working like a quarter-miler's after a tough 440. She looked to be about nineteen years old and not too smart about taking care of herself. Her skin was smeared with a brownish dye; sweat, trickling down her body, had left dirty-white streaks behind.

Her eyes were closed with temporary fatigue, but as Ozzie leaned over the railing she suddenly opened them. They were dark but not warm; bright but unintelligent. They traveled over Ozzie's face as if to say, "Pay your nickel, Plowboy; this ain't a free show." Then they closed again, bringing the interview to an abrupt close as far as she was concerned.

Ozzie had a better idea. Leaving the tent, he leaped across the tangle of stakes and tent ropes until he came to the back entrance of Sultana's dressing room. The back flap of the tent was unguarded. Ozzie pushed it open and gave a low whistle; the girl, still resting on one elbow, turned her head and gave him back a hostile stare. Farm boys meant nothing in her life and she managed to convey that fact without words. At which point Ozzie held out his bottle, smiled and said, "You must be thirsty. Have a drink?"

The girl's eyes remained unencouraging, but she stuck out a hand for the bottle. Her hand symbolized the rest of her body: it was much too dirty, it was sensuously modeled and the nails were glazed with a deep red polish. Without affectations of nicety she put the bottle to her lips and gurgled it down. The drink softened her up a little.

"How'd you know ah needed something like that?" Her voice was like the rest of her, an intoxicant with a Deep South drawl.

"Because I watched you do your stuff for an hour and never saw you take a drink. It made me thirsty to watch you, so I figured you must be pretty dry yourself."

"So you'all's feelin' kinda thirsty, huh? So whatcha goin' to do when ah polish off this pint?"

"I've got a case of the stuff in the back of my buggy."

It was true. Ozzie was supposed to deliver a case of Old Landmark at the Railway Express station, but for a consideration, he was perfectly willing to break the sealed box.

"How about me coming around tonight after your last dance? We could take a ride out into the country, get plastered n' everything."

"What you-all mean by everythin'?"

"Why a-ah music." Ozzie improvised fast. "Honey, I got a trombone in the back of my buggy that'll bring the moon down right into your lap."

"You play a slide horn?"

"Wait till you hear."

By her intonation Princess Sultana (square name Lila-Mae Busby) exposed a not-uncommon flaw. She liked horn players. She liked good whiskey. She liked the prospect of driving out into the country under a full moon. Half an hour later, while Mr. and Mrs. Dunleavy counted up the night's receipts ($4.15), Lila-Mae Busby was driving toward the Ohio River with six ounces of Old Landmark irrigating the membranes of a dream come true.

The August moon helped. The owner of the horse and buggy was driving with one hand, and the other was . . .

"Where's that slide horn you was talkin' about?" suggested Lila-Mae.

A command performance. Princess Sultana was asking Ozzie to play his trombone. His mother had never asked him, his father was too busy, Quincia wasn't interested, but here beside him, leaning against his shoulder in fact, her lovely legs braced against the dashboard, this refugee from a Persian harem was displaying interest in his musical ability! Flourish of trumpets. A long Mama-Papa roll announced the entrance of Duke "Ozzie" Woodhull. Silent all, while the virtuoso placed the mouthpiece to his lips, drew a bead on the fireball moon and played. He played like ninety violins tucked under ninety cast-iron chins. He bit off notes that never were bitten, executed impossible feats of triple-tongueing. Ozzie ripped off whole passages from *Die Walküre*, played *maestoso* passages, modulated into that ever-betwitching little number "The Last Rose of Summer" and wound up with the high-wire eight-bar passage from Sousa's "High School Cadets," which seemed simple now. . . . Perhaps the whiskey helped.

"Ah can't *stand* it, you play so beautiful!" Lila-Mae's fingers were inside his shirt. Her fingers were . . .

"Ah jus' feel like wallowing in a corn furrow between the big stalks. You feel thattaway?"

They wallowed. They drank. They reached up and touched the moon's rim. And when there wasn't any moon, they slept. In a furrow, on the ground, between giant corn stalks, for the first time in her life, Lila-Mae Busby got her fill of four-year-old whiskey; and for the first time in his life, Osgood Woodhull got his fill of a nineteen-year-old girl.

Dawn brought no guilt, no headache, no doubt. There was only one thing they could do. They must keep on doing what they had done all night. In order to bring this about, Lila-Mae Busby convinced Solomon Dunleavy that this here man I love either becomes an employee of the crummiest show on earth or els't I don't show.

Needing a trombonist, Dunleavy gave Ozzie the job. The boy sold his horse and buggy to Timmins' Livery Stable for $75.00. "Tell my old man I've decided to strike out for myself."

For many years thereafter Ozzie slept and boozed exclusively in the company of Princess Sultana. And for a better-matched pair of human beings, you'd have to travel a long day's journey.

EVERLASTING (1899)

"TO EVERY THING THERE IS A SEASON," says Ecclesiastes at the beginning of Chapter 3; and the next eight verses are the sum of complementary meaning. Quincia Woodhull knew them by heart. "A time to get and a time to lose; a time to keep and a time to cast away; a time to rend and a time to sew; a time to keep silence and a time to speak."

She had kept her silence for twenty years and now she decided it was time to speak. Or write, rather. With the fountain pen that Anson had given her as a graduation present from the State University in June 1899, Quince made a trial draft of a letter born of conscience and maturity. Four years ago she would have addressed the letter to Frances Bushnell, from whose lips sprang the evangelical fire. But Frances Bushnell, champion of American womanhood, had been dead these twelve months; it was to Mary Hunter, then, her successor, that Quincia penned her letter:

DEAR MISS HUNTER:

I am twenty years old, a graduate of Indiana State University. For the past three years—ever since hearing Frances Bushnell speak at the Baptist Church in Landmark, Indiana, I have been a wearer of the White Rosette, a subscriber to the W.C.T.U. magazine, as well as other Temperance periodicals.

I am deeply interested in the crusade to abolish the manufacture and sale of intoxicating liquors, and am willing to devote my life to Temperance work in any capacity for which you may think me fitted.

This letter, written in my own hand, will give you some idea of my penmanship and educational background. I am burning to take part in the anti-liquor crusade and could have no fonder hope than to follow you in some minor capacity.

I would be willing to work for the minimum wage offered by your organization. Hoping for the courtesy of a reply at your earliest convenience, I am,

Very sincerely yours,
QUINCIA WOODHULL

Two weeks later, Quincia received a brief note offering her a position as copyist in the mailing division of the W.C.T.U. at a salary of $9.00 a week. All that remained now was to tell Father and Mother. Zarah took the news calmly. "For a long time I've known that you've been in the Temperance Movement. Ordinarily, I'd urge you to follow your own inclination in this matter, but I must point out to you, Quincia, that your father will be deeply hurt."

Zarah laid aside her sewing and continued. "It seems to be a part of nature's plan that girls should hurt their fathers, whether for some other man or for a career scarcely makes any difference. I hurt my father when I married Anson Woodhull, but fathers can stand it. They go on living somehow." A final plea: "Speak gently to him, Quince."

How else?

To oppose one's father, to say, "Only Begetter, Source of My Being, Earthly Surrogate of Him which art in heaven" —to say these things without anger—then add, "I must leave your house; not for the comfort of human love but for an ideal principle; I must go far away, fight against the traffic in the thing you are making"—such statements or even thoughts like these require a special kind of courage. And yet Quincia Woodhull, who had given up the joy of plucking wildflowers because of the fancied hurt their stems might suffer, Quincia, who shuddered at the combat of wasp and spider, who wept when unconsciously she tread upon the earthworm, this sensitive, loving girl was obliged by conscience and conviction to hurt the man she loved most.

There were alternatives to the direct thrust. One could simply pack a bag, depart suddenly, secretly; leave a note or send a letter saying, "Forgive me, Father. I know you will understand my motives." But this would be the coward's kiss, treachery by default. In Quincia's heart and under Anglo-Saxon law, the accuser must face the accused; a fearful proviso, especially when the accuser has known nothing but kindness. In the tribunal of her twenty-year-old heart, Quincia prepared her case.

Quincia ascended the broad staircase toward that second-floor sanctuary—half den, half office—that her father had fashioned for himself. Zarah's advice—"Choose your time and place" buoyed up her sinking resolution. This *was* the time, and what better place could be chosen than the lair of the house-slippered lion-father? At ease among his pipes and papers. Tobacco was supposed to be the shrub of evil, but the scent of rough-cut Burley, becoming stronger as she approached Anson's door, seemed at this moment like incense, male, that she would never smell again.

"Dear Lord," she prayed at the door, "grant that my voice be free of censure and that my words be received with understanding."

Quincia's prayer was answered. Her words fell gently as she recited the simple fact of her decision. How bare the recital seemed. How much easier it would have been to kneel, press her forehead against Anson's long thigh and sob out, as in a confessional, the tale of conflict and remorse. Had she done so, oh, surely, fatally to her purpose, the mutual fondling would have begun. Quincia not only set the tone of the interview but by some strength of character kept it at exactly the right level. She showed Anson a copy of the letter she had written to Mary Hunter and Mrs. Hunter's reply.

He studied the documents, then set them aside much in the manner of a judge who had noted the exhibits, marked them and reserves decision.

When a father and daughter love equally, the advantage lies cruelly on the father's side. He can use it to bribe or beguile the unformed soul. Had Anson but stretched out his hand, swept his too-tall daughter into his arms, run his fingers through the roots of her hair, pleaded for mercy, an extension of time, Quincia's will might have crumpled under the assault because that in part was what she wanted.

She had spent her life as a dim star in the family constellation, outshone by personalities of greater magnitude—Zarah, Laly, yes, even Chance. Never had she been first, best loved, handsomest. Twenty years of tagging behind, plus the daily evidence of her dressing-room mirror, and who wouldn't succumb to affirmations of love openly declared and reinforced with binding arms and possessive kisses?

Intuitively, Anson knew this and refrained from wooing his daughter. What purpose would be gained by persuading Quince to give up her chosen career? He would miss this tall, dignified girl; her absence would leave an empty place in his house and heart. Yet he must test her.

"How long have you felt this way, Quince?"

"Ever since I knew what whiskey was, and what it did to people."

"What does it do, Quince?" Anson's probe struck the solid flint of his daughter's character, and but for Quincia's tact, sparks might have flown.

Gently she turned the query aside. "I would never presume to instruct you, Father. My views concerning whiskey would cause added pain."

"Thank you, Quincia, for your restraint. But truly now, I *want* to hear you state the case against whiskey. I know all the phrases: 'Whiskey poisons a man's soul, wrecks his body, saps his will.' I put it to you, Daughter, does whiskey do these things to men? Or do men *use* whiskey to do these things to themselves?"

"I don't know enough about men."

"Then let me tell you about a man." Anson rose from his chair and turned his back thoughtfully as if trying to recapture a certain moment of the past. "Myself. Do you remember the game we used to play when you were children? We played it after supper and it was called 'What You Put in the Old Man's Soup.'"

"I remember, Father."

"Well, one night, when you were a very little girl, I asked you, 'What do *you* put in the old man's soup?' and you said, 'Everlasting.' It was the name of a flower; remember?"

"Yes."

"Then I asked, 'If you were going on a long journey far from home and could never come back, never never—even though you wanted to—whom would you take with you, *me* or Everlasting?'"

At the memory invoked by Anson, Quincia burst into tears. "I said I'd take *you*, Daddy. But I was a little girl then."

"You're still my little girl."

Quincia steeled her soul against her loved and loving father. "I am a woman now. I must take the path that conscience points out to me." She dried her eyes. "And I must follow it to *Everlasting Life*."

THE ANTHONY BOX

THE POSSESSION OF OCCULT POWERS may prove ruinous to all but the strongest of characters; Arthur Coplestone's minor, yet genuine, power of hypnotism had tempted him into the dim regions of spirit photography. In 1900, after four years of marriage to Laly Woodhull, it led him into a poorly lighted studio on one of the dreariest side streets of St. Louis. With his wife and young daughter he occupied two rooms in a building managed by Maktoub Kazanjian, a no-goodnik in any language.

Under his management the tenants were allowed to deteriorate along with the building, in whatever direction they pleased, so long as they paid the minimum rent of $12.00 per month. The first floor was shared by the Acme Tonsorial Parlor, a three-table pool room and J. Twombly, Printer. From the second-floor corner, a gigantic gold tooth announced to the illiterate: Teeth Pulled Here. And on the third floor, its hallway lighted by a single gas jet, one came to the ground-glass door bearing the legend:

ARTHUR COPLESTONE
Occult Photography a Specialty

Tired of waiting for "sitters" that failed to come, Arthur had set himself up in the vastly more exciting business of faking likenesses of the departed dead. He inserted an advertisement in the St. Louis *Gazette:* "Get in Touch with your Departed Loved Ones." The ad brought in a trickle of customers, eager and willing to be gulled at prices ranging from $2.00 to $10.00.

To Laly's objections, Arthur had pointed out (and truly) that spirit photography was enjoying a vogue in England under the patronage of Sir Oliver Lodge and the Society for Psychical Research. Quite by accident, a pamphlet of the society had fallen into Arthur's hands scarcely a year after his marriage to Laly Woodhull. Arthur was particularly fascinated by an article entitled "The Unexplained Case of Mrs. Ruxton." Mrs. Ruxton, having lost her son in a lignite explosion aboard the H.M.S. *Triton,* wished naturally to communicate with his "discarnate" spirit. Threepenny postage stamps having no validity in that bourn from which no man returneth, Mrs. Ruxton betook herself to the village photographer, one Albert Bell, a man of honest repute, who took pictures with an old-fashioned tripod-and-bellows square camera. In the finished photo of Mrs. Ruxton a white disk appeared over her left shoulder. Under microscopic scrutiny, the disk revealed a startling resemblance of Alfred's features.

Talk about repercussions in a lignite laboratory! The honest, ignorant photographer of Finchingfield received a summons from the Society for Psychical Research. Appearing before them, he succeeded in obtaining, under the most rigid scientific controls, a series of astounding pictures in which the faces of loved ones long departed were recognized.

"Why, yes, it's Henry!"; "Genevieve, my beloved!"; "Bless me—Soamesby to the buttons" were some of the expressions uttered by interested parties who sat for Mr. Bell's broken-legged camera.

On the strength of the Ruxton article, Arthur had become a regular subscriber to the *Quarterly for Psychic Research* (6s 5d per annum). At the end of six months, he abandoned legitimate photography and began coaching Laly in the role of sympathetic receptionist. Her job, he explained, was to hold preliminary interviews with grief-stricken parents, husbands and wives, eliciting as much information as possible about the physiognomy of the deceased.

"You're supposed to be an actress," snapped Arthur. His contemptuous reference was to the soubrette parts that Laly had played with the Maskers Company—a dramatic club specializing in Shakespearean and Restoration comedies. The birth of Haila three years before had prevented Laly from accepting anything but minor roles with the Maskers. In Congreve's *The Way of the World,* she had played Mincing, a servant to Mrs. Millamant while understudying Millamant herself. When offered the leading role of Portia in *The Merchant of Venice,* Laly had consciously sacrificed this juicy part for the less-exacting role of Nerissa. Even so, she had been obliged to leave Haila in the care of Myrza, the Crystal-

Ball Gazer down the hall, and now a would-be Millamant-Portia-Angelica was being asked to waste her fragrance on Arthur's stupid clientele or ask her father for another sizable check.

Laly chose to waste her fragrance.

And this was the way it went:

"You say, Mrs. Nutter, that little Robert was three years old when he inserted his head into the goldfish bowl and thus came to an untimely death?"

"Lacking two months of three years," corrected Mrs. Nutter. "I remember, because I had just put him on Maltina."

"Excellent. I feed it to my own darling child. Now, Mrs. Nutter, have you any memento of little Robert?"

Baby ringlets, wrapped in tissue paper, would be produced. Blond, male, three years old. How much evidence does a smart photographer need? Arthur would touch up one corner of a plate with a composite portrait of all blue-eyed little darlings who ever drowned themselves in goldfish bowls (being careful, of course, to muffle their features in ectoplasmic fluff—*everything* was fluffed up with ectoplasm). Then, after a plea to Robert, Gwynne, John, Peter, Paul or Mark, as the case might be, he went into his "Chladni once, Chladni twice" routine, snapped the bulb, a failure the first time perhaps but oftener a success; and there, after a short wait, Mrs. Nutter would be shown a wet proof of her Robert.

"My babe-ling! My very own! Print me up a dozen, Mr. Coplestone."

"Cabinet size of course, Mrs. Nutter? That will be eighteen dollars. I myself am not permitted to handle money. Please pay my wife as you leave."

Cheeks burning with shame, Laly took the money. Alone with her husband, she protested, "How can you humbug these poor people?"

To which Arthur always replied, "Write your father for more money."

"He's already given us seven thousand dollars, Arthur. Five thousand when we were married, and two thousand for your experiments with the motion-picture camera. I *can't* ask him for any more."

"He can well afford it."

"That's not the question." Laly was pleading now. "How can you, a truly talented photographer, a man who believes in the possibilties of the camera—how can *you* afford to soil yourself by dabbling in fraud and deceit?"

Arthur slapped the table with the latest issue of the *Psychic Quarterly*. "Dabble? Deceit? The leading scientists in England are taking part in the great new experiment of spiritualism. They are pioneering in infra-red photography. Look at this list of contributors: Sir William Crookes, the inventor of the Crookes tube, Sir Oliver Lodge, Conan Doyle . . ."

"I've read the articles," said Laly. "No one can say whether the people who wrote them are right or wrong in their beliefs. But I know this: their experiments were carefully guarded and scientifically controlled. Does any such control exist here in St. Louis? No! Were you exercising truly psychic powers when you touched up the Nutter plate? Answer me!"

"Do you doubt my psychic powers?" Vanity and the wish to impose his will on Laly, to subjugate and silence her forever, led Arthur Coplestone into a fatal mistake. He lifted his left hand, not menacingly, but as one who proffers sedation to a troubled mind.

"Sit down, Laly. I'll put you into a calmer frame of mind." Purringly, diminuendo, his voice trailed off. "Lambda, who is speaking to you now?"

"My husband."

"You must co-operate, Lambda." Arthur attempted to be patient. "We are in the gazebo. Focus your attention upon the eye of my serpent ring. Let your hands droop at your sides."

Laly let her hands droop.

"Ah, that's better. Now will you write to your father asking him for another five thousand?"

Laly was out of her chair in a flash. "Arthur Coplestone, you couldn't put me into a trance the best day you ever lived. All the *lambda lambda* business from here to hell is a waste of time. You just don't entrance me."

"Your mother found me irresistible."

"What do you mean?"

Arthur laughed. "She folded like a fifty-cent umbrella when I threw a . . . a pass at and into her . . . ah . . . matron virtue."

"My mother wouldn't let you lay a finger on her."

"No? Then my Zeiss pocket-camera lens needs regrinding." Arthur selected an envelope from his files. "Here's a picture of *La Belle Dame Woodhull couchante.* Full exposure. Recognize anything? Vinaigrette? Dropped handkerchief, *peut-être?* Naturally the center of interest is that delicate *bocage,* adrip with do-it-to-me dew."

Laly snatched the picture. She glanced, saw, groaned. "Oh-h! It can't be! You caught her sleeping."

"No, she was quite awake—at first. Uttered some charming obscenities. Amazing technique, too. As I recall, she took the high-hoop leap twice in ten minutes; then, all passion spent, modulated into a docile serenity. I gave her a mere whiff of canister, reserving my grape shot for a late date in the gazebo."

"You crawling bastard." Laly shredded the picture.

"Tear it, burn it; I have the negative. May use it some time. Anyway, Mama's been well etched into your retina. If thine eye offend thee, pluck it out—optic nerve and all."

For the next five minutes the studio was an artillery range—with Arthur as target for everything that Laly could lift and throw—including a vocabulary of black-and-yellow names. Under this barrage, Arthur retreated with his best camera, leaving Laly with eighty-five cents, a three-year-old daughter, a month's back rent, an Anthony box camera and a crumpled horoscope written (how long ago?) by a former member of the Astral Society who, in a moment of illumination, had said, among other things:

> Women born on your birthday (July 7) are very handsome, with regal figures and luminous eyes that are most attractive to the opposite sex. . . . You can be a tremendous success as an actress if you will overcome certain obstacles in your environment. Believe in yourself; dare follow your star, and you will achieve the destiny that the future has in store for you.

That afternoon, while Laly was trying to visualize just what the future had in store for her, she heard a knock at the door. It was Maktoub Kazanjian, and, not to put too fine a point on the matter, he wanted his rent.

"God knows you deserve it," said Laly. She opened her pocketbook. "Will eighty-five cents help? It's all I have."

Maktoub Kazanjian—a Moslem version of Cruikshank's Fagin—waved aside the loose change and wiped his watery eyes with one of the silk handkerchiefs dangling from his coat pocket. He had the Armenian talent for gathering figs from thistles, and here was a luscious fig waiting to be plucked, processed and merchandised. Not once, but a thousand times. Circumstance had made Kazanjian a landlord. At heart he was a merchandiser. He dealt largely on the small-installment plan. For twenty-five cents down—no signatures, no collateral required—he would sell anything from a priceless Bokhara to a genuine Old Master, chiefly Italian (but Flemish if the customer liked Flemish). Between whiles he handled oddments of jewelry, opium, rosary beads (pearl, amethyst—name any stone), and phials of exotic perfume which he would produce from the pockets of his long, black gabardine coat or the crown of his flattish hat.

In the course of his dealings he had collected a catalogue of prospective buyers who would snap at anything from a Limoges tea set to a corrugated lingam. In only one department of his vast warehouse (situation unknown) did Kazanjian lack merchandise. He had been loath to traffic in this particular commodity because The Prophet had inveighed long ago against contact, commercial or otherwise, with infidel flesh. Due to the inevitable withering of certain glands, plus the injunctions of the Koran, Kazanjian himself entertained no desires other than mercantile toward the distressed, insolvent and luscious piece of woman flesh standing before him. What a source of income! Properly tutored and given the setting that any gem requires, this girl with the wheat-colored hair might prove more profitable than a license to print twenty-dollar bills!

Gazing around the barren studio, Mr. Kazanjian tested his client's attitude toward doing fancy work on mattresses.

"So your cash position is weak!" Merely by turning his palms outward, Maktoub Kazanjian expressed his willingness to be crucified along with Laly for a 50 per cent rakedown. "Is that any reason for evicting a young woman loaded with assets?"

To suggest that these assets should be guarded by a strong new bolt, Mr. Kazanjian pulled the very article from his voluminous coat pocket, held it in place against the door jamb, and waited for Laly to register. No register. How in the name of Allah's abacus did these American Protestants ever gain control of a great continent? Quite apart from this metaphysical question, Mr. Kazanjian knew that the clients in his stud book would expect a more encouraging approach to the blond Mystery of Mysteries traditionally preferred by gentlemen. Mr. Kazanjian found himself somewhat in the position of an impresario who needed a coach of the first magnitude to buff up the talents of a young star who didn't know enough to get off the horizon.

On the back of a greasy card, he scribbled a name and address: Mme. Lucienne, 225 Wharf Street. "Call on this lady tomorrow before two in the afternoon. After that hour she is sometimes . . . professionally occupied. May Allah go with you," he said, sidling toward the door.

The interview took place on schedule in the apartment of Mme. Lucienne Bisguier, survivor of fifty thousand encounters with cash customers and still able, at forty-one, to provide solace for a select "past-sixty" clientele. Her once marvelous strawberry hair had been touched up with henna and the original upper row dental pearls was now merely an expensive set of crockery. Comfort, not speed, was suggested by a *rondeur* of hip and bosom made fashionable by The Jersey Lily and Ada Bailey; a green satin dress was slashed from ankle to knee for mobility and display.

Mme. Lucienne's sitting room was a triumph of the velvet portiere period—an intermingling of feminine froufrou, *chinois* screens, samovars, chafing dishes, epergnes and girandoles, figurines and the ever-symbolic conch shell. Her mantelpiece was freighted with photographs, an ormolu clock and a glazed incense burner, especially designed for cremating the souls of departed rose petals. But the real tip-off on Mme. Lucienne's profession was the number and variety of lamps with which she could achieve any degree or color of illumination. There were lamps like pagodas, obelisks; there were lamps with beaded shades, floor lamps, table lamps, hanging lamps, pink, apricot, nectarine lamps—yes, and for the benefit of clients with certain peculiarities, Mme. Lucienne had a green-shaded lamp that cast a cadaverish hue over the proceedings.

As Laly entered, nothing more sinister than an early-afternoon sun lighted the bay window alcove, where a potted philodendron stood atop an octagonal marble table flanked by two plush armchairs. Lucienne motioned her guest toward the chair facing the sun and scrutinized her with the eyes of a woman who had seen hundreds of her sisters go forth to do battle with the beloved adversary, Man. How many had been trampled underfoot in that battle? How few had mastered the techniques necessary for survival? How much experience lay behind the aquamarine enigma of Laly's eyes? How many hands had pulled the pins out of her wheat-sheaf hair? Searched under her out-of-season woolen skirt (probably the only one she owned)? Did her knees open easily? Could she be *taught* to open them easily? It was Lucienne's task to appraise (for the fee already paid by Kazanjian) the attitude, durability and potential earning power of the superbly poised young woman who sat opposite her.

Kazanjian's briefing had been helpful—to a degree. On the surface, Laly's plight was both classic and commonplace; she was the abandoned wife of a no-good husband; mother of a little girl and, oh, yes, she needed money. Perfect conformity to the pattern. But at a point yet to be discovered, the pattern had been obscured by a rich complexity of character. Bone, not gristle, supported this girl's frame; flesh instead of blubber formed her uncorseted contour; she was strung with piano wires instead of nerves, yet each wire was responsive, keyed to concert pitch, and capable of producing a full ten-fingered chord. Or, to change the figure, all her buttons were in place, and all waiting to be pressed, too. But where was the *anxiety* button (thought Lucienne) which, if touched, caused so many girls to seek refuge in nail-biting, gum-chewing, eye-business, facial tics and a thousand other give-away manifestations of the round-heeled sisterhood?

Was this particular Miss Muffet naïve, afraid of, or hostile to, the proposals that she would hear in the course of the next half hour?

Lucienne made the always permissible opening: "Will you have a cup of tea?"

"Yes, thank you," said Laly. "Tea would be very nice."

"Your diction is excellent. Are you an actress? At liberty, perhaps?"

"Yes, I'm an actress and I'm quite at liberty."

To test the common honesty of the statement, Lucienne said, "Use your handkerchief in the manner of Rachel."

Smiling, Laly dabbed delicately at her nostrils.

"Superb. Now let me hear your Millamant—you know, the scene where Congreve's heroine is deciding whether her lover—what's his name?"

"Mirabelle. Act Four, Scene One." Laly took off in the Bracegirdle manner.

Ah—my dear liberty, shall I leave thee? My faithful solitude, my darling contemplation, must I bid you then *adieu?* Ah-h, *adieu*—my morning thoughts, agreeable wakings, indolent slumbers, all ye *douceurs,* ye *sommeils du matin, adieu?*—I can't do't, 'tis more than impossible . . .

"Pick it up at 'Liberty to pay visits,'" said Lucienne. Laly corrected her.

Liberty to pay *and receive* visits, to and from whom I please; to write and receive letters, without interrogatories or wry faces on your part; to wear what I please; and choose conversation with regard to my own taste; come to dinner when I please; dine in my dressing room when I'm out of humour; to have my closet inviolate; to be sole empress of my tea table, which you must never presume to approach without first asking leave.

Lucienne wrapped up the scene: "Which would you rather do: be sole empress of your tea table or make two hundred a week?"

"Two hundred dollars a week! How? Where could I possibly earn that much?"

I'd better play this *dolce,* thought Lucienne. She crossed the room and fingered the tasseled knot of a velvet rope. "You said you were an actress. Well, every actress needs a stage." Lucienne tugged at the velvet knot; portieres parting disclosed an oversized bed. "Here's your stage, dearie. All you have to do is climb onto it and turn in a good performance, for a solo audience. He won't always be the *best* audience; most times his only recommendation will be the ten dollars you collect before the show goes on. You're young, attractive, *smart;* you'll get plenty of action from the select clientele in Kazanjian's stud book."

Lucienne saw the heavy tears welling into Laly's eyes.

"I know. It'll be rugged at first." La Bisguier knew—or remembered. "No nice girl likes to take off her clothes in front of a perfect stranger—and most of them aren't so perfect either. But it's like playing Ophelia. When I was seventeen, I played Ophelia two hundred nights on the road and got so goddamned sick of her after the first week that I wanted to throw up. But no one out front could tell—they didn't care—all they wanted was a good performance. And that's what you've got to give, Honey. Why, with that balcony of yours, you could pack in ten, twelve audiences a day and be playing—ha, ha—to Standing Room Only."

Tears drawn from the deepest springs of Laly's selfhood washed away the box-office bribe. Two hundred dollars a week with all its *douceurs,* and indolent surrenders. Attractive . . . but impossible!

"I can't do it," she sobbed. "I couldn't let a man touch me unless—it sounds foolish, perhaps—unless I loved him."

Lucienne's bed vanished at a tug of the velvet cord. "Don't feel upset, child. Like Oscar Wilde said about writing sonnets, 'It's either easy or impossible.' Me, I like sonnets. Toss them off in three minutes. Just lucky, I guess. Let's have another cup of Suchong before I roll out Proposition B. If it fails to amuse, you can always fall back on nice steady work as a sewing-machine operator in one of our local sweatshops. Fifteen cents an hour and always the chance that the boss will invite you off the floor for a stand-up séance in the mop closet."

Lucienne snapped open a small cloisonné watch suspended from a fleur-de-lis pin under her left shoulder. "I have a matinee at three, so you'll excuse me for being brisk. To the point. Kazanjian tells me that you have a camera."

"Yes, I have."

"Do you know how to take pictures, develop plates and all that?"

"Yes."

"And would you have any objection to taking pictures of an attractive young female in a series of 'art poses'?"

"Would the model be . . . draped?"

"Decreasingly so. You would receive a dollar per pose in addition to the cost of the plates."

The Chinese gong over Lucienne's door went into a coded carillon:

> *bong*
> *bing   bing*
> *Bong   Bong*

"Punctuality, thy name is Poindexter," said Lucienne. "Fly,

fly, child, and don't let yourself be seduced by the massively endowed old lecher wheezing in the hallway."

Maktoub Kazanjian himself helped Laly get the Anthony camera, together with its tripod, screens and flash pan, into a cab next morning. Ardor for the earned dollar made the photographer punctual; unaided, she carried her apparatus upstairs in three trips while Lucienne fortified by black coffee, plunged into her habitual cold tub.

At eleven-thirty, with the camera, photographer and director ready for action, the model hadn't yet appeared. Noon. Still no model.

"To hell with her," snapped Lucienne. "I'll go through the routine myself. Can you get a hazy effect with that camera?"

"I can get any effect you want."

"Curtain in five minutes. All-star cast featuring Madame Lucienne Bisguier in her one hundred thousandth performance of Keyhole Fantasy." Lucienne's gaiety, the mock modesty of her first poses and the magnificent abandon of this woman nearly twice her age swept Laly into a sense of shared adventure. Working with Lucienne was fun—and how often does one have fun? As for the poses, they were tantalizing revelations of the mystery, never wholly revealed, that lies between a woman fully gowned and that same woman skillfully working her way to nudity.

"Take this one in profile." Lucienne, corseted à la Black Crook, wearing French high heels, opera-length stockings, began the ceremonial unclasping of the garter.

To catch the nuance of femininity suggested by Lucienne stretched Laly's technique and imagination. Then came a sequence of provocative quarter-turnings and modulations (the term *slow motion* hadn't yet been invented) that ended with Lucienne standing back to the camera, hands clasped at the nape of her neck.

> bong
>   bing   bing
> Bong   Bong

"Good heavens!" exclaimed Lucienne. "That's Charlie. It must be three o'clock."

The sequence of ideas puzzled Laly. "How do you know it's Charlie?"

"Because it's Wednesday—three o'clock—who else could it

be?" Lucienne pressed the buzzer releasing the front door and slipped into a quilted peignoir.

"Charlie likes me in a receptive mood," she explained. "I'd ask you to join us in a threesome—oh, Charlie's the boy for his *divertissements*—but you wouldn't have enough patience. So gather up your plates and out the door with you."

"When shall I deliver the proofs?"

"Tomorrow. Cash on the barrelhead."

Laly, closing the back door softly, heard Lucienne go into her ten-dollar routine. "*Sharlee, Sharlee*, it has been three days. You have anozza mistress."

Laly's first act on returning home was to regain physical possession of Haila. Her sense of guilt at abandoning the child even for a few hours had been mounting all afternoon. Only mothers are plagued with this anxiety. Nothing will relieve it but fierce, tender hugging and kissing, not particularly serviceable to the child, but as needful as tears to the eternal Mater Lachrymosa.

She plied Myrza with queries: "Did she cry? Did she miss me? Did she drink her milk?"

And Myrza, knowing that babies have lived—even managed to enjoy living—without a mother's attention, answered Yes to everything.

"Thank you, Myrza." Laly fumbled in her coin purse for a half dollar, but the Crystal Gazer waved it aside, "Should I who never had a baby take money for being a little-while mother?" She pointed to the crystal ball on her table. "I accept money only for peering into the future. Come back when you have put Haila to sleep."

Without clairvoyance, Laly could see that Myrza needed the half dollar. "I've a great deal of work to do first; I'll come back later this evening."

"Any time." Since Myrza dealt in nothing but the future, there was no hurry.

The ritual of feeding Haila, scrubbing her gently, putting her to bed, repeating Longfellow's "I shot an arrow into the air," standard diet for tiny elocutionists, occupied two precious hours of Laly's time. It was well past six o'clock when she entered the darkroom to develop the photographs she had taken that afternoon. When immersed in a bath of developing solution, the sensitized plates began to glow dimly: black where white should be, and vice versa. She set up the plates to dry. By the next morning they would be ready for printing up in rough proof for Lucienne's approval.

She brewed a cup of tea and munched on a day-before-yesterday's roll. At 11:15 she surveyed her "wash"; forty plates altogether; if they came out well Laly would get forty dollars. Why, if she could have even two days a month like this one, her future would take care of itself.

Future! Future? Repentantly her promise to Myrza, "I'll be back later," came to mind. It was eleven-thirty now. Would Myrza be awake at this hour? Laly locked her studio, tiptoed down the hall and gently knocked on Myrza's door.

"Myrza, are you awake?"

Like the eye that watcheth over Israel, Myrza, descendant of Nostradamus, neither slumbered nor slept, nor even bothered to take her clothes off.

"Come in."

Laly opened the door on a scene of dedicated solitude (quite different from loneliness) lighted only by the faint flicker of a candle. In her rocking chair, shoulders wrapped in a gypsy shawl, Myrza tranquilly waited out the one hundred thousandth vigil of her priestess life.

"Don't you ever feel lonely, Myrza?"

"The more the solitude grows, the less loneliness one feels. A German poet, Goethe, I think—what difference does it make?—was borrowing from my great-great-grandfather when he said, 'Character is formed in society; genius in solitude.' And my genius reaches a peak when the hour falls from twelve to one. Unfortunately, few customers find me at my best."

Laly had heard, during her four years with Arthur Cople-stone, so much sententiousness parading as wisdom, had seen so much claptrap passed off under the name *occult*, that she was oversensitized perhaps to any manifestation of occultism. Yet she also realized that Arthur Coplestone, despite his fakery, actually did possess certain gifts denied to ordinary men. That he had elected to abuse these gifts, that they had undermined his character, had not shaken the belief which she now expressed to the woman who held out her palm for the traditional crossing with silver.

"Myrza," she began, "I know that certain people possess, in varying degrees, powers beyond normal understanding. My husband possessed such powers."

"Your husband misused his gift." A declarative sentence

without moral overtones or change of expression. Undeniable, all-inclusive, damning, true.

"Tell me, Myrza, do you have the true gift of divination?"

Myrza accepted Laly's silver coin, slipped it into a wallet secreted somewhere in the voluminous folds of her dress, then presented her credentials. "On my mother's side I stand in direct descent from Nostradamus. From her I inherited the gift of crystal gazing. It is an unprofitable talent, as you see. Worse, it is a burden always to be peering into the future and doomed, a thousand times a year, to see *nothing*. Most people don't have any future. For these I put together some simple story: a husband will stop drinking; money will come across the water; a man is about to enter their life. You see, I cannot compete with the grand promises made by the churches, so I deal in comforting trifles. Without such comfort how would people have the courage to go on living?"

> *To-morrow, and to-morrow, and to-morrow*
> *Creeps in this petty pace from day to day,*
> *To the last syllable of recorded time;*
> *And all our yesterdays have lighted fools*
> *The way to dusty death.*

No doubt about it, Myrza was speaking in the great tradition.

"What do you see when you look into your crystal?"

"Either light or shadow—if there is *anything* to be seen. Perhaps in a thousand lives there will be one or two on whom even a splintered shadow of destiny falls." Myrza paused. "One in ten thousand bears the *sigla* of Light. I am the proof of what I say. Even in my hours of illumination I see nothing of my own future in that ball."

"What do you see for me?"

Myrza's shawl became a sibylline mantle as she gazed into the crystal glass.

"*Nostradamus*, shield us! Over your head a nimbus glows. It is a halo. The brightest I have ever seen."

"When will other people begin to see it?"

"Soon. Someone caught a glimpse of it today. A woman. You made a decision regarding her. Afterward . . . My vision blurs. . . . I do not know the details, but—" she spoke triumphantly— "you laughed."

"For the first time in years."

"Wait. Wait. Within a few weeks, you will make a still more important decision. *Ai-eee.*" Terror shook Myrza's grisly larynx. "For the first time I see my own future. I am a shadow . . . a dark moon, rimmed by a fingernail of light—a reflection of you."

Fatigue, the excitement of the day, the memory of laughter with Lucienne, knowledge that she had seen the pendulum of experience swing from Lucienne's controlled sensuality to pure manifestation of spirit made Laly feel lighthearted, generous.

"If I have any light to shed, you're welcome to a fingernail's worth, Myrza. Thanks for the reading."

Down the dark hallway a very real halo of light lay sleeping. Laly listened to her child's breathing and resisted the impulse to waken her.

"I shot an arrow into the air," she murmured, and five minutes later slipped into the feathery abyss of sleep.

Lucienne was delighted by the photographic proofs that Laly brought to her on the following day. Natural human vanity at the sight of her long, perfectly modeled legs, high waist and full bust that dared meet the challenge of a profile shot caused her to exclaim, "Why, these are the best pictures I've ever had! Is it me or the camera?"

"It's a good camera," Laly admitted, "but the subject matter is exceptional." Unreserved admiration shone in Laly's eyes. "You make everything seem so mysterious and beautiful. A great deal of thought and experience must have gone into these poses."

Lucienne took time out to correct her protégée. "No. Thought and experience are useless until imagination takes over. And what was I imagining when I unhooked the top stud of that black corset? It's not exactly a Protestant married woman's pose, would you say?"

"Just the opposite."

"Right. I was imagining something that doesn't occur in actual life. I was projecting a vision that most men, poor bastards, go to their graves dreaming of. The overture that few women don't dare, or care, to make." Genuine pity for the human condition—male, female, separate or together, with special emphasis on the shabby poverty of their sexual expression—pitched Lucienne's voice to a key of indignation. "Why ninety-nine and forty-four one hundredths per cent of our pure American womanhood doesn't realize the sheer buying power of the itty-bitty, not so pretty, but, oh, so comfy, umphy-bumphy shelter under their delta that makes a man feel as though he could support an army." She put on the air brakes—*whoooosh*. Her nostrils flared at the notion of the wattage going to waste all over the place. "Print up these pictures on glossy paper and we'll start an educational campaign that'll sweep the country."

Laly had never witnessed such a blaze of temperament. Anger and the authority to express anger; passion and the ability to project it in language that combined fury for the ideal with contempt for the actual—how did one come by these priceless gifts?

"Mrs. Siddons must have been like you."

"Siddons wasn't always being interrupted by that god-damned

> bong
>   bing   bing
>   Bong   Bong."

Lucienne went through the motions of being a Chinese pagoda, a Moorish mosque and came out on the true-blue Liberty Bell note.

"Here's twenty dollars in advance, the rest payable when the job is finished, and plenty more work if you want it. Any questions before the Chinese gong goes off again?"

"Yes." Laly selected the final picture of the series. "Do you want me to rub out these tiny letters, 'D.F.'?"

Lucienne inspected the scarcely discernible evidence of an experience that she wished both to remember and to forget.

"Don't bother. They won't be noticed. The slobs that buy Kazanjian's rifflebooks can't read, anyway."

During the next few weeks, the Anthony box camera brought in a steady income. Laly spent the morning and early afternoon taking pictures of Lucienne and other less-talented models in poses that went into general circulation as rifflebooks, retailing at a dollar a piece and evidently much in demand.

In Lucienne's apartment, flesh was a "commodity"—salable to any properly accredited customer who had an appetite for top-quality merchandise. Time and again Lucienne held out the lure of ready money, much-needed money for a much-loved Haila.

"It's yours for the having, dearie, if you'll only lay aside certain dainty misapprehensions concerning that little muff of yours. You could earn ten times, twenty times, as much as that box camera will bring in. You'd be a sensation. Think it over."

That night Laly discussed the proposition with Myrza. The crystal gazer was realistic in the Old-World manner. "There is a long tradition of actresses who were courtesans," she began. "The two oldest professions in the world twine naturally around each other. Some women can manage the matter quite easily." Myrza gazed into her glass ball. "But if you begin taking on men promiscuously the nimbus over your head will vanish. Already the luster is dimming. Worse, your daughter whimpers for you during your absence—a bad sign. Children know. You must weld a stronger link of security between you and your baby."

"How, Myrza, how? Look deeply into your glass. Tell me what you see."

The faded Romany princess passed her hand over weary eyes. "I see only a blur. Perhaps it will clear up. For the immediate present, you have two choices.

"Tell me, Myrza, what are they?"

"Either you must keep on doing what you're doing or go home to your people."

"I can't go home." Laly dared not tell Myrza about Zarah *couchante.*

"Why not? It would be no disgrace to return."

Bitter tears of rage and frustration gushed down Laly's cheeks. "Going home would mean an admission of failure, the end of my ambition for the stage."

There must be a conspiracy in the world, thought Laly; a conspiracy against love, talent and beauty—else I should not be weeping in this mean chamber tonight.

"I will keep on with what I am doing," she said, drying her eyes.

She continued to take pictures of Lucienne and various other models. She became increasingly expert with the Anthony box camera—so expert, in fact, and so professionally detached from the subject matter that Lucienne tried to persuade her into taking a "duo."

"What's a 'duo'?" asked Laly.

" 'Duo' means two. Like the Bible says, 'man and woman,'

He created them both. That's a 'duo.' I've got a local Eve who's willing to go the distance with a grease-ball Adam. It means two dollars a shot for you."

"Sorry," said Laly. "I can't do it."

Lucienne threw up her hands in desperation. "Kid, you get sorry too easy for this kind of business. Back you go—camera and all—to Kazanjian."

Laly's refusal to plunge deeper into the mire of pornography qualified her to become the missing cog in Maktoub Kazanjian's GRAND DESIGN. Devious at heart but direct in method, he aspired to make money by the simple expedient of printing it. For this purpose he had bought a special press and installed it in the cellar of his building. Living off his bounty was one Joe McPartland, a photoengraver, whose zest for making ten-dollar bills had already won him a penitentiary sentence. Although eager to try again, McPartland explained he must first have an enlarged photographic facsimile of the genuine article. But where in all St. Louis could Kazanjian find a reputable photographer who would lend his camera to such a plan? Why, he had one on the third floor of his own building—an innocent non-Moslem female desperately in need of cash.

Characteristically, the landlord avoided the straightforward proposition. He would be oblique, devious, creative, make an appeal to the girl's finer sensibilities by lifting the whole business onto the plane of Art.

He tapped gently on Laly's door. When she opened it, Kazanjian faced the East, salaamed, snuffled and came back with a message from the Orient. "The Prophet informs me that the human figure, undraped, has limited interest for the Enlightened."

"The Prophet and I must be getting our information from the same agency," said Laly.

"But in the case of art objects—pictures, statues, vases—these are legitimate subjects for your camera, are they not?"

"Of course. With my studio lights, I can photograph anything."

"Actual size or larger?"

"Larger, smaller, any size."

Kazanjian became a camel-driver beholding an oasis in the middle distance. "You come at a time when my figs are still green. Allah be praised for your benevolence." From beneath his voluminous garment, he produced a miniature bronze statue that Laly recognized as the Discobolus. "Could you take a picture of this?"

"Easily. In five minutes. It would take some time to develop and print it."

"For this small favor, you shall have payment in advance." Kazanjian handed her a dollar bill. "In my vast warehouses of art," he explained, "I have some hundreds of canvases and statues that should be photographed for cataloguing purposes. You may count on a steady income from me hereafter." As an afterthought, he added, "Strictly according to the Koran."

Kazanjian kept his promise. Such a parade of false, dubious, obscure and unsigned canvases passed before the lens of the Anthony box: Velásquez, Breughel, Bellini, Cranach, Tiepolo, Ingres, Watteau, Eakins (thank God for Eakins), Courbet, Constable and Gainsborough. The Moslem swore by Mohammed that they were all genuine. Genuine or fake, it made little difference to Laly. Her accumulation of dollar bills increased until she had almost enough money for her train fare to New York.

At this point, the landlord-connoisseur invited her to participate in his deeper thinking. "My object," he began, "is twofold: first, I wish to make a catalogue of all the pictures in my warehouse. After the catalogue is completed, I propose to hold a vast exhibition, to which the multitude may come. Not merely to gaze, but to buy at ten dollars a picture."

Balko-Mediterranean oiliness oozed from Maktoub Kazanjian. "To acquaint the public with my plan, I propose to make a huge placard stating in simple terms that I, Maktoub Kazanjian, thankful for the blessings showered upon me by America, am offering my entire collection of art treasures at ten dollars apiece—one to a customer."

A mucilaginous postnasal drip caused Maktoub Kazanjian to dirty another of the colored handkerchiefs dangling from various pockets. "As proof positive of my good faith, I intend to place at the center of the placard a replica of a mint-fresh ten-dollar bill. Here is the bill itself." Mr. Kazanjian produced the very article, mint fresh, uncrumpled.

Laly photographed the bill, enlarged the print and thought nothing more about it until, a week later, Myrza asked, "Did you take a picture of some paper money for Kazanjian recently?"

"Yes. He broke down and gave me the ten-dollar bill."

"Nostradamus, shield this innocent child!"

"Have I done something wrong, Myrza?"

"You have committed the high crime of reproducing in pictorial form a piece of United States money. Last night I heard the *thump, thump, thump* of a heavy press somewhere in the cellar. Dress Haila at once. If we move rapidly we can slip through the meshes of the net."

"What net?"

"Ask no questions. Come."

"But my camera!"

"Leave it as evidence against the evil man who tempted you into this thing. Walk quietly beside me toward the river. A boat will be waiting."

"Where are we going?"

"Keep on walking. Put this shawl over your head. Stoop a bit, Laly. Be a gypsy's daughter for a little while."

Maktoub Kazanjian, who dealt in many commodities, Lucienne Bisguier, who dealt in one, together with a haul of engravers, intermediaries and passers, received indeterminate sentences of five years and upward for the felony of counterfeiting.

But Laly Coplestone, wearing the shawl of a Romany princess, simply disappeared into the void of Missing Persons.

THE SPORTING THING (1901)

CHANCE WOODHULL's baseball team needed uniforms. Aided by Wayland Towner, Wampum Bearer, Chance promoted a Grand Raffle.

Wayland Towner, son of Landmark's leading apothecary, had captured Chance's imagination on the first day they had hung their caps side by side in the coat room of the Sycamore Academy. Now, ten years later, Way and Chance shared a joint perfection, too young for flaws, not old enough to realize that flaws existed. If Chance's shoulders were perhaps a trifle broader, Way's figure was more lithe. In any company of boys, Way Towner's competitive energy would have established him as captain; yet in the affairs of the Defiance A.C. he subordinated himself without envy to the role of lieutenant.

"Here's how it goes, Way," explained Chance. "We print

up three hundred tickets, offering a two fifty gold piece as a prize. Then all of us'll get together and sell the tickets at ten cents apiece. That'll give us thirty dollars, won't it?"

"Sounds like good fifth-grade mathematics to me," said Towner.

The tickets being printed and sold—not without some resistance on the part of churchgoers—the members of the Defiance A.C. foregathered in the loft of the Woodhull carriage house to inspect the "Sears, Roebuck offer."

Baseball Uniforms

First-grade quality wool, in choice of white, gray or blue. Big-League styling throughout. Pants, half-sleeve jumper, cap and stockings.
Complete as illustrated $2.75
Spiked shoes (optional) $1.50
Send us the measurements of your players together with money order. Delivery guaranteed within two weeks.

Because only Towner and Chance could afford the luxury of spiked shoes, Chance applied to the source of all bounty, his father. "The rest of my team needs spikes," he said.

Anson had never heard of spikes. "What are they?" he asked.

"They're steel cleats fastened to the sole of each shoe," explained Chance. "All the Big-League teams wear them. They give you better footing, more speed."

Pleased by his son's initiative in engineering the complicated Raffle-Uniform business thus far, Anson inquired, "How much would it cost to outfit the entire team with spiked shoes?"

Thirteen dollars and fifty cents."

Anson's inquiry was prompted neither by penury nor the fear of overindulging his son. He wanted to know if Chance realized that thirteen dollars and fifty cents represented a week's salary, a *good* salary, to millions of American laborers. Obviously, the lad didn't. Well, why should he? The aspiration for Big-League status (call it perfectibility, competitive fire, the dream of an adolescent virtuoso—call it what you will) rayed out of the boy with plumber's torch intensity.

Good—good.

"I guess I can finance the spiked-shoe part of the deal all right." Anson handed his son fifteen dollars. "While you're at it, get a couple of bats."

Gratitude has been defined as the "lively expectation of favors still to be received." There was no calculation in the wet "thank you" kiss that Chance planted on Anson's cheek.

Ten days afterward a great box bearing the Sears, Roebuck stencil was delivered to Mr. Chance Woodhull, c/o Defiance A.C., Landmark, Indiana. The Grand Sachem assembled his tribe; the carton was opened—and, oh! heart's desire and boyish dream come true—there lay nine baseball uniforms, pin-striped with crimson thread. Each blouse bore the block-letter legend "Defiance A.C." There were nine pairs of woolen stockings encircled at the calf with a wide crimson band— just like the Cincinnati Red-Legs. Yes, and nine pairs of light-weight leathern shoes, each bearing on its sole a triangular steel cleat, as sharp as a razor.

Elwood Hosmer wept openly. Goober Smith blubbered. In fact, there wasn't a dry eye in the Woodhull carriage house as each boy tried on his uniform.

"All we've got to do now," announced Chance, "is to beat every team in Landmark County. We'll practice twice a day on the academy field. Townie here has a schedule all lined up for Saturday-morning games."

Could it be possible that the uniforms pumped new voltage and a sense of team-play into the Defiance nine? It certainly seemed so when they beat the Peasely Public School 11-2, and trounced a Racer Dam outfit 14-6. Chance was putting a real hop on his fast ball and had a round-house curve that any bush-league batter could have knocked into the next township. Nothing so good as a bush-league batter existed in Landmark County. For it so happens that Nature places her fourteen-year-old pitchers several notches higher than batsmen of the same age. (Never ask why.)

Tirelessly, the battery of Woodhull and Towner practiced their specialized arts of pitching and catching. Way Towner could throw to any base with a flick of his supple arm. Elwood Hosmer, first base, was a "tower of strength"—as the sports writers say—and could sock that old apple a country mile— *iffen* he happened to connect. Goober Smith (s.s.) and

Charlie Pike (2nd b.) gave reasonable facsimiles of a maneuver later perfectd by Messrs. Tinker, Evans and Chance. Because Connie Mack's $100,000 infield was still a gleam in the McGillicuddy eye, no basis for comparison (or contrast) could be found in the Defiance A.C. Nevertheless, it put together a string of six consecutive victories during the summer of 1901. The only team yet to be played was the Hinkeydinks, a tough-knuckled crew led by Digger Magoffin.

The phials of Hinkeydink wrath sizzled when Digger Magoffin lipread the following squib in the Landmark *Cornet:*

> By trouncing all comers in convincing fashion, the Defiance A.C., made up of youngsters from the Sycamore Academy, is making a strong bid for the 13-14-year-old championship of Landmark County. Teams desiring games with this snappy, uniformed club should communicate with Chance Woodhull, c/o this office.

Next day Chance Woodhull received a communication, or summons rather, from the Hinkeydink captain, Digger Magoffin. An imperious jerk of the Magoffin thumb, followed by a "P-sst, hey you!" halted Chance and Wayland Towner as they passed Timmins' Livery Stable.

"Hear you're claimin' the champeenship," said Digger.

"That's right."

Magoffin snapped a cigarette butt past Chance's ear. "Nobody's goin' to be champeens around here till they play the Hinkeydinks."

"Fair enough," said Chance. "We'll play you a week from Saturday."

The game between the Hinkeydinks and the Defiance A.C. was played on Rossman's Pasture, a field liberally strewn with rocks and cow flops, adjacent to the village dump. The only spectators at the game were six disgruntled cows who had been shooed into an orchard of withered apple trees—and twelve-year-old Amy Towner straddling a bough overlooking the improvised baseball diamond. Secretly she had climbed the tree and hidden herself in its foliage so that she might watch what happened when big boys played together. Amy understood nothing about baseball. She wondered why her brother and Chance Woodhull had been so grim as they laced on their spiked shoes that morning; and she had come for the purpose of finding out—if possible—why these two magnificent heroes (Chance seemed especially heroic to her) should condescend to play the loathsome Hinkeydinks. She disliked Digger Magoffin's insolent manner of addressing Chance as "Holler-Boy" when the Defiance A.C. captain shouted encouragement to his teammates during pregame warm-up.

Amy was going to see a great deal that she didn't like, or understand, in the next couple of hours.

Marked by the usual number of wild throws, booted grounders and fumbled flies, the game was a free-scoring affair. In the bottom of the seventh inning, the score stood: Defiance A.C. 13, Hinkeydinks 12. With bases loaded, Digger Magoffin stepped up swinging three bats. Contemptuously he let the first pitch cut the heart of the plate.

"Strike One," cried Fatso Devlin, the umpire of Magoffin's choice.

"Dig the mush out of your eyes, Fatso," warned Digger. Fatso's eyesight rapidly improved. "Ball one . . . ball two . . . ball three. . . ." On the next pitch Chance threw his slow curve; it sailed up big as a cantaloupe, and the Digger lined a tremendous foul down the left field line. *Strike two.*

This classic count pleased the Digger. Bases full, pitcher in the hole, slugger at bat. Magoffin chose to play the scene for comedy. He whispered to the Hinkeydink batboy, who sped to the adjoining dump and returned with a long-necked square bottle.

Discarding his bat, Magoffin gripped the empty whiskey bottle by its neck and held it firmly over the plate like a bat. "You don't need no fast ball, Holler-Boy," he said to Chance. "Spikes and new uniforms won't help none now. Just break the bottle and I'm out."

Chance recognized the bottle. Once it had held a full quart of Old Landmark, his father's whiskey. Now it was a target that he must shatter to fragments, else another run would be forced in. He tugged at the visor of his cap and went into his wind-up. As the ball left his hand he knew it was a legitimate strike, but it missed the bottle by inches.

Hoots of derision rose from the Hinkeydinks as Digger Magoffin, bottle in hand, trotted down to first base. There, with mock modesty, he turned his back to the playing field and relieved the strain on his kidneys by half filling the Old Landmark bottle.

"Tain't four years old, but it'll splash just as good," he

said, hurling the container onto the dump. Amy, in the tree, shut her eyes. Was this the way big boys acted?

The incident unnerved Chance. Two more runs crossed the plate before he retired the side.

Between innings Way Towner gave his battery mate a fire-breathing pep talk. "We can still win. Magoffin's so busy showing off he'll get careless."

Either carelessness or a wicked delight in terrorizing his opponents caused Digger to hit the first two Defiance batters with his fast ball. Anyway it cost him three runs when Towner cleaned the bases with a homer, thereby putting his club ahead 16-15.

Coming up for the last raps in the ninth, the Hinkeydinks were still trailing. With two out, Magoffin stepped to the plate. No goat-getting this time. He rubbed his hands in the dirt, pointed to right field and announced, "I'll put it there. Way out."

He did—but not quite as deep as he planned. Goober Smith knocked the drive down with his glove, picked it up and pegged for home. Towner threw aside his mask, took the ball on its first bounce, and slapped it into Magoffin's rump as he slid for the plate.

Fatso Devlin, mourning the day his mother bore him, was obliged to cry, "You're out."

The game was over; Defiance A.C. 16; Hinkeydinks 15. Only a reversal of the umpire's decision could change the final score. Magoffin, leaping to his feet, demanded such a reversal. He doubled his fist and held it under Fatso's nose. "Now tell 'em again, you cock-eyed bastard, was I out or safe?"

Towner interrupted crisply. "You were out a mile, Magoffin."

"Who says so?"

"Your own umpire says so. *I* say so. I put the ball onto you and I ought to know."

Towner's coolness was like water to a hydrophobic pup. The fist that had threatened Fatso came up without warning and Towner reeled backward from a brutal blow on the chin. The Digger started another punch but it never landed. Chance Woodhull grabbed his arm and spun the Hinkeydink captain around.

"Look here, Magoffin, if you want to fight, take someone your size. Lay off my catcher, hear! The game's over. We won sixteen to fifteen."

Digger wrenched his arm loose and surveyed his new prey. Nothing could have pleased him more than Woodhull's interference, Here was the bird he really wanted to pick clean! Positive pleasure flamed in his eyes as he growled. "Holler-Boy protectin' his players again, I see."

With a sudden motion Digger jerked the visor of Chance's cap over his eyes, then dropped him to the ground with a belt on the jaw.

By neither training nor temperament was Chance Woodhull quarrelsome. Competitive, yes. He burned with a passion to excel at games, but in his code of sportsmanship there had never been any occasion for violence. Now his system of values had been challenged by another, more brutal system. His affectionate attempt to protect Wayland Towner had drawn upon himself a terrible consequence. That he was no match for Magoffin either in size or weight made little difference. Under pain of cowardice he must take a beating from the Hinkeydink captain.

For the first time in his life Chance felt the world's bitter unfairness. Tears welled into his brown eyes, ran down his young cheeks.

"Cryin' won't help none. Stand up and take your lickin'."

Chance rose to one knee, a position of conceded safety among sportsmen. Barely had he reached his feet when Magoffin came in like a freckled rhinoceros, jolting hard rights and lefts to Chance's head and body. Sheer agility enabled Chance to avoid some of Magoffin's punches, but in three minutes he was knocked down twice. Blood streamed from his nose; he could taste it trickling down his throat. His right eye was puffy, almost closed by the tattoo of Digger's granite knuckles. It was harder to get up after each knockdown. Why should he get up at all?

Well, you *had* to. Otherwise Magoffin's run would count. You had to keep on protesting.

Bang. A crushing left to the chin. Chance went down again. Up . . . up . . . Wobbling, he rose.

Bang. Bang. A one-two combination sent him down again.

Up, up, up. Chance felt the end coming. Yet so long as he could lift his hands, the unequal fight must drag on. By the rules, no one could stop it. No one dared to. No one did.

Cruelty among boys has its degrees of refinement. Magoffin, tiring of the comparatively tame sport of knocking Chance down at will, decided to add a touch of exhibitionism to the show. The instinct that had prompted him to appear at the plate with a whiskey bottle swelled within him now. The bottle trick would pale in comparison with the exploit he had in mind.

"Looka here, Woodhull, you don't seem to be hittin' nothin' but the ground. I'm gonna make you a fair and square proposition. I'll drop my hands like this [Magoffin's gorilla arms sagged to his knees], then stick out my jaw, and let you whang at it till you're tired."

Merriment convulsed the Hinkeydinks as their dauntless captain thrust out his naked jaw. "C'mon, Holler-Boy, take a good swing."

The offer was tempting. There was Magoffin's chin, taunting, wide open. But what would it prove, Chance thought, if he knocked Magoffin out with a free punch? He shook his head. "I couldn't hit a man with his hands down."

"Then the massacree will continue." Magoffin held up a bloody fist. "I don't want to waste no more punches." He gave his victim a choice.

"Do you want this in the face or belly?"

Actually it took three more punches to knock Chance out. As he lay on the ground, he heard far-off voices.

"Holler-Boy won't talk it up no more."

"Out stiffer'n a mackerel."

"Get the water bucket." That would be Wayland Towner's voice.

"Don't need no bucket." Magoffin speaking. "This'll bring him around."

Laughter. Then Chance felt a stinging stream, warm, ammonial, sharp, playing over his face. He opened his good eye and saw the legs of a forked colossus standing over him. From the fork of the colossus a loathesome drench was streaming.

The acid stream burned away the varnish of sportsmanship and penetrated to tissues of savagery beneath the civilized surface. Chance rolled over and leaped to his feet. No defensive dodging now; no more boyish offerings on the altar of sportsmanship. This was the death grapple and it was Magoffin who would die!

He drove his baseball spikes into Magoffin's naked foot, and as the colossus went down in howling anguish a triple stream of blood spurting from his bare foot, Chance kicked him in the groin.

"*Ugh.*" Digger's legs jackknifed in pain as he writhed on the ground. With bare hands, Chance went for his enemy's throat. He dug his thumbs into the ringed gristle of Magoffin's windpipe and tightened his strangle hold until Digger's eyes bulged. He lifted Magoffin's head from the ground and hammered it onto a rock that had recently been part of a playing field and, before that, a cow pasture.

Fairly fresh evidence of its cow pasture phase lay close by. Chance released his hold on Digger's windpipe and scooped up a handful of cow dung. The Hinkeydink captain had offered him a choice. Chance would return the courtesy now. With his spiked shoe over Magoffin's face, he said, "Which will you take?"

Digger, half-conscious, saw the triangular steel cleat directly above his eyes. All the Hinkeydinks saw it. All the Defiance players saw it. From her perch in the apple tree, Amy Towner saw it, too. The horror of the thing about to happen outweighed all the unbelievable horrors that had preceded it. Her feminine instinct to prevent the maiming of a human face with steel prompted her to cry out, "*No! No! Chance. Don't.*"

Any twelve-year-old girl would be forgiven if, in a voice high-pitched with agony, she had uttered such a plea. But Amy Towner wasn't *any* girl. Her special characteristic was her capacity to learn from the actions of those strange, marvelous, resilient, aggressive creatures called "boys." How different they were from girls! Could she, Amy Towner, get off the ground as Chance Woodhull had? Turn prostrate defeat into triumphant vengeance? No! Had she interposed when Chance was lying helpless on the ground? No. Should she stay him now in his moment of satisfaction over a brutal opponent? No. Should she reveal her presence in the apple tree? Again no.

The only thing that Amy Towner could do was to stuff her fist into her mouth, choke down the feminine cry for quarter where no quarter had been given and turn her streaming eyes away from a spectacle of the boy she loved and knew to be gentle descending, at the moment, into ugly brutehood.

Actually, Chance was saved from the descent by Wayland Towner. Way broke through the barrier of murderous rage encircling Chance, first with a sharp "Hey, that's enough," then, by the physical act of pulling his teammate aside. Sanity flowed back into Chance's blood stream. He could not slash

Magoffin with his spikes. Instead, he slapped the cow dung into Digger's face.

"We won, Magoffin, sixteen to fifteen. That's official; you hear. Dig that mush out of your mouth and answer me!"

Mush was a euphemism for the stuff in Magoffin's mouth. But he answered. And his answer was the equivalent of "yes."

News of the ghastly fist fight reached Zarah from feminine sources. Amy Towner had sobbed out the whole story to her mother. "Oh, it was terrible. Magoffin knocked him down five times." (Amy couldn't bring herself to report the shameful drench that turned the tide of battle.) Mrs. Towner thought it only her duty to run right over and report the incident (Greek messenger style along with some marginalia concerning the social status of the Hinkeydinks) to her *dear* friend, Mrs. Woodhull.

"He's down at the pharmacy right now," said Alice. "Charles is patching him up with arnica and witch hazel."

These sovereign remedies could not conceal the damage that Magoffin's knuckles had inflicted on Zarah's younger son. Attempting to climb the back stairs, he heard his mother call.

"How did the baseball game come out?"

"We won, sixteen to fifteen."

Zarah summoned him and saw for herself the puffy lips, gouged cheeks, the blackened eye that the Hinkeydink captain had inflicted with his battering fists. Bad enough. But it was the broken tooth, the beautiful incisor snapped off forever, that justified a decision that had long been forming in Zarah's mind.

Chance *must* go away to school.

Zarah waited until she and Anson were sharing the parlor hour—that inviolable, mutually wished-for, evening ritual; the dahlia lamp still cast a pink glow over the Boston rocker on which Zarah sat embroidering (with the help of presbyopic lenses) the initial *C* on her son's handkerchief.

"Anson, I'd like to talk to you about Chance's education."

"By all means, dear. You know more about these matters than I do."

For the next five minutes, Zarah presented a bill of indictment against Clavering's *ratio studiorum*. *Primo*, the man had no Latin; *secundo*, mathematics stopped short at fractions; *tertio*, foreign languages weren't taught, and American history faded into a blur after the administration of James K. Polk. As for world literature . . . Zarah removed her pince-nez, rubbed her tired eyes. "Chance will never be accepted at Harvard on the strength of Clavering's curriculum."

"What do you propose?"

"I've been thinking that he should go to one of the good eastern schools. Groton, Andover, Exeter. Two years at a first-rate prep school would guarantee his acceptance at Harvard."

Anson knocked the ashes from his pipe. "He's pretty young to be leaving home."

Who knows better than I? thought Zarah. Who'll miss him more? His whistling, his adolescent enthusiasms, his love of fresh bread; my delight at seeing him butter the heel of a loaf fresh from the oven. Yet as she remembered the signs of provincialism that were already showing in his speech and carriage, she submerged the selfish desire to keep him at her side.

"I hear he made Magoffin holler quits in a fight today," said Anson.

"Suppose he did." Zarah dismissed the victory. "Do we want to bring him up as a rube, a fist-fighter competing with towboat bullies? Think, Anson. This wonderful son of ours— the last of our children—this good-looking, fierce, intelligent boy will one day be a man. And what kind of a man will he be?"

"He'll be your son and mine—no matter where we send him to school."

"The 'argument from heredity' isn't enough. I hope he'll be as good a man as you, Anson, but environment, culture, call it what you will—these things enter the picture, too. I'll write to Cousin Lyman tomorrow."

Cousin Lyman's reply was most comforting. He agreed that Chance should attend an eastern preparatory school but pointed out that it was a bit late in the year to make application to Groton or Andover. "There's an excellent school at Uxbridge, Massachusetts, St. Brede's. Its headmaster, Dr. Loring, is a close friend of mine. From Uxbridge to Cambridge is a short and certain step."

So Chance was packed off to St. Brede's, where, after a light sandpapering, he received the unmistakable patina of a first-rate prep school. He lost a year because of his deficiency in Latin. He did not distinguish himself at St. Brede's, won no medals, but learned to wear the proper school tie without self-consciousness and became in due time a candidate for matriculation at Harvard.

8.

THE NINTH STATION

As THE NEW CENTURY left the shell of its low-vaulted past, great was Oliver C. Treadgood in the Anti-Saloon League councils. (*Saloon* is the key word here.) In great industrial centers of the East and Middle West, the barroom still flourished. The weed-killing spray of moral suasion, the thunderous disapproval of pulpit and counting house, the wails and promises of reform rising from the throats of forty million yet-to-be-enfranchised women, the bitter tears of wives who saw their husbands reel through swinging doors, stinking, brutal and penniless after a Saturday-night debauch—none of these, singly or together, had succeeded in uprooting the Saloon.

There it stood on the corner, or three to a block, in the poorest sections of town. Its customers were, of double necessity, beer drinkers. Most of them couldn't afford to buy whiskey; and it seems that the sheer liquid volume that accompanies beer-drinking made a three-way appeal to gullet, bladder and urethra—all very pleasing to a working man who might just conceivably find himself in need of a foaming eighteen-ounce seidel (or maybe five or six of same) before going home to greet the wife of his bosom who had worn her little calico number through a long, hot day at the cook stove (yes, and many days before that, too), armpits studiously neglected the while, to counteract a husbandly breath heavy with unoxidized alcohol. Considering the human situation, it remains something of marvel that so many persons stayed sober, industrious and out of jail. Nevertheless, it was the sheer intake and output of beer in and about the premises that gave the saloon its bad name and worse smell.

Only the Whirlwind of the Lord could cleanse the atmosphere. Puffing out his cheeks, Oliver C. Treadgood began to let the Lord's Voice be heard.

Among the other chores that Oliver Treadgood took upon himself was the formation of a publishing house, the Anti-Saloon League Press, Inc. With monies solicited from churches, industrial leaders and employers generally (not forgetting the widow's mite and the little brown piggy bank), Ollie purchased a battery of flat-bed presses and began turning out Anti-Saloon propaganda by the long ton. Textbooks, pamphlets, tracts, a weekly newspaper, a monthly magazine, sprang to life under his touch. Publisher, editor, circulation manager and editorial supervisor, Ollie became the spokesman of the Dry Movement.

"Get to the schoolchildren," he told his editors. But before the children could be reached Ollie had to cajole, threaten and coerce state legislatures to pass mandatory laws requiring that every textbook on hygiene contain powerful and repeated proofs that alcohol was *The Bane*. Penny-a-line Ph.D.'s solemnly advised young readers that Alcohol was a Poison that polluted the mind, stunted the body, impaired judgment, undermined character, caused idiocy, premature baldness, *ejaculatio praecox*, bleeding ulcers, constipation, acne, warts (or hair) on the palm of the hands and Shame in the Presence of a Fine Woman. Grave scientists longing for a fast buck sat around devising experiments to prove that Eskimo dogs quailed at the sight of a whiskey bottle and that green lizards turned pale at the first whiff of gin. Elephants' knees had been known to buckle when the animals were stabled alongside empty beer barrels.

Not creative himself, Treadgood engaged hack writers to turn out Dry Literature for consumption in grade schools, at lodge meetings, or wherever Anti-Saloon League members foregathered to scotch the Big Wrong.

Since it was humanly impossible to read, let alone write, the millions of words that rolled off the Anti-Saloon presses, Treadgood delegated much of this work to subordinates, either voluntary amateurs or underpaid hacks. Among the latter was a certain Bertram Whelk, who could write better, and sometimes faster, than a Blake archangel could fly. Scrutinizing Whelk's testimonials, Treadgood found them "spotty." The man had an A.B. from Amherst and had served as a press agent for Richard Mansfield. To complicate the picture, Whelk had also published a volume of poetry entitled *Only an Asterisk.* Somehow it didn't add up; but, given a trial spin, Whelk knocked off a red-hot philippic against the swinging door, the sawdust floor, the foaming mug and cuspidor.

"S-a-a-y," exclaimed Ollie. The man's virtuosity stuck out like a giant cucumber in a bottle of Baptist gherkins. Only trouble was Whelk wanted sixty-five dollars a month. Treadgood, emulating the Mayor of Hamelin, said, "Come, take fifty with fringe benefits, including a milk-and-graham-cracker lunch and a bean supper at the Y.M.C.A. every Saturday night." Done and done.

It was Whelk's job to keep the *Anti-Saloon Advocate* (a weekly) chock-a-block full of up-to-the minute shoulder-to-the-wheel, chin-up editorials, articles, storyettes and playlets aimed at the whites of the enemy's eyes. By writing nine tenths of the material himself, Whelk tripled the *Advocate's* circulation to 150,000 copies and won quotes from Alabama to Georgia. Still, Treadgood distrusted the fellow. More than once, Ollie blue-penciled questionable items that reeked not so much of midnight oil as something else that came in bottles (and not vanilla pop, either). Fact was, Whelk turned out to be a wino. After several warnings, Treadgood gave his nip-happy editor the heave-ho—without so much as a week's severance pay.

Hell hath no fury like a wino scorned! Just as Treadgood was mounting the podium in Dill, Kansas, for a Temperance lecture, someone handed him an envelope containing press proofs of the most recent issue of the *Advocate.* The date happened to be April 1, 1905, and Whelk's swan song as editor proved to be an April-foolerino of the first magnitudinorum. While the chairman hoisted his sails for an introductory cruise around the Cape of Good Hope, Treadgood opened the envelope.

Examining the proofs, he cried out, "That perfidious bastard" (or maybe he said "dastard"), shoved a *Stop Press* telegram into the hands of Mrs. Hattie McGargle, the 250-pound committee woman sitting beside him, and yelled, "Get this to the nearest Western Union office."

Hattie got it to the office, then had a heart attack. Faithful Hattie! Not so lucky Treadgood! His telegram arrived just too late; the first run-off of 5,000 copies had been shipped out.

Although many of them were reclaimed, 836 got into circulation and became collectors' items—chiefly on acount of the front-page playlet, entitled:

THE BROKEN PLEDGE

Place: MILLTOWN, U.S.A.

Time: THE PRESENT

(Cast of Characters)

NOLLY PRATT: Student for the Ministry, ardent member of the Anti-Saloon League, a clean-living youth of twenty, who has spent his day in the performance of good works: viz., reading his Bible, planting wisteria in the back yard, whitewashing the dog house, bringing jellied broth to destitute neighbors, etc., etc.

Nolly is twin brother to

ROLLY PRATT: A working stiff who entertains "moderate" ideas concerning the use of alcohol. (How wrong can a guy be?) He has been seen on occasions leaving McGuirk's saloon, after quaffing a glass of beer. Recently, however, Rolly, convinced that he is treading the rim of abyss, has been persuaded by Nolly to take the Pledge.

MOLLY PRATT: Mother of the twins, widow, a stout wearer of the White Rosette, but still able to keep time on her Ostermoor. Her chief mode of support is concealed by a neat housedress of much-mended velvet, trimmed with rhinestones and snippets of ermine.

The action takes place on the porch of the Pratt home, conspicuously well kept in a rum-dum neighborhood. On adjoining doorsteps drunks are sleeping off a Saturday-to-Monday jag.

The play begins with Nolly tugging at an imaginary bell rope dangling from a nonexistent belfry without a bell. He is wearing sandpaper mitts, not to obtain a firmer hold on the dangling bell pull, but for reasons to be disclosed later in the play.

Nolly's creditable attempts to produce carillon effects with these figments of fantasy are offset by a limited vocabulary, a dearth of ideas and an utter ignorance of prosody. His complexion shows the ravages of impetigo superinduced by clinical causes often linked together as "Froelich's Syndrome" (q.v.).The meanest jongleur in the train of Henry the Dullard could have given our Hero cards, spades and Big Cassino in the art of fashioning a fol-de-rol-lay *suitable for court usage. Gong-lover despite all. Nolly makes a couple of false starts with bell rope, then comes clean with a rendition of verses bearing an eerie resemblance to "My Country, 'Tis of Thee."*

> Trem-ble King Al-co-hol
>   Gib-bons' "De-cline and Fall"
>   For you was writ!
> Soon will lat-rines be dried
>   Of beer, the brew-er's pride
> While brewers, by dry sewers' side
>   Sui-i-cide com-mit.

(He sees Rolly. Greets him, hand on bell rope, with improvisatore *couplet.)*

> Come, new-pledged brother, let us jerk
>   Death to the dram shop of McGuirk.

ROLLY: *(Irritable after his fourteen-hour stint in the steel mill.)* Lay off McGuirk. He's not a bad fellow.

NOLLY: You defend the debaucheries debouching from the distended bladders of debauchées frequenting his saloon?

ROLLY: Unmix those metaphors. Clean up your etymology. Don't confuse accidental odors with primary essences. I merely hold that a glass of malted beverage, sipped in moderation, will uplift a man's spirits. Like they say in Maine, "You can't fish through the ice all winter."

NOLLY: *(Earnestly.)* New-Pledged Brother, I fear that your argument is crusted over by chancrous error. If, by malted beverage, you mean beer or ale, may I point out that Candor denies them the name of refreshment. Alcohol, whether malted or distilled, is yet the Enemy.

It stunts the body, pollutes the mind, tans the liver, causes lost virility and—as Shakespeare says—"Leads onward to excess."

ROLLY: (*Corrects misquote; then lapses into gloomy silence.*)

NOLLY: (*Rousing his twin brother by pointing to a man coming toward them with a bad case of jim-jams.*) Mark the unsteady gait of yon Fergus Kilpatrick. 'Tis but the beginning, Rolly. Next week Fergus will be evicted by the landlord; his eight children will become orph—I mean, public charges—and Heaven only knows what fate awaits his wife.

ROLLY: Don't worry about Fergus. He's been hitting the hard stuff since the tender age of three. Maybe he's tired.

NOLLY: (*Interrupting.*) Permit me to go on. If our honest laboring friend really wishes to refresh himself, why doesn't he squeeze the juice of a wholesome fresh lemon into a glass of tap water? Some sugar is permitted. If fresh lemons are not available, let him crush seasonal fruit or berries—pawpaw, banana or a sprig of mint, admittedly the heart of the julep. Stimulated by the acid tartness, Fergus would stride into his garden refreshed and delve in the earth surrounded by loving wife and smiling children.

ROLLY: (*Explaining the facts of life patiently to his brother.*) Well, in the first place, the kids aren't his; in the second place, they're up to their armpits in customers and, third, Mrs. Kilpatrick finds her kitchen bar trade much more pleasant and profitable than delving into the old gravel pit with Fergus.

NOLLY: (*More in sorrow than anger.*) I fear this neighborhood is running down.

ROLLY: (*Taking pencil from pocket.*) Let me give you the rundown on the rundown. Now, those eight kids you mentioned. Fergus' wife gets them from the orphanage. The state pays her two dollars apiece for their board and room—and, boy, do they earn their keep! You see, the mill extends the services of these specially trained young females as a kind of fringe benefit to unmarried Junior Executives. Naturally the mill kicks

in and pays Mrs. Kilpatrick a good salary for acting
as Mother Superior, so to speak, to a bunch of wayward but attractive young brats. Ever notice that red-
headed number named Ethyl? Jail bait, eh? But the
mill's got it fixed up with the D.A. so that any charges,
if brought, will be quashed, *nol prossed.* And if any
Junior Exec wants a change of luck, he asks for that
suspiciously dark-skinned girl, luscious Creole, named
Methyl.

NOLLY: Do you mean that these children are not the conjugal
fruit of Fergus and his wife?

ROLLY: Butt-wise, Noll. Con the chronology. A married couple doesn't have eight kids all at once fifteen years
ago. Wish I had a fringe benefit like Ethyl. Then,
there's Butyl—you know the one with the plushy seat.
She'll be making big money in Chicago if she ever
screws her way out of debt with Madame Kilpatrick.

NOLLY: (*Aghast.*) But what does Fergus say about all this?

ROLLY: Say? Like any sensible man who's wanted as a
procurer in twenty-six Dry states, he keeps his mouth
shut.

NOLLY: Such being the facts, why isn't he thrown into the
local Bastille?

ROLLY: Simple. Fergus is Oliver C. Treadgood's brother-in-
law.

NOLLY: (*Collapsing on doorstep.*) I must transmit these facts
to Mr. Treadgood at once. He will, of course, enter a
blanket denial. (*Looks suspiciously at Rolly.*) Are you
quite certain that you didn't stop at McGuirk's swinging door on the way home?

ROLLY: (*Offhand.*) Just for a spottle of the foamy.

NOLLY: Honor bright? Don't you mean a *ploc-ploc*-spottle?

ROLLY: Well a *ploc,* maybe.

NOLLY: (*Clutching his brother by both lapels.*) But your
pledge, man, your *pledge.* You back-slider.

ROLLY: F— my pledge! (*Knocks brother on prat with rude
blow.*) Who's back-sliding now?

MRS. PRATT: (*Listening from window, nipping the while from her bottle of Peruna, sovereign remedy for dandruff, dia-betes, and dys-men-o-rrhea.*) Birds in their nest should agree. Boys, let us reason together in prayer.

ROLLY: (*Consulting his Ingersoll.*) Sorry, Mother. I'm expected at the home of a blond but cleanly gentlewoman who caters to a select clientele at fifty cents a crack. (*Exits.*)

NOLLY: (*Aside.*) Crack of Doom!

MRS. PRATT: (*Philosophic; cheerful.*) No, Nolly. As I always said when your dear father went out for an evening's pleasure, "Better the BROTHEL than the BAR." But what is this? The Reverend Snavely seems to be paying me a pastoral call.

NOLLY: (*Rubbing sandpaper mitts together twittingly.*) Three times this week, Mother. I believe the Reverend Snavely is trying to get into your good gracious.

MRS. PRATT: Fie, lad. The Reverend Snavely merely comes to succor me in my bereavement. (*Slips Nolly a half dollar.*) Run down to the a-poth-e-cary and ask him to freshen up my tired old bottle of Peruna with a spottle of C_2H_5OH. If you don't remember the formula, just ask for Ethyl. Meanwhile, I must slip into something more appropriate. (*Exits into house.*)

REV. SNAVELY: (*Gravely.*) Good evening, Nolly. How are the sandpaper mitts working out?

NOLLY: Sometimes they slip off during the night.

REV. SNAVELY: Persevere, my boy, else we may be obliged to fall back on saltpeter and handcuffs. (*Changing to another subject.*) I trust I shall find your mother in good spirits.

NOLLY: (*Pettishly*) I don't know what you'll find her in.
As Reverend Snavely enters the Pratt dwelling place, Nolly stands on the porch, momentarily disconsolate. Visions assail him from all sides. On the right he sees a battlefield (Waterloo, Armageddon, Chickamauga?) on which wounded men are being succored by hordes

of cleanly gentlewomen—blondes, brunettes, titian-haired, who press fresh fruits—pawpaws, guavas, and other seasonable delicacies—against parching mouths. From the left appears a cloud of shufflers, dragging ball and chain, led by a skeletal figure bearing aloft the emblem "Solitary Vice."

Drunks arise from neighboring doorsteps and perform cancan in a mocking circle around Nolly holding Peruna bottle in hand. His virtue (and reason) are saved by apparition of Oliver C. Treadgood wearing plumed casque, Dry Lance at the ready, followed by numberless hosts of Anti-Saloon League Dry Workers. The sound of their marching feet drowns out the rhythmic thump-thump-thump *of Ostermoor within. Treadgood tips Nolly the wink as he passes. Nolly resolutely tightens sandpaper mitts and begins jerking at imaginary bell rope dangling from invisible belfry.*

(Tune of "Tramp, Tramp, Tramp.")	Tread-tread-tread the Drys are marching 'Gainst the brothel and spittoon Let us boycott swinging doors And promiscuous amours While we frig-a-jig the enemy

SALOON!

Ostermoor tempo slows down poco a poco. *Complete silence.*

NOLLY: (*Gazing at empty Peruna bottle in his hand.*) Mother will be needing her medicine any moment now. What was that formula she gave me? (*While Nolly racks his brain, Ethyl Kilpatrick appears in the back yard for breather. As she performs a series of handstands for relaxation, Nolly observes that her fringe benefit is the gen-u-wine strawberry article. Memory refreshed, he cries out:*) Just ask for Eth-yl! (*Exits to A-poth-e-cary.*)

QUICK CURTAIN

Talk about the hornets that stung Io's udders, by Jove! Treadgood itched, scratched, dodged, uttered blanket denials to the press, and accused Whelk of criminal libel, defamation of character, conspiracy to defraud, misuse of the U.S. mails and theft of office supplies, including a box of Zymole Trokeys. He demanded that Whelk be arrested forthwith, held without bail, tried by a jury composed of Anti-Saloon League members, sentenced to surgical sterilization and thirty years on the rock pile.

To no avail. An eastern news syndicate reprinted *The Broken Pledge* in three hundred and forty-two papers. When the bloodhounds finally caught up with Whelk in the bayou regions of Louisiana, he was found to possess no assets other than the two infant blackamoors he was carrying in his arms. Luckily he won his fight for extradition, was returned to Ohio, where he got off with a sentence for petty larceny, and later became a prominent script writer in Hollywood.

Meanwhile, Treadgood spent a bad two weeks sweating it out in Washington, D.C., where the top brass of the Anti-Saloon League reappraised his usefulness to the movement.

Commentators jeered, brewing interests leered, cartoonists smeared. But in the end Ollie was cleared. At the suggestion of the national committee, he dropped his publishing activities and focused his attention upon the ever-increasing number of lawsuits brought by the league against violators of existing state liquor laws.

Treadgood ran scared for a while. Thrice had the Lord reprimanded his servant; thrice had the servant fallen; thrice the Molder of Destinies had given Ollie another chance. Penitently, remorselessly, Treadgood surged forward, the better to purge himself by "good works."

9.

PARADINE ROW

WHEN A GAMBLER LOSES his fingertips and the sight of
one eye, he usually becomes just another card player out
of work. Take for example the case of Mr. Damon Frye. For
many years he had earned his keep (and a little extra) by
performing various odd jobs along the Cincinnati waterfront.
Nothing spectacular: a little opium-smuggling, some traffic
in bull whips, a term as spieler for Dreadnaught Dan's Tat-
tooing Parlor, a brief and not unlucrative period of "passing
the queer," which led, in turn, to the counterfeiting of those
green-strip stamps certifying that the whiskey in "this yhere
barrel" was the genuine bonded article. *Yes, sir.*

Plus a couple of sure-fire side lines. Did a perfectly
respectable merchant wish to meet an attractive minor of
either sex under conditions guaranteeing anonymity and satisfaction? Let him but answer the inconspicuous two-liner in
the Cincinnati *Courier:*

> Aladdin's Lamp at your disposal. Fees
> moderate. Address in confidence Box D.F.

Cincinnati wasn't the *only* city where a man wearing black
silk gloves and eye patch could glide through the weir of
convention simply by kicking in to the local boss. Quite possibly there were other sinks of munictpal corruption in the
United States. It so happened Damon Frye preferred the soil,
shall we say, of a city that had started out to be the Athens
of America and had become, under the personal supervision of
Boss Cox, just a City That Had Lost Its Way.

Probably in no other climate could a man with Damon

Frye's special gifts lay one little shinplaster on top of another and emerge (under the name of Dorian Frey) as landlord, proprietor and impresario of a seemingly respectable three-story brick dwelling at No. 72 Paradine Row. Few men in Cincinnati, or anywhere else, possessed Dorian Frey's power of gazing into the human psyche, seeing what was needed—oh, so pitifully needed—then fulfilling those needs at a price well within the reach of those able to pay.

By the year 1900 Mr. Frey was a kind of black-gloved Prospero who, by the wave of wand, could summon up Pleasure—Illicit, Diverse or Perfectly Normal. Much that went on within the walls of No. 72 was quite normal in the Sadie Hawkins tradition. Frey became a champion of inarticulate womanhood when he inserted a three-line ad in the Cincinnati *Courier:*

> Juliets past thirty-five. Don't despair.
> Romeo awaits you. Matinee or evening.
> Discretion paramount. Address D.F.

The response was phenomenal. So numerous were the local "Juliets" answering Frey's ad that he engaged a stable of lusty studs (willing to work for $25.00 per week, plus room and board), fine, upstanding fellows, reasonably free from communicable disease, clothed them like gentlemen and kept his charges on a high-potency diet while tutoring them in the fundamentals of venery. Viz: (1) feign involvement of the heart by offering nosegay of wax violets; (2) give customer a pet name; (3) wait until she moans for it; (4) hold fire until you see the whites of her eyes; (5) tell her she's wonderful as is, but has outstanding possibilities for future development; (5) plead for encore . . . *but soon;* (7) and this above all: don't be, or remotely appear to be, overfastidious.

To which Dorian Frey added the pastoral injunction "All monies, including personal gratuities, shall be turned over to the Proprietor. Your integrity in this matter will be tested by 'spotters.' Double-cross me, boys, and you'll be found floating in the canal. Loyalty Up, Loyalty Down."

Feminine customers who just conceivably found themselves a couple of months overdue became an extra source of income. Fee $50.00 in advance. "Our Dr. Schmalzenburger—3rd floor, rear—best in the business." Getting girls into trouble and then getting them out of trouble—all-ee same-ee—without question of race, creed or social status.

Ten or fifteen customers a day, seven days a week (yes, some of the Juliets found themselves with nothing but time on their hands after Sunday dinner) meant a gross take of approximately $750 per week. Cost of daily ad in the *Courier*, salaries, kick-in to Boss Cox, and Frey's net was around $400 a week without lifting so much as a finger.

His ability to make an immodest profit by exploiting perfectly normal instincts enabled him to soar into the higher income brackets and, incidentally, confer a benefit on mankind. Knowing as he did that the eye had supplanted certain other organs in this civilization of ours, he caused peepholes to be drilled in the walls of secret chambers in his house. By applying one's eye to a peephole @ $5.00 a peep, a customer could avoid paternity suits, social disease and go away stimulated by what he saw. Quick turnover' too. One exhibition could be viewed by twenty customers, some of whom might drift into other chambers with "ideas."

Frey was a great hand for combining the comic with the lewd. For this purpose he found two faithful St. Bernards—solemn dogs even at the crest of fulfillment with, say, a buxom mulatto. The girls got $10 and the dogs the usual bone. On this division of spoils the girls prospered but the St. Bernards went to premature graves within a year. Frey tried Dalmatians—with spotty results.

For the benefit of his peephole pupils, Frey introduced the mode *soixante-neuf*. It caught on, became a daisy chain. The chain is still spreading. Naturally . . .

Natural or not, Mr. Frey's activities were no substitute for his first, original love, cards. No gambler truly loves anything but the "rigors of the game," a flashy wardrobe and an adversary carrying an equal weight of metal. Mr. Frey's closetful of elegant apparel and hand-sewn boots could not, now or ever, appease his twenty-year hunger for the unpredictable fall of cards dealt by a shrewd opponent. But because Mr. Frey's finger stubs (always encased in black silk gloves) were barely able to hold the beloved pack of cards, much less deal them, all else was mockery, jest and gall.

Although the establishment at No. 72 Paradine Row was netting $20,000 a year (more than he ever made as a gambler), Frey was verging toward the melancholy superinduced by the knowledge that his talent for Evil might go to the grave unused.

Sipping a thimbleful of bourbon in Foucar's one chilly November afternoon in 1903, he felt himself slipping into a mood of self-pity. Is it my fate, he thought, to pimp and pander to the appetites of these clowns about me? Surely I was made to trace a design grander, more complex, than the poor sexual squirmings taking place under my roof. Show me the deeper trench, the cloacal fountain source where I can fittingly take my stand.

Frey was addressing no deity other than his own image reflected in the bar mirror. He saw there a face unmarked by conscience, regret or (save for the black eye patch) even the passage of time. A gymnast regime and the iron fingers of a professional masseuse had kept Frey's body in a state of seeming youthfulness. Self-denial where food and whiskey were concerned gave his olive skin an almost ascetic purity. When necessary Frey could make his luminous right eye flash like a gun flint; most of the time, however, he kept the eyeball itself and the emotions behind it veiled by agate indifference or half-lidded contempt for the creatures he encountered in the ordinary way of business.

A second image appeared in the mirror and a voice was saying, "Eyeless in Gaza . . . eh?"

The proprietor of No. 72 Paradine felt the shrewd jostle. Among the infinite permutations of chance, this stranger had chosen precisely the proper tag line. No matter. He must be chastised.

"How does it happen," asked Frey, "that a man with your insight is wearing a soiled pongee suit and dirty tennis shoes at this time of year?"

"I'm a grasshopper who has decided to join forces with Mr. Ant himself."

"Your self-assurance leads me to think that you have a good hole card. From where I sit your hand isn't impressive." Compassion and a minim of interest prompted Frey to ask, "Will you have a drink? Whiskey, they say, is an invisible overcoat."

"But not invisible gloves, I gather."

"Poverty has made you keen."

"Prosperity will make me keener. Shall we drink to our mutual prosperity?"

For the first time in twenty-five years Dorian Frey felt

himself confronted by an equal. A younger, poorly clad, advantage-conscious, cooler-nerved opponent who apparently held aces back to back. The in-fighting continued.

"Shall we exchange business cards?" asked Frey.

"Unfortunately the kind of business I'm in couldn't be printed on a card. My name is Arthur Coplestone and I have reason to believe that you will be interested in this little black box that I've invented."

"What does your little black box do?"

"It takes pictures." Arthur Coplestone paused. "In the dark."

"In the dark?"

"*In the dark.*"

That evening Arthur Coplestone demonstrated the possibilities of his little black box by placing it against a certain peephole. He snapped a shutter and, after a brief chemical processing, showed Mr. Frey an infrared photograph of what was being done to a socially prominent matron by one of Mr. Frey's hired men.

A second shot, profile, registered ecstatic expression of payee receiving the "goods."

"Well-a-well," mused Frye. "What a sordid tale the infrared end of the spectrum can tell."

Coplestone's ability to invade darkness and come back with visible evidence of what was happening therein was certainly worth something. The asking price seemed steep, but after a brief haggle Frey paid it. What he actually bought was not limited to the black box. Frey gave Arthur Coplestone a 50 per cent interest in Paradine; in return Arthur Coplestone delivered up his entire resources to Mr. Dorian Frey.

What a deal it turned out to be!

Working together in complete unison of spirit, the proprietors of 72 Paradine Row focused their combined talents on a single objective: the establishment of a clearing house for all kinds of information about almost everyone you could mention. This information (most of it damaging) came in from a number of sources, but chiefly from persons who, lolling in a barbershop or poolroom, happened to pick up a copy of *Spicy Stories* and read the following little teaser:

Highest prices paid for "hot tips"

regarding prominent personages in
your neighborhood. Address in
confidence BOX D.F., Cincinnati, O.

The steel filing cabinets at 72 Paradine Row became longer
and taller with the years. Never once did Messrs. Frey and
Coplestone use their material for purposes of blackmail. Conceivably they might have squeezed a supplementary flow of
gold into their coffers from this source. The gold flowed in
anyway *(just as Dorian had planned)* from springs best described as "interested parties." Did a husband come, hat in
hand, begging for information about his wife? For a fee he
was permitted to pore over the dossier, select the material
best suited to his needs and pay accordingly.

Any juryman knows that one picture of a wife with her
clothes in disarray is worth a thousand pages of testimony.

Since no chain of evidence is stronger than its weakest link,
a pictorial record was kept on every client that passed in and
out of the portals of No. 72 Paradine Row. Betweenwhiles,
Arthur's infrared camera took over. The serpents of Laocoön
never entangled their victims in a tighter hold. And there at
the center of the operation sat Mr. Dorian Frey waiting . . .
waiting . . . waiting for the "interested party"—a husband, a
wife, a father bent on justice or revenge.

A Good Government candidate for Mayor of Cincinnati
was ruined by a series of such pictures. Boss Cox merely
showed the aspiring candidate the photos and, in a burst of
magnanimity, tore them up when Mr. Good Government retired from the race.

But the best customer of all was the Anti-Saloon League.
You see, Oliver (Oom) Treadgood, preparing for the Dry
Trek, was eager to pay for testimony (verbal, literary or pictorial) that might prove useful in persuading the Wet representatives in a state legislature to see through a glass Dry-ly—
else swallow a peck of private dirt in public.

Ollie was interested in lewd photos, incriminating letters,
photostats of hotel registers, or other bits of skeletal debris
that might be found in almost any closet. Did a young Congressman still wet behind the ears sally forth from his third-
rate hotel for a brisk walk along F Street after a hard day
in the committee room? Was he accosted by a lady of the
evening, handbag idly swinging? And did he accept her offer
of a quickie for cash consideration in some adjacent hallway?

Well, if he did—or even if he didn't—he'd receive a letter shortly thereafter summoning him into the presence of a certain Mr. Oom, a sawed-off Sunday-schoolish josser, benign, fatherly, who would, in the course of his admonishments, produce some kind of document (the photostat of a hotel register, *vielleicht?*). Ofttimes evidence all too human, a handbag swinger bearing news of an impending paternity suit, might shyly admit that she was a high-school girl from Chillicothe, lacking power of consent by reason of her tender years. So what could a chap do but accept the kindly intervention of Mr. Oom Treadgood?

"Nothing to worry about, son," advised Ollie. "Forget the whole business. That girl's testimony about you pouring a pint of Old Belrose into her bloomers won't hold water. Drop in any time. Remember, Uncle Treadgood is watching your vote."

The night hath a thousand eyes. Aided by Messrs. Frey and Coplestone, Treadgood's eyes became as numberless as the mosquitoes in a Louisiana bayou.

Bayou, say you . . . ?

10.

TOBY SHOW

The distance between Times Square, Manhattan, and Hoke Pompsey's Toby Show in Tiberia, Louisiana, is eighteen hundred miles. But the distance from Tiberia, Louisiana, to Times Square is eighteen hundred miles raised to the ninety-ninth power—and uphill all the way. Not even Laly Coplestone (born Woodhull), professionally billed as Geraldine Haste, could extricate herself from the muddy ooze that sucks Toby Show actresses in one direction—down.

A Toby Show, in case someone isn't familiar with the genre, is a form of hedgerow entertainment that once flourished in regions where troupers playing *Ten Nights in a Barroom* disdained to enter. The tried-and-true theme of every Toby Show (including Hoke Pompsey's) is the eternal struggle between Urban Villainy and Bumpkin Virtue—a struggle wherein city-type cad (sideburns, Ascot tie and flashy diamond stick-pin) always gets a fistful of knuckles smacked into his kisser by Rural Hero.

Mr. Hoke Pompsey achieved this desirable end with a minimum of stage machinery and a cast of five. Pompsey himself played a thoroughly detestable villain both on and off stage. His son, H. Pompsey, Jr., hero-type chap, had good knuckles, a pow'ful back and a mop of tow-colored hair inherited from his poor mother, who, at the age of thirty-six, gave up pulling at the tug straps, lay down on her shelflike bunk and drank herself to death with a saturated solution of oxalic acid, ordinarily used in cleaning harnesses.

Her successor, the second Mrs. Pompsey, had amassed enough circumstantial evidence on her husband to keep him behind bars for ninety-nine years—"*iffen* he made a single, solitary false move." Now, since all Pompsey's moves were false—as false as the labels on the bottles of Stifferino that he sold between shows—Mrs. Pompsey must have been speaking with special reference to her husband's nickering for the person of his ingénue, Laly Coplestone.

The machinery carried by Pompsey's Show consisted of a circular saw turned by a hand crank backstage, a length of wooden railroad track for audiences that knew what a railroad was, and a miniature belfry to which the heroine climbed for sanctuary while the villain still pursued her with a lighted stick of dynamite or some other easily recognized symbol of his intention. An ever-popular version centered around the "Curfew Shall Not Ring Tonight" situation, in which the heroine latched onto the bell tongue so that the executioner (sheriff, hangman) was obliged to *dee-lay* kicking the barrel out from under the hero for whom the bell wasn't going to toll that pertikler night, anyway. The hero wore butternut jeans and the heroine was a trusting barefoot girl. Her pitiful pleas of "No, no, a thousand times no" were without power to soften the *diableries* of the fiend incarnate who held her in a bowling-ball grip. Just when Evil was about to pick up the marbles, the hero stepped forward, bade the villain "Stand back," and knocked him rump-over-tea-kettle into the next performance.

As Minerva Higginson used to say in quite another context, "Virtue may be assailed but never hurt."

Laly Coplestone, having played the trusting heroine in

three hundred and fifty hamlets up and down both banks of the Lower Mississippi, was sick unto vomiting of the hazards she ran on and off stage. Both were routine in nature. Twice every evening, she uttered her "No, no, a thousand times no!" to a paying audience; and twice every night (three times on Sunday) she fended off the strictly-for-free advances of Hoke Pompsey, Sr. or Jr., depending on where the second Mrs. Pompsey happened to be.

In moments of leisure, Laly wondered how a fully grown woman—talented, intelligent, good looking—could contrive to weave such a web of futility around herself. With New York City as her goal, why could she get no farther than Paris (Arkansas), Vienna (Mississippi), or Shagreen (Louisiana)? Did the itinerary make sense? No! The wages? (Four dollars a week.) Again, no.

Laly's sole prop, guide and guardian was Myrza. Billed as "Keeper of the Crystal Ball," Myrza more than paid her way on the Pompsey circuit. It was Myrza—in communication with some occult power—who had led Laly out of danger into a land strangely resembling the Nile Delta. Together they traveled up, down and across a desolate bayou region in a caboose-like structure divided sectionally into three compartments. Mr. and Mrs. Pompsey occupied the first compartment; Hoke Jr. and "machinery" rode in mid-section; Myrza, Laly and Haila occupied bunks in the rear.

Myrza fended off the advances of Pompsey, Sr. and Jr., boiled the drinking water, sponged Laly down with witch hazel after every performance. Under Myrza's gentle massage, Laly could almost forget the hazards hedging about the body of a Toby Show ingénue. Sometimes she dozed, dreaming of Broadway and the applause of vast audiences. Sometimes she dreamed of home. Then, sweating with grief, Laly would awaken to see Myrza, the "little-while mother," sleeplessly crooning over a baby not her own. Unbelievably maternal, this crystal-gazer. Was she a virgin perhaps? Womanlike, Laly pondered the question. Then, waking one night, she saw in Myrza's face (was it a trick of moonlight piercing the barred window?) the remnants of a beauty that, at one time or another, must have felt its power over men.

"Were you ever married, Myrza?"

"In a way—many times."

"What do you mean by that?"

Exposition, unmarred by apology, was the chief note in

Myrza's reply. "Under the code of my Romany tribe, I, the daughter of a prince, inherited certain responsibilities. Imagine to yourself a situation in which the 'Law of the First Night' is reversed. Tradition required me to testify in the presence of my tribe assembled that the would-be husband of another was truly potent. In that ritualistic sense I was married countless times before the age of twenty."

"Did you . . . enjoy it—I mean, being a wife for a single night?"

"One never questions Necessity." Remembrance and quiet pride untinged by vanity lived again in the exiled princess. "Once—I was fully grown at the time—the women of my tribe were stricken by a pestilential flux. I alone was spared. It became my duty to portion out feminine mercy to all who claimed their due."

"Did you like that?" asked Laly.

"I can say only this: No one suffered beyond mortal endurance. As for myself, I can only say I sometimes regret that I used the secret lore possessed by women of my rank to avoid bearing a child whose father I could never know."

The elastic fabric of Myrza's morality enabled Laly to regard herself as a thread—an untarnished thread—in the durable stuff which, from the beginning of time, has made women—women.

A closer relationship sprang up between Laly and Myrza. They shared each other's burdens. No longer content to play the queen-bee role—served, petted even, by the Keeper of the Crystal Ball—Laly took on the duties of body servant to Myrza. One night in the stifling heat of a nameless swamp, she said to the Romany princess, "It's my turn to rub *you* down. Take off your clothes."

Myrza smiled. Then with no trace of false modesty, she let her voluminous robe sink to the floor. Silently, she lay face downward on her narrow bunk. Age had inevitably softened the muscle tone of her flesh, but its Velásquez contours brought ungrudging admiration from the younger woman.

"Why, Myrza, I never knew how beautiful you were!"

"You have never seen me unclothed." The Crystal Gazer became a great actress throwing away a line. "The Romany costume is designed to conceal or flatter a woman's figure, according to her needs."

"It certainly concealed yours."

"That's why I wear it, child. In the midst of enemies, one must move under cover."

Toby Show tradition permitted little cover for its heroine. Laly's onstage costume—a sleeveless flour sack—was calculated to show one thing only: beauty in distress. Night after night, the distress became increasingly acute—to the elder Pompsey. "I just can't stand it much longer," he confided to Nebo, the spavined mare that had uncomplainingly taken her master's boot, whip, bounty and confidences for the past ten years. "One of these days a seam's goin' to bust around here."

The specific seam that Pompsey had in mind ran longitudinally from his ingénue's auxillary hollow to a point just beneath her popliteal arch (which includes just about everything). Only the vigilance of Mrs. Pompsey, some rather unfilial competition from Hoke, Jr., and Myrza's sleepless eyes kept Pompsey in the fantasy phase of operation.

"Somethin's got to give," he warned Nebo.

Something did give. Little Haila fell ill.

"Skitters," Pompsey called it. "Everyone gets skitters down thisaway. Give her some paregoric."

The only available medicine failed to relieve Haila's illness.

"My child needs real medical care," said Laly. "Where is the nearest hospital?"

Pompsey consulted his schedule, immutably recorded on the back cover of *Tent Show*. "Let's see now. We play Fickenberg, Lues, Yaws and L'Ordure on the east side of the river. Sorry—they ain't no hospitals along this bank."

Pompsey made an offer unparalleled in Toby Show annals. "I'd be willing to skip L'Ordure and take the west bank ferry to Meritrix—they's a Spanish mission hospital there." He qualified his magnanimity by adding, "*If* a certain party in this outfit played like she wuz agreeable."

Laly spoke with a mother's desperation. "After my child is in a hospital, I'll be agreeable to anything."

" 'Twon't do. You've got to start being agreeable tonight." Pompsey handed his ingénue a phial of blowsy perfume. "Douse this stuff liberal over yourself so's I'll know which bunk you're in. Leave your door unbolted and don't make a sound. Mrs. P. has ears in her hind axle."

Distracted, her eyes red with weeping, Laly told Myrza of Pompsey's ultimatum.

"So. Push has come to Shove. I wondered how long we could hold him off." Myrza extended her hand. "The phial, Laly." She shrugged. "What difference does it make to me?"

At midnight, under pretense of medicining Nebo's colic, Mr. Pompsey gulped down a pint of Stifferino, then lifted the hasp of the rear compartment. In the darkness he felt his way toward a highly scented female in the lower bunk. Without a single cavalier caress, he pigged away at his victim, who by a species of exotic hip-swaying egged him toward an all too sudden goal.

Gasping and rubbery-kneed, Jack-rabbit Pompsey heard a contemptuous bolt slam behind him. "Cert'ny knows her biz-ness," he confided to the murky sky. "Which is it—the Stiff-erino, me, or her?"

Mr. Pompsey never knew that he had been victimized by a deceit first practiced in Genesis, Chapter 29, Verses 23-28. He never realized that Myrza was acting as understudy, stand-in and pushover for Laly Woodhull. The crystal gazer fulfilled her week in accordance with Old Testament usage. Then, with Haila safely in the Spanish mission hospital, a series of ominous portents began to appear in Pompsey's mid-night heaven.

First, he found the rear section of the caboose firmly locked against his tomcat prowlings. (He couldn't expostulate or even whine lest Mrs. Pompsey hear.) Next, faithful Nebo, wearied by pulling the Pompsey troupe through ever-deepen-ing mud, collapsed. Pompsey's tried-and-true system—i.e., kicking her first in the ribs, then in the teeth—failed to revive the critter. Nebo was just plain and permanently dead. What to do? Pertick'ly when the Father of Waters started to chastise Pompsey—along with everything else in the Delta region—in a truly fearsome display of fluminal wrath.

What to do? Had Hoke Pompsey been cast in the mold of Leif Ericson (which he wasn't), had he possessed ten times the fortitude of Marquette and Joliet (which he didn't), there was still nothing he could have done to save his troupe. In certain moods Ol' Man River doesn't *intend* anyone to be saved. And the mood was on him now. Pompsey issued the only possible order: "Ev'yone for hisself. If we all ain't drowned, let's meet at L'Ordure two weeks from tomorrow."

Somewhere in the heart of this Toby Show villain throbbed an echo of a grand tradition.

"Show must go on," he cried, shinnying up a live oak.

At the moment, Laly Woodhull couldn't remember why.

On Anson's desk as of October 1903 lay six letters, each addressed to Mrs. Arthur Coplestone, 3021 River Avenue, St. Louis, and each bearing the ominous rubber stamp "NOT AT THIS ADDRESS." The most recent letter, containing a $500 bill, had been sent by registered mail; it, too, had been returned. Anson slit the envelope and reread his letter.

DARLING DAUGHTER:

I am greatly worried about your silence. Am sending you the enclosed money in case it may come in handy or that you may be in difficulty of some kind that you don't care to mention. If more is needed, just let me know. It won't make any difference. Just so long as my dear Laly answers her

LOVING
FATHER

In 1903 there existed none of the machinery that today locates 30,000 missing persons annually. Federal bureaus were interested in tracing only fugitives from justice. A private person usually made inquiries at the last known address of the missing person, pieced together (if possible) the motive of his or her disappearance and returned home empty-handed, silent, weighed down by grief.

Anson re-examined the collection of letters. If Laly wasn't at this address, where was she? What possible motive could prevent her from making her whereabouts known? Was she in prison? Was she *alive?*

Anson rose from his desk. "I must go in person to find my Laly. I will go alone. Now."

First stop, St. Louis. The run-down building at 3021 River Avenue now belonged to another landlord. A peanut-cracker, a surly, gooberish fellow.

"Don't know nothin' about the person you're lookin' for." He popped a peanut into his mouth. "Never heard of her."

"How long have you owned this building?"

"Long enough to know the tenants don't pay their rent. There oughta be a law that'd send them to jail, like the last crook who owned it."

"Crook?" A clue. "He's the man I'm looking for," said Anson. "What kind of crime did he commit?"

"All kinds. P'leece'll tell you."

At police headquarters the answer was "no jurisdiction." "Us local cops step aside when the Treasury agents step in. They're rat-bane to counterfeiters," said Captain Bradley.

"My daughter a counterfeiter?"

"That was the charge."

"Haven't you *any* record?" Anson threw the whole weight of his personality into the question.

"We don't keep records of Federal cases. My advice, sir, is that you go directly to Washington."

So Anson went to Washington with two questions uppermost in his mind: Where is my daughter? and What is the charge against her? He put the questions to Representative Alpheus Hinckley. Hinckley didn't know the answers so he gave Anson a note to Senator Barlow Grimshaw. Grimshaw didn't know either, but he passed the buck by writing a letter to the Secretary of the Treasury.

In the gloomy Treasury Building a curtly efficient undersecretary made a penciled memo on Senator Grimshaw's note and dispatched Anson to a tiny cubbyhole of an office occupied by one J. K. Fimister, Agency Chief in Charge of Counterfeiting.

Fimister wasn't really an agency chief. He was a born rubber-hose detective who proceeded on the assumption that everyone was guilty as all hell.

"You the girl's father?" Fimister's question was an accusation.

"I am." Anson offered his business card.

"This daughter of yours—did she run away from home?"

"No, she was duly married seven years ago, to a man named Arthur Coplestone."

"Then her legal name is Coplestone? Why in hell didn't you say so?" Fimister's slow burn yielded to his professional vanity at remembering names. "Coplestone, Coplestone, yeah —rings a bell—photographer, wasn't he?"

"Yes."

"Not exactly a law-abiding citizen, would you say?"

"Apart from abandoning my daughter, I know nothing that makes me think Coplestone a criminal."

"How do you know he abandoned your daughter? She might be with him right now."

"I hadn't considered the possibility. I hardly think she is."

"Well, she ain't. This handbill contains the grist of the matter." From his file, Fimister gave Anson one of those fearful notices, beginning

WANTED

Eulalia (Laly) Coplestone, married, white, age twenty-six. Height: 5'5". Well built, good looking. Blue-green eyes.

This woman was last seen boarding a train south of New Orleans, dressed in gypsy costume. She was accompanied by her small daughter and a crystal gazer named Myrza. The wanted person has theatrical ambitions. Law-enforcement officers may find her playing small tent show circuits, repertory, etc.

Testimony given by other members of the counterfeiting ring (Maktoub Kazanjian, Joseph McPartland, Lucienne Bisquier, *et al.*) indicates that Eulalia Coplestone was the photographer who took the picture of a genuine ten-dollar bill which later served as the basis for a copper-plate engraving made by J. McPartland.

Although an Anthony box camera bearing a brass plate engraved with the name "Arthur Coplestone" was seized during the raid, Coplestone was able to prove that he was in no way connected with the counterfeiting ring operating in St. Louis. After intensive questioning he was released.

Present whereabouts of Eulalia Coplestone: Unknown.

$500 reward for information leading to her apprehension and conviction.

It was Anson's turn to ask a few questions. "Who saw my daughter boarding a train south of New Orleans?"

"That comes under the head of 'Confidential Information.'" Fimister spoke off the record for a moment. "You'd be surprised how many guys hang around depots for fifty cents a day."

"Why don't you go into the region and bring her out?"

"Budgetary considerations affecting available personnel might be one answer." Fimister rose from his desk and walked toward a large wall map of the United States. He pointed to an area where the Father of Waters debouches into the Gulf of Mexico. "Guess you've never been in this neck of the woods, Mr. Woodhull. No reason why you should. People with all their buttons in place stay away from it—for the simple reason, and I hate to tell you this, that scarcely no one ever comes out."

"If my daughter is alive, I'll get her out of there."

"She'll still be facing a ten-year sentence," said Fimister, "unless—" With a meaty forefinger the agency chief drew an imaginary figure eight backward and forward on the Coplestone dossier.

"Unless what?" asked Anson.

"Unless a couple of other guys, named Hennessey and Dooley, say—" Fimister made it perfectly clear that he was being jocular—"found themselves in the respective positions now occupied by you and me. Take it now that I'm Hennessey suffering from a bad case of stricture contracted while sowing a wild oat in my youth. Just as I'm starting for the men's lavatory six or seven hundred yards down the corridor, who should walk in but a man named Dooley. Now this Dooley wants to see a particular file. He wants to see it bad. Almost as bad as I want to go to the men's room. I lay the file on my desk so's this Dooley person can inspect it during my brief absence."

Fimister timed the going and returning of his alter ego, Hennessey. "Round trip, twelve to fifteen minutes. Dooley inspects file, selects documents as may appeal to him, leaving behind a paper bag containing some pep'mints and a roll of old hundred-dollar bills aggregating somewhere in the vicinity of six, seven thousand dollars."

He added a footnote of explanation. "Course, it couldn't happen to Fimister and Woodhull. Neither of us would want to have a thing like that on our conscience, would we now?"

"I wouldn't," said Anson, rising to go. "But a friend of mine might know a fellow—his name wouldn't be Dooley, though."

"And mine ain't Hennessey," said Fimister, laughing.

Anson repeated the parable of Hennessey and Dooley to his friend Charles Moerlein.

"I don't know any Dooleys, either," said Moerlein thoughtfully, "but I have a friend who might give a good impersonation of Dooley. Now you go home, Anse. Take a rest. Leave the matter in my hands. The thing is as good as Dunne."

The man elected by Charles Moerlein to play the part of Dooley was, among other things, a murderer, the keeper of a high-class brothel and, generally speaking, a wearer of the Triple Cross with Box and Cox ramifications. His physical resemblance to Edgar Allan Poe, diminished by the black patch worn over one eye, was heightened by his affectation of black silk gloves, a stock collar, lavender tie and the mysterious manner in which he conducted his private operations in full view of the public. For the past ten years he had run a daily two-line ad in the Cincinnati *Courier*:

> Discretion Paramount. Privacy Guaranteed.
> No commission too delicate. Address Box D.F.

The D.F. stood for Daniel Freiberg, Damon Frye or Dorian Frey according to the nature of the business involved. He made a pleasant back-bar companion at the Hotel Sinton, where he now discussed with Charles Moerlein the case of certain archives which had better turn up as MISSING.

"Offhand, I can't say how these documents should be processed," said Freiberg. "It will be necessary to make an exploratory trip to Washington."

"Will ten thousand dollars cover the matter?"

"Easily. Federal employees are grossly underpaid. For five thousand dollars some of them would destroy the Declaration of Independence—or hand over the file on Martin Van Buren. In the event that I run into a bureau chief, it will be advantageous to have cash in the entire amount."

"How long will your investigation take?"

"Twenty days, perhaps."

"Ten days," said Moerlein, "and an extra thousand dollars per day if the contract is fulfilled ahead of time."

Freiberg made a profound bow. "You have involved my heels, heart and mind—everything but my fingertips." The Poe facsimile scrutinized his black silk gloves. "Maskers and mourners," he murmured, "or as Hamlet says, 'pickers and stealers.'"

Charles Moerlein was happy to pay Freiberg an additional three thousand dollars when they met a week later in a private room off the Sinton Bar.

"The complete file in triplicate," said Freiberg triumphantly.

"No other papers exist?"

"Not a scrap."

"The government has no case, then, against this poor child?"

"In my considered opinion, it has not."

Regard for Freiberg's professional methods put an end to Moerlein's questioning. "I am greatly obliged to you, Daniel," he said.

"Nor am I lacking in gratitude," said Freiberg. "May I be of further service?"

"No. There's a younger man in the wings. He has been waiting a long time."

"Youth has much to recommend it," said Freiberg. "As a younger man I made a . . . ah . . . spiritual retreat into the heart of this region." With a pencil between his finger stubs, Freiberg crosshatched the east bank of the Mississippi Delta and indicated with an X the precise location of his refuge. "Served a term as pastor to a colored flock there. Splinter denomination—Two-Seeds-in-One-Spirit. It was 'Hallelujah, Brother; Amen, Sister' for more than a year. I preached not only faith but good works—funds from the Robin Hood Foundation enabled me to tack a new belfry onto a leprous Go-Meetin' House."

"No."

"Yes. My congregation later salvaged a bell from a Spanish basilica overgrown with jungle foliage. Against my better judgment—that bell was a huge bronze affair—I let them hang it in the belfry. Nature's acoustics gave that bell a sub-aqueous tongue—B-O-N-G—which proved highly attractive to the bayou folkses. Once I preached to ninety brethren."

"No."

"Yes. Collected eighty-nine cents. Don't tell me there's no money in salvation work."

Freiberg added a marginal note. "Odd thing about L'Ordure—that was the name of my parish. At flood times—I mean during 'high water'—Ol' Man River headed straight toward my church with the obvious intention of grinding it to silt. Then—I've *seen* this happen—the river managed to get itself seduced (there's no other word for it) by a treacherous side slip of Mother Earth. She sort of pulled away. I once slapped a woman for just such a performance. On a miniature scale, you understand." Freiberg rose from his chair. "Yes, I'll bet that bell is still tolling shrimp-pickers o'er the lea. Please ask your young emissary to give its rope an affectionate yank for old time's sake."

"I shall give him full instructions," said Moerlein, "including this excellent artillery map that you sketched while talking."

Sending Richmond Plaskett to Laly's rescue was a concept in the best Toby Show tradition. With Love, Wealth and Bribery conjoining, it seemed not unlikely that Laly Woodhull—gifted, long lost and located at last—would soon be among her own people.

Reb was thirty-one now, unmarried, a natural light-heavyweight, an ascetic *cum laude;* possessor of six tailor-made suits, thirty starched collars (remember the Belmont?), an equal number of silk shirts with French cuffs fastened by fourteen-carat-gold links; four pairs of black low-cuts (later to be known as "oxfords"); a twenty-three-jeweled Waltham watch; fingers unencumbered by rings; a set of teeth that had yet to feel the *b-rrr* of a dentist's drill; brownish hair parted on the left side, and gray-blue eyes. He was a quiet-spoken salesman who could make six calls a day and get an order 75 per cent of the time.

Mr. Richmond Plaskett was, in short, a finely minted coin of high value. By training, experience, observation and common sense, he knew what was being worn, said, thought and bought (with special reference to whiskey) in the principal cities lying like a Golden Ellipse tipped diagonally athwart the northeast central quadrant of the United States: New York, Cleveland, Detroit, Chicago, Pittsburgh, Philadelphia and Boston. . . . In 1903 the man who had come into Anson Woodhull's life as a freckle-faced, shoeless pig-drover, armed only with a slingshot, was now General Manager, Director of Sales and a 10 per cent shareholder in the Old Landmark Distillery.

For most of his life Richmond Plaskett had been in love with Laly Woodhull. Ever since Anson had "put him on the road," he had traveled up, down, across and athwart the United States searching for the only woman he would ever love. Down what street did she walk? Who employed her? Was she happy? Prosperous? Ill, destitute? Was she still alive? Why didn't she write? What set of circumstances, barring death, could have prevented his proud, wonderful Laly from crying, "Here I am!" What paralysis of will or emotion had laid its shackles on Laly's desire to make her whereabouts known to those—including Reb Plaskett—who loved her?

Like heavy waters falling on a mill wheel which, for all its turning, could not grind out an answer, these questions had fallen remorselessly, unceasingly on Reb Plaskett's life. They drove his tireless legs along strange sidewalks seeking a glimpse of a lost face, a face never to be forgotten, forever to be remembered. Microscopic scrutiny of telephone books and city directories in thirty states had yielded nothing.

Dead end. Silence. Years made for love, wasted in waiting, searching, hoping and longing for that brave, wonderful, bossy, ambitious, proud, emphatically not-to-be-duplicated Laly.

And now—news of her whereabouts from Charles Moerlein. Detailed information in the form of maps, geodetic descriptions, together with a current copy of *Tent Show*—a typographical horror perpetrated on flimsy wood pulp. But there on the back page was Hoke Pompsey's advertisement. Mr. Pompsey sent his regards to Broadway and told all the folks on Forty-second Street just when he'd be playing where.

"Vanity sits in strange quarters, Reb," said Charles Moerlein. "Hoke Pompsey is leading us right into his camp. Take it from here, boy. Bring Laly back with you."

"I'd walk through live coals to get her," said Reb.

Not live coals, but the longest, wildest, most treacherous river in the world—colloquially known as the "Father of Waters"—stood between Richmond Plaskett and Laly Woodhull. Now, concerning the Father of Waters. It has two parents: one a clear, cold lake in northern Minnesota; the other a dancing fountain in the Rocky Mountains, eight thousand feet above sea level. These sources merge when the Mississippi allows itself to be polluted by "Big Muddy"—the Missouri—twenty miles above St. Louis. At this point the Father of Waters becomes merciless; his chief function is collecting tribute from fluminal deities of lesser rank—Chippewa, Minnesota, Wisconsin, Illinois, Platte, Ohio and Arkansas—which, together with their uncounted tributaries, drain the heartland of America.

Under normal circumstances the Father of Waters swirls along with a sullen foreknowledge of the humiliation that awaits him when, having traveled four thousand miles, he finds himself ignominiously sucked into a mysterious delta which feeds the ocean. There are times, however, when, swollen with insistent flood waters, the Mississippi is master of a region into which the will of Jehovah concerning the division of land and water has not yet penetrated. Such times occur when the ice-bound tributaries of the Mississippi (particularly those on the north bank of the Ohio) melt under the touch of a January thaw. Then, hamlets, villages and counties, together with their man-made structures, human inhabitants, stumps of mighty trees and hordes of frightened animals, are swept seaward while the Father of Waters wreaks wanton vengeance upon everything that opposes his tyranny.

The higher, more desirable ground along both banks of the Mississippi is held by white folks who have learned the art of making temporary sandbag levees (with the aid of their nonwhite brothers) against incursions of the brown god. Rarely are these incursions dignified by the name "flood." "High water" is the colloquialism of choice among property owners and local officials. News of approaching "high water" is usually telegraphed downriver a day or so ahead of the swirling flood-crest; and when such news reaches a little town, all hands, black and white, join temporarily in common brotherhood against the invader. The white hands hold shotguns to guarantee a full twenty hours of sand-baggery *per diem* by the blacks.

The Mississippi code of honor requires that such information be transmitted as soon as received. Accordingly Clint Fisher, the telegraph dispatcher at Cairo, Illinois, stayed up late one night in February 1904 to keep his unseen audience apprised that "high water" was coming like Sam Hill from all directions. Curtly and succinctly Clint tapped out the facts. The Ohio River was fifty feet above mean average height as it tore past Cincinnati. East St. Louis was under water. And Old Man River, no longer a muddy shuffler, was racing southward at an estimated speed of twelve miles per hour. No apologies, no explanations. Just the facts.

Reb Plaskett first heard about these fluminal complications when the *Thunderbolt* heaved into its southern terminal at Duraus, La.

"High Water on the way," announced the stationmaster.

When Reb asked for specific information as to the whereabouts of a river town called L'Ordure, the man pointed south. "Foller your nose. Jes' remember that the crest of high water is about fifty miles north—and mister, it's *high*."

So it came down to this: Reb must cover five miles on foot while the Father of Waters traveled ten times that distance along his own channel. Reb started running toward the river.

"Please, God, let me reach her," he prayed. As the water deepened, he tore off his coat and shoes. Now, swimming, he encountered a host of small aquatic animals—muskrats, raccoons and frightened birds moving in the opposite direction. The instinct that had driven them away from the flood served as a compass needle for the man looking for his childhood sweetheart. A mud hole tugged at his feet. He kicked himself free. He was swimming now through an aqueous haze under the boughs of overhanging cypresses. The rising mists created a scrim curtain, and somewhere behind that curtain was Laly Woodhull.

Mud-slimed, Reb emerged from the watery jungle and found himself climbing up a masonry escarpment, seemingly the wall of an old cathedral, solid enough to have served as a dike in previous floods. On this perilous bluff, fifty feet above the river, he beheld a fearful pageant: a watery universe stretching to the horizon, bearing on its surface the trophies and debris of a land already conquered.

Shanties, church spires, barns, pigs, horses, silos, wharf spiles torn from their man-made caissons, huge trees uprooted by a force more impatient than Time. Men and women clinging to housetops. A flotsam universe whipped seaward by the advance guard of the Flood King who had lost all but a final semblance of control over his own destiny.

Reb recognized that the sight directly under his eyes was merely a light-cavalry skirmish, clearing the path for the heavier thrust upstream. He noticed that the objects in midriver were being propelled at a rate nearly double the speed of those directly below him. Lower land on the Louisiana side of the river was tempting the Father of Waters to wheel away from the western bank and curve into the trap that gravity had baited for him. The flanking order trumpeted its will to every droplet under its command: *Hear this!*

The gigantic maneuver began. *By the right flank, huup! By squadrons, platoons, battalions, companies and regiments, turn! By divisions, you armies of destruction, wheel! Corps of desolation, deploy! By kingdoms, dominions and empires, wheel and turn away!*

Awed by the cyclorama of a natural power deploying its forces, Reb was shaken into consciousness of his own peril by the quaking of the escarpment under his feet. The dike, eroded at its base, was no longer a platform of safety. Yet should be abandon it? By every earth-taught precept Reb hesitated before diving into the flood. On what sunken spike might he be impaled? No time for adjudicating values or weighing risks. An instinctual precept older than earth bade him take sides with the winning element. He leaped into the flood, plumbed its depth, shot upward exultantly. If, to gain Laly, he must return through thousands of centuries to a medium from which the human race had climbed, he was willing to do so.

"Ye must be born again of Water," sayeth the Lord.

Triumphant in his rebirth, Reb snatched at a slow-turning scow, clambered over the side, fitted the idle oar into its semilune and became, if not master of all he surveyed, at least a manageable portion of it. The rising water told him that the flood crest was approaching. In less than ten minutes the Father of Waters would mete out vengeance to those who had failed to wheel at his command.

Bong-ng-g! A lugubrious chime, heavier than the clanging of marine buoys, struck the alerted timpani of Reb's ears. *Bong-ng-g!* Might it not be the reverberation of the bronze bell hanging in the L'Ordure belfry?

Through cupped hands, Reb megaphoned a name that he had so often uttered in loneliness. "Laly! Laly Woodhull!"

"Bong-ng-g!"

"Where are you, Laly? Speak to me! Tell Reb where you are."

Then he saw her, leaning out from the cupola of an unpainted belfry. Behind her a bell was tolling in the best tradition of Toby Show improbability.

Bong-ng-g! Bong-ng-g!

No Toby Show hero ever had such an opportunity to become the perfect agent of deliverance. Unfamiliar with the oft-told tale of the wronged heroine pursued by the ruthless villain, Reb sculled toward the belfry. The intent of the young helmsman was to throw his craft broadside against the bell tower. Good tactics. Nice boat handling. With a sweep of his long oar, he succeeded in his maneuver. At face level, Reb saw the woman he loved. She was barely two feet away. He stretched his arms wide.

"Climb over the balcony. Jump, Laly! Do as I tell you!"

Frantic, disheveled, crazed by the prospect of imminent destruction, Laly failed to recognize Reb's countenance or intention. Hands clutching at her breasts, she became the eternal symbol of outraged womanhood, pledged by the Toby

Show Code to repel the advances of the villain who still pursued her. Demented, Laly went into her act.

"*No, no, a thousand times no!*" she cried.

The flimsy superstructure of the bell tower gave way under the crushing pressure of Reb's scow. The heft of the bell was decisive and the tower sank beneath the surface.

Reb's scow passed over the spot where Laly went down.

Not prancing, not glancing, not dancing—as befitted Laly Woodhull's end—but with a sullen, arbitrary, sadistic roar, the river made a little vortex, then drove onward.

And this way the waters came down at L'Ordure.

Grief-stricken, Richmond Plaskett returned to Landmark. "I saw her face to face," he told Anson. "She was almost in my arms." Reb dashed tears from his eyes. "Why, *why* couldn't I save her, Mr. Woodhull?"

Anson pondered the question. "Don't blame yourself, Reb. I couldn't save her; Charles Moerlein couldn't save her; you couldn't save her. Now, if three good men—aided, as I gather, by the powerful support of a bad man—were unable to save Laly—" Anson paused before putting the thoughts into words —"some Force that we don't know about, that we'll never know about, must have been working for Laly's destruction."

Zarah passed through a private agony of self-recrimination. It was I, she thought, who made it impossible for Laly to be saved. God forgive me for competing with my own child. Laly was the woman I tried to be. I might have lived again in Laly. Instead, I chilled her budding talents, came over her with cruelty. Had I but encouraged her, sympathized, taken her into my arms. Oh, ye mothers, be warned in time. Look girlward, see your own past dewy with morning promise—and remember!

Zarah's grief was assuaged some months later when, accompanied by Solange, she claimed her granddaughter at the Spanish Mission Hospital. Life was giving Zarah a second chance, a chance to allow Haila to become the thing that neither Laly nor Laly's mother had been: a lovely girl, gifted, talented and encouraged to develop her personality in an atmosphere of love.

11.

THE HARVARD YARD

HARVARD SQUARE as of September 1904 had ceased to be
the Sabine Farm of Quintus Flaccus (Owen to you)
Wister, approached by horse cars over a chain-operated draw-
bridge. Not yet had it become a grid of tormenting cross-
currents set in motion by George Weller in *Not to Eat, Not
to Love*. It was, among other things, the terminus of a square-
wheeled trolley car, appropriately crimson as to color, that
shuttled back and forth between Boston and the groves of
Academe, where the motorman could take a puff at his old
dudeen while the conductor "cooled his parch" with a glass
of lemonade from the fruit store of P. Stokyopoulos before
switching the trolley roller from stem to stern.

Few signs gave evidence that the square, like the college,
was entering a new era. Vic Kennard's famous drop kick
against Yale was not yet the sole topic of conversation. Along
Brattle Street the first automobile had yet to park. To the
clop-clop of horse-drawn vehicles, the age of Eliot, Eliot the
Great Elector, Eliot of the mutton-chop whiskers, strawberry
birthmark and Augustan purpose, was drawing toward a close.
The *Drang nach Suden*—the movement away from classic,
plumbingless dormitories in the Yard—was already well advanced. But the Widener Library, the Model-T Ford, the
Lafayette Escadrille, many marriages, births, deaths and
bequests—ah, those undreamed-of millions—lay shrouded in
the future as the Freshman class of 1904 tried to lay hands on
its baggage piled barricade-high in the Square.

Chance Woodhull was among the lucky few who found it
unnecessary to take part in the battle of the baggage. By
prearrangement with American Express deities, his trunk,

bearing a St. Brede's sticker, and a new calfskin suitcase had been picked up at the home of Dr. Lyman Allston and delivered to C.A. Woodhull, Suite 2A, Apsworth Hall, Cambridge.

After breakfasting with Cousin Lyman and accepting the twenty-dollar tip always permissible between any student and any relative, Chance stood for a moment on the sunlit stoop of Dr. Allston's home on Marlborough Street, descended its brownstone steps and ran northward along Marlborough, noting in his flight the cross-streets named after British earldoms: Dartmouth, Exeter, Fairfax, Gloucester and Hereford. Then suddenly came Massachusetts Avenue and a crimson trolley car careening along at a speed of four miles an hour.

Pity the young man who has never leaped aboard a moving trolley!

Gathering momentum on the slight downward slope, the ark on wheels lifted its speed to seven miles an hour as it descended into an anonymous part of the world now covered by a magnificent layout known as M.I.T.

When the trolley came to a grinding halt in Harvard Square, the morning mounds of baggage had been worn down to a midday peneplain. Attracted by the whistle of a peanut stand in front of P. Stokyopoulos' fruit store, Chance refreshed himself with two delicacies indigenous to Boston and environs: a pickle-lime (obtained by thrusting his hand into a globular glass jar) and a five-cent bag of dulse, a reddish kind of seaweed, very salty, chock-a-block full of iodine and habit-forming once you got used to it.

At one o'clock he started meandering along Mt. Auburn Street trying to relocate Apsworth Hall, where he was awaited by roommates-to-be: Jimmy Stothart and Charles Coddington, both St. Brede boys; and a third fellow named Holliwell or Hallowell who had just finished choiring in that most seraphic of prep schools—Groton. This Groton Archangel was reputed to know fifty-one Vincent Club girls by their first names. Top that!

To contrast the magnificence of the Gold Coast dormitories with the chilly hutches in the Yard, Chance took to the middle of the street and gazed up at the apartments on either side. Some were four stories high! Craning his neck, munching dulse and shuffling—country style, through occasional deposits of horse manure—Chance was imagining what college life would be like when he heard a familiar voice from the second-story window of an imposing apartment.

"Dulse addict, this way! On the double!" It was Jimmy Stothart's voice—ribald, diaphragmatic and good to hear. In a punier register Charles Coddington, Boston born, gave a fair-to-middling example of what Milton Academy can do for the voice box of a day-school inmate.

"Advance, Corinthian, and show your testimonials."

Chance took the steps of Apsworth three at a bound. The door of 2A swung open; Stothart and Coddington began pummeling him about the head and body.

"Grasshopper, grasshopper, give me some molasses and I'll let you go." That was tub-chested Stothart hugging—no, squeezing—his prep-school roommate.

Chance squeezed back. "Address me as Mister Woodhull, you butter-whelk." He poked Stothart's belly. "What's this—lard?"

"*O-w-w-l*, you fearful Hackenschmidt. Leggo my short ribs."

A third roommate-to-be extended a slim pale hand. "My name is A. D. Hallowell. *A* for Ames; *D* for Dexter. At Groton they called me Deck."

On deck, below deck, top deck, hit the deck. Which? Chance wondered. To judge by Hallowell's blond hair, wavy, silken, beautifully barbered, together with subcutaneous complexities on the bluish side and an indefinably patronizing manner, A. Dexter Hallowell might have been any or all of these.

Chance cut through the superfine fabric with a light blade. "I'm C. A. Woodhull. *C* for Chance. *A* for Adams."

"The Quincy Adamses?" asked Hallowell.

"Collaterally. Does it matter?"

Hallowell nodded. "Other things being equal, it certainly wouldn't hurt a new man to claim Henry, Charles Francis, John and John Quincy as his antecedents."

"They're on my mother's side." Chance wanted to make everything perfectly clear. "My Father is a whiskey-maker from Indiana. Grandfather ditto. Had an Uncle Platt who managed to get himself eaten by wild dogs. Cancellation rules the nation."

"At Harvard we cancel out everyone but the top tens," said Hallowell.

A brick-red flush started to climb up Chance's neck. Stothart cooled it with a footnote of explanation. "Simmer down, Woodhull. Deck stems from the Groton branch of God. In some circles the Lord's Prayer begins: 'Our Father which art in Heaven, Hallowell be Thy name.' Atch-kay?"

"I catch. Where I come from, we pray: '*Woodhull* spare that family tree, touch not a single bough.'"

Hallowell acknowledged the touch with a flash of opalescent uppers. "I suggest, gentlemen, that we dissolve into a Committee of the Whole. There's *so* much to be done—organizational work, you know."

Like four colonels of a banana republic they lounged in various attitudes around a big fumed-oak table. Hallowell tapped an invisible gavel. A real take-charge guy, thought Chance.

"Now here's the way it's going to be," said Hallowell. "You understand, of course, that I'm speaking at second hand. My brother Amory, Class of ninety-six—he'll be an Overseer one of these days—gave me a copy of the blueprint that made him president of his class and, oh, a lot of other things too numerous to mention."

Long study of Big Brother's blueprint had apparently given Deck Hallowell a master key to the enigma of Fair Harvard. "I watched the baggage fracas in the Square today," he began, "and found the incoming class distressingly negative. Ninety-five per cent of them might have gone to Tufts, Trinity or Lehigh and never been missed. They won't even *suspect* what goes on at the center of power and influence here. They'll mill about, commute to Chelsea, Dorchester, Mattapan, get degrees leading to dentistry, salesmanship or ethical embalming. Imagine! They'll munch on the parched corn of Eliot's Inaugural delivered forty-five years ago, savoring such tidbits as 'The poverty of scholars is of inestimable worth in this money-getting nation,' *et cetera ad nauseam.*"

Hallowell's eyes narrowed like those of an overbred collie. "Meanwhile, *we*—meaning Coddington, Stothart, Woodhull and Yours-in-the-Bond—will seize the baton of command and emerge as the Quadrumvirate. We'll take over this ancient and very desirable piece of academic real estate known as the College and *run* it—as it should be, always has been, and always will be, run."

Chance entered a whimsical demurrer. "You don't mean that we'll play Yale, just the four of us, all by ourselves?"

"No. But we'll name the captain of the team that *does* play

Yale. Yes, and captain of the varsity crew. We'll pick the editor of the *Crimson* and monthly. Our man—one of us, possibly—will be president of the Senior class. We'll name the Upper Tens—chaps that we can introduce to our sisters. And finally—" Hallowell couldn't go much further—"we'll control Porcellian."

"No opposition?" asked Stothart.

"Some. But remember what George Meredith says in *The Egoist:* 'Aristocracy lives by the knife.' We've got the temper and material right here in this room. We'll divide, conquer, and share the spoils. We'll snub, cut and ignore. How? Simple! The snub direct, the cut intentional."

Chance shifted his weight from rump to elbow. "That'll leave us talking to ourselves."

Hallowell applied the crusher. "That's how the present incumbents—Sloane, Frothingham, Sears and Draper—operate. They've divided this college into baronial fiefs—for social purposes, I mean. No one gets a bid to a Boston party unless his name is proposed by Sloane. Frothingham takes the North Shore—the big houses in Manchester, Marblehead and Prides Crossing. Sears's territory extends as far south as Cohasset. Draper is still in training. Watch these men, Woodhull. You too, Stothart. Coddington doesn't need any coaching. He was born on the slope of Beacon Hill and I don't mean the water slope."

"Point of order," said Chance. "I wasn't born on either slope so I'll need some guidance. Suppose I run into a couple of fellows named Rabinowitz and Gilhooley. Let's go so far as to say I *like* them. What's the rule, coach?"

"The rule," said Hallowell, "is that Rabinowitz and Gilhooley do not exist."

His *diktat* was shattered by a heavy knock at the door.

"Open!" (Field Marshal Sloane speaking.)

"Come in," said Chance.

"Open the door, I said."

"It's Storrow Sloane," whispered Hallowell. "We'd better let him in."

"We've asked him in," said Chance. "He can turn a doorknob, can't he?"

An ague of indecision seemed to paralyze Hallowell's power drive. "But he told us to open the door."

"Well, then, in the name of common hospitality, I'll open it for him." Chance turned the knob and there in doorway stood

Seniors Sloane and Frothingham, seconded by Messrs. Draper and Sears.

Storrow Sloane's jockey size and lascivious wit had won for him the double distinction of being editor of the *Lampoon* and coxswain of the Varsity Crew. He was wearing a bowler hat, pegged-top trousers, a gray ascot and morning coat. He strolled to the center of the room and beckoned his retainers to assume supporting posts. Long accustomed to bullying larger men (three years as cox had given him plenty of practice), he squared off and announced the purpose of his visit.

"We are the Governing Board of the Intramural Coalition against Coition in the Normal Position." He severely admonished two members of the board who appeared to be playing footsie with each other. "Fellows, let's suspend all display of gherkin emotion while I quiz this candidate for emission." He addressed Woodhull. "You, sir, are you with us or against us?"

Chance munched a dulse leaf contemplatively. "Most people like it the Mama-Papa way. Still, there's much to be said for the 'Lazy Frenchman,' the 'Grecian Yearn' and some sixty-nine other variations—so I'm told. Have some dulse?"

Sloane patted down his rising codfish lunch. "You haven't answered my question."

"Well, as Christ says, when men question you, answer them 'Yea' or 'Nay,'" Chance emitted a dulsified "Na-ay."

"Give him ten demerits for talking with his mouth full," said Sloane. Draper entered the demerits on the record.

"Unbutton your blazer," ordered Sloane.

In the role of a stable boy pulling his forelock to the Lord of the Manor, Chance obeyed.

"Braces *and* belt, eh? You've been peeking at my page proofs of *Lampoon*," said Sloane. He pulled some inky sheets from his inner pocket and pointed to a collegiate spoof of a standard two-line joke.

> POP: *A man who wears both belt and braces.*
> SMALL BOY: *Pop, what's a pessimist?*

"You've got things upside down," said Chance. "I expect to grow another inch or two so I bought these flannel trousers a bit long. Naturally, I hist them up with braces."

"The committee frowns on braces," said Sloane, opening his jacket. "I, as chairman, wear only a belt."

"*Tutti giusti!* Including your hard hat." Chance tapped the crown of Sloane's bowler.

"Why, this is a genuine Delano. Famous School Street hatter."

"Make a note, Jimmy," said Chance. "Cut Delano."

Hallowell shuddered at his roommate's *lèse majesté*. Why, the man was committing social suicide. Worse yet, he was blackening Deck Hallowell with the tar brush of association.

"You seem to possess a kind of rude native wit," said Sloane. "Sharpen it by characterizing—in three words—a statement recently made by President Eliot. I quote: 'Every Harvard man cannot be an athlete, but we can all be athletic supporters.' "

Chance shook his head gravely. "Sounds too cocksure."

Sloane patted the palms of his hands together approvingly.

"One further test remains. The all-revealing handshake." He turned to his retainers. "Gentlemen, perform your duty."

Messrs. Frothingham, Sears and Draper offered Chance four fingers of their right hands. Sloane did likewise.

"H-m-m-m-m. The committee will now withdraw for conference." They whispered together in a corner of the room for some thirty seconds, then formed a ring around Chance.

"You have passed the test with distinction," said the chairman. "The members of my committee are amazed by the lack of hair, warts or excessive perspiration on the palm of your hand. How do you account for this singular freedom from the clinical tokens that betray, alas, only too well, the habit we are combatting in the college?"

"Simple foresight on the part of my parents," said Chance. "At fourteen, they gave me a French governess—*très jeune, agréable* and accomplished in her profession." He glanced at his watch. "Two o'clock. Dear faithful girl, she's waiting for me now at the Hotel Vendome."

"Hotel Vendome!" cried Sloane. "Why, my Aunt Seraphina lives there."

"Warn her against my tutoress—she's double-gaited. Been mentioned in the wills of several elderly ladies."

"Good God!" Sloane lifted his invocation to protect his aunt and the clause mentioning Sloane in her will. Perspiring, the chairman stepped aside and Frothingham took over the questioning.

"This French tutoress of yours. As one man to another, how often do you take advantage of . . . ah . . . that is . . . how many times a week do you . . . um . . . ?" Strict interpretation of the Harvard code placed certain words off bounds.

Chance took the fine, clean-living stance. "I think a growing boy shouldn't rap it oftener than twice a day."

"Twice a day! Say, what do you do between times?"

Chance pointed at Sloane. "I walk around like him."

The expected laugh didn't come from any member of the Coalition against Coition in the Normal Position. It was Jimmy Stothart who gave way to yahoo mirth; Charlie Coddington's obbligato was Milton Academy's equivalent of a guffaw.

Sloane switched his glance for a split second to this irreverent duo. Just long enough for Chance to jam the chairman's bowler over his ears and unloosen his belt buckle. Sloane's trousers fell to the floor, revealing an ornate pair of lavender shorts with a quivering pink prepuce sticking out at half-mast between the second and third buttons.

The undertow of laughter tumbled everyone, including Storrow Sloane, into postures of antic hilarity. Even Deck Hallowell laughed. He couldn't help it.

There was a great deal more that Hallowell couldn't help. The "here's-the-way-it's-going-to-be" seraph from Groton was obliged to admit that Chance Woodhull personified Prexy Eliot's "young man of unusual temperament, who must be accepted, welcomed, included, yea hailed, by any dynasty that hoped to reign."

With no feeling of ambivalence Chance walked in ways prescribed by The Great Elector, Pudding, Dickey and ultimately Porcellian. At the same time he walked in his own way and discovered that Rabinowitz and Gilhooley *did exist*—not only existed but enriched Chance Woodhull and Harvard College by the fact of their existence. He read Owen Wister's *Philosophy 4* and spat on the purebred Anglo-Saxon prigs who inhabited its pages. He read Charles Flaundrau's *Diary of a Freshman*, published in 1900, and was alternately charmed and depressed by its naïveté—an innocence forever fled, uncapturable by present or future generations of Harvard's sons.

Of the many people and experiences that transformed Chance Woodhull from an eighteen-year-old fledgling into a Harvard Senior—with all the privileges and exemptions accruing thereto—only Chance himself could tell. Many hours, happy at the time, were pebbles dropped into the urn of forgetfulness. Others were unforgettable.

For example:

The engagement of his entire physical and nervous system in learning how to handle the long sweep that won him a place in the Freshman Boat. The complicated forward maneuver of thrust and catch (careful not to catch a crab); the long backward pull, the feathery movement of wrists at the moment of recovery. *Repetando,* metronome fashion, thirty-two, thirty-four, thirty-six, yes, even forty times a minute—for a mile, two miles—and if you made the Varsity Boat—four miles, while the cox whipped you with brutal exhortations to "put your ass" into it. Indelible, once learned, never to be forgotten.

As William James said, "We learn to skate in summer and swim [or row] in winter."

In the summer of 1905 Chance fell in love with Amy Towner. Setting a stage on which he could be alone with his girl, he saved up the enormous sum of sixty dollars and became the owner of a genuine Old Town canoe, eighteen feet in length and fire-engine red. Swift as a pickerel it was; seasoned hickory and straight-grained ash made it a marvel of strength and lightness. The canoe was equipped with two paddles, a quilted canvas mat and a most imaginative rack for sofa cushions which, when properly placed, would induce a feeling of luxurious indolence in any girl fortunate enough to be asked for a cruise around the fringes of Brimmer Pond.

During that long summer vacation Chance had a hundred daily opportunities to talk with Amy, walk with her, swing her sky high—well, at least into the sycamore leaves—on the rope swing that he and Way Towner had built for the express purpose of "double-pumping," a feat requiring special skill.

Ever since their early teens, Chance and Amy had been circling around each other like a pair of binary stars held in a predestined orbit. Stars may circle so and be content; but not this young man and this young woman, whose sole desire and need was fusion.

If Amy Towner had not possessed in female form the spark that caused her big brother, Way, to burn with a special glow for Chance Woodhull; were she not fully charged with an identical current, perhaps Chance might never have noticed her. There were so many girls clamoring for Chance's attention. Big girls, fully developed women at sixteen. Good girls. Pretty girls. Fine girls, all of them. There were flaunting girls, taunting girls, boy-wanting girls. Probably fifty or sixty altogether in the Landmark garden. How could slender-stemmed, black-eyed Amy merely by nodding innocently, lowering her eyelids, or lifting them as the occasion required—how could this 107-pound package of first love succeed in binding with unbreakable withes a passionate young bullock without fearing his horns—in fact, waiting to be gored by same, and willing to wait longer if necessary?

According to all the rules it would be necessary to wait longer.

This much Chance and Amy discovered while a July evening perfumed Brimmer Pond with musk of midsummer. The time for preliminaries had long passed; the hour cried "now," but the only permitted response was the mouth-to-mouth acknowledgment that "now" would expand into a future of unimaginable fulfillment and mutual possession.

"Not yet, not yet, Chance."

"When, darling?"

"Not for years, years. Not till you finish college."

"Amy, Amy . . ."

And thus it went, with Amy, the slender young bull-priestess both inviting and averting the fatal stroke.

That such things should be; that a nineteen-year-old boy and a sixteen-year-old girl could lie beside each other in a red canoe, knowing by every sign and aspect that they were on-rushing fragments of an ideal dream yet to be realized—this is a triumph not to be credited to the gods of morality or convention.

When Love makes its presence felt, why invoke lesser deities?

The Wednesday evenings in Hollis with "Copey" reading or talking, honoring the English language as a great king might honor the sire who gave him birth, ennobled his youth, and brought him his academic throne, were certainly unforgettable.

Hail to thee, blithe spirit . . . Thou still unravished bride of quietness . . . That time of year thou mayst in me behold . . . Tears in his eyes, distraction in his aspect . . .

Then came an evening when Copey said, "Gentlemen, I should like to read from a living classic—President Eliot's

Inaugural delivered in 1869. It is my considered judgment that Mr. Eliot's words are as true today as in that older time." Then he read:

> Harvard College is sometimes reproached with being aristocratic. If by aristocracy be meant a stupid and pretentious caste, founded on wealth and birth, no charge could be more preposterous: the College is intensely American and democratic in temper. But there is an aristocracy to which the sons of Harvard belong, and will ever aspire to belong: the aristocracy which excels in manly sports, carries off the honors and prizes of the learned professions, and bears itself with distinction in all fields of intellectual labor and combat.

A voice (Hallowell's) from the shadows: "I had always thought, Professor, that the ideas in the Inaugural had become somewhat archaic."

Copey paused. "Do you think so *now?*" he asked.

Letters from Amy Towner—delicate streamers floating upward from the depth of a woman's heart. "I walk, move, dream through an aqueous haze. I am permeated, drenched, surrounded, engulfed by thoughts of you, my very dear one. I look forward to the long summer holidays when you will return to Landmark. I look forward to the years beyond, when my whole being can dissolve into a woman's 'Yes.'"

Associate Professor Thurlow's biting comment on Harvard's motto *Veritas:*

"I need not remind you, gentlemen, that the word *Veritas* was once removed from the Harvard seal and replaced only after an intramural battle during which, I believe, a couple of presidents were killed. Such thoughts may tend to shake the foundations of your trust in the richest and oldest academic institution in the United States. On the other hand, to translate *Veritas* literally as 'Truth' would be an act of consummate idiocy. Let us consider *Veritas* then as a convenient and highly serviceable catch-all—a kind of synecdoche, a figure of rhetoric in which a part is substituted for the whole. Thus, 'fifty sail' for 'fifty ships.' Or am I thinking of metonymy? When we refer to the cup that cheers, do we mean the cup itself or the liquor it contains? In the case of *Veritas*, I lean toward metonymy as the trope of choice. The container for the thing contained. How frightful, really, to be confronted by this many-headed monster, when for all intents and purposes we daily contemplate the word *Veritas* on our university seal without the hemidemisemi of a quiver."

The Vincent Club stag line. Young men in "full fig"—tails, white ties and white gloves. The ideal proportion was considered to be three men for every girl. Actually, all the young men were waiting to cut in on Stacey Slater—Stacey of the butterscotch hair, and eyes that struck you like a knout, raising weals of lust that couldn't, under the Harvard code, be medicined. Stacey shouldn't have been allowed out, but she got out anyway, and tempted the man of her passing fancy to break the code—as strict as Benedictine Rule—concerning chastity.

During Chance's Sophomore year, Stacey invited him to her father's estate at Prides Crossing. There she showed him the seven wonders of wealth, including a stable of thoroughbred horses. The stable odors were an aphrodisiac to her; she kept nuzzling up to Chance like a mare in rut; her fingers were all over him.

"Come into the tackroom," she whispered. "I'll show you our collection of whips, boots and saddles."

Inside the tackroom she threw herself down on a groom's cot in writhing desperation. Chance, nineteen, had never witnessed such an exhibition; Stacey's excitement was contagious. How was one supposed to act in a situation like this?

Stacey answered the question by rolling over on her back and gazing up at the tall young man standing over her. "You begin by unfastening my skirt," she said. "No, I'll make things easy for you; I'll lift it myself."

She was a true piece of butterscotch all right, ready and willing to melt in Chance's mouth. Or vice versa.

"*Once* doesn't count," she coaxed.

In Owen Wister's book, true-blue (pardon me—red-blooded) Harvard chaps didn't "do it" even once. But you see, Chance wasn't the Wister type.

Underneath the complacent academic surface of Cambridge, a renaissance was stirring. In the lectures of Santayana, Münsterberg, Copeland, William James and others, Chance felt the faintly stirring zephyrs that preceded the hurricane of ideas in classes prior to World War I. For the most part, the college lay in the trough of a ground swell, unmoved and unmoving. Teddy Roosevelt was wielding his Big Stick against "malefactors of great wealth"; muckrakers exposed graft in municipal politics; circulation-minded editors unveiled working conditions in mines, sweatshops, and meatpacking plants.

The favored young men who constituted the upper 5 per cent of the Harvard student body knew little and cared less about those abuses. Between lectures and proms, between the annual game with Yale and occasional trips to Quilty Curnayne's Esperanto Bar in Boston, there existed little opportunity for thinking about such matters.

The Harvard Yard, like every other campus, formed a protective capsule around its young men. It armored them with an impenetrable chain mail, each link stamped with the word *Veritas.*

During summer vacations Chance returned to Landmark to work in his father's distillery. Few whiskey-makers have ever been tutored by better instructors. From Anson he learned the secrets of mashing, fermenting and distillation.

"It might be a good idea for you to study chemistry," suggested Anson.

Dr. George Washington Waley, making his annual round of inspection, seconded Anson's motion. "Whiskey is an enigma so complex that only a chemist can glimpse the heart of it." Waley grasped young Woodhull by the hand. "Do as your father bids you. As Ralph Waldo Emerson said in quite another connection, 'I greet you at the beginning of a great career.'"

Chemistry came easily to Chance. He enjoyed working with test tubes and unknown substances. In his junior year he was permitted to make an independent analysis of the carbon-hydrogen-oxygen chain that lies at the heart of whiskey. He sent a copy of his term paper to George Washington Waley and received the accolade of Waley's "well done."

But if chemistry came easily, philosophy did not. Of all Chance's professors, Otho Purington's philosophic discourses seemed the least intelligible. Chance wasn't the only person who found Purington opaque. As Santayana remarked, "Purington knows all the words but has forgotten the music."

One chilly morning in November 1907 Professor Purington

blandly ascended the steps of Emerson Hall, entered his classroom and gave full vent to his opacity by writing an examination on the blackboard. After checking the questions carefully, he left the room.

The exam ran as follows:

"If you were (1) Descartes (2) Kant (3) Hegel (4) Spinoza (5) Hume (6) Spencer (the student may select any five) with what arguments should you affirm or refute the following concepts:

> (a) Thales "Original stuff"
> (b) the "Eternal flux" of Heraclitus
> (c) Empedocles "Roots of things"
> (d) the "Four causes" of Aristotle
> (e) the "Demiurge of Plato"
> (f) the "Logos of Philo"
> (g) the "Three basic substances of Paracelsus."

On beholding the gruesome quiz, one member of the class fainted dead away; two were seized by motor paralysis; three had torrential nosebleeds from a surfeit of blood trying to reach their brains; four suffered from a peculiar form of non-Heraclitean flux which rendered them malodorous to their companions; and five fell into odd lots of strabismus, vertigo and St. Vitus's Dance. The only man who finished his paper was a chap named Leffingwell who came to a weird end as an entomologist. Bugs about bugs. The fate of others is unknown, but a fluxed-up trio of students named Coddington, Stothart and Woodhull raced to their rooms in Apsworth for relief and repairs.

They were all fine, clean-living fellows, yet on this particular occasion there seemed no alternative but to get drunk. And the drinking place of choice was Quilty Curnayne's Esperanto Bar.

THE ESPERANTO BAR

"ALL MEMBERS of the same club." That was the feeling you got in Quilty Curnayne's bar at 9 Province Court, Boston, and, make no mistake about it, that was the feeling Quilty intended you to get. He had the knack of setting a bottle in front of you and saying, "Your pleasure, gentlemen," as though you were the Speaker of the House having a friendly glass with the Ambassador from Rainingpouria. It isn't every man who knows the secret of honoring you and himself while serving whiskey at fifteen cents a drink, two for a quarter. But Quilty knew, and for many years his bar at 9 Province Court (just behind the Parker House) was a haven where men of all fates, hopes and anxieties could hail each other in the Esperanto of good-fellowship: *"Long life, Johnno; Skoal, Gunnar; Slanti, Kevin; Sholom Aleichem, Abe. And to you Gus, Gesundheit."*

A hundred harmonious details had gone into creating the cheer-and-cheer-alike atmosphere of Quilty's bar. The length of the place was exactly right for its width; the green-shaded lamps cast an emerald glow neither too dim nor too bright and a clean rosiny odor rose from the sawdust on the floor. The bar itself was of Honduras mahogany (solid planks, no veneer) hand-rubbed to a fiddleback sheen. A rail of reddish brass ran around the upper edge of the bar at just the proper height for a confidential elbow. As for the foot rail, it was so perfectly gauged to the bend of your knee that you could stand first on one foot then on the other, until your body dropped its fleshly ballast and allowed you to float (without anyone's noticing it) an inch or two above the floor.

On walls of knotty pine, Quilty had hung a number of sporting prints all suggesting (and why not?) the age-old bond between honest liquor and virility at prime. Just inside the door was Aristides, the bay stallion, heavy-ballocked and deep through the heart, winner of the first Kentucky Derby. Next came a lithograph of Mike "Death" Dooley and Sailor Grogan, squaring off for their famous bare-knuckle battle at Swampscott Beach. Seventy-six rounds they had fought for a purse of fifty dollars! On the wall opposite the bar hung a handsome copper-plate engraving: *The Stag at Eve.* Having drunk his fill, this noble buck was scenting good news down the wind. Heaven help the solitary doe nibbling moss in his antlership's vicinity that night.

Every time Quilty's customers looked at those pictures they thanked their earthly father for giving that wonderful male twist to his conjuring wand when he performed the miracle of special creation back there, whenever it was.

No female ever entered Quilty's bar—none, that is, except Peachblossom, the luscious nude who hung in the oval gilt frame behind the bar. There she lay reclining on a cloud with nothing but the wisp of a mist to shield her from the other fellow's glances while she gazed, faithful in her fashion, at you alone. Quilty had paid $200 for that painting. If you hung a picture like that in your home or office, no one would understand. Peachblossom was part of the dream that hovered over Quilty's bar, inviting you to join her on a pink cloud of illusion, forget the world of categorical imperatives for an hour or two, and come back refreshed in time to catch the last trolley home.

Now as for the quality of the whiskey served in Quilty's bar. One could ask for any of the nationally advertised brands —Old Settler, Bald Eagle or Rosemere—but the tipple of choice was Quilty's bar whiskey bearing the label O.T.B. (Only the Best). As was the custom in those days, Quilty bought good rye and bourbon by the barrel, and kept a dozen or more barrels stored in his cellar. When business was quiet of an afternoon, he'd descend a narrow flight of steps, survey his stock and begin the ritual of mixing O.T.B. The procedure ran something like this:

He'd attach a rubber tube to various barrels and let fifteen or twenty gallons of good two-year-old whiskey flow into a huge vat, spotlessly clean, in the center of the cellar. To this he'd add a quantity of distilled water for the purpose of reducing the ardency of the original stuff. The rubber tube would now be attached to a barrel of "neutral spirits," considerably less expensive than whiskey, but eminently serviceable to the barkeep who wanted bulk and potency. Disdaining the use of a hydrometer ("Here's my hydrometer," Quilty often said, clicking his tongue against the roof of his mouth), the proprietor of the Esperanto Bar tested his mixture for its alcoholic proof, flavor and quality. Smacking his lips, he'd murmur, "Y—mm, the good craythur, O.T.B."

Next came the task of siphoning this concoction of whiskey, water and neutral spirits into freshly washed bottles. In matters of corks and labels, Quilty was a purist. Both had to be new, so that when he slid a bottle of O.T.B. across his bar, the customer could see with his own eyes that the goods were fresh and clean.

The artist satisfied, Quilty the businessman now figured his profit. Eighteen generous drinks to the quart; seventy-two drinks to the gallon; 3,600 to the barrel. Knock off a couple of hundred drinks on the house, sell the remainder at an average of twelve and one half cents a glass, and a tidy $500 would slide into Quilty's old-fashioned till. Good business. Not big, but good. O.T.B. was a popular and enduring blend—yet, as Quilty knew from experience, not one customer in a thousand, or one in a hundred thousand, knew or even cared what went into his bottles. All they wanted was a clean, tasty drink —something that gave them a slow aproach to satiety.

The fellows you met in Quilty's Saloon seemed a cut above the common run. Judges from Special Sessions would drop in to soften up their buckram bindings with a jigger or two of O.T.B. Beacon Hill barristers laid aside the dry-as-dust jargon of tort and replevin to wet their lips with some real high-proof evidence. State House politicians, newspaper reporters from Pi Alley, Ward 8 bagmen, paving contractors, police captains, wool-market speculators and Faneuil Hall produce brokers, together with a sprinkling of fight managers, traveling salesmen, gentleman jockeys, ship's officers and Harvard students, all drifted through the swinging doors of No. 9 to take part in the matinee or evening performance (as the case might be) of that continuous ever-changing drama entitled "Ten Thousand and One Nights in a Barroom." Admission free. Every man his own masker. All male cast. *Ici on parle Esperanto*. Standing room only.

The principal role in this never-twice-the-same drama was played by John the Incomparable, Duke of Usquebaugh and Lord of the Slightly-to-Leeward Islands—better known to his audience as Johnno Normile, dean of the Parker House cab-rank. The origins of this remarkable man were legendary. Rumor, issuing from a hawse hole of the S.S. *Hearsay* (flagship of the Old Canard Line) says that he was found by some Ostensian Brothers floating like Moses himself in a little boat moored among the rushes of the pond behind their monastery. Pinned to his swaddling rags was a letter, purportedly written by his mother, a hedgerow actress who had stooped to be conquered by a fox-hunting baronet whose name could be found in *Burke's Peerage*, if only she knew what name to look for. The Brothers, observing Johnno's brilliant parts, stuffed him with sound Latin and were preparing him for minor orders. But a Big Wind put an end to all that by blowing Johnno, piety and all, to Boston, where he was met at the dock by a man who offered him fifty cents a day for tearing down a Presbyterian Church. Land of opportunity! Later, Johnno served briefly as an undertaker's assistant but showed little skill at cadaver-palaver and went from job to job, always borrowing more than he saved, and spending more than he borrowed, until the lucky day came when his services as a repeater at the polls won him the badge of a licensed hackman. After that, it was merit, merit, all the way until he reached the peak of his profession—the cab-rank in front of the Parker House.

Leaning against the cab dispatcher's box at the corner of School and Tremont streets, Johnno cut a handsome figure in his bottle-green coat with silver buttons, buff-colored breeches and gloves to match, glossy top hat set at a Brummel rake on roached curls. His cavalry boots were always varnished as if for a Balaklava charge and he cracked a magnificent yellow whip as he tooled along Commonwealth Avenue behind his pair of matched bays. With elderly ladies he was faultless; in fact, ladies of all ages found him quick with the umbrella and otherwise accommodating. But the backbone and mainstay of Johnno's clientele were the college bloods who found themselves stranded outside the Parker House long after the last trolley car had left for Cambridge. They were his boys, his joys, and for a dollar he would drive them at any hour of the night across the dark moors lying between the Back Bay and the Harvard Yard.

In mild weather Johnno transported his diller-a-dollar scholars in a four-wheeled herdic with an elastic seating capacity ranging between five and sixteen, counting three on top, two hanging from the carriage lights, and the rest hopping on or off for a brain-cooling jog behind. With the coming of winter, Johnno brought out his famous "booby," a kind of snow-going dory on runners, with a hutchlike structure amidships, kept toasty warm by a wood-burning stove. Johnno the pilot sat well forward in the prow, bundled up in a multiplicity of capes, cardigans, shawls, earlaps, arctics, fur mittens and buffalo rugs. Then over the river and through the drifts to Holworthy Hall they'd go, with sparks flying out of the chimney and young gentlemen taking turns at the reins, lest their beloved Johnno catch his death of cold.

This, then, was the man who, during his hours of ease, trod the boards of Quilty's bar. Wherever Johnno stood, that was the center of the stage, and though many of Quilty's patrons could have bought and sold Johnno with the loose change in their fob pockets, none could match him—when his buskin mood was on—at telling a story. There was a great deal of storytelling in those days—a tale for every nostril and taste bud—spicy, succulent, scented, savory and sulphurous. There were Pat and Mike stories, Becky and Ike stories, Jack and Jill stories, Cock and Bull stories. Glass in hand, every man became his own Münchhausen, Casanova, or Joe Miller, and every saloon a Grand Vizier's palace. It was, in fact, the Augustan Age of storytelling, and Johnno Normile was master of them all.

Including that one about the fellow who wanted to be a lion tamer. How everyone laughed at the punch line: *"It'll be there, all right."*

When tale-telling palled, Johnno could freshen things up with the sweet breath of song. A fine baritone voice he had, rich but not suety, and his repertoire arched like a rainbow from twelfth-century Irish ballads right down to current music-hall hits. The numbers most in request, however, were two of his own compositions: "The Man on the Box" and "The Girl with the Hansom Behind." Though the titles remained constant and the theme never changed, the words were different every time, because Johnno carried a wild harp of improvisation somewhere about his large person. Had he been Homer, the world would have fifty different versions of that long stop-over on Circe's tight little island. And theologians can thank heaven that Johnno had nothing to do with the writing of Genesis, else how would anyone today know the true story of creation?

To this jongleur gift, Johnno added a talent sometimes found in those quick-change artists who pop behind a screen as Napoleon and come out as Simon Legree. This inferior breed requires machinery of one kind or another—wigs, tricornered hats, false beards and blue lights. But Johnno did it without props of any kind. Like Proteus, that shifty Old Man of the Sea, Johnno could change his personality into any shape he pleased. Mimicry wasn't the word for it; Johnno was the *Ding an Sich!* And what a range he had! One minute he'd be a river-boat gambler dealing himself a full house off the bottom of the pack; then the cards would be transformed into an ancient book of wisdom—the Torah perhaps, or a lost manuscript of Vesalius—with Johnno on the infallible side of the desk expounding some hitherto unrevealed truth of metaphysics or anatomy.

Because of his churchly background, Johnno was particularly good at burlesquing the clergy. His barbs were nonsectarian. Immensely tolerant, he'd bring tears to your eyes by enacting the poor sot who was taking The Pledge for the nineteenth time in front of the Virgin's statue. Snuffling into his sleeve, Johnno would beg for another chance,

"Let bygones be bygones, Holy Mother. I promise never to shame myself again in front of Maggie and our nine little bausheens crying for a crust of bread. And I'd prove it by lighting a candle, except the last dime I can lay my hands on is just enough for a hair of the dog. So take my word for this time, positively the last . . . Hail Mary, full of grace, intercede for me or I'm a gone goose, and blessed is the fruit of Thy Womb, Jesus."

Then Johnno would split your ribs portraying a deacon cozying up to the soprano in the choir loft.

"Let us reason together, Sister. The harvest is large but the reapers are few. So how about advancing the Lord's work with a teentsy, weensy nip of elderberry wine? Fortify yourself, Sister, for the labor ahead."

"Oh, Deacon" (falsetto) "what a big bottle you've got."

The Esperanto audience loved it, clamored for more.

As might be expected, a natural rivalry sprang up between Johnno and Quilty. Nothing overt; merely the type of thing that Irishmen use routinely in belittling each other. To cite an example; Johnno might drop in between fares, doff his hat to the proprietor and ask permission to relieve the strain on a weak tenant on a lower floor of the Temple. "Where's the Easiamento?" he'd whisper. Whereupon Quilty would point to a Brewster-green half door at the rear of his place and announce to all present, "There he goes. Look at the grandeur of him! He's one of the greatest peers of our time."

Sometimes Quilty rubbed it in by laying a century note on the bar and addressing the Normile directly. "You talk a good whiskey, Johnno, but would you undertake to cover this hundred-dollar bill by identifying three jiggers of whiskey that I'll pour for you?"

Whereupon Johnno would pull out a roll of bills big enough to plug a drain and go through the motions of balancing *Cash on Hand* against *Obligations Outstanding*. "This five hundred dollars I promised to the Cardinal as tithe money, payable at Michaelmas," he'd say. "And this cluster of twenties [all clipped together] represents overdue expenditures on Normile Castle in Tullybogs, Eire. Which leaves me with only one hundred and sixty dollars in petty cash for demand loans to any young Harvard gentleman who stands in need of same. Other than these little items, Quilty—" Johnno fumbled through his pockets—"I've nothing but a Canadian quarter and a dime plugged by Annie Oakley herself."

Johnno would look around the bar hopefully. "Perhaps some other gentleman in the audience would like to accommodate our host?"

Quilty's century note never did get covered. In fact, it narrowly escaped being blown away. One night in December 1907 a wind whistling down from the polar ice cap made a quick turn at the corner of Tremont and School streets, bored its way into the second alley on the right-hand side going down, and came to rest amid the sawdust of Quilty's saloon. It blew the century note off his bar and struck a chill into the hearts of some young Harvard gentlemen gathered around the base of the Normile banyan.

"The glacier is coming," they cried; "we must cross the wild fens lying between us and the Yard!"

Johnno accepted a nip of anti-glacial liquid and volunteered to take over the reins of the expedition. While the booby sped down Tremont Street, its chimney throwing off sparks, Johnno found himself inside the hutch basking in front of the stove and taking his turn at the bottle. (Heaven only knows who drove the horses that night.)

During that ride Johnno became what every man dreams of becoming: the complete Irishman. By turns he was authoritative, beguiling, convivial, dramatic, effusive, fantastic, germane, hortatory, ingratiating, judicial, kindly, lordlike, mnemonic, nobiliary, opulent, profound, quixotic, reminiscent, Socratic, tearful, understanding, vague, wily, Yorickish and Zodiacal. In short, *tout à fait* falling-down-drunk.

Peering through the frosted pane of his booby, Johnno saw that they were passing through a region infested by swamp angels, werewolves and, worst yet, trolley-car commuters. To exorcise these demons Johnno sounded off, *improvvisatore* fashion, in a song as fresh as a new leaf yet veined with presentiments of disaster.

"Hearken to me now," he cried. "I'll troll a stave for the company, and the title thereof—in case anyone should jump out from behind a lamp post and ask you—is 'A Chantey of Notorious Bibbers.' It's a monody or maybe a threnody. Vamp till ready, Maestro. *Um*-pah . . . *um*-pah . . . *ump*-dilly . . . *um*-pah."

Johnno took it from the top:

Plato was a bibulous Greek who loved the flowing bottle;
Herodotus was a thirsty cuss and so was Aristotle.

Cho.:

Sing ho! that Archipelago where mighty Attic thinkers
Invoked the grape to keep in shape and lampooned water
drinkers.

King Richard fought the heathen Turk along with his
Crusaders.
On wobbly legs they tippled kegs and hated lemonaders.

Cho.:

Sing ho! the gallant British King, sing ho! his lusty yeo-
men
Who felt the need of potent mead to make them better
bowmen.

Will Shakespeare loved to dip his pen in Mermaid Inn
Canary;
And Bobbie B. was boiled when he concoc-ted Highland
Mary.

Cho.:

Sing ho! the time when Pegasus at prime drank deep of
Helicon's sources;
The tipple consumed by contemporary bards is the color
of another horse's.

Dan Webster stoked his boilers with brown jugs of apple
cider
And won his claim to name and fame by op'ning the
spigot wider.

Cho.:

Sing ho! those spirited debates bereft of all restrictions
When senators carried on their hip the strength of
their convictions.

L'Envoi (lugubrioso)

Let's live and grow
On H_2O—
All other drinks
Are risky
And hist'ry is a record of
Good men gone wrong on
WHIS-KEY

Talk about freak explosions in a molasses factory! The walls of the booby buckled outward as Johnno's listeners fell into convulsions of laughter and flailed each other joyfully.

"Encore!" cried Stothart.

"Bis, bis!" shouted Woodhull.

Then and there Johnno was created Grand Templar of Minstrelsy—entitled to all the honors, exemptions, fees and emoluments pertaining thereto. Chance Woodhull was taking up a silver collection for his templarship when the booby took a high hoop leap over some fence or other, left the earth entirely and came down hutch side up, in front of Apsworth Hall. The intervention of St. Christopher saved Johnno and his passengers, but the booby was burned to a crisp when a coal popped out of its overturned stove and started a bonfire that lighted up Mt. Auburn Street for a glorious half hour.

Ah, well, Johnno's booby being made of mortal stuff had to end one way or another. But his song rose Phoenixlike from the ashes and flew on Pentecostal tongues around the Yard. A destiny high enough, one might think, for a piece of random verse. But you can't keep a good rhyme from rolling. One Easter morning it arose, pushed back a brick and started making the rounds of other colleges. Like the apple pie in Mother Goose, Johnno's song soon had a whole alphabet of universities clamoring for possession. Amherst angled for it, Bryn Mawr bedizened it, Cornell chortled at it, Fordham fought for it, Goucher garbled it and Haverford howled at it. While Harvard hung onto it, Michigan mythed it, Oglethorpe ogled it, Smith simpered at it, Vassar vaunted it, Wesleyan wanted it, and Yale yammered for it. Letters from Harvard alumni were received by the editor of the *Crimson*. These fine old vatted specimens expressed indignation that a piece of Harvard property should be appropriated by other colleges. Here's a typical letter:

THE EDITOR:

Might it not be a good idea—even though some expense were incurred—to publish the circumstances surrounding the origin of this piece of Harvardiana so baldly and boldly put to use by other so-called institutions of learning?

The letter was signed *Veritas*.

No, *Veritas*, it would not be a good idea. Johnno's song

gushed from the rock of folklore and poured (is still pouring) in a crystalline stream across a poetry-parched terrain. It's as permanent and all-pervasive as the *que* in *Filioque*, and ranks with the story about the man who wanted to be a lion tamer.

Who owns these things, anyway?

Eventually the Quadrumvirate reigned pretty much as Hallowell had predicted. Hallowell himself was allowed to pull a few plums from an infinitesimal wedge of the great Harvard pie. Behind the closed door of Porcellian, he took part in naming the captains of crew and football. But even without Hallowell's nod, Chance would have become—as he *did* become—captain and No. 2 oar in the Varsity shell.

In the previous year, Yale had swamped Harvard in its home waters. Thirsting for revenge, the Harvard crew lowered its shell into the Connecticut River at New London. Seven members of the crew averaged 185 pounds: the cox'n, Eddy Hochheimer, was a pint-sized mixture of larynx and nerve who had been picked from the culls by Woodhull himself.

One day, during spring practice, Chance heard Hock (as he was called) invoking strange deities as he sat in the stern of the Junior boat and squirted pure vitriol over the seven bulkier bodies toiling at their sweeps. Hock's language wasn't fit to eat—so he chewed tobacco. But his rudder tactics, his sense of wind, tide and timing made a mediocre crew seem and *row* approximately 25 per cent better than they actually were.

"Where did you learn about wind and tides?" Chance asked him.

"Sailing on the Ohio," said Hock.

"Whereabouts on the Ohio?"

"Cincinnati."

At Chance's suggestion, Hock was given a try-out in practice. He did everything but throw cayenne pepper into the eyes of the veteran stroke. Hock got the boat away faster and kept it out in front better than the Porcellian nominee. Chance threw the weight of his captaincy into the battle and Hock was cox.

That race against Yale was probably the weirdest ever rowed. Look it up in the record book. See for yourself how after a couple of false starts a certain stroke who shall be nameless here collapsed and pitched forward, an inert blond baggage at Hock's feet. Fortunately, Harvard happened to be in the lead.

Yale took legitimate advantage of the mishap and drew abreast of the Harvard shell and threatened to pass. Little Hock broke every rule in the book. To begin with, he took charge.

"Woodhull, you're stroke now. Hit it up to thirty-eight." He spat a stream of tobacco juice straight into Chance's eye. "I said thirty-eight, you *goy;* pull, you Porcellian *schweinerei,* you Christ-lovers." More tobacco juice. With a half mile to go, Hock lifted the beat to forty. "Now, you Nordic nudniks—get your ass into it!" The Harvard boat drew ahead of Yale and finished three lengths in the lead. Time: 20:21. Captain Woodhull, No. 2, was splattered from head to foot with tobacco juice.

According to tradition, the entire crew participates in tossing the winning cox into the river. This time Chance held his crewmates back.

"He's mine," he growled. Seizing Hock by both wrists, he whirled him around thrice, like a hammer thrower, and tossed him thirty feet from the pier. Hock dog-paddled back, grinning as he came. Chance pulled him out of the water, and they kissed each other. Just like Frenchmen.

Academically, Chance was graduated in the middle third of his class—a creditable position. Socially and athletically he was the *Homomagnus* of the Harvard Yard—captain of crew, a member of Porcellian, vice-president of his class. Although Cambridge had put its inimitable stamp on him, Chance had no difficulty in arriving at a decision about his life's work. He was neither an intellectual nor an artist. At heart he was a businessman, a product of the age in which he lived. Where could he find a better opportunity than in his father's distillery? He looked forward to life in a growing midwestern town, and more than anything else he wanted to marry Amy Towner as soon as possible.

But first, Commencement.

On the night before Commencement, Chance dined with his mother and father at the Somerset. Jimmy Stothart, Charlie Coddington and others in the upper tens paid homage to Anson and Zarah. Things were pretty wet—champagne mostly —and the wetness generated a special warmth, comparable perhaps to a certain farewell party given by a non-Harvard man, name of Washington, to the generals who had supported him during a long and dubious war. No breaking down of form, you understand; just a temporary loosening of the stays. Because everyone in the Somerset dining room "belonged" (heaven only knows how the rest of the class spent the evening), the emotional temperature rose to almost human cordiality.

For Zarah, the dinner was a complete triumph of everything she had hoped and planned for her son. The boy himself—no longer a boy, Chance had just passed his twenty-second birthday—had fulfilled the early promises of leadership and manliness. He was something new in the world. It helps to be tall, thought Zarah. Her boy stood six feet one in his crew socks. Evening dress, perfection; diction, flawless; the way he parted his hair—the color of that hair (a true chestnut) —dreamy. Chance had always given the impression of being effortless in anything he attempted. Add a special quality of grace and something of my own beauty (she thought), and there he stands for all the world to admire and imitate.

Like every mother, Zarah remembered him as a softhearted boy overflowing with generosity and imagination, fond of animals, obedient, well mannered, girl-loving and having a certain way in handling them. Somewhere along the line, Chance had acquired an intellectual and physical hardness; it shone in the enamel of his teeth and rayed forth from a pair of particularly handsome brown eyes.

A part of Zarah—the Brattle Street part—had hoped that Chance would remain in the East, follow one of the professions, marry a Vincent Club girl—preferably rich—with an estate at Prides Crossing, a city house on Commonwealth Avenue. Chance's decision to become a distiller had not wholly pleased her. Whiskey-making seemed something of an anticlimax; Landmark would certainly impose limitations. But there were advantages. Zarah could see her boy every day. Compensation enough.

Nearly half of the people in the Somerset dining room held tickets for James K. Hackett's *Prisoner of Zenda*. Mr. Hackett's characterization seemed overromanticized to Zarah; yet because the affair had the flavor of a family party and because she was surrounded by Chance's young companions, Zarah found herself being escorted back to the Parker House by an escadrille of young men better looking and better bred than the members of Hackett's troupe. And now the young men were gathering around Anson, tempting him to visit a saloon.

"A saloon!" Zarah's eyebrows went up half an inch.

Chance explained. "Mother, the Esperanto Bar isn't an ordinary saloon. I've always wanted Father to see the place and meet its owner, Quilty Curnayne—a man who dispenses something more valuable than the stuff he sells. He's fabulous. It's just too bad that you're not a man tonight."

"I rest content. Your father seems eager to go. Bring him back at a reasonable hour."

Kisses, promises and guarantees of safe-conduct being exchanged, Anson and Chance, accompanied by some half dozen A.B.s soon-to-be, set out for the Esperanto Bar.

Quilty was his usual gentlemanly self, courteous, restrained, as he greeted the delegation. Chance introduced his father in a style befitting a son proud of his parent. Compliments were very much in order. Anson could truly say, "Mr. Curnayne, Chance has often spoken to me about your place—its perfections, atmosphere. My impression is that he failed to do it justice."

"Words seldom do justice to anything," Quilty replied. "I might tell you that you have a fine boy, Mr. Woodhull; it would be true, but only a small part of the truth." He made a collective wave of his hand at the young men in the Woodhull entourage. "This I can say: Harvard form doesn't permit them to test their capacity. Well, they're young yet. Give them ten or fifteen years and they'll be an asset, a decoration to any bar in the land."

He spoke directly to Anson. "Now, sir, what is your pleasure?"

"I've already had my quota for the evening," said Anson. "I understand, though, that your O.T.B. is well worth tasting. Serve it forth, if you will, to my guests."

"Not tonight, they're not," said Quilty. "The honor is mine. How could a Harvard Commencement commence at all, at all, unless it commenced in the Esperanto Bar?"

"Hear! Hear!" they cried.

Quilty poured drinks all around. They drank to *Veritas* and set down their glasses. Then Jimmy Stothart winked at Chance and the dipsy-doodle was in motion.

"Did I tell you, Father—" Chance spoke more audibly than was his custom—"that Quilty has been waiting thirty years for a man willing to cover his famous bet?"

"Another thirty I'll be waiting," said Quilty. He addressed his remarks to Anson. "It is my contention, sir, that only one man in a million would be willing to risk a hundred-dollar note in a bottless, fruitless, feckless, reckless attempt to identify the three jiggers of whiskey that I set before him."

"What do you mean by 'identify,' Mr. Curnayne?"

"I employ the term in its threefold sense." (To hear him, you'd think Quilty was speaking of the Trinity.) "*Primo*, he must name the type and quantity of cereal predominant in the mash. *Secundo*, he must estimate within a two-per-cent margin the alcoholic proof of the liquor. *Tertio*, I require the age of the liquor and the geographic location of the distillery that made it."

"One man in a million," mused Anson. "That's cutting it pretty fine. Assume that there are forty million males of drinking age in the United States. Am I to understand you as saying that only forty men in this country know what they're drinking?"

"That's not quite the drift of my meaning, sir. My statement ran: Not one man in a million would be willing to risk a hundred dollars to prove that he *knows* what he's drinking." Airy was the Curnayne. "I'm in no danger of losing my money."

Anson laid a century note on the bar. "To keep things perfectly clear, Mr. Curnayne, you should know that I am a distiller. Is your bet still open?"

Quilty covered Anson's money. The long-awaited contest was about to take place.

Quilty began by pouring three jiggers from three different bottles, concealing his motions under the bar. "Well, there they are, Mr. Woodhull. Take them in any order you choose."

Anson barely touched the first glass to his lips. "This is an excellent specimen of straight rye whiskey. It was made in Reading, Pennsylvania, bottled at one hundred and one proof." He sipped again. "Age: four years."

"To the whiskers!" cried Quilty, exhibiting the bottle from which the whiskey had been poured. "Reading Fancy is the brand name. Well, sir, you're a leg up on me."

Tasting the second jigger, Anson pondered in puzzlement, then sipped again. "H-mmm, the liquor in this glass is a typical bar whiskey of better-than-average quality. The man who concocted it took steps to guarantee flavor and fire power. In the process, he added a touch of beading oil. As to the exact proportions of the ingredients, I'd say—" Anson applied the calipers of exactitude—"I'd say that he mixed thirty-seven and one half per cent of a young Indiana bourbon, not more than eighteen months old, with sixty-two and one half per cent of ethyl alcohol—better known to the trade as 'neutral spirits.' We will refrain from mentioning the concocter's name."

"Ah, but you're the wizard one." Never the man to reveal a trade secret, Quilty failed to display the bottle of O.T.B. which he himself had made in his cellar.

Chance had never seen his father in this light: the deadshot connoisseur calling another man's tricks, giving them a habitation, a name and an age. He knew that Anson never drank except for experimental purposes. What a range of information he possessed concerning earths and the waters thereunder: cereals, chemistry, distillation, trade practice and tricks of the trade.

If only Johnno Normile could see this performance!

Still a third round to go. Depend on Quilty to set a difficult problem. The Esperanto Bar was hushed as Anson lifted the jigger and held the carnelian-colored liquor against the rays of a polished lamp reflector.

"By its ruby glow, this whiskey can have but one name." Authority, respect and a touch of envy were mingled in Anson's voice. He passed the jigger under his nostrils and inhaled deeply. "The aroma is a worthy companion to its color. What you have offered me, Mr. Curnayne, is a beautifully cured, fully ripened bourbon whiskey. Its name is Rosemere, the Queen of American bourbons. Only one man in the world could have made it—Mark Chadbourne. His distillery is in Nelson County, Kentucky, and he hoards every drop till it's eight years old."

"Winner by a knockout!" exclaimed Quilty. He gripped Anson's hand. "Mr. Woodhull, in all my experiences as a barkeep, I have never witnessed such an exhibition." He thrust the hundred-dollar bills toward Anson.

"I can't take your money, Mr. Curnayne. Suppose we make a joint contribution to some worthy cause."

The "worthy cause" was being debated when who should walk in but John the Incomparable, Forty-fourth Duke of Usquebaugh, Lord Lieutenant of the Parker House cab-rank.

"Johnno!" they cried. "Come join the circle. Too bad you missed the demonstration."

"I heard every word of it. Like a tobacco-store Indian I stood motionless in the shadows, betwitched with admiration at the unexampled virtuosity of this gentleman." He doffed his glossy hat to Anson. "I have but one question to ask: Would you permit an amateur to risk his money by identifying a fourth jigger of whiskey—the same to be produced by Prospero Curnayne?"

"I'm agreeable," said Anson.

Johnno peeled off ten gold bank notes. "Tenth Station. Our Lord is stripped of His clothing," he muttered. "Quilty, *a passado!*"

Thus challenged, the Esperanto barkeep performed a punto-reverso crisscross with Reynard-the-Fox ramifications. He removed a cork from a certain black bottle underneath the bar and was about to pour a jigger that would fix Johnno's wagon. But the Normile intercepted him. "A whiff of the stopple is all I need."

Quilty passed the cork under Johnno's nose, whereat the Duke of Usquebaugh reeled, regained his balance, and diagnosed, *viz.:* "This panther suffered from an enlarged prostate," said Johnno. "Seeking relief, he went to the well to make water but in his weakened condition fell among rectifiers. They catheterized him ninety-nine times, leaching each specimen through chloride of lime, then stored the stuff in an uncharred barrel, formerly used by Canadian fishermen in quest of hake, haddock and cod. One stave of that barrel was green spruce, hence the gummy residue; another stave was taken from an abandoned jakes in northern Alberta. After quick rectification it was offered to the public under the name of Parliament's Choice. Rejected by an outraged populace, it reappeared in paraffinated disguise as Whelk's Varnish Remover and All-Purpose Disinfectant." He offered the cork to Anson. "Will you test my findings, Doctor?"

Anson sniffed. "The money's yours, Johnno. How did you arrive at these conclusions?"

"By adhering to the law of mathematical progression."

"Could you demonstrate that?"

"With ease. On the abacus of my own ten fingers." Starting with his left thumb, Johnno began to climb the ladder of infinity. At each rung he paused to insert illustrative material. Thus:

"*One for the road.*" John the Incomparable, Duke of Usquebaugh, accepts stirrup cup from faithful retainer. Drinks same, and gallops off to the Hanging Assizes.

"*Two strikes.*" Johnno whiffs at roundhouse curve and glares mayhem at umpire.

"*Three balls.*" He enters pawnshop, offers watch, haggles, and departs murmuring anti-Semitisms.

"*Four, no more.*" Enacts temperate drinker, clean-living chap who can take it or leave it alone. "Thash all for tonight, boys. Little woman waiting at home, you know."

"*Five to go.*" Hits line for Harvard, demolishes entire Yale team, then kicks goal with cuspidor.

"*Six of one, half dozen of another.*" Johnno shrugs. "A hundred years from now we'll all be bald."

"*Seven?*" Which shall it be: the seven sorrowful mysteries or seven capital sins? Torn, Johnno contemplates the utterness of man's degradation, does a Veronica with his bandanna, and drowns sorrow with

"*Eight—make mine straight.*" Glances at label of bottle, grimaces. "This horse had diabetes."

"*Nine. Time to recline.*" Johnno leans like the Tower of Pisa, then falls onto sawdust-covered floor. He snores three times, and rises, glorious and immortal, at

"*Ten, begin again.*" Johnno lifts his own right hand and announces, "Winner and still champion."

Anson led the applause. Everyone but Quilty patted their palms together in the manner prescribed by Cardinal Richelieu: "*Surtout, pas de zèle.*"

Quilty tossed four one-hundred-dollar bills onto the bar. "Eschew the numerical, Johnno. Can you tick off in alphabetical order the names of twenty-six well-known whiskeys?"

"It'll pauperize you, but I can," said the Normile, "alpha to omega, and everything in between. Hold your watch on me, Mr. Woodhull. If I pause for more than two seconds, you and Quilty can share the money."

Anson pulled out his gold Elgin. "Ready . . . on your mark . . . *go!*"

At the signal, a cataract of names—humorous, colloquial and enigmatic—tumbled up from Johnno's voice box. "Ace High . . . Bottoms Up . . . Conquistador . . . Dealer's Choice . . . Ecce Homo . . . Fly in the Amber . . . Grampy's Favorite . . . Have Another . . . Idle Hour . . . Jacob's Ladder . . . King's Ransom . . . Long Rifle . . . Magnolia . . . None Such . . . Old

Pal . . . Prince Charming . . . Quaint Custom . . . *Requiescat in Pace* . . . Sweethearts Forever . . . Treasure Tit . . . Under the Rose . . . Vox Populi . . . Weathervane . . . XXX . . . Yours in the Bond . . . and Zaubermann's Fancy."

"Elapsed time, forty-one seconds," reported Anson. "A world's record for speed, Johnno."

"Speed is easy," said the Normile. "With the kind permission of this audience I shall now try for altitude." Stepping into the basket of his Celtic imagination, Johnno tossed a few sandbags over the side and went up flying. Scandian antithesis bore him aloft. Strike out that Norse allusion. Johnno was ascending in a Phaedrus chariot drawn by two horses. One of the horses was white, the other black. Skillfully he handled his contradictory steeds, giving free rein first to one, then the other. And from the zenith he called down to the earth-bound watchers below.

"Elixir and Opiate; Tonic and Pain-Killer; Running Riddle and Fluid Answer; Destroyer and Preserver; Universal Solvent and Mortal Stain; Setter-On of the Dream and Taker-Away of Performance; Joie de Vivre et Lachrymae Rerum; Symbol of the Ferment in This Valley of Fog, Mist and Tears; Phoenix of the Maize; Spiritus Frumenti; C_2H_5OH—Carbon, Oxygen and Hydrogen blended together in Aqueous Matrimony; Congeners Conjoined for Better or Worse (and who's to say?)." Johnno's voice rose in a triumphant paean. "I see it now: Nyanza falling from the Gates of Heaven, down Purgatorial Cliffs, seeping through Earth to make Lethe's Liniment—*Aqua Vitae, Uisque, Usquebaugh, Uisgebeatha, Water of Life*—WHISKEY!"

The Commencement procession next day was led jointly by Eliot, the Great Elector, now Emeritus, and A. Lawrence Lowell, the incoming President. Eliot's Valedictorian Address was duly printed in the Boston *Transcript;* but the greater stories—unprinted yet never to be forgotten—relate how Anson Woodhull demonstrated his peerless and respectful knowledge of a substance traditionally consumed by Americans in magnitudes approaching one hundred million gallons annually; and how Johnno Normile topped him in three sustained flights of fancy.

Harvard has had other presidents; the Esperanto Bar is no more. Quilty lies in Woburn Cemetery and Johnno drives an incorruptible booby through interstellar spaces. But the odd thing is, whiskey abides. It seems that Americans like to drink whiskey—even though only one man in a million knows what he's drinking and few have ever surpassed the Normile in celebrating its name.

PART FOUR

The
Rising
Gale

1.

EPITHALAMIUM

IN ITS BAREST FORM, marital union requires only a two-dollar license and a few words uttered by a Justice of the Peace. No explaining can explain, then, why so many nice girls, genuinely in love with attractive young men of their own station, should elect to undergo the ordeal of the "big wedding" with its tribal paraphernalia of dressmaker's fittings, bridesmaids, ushers, rehearsals, wedding breakfast and/or reception with the protracted agony attendant thereon.

Amy Towner didn't want that kind of a wedding. She would have married Chance Woodhull with a minimum of socio-legal machinery. But—apart from fixing the date (September 7, 1908)—she had little to say concerning the pomp and panoply surrounding her marriage. You see, it was a "county marriage" (which is probably the best reason for county government) attended by at least one tenth of Landmark's washed population.

Charles Towner, father of the bride, footed the bill. Wayland Towner, brother of the bride and a medical student at the University of Indiana, was Chance Woodhull's best man. Anson Woodhull, father of the bridegroom, gave the couple a title deed to a brand-new home on Echo Hill, the choicest and most recent suburb of Landmark. Charles and Solange Moerlein contributed a Stutz Bearcat, all wrapped up in white ribbon, together with a powder-blue check drawn to Amy Towner Woodhull in the amount of $1,000 and a sketchy road map indicating the location of Moerlein's hunting lodge in the Kentucky hill country.

Like a pair of mating robins, Amy and Chance disappeared into the forest.

Their first stop was halfway up an almost-mountain on the Kentucky bank of the Ohio. With his right hand Chance threw the bronze shifting lever into neutral. With his left he pulled the manual brake way back. The giant engine, still to be unhooded, was throbbing before them. Chance took Amy in his arms, scrutinized the unbelievably delicate and responsive face of his bride.

"Is all this mine?"

"All. More than you know. Always."

Virginal, breathlessly eager to become in fact as well as pledge the wife of the only man she had ever loved, Amy closed her eyes and took the first of those numberless kisses that punctuate the history of love.

They found Moerlein's hunting lodge early that evening.

Nothing that they said or did during the next ten days was different from what has been said or done by selected members of a privileged race. Only this: phantasies that once spilled over the gunwales of a red canoe became reality. Strength tested at sixteen by self-denial could be spent prodigally (now that Amy was nineteen and married) by the bull-priestess who, knowing nothing of the Cretan cult, was perfectly able to defend herself.

How does it happen that a hundred-and-twelve-pound girl with a twenty-inch waistline can subdue a wide-shouldered, six-foot, hundred-and-seventy-five-pound lover-husband at prime? Not only once, but every time they come together? This is one of love's mysteries. "Where the apple reddens, never pry."

Late in September they returned to the house on Echo Hill. The ritual of lifting Amy across the threshold of their new home was prolonged by a clinging of lips.

"Do I feel heavy, dear?"

"About as heavy as a snowflake. A good-sized grown-up *girl* snowflake—and to remove any hint of frigidity from the figure, about two hundred and thirteen degrees warmer."

"That's boiling."

"Well . . ." Chance set her down gently. "Simmer awhile till we look the place over."

What they found was a never-before-used house with a fieldstone fireplace in the living room; a kitchen filled with copper-bottomed kettles, cast-iron spiders; drawers cramful of knives, forks, spoons; and a lovely black stove, nickel trimmed. Then, of course, there was the big master bedroom where the master and his bride could celebrate the never-twice-the-same, habit-forming ritual that seemed to grow stronger all the time. Oh, yes, also a dining room. And, upstairs, two extra bedrooms for overnight guests.

Walking down a flight of cellar stairs, they saw a pair of built-in washtubs—the solid soapstone kind. Hard to imagine that bed linen, towels and articles of underclothing worn by two such perfect human beings would ever become soiled. But in case they did, there was a corrugated washboard, unwrapped cakes of yellow soap and bottles of bluing. Plenty of hot water—twenty gallons a minute—supplied by a coil arrangement attached to the huge coal-burning furnace with asbestos-covered ducts that carried heat to every room in the house.

"Everything is simply perfect." Amy twirled in ecstasy. "Who thought of all these things?"

"A couple of women named Alice Towner and Zarah Woodhull," said Chance. "Mothers just seem to know." He cupped Amy's heart breast. "But Nature so arranges things that they can't imagine."

"It would drive them crazy if they could."

Purple twilight was settling over the earth when Chance suggested that they test the echo that gave the hill its name.

"It lies right there," he said, pointing to a cleft in the woods, some fifty yards distant. "All you have to do is say something and it obligingly magnifies your voice."

"What shall I say?" asked Amy.

"Anything that occurs to you."

"The only thing that occurs to me is . . . you."

"Share me with the echo."

"I don't want to share you with anyone."

"You are turning out to be a very stubborn woman. Will you do me the honor of mentioning my name, in a tone slightly higher than a young wife uses in addressing her husband?"

Amy obliged. "Chance, darling" were the words she uttered.

Back they came—taking their time about—tremulous, vibrant, yearning, expectant, thrusting and eerie. *Chance, darling.*

"Did I say all that?" asked Amy.

"You did."

"It's your turn now."

Chance uttered his wife's name: *"Amy."*

Back came the echo: triumphant, possessive, masculine (oh, but dependent, too), loaded with secret overtones audible only in the voices of young lover-husbands. *Ai-mee.*

"Say," he added, "we'll have to be careful in using this thing. Other people might find out about us."

Amy agreed. "No one but ourselves must know."

Reporting for duty after his wedding trip, Chance found production seriously behind schedule. A noxious odor hung over the Old Landmark Distillery; no exhalation from a sick-room could be more loathsome.

Anson greeted his son affectionately. "Was it happy, Son?"

"Very happy, Father."

"I'm glad you're back. Two batches have gone sour on us, and I don't dare start another run until every pipe, fermenter and mash tub in the place has been inspected. The way Reb used to do it, before he went on the road. Just imagine that you're Reb Plaskett with a Harvard degree and a three-objective microscope. Will you do that, Chance?"

"I'll give it the old Plaskett try."

Like a diagnostician testing his patient for an unknown disease, Chance scraped specimens of mold from every aperture and container in the distillery. With a cotton swab at the end of a long wire, he went into a pipe knuckle; then, drawing the wire out, he placed the swab in a test tube, half filled with nutrient culture; labeled, corked and sealed it for future examination under his microscope.

Distilling operations were held up for three days while Chance collected specimens from the calcimined wooden fermenters and mash tubs. Chance placed smears of each specimen on sterile glass slides, then viewed them separately under the oil-immersion lens of his microscope. He discovered no disease organism until he came to a test tube marked "Pipe knuckle leading from Fermenter No. 1." Examining a smear of this material, he saw a terrible battle in progress on the glass slide. Rod-shaped bacilli, normal enough, were being consumed by armies of spiral-like organisms resembling minute boa constrictors. The dread spirochetes. Not the type that battens on human beings; rather, a distant cousin that thrives in cereal scum. Chance found these fatal organisms in three places. No wonder Old Landmark smelled sick!

The cure? Chance prescribed that the wooden converters be given new inner coats of formaldehyde. Within a week he banished the plague that had threatened his father's distillery. On October 7 he reported: "Production can begin again."

Anson's eyes and voice were grateful as he thanked the tall young lieutenant who was his son. How right Zarah had been about this boy, who could take an order, fulfill it and gain stature thereby. In the life of every father there comes a time when he values, *needs* a dependable subaltern. Anson, though still able to shoe a horse (or break one if need be), was frankly happy to lean a little on the special knowledge, fresh resourcefulness and good judgment of his son.

Chance had proved his worth in diagnosing and curing the malady that had attacked Old Landmark. Yet how much did he know about the graver illness that was threatening the whiskey industry itself? Because the proper study of fathers is their own children and because Anson wished his son and co-partner to be aware of the impending crisis in the whiskey business, he decided to give the boy a workout.

"Sit down, Chance. I'd like to bring you up to date on some of this typewritten correspondence and printed material concerning the Pure Food Law—particularly F.I.D. Sixty-Five. Ever hear of that?"

"No. What does it mean?"

"*F.I.D.* stands for 'Food Inspection Decision,' and Sixty-Five refers to one of George Washington Waley's decisions regarding adulterated whiskey."

With an incisiveness that Chance had never seen in any of his professors, Anson cut to the core of his subject. "By a proviso of the Pure Food Law, any manufacturer of food, drugs or whiskey whose goods are condemned by Dr. Waley as adulterated or misbranded, is permitted to carry an appeal to the Federal courts. It's a good proviso, in the best American tradition of checks and balances. Even an honest man like Waley, whose job is to enforce the Pure Food Law, might become dictatorial."

Anson filled his bo'sun pipe with home-grown Burley and lighted up. "Waley began tousling the rectifiers soon as the law went into effect. Boy, did he tousle them! T.R. grinned from ear to ear. And it seems that Waley also had the support of his departmental chief, the Secretary of Agriculture. I tell you, Chance, it made an honest distiller feel good all over to read Waley's ultimatum concerning the purity of whiskey."

Anson riffled through the papers on his desk. "Listen to

Waley reading the riot act to the rectifiers. 'By the authority vested in me under the Pure Food Law, I hereby declare that any mixture of neutral spirits and coloring matter shall be labeled *Imitation Whiskey.*'"

"Imitation whiskey! That must have made the rectifiers howl to high heaven."

"It did. The last time I saw Charlie Moerlein he told me that if Waley made F.I.D. Sixty-Five stick, it meant bankruptcy for the neutral-spirits crowd."

"Can Waley *make* it stick?" asked Chance.

"He's been going about it real businesslike. Sent his men into the field to collect evidence; analyzed the samples, and passed more than a dozen condemnatory judgments. He's got seven cases in the Federal courts right now. Here's a couple of typical cases."

Anson fished for his reading glasses and read:

Notice of Judgment. The United States of America. Libellant vs. 93 cases, containing 12 bottles each, of alleged Whiskey, C. Person's Sons, Defendants, before the Western District Court of New York, Case No. 79. Judge, the Hon. John R. Hazel.

This Whiskey was adjudged adulterated and misbranded and, under the law, the seized liquor was ordered to be destroyed or, after proper branding, delivered to the claimants under a bond of $2,000 that it would not be sold in contravention of the existing law. Date of judgment, August 27, 1908.

"A Daniel come to judgment!" exclaimed Chance.

Notice of Judgment. United States vs. 4 barrels of Liquid Purporting to be Whiskey. This case was brought in the District of Columbia, Case No. 790. The libel alleged that the product was colored and mixed by the addition of coloring matter, in a manner whereby its inferiority is concealed and in order to imitate old mature whiskey and whereby the said product does imitate and appear to be old mature whiskey.

"How's that strike you, boy?"

"It seems that the bamboozlers are getting it in the neck."

"So it seems." Anson puffed meditatively at his bo'sun. "But the sad truth is, they aren't! Their cases are on the docket, sure. I doubt if they'll ever come to trial."

"Why so liverish, Father William?"

"Glance at the headlines in today's Cincinnati *Courier;* then tell me how *you* feel."

Chance scanned the double-column streamer:

SECRETARY OF AGRICULTURE RESCINDS
FOOD INSPECTION DECISION 65

PLANS TO BRING NO FURTHER PUNITIVE
ACTION AGAINST RECTIFIERS

Chance laid aside the paper. "It puzzles me, Father. Why should Waley's own chief turn against him?"

Anson rose and gazed out of the window at his four warehouses loaded with honest whiskey mellowing in oaken casks. "I'm not a soothsayer and have no special information from Washington, so I'll put my suspicions in the form of a question." He turned to Chance. "Do you remember the parable of the Unjust Steward?"

"Vaguely. Wasn't he the fellow who went among his master's debtors and bade them to write down bills in their own favor?"

"That's the one. Now I don't know the Secretary of Agriculture, and maybe I'm doing him an injustice. But figure it out for yourself. Teddy's leaving office in a few months; his Cabinet goes with him. Now, mightn't it just be possible that one of these Cabinet members could be feathering a nest for himself in the Rectifiers' Lobby? I've seen ex-Cabinet members have a second coming as lobbyists with salaries ranging between fifty and one hundred thousand dollars. It's a routine step, and the present incumbent has made a good beginning by clamping a gag on our old friend Waley." Bitterness that Chance had never heard edged Anson's voice. "With Waley gagged, the Pure Food Law becomes a corpse. A two-year-old corpse. That baby never had a chance to grow up. It was strangled in its cradle."

"Exactly how does it affect us, Father?"

"If the Pure Food Law isn't enforced, Old Landmark will be back in the arena with lower-priced imitation whiskeys. But let's not hang crape on our sleeves yet. We've got a few shots left in our locker. . . . Ever hear of a fellow named Andrew Jackson Beane?"

"No. Is he one of Waley's men?"

"Not officially. This Andy Beane is an unreconstructed descendant of Old Hickory himself. I hired him as General Counsel for the Bonded Whiskey Institute." Anson listed Beane's qualifications: "The man knows whiskey; he's a bare-handed raccoon fighter in or out of court, and, last, he's a calendar-maker."

"A what?"

"Like I said, a calendar-maker. Prints them up six months ahead of time. Now, according to Beane's calendar, here's the schedule. Right after Election Day, the Bamboozlers will make strong representations to Washington, complaining that Waley's enforcement of the Pure Food Law is ruining their business. They'll ask for a hearing. Son, we'll receive a copy of their complaint a little after New Year's, 1909. Whereupon Andy Beane will write a letter to the Attorney General pointing out some home truths about due process of law. The Attorney General will fob the whole matter off onto an officer not mentioned in the Constitution—the Solicitor-General. We don't know his name yet because the incoming President hasn't appointed him."

Anson squinted past the 1908 calendar into the region of Things to Be. "Yep. Somewhere in these United States there's a man who'll be called in to referee a Fracas with a Foregone Conclusion. The firing will begin on or about April Fool's Day, 1909."

It all turned out just as Anson predicted. The rectifying crowd, groaning under the heft of Waley's hand, cried out to the new President, "Help! Save us!" Andrew Jackson Beane put the Attorney General on notice by pointing to seven cases yet to be adjudicated in the Federal courts. The incoming President . . . jovial chap, name of Taft, asked almost everyone for a definitive opinion. The Internal Revenue Department sighed, "No jurisdiction." The Attorney General, whose sworn duty is to advise the Executive arm, shied away in terror.

Whereat the President, not wishing to be annoyed by the hubbub outside his window, wrote a brief note to his Solicitor-General, the Honorable—yes, the Truly Honorable—Lewis Gifford.

DEAR GIFF:

Please look into this matter—some unfinished business from the last administration . . .

2.

WHAT IS WHISKEY?

THE HEARINGS

FEW WARDROBES WERE ever in such a curious state of imbalance as that of the Hon. Lewis Gifford, Solicitor-General of the United States. As of January 1, 1909, he owned fifteen pairs of striped trousers, twelve morning coats, eleven pearl-gray waistcoats, nine top hats, eight Homburgs, six Borsalino fedoras, five dinner jackets and four sets of tails. In his locker at the Burning Wood Tennis Club on the outskirts of Washington, D.C., he had ten pairs of white flannels, eight white cashmere sweaters and two dozen assorted tennis shoes. On summer weekends he wore a grommetless yachting cap, a Breton jersey and duck trousers while sailing on Chesapeake Bay. In autumn he alternated between a threadbare tweed shooting jacket with leather elbow pads and a marvelously woven Shetland with staghorn buttons. Corduroy pants and a two-thousand-dollar French shotgun completed his "Sunday-Hunter" attire while he ranged across his three-hundred-acre estate on the eastern shore of Maryland.

No one had ever caught Lewis Gifford wearing an ordinary sack suit. As Solicitor-General he had little occasion to wear such a plebeian garment. His official duties (not specifically mentioned in the Constitution) lay somewhere in the shadowy zone between Cabinet responsibility and Administration prominence—a zone perfectly suited to Lewis Gifford's private tastes, legal abilities and social preference. Groton and Harvard had given him inalienable rights to the best school ties: a correct and happy marriage to a Flagler had enabled him to purchase a desirable town house on Massachusetts Avenue. Fifteen years as legal adviser to various secretaries of state (with a four-year interregnum as Attorney-General of Maryland) had made him a knowledgeable spectator of the Washington scene—so knowledgeable, in fact, that William Howard Taft, scrutinizing the long list of eligibles for the Solicitor-Generalship, had said affably, "Giff's our man."

And so it happened that Lewis Gifford became, by presidential appointment, the second highest law officer in the United States. Every morning from Monday to Friday the Solicitor-General, attired in morning coat, pearl-gray waistcoat and jewelry to match, entered the gloomy portals of the Department of Justice Building, stepped into a birdcage elevator and was hydraulically hoisted at a speed of thirty feet a minute (the prevailing tempo of the age) to his offices on the third floor. He seldom spent more than three hours a day at his desk; no one expected a government official of Lewis Gifford's rank to wear out the sleeves of his coat, much less the fibers of his well-conditioned body and pleasant mind, in matters of routine detail. One's chief clerk did all that and quite competently, too.

After dictating six or seven letters and making a few high-level phone calls, the Solicitor-General lunched at the Cosmos Club. Then an afternoon of indoor tennis in the William Larned manner—considered stylish at the time—and so home for a nap. Afterward he would dress for dinner either at his own house or at the table of highly placed friends; in either case, Lewis Gifford's charm, wit and urbanity added flying buttresses to his fame as a conversationalist and dinner companion.

This highly civilized program was interrupted early in April 1909, when, riffling through his correspondence, he came across the following note written on White House stationery:

Dear Giff:
Please look into this matter—some unfinished business from the last administration. You will oblige me greatly by making the necessary arrangements for public hearings, etc., etc.

The note, initialed WHT, carried a postscript:

I enclose a copy of Executive Order 1061 which will bring you abreast of details and empower you to take whatever action seems necessary.

Reading the Executive Order, Lewis Gifford marveled briefly at its contents and implications. He then summoned his chief clerk, George Poyner, an alpaca-coated civil servant, and directed him to make all necessary arrangements for a Public Hearing on the manifestly absurd question "What is Whiskey?"

Poyner, a whiz-bang arranger, lost no time. Within twenty-four hours he laid a neatly typed agenda on the Solicitor-General's desk.

"For your guidance, sir," said Poyner, "I have listed the names of the principal witnesses and counsel for the contending parties. I have also taken the liberty of phrasing a letter of invitation to well-known members of the distilling industry."

"Excellent staff work, Poyner." The Solicitor-General glanced at the letter of invitation, initialed it and said, "Please expedite the typing and mailing of this letter to all interested parties."

By the end of the week George Poyner mailed out four hundred letters. One of them was addressed to Anson Woodhull, Landmark, Indiana.

Anson showed the letter to his son Chance. "A day or so behind Andy Beane's calendar. Not that it makes much difference. Zarah and Amy will love Mr. Lewis Gifford's note requesting the pleasure of their presence in Washington. It's been a hard winter and the girls deserve a party. Make reservations at the Willard, Son."

Chance made the reservations as directed. In his own mind he made another reservation: Would Amy, well along in pregnancy, be up to the strain and excitement of traveling? When he voiced this question to his wife, she threw her arms around him, laughed and exclaimed, "What an advantage, to have a son born in Washington. At the Willard, too! Why, it's barely a step to the White House. I'll do my very best to produce some Presidential timber for—" Amy peered into the future— "for 1960. Both parties will be needing a good candidate then."

The hearings began April 8, 1909 in the Committee Room adjoining the Solicitor-General's office, a narrow, high-ceilinged chamber combining the worst features of a squash court, Old Bailey and the hold of a ship. Its always dark interior was lighted by porthole windows and a huge crystal chandelier hanging like a stalactite from the ceiling. Down the center of the room ran a long oval table, and around this table—with the Damocletian chandelier suspended above their heads—sat the interested parties and their counsel.

Because the hearings were public, a small audience occupied the narrow balcony that clung like an eyelash to the east wall of the Committee Room. On a slightly raised dais at the north end of the chamber sat Lewis Gifford flanked by the lictor symbols of his authority—the American flag and the Department of Justice Seal. To his right, a witness chair; to his left, a linen-draped table on which some two hundred bottles of whiskey—presumably the exhibits in the case—had been arranged.

The time being 10:47 A.M., Lewis Gifford tapped the water pitcher on his desk with a brass-edged ruler and opened the meeting on a note of pleasant informality.

"Gentlemen, I think we are all familiar with the purpose of these proceedings. I take it that you are also conversant—more so, probably, than I—with the events leading to the issuance of this order. For the record, however, I propose to sketch briefly the causes that have brought us together.

"May I point out parenthetically that no one in this room is charged with any civil or criminal offense. This is an inquiry, not a trial. You have come here voluntarily at my invitation. No summons or subpoena has been served: witnesses will not be required to testify under oath. Although I shall preside, and may ask questions, I am neither judge nor prosecutor. My sole function is to elicit such information as you choose to give. Later, on the basis of information gathered here, I shall submit my recommendations to the President. It is unnecessary for me to add that I am in no sense *parti pris* to either side of this controversy. I come in to learn—and hope to leave instructed."

His exordium behind, Lewis Gifford plunged into the body of his remarks. "These hearings stem directly from the passage of the Pure Food and Drug Law enacted by the Congress in 1906. I shall not go into the provisions of that law except as it affects the labeling of a certain article entering interstate commerce—to wit, whiskey.

"On May fourteenth, nineteen hundred and eight, the Secretary of Agriculture issued a departmental decision ordering certain whiskey manufacturers to place prominently on their products the words *Imitation Whiskey* or *Compound*

Whiskey. Whereupon the makers of these whiskeys, having well-settled names in the trade, claimed that it was not the intention of Congress that such designations be made. They further claimed that their business, involving several hundred millions of capital, would be gravely damaged, possibly ruined, by such designations. They prayed that the order be rescinded. Straightway their plea for relief was met by a counter-petition from certain distillers of bonded whiskey who contended that they, and they alone, were entitled by law, and in fact, to label their goods as *whiskey*.

"In the light of these conflicting claims the President has ordered me to hear testimony on both sides of the question."

Conscious that he was making a longish speech, the Solicitor-General came to the heart of the matter. "May I direct your attention to three specific queries contained in the Executive Order 1061?"

I

What was the article called *whiskey* as known (1) to the manufacturers, (2) to the trade, (3) the consumers, at, and prior to, the date of the passage of the Pure Food Law?

II

What did the term *whiskey* include?

III

Was there included in the term *whiskey* any maximum or minimum of congeneric substances as necessary in order that distilled spirits should be properly designated *whiskey?*

"I must confess," said Lewis Gifford, "that on reading these questions for the first time I felt slightly bewildered. I had believed that the matter of "What is whiskey" had been well established by preceding generations of drinking men, and that the article commonly known as whiskey—bought, sold and consumed as whiskey—was . . . ah . . . indeed whiskey. [Laughter from audience.]

"I realize now, however, that the term *whiskey*, formerly regarded as part of the public domain, has become a disputed and immensely valuable piece of property. We must ask ourselves: Is any single group entitled to stake out an exclusive claim to this term and eject all other claimants as trespassers?

Has a hard-won and carefully cultivated field been invaded by late-comers with faulty or nonexistent claims to ownership? On the other hand, we must consider the possibility that economic hardship, injustice even, may result if a single group is allowed to monopolize the term *whiskey*.

"With these considerations in mind, gentlemen, I shall now impose silence on myself while learned counsel for each side presents his opening argument. It has been agreed that Mr. Polk Waram, counsel for Midwestern Distillers, shall speak first. . . . Mr. Waram."

Mr. Polk Waram, the ablest extant specimen of the genus corporation lawyer, arose and bowed with forensic courtesy to the chairman. Then, removing his gold pince-nez, he cast an eye of wintry displeasure at the half-filled balcony. Spectators? Most annoying! Mr. Waram's, regard for the public, or any splinter thereof, was low, *low*. A born Hamiltonian (with McKinley improvements), he had spent his life advising a corporate elite how best to milk and mulct, rule and overrule (constitutionally of course) that gullible, improvident, unwashed, be-damned and howling multitude—the public.

To Caesar's injunction "Divide and conquer," Mr. Waram had given the more modern reading "Combine and conquer." "Merge" was his watchword, "amalgamate" his motto. Polk Waram never claimed to be the inventor of the corporate engine, yet no one could deny that he had lifted it to juggernaut efficiency in the Supreme Court cases involving U.S. Metals, Inc., and, later, Consolidated Utilities. More recently he had provided the legal cement that bound thirty-five small distilleries into that huge monolith, Midwestern Distillers, the second largest producers of whiskey in the United States. And now, with thirty million gallons of whiskey pouring from Midwestern's stills every year, some Pure Food zealots were claiming that this vast gallonage wasn't whiskey at all!

For a fee of twenty-five thousand dollars, Mr. Waram proposed to put public interest in its properly subordinate place. He intended to show that Large Business, Inc., was concerned not so much with Pure Foodism as with a guaranteed return on its investment. Concerning the outcome of the present hearings he had no fear; he knew that the Time-Spirit was in his corner and that neither governmental decree nor popular opinion could halt the ever-widening combinations of plant and capital.

Overconfidence, however, was not likely to trip Polk

Waram. He never depended upon improvisation, and now, with his arguments carefully marshaled, he sounded the keynote of his case: "Mr. Solicitor-General: I find myself in agreement with your fair and penetrating statement of the problem before us. Both parties to this controversy are indeed seeking title to a piece of property. But in the interest of greater accuracy, I should like to change your metaphor of a 'carefully cultivated field' to that of a stream—or river perhaps—thronging with traffic. My clients do not claim title to *both* banks of that stream. We come here to establish our riparian rights, so to speak, to a single bank of that stream. We are content that the manufacturers of bonded whiskey should continue to sail their little boats on *their* side of the river if they will permit us to navigate our larger, more highly capitalized craft on *ours*.

"I bring up this matter of size—of big versus little—with no intent to scorn small independent distillers. But if volume of production constitutes a claim to the term *whiskey*, this hearing might adjourn without delay. A glance at the Internal Revenue figures for the preceding fiscal year discloses the fact that one hundred and two million gallons of an article made, sold and *taxed* as whiskey were produced in this country. Of that amount only nine million gallons—less than ten per cent—were straight whiskey. The remaining ninety-three million gallons were made by distillers who, under existing regulations, are being asked to label their product 'Imitation Whiskey.'"

Polk Waram waved the Internal Revenue Report like a banner of righteousness and went on: "This report reveals much that is germane to the issue before us. It reveals, for instance, that an overwhelming majority of the American people have rejected straight whiskey as the beverage of choice—a rejection, I may add, that has become increasingly marked during the past three decades. Many conclusions may be drawn therefrom; but the one conclusion that *cannot possibly be drawn* is that a product so widely in demand, so eagerly and repeatedly purchased in a free market, should be labeled an 'imitation' of anything else."

With forensic intent, Mr. Waram polished the lenses of his pince-nez. "The makers of straight whiskey will contend that their product alone can be called whiskey. It was always an audacious contention, confined to a few distillers in Kentucky. For many years it was a preposterous contention, unsupported by public demand and acceptance. But the passage of the Pure Food Law has put a seeming lever in the hands of these hitherto impotent men. They propose now to regulate themselves *into* prosperity, and their competitors—my clients—*out* of prosperity by denying the name *whiskey* to an alcoholic beverage that has proved entirely satisfactory to the vast bulk of the drinking population for the past thirty years."

Full pause. Modulation of voice to oracular level. "I venture to predict, Mr. Solicitor, that the whipping boy of this hearing will be a substance long and honorably known to the trade as 'neutral spirits.' My clients will be charged with the high crime of using this substance as the chief element in their whiskeys. To expose the falsity of this charge, I shall now attempt to set the matter in its true light and proper perspective."

Polk Waram was lucidity itself as he began his exposition. "Prior to eighteen seventy-five all whiskey was made by the pot-still method. Now it must be admitted that the pot still was a useful vessel—as serviceable and picturesque as the spinning wheel or covered wagon. Yet even the *best* whiskey made by this method was a coarse, rough-charactered liquor loaded with undesirable ingredients, then known as fusel oil. Old-time distillers knew nothing of chemistry. They merely knew that their whiskey had a rank odor and a nauseating taste, which they tried to remove or disguise by various clumsy expedients, such as leaching through charcoal. We should still be drinking these coarse, unpalatable whiskeys if, in the mid-seventies, science had not discovered the patent still. This remarkable invention made it possible to strip out the undesirable odor and taste of new whiskey and produce a virtually pure ethyl alcohol now known as neutral spirits. Thus, at a single bound, whiskey-making was lifted from a hit-or-miss operation to an exact science.

"Neutral spirits, made from the same cereal used by the old-type distiller, is ethyl alcohol wholly cleansed of the undesirable elements that plagued and tainted the pot-still product. Neutral spirits has no objectionable taste or odor. None whatsoever. And it is this perfected method of producing ethyl alcohol—the conceded base of *all* whiskey—that disturbs our pot-still friends."

Waram concluded his argument. "If, through stubbornness, they wish to ply their archaic craft on their side of the river, they are certain to suffer economic extinction. Meanwhile, we must not permit their dying gasps to divert our attention from the fact that scientific progress and popular demand—operative for thirty years, and still advancing—have given us a clear title to the term *whiskey*. Which, if I interpret the President's meaning correctly, is all that need be demonstrated."

Having hitched his case to the irreversible engines of Progress and Popularity, Polk Waram sat down.

Now arose Andrew Jackson Beane, Counsel for the straight-whiskey distillers. It suited Andy Beane at this moment to underscore the differences between Polk Waram and himself. Beane had never worn a frock coat or pleaded before the Supreme Court. Other lawyers might be better acquainted with the intricacies of corporate organization, but no one could match Beane's knowledge of common men and classic whiskey. As a barefoot boy in Tennessee, he had felt the viscous *sqush* of a sour-mash foreshot oozing between his toes. As his name suggested, he was a collateral descendant of Andrew Jackson and had inherited some of his ancestor's hatred of vested capital—*vested* meaning a silk-faced garment worn by the paunchy figures of Opper's cartoons.

In addressing Tennessee juries, Andy Beane liked to punctuate an argument by snapping his galluses with a large thumb. He was shrewd enough to know, however, that mere rusticity would not serve him in the present instance; yet as he began speaking, he retained the diction of a strayed homespun set down in the midst of urban sharpsters.

"Heard lawyers all my life set out to prove that the worst was the best. But never heard a lawyer claim that the best was the worst—that is, till counsel Waram got through telling us that neutral spirits ought to be called whiskey. Everyone knows that whiskey's a low-down thing reeking with fusel oil—congeners—like the President says. Neutral spirits, according to friend Waram, is the uncorrupted essence of the corn. Pure as a raindrop, dewier than dew. Seems to me that if neutral spirits is the wonderful stuff he says, more people ought to know its right name. 'Stead of that, learned counsel wants it to be advertised, labeled and sold as whiskey. Beats me why owners of a fine dog want to give it such a bad name."

Andy Beane, pondering this strange injustice, tried to think up possible reasons for it. "Can't be the makers of neutral spirits want to indooce trade. No, majority of drinkers don't like whiskey. Reject it ten to one. The people's choice is neutral spirits. Such being the fact, why doesn't high-priced counsel advise his clients to sell neutral spirits under its own name?"

Beane dropped the mask of irony and became the expositor of fact. "Mr. Solicitor, the grievous complaint we make is this: Deception and fraud are being practiced on the public by a few who claim that long usage entitles them to continue this fraud. If they were making spurious dollar bills, they'd be prosecuted as counterfeiters. In their defense they might claim that counterfeiting, too, has been practiced for a long time. But in my opinion—and the opinion of the U.S. Treasury—long and successful counterfeiting does not establish the right to continue criminal activity.

"May I pause a moment here to scrutinize the nature and origin of this remarkable stuff called 'neutral spirits'? What is it? The very name signifies its character. It has neither taste, smell, nor color. Its chief virtues are the cheapness and speed with which it can be produced. It can be made overnight. It can be made of anything—molasses, beets, watermelon, even sawdust. Not even the keenest chemical analysis can detect *what* it is made of. It can be made from moldy, rotten, mildewed or otherwise inferior grain; and these facts, too, will escape chemical analysis. Its approximate cost is less than ten cents a gallon. Yet this cheap, characterless product, diluted with water and artificially colored, is palmed off on the consumer as whiskey. Talk about counterfeiting!"

Beane snapped both galluses and went on: "The purpose of the Pure Food Law was to abolish such deceit. We shall introduce evidence to prove that the neutral spirits crowd—adulterators, false labelers—are engaged in systematic and highly profitable misrepresentations of their products at the expense of the makers of legitimate whiskey."

The Tennessee gallus-snapper vanished and in his place an indignant advocate was making a reasonable demand. "We do not ask for the confiscation or embarrassment of any business. We are content to sail our little boats on our side of the river if we can be assured that heavily armed raiders won't pirate our best asset—the proud name *whiskey*. We ask, in short, that any compound of neutral spirits and coloring matter be plainly marked for *what it is!*"

As Andy Beane sat down, no one in the room, including the Solicitor-General, doubted that Polk Waram would earn his fee the hard way. But not even the Solicitor-General, suggesting a recess for lunch, dreamed that the way would be so hard, so slow or so long.

Some intimation that the hearings would proceed at a dragging tempo was given by Polk Waram's first witness, Prof. Fergus McKittrick, a fierce Scots pedant afflicted with complete recall. The direct questioning, led by Mr. Waram, began with the usual preliminaries.

"What is your name and occupation?"

"My name is Fergus McKittrick—A.B., Edinburgh; M.A., Glasgow; Ph.D., University of London. I hold the title of Professor of Anthropology in the latter institution and am presently delivering the Adamson lectures at the University of Louisville."

"You say, Professor McKittrick, that you are a professor of anthropology. Of what does that science treat?"

"Anthropology is the science of man in general, with particular emphasis on human customs and social practices throughout the ages."

"Have your researches shown that these social practices include the consumption of alcoholic liquors?"

"Indisputably. From earliest times man has always used alcohol, either fermented or distilled, making it from such materials as were readily available. Communal drinking is the invariable accompaniment of primitive fertility rites and religious ceremonies. The Ubangi—"

Waram held up a curbing hand. "We shall come to the Ubangi later, Professor. Have you written on the subject of alcoholic beverages?"

"Extensively. My articles have appeared in *Lancet, The Anthropological Review, The Hibbert Journal,* to mention but three. I am, moreover, the author of innumerable pamphlets and brochures as well as a contributor to the Encyclopaedia Brit—"

"You have also published books, Professor?"

"I have." Fergus McKittrick held up a thickish tome. "This is my chief work, entitled *The History of Inebriating Liquors from Remote Antiquity to the Present Time.* It is substitled *A Philosophic and Scientific Treatise on the Use of Alcoholic Liquors by Egyptians, Greeks, Romans, Persians, Hollanders, Gaels, Celts, Scots and Skands; with Exploratory Excursions into the Lesser Antilles, Outer Hebrides and Colonial America."*

Lewis Gifford entered a dry demurrer. "This is all very edifying, Mr. Waram. But to expedite matters, may we not confine these hearings to a period somewhat later than . . . ah . . . the fall of the Roman empire?"

Polk Waram's pince-nez came off his high-bridge nose. "We deem it necessary, Mr. Solicitor, to show that distillation is a universal practice, with many varied methods and end products. Our intention is to demonstrate that no single group of persons enjoys, or has ever enjoyed, a monopoly on these practices."

Lewis Gifford nodded. "I have no desire, Mr. Waram, to prune away your privilege of introducing testimony that seems essential to you. You may proceed."

"Thank you, Mr. Solicitor. Now, Professor McKittrick, regretfully skipping your exhaustive chapters on *Brewed and Fermented Liquors*, will you turn to the section that treats of whiskey? Could you tell us something about the origin of this term?"

"Etymologically, orthographically or phonetically?"

"Mm-m . . . as you choose."

Fergus McKittrick submerged himself in the erudite pages of his *History*. "I find a passage in my Preface that rather happily conjoins the derivation and variant spellings of the word *whiskey*. I read:

> "The Latin epithet *aqua vitae*, the Gaelic term *uisge-beatha* (latterly spelled *usquebaugh*) and the modern word *whiskey* are, in point of fact, synonymous. *Aqua vitae* and *usquebaugh* (sometimes written *iskebaghah* or *isquebeoh*) stem from a common root. Since *isque* or *iske* means water, it appears evident that the word *whiskey* is only a slight alteration of the Gaelic form."

The Professor turned a page and continued:

> "The origin of the term *aqua vitae* as applied to exhilarating liquors is, on the basis of reasoning already advanced, not difficult to determine. Water, in the opinion of the ancient philosophers, constituted the basis of all matter; and Moses having written that the 'spirit of God moved upon the face of the waters,' it was inferred that a

living or prolific principle was thereby communicated. Hence the early Persians considered water the source of all bodies (*aqua omnia*) and the Koran states that 'God made every living thing of water'—a view shared by the Greek philosopher Thales. May not, therefore, the appellation *aqua vitae*, or 'water of life,' have been derived from the prevalent opinion that whiskey was adjudged to possess so many renovating and revivifying virtues?"

Rhetorical questions require no answer, and Fergus McKittrick was about to plunge forward when a hissing sound—low and ominous—startled the hearing. The hiss might have been caused by steam escaping from a radiator valve. Yet something about the sound (quite apart from its origin in the gallery) gave it the don't-tread-on-me quality of an angry snake. Since snakes were not ordinarily found in the Department of Justice Building, the Solicitor-General assumed that the hiss had come from human lips. Lifting his well-bred voice, he said, "Our guests and visitors will please observe the laws of courtesy by refraining from audible expressions of approval or disapproval. Counsel may resume his direct examination."

Waram's next question skillfully condensed McKittrick's previous testimony. "Then, in your opinion, Professor, the term *whiskey* is of extremely ancient origin and was probably brought to America by immigrants of Scotch or Irish origin?"

"No other view is tenable, sir."

"Now, in the course of your researches, did you find any single formula for making this alcoholic beverage traditionally known as usquebaugh, and in America as whiskey?"

"Many such formulas exist."

"Will you read us one?"

Professor McKittrick thumbed through his book. "I read from page two hundred and three: *Usquebaugh*—A Recipe for Making: Kentucky 1835. Eleven gallons grain spirit. Cloves, 2 ounces. Cinnamon, 2 ounces. Aniseed, 4 ounces. Caraway and coriander seed, each a quarter of a pound. Licorice, half a pound. Six pounds of sugar. Saffron, 2 ounces."

Polk Waram sharpened his point. "Why was the saffron used?"

"To give the beverage a light amber color. There's an old Irish saying: 'He's been sleeping in a sack of saffron.' Meaning, of course, that the person referred to was inebriated, or at least—"

"Y'mm . . . Very interesting. And why were these other spices and flavorings added?"

"To drown out the rank, nauseating character of the new spirits."

"Was it a general custom among early American whiskey-makers to color and flavor their product?"

"It was a widely practiced custom. They called it 'dulcifying.' Brown sugar, various sirups, peach juice, sherry and other ingredients were frequently used by early American distillers to make their whiskey palatable."

"Are any of these ingredients harmful to the human system?"

"I am not a physician, sir. In my opinion they seem quite innocent and harmless."

"One more question, Professor. Was it the custom among these early distillers to age their product for long periods in casks or barrels?"

"My researches show that they *put* it into barrels, but I have uncovered no evidence to show that it remained there very long."

Waram waited for the laughter to subside. "To summarize your testimony, Professor McKittrick, would it be fair to say that distillation is an ancient practice; that usquebaugh and its modern equivalent, whiskey, have been made with a variety of formulas; that in the past it has been flavored and colored by harmless ingredients; and, finally, that aging was not considered essential?"

"Yes, I think that is a fair summation, completely in accord with the facts." —

Polk Waram turned triumphantly to the Solicitor-General. "I have no further questions, sir."

Neither Lewis Gifford nor anyone else in the room expected Andy Beane to challenge the academic Scotsman; cross-examining such a witness would be like putting one's foot into a bear trap. The hearings were still in the skirmish stage, and Beane might well elect to lose the first round.

The Solicitor-General made a courteous gesture: "Mr. Beane, do you wish to exercise your privilege of cross-examination?"

The lanky Tennessean seemed not at all eager to tangle with the pedantic Scot. He was about to say, "No questions," when, on second thought, he decided to hazard a shot or two. Rural foot foremost, he gave the impression of a man scarcely knowing how to begin.

"Guess I owe you an apology, Professor, for not having read your history. A good deal of hard work must have gone into writing such a scholarly work."

McKittrick took his due complacently. "That is quite true. I spent ten years collecting the material and five more preparing it for publication."

"Don't doubt it. By the way, Professor, when and where was your book published?"

"As the title page indicates, it was brought out by the Royal Anthropological Press, London, nineteen hundred and five."

"Well, well, nineteen hundred and five. Rather an opportune time, wouldn't you say?"

"Opportune?" McKittrick bristled. "The force of your locution escapes me, sir. . . . Why should nineteen hundred and five be more opportune than any other year?"

Beane dropped his country-cousin mask. "You're the expert here, Professor. We'll come to the matter of opportunism later. For the present I'd like to ask you about this Royal Anthropo-something-or-other Press. Is it a commercial publishing house?"

"No, the press is a subsidiary of the Anthropological Society, which, like any other scientific institution, is supported by membership fees, as well as by grants and subsidies from various sources."

"Now, Professor, who was President of the Royal Anthropological Society between the years nineteen hundred and nineteen hundred and four?"

"I had that honor."

"And during this period was the society also honored by having on its board of directors the noble Lord Dissart? As a matter of fact, wasn't this distinguished nobleman the chairman of your board?"

"Yes, I believe he was."

"Is Lord Dissart an anthropologist?"

McKittrick inserted a bony forefinger between his collar and Adam's apple. "No, Lord Dissart is an eminently successful businessman to whom I—the society, that is—appealed for advice in straightening out our rather complicated financial affairs. We scientists, you know . . . " The Professor's smile displayed a set of abominably ill-fitting dentures.

"I quite understand. Now, Professor, in what line of business has this nobleman won particular distinction? Is he by any chance the same Lord Dissart who produces the world-famous White Unicorn Scotch whiskey?"

Waram was on his feet with an objection. "I see no point, Mr. Solicitor, in traversing the highways and byways of British nobility in an attempt to discredit this witness. What is the purpose of Mr. Beane's excursion?"

Andy Beane seemed to be enjoying himself. "Mr. Waram will discover the purpose of my excursion when we leave the highways and get into the byways of Lord Dissart's connection with this supposedly scientific *History of Inebriating Liquors.*"

"You cannot prove any such connection," thundered Waram.

"No? I've already proved that you get jumpety as a treed coon when Lord Dissart's name is mentioned." Andy Beane turned to McKittrick. "Professor, how far had you progressed with your history when Lord Dissart became chairman of the Anthropological Society?"

"My manuscript was nearly completed."

"Now I put it to you, Professor. At some period, say around nineteen hundred and three or four, didn't you show the manuscript of your history to Lord Dissart? I don't say it was dishonorable. But you showed it to him. And didn't Lord Dissart subsidize, finance or otherwise defray the costs of publishing your book?"

McKittrick's dignity as a scholar asserted itself. "I would prefer to say that Lord Dissart made a generous contribution to the furtherance of scientific knowledge."

Beane grinned. "I'll be content with that answer. Now we come to the question 'To what *special* use did this noble Briton put your so-called work of science?' Of course, I understand it was distributed among libraries and institutions of higher learning. But, isn't it true, McKittrick, that Lord Dissart used you *and* your book as tools in his successful scheme to monopolize the British whiskey trade?"

The Solicitor-General, perplexed by the direction of Beane's cross-examination, interposed a question. "Will the learned counselor enlighten us as to the facts underlying this alleged 'scheme' of Lord Dissart's?"

"Be glad to, sir. For many years prior to nineteen hundred and five, the English whiskey trade was in a state of mounting tension—closely resembling the turmoil that now exists in our own country. Small, independent makers of straight malt whiskey were being forced to the wall by a cartel known as Distillers, Limited. This cartel, with Lord Dissart as its presiding genius, had flooded the market—domestic and foreign —with compounds of neutral spirits, artificially colored or flavored with small amounts of straight Scotch whiskey. The conflict came to a head in a law suit brought against Lord Dissart's syndicate by a group of independent distillers. A Royal Commission was appointed—" Andrew Beane shot a long finger at Professor McKittrick—"and this man was the chief scientific witness for the Dissart group."

The Solicitor-General asked the witness a simple question: "Is this true, Professor?"

"It is true that I did testify. I think, however, that Mr. Beane places undue emphasis on the value of my testimony."

"Undue emphasis, eh?" Andy Beane produced a newspaper. "I hold in my hand a copy of the London *Times* dated May second, nineteen hundred and five. I read from the report:

"Lord Justice R. B. Fulham, presiding over the Royal Commission on Whiskey Manufacture, and his colleagues appeared to be deeply impressed by the testimony of Professor McKittrick. Reading from his recently published *History of Inebriating Liquors*, he established that the terms *usquebaugh* and *whiskey* have a common root, that distilling practices vary widely . . ."

Mr. Polk Waram slapped the counsel table with the flat of his hand. "I move, Mr. Solicitor-General, that the preceding remarks be stricken from the record as incompetent, immaterial and irrelevant. The United States is not bound by the decision of a British court, nor are we concerned here with the practices of English distillers."

Andy Beane slapped, not the table, but his thigh. Laughter convulsed him. "I agree with the statements just made by learned counsel," said Beane. "The United States is *not* bound by the decision of a British court. Nor are *we*—" Beane included the entire audience in a sweep of his long arm— "concerned with the practices of British distillers. But you—"

the lanky Tennessean gazed straight at Waram—"*You are!*"

A tumult of voices rattled the crystal chandelier. The Solicitor-General waited for Waram's retort. It came splutteringly from dark-cherry jowls.

"I protest against these diversionary and malicious tactics," said Waram. "It is a matter of common knowledge that I number among my clients Distillers, Limited, of England. I am exceedingly proud of my professional connections with Lord Dissart and his associates—"

"Are you equally proud," asked Beane, "of tempting Fergus McKittrick to these shores and into these hearings, by offering him the Adamson Fellowship at the University of Louisville?" There was a mean backlash to Andy Beane's query.

Waram took the lash unflinchingly. "Professor McKittrick would add distinction to any institution of learning."

In a stand-off between Waram and Beane, the session ended. Lewis Gifford tapped his water pitcher with the brass-edged ruler and made faint sounds resembling "The meeting is adjourned."

Next morning, the hearings opened on a quieter note with the testimony of Charles Moerlein, president of Midwestern Distillers. At sixty, Moerlein was several times a millionaire; but fate in the form of diabetes—a then incurable disease—had wasted his once-robust frame. As he took the witness chair, he smiled up at Solange in the gallery and received an encouraging little wave from her lace handkerchief.

Polk Waram began direct examination with the deference due a distinguished witness.

"Mr. Moerlein, how long have you been in the whiskey business?"

"More than forty-five years."

"You are president, I believe, of Midwestern Distillers?"

"I am."

"Can you give us some idea of the size and scope of your organization?"

"Midwestern Distillers and its subsidiary companies are the second largest makers of whiskey in the United States. Last year our gross sales amounted to sixty million dollars. On which we paid seven million in Federal taxes."

"Now, Mr. Moerlein, do you recognize among the exhibits on the table here any of your products?"

"Yes, I see bottles of Old Settler and Champion."

"I call your attention, Mr. Moerlein, to this bottle of Old Settler. Could you, without revealing any trade secrets, tell us what it contains?"

"No trade secrets are involved. Old Settler is composed of eighty-five per cent neutral spirits blended with fifteen per cent straight whiskey."

Interruption from Andrew Beane. "I object to Mr. Moerlein's use of the word *blend*. A blend is a mixture of *like* substances. Old Settler is a mingling of *unlike* substances—namely, neutral spirits and whiskey—and should therefore be referred to as a 'mixture.'"

SOLICITOR-GENERAL: "No one has yet proved that neutral spirits and whiskey are *unlike* substances, Mr. Beane. If you wish, you may bring the matter up in your cross-examination. Proceed, Mr. Waram."

WARAM: "Now, Mr. Moerlein, when a wholesaler orders a case or carload of Old Settler from you, how is it invoiced?"

"As whiskey."

"And when the retailer sells it to the ultimate consumer, what is it sold as?"

"Whiskey."

"How long has Old Settler been on the market?"

"For thirty-one years."

"And during all that time no one has ever objected to its being called whiskey?"

"No one. That is, not until the recent agitation."

"Would your business be adversely affected if you were obliged to label Old Settler as 'Imitation Whiskey'?"

"We'd be ruined. That is why we petitioned the President for a hearing on this matter."

"Do you feel that you are deceiving the consumer when you label Old Settler as whiskey?"

"I never knowingly deceived anyone in my life. In labeling Old Settler as whiskey, I merely followed a well-established tradition."

"I quite believe it, Mr. Moerlein. Now, I call your attention to this bottle of colorless liquid labeled Champion Whiskey. What are its ingredients?"

"Champion is a mixture of neutral spirits and distilled water. No flavoring or coloring matter have been added. It is called white whiskey and it is very popular in some parts of the country."

Lewis Gifford interrupted with a question. "I am somewhat

puzzled by the term *white whiskey*, Mr. Moerlein. In what respects does it differ from the beverage that many of my southern friends refer to as White Lightning. White Mule or, when they wish to be especially facetious, Skull-Popper?"

Moerlein smiled at the naïveté of the question. "Why, there is all the difference in the world, sir. White Lightning, or Skull-Popper, is a new, brutal corn whiskey made in a pot still. Its smell and taste would nullify the odor of a pigsty at a hundred yards. But Champion Whiskey, being pure neutral spirits cleansed of all congeners, is utterly free of these objectionable qualities. Chemically, Champion Whiskey is the purest drink on the market."

"You make it all sound rather antiseptic, Mr. Moerlein," said Gifford. "I have no further questions."

Polk Waram summed up in his best Q.E.D. manner. "I believe we have demonstrated, Mr. Solicitor-General, that both of the alcoholic beverages produced by Midwestern Distillers have been known to the trade and to the public as whiskey for the past thirty years—a sufficient length of time, you will agree, to establish their right to be called whiskey, which is all that the President has asked us to do."

It was Andy Beane's turn to cross-examine. He began with a compliment to the witness. "You've been mighty frank on some points, Mr. Moerlein. I like to work with a man who has nothing to hide and no disposition to hide it. Now, to go back a little. When you were describing that mountaineer drink called White Lightning or Skull-Popper you used the word *new*. It sure is new—you were right about that." Beane picked up a bottle of Old Settler. "I suppose this stuff is aged?"

"There is no need for aging it. When neutral spirits come from the still, they're as pure as they'll ever be. No curing process is necessary."

"Hm—m. Then it's possible to distill Old Settler on Tuesday and sell it on Wednesday?"

"Theoretically, yes."

"This quick turnover gives you quite an advantage—financially, that is—over the distiller who ages his whiskey four years or more?"

"Such savings are passed along to the consumer in the form of reduced prices. That's the modern notion on which our business is founded."

"Oh, it's modern enough. No one can say that your manu-

facturing and merchandising methods aren't right up to date.
New as a pin. Such being the case, why don't you rebaptize
this bottle of whiskey and call it *New* Settler? Just to keep
abreast of the times, I mean."

Waram interposed. "This line of questioning is ridiculous,
Mr. Solicitor. It invades the maker's right of naming his product as he pleases. The maker of the Speedwell automobile
and the proprietor of the Up-to-Date Department Store are
permitted to exercise their imagination in choosing whatever
names appeal to them."

Andy Beane liked the ground chosen by his opponent.
"Counselor Waram's hit the nail right on the head. In every
other line of business, the manufacturer tries to give the impression that his product is something new and improved—
just a little bit ahead of everything else in that field. But Mr.
Moerlein does just the opposite. He wants to give the impression, one way or another, that his whiskey is as old as
the hills. He and his associates call their product Charter
Oak, Ancient Tubbe, Old Settler and so on. How does the
witness explain this passion for antiquity in a brand-new
product?"

"I offer no explanation other than the one suggested by Mr.
Waram. I have the right to call my product anything I
choose."

"But you said back there that you had never deceived anyone in your whole life. Aren't you deceiving the consumer
when you imply that this new-born whiskey of yours is as old
as Plymouth Rock? Aren't you trading on a belief, long established in the public mind, that whiskey should be an aged
and venerable thing?"

"I am not called upon to read the public mind," said Moerlein wearily.

"Well, then, let's leave the public out of it. They've been
left out so long it won't make any difference here. Suppose
now that I address you not as the president of Midwestern
Distillers but as one man to another. Let us suppose further
that a dear friend of yours visits you at your home. Your
friend is a man of educated taste, someone whose knowledge
of whiskey matches your own. From which of these bottles,
Old Settler, or Champion, would you pour him a token glass
of hospitality?"

Waram sprang to his client's defense. "I fail to see the
relevancy of this question, Mr. Solicitor. The President's di-

rective asks, 'How was the term *whiskey* understood by the trade and the public?' There is no suggestion that we go into the matter of what one man serves another in the privacy of his home."

SOLICITOR-GENERAL: "The point is well taken. Mr. Beane, could you possibly manage to rephrase your question?"

"Be glad to. Mr. Moerlein, I see an old friend of yours, Mr. Anson Woodhull, sitting in this room. Mr. Woodhull is a member of the whiskey trade. I guess that qualifies him. Now, which of these two whiskeys would you offer him if he came to visit you?"

"In deference to Mr. Woodhull, I might offer him some of his own excellent whiskey—Old Landmark."

"That's all I wanted to know. When it comes to selling whiskey to an ignorant public, you unhesitatingly offer them Old Settler or Champion. But wouldn't a blush of embarrassment rise to your cheek if you offered Mr. Woodhull any of these unaged, adulterated *imitations* of the genuine article?"

A blush of embarrassment?

An undertow of weariness laid bare the reef of compromise that underlay Charles Moerlein's life. Beane's question recalled his first meeting with Anson Woodhull on a day of snow. Together they had entered Anson's cellar, shared the delight of finding each other across the rim of a Mason jar half filled with a ruby liquor. They had savored its rarity, agreeing that time and care alone could ripen a noble whiskey. Anson had gone on making an honest product, kept his austere integrity. But what had happened to Charles Moerlein, who, knowing the better way, had consciously elected the cheaper, quicker path to fortune?

What indeed? Where now was that earlier sense of exaltation and personal responsibility that he had once known? Charles Moerlein, sitting in the witness chair, would have been grateful now for a tingling flush of blood to his once-florid cheek. But even his blood had become gray and his tired heart could scarcely keep it flowing to his brain.

Still, he must answer his inquisitor. In a low, feelingless voice Moerlein said, "Nothing in the President's directive requires me to blush, Mr. Beane. If you will excuse me, I have lost the power to blush at anything."

Day after day the testimony poured in. Much of it was

irrelevant, repetitious—and downright contradictory. On every important point experts clashed and doctors differed; scientists knew nothing about practical distillation and distillers knew less about chemistry. A fog of confusion hovered over the hearings. The definition of whiskey varied with the definer. Apparently there were a thousand different formulas for making it and an infinite number of variations at every step in its making. Even the orthography varied. British and Canadian distillers spelled it *whisky;* American custom preferred to add an *e*.

For the next week Lewis Gifford did some strenuous homework on the transcript of the testimony. The technical aspects of the problem were puzzling enough, but even more baffling was the apparently simple question "What did the trade and public think whiskey to be?" According to Socrates, if you wanted information about saddles, you went to a saddlemaker. Alas for the Socratic method! It just didn't work when applied to whiskey-making. Regard, for instance, the stenographic transcript of Mr. William Hines, a wholesale liquor dealer in Rochester, New York. Mr. Hines had been interrogated by the Solicitor-General himself, and here is a question-and-answer copy of their dialogue.

Q. "How long have you been in the liquor business, Mr. Hines?"

A. "Thirty-five years."

Q. "Do you deal largely?"

A. "Over a million dollars a year."

Q. "From your long experience, Mr. Hines, have you formed any opinion as to what retailers know about whiskey?"

A. "They know nothing, sir."

Q. "Do they know the difference between straight whiskey and blended whiskey?"

A. "They know only what they read on the label."

Q. "Do you handle many brands of whiskey, Mr. Hines?"

A. "All the leading brands."

Q. "You are familiar with Old Settler?"

A. "I sell thousands of cases of it a year."

Q. "How do you represent it to your customers?"

A. "As whiskey."

Q. "Has there ever been any complaint about its *not* being whiskey?"

A. "None that I've heard of."

Q. "Do you know how Old Settler is made?"

A. "No, sir. I simply buy it as whiskey and sell it as whiskey."

It seemed incredible to Lewis Gifford that a man should buy and sell thousands of cases of whiskey every year and—after thirty-five years—know nothing about the manufacture of the commodity he dealt in. Even more incredible was the ignorance among consumers. Here was the testimony of one Quilty Curnayne, proprietor of the Esperanto Bar in Boston.

Q. "How long have you been proprietor of the Esperanto Bar, Mr. Curnayne?"

A. "Close to forty years."

Q. "Have you any opinion as to the average consumer's knowledge concerning whiskey?"

A. "Well, sir, when it comes to whiskey, most men pride themselves on being experts. 'Tis a harmless human vanity. But it's been my observation that scarcely one man in a thousand knows what goes into a bottle—or comes out of it."

Q. "Could you honestly say, then, that your customers are in a state of total ignorance about whiskey?"

A. "I couldn't say that, sir. They know what they like. If I offered them a coarse, untasty whiskey, they'd go someplace else. But I've met only one man who'd take me up on my standing hundred-dollar bet—I mean, wager, sir."

Q. "And what is that wager, Mr. Curnayne?"

A. "Well, I pour three different kinds of whiskey into separate glasses. Then I lay a century note on the bar. If the man can identify each of the three drinks—and by identify, I mean the age, alcoholic proof and the type of grain used—he wins the hundred dollars. To date, I've had only one taker." He glanced at Anson Woodhull.

Q. "Would you be willing to submit to such a test yourself, Mr. Curnayne?"

A. "I'd have been willing twenty-five years ago, sir. But today, with all the dilutions and mixturing and flavorization that's going on, it'd be like playing against a stacked deck, with deuces wild and every other card a joker."

The figure seemed apposite to Lewis Gifford: the pages of testimony were becoming a cumulative, contradictory and irrational pack of cards in which treys and aces had an equal value. It was the Solicitor-General's problem to arrange the cards in some kind of rational order, to assign a proper value to each and come up with an answer to the President's "What is whiskey?"

Fortunately, Lewis Gifford was not required to consider the moral aspects of the question. The President had not asked: "Is whiskey good or bad for people?" And by tacit agreement the issue was never raised by any of the witnesses. Members of the working press never mentioned the matter in their coverage. But the Temperance press was having a field day. Under the caption "What is Whiskey?" the Anti-Saloon *Bulletin* jeered:

> It matters not the slightest whit to this journal or its readers which of the quarreling parties emerges victorious in the battle now raging at Washington. While the whiskey barons struggle for a monopoly (or shall we call it death grip?) of the saloon, the prize is being snatched from under them by the militant forces of the Anti-Saloon League. Let the whiskey crowd quibble and quarrel, let them make their "distinctions without a difference." Meanwhile, the growing majority of the American people are moving in an indignant phalanx against that crumbling institution, the Saloon.

Marked copies of this and similar fulminations were received by Lewis Gifford daily. Since they had no place in the official record, he consigned them, after careful reading, to his waste basket. Into a much larger basket he tossed hundreds of crank letters. Many of the letters were illiterate, some abusive, others threatening. A typical communication bearing a Washington, D.C., postmark ran as follows:

DEAR SIR:

What kind of a hearing is this any way, when all the witnesses utter nothing but false testimony about the nature of Strong Drink? Whiskey is the scourge of mankind. Alcohol in any form degrades the body, saps the will, and hovers like an incubus over our fair land. So why doesn't someone get up and say that whiskey is a POISON and ought to be labeled with the Skull and Crossbones, like other poisons? Instead of calling it Water of

Life, it ought to be called Water of Death. If someone doesn't speak up pretty quick, you'll be hearing from,

A WITNESS OF THE LORD

Lewis Gifford decided to drop a minatory word into the ear of Larry Gaines, the official doorkeeper. "Keep your eye peeled, Larry, for any weird characters who try to get in. We want this thing to go off quietly."

"I understand, sir."

"Have you noticed anything suspicious about the appearance or actions of any of the visitors?"

"Only one case, sir. There's a lady comes in sometimes—not every day—with a baby in her arms. At first I didn't want to let her in. 'Your baby might cry,' I said. 'Oh, no,' said she. 'He's a quiet one—bottle-fed.' So I let her in and there's never been any trouble."

Stepping out onto Massachusetts Avenue after the twenty-second day of the hearings, the Solicitor-General observed a picket line parading in front of the building. The pickets were a tight-lipped lot of females and each carried a placard bearing some Biblical inscription:

WOE TO THE DRUNKARDS, THEY SHALL BE TRAMPLED UNDER FOOT.

AS A THORN GOETH INTO THE HAND OF A DRUNKARD, SO IS WISDOM IN THE MOUTH OF FOOLS.

STRONG DRINK SHALL BE BITTER TO THEM THAT DRINK IT.

Despite these Biblical injunctions, Lewis Gifford hastened to the cozy bar of the Cosmos Club, where, asking for a bottle of bourbon, he poured himself a glass of excellent whiskey that could not possibly be described as bitter. Nor did it enter his hand as a thorn. It was, in fact, quite mellow, very satisfying and precisely the thing he needed to quiet his jangled nerves. He took another glass, neat, and captured thereby a sense of well-being that sustained him for the battle still ahead.

On the twenty-third day of the hearing, the date being May 2, Dr. George Washington Waley took the stand. The Solicitor-General himself undertook the questioning of this key witness, whose testimony was expected to provide a much-needed prop to the straight-whiskey side of the controversy.

"Dr. Waley, you are chief of the Bureau of Chemistry in the Department of Agriculture?"

"Yes. I have held that position for twenty-seven years."

"And you are charged with the administration of the Food and Drug Act?"

"That is true."

"Prior to the passage of the Act, had you made researches and examinations into the labeling of whiskey?"

"Yes. As a result of my investigations I have collected some four hundred specimens grossly misrepresented as whiskey."

Polk Waram rose to object. "May I point out that we have not as yet determined what whiskey is. Dr. Waley's use of the words *grossly misrepresented* is a matter of personal opinion."

"That is perfectly true, Mr. Waram," said Gifford. "But since we have permitted a wide latitude of opinions here, I think that Dr. Waley should be allowed to testify on his findings. Now, Doctor, how did you obtain these four hundred specimens?"

"We bought them in the open market. From retailers mostly."

"Now as to the labels. Have you found that they stated the truth?"

"Quite the contrary. Almost without exception they were outright falsifications. Here, for instance, is a bottle labeled *Oakmont Eight-Year-Old Pure Rye Whiskey*. On analysis, it proved to be nothing but neutral spirits, artificially colored and flavored."

Waley went on: "Here is another sample labeled *Old Maryland Whiskey. Aged in the Wood. Purity Guaranteed.* My examination of this product showed it to be unaged; both its flavor and color were artificially produced. Here is another sample: *Old Reliable Bourbon. Age and Purity Guaranteed.* It contained a large amount of glycerine and was artificially colored with caramel."

Waley flung out a scythelike arm. "I might go on indefinitely, Mr. Solicitor—but to what end? All these bottles contain liquids purposely misbranded to deceive the consumer. They are nothing but a museum of fraud."

"And what, in your opinion, Doctor, does the consumer believe whiskey to be?"

"The consumer believes that whiskey should be a distillate of fermented grains, containing all the volatile flavors, essential oils and other substances congeneric with ethyl alcohol.

The resultant product—to which nothing has been added or taken away—is stored in wood containers for a period of not less than four years. *That*, sir, is what the consumer thinks whiskey should be."

This pompous fiat brought a growl from Waram. Even the Solicitor-General was quizzical about this ideal statement. He wanted to ask, "Haven't we heard, Doctor, that the ordinary consumer has little knowledge of whiskey?" But this would be trenching on Waram's function as a cross-examiner. Accordingly, Lewis Gifford contented himself with asking, "You found that the consumer then regarded age as essential to whiskey?"

"Most decidedly. Age is the *sine qua non* of whiskey."

"Do you believe that the consumer regards a certain amount of congeneric products as necessary to whiskey?"

"I do. These congeneric substances, coming into contact with the wooden barrel, give whiskey its body, color and flavor."

"Have neutral spirits ever been regarded as whiskey?"

"Never. It has been *represented* as whiskey, and doubtless many uninformed persons have bought it as such—just as they bought adulterated maple sirup thinking it to be the genuine article. It was to put an end to this deception that the Pure Food Act was passed—and I intend to do everything within my power to enforce that law—"

Waram burst out. "I heartily wish that Dr. Waley would stop making speeches about maple sirup and what he intends to do with his exaggerated notion of his powers. Dr. Waley is a chemist. Let him testify as such."

SOLICITOR-GENERAL: "As a chemist, then, Dr. Waley, do you think that neutral spirits, uncolored, unflavored, deserves the name whiskey?"

"I do not. It is being *sold* as whiskey, but it is my duty under the law to expose it as an infamous deceit."

SOLICITOR-GENERAL: "Well, I think we've had enough testimony on that point, Doctor. Now, turning to a happier line of questioning. During your researches, have you ever found a whiskey that was truly labeled?"

"Several such whiskeys are on the market. I think specifically of Rosemere, an eight-year-old bourbon that complies with every specification of an excellent whiskey. Among other such whiskeys, I found Belle of Reading, a splendid Pennsylvania product; also Old Landmark, made in Indiana. These are all straight whiskeys, acknowledged, each in its own field, as a standard of excellence."

"Thank you, Dr. Waley. Your answers have been most responsive. I will now hand you over to the tender mercies of Mr. Waram."

Witness and cross-examiner, though facing each other at close range, were separated by polar distances in belief and temperament. They were, figuratively speaking, anchor men in the gigantic tug-of-war taking place in the United States: Waram, spokesman for entrenched capital, and Waley, champion of a long-beguiled public. In any arena—drawing room or public hearing—their views and personalities made them natural antagonists. Waram despised (and possibly underestimated) the gadfly bureaucrat who had dared sting Big Business. And Waley, beneath his buzzing, bureaucratic manner, was, in reality, the advance guard of a new moral order.

Waram opened with polite sarcasm. "Doctor, you said that you intend to 'enforce the law.' Exactly what law do you have in mind?"

"The Pure Food Act of nineteen hundred and six. Whiskey, as an article of interstate commerce, is specifically included in that law."

"We all know that, Doctor. But unfortunately it was never defined. We are here—or have you forgotten?—to frame a definition of what whiskey is."

"Whiskey has been quite adequately defined in a regulation issued by the Secretary of Agriculture."

"Ah-h! Now you are taking slightly lower ground. For a time I thought you were both houses of Congress. But as it turns out, you, a mere bureau chief in the Department of Agriculture, are attempting to give a departmental regulation the force of law. Does it not occur to you, Doctor, that you may be exceeding your authority when you try to regulate a billion-dollar industry out of existence?"

"I am not trying to regulate industry out of anything except dishonest practice. I am merely attempting—and will persevere in my attempts—to make the manufactures of spurious whiskey label their product for the thing it is. Naturally I expect opposition."

Waram's smile was wintry. "You have come to the right shop, Doctor. We are specialists in opposition—particularly when we encounter it in the form of arbitrary power."

Waram bore down on his witness with the crushing intent

of a steamroller: "In your previous testimony, weren't you rather offhand the other day when you condemned certain whiskeys as frauds? May I inquire as to the methods by which you slandered my clients in this outrageous fashion?"

"You may inquire. But since you are not a chemist, I must ask the Solicitor-General for a ruling as to your competency to understand my answers."

Lewis Gifford repressed a smile. "I myself am not a chemist, Dr. Waley. This serious defect in my education might conceivably disqualify me as referee in these hearings. But will you not grant me and Mr. Waram a modicum of . . . ah . . . hypothetical lay intelligence, capable of receiving instruction?"

"Gladly, sir. I merely wish to suggest that whiskey is a complex chemical enigma, and I have gone to great pains in my attempts to devise methods of cracking that enigma—especially as it concerns the age and purity of any given whiskey. I shall now state the importance of these tests in the following order: 1) total acidity; 2) esters; 3) solids; and 4) tannins—all expressed *in grams per liter.*"

Dr. Waley was pure benevolence as he turned to Polk Waram. "Does my answer make anything clearer to you?"

Since it was impossible for Waram to reply in the affirmative, he elected to attack the method and body of testimony offered by his bureaucratic adversary.

"Did you make these tests yourself, Dr. Waley? Have you personally analyzed the substances that you so readily condemned?"

"No. The principal work was done by two of my assistants: Mr. Coleman and Mr. Chiappe."

"Hah! So you are passing off as fact secondhand information. I must remind you, Doctor, that there exists a well-established abhorrence of hearsay testimony."

Waley, the old logician, put a headlock on his opponent and squeezed hard. "Within the past two minutes you have employed the term *slander,* Mr. Waram. Behind that term lies a long history of judicial decisions. You yourself did not render these decisions. You played no part in creating the truly terrifying idea that the spoken word can in certain instances constitute a crime per se. Or possibly I am wrong. Polk Waram may be the author of the Great Commandment against the 'bearing of false witness.' Did you write that

Commandment?" Waley's voice rose in Sinaic anger. "Do you accuse me of breaking it?"

In the silence that followed Waley's thunderclap, the bureau chief turned to Lewis Gifford. "I ask for a ruling, sir. Shall eight years of investigation by duly accredited scientists —checked by myself and other scientists of repute—shall these be characterized as 'hearsay testimony'?"

Lewis Gifford, born negotiator, poured the oil of his well-tempered soul over the troubled waters. "I am certain that Mr. Waram can rephrase his question or withdraw it altogether. For myself, I am perfectly willing to accept your testimony. In the interest of progress I suggest that these hearings proceed.

"I will venture to lead off with a question. Dr. Waley, your expression *grams per liter* puzzles me somewhat. Yet, according to the chart you have just submitted, it would appear that the combined elements that differentiate aged whiskey from unaged are approximately .095 grams per liter. Can you state that quantity in language understandable to Mr. Waram and myself?"

"Yes. The figure .095 is approximately the equivalent of ten drops to a quart."

The Solicitor-General's courteous "Thank you, Dr. Waley" needed to be driven home by Beane's relentless advocacy. Andy didn't need a sledge. One simple question did it: "And how many drops are there in a quart, Dr. Waley?"

"Fifteen thousand, three hundred and twenty."

"Do you contend, Doctor, that ten drops in fifteen thousand constitutes the difference between whiskey and non-whiskey?"

"I do so contend."

The Solicitor-General turned to Polk Waram. "Have you any further questions, sir?"

Polk Waram had neglected to consider the naked simplicity of Andy Beane's demonstration. Too late for improvisation now, "I shall be obliged to consult my experts," he huffed and sat down.

The dog fight between the two men lasted for three days. Waram's ruthless assault was met at every point by Waley's tooth-and-claw resistance, which at times took the form of resourceful counterattack. Waram's claim that "public usage" constituted a definition of whiskey was met by Waley's charge

The Rising Gale • 534

that the public had been misled by huge outlays of money on false advertising. Reformer Waley declared that government should and *must* halt such practices. Corporation counsel Waram branded this course as an unthinkable invasion of private enterprise. The two principals fought the social aspects of the question to an inconclusive and fatiguing draw.

And when they retired from the littered field, whiskey was still undefined.

Zarah and Amy Woodhull, sitting in the front row of the narrow gallery, watched Anson take the witness chair. The hearings, though protracted, had provided a wonderful excuse for a long holiday in Washington. Together with Solange, they had explored the shops on F Street and Pennsylvania Avenue, taken sight-seeing trips around the capital, and now both were ready to go home. The more so because Amy was expecting her baby soon and Chance was in Landmark taking charge of distilling operations.

Amy had listened with intense interest to the proceedings. Her concentration was interrupted by the cooing sounds made by a woman beside her. The woman had a baby in her arms; the baby's head was covered with a shawl. Both Zarah and Amy were so fascinated by the exchange of questions and answers that they temporarily forgot the woman.

Andrew Beane, depending heavily on his star witness, began the direct questioning.

"Please state your name, occupation and place of business."

"My name is Anson Woodhull. I make Old Landmark whiskey. My distilleries and warehouses are located in Landmark County, Indiana."

"Have you ever sold whiskey that was less than four years old, Mr. Woodhull?"

"Not under the name Old Landmark. Every drop of whiskey bearing my label is four years old."

"You regard age, then, as indispensable in the making of a fine whiskey?"

"Age is an important factor but by no means the only one. If your whiskey is poor, thin stuff to begin with, no amount of aging will ever give it character. Time alone doesn't guarantee *growth*. And it's growth—call it maturity if you prefer —that we look for in whiskey."

The Solicitor-General, listening intently, was fascinated by

Anson's conception of whiskey as a growing, evolving substance. For the first time he understood the difference between age and maturity. Age was merely a calendar term. Maturity, in whiskey as in people, was a goal that might or might not be achieved with the passage of time. To clarify this important train of thought, Lewis Gifford himself took over the questioning.

"What elements other than age enables whiskey to 'grow,' as you put it, Mr. Woodhull?"

The fruit of forty-five years' experience was in Anson's reply. "I'd say, sir, that whiskey must contain a certain minimum of congeneric substances when you put it into the barrel. Lacking this minimum, it will never reach maturity."

Lewis Gifford weighed his question. "What is the nature of these congeneric substances, Mr. Woodhull? Where do they come from? And why should their presence in such minute quantities be deemed essential to whiskey?"

Had Anson been queried concerning his beliefs in a deity, or the problem of Free Will versus Predestination, his answers could not have sprung from deeper levels. "I've thought about these matters for a long time, General, and because I am unable to testify as a scientist, I must speak in a kind of parable. Now, then, the presence of congeners in whiskey is comparable to what we call 'temper' in a man. In excessive amounts, temper is an ugly, undesirable trait. Yet if it is entirely eliminated in a man, a woman—or a whiskey—they become tame, flat, uninteresting. I hold that some untameable residue must remain in human beings—and in whiskey—for both their own sake and their effect upon each other. When deep speaks to deep, what voice is speaking? A mutual recognition takes place, and I suspect that this recognition springs from the existence of congeners in both parties." Anson continued. "I will go further, Mr. Solicitor-General, and say that congeners represent a trace of the old Adam in all of us. If whiskey were the tipple of angels or of gods, such traces might well be eliminated. But since it is consumed by mortal man, I think that some remnant of its mortality will always remain. Both men and whiskey are born with some such taint, which perhaps accounts for the affectionate bond between them."

Lewis Gifford wanted to add his "Hear, Hear," to the musketry of applause that rattled the crystal chandelier at the conclusion of Anson's remarks. As an impartial referee, the Solicitor-General was obliged instead to hand the witness over to Mr. Polk Waram for cross-examination.

While sizing up his man, Polk Waram permitted himself a bit of sarcasm. "Mr. Woodhull, we have been edified by your heroic sentiments as to the nature and function of whiskey, with pardonable emphasis on the virtues of Old Landmark. You admit quite readily, do you not, that you have made a better mousetrap?"

Anson's response was humorously good-tempered. "The world has not beaten a path to my door."

"Ah-h, a fellow Emersonian. Now suppose we forget the sage of Concord and come to the business at hand. My clients have been charged with the grave sin of omission by failing to mention on their label that their whiskey contains neutral spirits. You do not practice that kind of deception yourself, do you?"

"No."

"And you certainly do not mislabel your own whiskey?"

"I believe not."

"Well, we shall see about that. Now, Mr. Woodhull, do you recognize this object in my hands as a bottle of Old Landmark?"

"I do."

"Have you any objections to my reading aloud the printed matter on the label?"

"None at all."

Waram elaborately adjusted his pince-nez and read: *"Old Landmark Whiskey. Bottled in bond. Made by Anson Woodhull, Landmark, Indiana.* Now, sir, will you swear that your label states the truth, the whole truth, and nothing but the truth, concerning the contents of this bottle?"

Lewis Gifford interposed. "The witness is not obliged to swear, Mr. Waram. He is not under oath. I am sure that you can rephrase the question."

"Forgive me. In my zeal to obtain the strongest possible statement from this witness, possibly I overstepped. Well, now, Mr. Woodhull, do you *maintain*, do you declare and do you assert that you have honestly and truthfully labeled your bottle?"

"I do."

"Will you name the chief cereal from which this whiskey is made?"

"Old Landmark is made chiefly from corn."

"Corn?" Waram scrutinized the label with elaborate exaggeration. "That is curious. I see no mention of corn here. In your haste to appropriate the term *whiskey*, you have apparently omitted the word *corn*. Can you explain why?"

Anson felt the inquisitorial pinch. "It is common knowledge that Old Landmark is made from corn."

"Common knowledge? Come, sir! For weeks we have been hearing that scarcely one man in a thousand has the remotest idea of what he is drinking."

"Well, that one man must be the fellow who steps up and asks for Old Landmark."

Laughter from the audience annoyed Mr. Waram. He had been through a harrowing three weeks and his frayed nerves winced under the abrasive rub of laughter. He managed an appreciative smile and went on. "I am quite willing to believe that your product is made of corn. What puzzles me is why you don't state that fact clearly on the label."

Waram let his puzzlement travel about the room. "Do you fear the connotations that corn whiskey has in the public mind? You know the type of thing I mean. Moonshining. White Mule. Skull-Popper. Shooting revenue officers. Are you *ashamed* of the word *corn*, Mr. Woodhull?"

"I think it is one of the proudest words in the language."

"Then if it is such a proud word, why don't you print it on your label? Very powerful reasons must have influenced a man of your moral stature to practice so bald a deception. It *is* a deception, isn't it, Mr. Woodhull?"

Polk Waram, together with everyone else in the room, waited for Anson to squirm. Zarah, leaning over the gallery rail, wondered what reply her husband would make. In the thunder of expectant silence, only the maker of Old Landmark seemed unperturbed. He hefted his gold watch chain as if its solid metal were a talisman, and began: "It would be a bald deception, Mr. Waram, if I *did* use the word *corn* on my label. It is true that corn is an important ingredient in the making of Old Landmark. But the clear limestone water that constitutes fifty per cent of my whiskey is equally important. Then there is also the special strain of yeast, developed over a period of years—not to mention the rye and malted barley prepared in a special way. In addition, I have a particular method of mixing and fermenting these materials, then distilling them at the proper temperature. I suppose, too, that I might mention the skill and patience that governs the entire operation."

Anson shook his head as if to convey the hopelessness of giving these intangibles a name, or making Waram understand their importance. "The whiskey in my bottle cannot properly be called corn whiskey, or water whiskey or yeast whiskey, or charred-barrel whiskey, or skill-and-care whiskey. It is a unique substance, greater than, and different from, the sum of its original parts. It is, in short, Old Landmark Whiskey. I have stated that fact on my label and you will never wring from me the slightest admission that is should be labeled in any other way."

"That is a noble statement, sir. Quite transcendental. I will not further pursue the matter of labeling lest we should end up by calling your product 'Over-Soul Whiskey.'"

In a cooler moment Waram's judgment would have served him and his clients to better advantage. It was not considered good public policy to mention—or even admit—that ethyl alcohol had the peculiar power of causing drunkenness. In his present irritated state Waram brushed aside this taboo.

"Have you ever seen a man become intoxicated on a drink composed chiefly of neutral spirits?"

"I have."

Cadence of doom marked Waram's next question. "Have you ever seen a man get drunk on Old Landmark?"

The hearing became a tumult. Beane cried to Anson, "Don't answer that!"

Lewis Gifford's objection took a milder form. "What do you hope to prove by this line of questioning, Mr. Waram?"

The corporation counsel's jowls were the color of dark cherry. "Why, sir, simply this. Mr. Woodhull has come among us—'descended' is perhaps a more accurate word—bearing news of an Olympian liquor possessing the combined virtues of nectar and that elixir of life sought by philosophers. He has been permitted to contrast his Old Landmark whiskey, this Aristotelian essence, with other less expensive tipples. He refuses to admit that the two have anything in common. Now what I want to know is this: when a man drinks enough of Mr. Woodhull's whiskey, does it transform him into a god? Will it make him a philosopher? Or does Old Landmark share, with other less patrician whiskeys, the power of making a man *drunk?* That is the purpose of my question and I think it would create a vastly unjust impression if the witness fails to answer."

As an impartial referee, Lewis Gifford rendered judgment. "Neither the question nor any answer the witness may care to make will advance our inquiry, Mr. Counselor. I rule, therefore, that it should not be answered unless Mr. Woodhull chooses to do so."

"I have no objection to answering," said Anson.

"Then if the visitors in the gallery will be quiet, the stenographer will repeat the question."

"I will repeat the question myself," said Waram. "Now, sir, when I asked you, 'Have you ever seen a man get drunk on Old Landmark?' I didn't mean merely convivial, witty or lachrymose. What I mean is the ordinary, stupid, sodden, falling-down kind of drunkenness. And what is your answer to that, sir?"

"My answer is 'Yes.' Any alcoholic liquor, good or bad, if taken in excess, has the power of making a man drunk."

The forthright simplicity of Anson's reply checked Waram's aggression. His forward motion, indeed all his thought processes, came to a halt while he sought for a method of exploiting the witness's frank admission. The half second of silence that he required to gather himself for a new attack was broken by a hysterical shriek from the gallery. It was a female voice, maniacally uncontrolled, and it was followed by a shower of crashing glass as a heavy object struck the crystal chandelier.

Amy Woodhull saw the whole thing happen. The woman who had sat beside her during the hearings, cooing to a baby, suddenly rose, tore away the mothering shawl and exposed a grinning death's head.

"Hypocrites, murderers, liars!" she cried, wrenching the supposed head from her baby. She brandished the skull aloft. "*This* is the emblem that your bottles should carry!" Then she hurled the skull at the huge chandelier that hung from the ceiling.

Amid a shower of crashing glass the skull landed on the oval table in the center of the room and rolled onto the floor.

Larry Gaines, the doorkeeper, picked up the gruesome object and carried it to the Solicitor-General. In the cranial hollow lay a scroll of paper. Unfolding it, Lewis Gifford read:

Give Him Strong Drink Who Is About to Perish.

In the general hubbub that ensued, no one paid much

attention to Amy Woodhull. She collapsed against Zarah, murmuring, "I think I'm going to have the baby right now."

Which she proceeded to do.

THE SOLICITOR-GENERAL PROPOSES

IN HIS REPORT to the President the Solicitor-General made no reference to the death's-head incident or the birth of Amy Woodhull's son. Matters infinitely more complex absorbed Lewis Gifford as he attempted to impose form and meaning upon the mass of conflicting testimony taken during the past thirty days.

For the first time in his life this amiable man with the good legal mind found himself baffled by a problem that involved more than law with its outriggers of judicial precedent and departmental regulation. Entangled with the whole subject were problems of philology, orthography (was is spelled *whisky* or *whiskey?*) and differential usages of meaning. Why, the very *meaning* of meaning must be plucked from the twenty-five hundred pages of testimony—much of it contradictory, specious or born of ignorance. How distinguish between honest differences of opinion and special pleading? How reconcile deeply held convictions about the enforcement of the Pure Food Law with powerful commercial interests that cared nothing about "the greatest good for the greatest number"?

Well, no one could help Lewis Gifford now. The President had asked him to submit a report on the question "What is whiskey?" and the Solicitor-General must search deeply among the inconsistencies of supposed experts to give an answer that would conform not only to the facts but to the deeper necessities of clarity, logic and common usage.

By definition, an impossible task. By reason of his directive, inescapable. Lewis Gifford canceled all social appointments, locked the door of his book-lined study in the house on H Street and, like a latter-day Beowulf, plunged into the depthless tarn where Enigma lurked in her subaqueous den.

He forgot the emerald-green tennis courts at Burning Rock and the joy of driving an opponent through wider and wider arcs before placing the ball home for point, game and set. He forgot the blue waters of the Chesapeake where his yacht *Isabella* lay at anchor. His chair at the Cosmos Club stood empty at lunchtime. At supper parties, the fusee of laughter crackled less often because Giff was not there.

With a wooden pen holder as his lever, Lewis Gifford was sincerely attempting to lift the word *whiskey* into the light of truth. Emphatically, he was not concerned with the moral or physiological effects of whiskey on the human body, nor did the President's directive require that he pass judgment on those who made, sold or drank this alcoholic beverage. Rather—and this was the fascinating part of his task—the Solicitor-General must define the *isness*, the *whatness*, the *Ding an Sich* of an article of interstate commerce, a common, everyday article that had been taxed and trafficked in for centuries, without anyone every inquiring into its essential nature.

Odd. *Damned* odd.

For two weeks Lewis Gifford wrote, revised, discarded what he had written, then started all over again. And this, in part, is what the Solicitor-General finally said in his report to the President.

The questions which I have been called upon to consider have no answer in the Act of Congress known as the Pure Food Law. That statute deals with whiskey as well as food, drink, confectionery, condiments and drugs generally and prohibits their adulteration or misbranding. It does not, however, afford any means of determining the true nature or proper constituents of these articles. Before one can say whether an article is adulterated or misbranded, it is necessary first to know what the article really is in its true nature and ingredients. Concretely, before one can say whether the name *whiskey* is wrongly applied to a particular article, it is necessary first to ascertain what is properly called whiskey; and this must be ascertained outside the statute.

Nor do the questions which I have been called upon to answer relate at all to the relative excellence or merit of one or another article. The problem is not whether straight whiskey is better than a blend, or the reverse; or whether whiskey is better than alcohol; or whether whiskey or water is better. The sole problem is, what is whiskey in the general and true significance of that name?

Whiskey is not a natural product. It is always a thing

manufactured by man. Whether a thing be natural or artificial, however, its name is given to it by man; and accordingly *in this matter of names the actual usage of the people controls.* A name imports what the people understand by it. The questions in hand can be determined therefore only by endeavoring to ascertain the significance of the word *whiskey* in the public mind; and that depends upon intelligent public usage.

Having established a criterion of meaning based upon public usage, Gifford went on:

I turn now to the question which is perhaps of chief moment in the controversy over whiskey, viz., whether a so-called "neutral spirit"—i.e., a distillate from grain not substantially different from pure ethyl alcohol—may properly be called whiskey. I have found that such neutral spirits, when colored and flavored, have been actually called whiskey by manufacturers in their sales to retailers. Retail traders, in their dealings with one another and with consumers, have also called this article whiskey. But—

And here Lewis Gifford drove a painful splinter of fact into his argument:

. . . I have likewise found that this same neutral spirit was being sold by distillers to rectifiers as neutral spirits—not as whiskey. I have found that retail dealers seldom knew that they were receiving, and subsequently selling, neutral spirits. Nor has the generality of consumers known that they were buying a mere neutral spirit, colored and flavored, under the name of whiskey. Because of these facts, I am unable to accept the view that neutral spirits are entitled to the name *whiskey*. Nor is there any possible doubt that the public has been almost always ignorant that it was actually receiving neutral spirits, falsely labeled as whiskey.

Deep in his subject now, the Solicitor-General discussed the changes that had taken place in distillation since the invention of the continuous still. His reasoning took the form of a syllogism.

(1) The bulk of so-called whiskey produced in the U.S. during the past forty years is, in reality, ethyl alcohol artificially colored and flavored.

(2) Ethyl alcohol does not contain the chemical elements (congeners) which give whiskey its characteristic odor and flavor.

(3) The manufacturers of ethyl alcohol have not informed the consuming public of this change.

"In the absence of such knowledge," wrote Lewis Gifford, "the public must have supposed that they were still getting under the name of whiskey what they had previously gotten under that name."

How far, Lewis Gifford wondered, should he go in dividing responsibility for this fraud? Was it incumbent upon the rectifier—prior to the passage of the Pure Food Law—to educate an unsuspecting public as to the nature of the article sold as whiskey? No. The ancient rule of *caveat emptor* (let the buyer beware) could be applied with equal force to whiskey, fishing tackle or tennis balls. The graver fault lay embedded somewhere in the invincible ignorance of the consuming public. But this ignorance had been hammered home by the sledge of calculated deceit in the matter of labels and advertising. As a thorn goeth into the flesh, so had false notions festered—and been *encouraged* to fester—in the whiskey trade itself. Only the rectifier, according to the evidence, knew that his barrel contained neutral spirits. The jobber bought this article as whiskey and sold it to the retailer as whiskey. The retailer sold it to his customers as whiskey.

Clearly, it was the Solicitor-General's duty to point out the culpable source from which these errors flowed. Scathingly he indicted the rectifiers and thereby drove the first nail into his own coffin.

The next nail was a paragraph condemning the use of molasses and beet sugar as substitutes for grain in the manufacture of neutral spirits.

Either from fatigue or some astigmatic mote in his vision, Lewis Gifford asserted that a mixture of neutral spirits and whiskey containing a minimum of congeneric substances should be entitled to the name whiskey. And this, unfortunately, exposed him to the wrath of Dr. George Washington Waley.

Physically and mentally exhausted, the Solicitor-General dispatched his report to the President on May 24, 1909. That evening he complained of dizziness. "Might easily be ascribed to eyestrain, overwork, a dozen different causes," said Dr. Barlow. Secretly, the physician advised Isabel Gifford to take her husband away for a long rest.

Lewis Gifford and his wife spent a quiet summer cruising in the waters of Chesapeake Bay. Although the Solicitor-General managed to suppress the greater part of his official worries, Isabel's wifely intuition told her that the man she loved (and truly, too) was slowly disintegrating. His tanned cheeks were tautened like drum heads waiting, waiting, waiting—for what?

"Tell me, Lewis. What is really troubling you?"

"I am really troubled," said Lewis Gifford, "by the lack of common courtesy in an official superior who shall be nameless here. He didn't even acknowledge my report."

Lewis Gifford was destined to wait a long while for the official disposition of his report on "What is Whiskey?" Because it just so happened that "Big Lub's" character contained a vast gray emptiness into which he could drop everything that troubled him until pressure from interested parties brought it to the surface again.

Don't think that interested parties weren't trying to reach the President. Oh, they were really extending themselves. But in the year 1909, the jovial President of the United States decided to retreat into the vastness of his summer estate at Murray Bay, Canada. The official orders were "No Visitors." And when a President hangs out that "No Visitors" sign, a platoon of strong, silent men make it their business to see that the order is obeyed.

THE PRESIDENT DISPOSES

Mirror, mirror on the wall; who, among illustrious Cincinnatians, is the most illustrious of all?

If the mirror were a truth-telling glass the answer would have been, in 1909, "William Howard Taft," twenty-seventh President of the United States. Jurist, diplomat, administrator, Cabinet member, he had held just about every appointive office that the Grand Old Party could confer on an able member of its hierarchy. "Big Lub"—a boyhood nickname that had gradually modulated into Big Bill—began his career as Collector of Internal Revenue for the Ohio district, and in the scrupulous discharge of his duties, he had handed over some twenty million dollars in whiskey taxes to the Federal government. Later, he had served as Solicitor-General of his home state, as circuit judge, Governor of the Philippines and Secretary of War in the Cabinet of Roosevelt the first.

Strong-willed Presidents of the United States have generally managed to name their successors. And so it happened that the twenty-sixth President, loving his Secretary of War as a brother, handed Big Bill the Republican nomination with the hope (based on God knows what) that his nominee would carry out those measures of social reform and economic liberalism that lay fermenting dangerously in the American melting pot.

The better to give his hand-picked candidate a free rein, terrible Teddy had gone on a long safari to Africa. Whereupon the new Chief Executive began to display those deliberative symptoms of a man who would rather be Chief Justice than President. Since he was a staunch believer in the *status quo ante* (the mixture as before McKinley), his administration was regarded as one of those breathing spells—welcomed; indeed, necessary—after seven hectic years of agitation and reform. The Chief Executive set the tempo of his age by taking a long nap after luncheon, then playing a leisurely round of golf. All was indeed quiet along the Potomac. And in this somnolence the little foxes gnawed busily at our vines.

"Uncle Joe" Cannon, an unreconstructable vestige of the Reconstruction period, held the House of Representatives leashed like a beagle pack; in the Upper House, a powerful group of Senators formed a Palatine guard around the controls of money, lifted an unscalable tariff wall against importations. Monopoly and child labor flourished. Social legislation evaporated and the Pure Food Law went unenforced.

In this atmosphere of nonfeasance, the President turned his attention, late in June 1909, to the "What is Whiskey?" report submitted by his Solicitor-General. No public decision had ever received such unanimous condemnation as Lewis Gifford's earnest attempt to uncover the truth. Everybody, it seems, was dissatisfied; and each in turn made his dissatisfaction known to the President. Polk Waram objected in a strongly worded brief, and Mr. Waram's objection was sustained by Senator Foraker of Ohio—the very man who had appointed Big Lub as Collector of Internal Revenue in 1882. The Senator pointed out, and Big Lub well knew, that the huge rectifying business, centering in Cincinnati, contributed nearly one quarter of all Federal revenue to the national treasury. Should contributors so princely be obliged to place the word *Imitation* on the product they sold as whiskey? Unthinkable! Yet a terrible young lawyer from Tennessee, one Andrew Jackson Beane, had rounded up a contingent of Senators from Pennsylvania, Maryland and Kentucky. Beane's point was that an article grossly adulterated, composed largely of alcohol made from molasses, artificially colored and flavored, flagrantly misbranded, was still flooding the market under the name whiskey.

Respectful enough in voice and manner, Andy Beane had asked: "Does your administration wish to go on the record as destroying the Pure Food Law, Mr. President?"

William Howard Taft wished neither to destroy nor coddle the Pure Food Law. To begin with, it wasn't his baby; and, secondly, he didn't relish having his afternoon nap destroyed by the yowling of a brat left on his doorstep. As a jurist, he questioned the legitimacy of the Act itself. Did it lie within the purview of Congress, or the Department of Agriculture, or the Bureau of Chemistry to regulate what the American people should eat and drink? By temperament he had no wish to tamper with Lewis Gifford's findings and had sought to fob the whole matter off onto the Internal Revenue Bureau. Echo answered, "No jurisdiction here." Meanwhile public uproar and universal criticism of Gifford's report had obliged the portly, jovial incumbent of the White House to intervene as referee.

"I will hear the exceptions of all parties and render judgment," said the President.

It was a curious decision. While seven cases involving the nature of whiskey lay waiting in the dockets of Federal courts, Big Lub, against whose good name and spotless reputation no biographer has ever uttered a single syllable of condemnation, usurped the judicial function of the Supreme Court by acting as judge and jury in the rehearings that began in the White House late in June 1909. As a constitutional lawyer he could not take the view that the President's powers were unlimited. How he happened to be sitting as judge, jury and counsel in the whiskey rehearings will never be explained. But there he sat in the White House flanked by his Attorney General and Secretary of Agriculture. The Honorable Lewis Gifford was conspicuously absent.

"I believe," began the President, "that the Solicitor-General's report has the first indication of correctness in that there are exceptions from every side."

"Nobody satisfied," said Mr. Polk Waram, rising.

"Nobody satisfied," said Andrew Jackson Beane.

"Nobody satisfied," repeated the President. "You may proceed with your exceptions, Mr. Waram."

Six months later the twenty-seventh President of the United States overruled the most important findings of his own Solicitor-General and adopted many of the principles presented by the rectifiers. His biographers fail to mention why. But here is what Big Lub finally got around to saying:

"It is undoubtedly true that the liquor trade has been disgracefully full of frauds upon the public by false labels; but these frauds did not consist in palming off something which was not whiskey as whiskey, but in palming one kind of whiskey as another and better kind of whiskey. Whiskey made of rectified or redistilled or neutral spirits was often branded as bourbon or rye straight whiskey. The way to remedy this evil is not to attempt to change the meaning and scope of the term *whiskey*, accorded to it for one hundred years, and narrow it to include only straight whiskey; and there is nothing in the Pure Food Law that warrants the inference of such an intention by Congress. The way to do it is to require a branding in connection with the use of the term *whiskey* which will indicate just what kind of whiskey the package contains. Thus, straight whiskeys may be branded as such and may be accompanied by the legend *aged in wood*. Whiskey made from rectified, redistilled, or neutral spirits may be branded as whiskey made from rectified, redistilled, or neutral spirits, as the case may be. . . .

"The term *straight whiskey* is well understood in the trade and well understood by consumers. There is no reason, therefore, why those who make straight whiskey may not have the brand upon their barrels of straight whiskey with further descriptive terms such as *bourbon* or *rye whiskey*, as the composition of the grain used may justify, and they may properly add, if they choose, that it is aged in the wood.

"Those who make whiskey of rectified, redistilled, or neutral spirits cannot complain if, in order to prevent further frauds, they are required to use a brand which shall show exactly the kind of whiskey they are selling. For that reason it seems to me fair to require them to brand their product as 'whiskey made from rectified spirits,' or 'whiskey made from redistilled spirits,' or 'whiskey made from neutral spirits,' as the case may be; and if aged in the wood, as sometimes is the case with this class of whiskeys, they may add this fact."

Because the President did not mention exactly where the objectionable word *neutral spirit* should be displayed on the container, the rectifiers took advantage of this omission by pasting a small label on the back of the bottle, where it stands even to this day. Johnno Normile's testimony. "Not one man in a thousand knows what goes into a bottle and what comes out of it," still holds true. Other adulterators of food and drink followed the example of the rectifiers; gradually the Pure Food Act was virtually nullified.

And so the hearings ended with a compromise. Neither side was wholly victorious or utterly defeated. An industry divided against itself, and destined within a decade to perish, continued to provide strong waters to any and all who cared to drink whatever was offered them as whiskey.

The only immediate tragedy of the hearings was the unexplained death of Lewis Gifford.

Among the hobbies of the Solicitor-General was a fondness for ice-boating. On the morning of December 10—the day after the President's proclamation—Lewis Gifford raised the mainsail of his spidery craft and was last seen by Mr. Thomas Brainerd, a neighbor, scudding before the wind along a frozen inlet near his home on the eastern shore of Maryland. Brainerd states that he called out to his friend warning him of open water at the mouth of the inlet. Gifford raised a red-mittened hand in acknowledgment of the hail and seemingly tried to bring his craft about. Whether he misjudged the velocity of the wind, or whether he chose to hurtle into the icy waters of the bay and thus cool forever his burning sense of humiliation, will never be known.

For what profiteth it a man to be charming, courteous, patient, scholarly, a good doubles player, a loving husband and a seeker after truth, when he finds himself in water so deep, so frigid, so treacherous, that even the best school ties cannot prevail against it?

3.

ROSEMERE

BEFORE DR. BANTING and his colleagues blessed the world with their gift of insulin, diabetes had a fatal way with some two hundred and fifty thousand Americans every year. The disease was no respecter of age, race, social position or wealth; the only treatment amounted to virtual starvation; and because life requires food, sufferers from diabetes inevitably died in a state of comatose emaciation.

In the master bedroom of Vieuxtemps, Charles Moerlein lay dying of a disease that in 1912 could not be controlled. During the earlier courses of his illness he had lost fifty pounds. Now, with death closing in on him, Charles Moerlein did what every courageous man does: he faced the inevitable end with a certain tranquillity. Somewhere he had read Sir William Osler's aphorism: "In my fifty years of medical experience I have never witnessed an unhappy death." Moerlein did not intend to be the exception to Osler's rule of *tranquillitas*.

As the end neared, Charles Moerlein wound up the financial affairs attendant upon a rich man's death. His wife Solange would be the principal benefactor of Moerlein's Last Will and Testament; she had approved all of the minor bequests (and some not so minor) that Charles had made to his special charities and family retainers. Under the terms of Moerlein's will Solange would become the principal stockholder in Midwestern Distillers, Inc., with an assured income of $300,000 annually. Title to Vieuxtemps had long ago passed into her hands; she owned a portfolio of securities that might have aroused envy in a medium-sized investment company; in addition to some twenty thousand in ready cash sh* would become the beneficiary of a two-hundred-fifty-thousand-dollar life insurance policy.

At fifty-seven her luminous dark beauty, guarded at critical points by massage, cosmetic skill and natural muscle tone, had been silvered over lightly by the passage of years. A quarter century of marriage to Charles Moerlein had helped. Now the association with a tenderly loving husband was drawing to a close. The usual thoughts—How can I live without this man? What shall I do with the rest of my life?—were subordinated to sympathy for Charles himself. After all, it was Charles who was dying.

Uxorious men under sentence of death choose to have the beloved wife near them when the shadow falls. But before the shadow fell upon Charles Moerlein he wished to dispose of two confidential and quite disparate pieces of business. Only one man in the world could execute both of them, and that man's name was Anson Woodhull.

"Ask Anson if he will come to me," said Moerlein to his wife.

"Of course, darling."

Within six hours, the summons was fulfilled in the ageless person of the man Charles Moerlein had asked to see. Anson sat facing his bedridden friend, propped up on pillows. Both men kept the conversation at a nonsentimental level. They spoke of Big Lub's jovial nonfeasance as President; Boss Cox's misrule of Cincinnati; of Zarah and Chance, of the whiskey industry. Masculine, commonplace matters; thin ice above deep water.

It was Moerlein who broke through into the true business at hand.

"Anse, my doctor tells me I have three good months ahead of me. Not quite long enough to do the things I should have done or to omit the acts I should have omitted. Don't misunderstand me, Anse; I'm not afraid of dying." He stretched out a withered hand to his friend. "You gave me a priceless gift of happiness when you said, 'Yes, you may court Solange. The girl's heart is her own.' Anson, I owe you a great deal for that permission. More than I can ever tell."

"Don't forget, Charles, you made Solange happy too. She deserved an honorable, affectionate husband. No one owes anyone anything—so long as they give their best to each other."

A tide of reminiscence began to flood in from the past.

"Remember the day when I first drove into your yard in a hired rig?"

"I remember. It was a cold day. I was chopping cornstalks and had exactly nine dollars to my name."

"You treated me as though you had nine million dollars' worth of independence. And I'm selling you short at that figure."

"I was damn glad to get six hundred dollars for that whiskey."

"I was damn lucky to get the whiskey."

A feeble laugh was prelude to Moerlein's next remark.

"I thought then, and I think now, that your whiskey was as good as Rosemere. Old Mark Chadbourne echoed the same idea when he cast his vote for you at Chicago."

"Sad about Mark's passing. Well, he was pushing ninety. Even so Charles, try to imagine a world without Rosemere."

"That's what I'm coming to, Anse. One of the last things I did was to buy Rosemere from Mark's heirs. It seems they turned Baptistic. Their religious convictions, fired by the prospect of—well, I won't tell you how much I paid for it—gave me title to the Rosemere plant, its formula and that miraculous spring of limestone water gushing from the rock. Along with two thousand barrels of whiskey that must be eight years old by now."

"Come on, Charlie, how much did you pay for Rosemere?"

"Fifty dollars and sixty-five cents."

"You should apply for membership in the Ananias Club. Sorry I can't sponsor you."

The time for chaffing had passed. From beneath the coverlet of his bed, Moerlein drew a legal-size envelope and handed it to his friend. "Open it, Anse. Read what the paper says."

Anson opened the envelope and saw a document printed on vellum in Old English type.

TITLE OF CONVEYANCE

For considerations good and valuable, I, Charles Moerlein, being of sound mind and giving disposition, do bequeath, devise and give to Anson Woodhull the property formerly owned by the late Mark Chadbourne and used by him in the distillation of Rosemere, the acknowledged archetype of Bourbon Whiskey in the United States.

I make but one stipulation: that the aforementioned

Anson Woodhull produce a minimum of one hundred barrels of Rosemere annually, employing his known skills and science as distiller in the production thereof.

Anson protested. "Charles, I can't accept this property. It's the most valuable distillery in Kentucky. Why did you do a thing like this?"

"Call it atonement. Say that I realized all along the difference between the stuff I sold as whiskey and an honest straight product like Old Landmark. The fact is, Anse, I want Rosemere to keep on living—and you're the only man who can be trusted with the job. Make Rosemere a memorial to a friend named Charles Moerlein whose name was writ in water—and neutral spirits."

"I'll start the Rosemere plant going, Charles. You can depend upon that. Meanwhile, what can I give you—or do for you—in token of a friendship that has survived so many differences of opinion?"

Moerlein lowered his voice "There *is* something you can do for me, Anse. After I pass on, my lawyer will give you a sealed envelope containing the key to a safe-deposit box in the Atlas National Bank, together with power of attorney to open that box. I won't go into details. Enough to say that it all happened before I knew Solange."

The danger of getting lost among all his yesterdays bade Moerlein be brief. "In that safe-deposit box is a beautiful diamond. Sell it for whatever you can get and send the money to the person whose name and address are written on the small, brown envelope containing the stone. Will you do this for me, Anson?"

"It's done, Charles."

Moerlein's strength was ebbing. He murmured something unintelligible to his old friend—something about welcoming death if you have made your peace with life.

Barely a month later Charles Moerlein died of intercurrent pneumonia. Burial services were conducted by his fellow Masons; in their traditional manner, they placed a sprig of evergreen, a pinch of salt and a few grains of earth in the coffin of the deceased. Many things have been said about Masonry; but no intelligent criticism has ever been leveled at the hopeful, stinging, dust-unto-dust symbols employed by the Order in performing its final work of corporal mercy.

One hundred honorary pallbearers, constituting the elite of the business and professional set in Cincinnati, bore Charles Moerlein's body to a handsome mausoleum overlooking the city and the Ohio River, forever winding toward the sea.

In the first carriage rode Solange, veiled. Supporting Moerlein's widow in her hour of grief, Zarah and Anson rode in the same carriage. Behind them came Chance and Amy Woodhull, together with their two-year-old son Quin. For a complete list of the many others that followed—some in carriages, some in automobiles, some afoot—consult the Cincinnati *Courier* of April 23, 1912.

At the tail of the funeral cortege walked a man attired in the black costume of a professional mummer. He wore black gloves and a black patch over his right eye. As the first shovel of earth fell upon Moerlein's casket this mourner advanced unobtrusively to the edge of the grave and drew from his waistcoat pocket a couple of ordinary playing cards. One was the Ace of Diamonds, the other the King of Hearts. Kneeling, the better to solve in his own mind the enigma of Moerlein's total personality, the man hesitated between the two cards. Then, with bowed head, he dropped both of them into the oblong pit.

It would seem that no one has a monopoly on symbolism.

Selling a seven-carat diamond can be quite a problem, especially if the seller knows nothing about the diamond market or the potential value of the stone.

In complying with Charles Moerlein's expressed wish, Anson's first order of business was to determine the approximate worth of the square-cut diamond that he found in Moerlein's safe-deposit box. His line of reasoning took the form of a Socratic dialogue:

Q. If this diamond were a horse and you didn't know anything about horses, to whom would you turn for knowledge?

A. To a horse-dealer, of course.

Q. Would you be satisfied with the opinion of a single horse-dealer?

A. No. I'd get two or three opinions, compare them, paying each an appraiser's fee.

Q. Good man. But this is a diamond, not a horse. Where then will you go for advice?

A. To the leading diamond merchants of Cincinnati.

Q. Excellent idea. Get going.

Consultation with three reputable diamond merchants cost Anson thirty dollars for appraisal fees and three days of precious time—time that might have been spent in staking out his claim to the Rosemere distillery. During these three days Anson learned many things about diamonds.

As one merchant explained: "This flawless white stone—it's a bit old fashioned in its cutting—probably retailed for ten thousand dollars. You are entitled to know that the retail price represents a one hundred per cent markup over the cost to the dealer, who may have carried it in his stock for a long time, waiting for just the right buyer. Now which do you want to know: the cost of this stone or its price?"

"I'll settle for the cost," said Anson.

"Oh, no, Mr. Woodhull. Theoretically you'd sell it for whatever the *least* interested party is willing to pay—unless you stumble by chance across the *most* interested party. In which case you could ask, and probably receive, nine or ten thousand dollars."

"Thank you," said Anson. He paid the appraisal fee, walked out of the shop, and decided that he, Anson Woodhull, was the most interested buyer in Cincinnati. Accordingly, he bought the stone as a gift for Zarah. With the proceeds of the sale he purchased a cashier's check for seven thousand five hundred dollars (a fair enough straddle between cost and selling price) at the Atlas National Bank. To complete his confidential mission, he then forwarded the check to the person whose name and address—written in Moerlein's own hand—were inscribed on the small brown envelope in which he found the stone.

Shortly afterward, a charwoman named Lucienne Bisguier received a cashier's check for seven thousand five hundred dollars drawn upon the Atlas National Bank of Cincinnati. Having lost her beauty, Lucienne could no longer ply her ancient profession even in the cheapest of brothels. She estimated that seven thousand five hundred dollars, if carefully spent, would last as long as she did. In a spirit of thanksgiving, she entered the Eglise de St. Charles, lighted a candle for *dix centimes*, said a little prayer, and blessed the memory of the man who had loved her in the springtime of her beauty.

Distrusting banks, Lucienne kept the money hidden in the mattress of her wretched lodging-house room. It is a sad commentary on the filial relationship that a worthless young man named Lucien Frye, having sponged off his mother for many years, should have slit open the mattress cover, stolen the money and vanished from that place.

Anson's search for the Rosemere distillery was a composite of Grail-quest wanderings, picaresque adventure and country-mile misdirection. Kentuckians, omniscient in all matters pertaining to bourbon, knew or had heard of the famous still. In an imprecise way *everyone* knew precisely where it was.

"Just over the county line"; "Sets on top of a hill"; "Lies deep in a holler"; "Why, sure, I helped Mark Chadbourne make his first batch of Rosemere. 'Scapes me where it was. Tell you, though—ask Colonel Wambsley Hyatt; he knows eve'ythin' 'bout Kentucky history."

Anson collected a saddlebag full of unhelpful "this-aways" and "that-aways." "Don't give up, Peary," he whispered to his horse. "We're not gaining on 'em, but thank God we're holding our own."

Even the Internal Revenue people couldn't say for certain where the still was to be found. The collector explained apologetically, "We've only one gauger in that region, and he lit out a couple days ago. Try the court house. Someone there ought to know."

At the court house an aged clerk named Tukey *did* know. "Problem is, how to head you." Tukey drew a compass rose. "*N*'s for north. That bein' so, you're practically at the place you want to go." Tukey drew a labyrinthine web with the stub of his pencil, then triumphantly marked the location of Rosemere with an X—the mathematical symbol for the thing yet to be found.

Sticking to Tukey's trail, Anson passed through a glade, a dell, a glen, a wooded piece, and after fourteen hours in the saddle he entered a dead-end ravine. The walls of the ravine were limestone outcroppings thinly carpeted by bushes. At the farther end of the hollow Anson saw a waterfall—a clear sheet of aquamarine descending without sound into the tarn below. Approaching the waterfall, he saw the figure of a burly man seated on a tree stump plucking industriously at a primitive zither. Softly the man played—so softly that Anson could hear neither the music nor the burden of his lay. Burden it must have been, to judge from the anguished heaving of the player's body, the distortion of his face, as he sang to himself the final variant on the saddest theme ever to issue from the general heart of man.

Why don't I hear the song? thought Anson. Not until he reached the waterfall did he realize that an aqueous barrier hung between himself and the singer. Anson measured the probable weight of falling water. "We'll risk it, Peary," he said to his horse. "On the gallop, boy!"

Peary plunged; they were through, barely dampened. Now Anson could hear folkish words and music, recounting the pathetic difficulties of one Mark Chadbourne in attempting to make St. Peter understand why Rosemere couldn't be made in a day less'n eight years. Somehow the Lord Himself became involved in the discussion. After a bit of chaffering, the Lord told Mark Chadbourne to stand back and watch a barrel of eight-year-old Rosemere materialize at His command.

TR-Rang, TR-Rang went the zither, followed by these words.

> *Now the Lord drew forth his miracle stick*
> *'Twas a won-der-ous thing to see,*
> *And he said in a high-ly commandatory voice.*
> *"Make Rosemere now for me."*

TR-Rang, TR-Rang.

> *Well, the miracle stick, it bent and strained*
> *To do as the Lord commanded*
> *But Rosemere takes eight years to make,*
> *So the Lord stood empty-handed.*

At this piece of unorthodox theology Peary snorted. The burly singer rose from his stump, walked around Anson and his horse, then passed judgment.

"You're a north bank character. C'n tell. Ridin' boots, beaver hat, buckskin gloves. Sometimes they wear black silk ones. You don't catch me dressin' that way."

"Maybe you're not dressing up to your part," said Anson. "How might you know what my part is?"

"Tinney, you're a national figure. Not on account of your fighting cocks; they didn't lift mortgages as promised in the contract. And not on account of your fisticuffs, either."

Anson continued. "No, Tinney, your reputation is built solid on the skill and care that you put into the making of Rose-mere."

Tinney was only half mollified. "Concedin' recent truths 'bout me and Rosemere, how come you know so much 'bout things that happened twenty-five, maybe thirty years ago?"

"I happen to know because I knocked you stiffer than a frozen mackerel in Jesse Rocamp's barn one night back there around eighteen eighty-six."

Figgatt's hand automatically rubbed the back of his skull. "Yeah, it rained next day. In wet weather the bump still raises up."

Anson told Figgatt briefly about Reb's slingshot; then, leap-ing from his saddle, he tapped a light left into Tinney's jaw. "Like to step a fast round with an old Indiana hand?"

The two men hugged each other like bears while the walls of the ravine almost buckled at their guffawing.

Then Anson showed Tinney the Title of Conveyance. "We're going to make Rosemere again, Tinney. Before we start, I'd like mighty well to look at the two thousand barrels nominated in this bond."

"Sorry, Mr. Woodhull. They ain't no two thousand barrels any more."

"What happened to them?"

Figgatt's recital was tragic. It told the story of a man wear-ing a black patch over his right eye. The man had presented to the Federal gauger warehouse receipts covering the whiskey. The gauger demanded payment of the excise tax and the man with the patch over his eye had paid off with cash.

"When did all this happen?" asked Anson.

"Yesterday, 'bout noon."

Dazed, Anson sat down on the zither player's stump. "Hand me that instrument, Tinney. Put my fingers on the saddest places there are. No, never mind. I couldn't strike notes sad enough. Hit the strings very melancholy, choose the most lamentifying words in the language."

Tinney started off with his usual "*Tr-rang! Tr-rang!*" then modulated into a piece of pure lyricism that expressed the universal, ever-constant struggle between the forces of good and evil:

> *Pull Devil, Pull Baker,*
> *The south wind yet blows;*

> *Come blight or come canker,*
> *Still reddens the rose.*

> *Count thee the bounty*
> *Of clover, of corn;*
> *Forgetful of threatful*
> *Hailstone and thorn.*

> *Pull Baker, Pull Devil,*
> *The harvest unwithered*
> *By weevil or Evil*
> *Stands up to be gathered.*

"The last catch didn't quite rhyme," he said despondently.

Anson arose from the stump. "Tinney, your song was marvelous. Did me a world of good. Show me the still, now."

"Tain't much to look at," said Figgatt.

And it wasn't. Anson poured fifty thousand dollars into the Rosemere plant, for repairs, new apparatus and seasoned cooperage. It took nearly a year to get the place in order. Then Tinney began making Rosemere, but as his song recounted, every drop took eight years in the making. By the time Rosemere ripened, history so arranged matters that Kentucky's boast and America's best bourbon became an article of contraband.

Thus, like every myth, Rosemere gave Anson no material benefit. Yet, a couple of other things got settled. Anson was elected president of the Straight-Whiskey-Makers Institute, a prestige position, without pay. Anson Woodhull traveled back and forth to Washington, bearing testimony in behalf of aged-in-the-wood whiskey as against the overnight rectified article. He spoke quietly, temperately and, in at least one instance, with a kind of dry humor. He was being questioned by Senator Filmore of Pennsylvania—a man who combined some knowledge and a great deal of curiosity in an attempt to define (as he put it) "the whiskeyness of whiskey."

"There's a rumor going about, Mr. Woodhull. Perhaps you've heard it. Some people say that the limestone fountain gushing out of the Rosemere ravine eventually finds its way *under* the Ohio River and into your creek. Have you any statement to make?"

"I've heard the rumor," said Anson, "but never had enough

ingenuity to prove it. Funny thing, though—funny thing about Quin's sailboat."

"Please elaborate."

"My grandson, Quin, sharp as a brier, likes to sail his little boat wherever he finds water. Just recently he was sailing it in the natural basin under our Rosemere waterfall. Came to me and said, 'Gramp, I've lost my boat.' 'How'd you lose it?' 'Well,' says Quin, 'I saw it whirled around and around in the middle of the Rosemere basin and then it seemed to get sucked down.'"

"How would you explain this phenomenon, Mr. Woodhull?"

"Easy enough to explain. Whirlpools might suck any little boat down. But what I can't explain, Senator—" Anson shook his head—"is how Quin's boat turned up a day or two later, sailing along, prim as the Mayflower, on the surface of Paddle Creek."

4.

THE IRON SHOE

"Landmark—The Fastest Growing County Seat in Southeastern Indiana"—was celebrating Old Home Week, a civic rite that, for better or worse, has vanished from the calendar of American folkways. God only knows what happened to Old Home Week; some suspect that it suffered a commercial change around 1914 and reappeared a decade later as Merchant's Week; others contend that the profit motive, wrapped in sheet-music nostalgia, *Gee, Ain't It Great to Meet a Pal from Your Home Town?* always existed in these affairs.

But away, *fauteuil* thimkerings. Just the facts. Like you were saying, ma'am. It was Old Home Week 1912 in Landmark, Indiana (pop. 6,019). Not a big place, but growing mighty fast. Had a Chamber of Commerce, a Carnegie Library and a new high school with the names of the architect and contractor chiseled right into the cornerstone. Plato, Aquinas,

Descartes and them bookaroo gents are okay, but in Landmark it's the Palmer Method, see? No C.P.A.'s or auditors need apply. You just kept books and you kept them in a neat, legible hand while sitting on a high stool for eleven dollars a week. Why, merely to think about all the pretty girls who sat on those stools trying to strike trial balances is to be full of leaden-eyed despairs. It's even worse when you think of the men with straw desk cuffs and green eye shades who spent their lives entering someone else's profits in someone else's ledgers.

The committee will please refrain from Unconstructive Criticism. Let's make a solid effort, chaps, to recapture the Old Home Week Spirit of those Make-Hay Days before the Income Tax infringed upon the Promise of American Life—before Trade-Unionism began to interfere with those basic tenets of *laissez faire*—you know, Freedom of Contract, full Responsibility of the Employer to hire and fire, Bank Failures at Discretion and Opportunity Unlimited. Turn backward, Time, in Thy Flight, and Show Us Old Home Week Just for Tonight.

Well, anyway, here's the program:

OLD HOME WEEK—LANDMARK, INDIANA

OFFICIAL PROGRAM

June 11, 1912

9 A.M.	Union Service First Methodist Church	Sermon "Our Full Duty as Citizens" by Rev. Llewellyn Makepeace Jones, LL.D., Chaplain, State University
10 A.M.	Athletic Events at High-School Grounds	Fat Men's 100-yd. Dash; 2-Legged Race; Greased Pig Contest
12 NOON	Baseball Game	Epworth League vs. Seventh-Day Adventists
2 P.M.	Grand Parade with Floats	From City Hall to Torrent Hook-and-Ladder Company and return *via* Canal Street
4 P.M.	Livestock Contest	Prizes for all classes

6 P.M.	Doughnut-Eating Contest	Boys under 12
8 P.M.	Marching Exhibition	Landmark Zouaves
9 P.M.	Concert and Fireworks	Torrent Hook-and-Ladder Brass Band

A full day; and as it turned out, a fine, clear day, blue-skied, fiesta-like. A meridian sun shone down on about seven thousand more-or-less innocent bystanders lining the sidewalks to catch a glimpse of the elaborate floats illustrating some phase of Landmark's historic past and industrial present.

Float No. 1. *Tableau vivant.* Early settler, flintlock at the ready to ward off attacks from Potawatomis, surrounded by wife at spinning wheel and eldest daughter churning butter while boy of twelve fishes in the emphatically not-to-be-imitated Hoosier manner, conical straw hat covering face. Everything true to life except the boy—and he will persist No Matter What.

Float No. 2. Sponsored by No-Wheez Cough Drops Co. A combination set showing herb women plucking medicaments from Nature's Pharmacopoeia. Dramatis personae: Miss Slippery Elm, Miss Horehound and Miss Cocillana, gathered around a papier-mâché replica of the company's founder, Salmon P. Cubberley, a benign old josher (as represented), mercifully gone to his grave, holding a parchment containing the original formula of No-Wheez, minus the cocaine. Behind him a niminy-piminy replica of laboratory conditions supposedly prevailing in the No-Wheez factory. Girls seated, stamping on spinet pedals while streams of golden cough drops flow into the packaged article. Any resemblance to fact purely coincidental. *Cheers.*

Next a steam calliope with an up-to-the-minute repertory: "All Night Long She Called Him 'Snookie-Ookums' "; "Come, Josephine, in My Flying Machine," and that boff hit (yes, and still good today) . . .

> Come on and hear
> Come on and hear
> Alexander's Ragtime Band

Hats off, young Irving Berlin is passing by. For the first time since the Civil War, America is singing in unison, and Land-mark sings too.

But soft, she comes, the Spirit of the Maize. Nubile, blond, the archetype of all midwestern dream girls, draped in the purest white lawn. Stacked like the Samothracean Nike, and no Bali bra for cleavage either; yet vestal somehow. Who is she? Don't tell me it's Sylvia Bierweiler, granddaughter of old Milt Bierweiler, former grain-sorter in the Old Landmark Distillery? Yep, it's Sylvia all right. How'd she get there?

Sylvia owed her place of prominence to Amy Woodhull. As originally conceived, the Old Landmark float depicted three men working a pot still under real-life conditions. Amy had lifted the whole concept into the realm of allegory by selecting the fairest of the village fair, Sylvia, coaching and robing her to represent Ceres as Ceres never was; standing with a cornucopia against a backdrop of tall corn.

"No mention of whiskey," advised Amy. "Just Sylvia, smil-ing at her own perfection, and we'll get First Prize."

Chance took Amy's advice and was amazed by the crowd's favorable reception. Mayor Peterson whispered, "Damn clever presentation."

The faintest of zephyrs rustled the hem of Slyvia's robe, defining the marvelous convexity of her sixteen-year-old *mons*. Soon would the swains commend Sylvia—and with reason.

Meanwhile, lovers of horseflesh could feast their eyes on the magnificent double team of Percherons drawing the Old Land-mark float. Such draft animals were not native to this soil. Sixteen and a half hands high they stood, with dappled-gray coats shining under a benevolent sun. Two mares and two stallions, the mares each weighing slightly more than a ton and the stallions slightly less. Into their manes and tails red ribbons had been braided. Spirited, elegant, docile, durable, these Percherons (imported by Anson Woodhull from France) could draw a loaded distillery wagon at a speed of fifteen miles an hour, day in, day out—ten hours a day. Their hoofs were impervious to equine diseases. They had been newly shod that day by Anson's own blacksmith. Each horseshoe measured nearly twelve inches across.

If the horse-drawn era *had* to pass, if the internal combus-tion engine seemed destined to take over the chore of trans-portation, what nobler examples of the age-old relationship of horse and man could be found?

Such was Anson Woodhull's thought as he watched his float trot past the reviewing stand.

Chance Woodhull had private reasons for thinking otherwise. Only this morning he had supervised the grooming and harnessing of the Percherons. Three of the horses were perfect specimens. Lyra and Nannie, lead horses, trustworthy mares, sound of wind and limb. Hector, the stallion, was a dependable off-horse. It was Ajax, the ridgeling, that worried Chance.

Now, a ridgeling, let it be known here, is a stallion in whom only a single testicle had descended; and such was Ajax. He could go to stud, yet Anson had given specific orders that no mare should be serviced by this animal lest his imperfection be transmitted to his get. As a result, Ajax tended to be irritable, downright cranky at times. Only when following Nannie, who drew him to her by a kind of natural selection, was Ajax docile and dependable. Because Nannie was not presently in rut, the half-stallion following her suffered none of the frustrations known to males of the human species.

Chance often allowed his own son Quin to play beneath the bellies of these Percherons—Lyra, Nannie and Hector. But Ajax, no. He was like a hang-fire cartridge. You could never tell. Today Ajax was behaving perfectly. The four Percherons moved the spectators to steady applause, and when the parade was over, the conferring judges awarded first prize to the Old Landmark float.

Now all that remained was to present a blue ribbon to Tim Hartwell, driver of the float.

"Let me give it to Tim." It seemed only fitting that Amy Woodhull should hand the blue rosette to the skillful driver. Timothy, smiling down at the pretty young woman, accepted the trophy and doffed his hat. General applause.

As Amy turned to her husband, the tip of her parasol accidentally flicked Ajax's rump. The ridgeling lashed out with his heavily shod rear hoof. It was an oblique, one might say almost calculated, kick, and it caught Amy full in the pelvic arch.

She crumpled to the turf and lay there unconscious.

Amy's brother, Dr. Wayland Towner, was the first to reach her side. Chance, who had been chatting with the mayor, shouldered his way through the crowd that always gathers around a stricken person. "Ambulance," "stretcher," "water," the usual stupid clamor of ignorant spectators went up. Wayland Towner on his knees whispered to Chance, "Get the crowd to stand back. Under no circumstances must she be moved until I make an examination."

The privileged hand of brother and physician searched underneath the voile of Amy's dress and came out dripping with blood. This was no simple breaking of one bone; even Wayland Towner's superficial examination told him that Amy had suffered a comminuted fracture of the pelvis—literally, a fragmentation of the four bones which interpose anatomically between spine and thighs, as a weight-bearing hinge.

Ajax's hoof had shattered the central region of Amy's womanhood. An arm, leg—even a rib cage could be mended—but where was the surgeon who could piece together the crushed and mutilated shards which, intact, had made Amy Towner's frame a mobile, beautiful, self-sustaining thing?

Training and temperament enabled Wayland Towner to suppress those premonitions of dread that Chance Woodhull in the midst of his immediate anguish could not feel.

Coolly, by the authority of his double office, Towner superintended the lifting of his sister onto a stretcher. Stethoscope at her heart, Way Towner heard the scarcely perceptible throbbing of Amy's heart. A good sign: the blood, leaving brain and extremities, lay in a vast abdominal reservoir where life makes its final stand. The heart, true to its primary wisdom, had temporarily relinquished its circulatory function.

With skillful fingers Towner twisted tourniquets high around Amy's thighs, plugged the sacred birth orifice with wads of cotton. An iron shoe that could pulverize the most massive bone in the human body was quite capable of causing internal hemorrhage. The horrible possibilities could not be confirmed until Wayland Towner had made a more complete examination in his office.

At the office, Dr. Charles McCausland, an older practitioner, stood at his young colleague's side while Way seized a pair of surgical shears and cut away Amy's dress and feminine gear. Bony fragments of the pubic arch had been driven deep into her bladder and uterus, destroying the trigonal mechanism which insures continence. Thank God the base of her spine seemed undamaged. With clamps, needles and thread, Wayland made internal repairs, palpated the liver and spleen for signs of hemorrhage and found none. He wheeled his X-ray machine into position and threw the switch. *B-zzz.*

The picture when developed resembled a gray and white kaleidoscope of broken bone fragments. Fortunately, the sacral end of the spine was intact; Amy might be able to move her legs, but the principal bones of her midriff had been broken like . . . like a vase. Only God could put these pieces together again, and Wayland Towner was not God.

If his sister Amy lived at all, she would be a helpless, hopeless cripple.

And now it became Towner's duty to communicate his findings to Amy's husband, Chance Woodhull, striding up and down in the outer office. Way Towner opened the door.

"Tell me, Way. For Christ's sake, tell me!"

"Sit down, Chance." For the first time in their long relationship, brown eyes could not look levelly at the blue eyes searching his face. "We can't be sure yet."

"Will she live?"

"Yes, she'll live." Spartan underemphasis. A Laconian speaking to his best friend.

"Don't tell me the rest, Way." Chance was biting the heavy knuckle at the root of his thumb. "What does it matter so long as she lives?"

Yet even as he spoke, Chance realized that his beautiful Amy, the vessel of singular devotion into which he had poured his whole heart, his only love, would never be able to . . .

But what did it matter—what did *anything* matter—so long as she lived!

Amy did live.

For the first six months she lived in a hospital bed while various orthopedic specialists examined, consulted and disagreed. All the science in the world couldn't restore the weight-bearing hinge of a young woman's body to its original function and grace. Sometime during the first six months, they broke the cast that had provided an artificial support for Amy's torso. More X-rays. *H-hmmm* . . . the bone fragments hadn't fused as the doctors had hoped. One daring surgeon— far in advance of his brethren—tried to join the pieces of Amy's pelvis together with aluminum wire. The metal corroded. Another still more daring operator excised portions of Amy's shinbones, pulverized them and hopefully strewed these deposits of living calcium into the cracks and fissures of the broken arch. The result could by no means be called satisfactory. The transplanted bone fragments did indeed fuse together, but not in the form of a normal female pelvis. Amy would, thereafter, remain rigid from the waist down. Rigid and twisted, too.

What does one do? Teach us, O Lord!

At first, Amy's fate seemed the heavier. It was *she* who suffered the physical pain; it was *she* who must be pushed about in a wheelchair. Not unnaturally, the young wife passed through a period of suicidal dejection. Chance caught her hoarding the daily morphine dosage that would put an end to her misery.

"You must not leave us, darling Amy," he begged. "Quin and I need you in our lives."

Despite the increased tenderness of her husband there were times when Amy fell into pits of bleak depression. Lost in a bottomless abyss, how could she respond when Chance or Quin smiled down at her? Only Chance's devotion and unfailing love brought her through the first year. Gradually an adjustment took place; despair became resignation, and this, by degrees, triumphed into acceptance.

Somewhere she had read a line from Thomas Aquinas: "Life must be lived even by those who lack the courage to live it."

Amy Towner Woodhull found within her own soul the courage to keep on living.

As the months went on, Chance began to suffer torments of sexual deprivation. At twenty-six he was at the peak of young manhood, deeply in love with his invalid wife. His whole nature revolted at the idea of marital infidelity. Recourse to brothels or casual affairs was distasteful to him, unthinkable. And yet, his state of unrelieved sexual tension mounted to an unbearable pitch.

Sleepless and desperate, he decided to find relief in whiskey. He would get drunk. Yes, God damn it, *stay* drunk if necessary. No better time or place to begin than this awful midnight hour. He tore the seal off a bottle of Old Landmark. What had Johnno Normile called whiskey? "Elixir and opiate." Well, let the opiate work now. He poured a tumblerful of the reddish-amber liquid (O! wise apothecary) and tried to swallow it at a single draught.

Old Landmark was good whiskey, ripe, mature and flavorful. The glass in his hand held a quarter pint of the best four-year-old whiskey in the United States. But after the first desperate gulp, Chance knew that it wouldn't solve his problems. "Winner by the glass, and loser by the bottle"—wasn't that something Johnno Normile had said? Anchor to windward, yes, but Key to the Cemetery, too. "Universal solvent, ah, how did the rest of it go? Mortal stain . . . Symbol of the ferment in this valley of fog, mist and tears. Carbon, oxygen and hydrogen, blended together in Aqueous Matrimony."

Matrimony! A sacrament bestowed by each of the married partners on the other. Is my relation to Amy still a sacrament? Chance wondered. Yes; read the contract, mister . . . *For better or worse . . . For richer or poorer . . . In sickness or in health . . .*

Noncancelable.

Water of Life, Water of Death, Usquebaugh . . . WHISKEY! Chance shattered the glass of Old Landmark against the tiled wall and watched the liquid stain begin its course downward to the ultimate sea. But it would not bring Chance Woodhull down with it. Stupefaction was a price that he was unwilling to pay. Grief, a ghastly domestic situation, the daily sight of a loved face, the memory of eyes closed and lips parted in ecstasy—all these were very much present in his life. But—and it was a *but* that needed some investigation—whiskey offered neither solace nor escape.

Half disappointed, he resolved to ask Wayland Towner why whiskey had failed to cheat so well as it was famed to do. Way's explanation was utterly devoid of the sentimental pap offered by reformers to suffering men and women in need of help and truth.

"No one can use whiskey excessively unless pre-existing conditions—usually traceable to an insecure childhood—are present. You, Chance, were conceived by a father and mother who loved each other. They transferred some of that love—not too much, just enough—to you. You were brought up in an atmosphere of security and fearlessness." Way smiled reminiscently. "Remember the day you got off the ground and shoved your spiked shoes into Magoffin's foot?"

"I remember . . . It wasn't exactly sporting."

"Sporting, hell! It was a triumph of life over death. That prostrate boy, you—" Towner's index finger jabbed Chance's breastbone—"refused to accept the enemy's will. And why did you refuse? Because you knew that you couldn't be beaten. Where did such knowledge come from?"

Towner answered his own question. "I'll tell you. It spurted out of Anson into Zarah. She carried you to term, fed you with the milk of her love. And I'm not talking literally, Chance. How could any man child who has drunk his fill from such a fountain—how could any boy who grew up in the presence of Anson Woodhull—I put it to you, how could such a person become a drunk?"

"Ozzie's doing pretty well," Chance pointed out.

"Woodhull, sometimes I think you ought to get a refund from Harvard. They didn't *learn* you nothing there, so don't try to come over a lad from Indiana U. with that *per accidentum* crap. The meanest farmer in Landmark County will tell you that every litter of pigs has a runtling that can't even latch onto the hind tit. Now, you priceless chunk of Porcellian, you don't claim to be a hind-tit runtling like Ozzie—or do you?"

Towner drove his argument home. "You tried to be one with that quart of Old Landmark. And what happened? The stuff didn't take hold. There was nothing for it to take hold of. No anxiety streamers carried over from childhood. Sorry, Woodhull, you couldn't be a drunk if you wanted to."

By an act of supreme identification, Wayland Towner became Chance Woodhull himself and spoke from an altitude that only perfect love can attain. A sudden access of coarseness grated his larynx. "Turn whoremaster. Try jerking off. Fuck bulls or bugger foxes. Make any arrangements you please. It won't make any difference to me, Chance."

Zarah and Anson, both deeply concerned—as much for Amy's comfort as for Chance's suffering—awaited his appeal for guidance and practical aid. They waited in vain. Womanlike, Zarah's tendency was to soothe, coddle her son by preparing special dishes, petting him like a child whenever he appeared in the house. Chance bore her attention passively, without interest; once he gritted his teeth to prevent snapping at her "Let me alone! You can't help me now!"

Zarah took the problem to Anson during the parlor hour that they still shared together.

Between the click of knitting needles, she asked her husband, "Have you given Chance the benefit of your advice?"

Anson laid aside his pipe. "Advice? *Advice?* Zarah, that's the last thing I'd presume to do. If Chance were an ordinary man, I'd tell him to get a girl friend. If he were an archangel, I'd tell him to float above the whole miserable mortal situation. But since our son is nothing but an extraordinary man, 'a special act of creation,' as you once called him, I'm not the one to un-special him by giving him ordinary advice. He'll do what he has to do, when he gets ready to do it. Just purl that into your muffler."

5.

THE EMBEZZLERS

IT WAS THROUGH SOLANGE that easement finally came.

A widow at fifty-seven, the mistress of Vieuxtemps was still a handsome woman. The years had sifted a fine powder of pearl over her hair and features as though to hush the cry of her first beauty. As she reclined on a chaise longue in a beautifully appointed room, half salon, half boudoir, Solange Moerlein might have been an American version of Récamier herself. Rich, poised, fulfilled by life, she listened sympathetically to Chance's tragic story. Sobbing, he knelt beside the chaise longue and buried his face in the shoulder of the woman peculiarly fitted to understand the torments of a Woodhull in love.

Another Woodhull had knelt beside her in similar fashion— how long ago? Solange remembered that terrible winter, buried under the drifts of thirty years, when this man's father, bereft and lonely, had said, "Look at me, Solange. . . . Look at me and understand." Could this boy, the son of that earlier Woodhull, learn to accept a solution that Anson had refused? She stroked Chance's auburn hair with a hand stiffened by arthritis but still soft with memories of love and use in the service of love.

A query still sharp after nearly thirty years of marriage to Charles Moerlein started an interior colloquy:

Did I ever really love anyone but Anson?

Yes, yes, I did love another, she thought. *Sad, is it not, Charles, that the answer should be so. That it will always be so. That custom and usage and habitude and propinquity and dearness, nearness and generosities—the rhythmic exchange of human kindness day after day, year after year, can blur the clear-cut image of one loved long ago.*

"It's not easy," she began, still stroking the hair that faintly reminded her of Zarah, "to suggest that love may be transferred gradually; that no love is unique. Love itself is the Necessity, an imperative denied only at the cost of life. It is the aching Now that assails us. I say *us*, meaning you, while thinking also of myself and probably everyone else in the world. Dolorous though one may be for perfection's sake, which of us does not accept the easier, nearer thing?"

Chance lifted his tear-stained face. "What are you trying to tell me, Aunt Solange? That I should be unfaithful to Amy?"

"I'm not talking about infidelity. Or Amy. I'm talking about you. Or, perhaps, I'm talking about myself if I *were you*."

"What would you do then?"

"I would let my Aunt Solange arrange matters for me. I'd make her deputy of my heart; give her powers of attorney in a province where she is more familiar than any man could possibly be."

Chance smiled for the first time. "Must I sign any papers?"

"Signatures are not necessary. The heart stands bond for itself."

With her lace handkerchief she dried the corners of his eyes. "Give me, say, two weeks. After all, one does not charge at a dove."

The name and whereabouts of this particular dove were not known exactly to Solange, yet she had a definite person in mind. On the previous evening she had entertained at dinner Judge Rainey and his wife, Harriet.. While lighting one of the English market Havanas, Judge Rainey told the dinner party about a disturbing—yes, a *rather* disturbing—duty that he had been obliged to perform that day.

"One of the most painful things that ever happened to me. Had to sentence a young man named Barrows for embezzlement."

"Embezzlement?" The term was unfamiliar to Solange.

"In the legal sense it means the fraudulent appropriation to one's own use of another's property. Carries a sentence of five years." The judge puffed his cigar meditatively while weighing the comparative values of the Sanctity of Property versus a goodly fraction of a man's life.

"This Barrows, damned attractive chap, was a teller at the Atlas Bank. Career ahead of him. Slated to be an officer, I was told. Well, he got mixed up with a gambling crowd; wildcat stocks; last-place nags—the usual thing. *In extremis*, he appropriates twenty-five hundred dollars of the bank's money, loses it and (here's the pathos) is unable to make restitution. That's embezzlement."

The judge savored his dollar cigar and downed a dollop of cognac. Plenty more where these came from. "Almost tempts one to become a cynic. How does Walter Savage Landor put it? 'Thou shalt not steal; an empty feat/ When 'tis more lucrative to cheat!' "

The poet-jurist made a Prospero circle with his Havana wand as though summoning up untold wealth from unrevealed deeps. "Landor was speaking in a large way, I gather."

Harriet interrupted before dear Ambrose should reveal too much. "Barrows' wife was an extraordinary girl. Spoke French. Played the piano and made a better-than-ordinary fourth at whist. I was sorry to lose her as governess for our children when she married Barrows. What on earth will she do now"— Harriet shuddered—"the wife of a convict?"

Solange knew very well what Rena Barrows would do.

A cleverly worded advertisement in the Cincinnati *Enquirer* set the preliminary snare:

Wanted: Lady's companion. Cultivated. Middle twenties. Able to speak French and play piano. Liberal compensation. No followers. Box 81 X.

A score of applicants answered Solange's ad. Sifting from among them she selected an attractive young woman who, in build and coloring, might have been Solange's own daughter. To test her, the interview was conducted in French.

"Your name, my dear?"

"Rena Sandys." Rena had reverted to her maiden name and Solange was content not to explore her marital status.

"You have references?"

"Yes, Madame. I was formerly employed by Mrs. Ambrose Rainey."

"The wife of Judge Rainey? Excellent. Your duties will be very light," explained Solange. "I am fond of music—Chopin, Mozart. You will play for me and read a little. My eyes are failing and vanity prevents my use of those horrid things called 'spectacles.' Finally—and I cannot place too great emphasis on this point—you must *not* consider yourself a servant."

"I understand, Madame."

"You will receive a hundred and fifty dollars a month [this was three times the usual pay] and have your own apartment in the east wing of Vieuxtemps. Come, I will show you."

Solange led the way to the one-time Petunia wing (now redecorated) that she herself had occupied during the regime of Stella Battle. Rena was enchanted by the French doors of the sitting room; the onyx-and-gold bathroom fixtures and the triptych-mirrored dressing table. All remnants of the subdued, rather dowdy girl vanished as she pirouetted in the midst of her new-found private stage.

"You have excellent legs, my child," said Solange. "We must fit you out with a new wardrobe that will—what is the word they use now?—'project' you."

Intuitively the mistress of Vieuxtemps reconstructed the anatomy of her new companion. And her intuition was given physical substance when she supervised the modiste's fittings. With secret delight Solange set about transforming her companion from a dowdy governess into—what? a social ornament? Rather,

> An Image gay,
> To haunt, to startle and waylay.

Two weeks were spent in preparation. Then Solange sent out dinner cards to a small company including Chance.

Rena made modest contributions to the table talk, played Chopin's E-flat Nocturne thoughtfully; then, after an encore, blended into the drawing-room décor.

Next day Solange questioned her casually. "What did you think of my young friend, Mr. Woodhull?"

"I found him charming; he seems sad."

Solange sighed. "His domestic situation is tragic." In confidence she whispered of Amy's condition. "Bedridden; so beautiful, too."

Like an armorer honing a Damascene blade, Solange edged Rena's curiosity. Then (pleading arthritis) she kept her in virtual seclusion for another two weeks.

Who could estimate better than Solange the effect of mounting sexual tension on a woman's nervous system? Evidences of

Rena's tension became apparent—not in house-cat mewlings or scratchings for release at the back door, but in the savagery of her attack on the keys of the Steinway Grand. Farewell, "Moonlight Sonata." Rachmaninoff, stand from under!

Hearing Russian grandeur fill her drawing room till the walls threatened to buckle, Solange knew that another dinner party was indicated. This time a simple meal *à trois*. Candles, a bowl of gardenias—and Chance. Solange could see it all—feel it all —even the excruciating pain in her knuckles that would provide the excuse for an early withdrawal.

An element of surprise entered her plan when Chance, homeward bound from Louisville, stopped over at Vieuxtemps.

Chance Woodhull, traveling representative of Old Landmark, compelled to be away from home for days, weeks at a time; plentifully supplied with cash; by business necessity a frequenter of bars and cafés; this twenty-six-year-old ascetic by circumstance had been approached in every river port from Cincinnati to New Orleans with that most unbelievable of generosities: "Mister, for you I'd lift up my dress any time, free for nothing."

One had to be courteous, and the acceptable courtesy was: "Sorry. I have a sweetheart." How long could he go on repeating that fable, Chance wondered. I have no sweetheart, nor am I likely to have one while Amy lives. If she could be my sweetheart as once she was, I should not now be crossing this flagged terrace to visit Aunt Solange.

Aunt Solange? Or her companion, Rena Sandys, the girl who had walked toward him across the floor of sleep twice during the past three weeks.

Too weary for introspective musings, Chance let himself into Vieuxtemps with the golden key that Solange had given him. He climbed to his room on the second floor of the east wing, summoned Partridge and said, "Please tell Mrs. Moerlein that I have come to dine. I hope she has planned nothing social."

"To my knowledge, nothing, sir."

A bath, a nap; and on waking, a note from Solange tucked under his door:

DEAREST BOY:
So glad you are here. We dine on the terrace at seven-thirty.

SOLANGE

Within the hour he would see Rena Sandys. What color were her eyes? Her hair?

Rena Sandys' eyes were dark purple—nearly as black as Concord grapes; to be quite specific about her hair was impossible. It seemed to be a light brown illuminated by some golden hue, not truly definable as "blond." She had high cheekbones and a drum-head tautness of camellia skin, more desirable to the educated taste than apple-fresh convexities. Any suggestion of disembodiment was offset at the two places where woman becomes most feminine. While Rena Sandys sat managing her knife and fork in the continental manner, she could conceal her hips and bosom. Only in motion did this truth become apparent—that Solange's companion was no dove. Rather, a full-plumaged female capable of soaring beside the man of her choice.

Nothing that Chance had ever seen could equal the subdued *hauteur*—call it high style—of Rena's rising from the table and clearing her dress from the thousand possible entanglements that no lady's skirt ever gets entangled with; then, after entering the music room, of sitting down on a Louis Quatorze armchair. There was no hint of the *noli me tangere* affectation about her; only correctness—hiding what?

At Solange's request Rena played a mélange of Victor Herbert. In the midst of "Kiss Me Again," Solange rose with an apologetic "My arthritis is being naughty tonight." She spoke in French and used the word *méchante* to bridge the difficult chasm between the condition of her finger joints (which were, indeed, swollen with pain) and that delicious state of naughtiness that prompted her to leave Chance and Rena alone.

"May I help you in any way, Madame?"

"Only unhook me, my dear. One must never leave so attractive a man as Chance unattended for long." As Chance kissed her cheek, the love-conspirator murmured, "Are you staying the night, dear?"

"Some other time, perhaps. I must be in Landmark early tomorrow morning. Thank you, dear Solange: there will be other times. . . ."

Her hook-and-eye duties performed, Rena slowly descended the grand staircase of Vieuxtemps. Guiltless of any part in Solange's conspiracy, she could not fail to estimate the danger of being exposed to a full-blooded male for an entire evening, especially since her mistress had told her of Chance's domestic situation. Rena scarcely knew how much of herself she should offer this fresh-colored young man and decided to take refuge in the traditional courtesy that is at once permissive and unencouraging.

Chance, watching her enter the drawing room, felt almost protective toward the lovely young woman who had been snared for his pleasuring. His protectiveness (call it pity) made him unwilling to take advantage of her plight unless such advantage were canceled by Rena's expressed consent. Time was not of the essence, here. Intuitively he felt that Rena would keep. It was obvious, furthermore, that Rena considered herself under no obligation to accept his advances. Her independence revealed itself in their first conversational passage.

"Shall I continue playing the piano?" *De la musique avant toute chose.*

"If you will let me stand in the position of page-turner?"

"This music I have by heart," said Rena, fingering the opening bars of *"Für Elise."*

"Then play it so."

No rebuff given, taken or intended. *That strain again.* Neither sharp nor submissive. Sweet, yet not oversweet. *If music be the food of love . . .*

Rena played on. Chopin. Debussy.

Chopin, what were you really saying in those Nocturnes? Were you aware of the Illyrian law that forbade courtship with the aid of a lute? Et vous, *Debussy? Did no one ever serve you with a warrant for composing that deceptively innocent* "Pied dans la neige"? *Who made those footprints in the snow* et à quelle va-t-il? *Heh?*

The great clock of Vieuxtemps, which recorded the positions of Mars and Venus as well as U.S. Central time, bonged twelve.

"Midnight," exclaimed Chance. "Good heavens, where have the hours flown?"

Rena turned from the piano. The evening had indeed flown. She was safe (so long as she wanted to be) in the company of this young businessman who evidently knew a great deal more than his business.

"The hours will fly back . . . I hope," murmured Rena.

The hours did fly back. A dozen times, and not always to

the accompaniment of music or poetry. Between a man and a woman moving at an ever-increasing tempo toward the final intimacy there are truths that cry out for exchange. Long before the caresses begin, the heart must be laid bare.

No serious man (at least, not Chance Woodhull) would dream of taking on the responsibility of male love without an understanding of the cares and griefs that afflict the beloved. Solange had told him little about Rena. He knew nothing of her husband. It was Rena who told him that she was married to a man who had just begun a five-year sentence in the state penitentiary.

And why did she tell him? Because any honest woman about to give herself to a man wishes him to know everything that might later reach his ears as a hurt, surprise or shock.

"This is the ticket I wear," said Rena in effect. "I am the wife of a felon."

"And this is the ticket I wear," confessed Chance. "I am the husband of a wife irreparably ruined for love. I grieve first for her; and my grief may, at times, overshadow all other emotions."

"Give your grief its right name," whispered Rena. "Call it love."

"Love without fulfillment scarcely deserves the name."

Rena said, "I am very fond of you, Chance. But I have no wish to be used as an opiate for pain. Our situation being what it is, I think it best . . ."

Rena may have *thought* it best, but the blood has reasons that bypass the brain, or never reach it. Men know this and their knowledge has passed into coarse proverbial usage. Women know it too—fully as well as men. Time, place, man and woman in favorable conjunction—why bother with horoscopes? There is no need for spoken consent.

Rena Sandys' closed eyes, salt wet with mixed tears of joy and necessity; her warm mouth yielding gently at first, then not so gently, was signature enough for the contract voluntarily entered into with Chance Woodhull on a June evening in 1913. For considerations good and valuable—human comfort, mortal necessity, together with equal knowledge of, and participation in, the ecstasies and sorrows of illicit love—she gave him free access to her person and personality.

Such access once enjoyed cries out for frequent renewal when one is twenty-six. The interim is filled with longing; no distance seemed too great for Chance to travel; no deception too barefaced; no blade of conscience sharp enough to sever the withes that grow greener, stronger at every attempt to break them. At least it was so with Chance and Rena. Vieuxtemps became a haven for Anson Woodhull's son. The mistress of Vieuxtemps saw nothing, *knew everything*, without ever mentioning the matter. Vicariously, Solange had conquered the stern Woodhull morality that had deprived her of Anson's love at the height of her need! No dregs of rejection embittered her memory; rather, Solange was happy that Anson's son should find peace and comfort under her roof.

6.

WHIRLWIND OF THE LORD

November 10, 1913! That's the date to remember. 'Twas on that famous day and year that the mightiest Dry Convocation ever assembled in America convened while a blizzard raged through the city of Columbus, Ohio.

Nine hundred delegates representing the triple alliance against "King Alcohol" had met to discuss the question of unified leadership, hitherto lacking in the drive against the "Big Wrong." Intended as a peace pow-wow, the convention had degenerated into a dog fight. And the bone of contention was this: Who would act as Generalissimo of the Dry Forces in the approaching Armageddon? Should a leader be chosen from the W.C.T.U., the Prohibition Party, or the Anti-Saloon League?

Were Frances E. Bushnell alive and a man, she would, by deserts and ability have been the unanimous choice of the convention. But this noblest of American women, exemplar of personal purity, exponent of "moral suasion," President of the W.C.T.U. and originator of the White Rosette as symbol of Temperance, had been dead these many years. The White Rosette, a blossom that had held so much promise during the Eighties and Nineties, was now wilted. The W.C.T.U. faction, though numerous, could offer only Mary Hunter, a mannish champion of woman's rights. Her assistant, a willowy creature,

Quincia Woodhull by name, was recording secretary for the convention.

The Prohibition Party, with its long record of defeat at the polls, stood in the position of pretender to a crown it could not seize. In the preceding year (1912), its presidential candidate, Charles V. Berrington, a man of undoubted rectitude, temperamentally opposed to hoss-tradin', had taken a terrific beating at the polls.

And now while a blizzard raged outside Convention Hall, Columbus, Ohio, this same Charles V. Berrington rose to introduce the next speaker. Formal courtesy—no more—marked Berrington's voice and mien as he presented the spokesman for the Anti-Saloon League, Oliver C. Treadgood.

Standing five feet four inches in his bluchers, weighing one hundred twenty-nine pounds, with a Bible in his hip pocket, Treadgood advanced to the podium. His watery blue eyes and rubbery features, dominated by a Mutt-and-Jeff mustache, seemed scarcely the equipment for one destined to fill a major niche in the Pantheon of American Mythology. Yet this runtling had already mopped up the State of Ohio and forced the passage of the Webb-Kenyon Act through Congress. He was a terrier to the brewers, a terror to distillers and a Constitutional attorney of the first rank. Oliver C. Treadgood had rendered tireless service to the Cause.

Why, then, should this Apostle of Righteousness be received so coolly by his audience?

Well, Oliver Cromwell Treadgood was a known habitual trickster, yet no one expected the trick that he now proceeded to pull on the delegates assembled.

He began to read droningly from a written manuscript. To judge from the thickness of his manuscript it would be a long speech and the delegates were weary of long speeches.

"Louder, louder," they cried from the back of the hall. Whereupon Oliver C. Treadgood took off his mask, threw the written speech aside and fired the shot heard round the world. *"I demand a Constitutional Amendment prohibiting the sale and manufacture of intoxicating liquors in the United States."*

Quincia Woodhull formed the shorthand characters representing "Constitutional Amendment" in her notebook, started to turn a leaf, then looked back at what she had written.

"Constitutional Amendment?" Had she heard the speaker correctly?

Charles V. Berrington, pallid with anger, reached for his

gavel. Had it been a tomahawk—had he been Pontiac—he would have sunk its edge into Treadgood's skull. But Berrington was not Pontiac; he was merely a badly defeated candidate for the Presidency of the United States, and as such he must sit in fuming impotence while a false Messiah seized control of the assembly.

By prearrangement (Ollie never left anything to chance) four hundred Anti-Saloon League delegates whipped out banners bearing the shibboleth "Constitutional Amendment" and staged a war-dance demonstration. Treadgood let them yip for two or three minutes, then held up a hand for silence and began to pour snake-oil oratory on troubled waters.

There was a need for such oratory. Two thirds of the convention, involved in local frays—high license, low license, county option, town option—hadn't been told of the giant step Treadgood intended to take. Many of them thought it untimely, ill-advised, unripe. Charles Berrington and his followers knew it to be treacherous.

Treadgood allayed each group in turn. First the Prohibition Party: "With all due respect to my fellow workers in the Prohibition Party, I'm obliged to point out that it's the hardest-luck third party that ever existed. It seemed to be getting somewhere in eighteen ninety-three, until the Populist crowd took over. Ran into Silver in eighteen ninety-six. In nineteen hundred, it elected a sheriff in Maine. [Laughter.] But he died. In nineteen hundred and four, they *almost* elected a Congressman in Minnesota. In nineteen hundred and eight, they wound up with two hundred and ten thousand votes. When last seen at the polls, Prohibition's coattails were hanging from the Bull Moose horns."

He concluded by saying, "No third party ever got anywhere in these United States, and the Prohibition Party is getting nowhere slower than most."

Treadgood tossed a sop to the W.C.T.U. "No one appreciates more than I do the spadework done by our noble sisters of the Christian Temperance Union. Education, prayer, personal visitation, fine examples of personal purity—all these are written into their record in letters of gold. Fine. But how did Mark Hanna treat Frances E. Bushnell when she tried to present a petition in 1893? He made her wait two hours in his anteroom filled with cigar-puffing henchmen; then he personally spat tobacco juice onto her shoe tops."

Treadgood waited for the acids of indignation to churn his

listeners' blood. "Now I'm not one to exalt my own horn, but I'll say this: no political boss ever squirted tobacco juice onto *my* shoe tops, while I dried up the State of Ohio." He recited Anti-Saloon League records of success during his incumbency as superintendent. "Seventy-eight counties." A note of boastfulness entered his voice. "Why, I bought some of those legislators for peanuts. Others cost more. Had to foreclose a few mortgages in critical places. The point is: we out-politicianed the professionals at their own game of bribery, threat and coercion. And if we join forces (by *we*, I mean the Anti-Saloon League, the Prohibition Party, the W.C.T.U., the church groups) that filthy institution, the saloon, supported by brewers, distillers and cuspidors will be blown off the face of our fair land."

It was Bryan's Cross of Gold speech focused like a burning glass on Dry tinder—and did it burn!

Among the first to shake Treadgood's hand in congratulation was the willowy recording secretary, Quincia Woodhull. "You have put new blood into our movement by placing it on a Constitutional level," she said.

"Why, thank you very much, Miss Woodhull." Ollie appraised her possibilities and decided to explore them further when a swirl of delegates swept him away on their shoulders.

Quincia withdrew to the double room in the Crescent Hotel which served her and Mary Hunter both as office and sleeping quarters. For the recording secretary to the convention a tremendous job lay ahead; Quincia must transcribe her four books of stenographic notes into some thirty typewritten pages before midnight. She was finishing them late that evening when the new generalissimo knocked at her door.

The willowy object of Treadgood's desire, looking particularly attractive because she was on the verge of physical exhaustion, pulled a quilted dressing gown closer to her person as the Dry hero entered. Treadgood had expected to find Quincia alone; he had planned to ask her to come to Washington with him as his personal secretary. He had other plans for her too. . . .

All these evaporated when he saw Mary Hunter collating the pages from Quincia's typewriter. Nothing overt or unreasonable in the situation; but Treadgood guessed at a glance the quiet, unshakable nature of the relationship between these two women. He congratulated them for their services to the cause and retreated.

Later, falling off to sleep, he mused: Funny about some women. This Woodhull girl could have come to Washington with me, taken an active share in the work and glory of putting across the Eighteenth Amendment. I might even have grown to like her. It would have been a change from . . .

From . . .

7.

THE BROKEN CISTERN

ALL THE OMENS were bad.

In Europe the hundred-year *Pax Britannica* was about to be shattered by the flanking sweep of Von Schliefen's dead arm. All the King's horses and the blood of six million men would never put *that* egg together again. In Washington, a professional voice was indicting the wielders of America's money power. Too late! The American people themselves seemed to be caught in a cross-rip of hysteria. And the third wave of Prohibition was mounting, mounting, mounting toward a Constitutional Amendment—already written—forbidding the manufacture and sale of spirituous liquors . . . just as Oliver C. Treadgood had planned it.

Unscrupulous, opportunistic, Oliver Cromwell Treadgood, captain of the Anti-Saloon forces, smilingly surveyed the scene from his office on Capitol Hill. His files were loaded with shrapnel dossiers covering the activities of every Senator and Representative; his fisc was swollen with contributions; everything was grist to the mill that had ground exceeding slow for nearly a century and was now slipping into high gear to pulverize the Big Wrong. By 1913 he had twenty-one states in his pocket; in that year the Webb-Kenyon Act made it illegal to ship liquor into these states. The distilling industry began to feel the pinch of Treadgoodism.

Chance Woodhull's life turned now on three faulty bearings: his stricken wife, a threatened business and his illicit love for Rena Sandys.

At home he was tenderly solicitous of Amy. Because her legs were immobilized he would lift her in his strong arms, carry her downstairs and place her in a specially constructed wheelchair. Hour after hour he pushed the chair up and down the long alley of maples curving up from the county road to the verandah of their house on Echo Hill. Slowly, slowly, past the lily pond, deceptively tranquil, with a teeming life of its own.

Such a cycle of sound and color; the peepers of springtime became the bass-croaking September bullfrogs; the shoals of minnows darting like underwater shadows grew up to be sticklebacks—at least that was the name Quin gave them. Then the wonderful flowering of floating green islands—the loveliest of parasites, pond lilies. The pond was a cosmos in perfect balance. Disturb that balance by removing a single bullfrog and weeds would grow rankly. If you destroyed the weeds, the little black flies couldn't make their home among them; and if there were no black flies the frogs would perish and the minnows die of starvation. So one had better leave the pond to itself. Enough to watch its changing phases that always ended with withered sedge, squadrons of wild ducks flying southward, and then the film of thin ice, thickening until snow obliterated the pond. Then a January thaw, a day or two while spring, that spinner of green joy, wove its first threads and the peepers came in with a false chorus of hope.

Chance explained as much of this cycle as Amy cared to hear. Emaciated now, supported only by faith in her husband's love, Amy at twenty-six seemed almost too frail to bear anything heavier than the repetition of certain phrases. *I do love you, darling, I do, I do. You must live for my sake . . . and for Quin's.* They must be repeated. Amy lived by them.

Quin was going on six now. Though not physically rugged, he burned with emulative fire, imitated Chance and competed with him for Amy's attention. Whenever Chance pushed Amy's wheelchair, Quin wanted to push it too. Because the handles of the wheelchair were too high for him, Chance built a crossbar, lower down, so that Quin might assist in the proprietary duty of wheeling his mother.

"Do you feel me pushing, Mother?"

"Very distinctly, Quin."

"Am I pushing too hard, or not hard enough?"

"You're pushing just right, Son."

"Hear that, Daddy? Soon I can push Mother alone. Right now it's more fun doing it together."

Every day, at the loneliest hour of the day, Chance was faced by a cruel choice: should he turn northward to Cincinnati and Rena Sandys, or south to the remnants of his stricken Amy? Oftenest he turned south, and a few moments later would approach the gravelly driveway leading past the little pond and enter his house.

Quin was always the first to greet him. As the summer days grew shorter, he ran toward Chance swinging a little lantern in the darkness, wearing a miniature oilskin coat and fishermans' hat if it rained. But always he ran with arms outflung, golden curls flying into arms that scooped him up and set him on Chance's shoulders. Sometimes he held the boy in the angle of his arm, crying, "Pigs for sale. Anyone want to buy a pig?" and carried him into the house.

Next came the ritual of washing up, putting on the mask of cheerfulness, before knocking at Amy's door. Everything had been done by Nurse Watkins to make her patient as attractive as possible. Propped against pillows, wearing a light-pink bed jacket, a mop of curls caught up with a silk ribbon at the nape of her neck; cheekbones discreetly touched with a rabbit's foot and the pallor of lips hidden by the faintest application of geranium cream rouge; her eyes bright with anticipation, Amy was still beautiful from the waist up.

Her tragedy hidden by blankets and counterpane was not detectable to the eyes. But no fumigant yet devised, not all the perfumes in Araby, could drown out the cloacal odor issuing from her broken body. Pity, tenderness, love—combined—could not make Chance's nostrils impervious to the fetor hanging about the body of this innocent, blameless girl.

The ordeal by smell! Physicians and nurses might become professionally accustomed to it, but where is the lover-husband, who is he that can make even the pretense of not noticing?

It was Chance's fate, his duty, to inhale at close range excremental odors issuing from his wife's body. Odors plugged at the source in Amy's case by skillful nurses working on a two-platoon shift. The nurses did their job well; they repeated it frequently; they made light of it, but Amy knew that Chance knew. . . .

And what did they speak of—this condemned pair? Chance did most of the talking. It was his custom to gather up, during the day, a little bouquet of happenings in the outer world and present these blossoms, such as they were, one at a time to the woman whose world was populated by only her husband and her little boy.

"You must be hungry, darling. It's after seven and you haven't had your dinner yet." Amy knew better than to ask him to share a tray. Chance had tried it once; the odor of illness gagged him; when Death puts its finger into food only the living dead can eat thereof.

Hungry, worn by the day, and without prospect of joy during the night to come, Chance usually dined alone, until Quin, marking his sixth birthday, claimed a son's right to sit at the table with his father. The child, as Chance discovered, possessed a charm oscillating on its own little arc between extreme intelligence and a tendency to Robin Goodfellow impishness. His first trick involved the transfer of a strawberry tartlet from Chance's plate to his own mouth.

"Look, Daddy," he whispered, "see the funny wart on Mrs. Masterson's nose."

Chance bent a fractional gaze upon the housekeeper. Saw no wart on her nose. Then turned to his son, whose cheeks were oddly distended while he tried to gulp down the tart he had filched from his father's plate. With the evidence still in his mouth. Quin's eyes registered innocence of the "Who, me?" variety.

They exchanged stares. Blandly. No charge was made, no excuse offered, the evidence destroyed.

Quin's mental agility was beyond question. After playing six games of chess, with dear gullible Daddy acting as instructor, Quin put over a Scholar's Mate—a pit into which no grown man likes to stumble. After two tries at ticktacktoe, he beat Chance continually. With checkers he was all over the board.

"How come ye so, Daddy?"

"How come *ye* so, you unfilial young pirate?"

The game that Quin liked best of all was the game every boy child likes best of all—being tossed high into the air knowing that you would be caught just before your forehead bumped the floor. Snap the whip, meaning that Daddy grabs you by the ankle and swings you about like a lariat, passes you between Colossus-like legs and then hangs you up on a coat hook.

"Take me down, Daddy. I'm not a coat; I'm an umbrella today," said Quin.

Chance longed to see Rena Sandys. He would hold the longing at bay until Rena's claim upon him became imperative. On pretext of business, he sometimes took the northward turn at the end of Canal Street and followed the Ohio into the Queen City.

When Rena would see him, her joy would be salve for Chance's guilt. "It's been so long," she would cry. "I pace up and down the terrace until Solange thinks I shall go crazy. There are times when I think so myself." She would look up at him. "And such a time is now."

The evening would begin with the usual after-dinner amenities. By a nod of his head Chance would inform Rena that he was staying overnight. On these occasions she could control herself for nearly ten minutes after unhooking Solange. Then, descending the stairs with the ferocity of a leopardess, she would attack the piano, pretending to ignore Chance's presence. Always he assumed the position of page-turner, out-playing Rena at her own game of teasing until she would murmur, "Tell me to stop playing."

"Stop playing, Sweet."

"But the music says *sostenuto*."

"Then sustain it."

"In mercy, Chance."

"Go, then. I'll take two turns about the house. In exactly four minutes . . ."

Amy struggled against a melancholy induced by her hopeless illness. She attempted to be cheerful and confided to Chance that one of her chief sources of strength was her perfect faith in his unwavering love and fidelity.

On a September afternoon in 1916, Amy was sitting in her wheelchair underneath the elm that shaded her home. She was in a mood of temporary depression; the beauty of the day, the free-moving clouds and the rustling of leaves overhead filled her with grief and self-pity. How easy, she thought, to start the wheelchair rolling downhill into the pond at the bottom of the slope. She manipulated her chair into position; then dismissed the suicidal temptation as Quin came running toward her.

I have so much to live for! thought Amy. A son, a wonderful husband who will soon be coming home to fondle and encourage me. She banished the idea of suicide.

"Will Daddy be coming home soon?" asked Quinn.

"Any moment now."

Quin, filled with a desire to assert his proprietary role before his father's arrival, went behind Amy's chair and pushed at the crossbar. He intended to wheel his mother toward the house; actually the chair started rolling downhill.

"Mama, Mama," cried the little boy, racing after the chair. He stumbled and fell as the chair bounced downhill.

Chance, arriving soon afterward, found Quin stunned and bleeding on the slope. Some time elapsed before Chance noticed the handles of Amy's wheelchair barely visible above the surface of the lilies in the pond below.

She had been drowned.

After Amy's funeral, Chance and his seven-year-old son moved into the big house with Anson and Zarah. For a second time in her life Zarah found herself being a grandmother, not the doughnut-making, cookie-jar type so dear to American hearts. Instead, she became a wise listener to the motions of Quin's tremulous heart—a heart that doubled its tempo if a starling flew into the conservatory while he helped Zarah fill flower pots with fresh loam. Zarah learned that she must make no sudden movement in Quin's presence. "He panics easily," she told Anson.

"Most people panic when they're afraid. The only cure for fear is . . . " Anson let the unfinished sentence trail off.

"Why don't you say 'love'?"

" 'Love' isn't something you *say*. You've got to *be* it for Quin."

All day long in a thousand ways Zarah filled Quin's active mind with the stored-up riches of her own, participating in the skyey flights of his imagination. She taught him how to paint, read and speak French, how to play the piano, told him the greatest stories ranging from the usual Daniel Boone, Robin Hood fare to the noblest tales conceived by poets, Roland at Roncesvalles, the exploits of Lancelot and the Round Table brotherhood. At the age of six, Quin read for himself the story of Robinson Crusoe. His comment was: "Say, this is the best story I ever read."

"It's the best story ever written," said Zarah.

"You mean there aren't more stories like this?"

"Very few."

"Guess I'll read it again."

No quantity of reading could protect Quin from the dreams that swarmed over him at night. They glided up to his bed on a wheelchair with soundless axles.

"Mama! Mama! . . . I didn't mean to—oh!"

Zarah suggested that the boy's bed be placed in Chance's room. Constructive idea, except . . . except . . . every dreamer always dreams his own dreams, and no one can protect him when he lies nakedly exposed.

Chance, picking up his son one night, felt the beaded perspiration and smelled the odor of fear. "Where do the dreams come from, Quin? Where do you seem to be while you're dreaming?"

"I'm in the house on Echo Hill. The dreams come out of Mama's room; then they climb the stairs to get me."

The house on Echo Hill had stood empty, unoccupied, since Amy's death. No one lived there any more. In the secret places of his own heart, Chance had decided that no one would ever live there again. People wanted to buy the place. Wilmer Stires came in two or three times a month with a new offer.

"It's not for sale," said Chance.

"Well, rent it, then. You could realize fifty or sixty dollars a month on your investment."

"I'm not interested. I have other plans for it."

When, and by what species of insight, would this loathsome Stires creature—Landmark's leading realtor—grasp the idea that the tabernacle built especially for Amy would never be sullied by common occupancy?

Around the first of November Chance received from Mr. Wilmer Stires a new fire insurance policy and a brief note calling his attention to the fact that the old policy was about to expire. "A check in the amount of $45.00 would be appreciated."

Chance never wrote or contemplated writing such a check. A month later, Mr. Stires put in a personal appearance. "I've taken over the Northern Valley Insurance Agency," he announced. "According to the books, your fire insurance expires as of December tenth."

"Let it expire. Good day, sir."

Can a Christian mind conceive the wanton and deliberate

action of a man who chooses to let his fire insurance expire?

Thus, Stires. And to give credit for a certain kind of thinking, he was right.

Chance Woodhull's thinking lay in another direction—a ghostly plan of exorcism. Call it burned sacrifice, cleaning the altar.

On a night of whirling snow, Chance opened the back door of the house on Echo Hill. Neat, clean, as the perfect altar should be. Chance sloshed the contents of a ten-gallon can of gasoline over the carpet and walls. Up the stairwell leading to Quin's bedroom, he broke open all windows in the upper part of the house. With the remaining gasoline he anointed his marriage bed. Leaving the house, he locked the back door, kicked open a windowpane.

Standing bareheaded in the snowstorm—each flake sliding to earth amidst the uncaring multitude of its kind—Chance lighted a wad of cotton waste and flung the incendiary torch through the broken window into his house.

Bang! The house went up like the top of a volcano in eruption.

"Consume to ashes, Lord, this house. I ask it not in atonement for my own sins, or in memory of my beloved Amy; I ask it for Quin. Let your vengeance fall on me, not on my son. With malice unequal to yours, I make this house of love a charred pyre."

Suttee in reverse? No, one needn't seek explanation in exotic religions. Chance Woodhull shouted down the wind: "*Aim-ee, Aim-ee!*"

Hearing the pitch of terror in his own voice, he lowered it by an octave.

"AIM-EE, AIM-EE!"

Once more from the profoundest register of grief, he cried, "AIM-EE!"

A groan, orphaned by the begetting storm in which Chance Woodhull's voice and dream-haunted son were no more important than the snowflakes gliding earthward.

The snow, falling steadily, covered all tracks of Chance Woodhull's automobile. No one had witnessed his deed. Besides, who *cares* if a man chooses to burn down his own house?

Well, Wilmer Stires for one.

He had lost an insurance premium and a potential sale. Not conspicuously imaginative in other fields, Wilmer—a practical man—was obliged to consider the hazard of wind-blown sparks. *Ever let the fancy roam.* Now, take it that the wind had been blowing the other way; one of the sparks might have fallen on the shingled roof of Stires' own home. Giving his fancy free rein, why, gosh, Wilmer saw the headlines: COUNTY SEAT WIPED OUT BY GENERAL CONFLAGRATION.

Yessir. And the whole thing had been started by a distiller, one of those whiskey-making Woodhulls—none of them much good. That trollop—what was her name? Yeah, Laly, the one with the big tits—she slapped him dizzy when he tried to make a well-intentioned, exploratory feel.

And coming right down to events of recent date, Chance Woodhull had been seen, less'n six months ago, riding in an open car with a woman who was the wife of a convicted embezzler. By adding the rumor of adultery to suspected arson, Wilmer knew he had the makings of a negotiable instrument.

While waiting for a haircut in the Landmark Tonsorial Parlor, Wilmer dipped into the pile of horny magazines and found the very market he was looking for.

Spicy Stories pays highest prices for hot tips on real-life characters. Sources of information respected. Utmost confidence. Address Box D.F., Cincinnati, Ohio.

Wilmer risked a two-cent stamp and received a wire from D.F.

DEFINITELY INTERESTED. WILL PAY TWENTY-FIVE DOLLARS FOR COMPLETE DETAILS.

REPRISE (1917)

At sixty-five Anson Woodhull might be classified as a legitimate source of concern to actuaries—those busy little nippers who work in glass-partitioned lofts of insurance companies computing the life expectancy of their policy-holders. Barring accident, cardiac failure and a few other delicacies so dear to the actuarial table, Anson Woodhull looked as though he were built to beat the system (which in life-insurance terms means that a man must be "96" old before he collects).

Sound of wind and limb, still able to shoe a horse, or, if need be, tame it; retaining the color of a man exposed to outdoors; growing handsomer each year in the inimitable spare tradition that America valued in her frontiersman.

To preserve at its prime the image of the man they both loved, Chance and his mother conspired with the best living American portraitist, Theodor van Ruysdael, to paint a portrait of Anson on his sixty-fifth birthday. Not in vain had Van Ruysdael studied the canvases of Thomas Eakins and Rembrandt before Eakins was. Not a flatterer of the Sargent school, Van Ruysdael mixed ochers and umbers to produce a full-length portrait of America's Transitional Man. Standing, right hand on a ledger, left thumb hooked through the heavy watch chain—the portrait was a miraculous saga of that traverse between landsman and merchant suggesting every step of the passage from plow to counting house. Individual, yet of a type too, Anson emerged as the timeless yea-sayer to Life with something of the Mosaic lawgiver and a hint of Blake archangel in the man of graying hair and long-boned jaw.

Zarah, beholding the finished picture, remembered Anson as she had first seen him. She remembered the interior voice that had warned: Beware, beware, his flashing eyes, his floating hair . . .

"Leave me alone for a little while with the portrait Chance," said Zarah. Then, seating herself in an armchair, she allowed associations of a lifetime free passage between the canvas mirage and the man whose weight she had borne on her body, heart and mind.

Was it possible that a man could change so little? Gain so much? Yet remain essentially the same after forty years? Would I come off so well under the brush of a master? And, finally, what would my life have been without this man whose face has occupied the center of my soul even when that soul itself was clouded; this man whose strength has flowed into me so often without loss to himself? Where but from him should I have gained the strength to meet the challenges and disappointments, defeats, never envisioned, not to be acknowledged as yet, that have broken me to his will and kept me whole thereby?

Once a flood of tears would have drowned Zarah in self-pity at her obscure fate and the bewildering failure of her children, except Chance. Like Ruth she would always stand amid alien corn.

> *Forsaking all others*
> *Wilt thou cleave to this man?*

Forsaking all others? Brattle Street dust was no richer than that of Landmark. Where else could she have taken her stand? Who but Anson could have tolerated her queen-bee manner long enough to subdue it?

What though the offspring of this marriage were unworthy of the begetters? How pitiful the myth that made children the measure and proof of love? God bless this man Van Ruysdael. Heap up riches, honor, recognition, social preferment, add a family of prosperous, successful children. What did anything matter when compared to the truth that she had been, was, always would be Anson Woodhull's wife?

Love is a wet thing. Some of its wetness collected at the outer corner of Zarah's eyes and streamed down her face in a proud, thin trickle.

8.

DOSSIER VS. DOSSIER

THE WAR TO END WARS began (need the date be mentioned?) on April 6, 1917. Anson Woodhull, returning from his distillery in a drizzling rain that day, caught a cold—the first in ten years. Because he didn't respond to the usual home treatment, Zarah summoned Dr. Wayland Towner. Way went over the patient with the meticulous skill of a born internist. He didn't like some of his findings. The heart sounds for instance: feeble. Blood pressure: 95 over 70. He prescribed bed rest, alcohol rubs—the usual supportive measures. A week later, after making two intermediate calls, Wayland Towner became gravely concerned.

"How do you feel, Mr. Woodhull?"

"Weak. Tired. Food nauseates me."

"Do you mind if I watch you take your next tray?"

Neither Anson nor Zarah had any objection to the young

physician's solicitude as he observed Anson toy with a couple of poached eggs on toast.

"Have you always used so much salt on your food?" asked Towner after his patient had emptied nearly half the salt shaker on his simple meal.

"No. Recently I seem to feel the need of . . . well, I suppose you'd call it an excessive amount of salt."

That was the tip-off. Towner examined his patient's tongue and lower inside membrane of his eyeballs. Both were brownish.

Wayland called Chance into his office. "Sit down, Sachem. Your Wampum-bearer brings grave tidings. I hope I'm wrong, Chance, but I think your father's life expectancy is somewhere between six months and a year. It wouldn't be fair if I didn't tell you."

"What are you talking about, Way? Three weeks ago Anson was a pillar of manhood at prime. What happened?"

Towner answered with another question. "Have you noticed the brownish discoloration on the back of your father's hands?"

"No."

"The darkly pigmented freckles at the corner of his eyes?"

"Well, his complexion isn't what it used to be. Neither is mine. Or yours, for that matter."

"Listen, Chance, I'm not joking. Your father has Addison's disease. It's a malady that strikes men after sixty. Rare: three cases in one hundred thousand. The signs and symptoms are prolonged and increasing fatigue following upper-respiratory infection; marked discoloration of the skin—usually brownish gray with quite noticeable bands of yellow across the back of the hands and elbows."

"What causes the disease, Way?"

"Atrophy of the suprarenal gland. The adrenals, as they're usually called, are little tri-cornered energy batteries that sit on top of the kidney." Towner drew a simple diagram. "Their function is to release glycogen or blood sugar stored up in the liver. When the adrenals fail, as they do in Addison's disease—whether from tuberculosis, lues, or just plain atrophy —the patient hasn't any apparatus for shooting up his energy. He gets weaker and weaker. Sometimes intercurrent pneumonia makes its fatal onslaught; usually, however, the heart just can't pump enough blood to the body."

"What's the cure?" asked Chance hopefully.

"There isn't any. We can keep the blood pressure up by heavy doses of sodium chloride, guard the patient against physical or mental strain, tie him in bed. But these are only supportive measures. A man with Addison's disease must prepare for the end."

"Can't we call in specialists—have a consultation?"

"Sure we can." Towner wrote down the names of three physicians in Cincinnati and Cleveland. "Call in any or all of these. I'll be damned glad if they spit in my eye and tell me I'm wrong."

Chance summoned all three. One said .six months. The second said nine. The third, having actually seen a case of Addison's disease (Addison himself saw only one), held out the frail hope of remission, by which he meant an abatement or cessation of the acute symptoms. All three accepted the one-hundred-dollar bill, plus expenses, paid them by a desperately wretched son.

Six months . . . nine months . . . maybe a year.

"And I was just beginning to know him," said Chance to Zarah.

"I was just beginning to love him."

Both were echoing the sentiments of Thomas Aquinas, who, after attempting to define the Father, decided that the better—indeed, the only possible—wisdom was to love Him.

Even the strongest love is unable to reverse the wasting process of Addison's disease. Gaunt, doomed, and conscious of his doom, Anson lay in his great bed, patiently awaiting the premature coming of death.

Midsummer 1917. America was being called in to redress the balance of Europe. And Andrew Jackson Beane, General Counsel for the Straight-Whiskey-Makers Institute, was looking for a man willing and able to stand up against the forces of Treadgoodism. Instinct led him to Landmark and into the presence of Anson Woodhull. A glance at Anson's wasted frame told Beane that the maker of Old Landmark and Rosemere would never again leave his bed.

"I just happened to be passing through and wanted to pay my respects," said Andy. "Old time's sake, you know."

Anson managed a sepulchral smile. "Nice of you to come."

Standing on the steps of the front porch with Zarah, Beane paid his respects to the widow soon-to-be. "Your husband's character was the best recommendation the whiskey trade ever had," he said. "The question now is, ma'am: Where can we find a reasonable facsimile thereof?"

"You haven't seen our son, Chance," said Zarah quietly.

"Where can I find him?"

"At the distillery."

In the person, voice and bearing of Chance Woodhull, Andy Beane saw the fulfillment of an obscure prophecy made in the *North American Review* in November 1876. In an article entitled "The Great American Confluence," a forgotten professor of philosophy had said, "The fusion of East and West will produce a new American type."

Chance Woodhull *was* a new type in the world, unbelievably rare (and tough) by birth, produced by the cross-fertilization of Hoosier, Harvard and Hellas. He resembled neither Anson nor Zarah; this twenty-nine-year-old man possessed Anson's length of thigh and cannon bone (seconded by Zarah's), but where his father's rib cage tended to be flat, the son's chest, indeed the whole upper half of his body, was an upended three-dimensional triangle topped by an Apollonian head. Most surprising of all was the expression of patient sorrow on a face originally intended to reflect the fuller satisfactions, whatever they might be, of joy, love and power.

The good-looking young bridegroom that Andy Beane remembered at the whiskey hearings was a man who, after looking straight into Medusa's eyes, had refused to become stone.

"I'm surprised that you remembered me," said Beane.

"How could I forget the way you wrapped up Professor Fergus McKittrick, sometime professor of something-or-other at Dissart U.?" Chance mimicked Beane's intonation: "Was Lord Dissart an anthropologist?"; then he modulated into McKittrick's servile, belly-crawling, "Why, no. The noble lord was a man of wide interest and large affairs who graciously guided the society through a time of trouble."

"Where'd you get that verbatim account?" asked Beane.

From a small bookshelf Chance pulled down a bound copy of the whiskey hearings.

"If you want a lesson in triple-tonguing, Andy, you should read this quaint volume, thirteen hundred pages of testimony —most of it incompetent, irrelevant, contradictory. It rather reminds me of Browning's 'Ring and the Book.' You're familiar with the work, of course." Quintessential extract of Harvard priggishness, 199-proof contempt for the ordinary race of men and a philosophically detached attitude toward the conspirators that govern human affairs were conveyed in Chance's question.

Ten years of gutter-wrestling with the enemies of straight whiskey had calloused the nerve endings of Andy Beane's touchiness. He delighted in the prospect of rumpling up this good-looking young man and transforming him thereby into a serviceable tool.

Flipping through the pages of the volume on the "What is Whiskey?" hearing, he struck the compassionate note. "Poor Gifford."

"Poor Waley," said Chance.

"Poor us." Beane brought the case into contemporary focus.

"Hallelujah, Brother Beane. Let us reason together. Have a drink?" Chance ripped the green revenue stamp off a fresh quart of Old Landmark.

"You a corn-liquor addict?"

Remembering Anson in his finest hour, Chance quoted him almost verbatim, "It is not corn whiskey, Mr. Waram, nor limestone whiskey, nor skill-and-care whiskey. I would be perverting the truth if I called it anything but Old Landmark whiskey."

They drank to that.

The acting president of Old Landmark Distilleries gave off with his deepest chest tones. "I am a busy man, Mr. Beane. How may I serve you?"

"I've been instructed by the Whiskey-Makers Institute to find a spokesman for the whiskey industry on the Food Conservation Bill. What we're looking for is a man of character. Brains won't hurt none. Naturally, I called upon your father."

"Naturally." No humor now.

"It appears that your father won't be strong enough to make the trip."

"That's right."

Testing, testing, Beane inserted the thin edge of his wedge. "Would you be willing to take his place?"

Chance gazed pityingly at the Tennessee gallus-snapper. "Andy. Be your age. As a trial lawyer, give me six good reasons why I'm not the best man for the job."

"Must I be frank?"

"You'll go through that door ass-over-tea-kettle if you aren't."

"Well, for one thing you don't act, speak or look like an underdog."

"Poor show, Andy. Weak, weak."

The professional gutter-wrestler found himself being taken from behind as Chance went on, "I could give the best dog-gone imitation of underdoggery you ever saw. Cringe, whine, lick Treadgood's boots. Get into deeper material, Counselor."

"Deeper material?"

"Must I give the old master a boxing lesson? Start thinking like Treadgood."

"That's pretty dirty thinking."

"Get dirty, then. Ask me about my draft classification. Probe into my adulterous relationship with the wife of an embezzler. Produce photostatic copies of hotel registers. *Sub-peeny* my bank account, show checks written to one who shall be nameless here. And while you're about it, ask me if I've stopped being a house-burner, imperiling adjacent property?"

Chance shook his head. "I'm disappointed in you, Andy. You've been eatin' too high off the hog. Beane, get your wind up. Ask me if my wife was pushed to her death in a wheel-chair so that I could marry an adulterous partner. That's the kind of question Treadgood's going to ask me.'

Beane knew he had a witness. "You're right. Treadgood will ask some mighty embarrassing questions. But I've got a couple fuses of cordite—" Andy indicated his satchel—"that'll crack the hinges off the secret life of Oliver C. Treadgood."

"I'm not particularly interested in exposing another man's life."

"You won't have to. Take my word for it. When the proper time comes—and by *proper time,* I mean when Treadgood begins weaseling into your personal affairs—I'll nudge you with my elbow. 'Give him to me,' I'll say. 'This weasel I must skin for myself.'"

The defender of straight whiskeys, past and present, rammed two great fists into the pockets of his baggy trousers. "I'd die happy if I could take Treadgood's pelt off raw."

"I didn't know you were a sadist, Andy. But if you're really in a skinnin' mood, I'm willing to bait your trap for Treadgood."

Both men laughed, shook hands. "It'll be fun," they said simultaneously.

"Even if we lose?" asked Beane.

"Even if we lose," said Chance.

June 1917. *All quiet along the Potomac.* Stagnant almost, as befits a river in its season of low water. When a hot, on-shore breeze wafted into the capital, it carried a pluff-mud odor of encroaching death. No one seemed to notice. Ordinarily the capital was deserted at this time of year. But in this particular June, both houses of Congress sat in sweltering session ramming through emergency wartime legislation. The Capitol itself became a gigantic carousel with everyone grabbing for the brass ring. Bankers, national and international, manufacturers (you name it, we've got it), salesmen, big, little and medium-sized, and, *ha, ha, ha* lobbyists actually working at their trade, giving sardonic proof of Newton's first law of motion: *Bodies at rest tend to remain at rest until operated on by some outside force.* And when that outside force happens to be war, and when that war happens to be the War to End Wars, the result is bound to be confusion massively confounded, with every hotel room occupied.

Occupied? At the Willard they were sleeping six in a room and the cots in the hallways made the place look like an emergency hospital. Andy Beane and his prize witness were lucky to get lodgings in a private attic on "H" Street. Under the eaves, one bathroom for thirty people, price $10.00 a day, temperature 105°F.

"There's a war on," said the proprietor. No hint of apology.

"I know," said Beane, "and if it lasts long enough, you're going to get your mortgage paid off."

He turned to Chance. "Colonel, shall we pause for a mint julep, or proceed at once to the ho' house?" Which was Andy Beane's periphrastic way of stating the problem in its irreducible terms.

They proceeded to the hearings.

The hearings on the Food Conservation Bill, held in the Senate caucus chamber while July sweltered toward its end, were staged, directed and dominated by the personality of the Dry impresario Oliver C. Treadgood. Acting as a special counsel for the committee, Treadgood had invited prominent persons to speak their prearranged pieces in five-minute periods.

A parade of singlehearted patriots marched with banners across the floor of the caucus chamber, each speaker pausing long enough to emphasize, with clenched fists, flashing eye or apt locution, the Necessity, the Overriding Necessity, the

God-Help-Us-If-We-Don't Necessity of Conserving Food-stuffs while our boys were fighting the War to End Wars. Over there.

Over here, Oliver C. Treadgood, with a Dry majority in both houses, was going through the preparatory motions of slipping Somebody a perfectly Constitutional Mickey Finn while that Somebody was under the influence of Southern Wisteria, Wartime Hysteria and the puritanic prospect of a life growing drearier and drearier.

Treadgood's first overt act had been to guarantee the un-stained purity of America's Armed Forces. *Pas de vin, pas de guerre* was proof (he said) of Gallic laxity on the field of Mars. Just how those gray-coated poilus succeeded in holding back the Hun was explained by a kind of paranoiac logic. The Hun, it seemed, took beer with his meals! To break the stale-mate of Europe's trenches, Treadgood proposed that no en-listed crusader in the A.E.F. should be permitted to blow the froth off a seidel or tug at a pintie of the Craythur while en-gaged in a sacred mission that might, incidentally, entail be-ing gassed, hung up on a barbed wire, shot at and sometimes decapitated, disemboweled or otherwise inconvenienced by odd-shaped bits of shrapnel. Ergo, no booze for our Crusaders.

This piece of Plumed-Knight strategy was merely the curtain-raiser to the main event, the enactment of a Consti-tutional Amendment. But complications set in. You see, the President asked Mr. Treadgood to hold off his Dry legislation until certain other matters—the financing of a first-class war, the seizure of railways, factories, mines, the drafting of six million men—things like that—should be taken care of.

From his station of power in the Bliss Building on Capitol Hill, Ollie made voluntary concessions to the President. "Patriotism comes first," announced Treadgood deferentially. Everything thereafter was simply a matter of cutting the Wets to pieces. And the present hearings on the Conservation of Food were merely a *démarche* calculated to identify Pro-hibition with Patriotism.

A God-marked and constructive idea. In the best tradition of American fairplay, telegrams had been sent to the leading brewers and distillers inviting them to state their side of the question if, in their opinion, they had any side. The telegram was signed by the leading Dry in the upper chamber, Senator Morris L. Sheppard, but the voice was that of Oliver C. Treadgood marching straight on the Wet camp.

The brewers decided to sit this one out.

At a time when German measles had suffered a submarine change and emerged as Liberty measles, what would happen to a brewer who stood up in the Senate hearings and shouted *"Hopf und Malz, Gott erhalts"*? An overweening emperor had already associated himself with the Deity; moreover, hops and malt were cereals—foodstuffs. The brewers decided not to show up at hearings that were bound to end as a Tyburn Hill lynching.

In setting the stage, Treadgood out-Belasco-ed the master himself. In the well of the caucus chamber he caused a portable gangplank to be erected, and the timbers thereof, bunting-wrapped, struck the red-white-and-blue keynote of the proceedings. One by one, prominent Drys climbed the steps of this gangplank, paused on the platform, where, practically smothered in billows of stars and stripes (kept in motion by a small electric fan), they recited their lines. Such true-blue, simon-pure, Simple-Simon lines you never did hear. Alcohol wasn't mentioned. No one stooped to flay the whiskey-makers. Treadgood put the whole matter on the positive, affirmational level of patriotism. Foodstuffs rode again with Paul Revere, stood beside John Paul Jones on the quarter-deck of *Bonhomme Richard.* By a species of metempsychosis, Barbara Frietchie became "the spirit of the maize," and anyone who sniped at her old gray head was riddlin' his country's flag instead.

Specifically now:

A distinguished clergyman, former Rhodes Scholar and national secretary of the Y.M.C.A. assured the committee that "France, bled white, prostrate, is begging us to repay the ancient debt—*souvenez-vous,* Lafayette—not with gunpowder but with freight cars brimming with wheat. Six loaves of bread are the equivalent of one bayonet," he said.

An investment broker, morning-frocked, laid aside his interest in tax-exempt securities and became one of the People. "Only by tightening our belts can we earn the proud name 'patriot.'"

A dedicated public-school teacher (third grade), Beloit (Illinois), contributed her threepenny bit by telling the committee: "Last Tuesday, one of my little prattlers popped up with a truly original, all-her-own idea: that *Constitution* should be spelled *Corn-stitution.*"

Tears in his eyes, a smile quivering underneath his inquisitorial mustache, Treadgood led the applause.

An ex-governor of Iowa, now lobbyist at large for the milling interests, proposed that everyone in the United States who could *write* (no snobbishness, please) should sign his letters "Sin*cereally* yours."

The president of the Women's Associated Clubs of America assured all within hearing distance that "If Christ were on earth today, as in that yesteryear when He in sandal shoon preached to the multitudes, he would now tack another beatitude onto his Sermon on the Mount, viz: 'Blessed are the conservers of food, for they shall be called the Saviors of Democracy.' " Then the noted feminist added, "We are prepared to meet every wet dollar with a dry woman."

If a witness were particularly prominent (say a bishop or president of a life insurance company) Treadgood might underscore the testimony by tossing in a question or two. "Is it your considered opinion, Sir [or Excellency], that the conservation of food is our nation's first line of defense against the Hun?"

"Indubitably, Mr. Treadgood."

Benign, reverent, deeply moved, Treadgood would then boot the witness off the stand with a *pro-forma* expression of gratitude. "On behalf of the committee and, behind them, the men, women and children of these United States, I extend my thanks. Next witness."

Amazed by the docility of the witnesses, Chance Woodhull studied the scene taking place under his eyes.

"Is this a typical Senate hearing?" he asked Beane. "Do facts and figures ever get on the record?"

"Usually the opposition gets a word in. I've watched hearings that were real coon fights. Just you wait and watch. The locomotive in trousers may develop a hot box. Keep sniffin'."

Toward the end of the first day, searching (or sniffin', as Beane put it) for a weak spot in Treadgood's line-up, Chance found an unguarded postern in the person of Pat Neely, official recorder of the hearings. He observed Neely's pitiful eagerness to obtain from witnesses a written copy of their remarks. Two or three times he caught Pat Neely sliding off into a half doze while still going through the automatic motions of transforming sound waves into whiploop hieroglyphics that had served him well for the past forty-five years in the Civil Service of his country.

Chance nudged Beane. "Watch the court stenographer. He seems punchy to me."

Andy confirmed the diagnosis. "Poor Pat. He was a fair-to-good court stenographer in his day, back there—whenever it was. Treadgood fished him out of retirement to serve in the war-emergency pool of stenographers."

Poor Pat indeed, thought Chance. He doesn't deserve what's going to happen to him.

The second day was a repetition of the first. Treadgood's witnesses, linked each to each in patriotic harmony, made protestations, long drawn out, that food was our first line of defense, etc., etc.

In timing only did Treadgood overplay his hand. Eager to stuff the record with Dry testimony, he invited too many Witnesses for the Cause. Even by cutting them down to three minutes each, the allotted two days had nearly elapsed. It was 3:30 P.M. when the Hon. Morris L. Sheppard popped a Smith Brothers Cough Drop into his mouth and tapped his deacon's gavel.

"The scheduled business of the Senate is heavy. Time is short and the emergency great. These hearings shall be concluded as of today. In the remaining half hour the committee will entertain expressions of opinion from the opponents of the proposed bill."

The only opposition appeared from an expected quarter. Oliver C. Treadgood, knowing in advance all that could be known about Mr. Chance Woodhull, licked his chops in anticipation of the Torquemada cross-examination that would nail—well, let's give it the proper word, *screw*—this popinjay to the cross.

The atmosphere of the caucus chamber was wilting. Senatorial shirts were glued to perspiring backs. No waving of palmetto-leaf fans would cool their brows. During the noon recess Chance had slipped away for a shower, fresh linen. He looked unbelievably cool as he mounted the gangplank and gave the committee the full benefit of his personality, crisp attire and well-scrubbed physical charm. A latter-day Cicero who had laid aside his toga for a pair of beautifully pressed French flannel trousers, white canvas-topped shoes and the seersucker coat with fly back—summertime tabard of Cambridge men everywhere.

Without impertinence, he was insolent in the calculated manner of a title-holder who would, when he got ready, knock a local boy through the ropes. With an inclination of his head, he addressed Senator Sheppard.

"Mr. Chairman." To each member he paid obeisance. He turned to Treadgood, glanced at Pat Neely and took another turn around the platform. The clock now registered three-forty.

"Quit stalling," snapped Treadgood. "You've got exactly thirteen minutes."

"Nathan Hale covered the ground in thirteen words."

Elegantly remote, full brother to Count L'Isle Adam leading a deep-sea tortoise on a silken thread down Boulevard Hausmann, Chance Woodhull laid both hands lightly on the rail of the gangplank, leaned patronizingly forward and went into the speaking part of his act.

"Gentlemen: You essay to assess the unassayable—to wit, the esteem shown in all parts of our country for an industry that you now attempt to appraise, not in the style of our fore-bearing founding fathers but, alas, in the less elastic manner befitting a Hanging Assizes."

A titter broke out in the press box. Chance quelled it with a half turn of his head; he was playing for bigger game than a few appreciative reporters.

"Support, if you will, venerable sirs, this policy of horse-pistoling Freedom as she walks toward a shameful urn, all unguarded, unshriven and unannaled.

"That's my exordium," he announced. "Would you mind having the stenographer read it back to me?"

Senator Sheppard bristled. "Do you question the competence of our official recorder?"

"I question no man's competence. Since I'm speaking without notes, I wish to be certain that my remarks are being correctly recorded."

Senator Sheppard leaned over his desk and tapped his gavel lightly against the bald scalp of poor Pat Neely. "Wake up, Pat. Read back what the witness just said."

Like a weary prize fighter, Neely had been making a pre-Pitman record of the chief consonantal sounds uttered by the speaker. He now attempted an oral transcription of the characters on his page. And this is what came out:

"Gentlemen: The United States of America has two steamships, nonsalable or maybe nonsailable (I can't make out which), steamed by half-wits through all parts of the country, not in the style of our fur-bearing founding fathers, but more—" Pat's eyeglasses were blurry—"in the manner of a lass with an elastic hanging ass fitting many sizes."

Treadgood gazed about in bewilderment. Instinct said, "Pounce." Echo answered, "Where?"

The chamber was filled with Chance Woodhull's imperious voice. "I demand a respectful silence while the court stenographer engages in his life-and-death struggle with the English language!"

Neely struggled on. "Support if you will, venereal sores, this policy of horse piss . . . tolling Freedom toward a shameful urinal, without any garters . . . and shivering like Hell."

A surf of laughter breaking high in the chamber washed the committee with a refreshing salt spray, then sucked the proceedings down in its undertow.

"You essay . . . ha, ha, HA. U.S.A. . . . to assess . . . TWO *s.s. . . . two steamships . . . ho, ha, HO . . . the unassayable . . . unsalable or unsailable. Ha! Ha! Ha! HA!"*

The gavel dropped from Senator Sheppard's helpless hand. Senator Bisby, the only Wet member of the committee, slid off his chair, screaming, "The lass with the elastic hanging ass fitting many sizes."

Treadgood struggled against the tide. He seized the Chairman's gavel and banged for order. "Stop it. Stop it, I say. Stop this unseemly laughter. The dignity of the United States Senate has been affronted by . . . by . . ."

By whom?

Chance Woodhull, lenient, forbearing, contemplated the upper-right-hand corner of infinity and brought back an answer. "The dignity of the United States has been affronted by you, Mr. Treadgood, when you engaged a weary, incompetent old man as the official recorder of these proceedings." Like a pillar of wrath, Chance bore down on the Committee Counsel. "Since we are making history here this afternoon, I refuse to testify further unless you can produce a stenographer of proved competence."

With the hands of the clock at 3:55, Treadgood went into a whispered huddle with Senator Sheppard. Odd that Ollie should plead the constitutional rights of a whiskey-maker. But he longed to bring his dossier into play against this Harvard Squirt.

"Considering the lateness of the hour, the heat of the day, the momentary lapse of our stenographer and the difficulty of replacing him today, the committee adjourns the hearings until tomorrow at nine-thirty A.M." Thus the chairman.

Andy Beane clamped a bear hug around his witness and murmured ecstatic hillbillyisms into Chance's ear. "Great showers of eagle-dung! You smacked it right into their whiskers."

The Harvard squirt (still wet behind the ears because of his addiction to cold showers) took the stand at 9:30 A.M. the following day. The witness didn't quite fit into the pigeonhole assigned by Treadgood to distillers, besmirchers of Old Glory, convicted felons and the like. This young fellow was begging for a touch of the bull whip. To oblige him, Treadgood had greased up his "persuader"—a dossier that would make his victim dance, squirm and holler "Uncle" during the cross-examination ahead.

Chance's opening material was straightforward, factual, his manner serious. "Gentlemen," he began, "I propose to lay before you a few pertinent statistics. I hope that the novelty of my approach, although at some variance with the testimony of the preceding witnesses, will not utterly disconcert you. The statistics are not of my invention; they appear in the *United States Statistical Abstract* for the year 1916 and constitute, so far as I know, the only legitimate approach to an issue which has been somewhat beclouded by oratory, emotionalism and cant.

"I shall use round numbers—but those numbers, gentlemen, will demonstrate that the stones of the distilling industry grind 'exceeding small.'"

He consulted a few outlying notes. "In the year nineteen-sixteen, the croplands of the United States yielded approximately two and one quarter billion bushels of corn. The mean average market price was seventy-five cents per bushel. Anyone who had seventy-five cents could purchase a bushel of corn. Apparently there was no shortage of corn because the year-end stocks amounted to three hundred and fifty million bushels. And this, mind you, in face of the fact that we exported four hundred million bushels of corn to our Allies and customers in other parts of the world."

Chance laid aside his notes and continued. "You are entitled to ask: 'How much of this corn actually became whiskey? I can best answer by telling you that a single bushel of corn produces four gallons of whiskey. Last year the straight-whiskey industry produced exactly sixteen million gallons of new spirits, which means—if figures mean anything to this committee—that the makers of bourbon whiskey used approximately four million bushels of corn. Expressed in per cent of the total crop, it would appear, Mr. Chairman, that my section of the industry (I do not speak for the brewers or any other branch) drew from the nation's granary something less than four tenths of one per cent.

"No sane person can argue that this infinitesimal portion can impede the war effort. Rats ate more corn than the stills of this country consumed. No, there must be, indeed there is, some reason, some very *powerful* reason for denying to distillers their traditional portion of the nation's cereal crop."

He glanced briefly at Treadgood. "There has been much talk about breadstuffs and rightfully so, because bread, whether in war or peace, is indispensable to life. Now I put it bluntly, gentlemen: The bread on which the people of the United States have gained their heroic stature—or lacking which they had become rachitic and undernourished—is made of flour. This flour is derived not from corn but from wheat. Does it not seem strange that a cereal which is the basic material of bourbon whiskey should be singled out for confiscation? Will cornmeal turn the tide of Europe's battle? Can Victory on the field of Mars be endangered, retarded, or in any way affected by four million bushels of corn?

"As a member of an honorable industry, I feel it is my duty to point out alternative measures. If we would increase by a single slice the daily bread rations of the submerged third of our ill-fed population; if we would pour richer treasures into the granaries of England and France, two steps are necessary: *first*, let the Fertilizer Monopoly reduce its prices; *second*, lower the tariff schedules rammed through Congress by Milling and Packing interests. Let wheat pour in from Canada, beef from the Argentine."

Chance paused with forensic intent. "But no. Why tamper with commerce when it is so much easier, so much more patriotic, to have wheatless, meatless, yes, and as it would seem, whiskey-less days?

"To sum up: Last year the United States produced two and a half billion bushels of corn. The distillers of straight whiskey converted four million bushels of this corn into whiskey. I say that the exigencies of war should not permit Dry fanatics to don the mantle of patriotism. I predict that this mantle will be twitched from their shoulders by an outraged people. If this be treason, make the most of it."

Chance Woodhull sat down. He had made the only true statement that could possibly be made to the committee.

And now arose Oliver C. Treadgood, who on his droopy mustaches alone could have been elected Sunday-School Teacher of the Year. Throw in a pair of thick-lensed glasses and a peering concern for the spiritual welfare of the witness, as he began: "How old are you, Mr. Woodhull?"

"Thirty-one."

"Been wounded in military service?"

"No."

"Let's see your draft card."

Chance gave his draft card to a committee attendant, who passed it to Treadgood.

"See you've managed to get a deferred classification. How'd you arrange that?"

"I had no hand in arranging it. On the illness of my father, I became acting president of the Old Landmark Distillery, sole manager of my family interests and the only living parent of an eight-year-old son."

Treadgood changed his tack. "You said back there awhile that there was nothing especially immoral about whiskey-making. Do you contend that the manufacture and sale of inebriating liquors does not impair morals?"

"I do so contend. The making of whiskey is an honorable business, older than the Constitution."

"Do you contend that a fam'ly engaged for the past sixty years in whiskey-making can escape the prophecy in Luke, 'Give him strong drink who is about to perish'? Ever hear that before?"

"I am acquainted with the quotation, Mr. Treadgood."

"You may be acquainted, but you don't sound *convinced*. Well, I'm not surprised—" Treadgood turned the pages of his dossier—"when I examine the record of mortal turpitude beginning wa-ay back before you were born. Time won't permit a *dee-tailed* scrutiny of your family tree, so I'll pass over the fact that Platt Woodhull, uncle on your father's side, was a professional gambler, a forger and part-time brothel-keeper. 'Twoundn't be fair to your ma if I told the committee how the fumes of whiskey drove her crazy and that she entered into a relationship—"

Beane drew Chance back into his chair. "Mr. Chairman, I

advise counsel not to finish that sentence," he said, rising. "In all my years as a lawyer, I have never heard such wanton, base and baseless slanders as those uttered by your counsel. Under rules of civil procedure he would be rebuked by the presiding judge. I demand that you remind him that these hearings turn on the Conservation of Food."

Senator Sheppard wouldn't dare remind Treadgood that his fly was unbuttoned. He rendered judgment.

"It's my opinion, Counselor, that the witness opened the door to this . . . ah . . . hm . . . cross-examination by saying that whiskey-making was an honorable occupation."

"Thank you, Senator," intoned Treadgood. "I've got other little items here that have a direct bearing on the morality or lack of same that's bound up with whiskey-making." He picked up a heavily bound volume. "It has pleased the witness to quote from governmental sources. I'm just taking a leaf from his book in referring to a piece of testimony in the 'What Is Whiskey?' hearings printed by the U.S. Government in 1909. Let me fill in the background for the record. Anson Woodhull, father of this witness, is attempting to explain the presence of something called 'congeners' in whiskey. He says, and I quote:

> "Congeners represent a trace of the Old Adam in all of us. If whiskey were the tipple of angels or of gods, such traces might well be eliminated. But since it is consumed by mortal man, I think that some remnant of its mortality will always remain. Both men and whiskey are born with some such taint, which, in my opinion, accounts for the affectionate bond between them."

Treadgood slapped the heavy book shut. "Now, Junior, you just heard what your pa said. 'There's a taint about whiskey, a trace of the Old Adam,' he calls it. Care to enter a demurrer?"

"If that's what my father said—it must be true."

Mr. Oom pontificated. "Only bears out my contention that as the tree's inclined so's the twig bent. Let's have a look at some other bent twigs on this whiskey-inclined tree. You have a brother named Osgood, don't you?"

"I do."

"Know where he is now?"

"I do not."

"It might interest you to hear that he was tarred, feathered and lynched for alienatin' the affections of the dirt farmer's daughter with a musical instrument—to wit, a slide trombone. Well, let me read the deposition duly made by proper authorities: 'The aforesaid Osgood Woodhull caused Lottie May Semple to leave her father's home in Macon County, Georgia, and thereafter committed acts of sexual violence upon her person without Lottie May's consent, she being not quite full-witted anyway, and that in consequence thereof the aforesaid Osgood Woodhull was tarred, feathered and hung by the neck until dead by a posse of indignant husbands and brothers on or about July 15, 1911.'"

Chance bowed his head. "Poor Ozzie. *Requiescat in pace.*"

Treadgood fished among his papers. "Did you have a sister who went by the name of Lally?"

"Her name was Eulalia."

"Married a fellow named Coplestone back there in ninety-six? Photographer, warn't he?"

"Yes."

"He taught your sister, his wife, a lot of photographic tricks —such as taking pictures of twenty-dollar bills, later to be used in printing counterfeit money?"

"I have only your word for that."

"Whatever became of Laly after she *ee*-luded U.S. agents looking for her?

"Laly was drowned—to the best of my knowledge—in a Mississippi flood."

Treadgood's voice rose in Sinaic thunder. "Who filched the records of her case from the U.S. files?"

"I am not the custodian of those files," said Chance quietly.

High in the chamber sat a gentleman wearing a black patch over his right eye. Black silk gloves encased his fingertips. He smiled—a benevolent, relishful smile—as he remembered filching these very records and receiving thirteen thousand dollars for same from Charles Moerlein in 1904. Plus a fat bonus from Oliver C. Treadgood for the same material ten years later.

More profitable than filling an inside straight, eh? Wouldn't you say? Yeah, brother. Amen. Discretion Paramount. Halle-lujah.

"Looking into your family record, I must say it doesn't give off a savory *bo-kay*. Isn't that the word you use in distilling?"

"We pronounce it with a *boo*," said Chance.

"Coming down to modern times, now, did you formerly

own a dwelling house on the outskirts of Landmark, Indiana?"

"I did."

"Was this property ever insured?"

"At one time it was insured for ten thousand dollars."

"But you let the insurance lapse."

"That is true."

"Shortly after the expiration of the insurance did a fire of incendiary origin burn your house to the ground?"

Beane rose with an objection. "Mr. Chairman, the word *incendiary* is inadmissible, irrelevant and unfounded in fact. Unless Mr. Treadgood possesses evidence to the contrary, I move that he rephrase the question."

Like a squid who has sufficiently blackened the waters, Treadgood seemed satisfied to let the implication stand. He wiped his droopy-drawers mustache on the back of his hand and went for his enemy's scrotum.

"I hate to ask you this question, Mr. Woodhull, and maybe your counsel will advise you not to answer. Anyway, it's my bounden duty to put it. The Anti-Saloon League expects every man to do his duty."

With an avuncular shaking of his head at the decadence of the younger generation, Treadgood fished among the papers in his brief case.

Dossier vs. dossier.

Chance knew the nature of the question that Treadgood was about to ask. Without knowledge of the stopper in Andy Beane's possession, he was quite willing to reply with a simple "Yes."

The question fell. "Did you, Chance Woodhull, a leader of the distilling industry, live, during the last three years of your marriage, in a state of chronic adultery with the wife of a convicted felon?"

Andy Beane whispered, "He's mine now. Give him to me."

"Take him."

Andrew Jackson Beane repressed the killer instinct churning in his blood. "Mr. Chairman," he began in a parliamentary tone, "my client is quite willing to answer the question, *if—*" Andy Beane's long forefinger shot out at Treadgood—"if counsel for your committee will reply to a single query all typed up neat and specific on this little piece of onion-skin paper." Bean cozened his man. "You're quite a jackknife trader, Mr. Treadgood. Care to trade your entire dossier against an itsy-bitsy piece of mine? A piece no bigger'n a baby's hair ribbon?"

Senator Sheppard adjudicated. "This is not a trading post. Our counsel is under no obligation to answer any questions. He may, however, use his own discretion in the matter."

With a Dry majority in both houses, a packed committee under his thumb and a Constitutional Amendment well within his grasp, Treadgood's pride tempted him toward the brink of overweaningness.

"I'm sure I can answer counsel's question—whatever it may be—to the satisfaction of all parties."

Beane dug thumb and forefinger into the man's windpipe. "My question will be so damaging to Mr. Treadgood that even if it is stricken from the record of these privileged hearings—I dare not utter it orally. Nor, under penalty of the law of libel, may I disclose the nature of my question to anyone else. I must therefore deliver this slip of paper to the General Counsel of the Anti-Saloon League. I fold it so. Twice I fold it, lest another eye should read the typewritten question. No one but myself knows what is on this paper. My client does not know. If any other person than Oliver C. Treadgood should read what is written thereon, I stand guilty of criminal libel."

Advancing upon Treadgood, Beane paused in mid-course. "It is only fair to remind the committee that this piece of jackknife trading hinges upon the last question that Treadgood directed at my client. Will the Chairman please have the stenographer read the question?"

The court reporter, fresh, alert, read:

Q. "*Did you, Chance Woodhull, a leader of the distilling industry, live, during the last three years of your marriage, in a state of chronic adultery with the wife of a convicted felon?*"

Beane pressed the gimlet home. "Is that the question you asked, Mr. Treadgood?"

"Yes."

"I now give you the opportunity to withdraw the question."

"And I refuse. No one in these parts is going to intimidate me."

"I congratulate you, sir. You have taken a bold stand. In fact, you have stepped onto the barrel head which I will now boot out from under you. The first boot," Beane continued, "comes to you in the form of a simple question: Did you formerly hold an Embalmer's License in three states?"

"It is a matter of common knowledge that I did."

"Such being the case, please read this question." Beane thrust the slip of paper into Treadgood's hand and stood barely a foot from the Dry leader, threatening him with his physical bulk.

Treadgood unfolded the slip of paper and saw these words:

Are you prepared to swear before God and your own conscience that you have never violated the high ethical standards imposed upon its members by the National Association of Embalmers?

High in the chamber sat a gentleman well along in years, to judge by his silver hair. Apparently he was still able to relish the spectacle of an Irresistible Force (one Andy Beane) moving toward a hitherto Indestructible Object (one Oliver C. Treadgood). The Irresistible Force carried a tiny piece of onion-skin paper between his thumb and forefinger and the information on that piece of paper had been supplied by silver-haired Mr. Discretion Paramount himself.

Dossier vs. dossier.

Whey-faced and trembling, Treadgood gasped for the precious ounce of oxygen that would bring the blood back to his brain. He looked like a sculpin with spectacles as he stammered, "I . . . I . . . I."

"Well—" Beane gazed straight into the sculpin's mouth—"what are you 'I . . . I . . . I'ing' about?"

"I withdraw the qu . . . qu . . . question."

"On what grounds?" snapped Beane.

Blood was flowing back now into Treadgood's brain.

"On the grounds that it is irrelevant, incompetent and immaterial."

Treadgood's universe was spinning. The Dry tower was leaning perilously; the typewritten slip of paper fluttered to the floor.

"Watch that slip of paper," warned Beane. "Pick it up, man. If anyone sees it, we're both ruined. Tear it up, I say."

In a semihypnotic state, Treadgood shredded the slip of paper.

Beane handed him a glass of water. "Here, wash the evidence down with this."

—Gaggingly, Treadgood obeyed.

"Watch your bowel movements for the next couple of

days," advised Beane. "We wouldn't want any of this evidence
to fall into the hands of a coprophiliac, would we?"

In spite of counsel's utter collapse, the committee voted
unanimously to present a bill to the Senate prohibiting the use
of cereals in the manufacture of intoxicating liquors. The
Lever Bill passed the Senate; while Anson Woodhull lay dying, legal distillation of whiskey (except for medicinal purposes) ended in the United States.

Properly viewed, the Lever Law—more generally known as
the Food Conservation Law—was an exhibition of Treadgoodism nearing its peak. It had no bearing on the outcome of the
War to End Wars; it was merely another step—a giant stride,
if you will—toward the Eighteenth Amendment.

Ironic(wasn't it?) that the war in Europe ended—rather
victoriously for our side, too—thirteen months before the Eighteenth Amendment went into effect!

9.

FULL CIRCLE

RETURNING TO LANDMARK, Chance entered the house
where his father lay dying. The cruel disease that had
stricken Anson in his prime was closing in for the kill. The
pigmented freckles were larger, darker now; yellowish-brown
stripes flaunted across Anson's hands and once-ruddy face.
Pallid, gaunt, he managed a feeble smile in addressing his
son.

"They did us in for sure, boy. From what Zarah tells me,
you gave 'em a hard time."

"I made the old Merriwell try. At one point we had Treadgood kicking from behind his own goal posts." The temptation to break down, to kneel beside Anson and weep with
foreknowledge of grief, almost overcame the thirty-one-year-
old heir to a dynasty in the dust.

"We're still permitted to sell our whiskey to properly accredited pharmaceutical houses," he said cheerfully. "I've brought the inventory sheets and a list of possible customers."

"Draw up a chair, son. Read the figures to me."

To save Anson's strength, Chance condensed his report. "In warehouse number one we have two thousand barrels of four-year-old whiskey. At an estimated selling price of three dollars a gallon, excise tax paid, that should net us around two hundred thousand dollars."

"Enough to buy Zarah an annuity. Earmark that money for your mother, Chance."

"It is so marked, Father." Chance proceeded with the inventory. "In warehouse number two there's another thousand barrels of whiskey between one and three years old."

"Age won't count any more. Sell it for a dollar a gallon——or let it stay in the warehouse. Let it stay in with the understanding that the purchaser will pay the excise on withdrawal." Anson spoke definitively. "This money I want you to keep for yourself."

"Thank you, Father."

Order of the Day: Sell!

Execution of Order: Get in touch with President of Allied Pharmaceuticals, Inc. Headquarters, Cincinnati.

Cincinnati . . . Vieuxtemps . . . Rena Sandys . . .

Is it possible for a man to associate thoughts of love with imperative business negotiations? Can the face of a mistress replace the gaunt visage of a dying father? Yes, such things are possible. Even to a good son. Especially if he hasn't seen his sweetheart for nearly three weeks. And particularly if he wants her to become his wife.

The biologic element in that infinitely complex man-and-woman relationship called love has been given more credit than it deserves. No one can say what fractional part it plays; but this much is certain: the impetus that drives a fully matured man toward an emotional equal may be compounded of frustration, unshed tears, failure in the world's eye, and a kind of weary, empty-handed, full-hearted home-coming to the waiting loved one. She will know what to do, where to begin, how to mend. Out of the surplus generated by her own need she will make good all the deficiencies of life. She will be understanding, patient; docile if need be; dominant in her own good time. She will be everything that a long line of Western poets, painters and novelists has promised that she will be.

Or in certain situations, she may assert her privilege to be none of these things.

Rena Sandys had yet to fail in being (or becoming) everything that Chance asked or expected of her. Never once in their long and passionate relationship had she denied him ready access to her person; there she was—his for the taking, a sedative draught if that were his need; a powder train waiting to be ignited; a sensory delight, warm, resilient, tirelessly responsive to the searching hands; no apparition, no phantasy, no celluloid imitation of a woman, nor complaisant doxy either. Rena played for high emotional stakes and paid off at odds of ten-to-one.

Chance, on his part, never underestimated the value of Rena's gift. He knew that she loved him, that her love was prizable; that she was not a simple woman, that she placed a proper value on devotion freely offered. Jealousy and suspicion were beneath him; temperamentally he was unable to believe that his love for Rena could go unrequited. And this combination had tricked him into the habit—the very dangerous habit—of taking her for granted. She was a fixed star in his life; indeed, since Amy's death, the only star. What more could a woman ask than to be loved by Chance Woodhull? Marriage? Not unthinkable if you took time to think about it. What about her husband—Barrows? Until the Senate hearings Barrows had always been a vague unreality. Treadgood's question: "Did you . . . live, during the last three years of your marriage, in a state of chronic adultery with the wife of a convicted felon?" brought the problem into the forefront of Chance's mind. He consulted a lawyer, learned that felony constituted grounds for divorce. At some convenient future date the technicalities could be ironed out.

First, Rena's consent had to be won. Chance needed that consent now—this very night. But by some freak of circumstance Rena was being, of all things, difficult. She was nervous and preoccupied at dinner; Solange, attributing her companion's fidgety behavior to natural causes (sexual deprivation ranked as a natural cause), had left Rena and Chance in the music room. Rena would be "taken care of" by taking care of Chance. The mistress of Vieuxtemps whispered, "Don't prolong the piano playing." Whether because of Solange's advice or some other contributing cause, Rena stopped in the middle of a Chopin nocturne, rose distractedly and ran upstairs. In the approved "don't be too eager about it" manner of the accepted lover, Chance took his customary four-minute stroll around the terrace, then went up by the stone steps leading to Rena's balcony.

Through the curtained window he saw his sweetheart preparing for the rite of love. Which is to say that Rena was tearing her clothes off, frantically. There she stood profiled—"Beauty's self," now that her robes were gone. But what was Beauty doing? She was taking a bottle of Rosemere from the top drawer of her bureau, pouring a tumblerful, neat. Chance knew that Rena seldom drank. He had never seen her finish a drink. But she finished this one, shivered at the jolt of it, then began a leopardess striding of her boudoir jungle.

Chance opened the French door and caught her in his arms. Or had she walked into them? Such details are lost when the broad, deep onrushing surf breaks against the beach. "It is the falling wave that has the power." And which was wave and which was beach, and exactly where the undertow, a gritty mixture of sand, salt, water and gravity, takes hold—who can filter out, catalogue, place in sequence the order of these events when they are followed by the most outrageous statement that a woman can utter?

"Take your fill of me. This is our last night together."

"What?" (It was a brutal *what*.)

"My husband is being released from prison tomorrow."

"I thought—" Chance could have bitten off his tongue at the implication of the words.

Rena sprang out of bed, switched on the night lamp. "I know what you thought. You thought that I—this body of mine and everything inside it—belonged to you for five uninterrupted years. Now, because my husband is being paroled on his deathbed, it turns out to be only four and a half years. You feel cheated of your six months. Can't you read? See the ticket around my neck! I am the wife of a convicted felon."

"I want you to be *my* wife. Felony is grounds for divorce."

"But a dying felon, ah!—that's different. A man who has rotted for four and a half years in prison. Can I desert him now?"

"Desert *him!* How can you desert *me?*" He lunged at her with strangling intent.

"Keep your hands away from my throat. Did I try to choke *you* while your wife stood between us? Is my sense of duty less binding than yours?" She gave him the knuckles of both hands. "Why did you wait so long before asking me to marry

you? Oh—" she groaned at the thought of the tragic delay—
"who would choose to leave Chance Woodhull, most beautiful
of men, and go to a living corpse? I do not choose to leave
you, but I must. I could forgive everything you have done or
failed to do and think it no hardship to live out my whole
life without hope or desire of social recognition or legal status.
I had Chance Woodhull, and he was the only thing that
mattered. I gave and I took, and I would keep on giving and
taking, because . . . because I can never love anyone but you.
Never, never, never *ever*, never anyone but you. Does that
make you feel any better?"

"No. I cannot keep on living without you."

"You will go on living. You are the Way and the Life. It is
I who am condemned to death."

"Not yet." Chance had her under his mouth now. "Once
more, darling," he pleaded.

Making love for the last time is not a happy business.

While Rena slept, Chance rose and dressed quietly, wrote
a check for five thousand dollars payable to Rena Sandys.
Then, in the first day shallows of the sun, he left Vieuxtemps,
registered at the Hotel Sinton, and make his presence known
to Mr. Julius Hochheimer.

The president of Allied Pharmaceuticals turned out to be
one of those elusive customers who tire an opponent by giving
him the full run-around treatment before entering the ring.
Mr. Hochheimer dealt largely; he bought whiskey by the
carload and stored it away for the inevitable rise in price.
But he also dealt (as Chance discovered) through a screen of
subalterns, all of whom lacked the authority to say either yes
or no. The word seemed to be that Mr. Hochheimer was out
of town yet at the same time definitely interested.

Chief among these subordinates was a male secretary
named Albrecht who possessed a positive talent for not knowing the exact day when his chief might return. "If you care
to leave your name and telephone number, Mr. Hochheimer
will get in touch with you at your earliest convenience" was as
far as Mr. Albrecht seemed willing or able to go.

For three wretched days, Chance lay face downward on his
bed in the hotel suite, alternately grieving for Rena and waiting for Mr. Hochheimer to materialize. On September 14 he
wrote a brief note to the man behind the screen:

Are you prepared to make a firm offer for 100,000 gallons of aged Old Landmark? I am in a position to sell. Would appreciate the courtesy of a reply.

Back came an answer on Mr. Hochheimer's personal stationery.

Heavy previous commitments render it impossible to make offer. Price considerations may prove an influencing factor. Will be honored to discuss terms with you 10 A.M., tomorrow, at my office.

The Allied Pharmaceutical building on Grove Street was one of the most modern structures in Cincinnati. The prevailing atmosphere, beginning with the receptionist, was a combination of utter indifference and predatory strength waiting to take advantage of harassed distillers pressed for cash and without legal outlets for their product. The outer office of the president was filled with nervous whiskey-makers whose means of existence had been nullified by law. Of course, they could go to New York or Chicago with their product; Allied Pharmaceuticals wasn't the only firm empowered to buy whiskey for medicinal purposes. Chance watched a procession of older men walk into Mr. Hochheimer's office and emerge with a beaten air of desperation. Never had whiskey or anything else been sold in a market so favorable to the buyer. Mr. Hochheimer had determined to clamp a forty per cent corner on the medicinal whiskey; he possessed the millions to do it with—and on this particular morning he was clamping hard.

When Chance Woodhull entered the president's office, Old Landmark was worth only what Mr. Hochheimer might elect to pay. The president of Allied Pharmaceuticals sat behind a small regency desk. He was wearing a morning coat, a Prince Albert collar and a waistcoat with white piping. Without looking up from a small tidy pile of warehouse receipts, he waved his hand at an armchair. "Please be seated," he said.

It was Hochheimer all the way. Except for a silver-framed photograph of a young man on the mantelpiece behind the president's desk. The young man in the photograph was wearing the not-to-be-duplicated summer uniform of Harvard men everywhere: a rumpled seersucker suit and a pair of white linen-topped shoes. Chance recognized him as coxswain of the crew that had beaten Yale in his senior year.

"It's Eddy," he exclaimed. "Eddy to the buttons!"

"Do you know my son, Edward?" asked Hochheimer.

"*Know* him! I personally tossed him into the drink at New London in nineteen hundred and eight. That was the year our crew beat Yale, and Mr. Hochheimer, it was your son Eddy who won for us. He told me to lift the stroke to forty at the three-mile mark. I thought he was crazy, but the rule at Harvard is 'Do as the coxswain says', so I lifted the stroke to *forty* and we pulled out half a length ahead."

"*You* . . . you were the stroke of the Harvard crew?"

"During that race I was."

Julius Hochheimer rose, grasped Chance by the hand. "Edward has often spoken of your many kindnesses to him. If I remember correctly, he accompanied you on the famous sleigh ride in Johnno Normile's Booby."

"Eddy and I pulled Johnno out of the flames," lied Chance.

The rehearsal of these intimacies between his jockey-sized son and the maker of Old Landmark brought Mr. Hochheimer's pocket handkerchief to the vicinity of his eyes. It did more. It atrophied the bargaining nerve in the *ausgekochte Kaufmann* in Hochheimer. He pressed one of the pearl buttons on his desk. A subaltern appeared in the doorway.

"*Zwei Kaffee, aber schnell,* Herr Albrecht. This morning I do business with an old Harvard chum of my son Edward!"

Otto Albrecht never came nearer to having a stroke. "*Sofort,* Herr Aufsichtsrat.*"

Over the coffee, served in Meissen porcelain, Mr. Hochheimer made a firm offer of seventy-five dollars a barrel for Woodhull's complete stock of Old Landmark.

"Allied Pharmaceuticals will, of course, pay the excise?" suggested Chance.

"But that is understood."

For a quick, clean profitable piece of business Hochheimer's offer couldn't be surpassed. Chance left the Allied Pharmaceutical building with a check for two hundred and twenty thousand dollars. Mr. Hochheimer accompanied him to the very door of the building's entrance.

"Where is Edward now?" inquired Chance. "I'd like to see him again."

"He is in the Office of the Alien Property Custodian in Washington."

Otto Albrecht came running toward his employer with a telegram. "Herr Hochheimer, this wire is addressed to your guest, Mr. Woodhull."

"My father is very ill," explained Chance. "I left word at the Sinton that if any messages arrived for me they should be forwarded. You will excuse me, sir, if I read the wire."

The telegram was a signal announcing Anson's end.

YOUR FATHER'S BLOOD PRESSURE OMINOUSLY LOW. ADVISE RETURN HOME IMMEDIATELY.

WAYLAND TOWNER

The Packard could do seventy-five miles an hour; Chance asked for eighty—and got it. In the thirty-six-minute eternity that elapsed before he bounded up the front steps of his father's house, Chance reviewed the flawless relationship that had always existed between himself and the man who had been his teacher, banker, friend and father without ever resorting to the "argument from authority."

So far as Chance knew, his father had never consciously exercised authority over anyone. He didn't have to. Nineteen hundred years of Western civilization, with special emphasis on its American aspects (specifically Indiana), had gone into Anson Woodhull's making. Barring the accident of cancer and that infinitely rarer malady known as Addison's disease, Anson Woodhull might reasonably have looked forward to another twenty years of vigorous activity.

It is I who have lost those twenty years, thought Chance. He felt like a mariner who, navigating by Polaris, sees only an empty coalsack in the sky overhead. Then came the still more terrifying thought: From this time forward, *you* must be Polaris.

Chance began to weep—"No, no," he whimpered, "I can never take his place."

Rolling up the crushed stone driveway, he saw Wayland Towner on the front steps, smoking a quite unprofessional cigarette.

"You're one minute early, Sachem. I thought I could sneak in two inches of this Sweet Caporal. In fact, I'll finish it while briefing you on your father's condition."

"Skip the technicalities, Way. How long will he live?"

"Twenty-four hours, maybe. I guess that's all you need to know."

In the hallway Chance embraced his mother, comforting her with arms nearly as strong as Anson's had been at prime.

"Way tells me the time is short. Father may have something special to tell me. You don't mind my going in alone, Mother?"

"Not at all, son. Your father can die in my arms without saying anything. Go in while he is still lucid."

Hesitant as a boy, Chance stood at the foot of his father's bed. Gaunt, propped up by pillows, vision dimming, Anson felt his son's presence.

"Come closer, lad, so that I can see you. My eyesight isn't what it used to be."

Kneeling like a penitential, Chance brought his face into Anson's line of vision. "Here I am, Father. Touch me. So . . . On the cheek."

By a species of homeopathic magic, something of the younger man's strength was transferred to Anson.

"I feel a whole lot better already. . . . Now listen, son. You know our family burying ground. You've been there with me . . ."

"Yes."

"I want to be buried there. A little bit down from my father and mother—facing the river."

"It shall be as you say, Father."

"The next part is hard to explain."

"Tell me, what it is, Father?"

"Chance, I want you to dig my grave for me. All by yourself. It'll be hard work. You may not understand now why I ask this of you, but it will all come clear when the work is done. Dig deep against frost and wolves. Think of me while you dig. If there is any fear or grief in you, *work* it out. Mark me, Chance: this is the sum of everything I can leave you. *In the work is the solution!* There is no other knowledge. No other freedom than . . . than . . ."

Coma drew its curtain.

Digging Anson's grave was the hardest manual labor that Chance had ever performed. He began by sinking his pickax into the yellowish-brown loess, one of America's typical soils—neither clay, nor marl, nor sand, nor loam, but a mixture of all these laid down billions of years ago, along the northern bank of the Ohio River. With his pickax Chance broke up an area eight feet long and five feet wide. Plumb lines pegged into the earth guided the first phase of the labor. Now the long-handled shovel came into play, as Chance scooped out Anson's final resting place. Some three feet down he encountered an edge of terminal moraine thrust up by the last glacier. Boulders! Neither pick nor shovel could prevail against them. Bare-handed, Chance wrestled huge stones from their glaciated bed, uprooted hundred-pound rocks to make way for his father's body and tossed them to the top of the grave.

Now again, the long-handled shovel. Now again the pick. Shovel and pick, pick and shovel, shovel, pick, lift, heave . . .

In the work is the solution. So his father had promised. But after laboring ten hours, the grave was only half dug. Tomorrow, people would come to Anson's funeral and see his son toiling at an unfinished task. "Shame, shame!" they would cry. And rightly. The father had said, "I want you to dig my grave for me," and the son had given his word that it should be done. Well, then, in God's name, do it! Dig deep against frost and wolves. Dig now, before tomorrow comes, but dig, Goddammit—pick and dig, grapple bare-handed with boulders, sweat and cry, "*How long, oh, Lord,*" until you fall down with exhaustion in the bottom of a trench deeper than yourself and, lying on your back, look upward at a rectangular slice of star-studded sky. And at the center of what you see, Polaris glistens, whirling the Wain around like a sidereal trinket on a magnetic stick.

"*It will all come clear when the work is done.*"

Climbing out of the pit he had dug for his father, Chance dimly guessed at the meaning of Anson's words.

Concealing bandaged hands behind his back, Chance entered Zarah's room. "Have you any special wishes concerning Father's burial?" he asked.

"Yes." Zarah was dry-eyed and definite. "I want it to be an unblemished piece of Americana with Indiana overtones. Keep it simple, son—as it must have been before undertakers, clergymen and civic organizations took charge."

"I promise you. This will be kept pure."

And so indeed it was. A few friends and neighbors stood in the deep grass sloping toward the river.

Anson's casket, borne on the shoulders of Chance, Reb, Wool Hamer and Tinney Figgatt, descended the slope to the new-made grave. Hands skillful in the use of ropes lowered Anson's remains into their final resting place. Exercising his privilege as master of ceremonies, Chance solicited remarks from any who wished to speak. He called them by name.

"Dear Quincia, will you speak?"

"Forgive me, Chance. I have nothing but tears."

"Reb? . . . Wool? . . . Tinney? . . . Have you no words for this man?"

All shook their heads.

Chance turned to Zarah. "You, Mother? You who knew him best. Speak for all of us."

"Since you ask it, son, I will." Zarah threw back her mourning veil, approached the edge of the grave, gazed about the field of waving grass, the pine boughs overhead and the blue Indiana sky above.

"Nature has decreed that the wisdom, tolerance and fortitude accumulated during the lifetime of one individual cannot be transferred to those he leaves behind. It is a wise provision. Which of us, singly or together, could bear the crushing burden of Anson Woodhull's greatness?

"From the moment of our first meeting, I knew he would outmatch me. He did. It chafed me to pass under his yoke. There were times when I resented his superiority and strove against it. Foolish, foolish. There is no cure for superiority but love. I am blessed among women to have learned the dimensions of the temple."

Zarah fell to her knees. "Only this, Lord: do not measure me in the same magnitudes."

Rising, she resurveyed the earth, the middle spaces above the earth, and the waters below.

"Come, Quincia; come, Chance. I need both of you very much." She gazed backward only once. "Let the wind be his anthem. The river his elegy."

FOOL'S MATE

IN AN UPPER ROOM of his establishment at 72 Paradine, Mr. Damon Frye lay on a monastic iron bed, burnishing the pieces of a small, intricate plot. The plot was a bomb and Damon Frye planned to chuck it at his partner and disciple, one Arthur Coplestone. The better to fan the dying coals of his genius, Mr. Frye opened an envelope and read a document entitled "Last Will and Testament"—a simple instrument which assigned, bequeathed and *devised* (how right these lawyers are) all of Mr. Frye's property to the above-mentioned Arthur Coplestone. A harmless little codicil stipulated that in the unlikely event of Coplestone's death, the properties should be divided evenly among those residents of Cincinnati who could prove themselves to be blind in one eye and lacking the metacarpal joints of both hands.

"How positively macabre," Arthur had said, on reading the codicil. It became even more macabre when Frye discovered (by chance) that the illuminated hands of a gift watch from Arthur contained enough radioactive substance to bore a hole straight through the spleen of him who wore it.

How sharper than a serpent's tooth it is to have an ungrateful disciple!

Time being short, the master of 72 Paradine spun at triple speed. His plan required that Arthur be (a) mutilated, (b) killed and (c) sent to his eternal reward by persons possessing the nerve, will and cue for passion. It was important also that Arthur should not suspect until very late in the game that he had been lured into a Fool's Mate. His awareness of treachery must come upon him as the cruelest cut of all.

It occurred to Mr. Frye that Arthur needn't have bothered about the radioactive paint. He was bored unto weariness by his no longer promising pupil. Coplestone's unimaginative handling of Evil made him an unworthy heir to the riches heaped up by his mentor. Arthur's preoccupation with sex—revolting. At forty-five a man should be able to go about the day's business, gathering up warehouse receipts for whiskey, forging them if necessary, bribing Federal gaugers, etc., without listening for the rustle of an extramarital skirt.

There's no *mischief* in the man, thought Frye.

With affairs in this posture, Mr. Frye leafed through a recent copy of the Cincinnati *Courier*, seeking solace that only the obituary column can provide. And here he read a condensed account concerning the death and interment of Anson Woodhull, distiller, of Landmark, Indiana.

". . . He is survived by his widow, a daughter, Quincia, and a son, Chance."

Mr. Frye remembered Chance's performance at the Senate hearings on the food conservation bill. What a terrific show the youngster had put on—spotting the flaw in Treadgood's lineup, then breaking through with that fantastic piece of double-talk about the lass with an elastic ass fitting many sizes. It had knocked the committee off its hassock. Chance Woodhull, the perfect piece of TNT with a built-in detonator, complied at all points with Mr. Frye's specifications.

One question remained: How much did Arthur Coplestone know about the man who would kill him?

Frye clipped the obit and explored the matter that evening. Quite casually, he passed the clipping to his associate.

"Well, well," said Arthur. "One more unfortunate gone to his grave."

"Weren't you married at one time to his daughter?"

"Yes, back there, whenever it was. A stubborn girl. Came to no good end."

"As I recall—" Frye went through the motions of skull-tapping—"you once took a picture of Mrs. Woodhull in a pose *très piquante*."

"So I did. Never was able to find a place for it."

"You mean," said Frye, "that her husband would have killed you. Well, he's gone now, and what do we discover? A widow, loaded, vulnerable, defenseless. Excuse me for sounding testy, Arthur, but you really do not put the pieces of eight together properly. Concentrate! Take the strain off your seminal vesicles a while. Present me with a plan!"

"I could go out there, apply the thumbscrews."

"Middle and end game are well conceived. Opening, not quite satisfactory. It's uncouth to force one's attentions upon a lady without giving notice. Write her a note. Something in the *simpatico* vein. 'My dear Madam, in this hour of bereavement, may I extend, et cetera, et cetera.' Modulate gradually into recollection of her loveliness unveiled. Suggest that your present financial stringency might be relieved if . . . No threats; nothing that might be misconstrued as blackmail. Do you take my meaning, Arthur?"

"I do, Damon. I shall write the lady this very evening."

Twenty-four hours later, Zarah Woodhull received a letter from Cincinnati. It was written with green ink on mauve paper. She read the letter, girded up her matron strength and decided to lay the matter squarely before her son.

"Do you recognize the handwriting on this envelope?" she asked.

"Shades of Aubrey Beardsley! Green ink on mauve paper. Sprigged serifs! Who in the world writes like this today?"

"Arthur Coplestone—Laly's former husband. Read what he says."

Chance read:

MY DEAR MRS. WOODHULL,

You will perhaps remember me as the husband of your daughter, Eulalia. Ever since our unfortunate estrangement I have diligently sought information regarding Laly's whereabouts. My object has always been a reconciliation and a renewal of our marriage relationship.

Pardon me for intruding upon your personal grief at the loss of your husband. His passing was brought to my attention by the public press. Meanwhile, may I hope that you will bring this letter to the attention of your daughter—co-heiress, as I surmise, to the Woodhull estate.

Be assured, Madam, of my unwavering sympathy and affection, renewed, indeed reborn, every time I permit the pleasure of remembering our once tender relationship.

Chance started to read the letter again. "What a farrago of nonsense! This man is a canting knave!"

"He is all that—and more," said Zarah.

Chance heard the overtone of dread in his mother's voice. Was it possible that Arthur Coplestone possessed evidence—written or photographic—suppressed during Anson's lifetime and brought forward now in the belief that Zarah was a defenseless widow? Treadgood's insinuations at the Food Bill hearing—" *'Twouldn't be fair to your ma if I told the Committee . . . that she entered into a relationship . . .'*"—echoed through Chance's mind. Andy Beane had refused to tell him the nature of that relationship. "Red-herring stuff," Beane had said. Chance had been content then to let the matter pass. Never would he judge his mother's action, whatever it may have been. And now, seeing her obvious disturbance, his sole impulse was to protect her.

"Have you any reason to be afraid of this man, Mother? I don't want to know the reason. Just answer me—yes or no?"

"Yes, son."

"Would you feel happier if he were to . . . disappear permanently?"

"Yes."

"Good. Take this pen and sign your name to a piece of your personal stationery. Leave the rest to me."

By return mail, Arthur Coplestone received a perfumed envelope containing a piece of notepaper and a new thousand-dollar bill. Although the typewritten note had been dictated to a social secretary, its tone was unmistakably warm. Phrases sprang up from the page: "Your letter touched me deeply. Tender recollections . . . Please accept enclosure as an earnest of my continuing regard."

Arthur showed both the note and the thousand-dollar bill to the frail personification of Evil lying upstairs.

"Aces over tits!" exclaimed Frye. "Let me break that treasury note into bills of smaller denomination." He counted off four one-hundred-dollar bills and handed them to his business associate. "I'm deducting the fifty per cent you held out on me in the Butts affair," he explained. "Read me the last paragraph again."

Arthur read:

"Laly died with your name upon her lips. She named you as principal beneficiary of her estate. Will you, at your convenience, present yourself at my home. A car and chauffeur will meet you at our station.

"Until our next,

"ZARAH."

"That strain again. It hath a deceptively dying fall. I advise you to go armed. Merely insurance. Here is my revolver, a thirty-two Smith & Wesson. If in doubt, aim, pull the trigger, and hasten back to your devoted friend, Damon."

"How much do you think I should ask for this little art pose?" asked Coplestone.

"Let me take a good look at it. . . . A triumph of vision and design. Considering the factors involved, I think that twenty-five thousand dollars would be a not unrealistic figure."

Chance Woodhull greeted the fleshy man who stepped off the C & O Express. "Arthur," he cried. "I'd recognize you at sight. How good of you to come! That's my Packard throbbing at the end of the platform."

"You're not a little boy watching for the birdie any more," said Arthur.

"At thirty-one the birdie has been seen. Please precede me."

"Your manners are still impeccable. I remember an evening—how long ago, when you picked up your mother's handkerchief? Is your mother well?"

"Radiant. Mysteriously radiant. I chaffed her about it this morning. Would you believe me, sir—but, no, I'm prejudiced. I think Mother is the most beautiful woman in the world. Incidentally, she asked me to bring you to the distillery."

"Oh?"

"The Federal people required her presence there this morning. I gather that she plans to spend the afternoon exchanging memories with you."

"That will be very pleasant," said Arthur. "Do you always drive at this rate of speed?"

"A Prix de Rome hangover. But here we are." Chance braked the Packard suddenly, dashing Arthur against the windshield.

"Sorry. Are you stunned?"

"No, just a bit dizzy."

"It will wear off. This way." He led Arthur toward a high-peaked building with sliding doors. "This was formerly a barn. Note the handadzed timbers overhead. There are barn swallows up there. Watch for the birdie, Arthur."

While Arthur watched for the birdie, Chance Woodhull closed the sliding panels of the barn and secured them with a cast-iron hasp. "Now, sir, we are alone. We shall spend the afternoon together. Afterward you will meet Zarah. Be seated while I outline in a general way the program that will occupy us until evening."

"Until evening? Your mother—Mrs. Woodhull—said that a few minutes would suffice."

"Mother said that because I told her to say it. Mother and I see eye to eye on most matters. She brings her problems to me and I dispose of them. Now, sir, I direct your attention to the array of edged tools on this side of the barn: axes, hatchets, chisels, hammers, all neatly fitted in leathern sockets. I will demonstrate how easily this hatchet comes out. Run your finger along its edge."

"I'd rather not."

"As you wish. Arthur, this armory of steel is yours. In attacking me, feel free to select any tool that strikes your fancy. Under our ground rules, I have no weapons other than my fists." Chance held up his two hands. "Oh, yes, and my size eleven feet. My intention is to beat you into a swollen pulp."

"Bbbbbb-but why?" stammered Arthur.

"Because I hear Laly crying out, 'Avenge me, Dear Brother.' Because my sainted mother whispers, 'Destroy him, son,' Now stand up, Arthur. Take off your jacket and defend yourself."

"I don't like your ground rules or your game. We'll play it my way." Arthur drew his thirty-two revolver. "Open that door."

"Don't bark unless you can bite. The sound of a pistol shot would bring friends on the dead run. You would be apprehended, destroyed by passionate hands. I advise you to toss your revolver into the hayloft."

"I advise *you* to open that door. In ten seconds I start shooting."

"Shoot away. Pistol fire is notoriously inaccurate. You couldn't possibly hit me in a vital spot."

Arthur followed Frye's directions: "Aim and pull trigger." He pulled the trigger. It made a clicking sound. Again. Another clicking sound. At the third metallic click, Arthur became aware of the fierce simplicity and beauty of Frye's plan.

"Your revolver doesn't seem to work," said Chance. "Let me fix it." He broke the gun, spun its cylinder. "Why, someone has slipped you the wrong ammunition, Arthur. This is a center-fire revolver and these bullets—see, they are marked 'rim fire.' You have been led down a long alley, seduced, betrayed. Have you any idea who did these things?"

"Damon—Oh-h-h . . ."

"I detect an *et tu Brute* sadness in your voice. On your past record you probably deserved it. Now, as an earnest of what you may expect for the future, let this left jab draw a bit of claret. You really must attempt to seize an edged tool, Arthur, or the afternoon will be very dull."

Arthur made a dash for a long-handled ax. He almost got it out of its leathern thong when Chance kicked him in the groin.

"Ugh!" Coplestone fell to the floor. His head struck a rough, hard plank. He passed out.

Chance brought him to with a pail full of water. "Up again, Arthur. It will be up and down, all afternoon. I am not an expert boxer. I shall do my best to close your eyes, puff out your cheeks, break a few teeth; I'll watch you vomit, haul you up again, and paste you silly. At three o'clock I shall be relieved by Mr. Reb Plaskett. He has asked permission to put over the KO. He has been waiting twenty-one years for this opportunity."

"Who is Reb Plaskett?"

"He was Laly's sweetheart. He loved her. He still loves her. In due time you will discover his passion for her."

During the next two hours, Chance Woodhull punched himself out. He was relieved on schedule by Mr. Richmond Plaskett, who systematically broke every bone in Arthur Coplestone's face.

It was evening when Arthur died of exhaustion. Chance emptied the contents of Arthur's pockets into a briefcase. Darkness lay upon the earth while he and Reb tied Arthur Coplestone's feet to the rear axle of the Packard.

"Hop in, Reb. We'll drag him down to the willows by the river's edge."

They did exactly that. They did more. They punctured Arthur Coplestone's abdominal organs with edged tools. A necessary step because, you see, that's where the gas forms, and it's the gas that brings dead men to the surface.

Zarah heard Chance enter the house at nine o'clock.

"The gentleman addicted to green ink and mauve paper has been dispatched via river freight to the Delta. Possibly he may meet Laly there, but he will never write you or trouble you again. His personal effects—with the exception of a revolver that must be returned to its owner—are in this briefcase."

In an upper room of his establishment at 72 Paradine, Mr. Damon Frye lay on a monastic iron bed twirling the cylinder of a thirty-two-caliber revolver that he had received via American Express that morning. The package in which the revolver came bore no return address, but Mr. Frye recognized the master hand of its sender. The returned weapon was a signal saying, "Mission completed." Dead Arthur had been properly put away and now Mr. Frye was training a new candidate to replace his former partner. The new candidate's name was Lucien Frederick, recently released from police custody in Quebec. Incidentally, Lucien Frederick was Frye's own son, and the master of 72 Paradine had drawn up a new will bequeathing, giving and devising all his property to his long-lost baby boy.

"Now, Lucien," said Frye, "this business we're in requires a certain amount of nerve. You'll be jostled to death by competitors and rivals, unless you can display, when the case demands it, an unmatchable reserve of nerve power."

"I quite understand, Father." Lucien's dark eyes glowed with pleasure at the prospect of backlashing competition. He was a handsome young man, taller than his father. A neophyte, eager to learn.

"But do you really understand what I mean by 'nerve'? Take this revolver, for example. I will remove one cartridge and spin the cylinder. So. Now, Lucien, have you enough nerve to place this revolver to your temple and pull the trigger?"

The younger man hesitated, hung off.

"Come, lad. Let me show you how it's done. Example is the best preceptor."

Mr. Frye placed the muzzle of the revolver against his fine-veined temple and pulled the trigger.

Bang!

A bullet entered his brain, and Mr. Frye was dead, quite dead.

A police captain, investigating the case, scrutinized the death weapon. "Well, well," he remarked. "Some clever person, identity unknown, has soldered a new pin onto the hammer. Originally this seems to have been a center-fire gun. Now it can detonate rim-fire cartridges. Artful chap, whoever he was."

10.

LE PETIT MORT

EVERY LANGUAGE KNOWS IT by a different name: in French, it is *le petit mort;* in German, *das ewige Nein;* in English, the "Everlasting No." Mystics call it the "period of aridity"; psychoanalysts prefer the term "acute depression." Under whatever name, it is a malady that often strikes men at a point in their middle-thirties when, their first strength waning, initial momentum lost, they must either summon up fresh psychic reserves or sink into a paralytic sea.

At such times, a family, a home, the necessity of earning a livelihood, of keeping a roof over a wife and children serve as an impetus. A good job, money in the bank or an insurance policy to borrow against are withes that bind together the lictor rods of personality. In tribal societies the stronger carry (or sometimes kill) the weaker. Often enough a wife steps forward to cover her husband during this period of transition. Pride in past performance, the laughter of budding children—even a clandestine love affair—can prop up a man's self-esteem, enable him to go through the motions of coming out for the next round.

For thirteen months following Anson's death, Chance went through all the motions. As executor of his father's estate, he bought an annuity that yielded Zarah nearly ten thousand dollars a year; paid Reb Plaskett another twenty-five thousand; and deposited ten thousand dollars in Quin's name, with Wayland Towner as trustee. The payment of inheritance and excise taxes; the closing down of the Rosemere and Old Landmark plants *seemed* like activities. Actually, Chance performed them while treading the brink of uncaringness. He had expected to feel physical pain while padlocking the high-peaked barn where the now-useless distilling apparatus lay stored. But he felt nothing, and it was this mounting sense of nothingness, compounded of a thousand disappointments, failures, regrets—yes, and loves too—that had driven him from his father's house, from Landmark and all its indicting memories, to New York City.

In November and December 1918, New York was a city of parades and martial music. Divisions of armed men either marched *down* Fifth Avenue to embark for Europe or *up* Fifth like conquering heroes. Whether they marched up or down, the band played on. New York was a city overpopulated with men wearing Sam Browne belts; some of them actually carried swagger sticks. Hotel space was at a premium. What more natural, then, that a Harvard man should seek the seclusion that a college club grants? Which is exactly what Chance Woodhull did. With approximately five thousand dollars in his checking account, he engaged one of the less-expensive cubicles in the back of the club. By cutting expenses to a not-unreasonable two hundred and fifty dollars a month, Chance calculated that he could remain solvent until his psychic malaise had run its course.

As a place of residence, the Harvard Club possessed marked advantages: No. 27 West Forty-fourth Street was (still is) an excellent address; the elegant public rooms of the club were hung with oil portraits of former deans and past presidents gazing down from serene altitudes specially reserved for Harvard deities. The club possessed a complete library of Harvardiana together with other useful and entertaining works. There was a stand-up bar too, at which one could (and in many instances, *did*) renew, advantageously, those priceless relationships formed during undergraduate years.

If hopes are dupes, fears may be liars.

Wife, home, business, father, sweetheart—the supports that keep a man erect and moving forward, the internal braces that buttress the soul from within—of these, not one remained in Chance Woodhull's life. Through his curtain of cheap marquisette, sunlight never fell. The prevailing gloom wavered between grayness and pitch black. No vista of tree, hill or star; not even a reassuring glimpse of human chimney pots; only the blank dead-endness of a battleship-gray wall.

Chance Woodhull was neither disoriented nor troubled by hallucinations; his feelings of persecution were negligible; all sexual desire seemed to have ebbed away; there was no sign of physical deterioration (except pallor, perhaps) to be noted in his appearance. Every morning he held his face up to the mirror for an unwanted shave; once every two weeks he summoned Guido, the club barber, to cut his hair. For breakfast and dinner he called Room Service. Because whiskey had no effect on him he never drank. As for cigarettes, a pack might last two days. He read nothing but the morning paper, which informed him seriatim that President Wilson was being hailed in Europe by acclamations of battle-weary millions.

Chance's trouble came to this: he was suffering from an emotional apathy induced by the loss of everything that gives flavor, tone, zest, meaning and human warmth to life. Some atavistic wisdom (common to wolves, dogs, bison and men) warned him to conceal his wounds—indeed, his vulnerable body—lest he be torn apart by the pack. Therefore he stayed in his room. He would stay there until his capital was spent. Concerning the future he had no plans; the present was unproductive; but the past—ah, the past!

Chance Woodhull's past, immediate and remote, was like a phonograph record that kept on playing, sometimes loud, sometimes soft, but compulsively repetitive. The record had found an ideal audience—a man who simply lay with his hands behind his head and listened.

Anson spoke to him:

You may not understand now why I ask this of you, but everything will come clear after the job is done. In the work is the solution.

Mr. Julius Hochheimer was purring:

As president of Allied Pharmaceuticals, I offer you our check in the amount of $220,000. We are prepared to assume the payment of excise taxes, when due.

Rena Sandys was playing Chopin's Nocturne in F-Sharp Major:

In mercy, Chance, bid me stop playing. Come to me quickly. . . . This is the ticket I wear, "the wife of a felon." Give your grief its right name . . . call it "love." Be patient with me, oh, best and dearest of men. My husband is about to be released from the penitentiary. He is ill; it is my duty to go to him. Remember our three years together. . . . I shall never love anyone. . . . Goodbye. I wish . . . I wish . . . I wish . . .

The record had a way of running these words into distortions of Rena's voice while Chance buried his head in the pillow

Then a very small voice, a Robin Goodfellow voice, came in whispering:

Daddy, see the wart on Mrs. Masterson's nose. I'm not a raincoat today; I'm an umbrella. I didn't mean to, Daddy. Honest I didn't. I tried to be like you. Too soon, I guess. Take me with you, Father. It'll be so lonely here.

Every vowel has its own color. Was it Rimbaud who said that? No matter. Every word on the record evoked color, odor and a complete syntax of association. Pond musk, strongest of aphrodisiacs, and a red canoe gliding into an island of water lilies.

> *Not yet, Chance.*
> *When, Amy?*
> *AIM-EE! AIM-EE! AIM-EE!*

Echoes of an anguish lost in a universe of uncaring snowflakes.

> *Looka here, Woodhull—you don't seem to be hittin' nuthin' but the ground. . . . I'm gonna make you a fair 'n' square proposition. I'll drop my hands like this. Stick out my jaw and let you whang at it until you're tired.*

Voices scarcely recognizable came in from all points of the compass—wheedling voices, threatening voices, the voice of Andy Beane, of Oliver Treadgood—wheeling round and round in an endless *recititavo da Capo al Fine in cyclo cyclorum.*

Chance forgot to wind the gold Elgin he had inherited from Anson, and because his connection with the outer world of time and reality ceased to exist, he didn't bother to rewind it. Letters piled up on his bureau; letters from Zarah, Solange, Quin—yes, one from Rena Sandys. There was a telephone on the table beside his bed. Simply by lifting the receiver from its hook, he might have called up Jimmy Stothart or Charlie Coddington, whom he had glimpsed at the bar downstairs. *But what could he say to them?*

He lifted the phone only to say, "Room Service, please." And when a voice answered, "This is Room Service," Chance said, "Coffee, a cold roast beef sandwich, cigarettes."

Could life be content with these? *At thirty-two?*

Confronted by borderline cases, *le petit mort* sometimes summons in his Big Brother. Around Thanksgiving, 1919, Chance heard the Big Brother knock at his door, saw him glide into the room, sit in the sag-bottomed chair and hold out a familiar blue bottle containing bichloride of mercury tablets. (These tablets were the confection of choice in suicides attempted or successful in 1920.) Chance tentatively fingered the bottle and handed it back.

"Oral guilt isn't my problem," he said to his phantom visitor. "Consider the interview closed. Go away."

Practically the only voice originating outside the room was the cheerfully warm baritone of Perley Gibbons, the night clerk.

The conversations had begun when Perley called up from the switchboard saying, "Mr. Woodhull, a couple of gentlemen—Mr. Stothart and Mr. Coddington—are asking for you in the bar. What shall I tell them if they question me directly?"

"You may tell them," said Chance, "that Mr. Woodhull has accepted an important post in the consular services. Say that he's gone to—well, make it far enough away; preferably in South Africa."

"Thank you, Mr. Woodhull. I shall decorate my discourse with inventions suitable."

"May I inquire what your name is?"

"Gibbons—Perley Gibbons."

"Thank you, Gib—I mean, Perley, for being so thoughtfully intelligent about all this."

Thereafter the conversations between Chance and Perley grew longer and more intimate. "Did you say Friday's your day off?" asked Chance. "What do you do that day?"

"I'm a Curb operator, specializing in penny stocks. Last Friday, for instance, I bought one hundred shares of U.S. Nutmeg-Grater at two—two cents, that is. I sold it at three and picked up a nice ten-dollar profit."

"Where is this Golconda of yours?"

"At the corner of Broad and Wall. The financial district, sir."

"Why is it called the Curb?" asked Chance.

"Because," said Perley, "the trading is done outdoors. Men stand in the street and signal their orders to clerks seated in office windows above. The sign language is quite complicated, and since the contracts entered into are considered binding, a chap had better know the rules. Would you like to visit the Curb with me some Friday—take a gentlemanly flyer perhaps?"

"Your invitation is most attractive, Perley. I'm not quite up to accepting it yet."

Because Chance offered no further explanation, Night

Clerk Gibbons didn't press the point. "Is there anything I can do for you, Mr. Woodhull?"

Perley's resourceful handling of Messrs. Stothart and Coddington prompted Chance to ask a leading question. "Have you a typewriter, Perley?"

"A three-bank Corona, pretty well beat up. Why do you ask?"

"It occurred to me that you might cut a path through the mountain of letters that's gathering on my bureau."

"I've never answered anyone else's mail, but if you'll trust me I'll be glad to try."

"Good man. Send up one of the door boys and I'll start you off on a trial batch."

Perley Gibbons turned out to be a wizard letter writer, full of invention and discreet periphrasis—in short, the art of saying little while using many words. But the words Perley used were so contagious in their felicity that they left the recipient in little doubt concerning the whereabouts, glowing fortunes and still more roseate prospects of Yours Sincerely, cordially, affectionately, most affectionately, etc., Chance Woodhull. Why, the man was a ventriloquist, or the letter-writing equivalent thereof. With Quin he was a veteran father, full of inquiries and information about split-bamboo fishing rods, high-laced leather boots and, come Christmas, a bicycle. In corresponding with Wayland Towner, M.D., Perley half disclosed the secret nature of confidential missions to the stricken Levantines. Malnutrition endemic throughout the Near East. Funny thing, though. Albanians kept their teeth to a ripe age despite their limited larders. Am staying at the Harvard Club. Wonderful to feel myself amid familiar settings again. Zarah was handled with less clinical detail, but oh such a flood of warm apology about letters hung up at international boundary lines. Surprised she hadn't received the pearls from Bagdad. Solange received, among other things, a snapshot of Chance parading along the Ringstrasse, Vienna (try and find me in the crowd, ha, ha!).

The carbon copies of Perley's letters had a tonic effect on Chance. He remembered the story of a man confined in some medieval dungeon who, by making friends with a bluebottle fly, had been able to outlive the terrors of solitude. So little encouragement does Life need! And here, in the carbons of Perley's letters, Chance found not a bluebottle fly but an emotional and intellectual equal—a man gifted with imagination and compassion, a man unafraid to use these gifts in the service of love. Could Jimmy Stothart, Charlie Coddington, Deck Hallowell, taken separately or together, match this non-Harvard night clerk, this penny-stock trader, this respectful (though never servile) tongue-in-cheek kisser of the Blarney Stone?

No, no, a thousand times no.

Perley Gibbons's letters, together with their flood of happy replies, marked the beginning of Chance's will to live. But to live in the outer world, a man must have money, or at least credit. Chance had little of either. Examining the stubs in his checkbook in mid-December, 1919, he saw that he had a balance of six hundred and some odd dollars in his checking account—barely enough to pay his bill at the Harvard Club. True, there were literally dozens of friends who would advance him sums ranging between fifty and five hundred dollars. Merely by setting pen to paper he could ask the House Committee for an extension of credit—and, under the Harvard code, his request would be granted.

In his still convalescent state, Chance Woodhull might have asked for such an extension. Fortunately, he was spared this ignominy by the intervention of fate in the person of T. Higginson Sears.

There exists a type of person who always ends up as chairman of the House Committee. This man may be fairly said to embody Fiduciary Trust. He believes that everything should always be in *vollkommenster Ordnung*, and this Prussian concept, refined by contact with American business methods, has produced some real stinkers.

Mr. T. Higginson Sears, III, coming into the Chair of the House Committee late in November 1919, poured several hundred hours of his time and the full authority of his office into the thankless, never-to-be-compensated task of exploring every nook and cranny of the Edwardian structure officially in his care. He held long *causeries* with Mrs. Delia Drumgoole, housekeeper, concerning the disappearance (during the past nine months) of some three hundred and eighty fluffy bath towels, all bearing the Harvard seal. Mr. Sears was amazed to discover that this was par for the course. He determined to alter the course; in a single month—December 1919—the towel loss was slashed by a thumping fourteen.

Meanwhile Sears had activated the Collection of Past Due

House Accounts. Net gain: $1,309.82. In the process of collecting this important sum, eleven members had been dropped from the rolls. Obviously, the *T* in the chairman's name stood for "Thorough."

Shortly after New Year's Day 1920, Chairman Sears began investigating the personal habits of resident members. Among the oddities uncovered during this intensive probe was the fact that a Mr. Chauncey Adams Woodhull ('08) had been monopolizing room 57A for nearly a year while other more worthy members were being turned away for lack of space. There was a principle involved—the Aesopian principle of the *Ant vs. the Grasshopper.*

Woodhull's case clearly deserved further examination. The chairman began his investigation by cross-questioning Perley Gibbons, a personable young man (not Harvard, of course), who appreciated the honor of being paid twenty-two dollars a week for the privilege of associating with his betters.

"What does he do up there?" asked the chairman.

"Mr. Sears, I honestly can't tell you. He's quiet, never drinks or quarrels with any of the members. I speak to him occasionally when he asks for a package of cigarettes. I like the sound of his voice."

"Gibbons, are you concealing anything that the House Committee should know about this man? I need scarcely remind you that your first loyalty is to the club."

"I quite understand, Mr. Sears. But there's really nothing I can add to what I've already said."

"Does he use the phone for long-distance calls?"

"Not to my knowledge, sir."

"His checks—are they on a New York bank?"

"No. He banks with the Landmark National of Indiana. His contribution to the Christmas Fund was quite substantial."

"What, in your estimation, Gibbons, is 'a quite substantial contribution'?"

"I should call one hundred dollars substantial," said Gibbons. "That was the amount of Mr. Woodhull's contribution."

The chairman of the House Committee had thought his own check of fifty dollars rather princely. Yet here was a recluse doubling him. Probably making ducks and drakes of his capital. T. Higginson Sears III decided to do the really fine Harvard thing. He would visit Woodhull, explore his mind and, if the situation warranted, give him—well, let's not begin with preconceptions.

Preliminary news of the Visitation reached Inmate Woodhull the previous evening. Over the house phone Perley announced that Inspector General Sears would begin *Mopping Up* the fifth floor tomorrow.

Accordingly Chance was not unprepared when, shortly after dinner on January 13, 1920, Mr. Sears laid a set of genteel knuckles against the panel of Woodhull's door. He heard a well-modulated voice ask, "Friend or enemy? Come in." Upon opening the door, the chairman saw a man fully clothed, engaged in the quite unpurposeful activity of gazing at the ceiling. The room was in order; the man's face was shaved.

"Make yourself comfortable," said Chance. "Fellow member, I suppose."

"I happen to be chairman of the House Committee. My name is T. Higginson Sears."

"Any relation to Ozymandias?"

"O.Z.—who?"

Chance flung out a declamatory arm. *"Gaze on my works, ye mighty, and despair,"* he intoned, then sank back onto his pillow.

Mr. Sears sniffed. Not to labor the point, Sears was a compulsive sniffer. His nasal membranes (sprayed daily with chloretone) were constantly on the alert for the orange-sweet odor of unoxidized alcohol that betrayed—ah, so well—the excessive use of spirituous liquors. Perhaps he sniffed with the unconscious hope of detecting the after-fumes of cannabis or opium. If nothing more damaging could be sniffed at, Sears would settle for a whiff of Scandale, the perfume sometimes used in semi-private cases of transvestism (not confined to Harvard men, you understand), or, worse yet, the smuggling of women-in-men's clothing—onto the upper floors of the club. Sear's truest instinct, however, lay in his diagnostic power of smelling insolvency in its earliest stage—often thirty to sixty days in advance.

"Open the window," suggested Chance. "My eight-by-ten snuggery sometimes gets a bit stuffy."

Sears started to raise the lower half of the window.

"Not from the bottom, man," cried Chance. "I might jump out. Can't you see the headlines? *Incident at Harvard Club.*"

Sears slammed the window shut. Obviously an incipient case of financial stringency complicated by overtones of guilt. To guarantee collection of the man's House Account, Sears must proceed with caution.

"How do you feel, Mr. Woodhull?"

"I feel quiet," Chance said. "That is, I *felt* quiet until you came in here sniffing like a beagle."

"I do not sniff to amuse myself," said Sears. "But don't you think it rather strange for a man to lie looking at the ceiling for a whole year?"

"Frankly, no. I think that if everyone took a year off and did nothing but look at a ceiling, he might discover some pattern in the skein of circumstances that brought him to wherever he is—and eventually make some wise decision regarding his future."

"Are you prepared to make such a decision?"

Chance sat up on the side of his bed. "I'm getting ready to, Mr. Sears. For a year I've been gathering the necessary strength to break every thread of the old school tie that strangles when pulled too tight by weemsters."

"Weemsters? The force of your locution escapes me."

"Dessay. My son Quin, at the age of six, coined the word to describe persons with Parson Weems's preference for the maraschino of fancy as against the crab apple of truth. I find in 'weemster' overtones of weasel-worded Polonius; of Poor Richard, particularly when he speaks of thrift; of Ralph Waldo Emerson and a person unknown to fame—one Wilmer Stires. These people, sir, pry, spy, pontificate and pass judgment. They stick in their thumb, pull out a plum—why, they out-Horner Jack himself in crying, 'See what a good boy am I!' Proverbial wisdom befogs their gold-rimmed spectacles. They deal in wholesale cant—and the odd thing is, they find an audience of believers. Oliver C. Treadgood ranks high among the weemsters of our age. You, T. Higginson Sears, tracer of soiled linen, rate low, low."

At the mention of befogged spectacles, the chairman began polishing his own presbyopic lenses with a piece of tissue paper.

"You seem agitated, Mr. Woodhull."

"You're goddam right I'm agitated. Why shouldn't I be? Here I am, minding my own business, when Mr. Turnkey Sears knocks at my door and begins to sniff."

Chance was up now, the better to pin back the ears of his visitor. "Had you entered my room with Samaritan intent, hoping to bind up the wounds of one who didn't presume to whimper, get drunk, weep on club members' shoulders; were there a single drop of oil in your joints, which I predict will be calcined to chalk shortly now, I might have launched, managed, and financed—in part—your campaign for Overseer, Trustee or whatever the hell you're bucking for."

"Your sponsorship, Woodhull," said Sears dryly, "would blast, blight and utterly negate my nineteen years of dedicated service to our great university."

"Behold *Veritas* lying at the bottom of a teaspoon!" said Chance. He began tossing shirts, neckties and toilet articles into his suitcase. "Will you, before bringing my case to the attention of your distinguished committee, tell me the nature, date and enormity of my intramural crimes? Have I fallen down—stoned in the men's lavatory? Exposed myself indecently to fellow members? Have I failed to pay my bills when presented? Have I complained about the twenty-five-watt bulb allotted me for reading purposes? Hurled beer bottles, house crockery or myself into the areaway? No, Sears, I haven't broken a single rule. My only crime was to lie here like a mud scow full of dead fish, patiently waiting, waiting for the life tide to come again and float me off the bottom. Well, my fat, fecund friend, the tide has come in. I'm off, up and out through the portals of a club that has been cruel only to be kind."

"Before you go," said the chairman, "there is a little matter of your House Account." He presented a brown envelope fat with chits. "Shall we go over the items together?"

"Are you *serious*, Higgy? As one gentleman to another, I was prepared to take your word for the total." Chance became unexpectedly co-operative. "I see now that it will be most instructive to scrutinize—under the eyes of an expert scrutineer—exactly where my money has gone. Draw up a chair, Chairman. Make with that oversized Waterman of yours. Comfortable? Sufficient light?"

"I think I can manage." Sear's scrutiny disclosed some rather pertinent facts: First, that C. A. Woodhull had signed a Christmas Contribution slip in the amount of one hundred dollars. *Ha!* Second, his semiannual dues (payable in advance) hadn't been paid. *Ha!* again. The chairman began to feel solid ground beneath his feet. Technically, C. A. Woodhull was a delinquent. As such, he could be dropped from the rolls. And T. Higginson Sears was quite ready to drop him.

"Your total indebtedness, already overdue, is $588.91," announced the chairman. "Unless you discharge this obligation"

—Sears stretched the quality of mercy—"*within twenty-four hours,* all club privileges will be denied you."

That hurt! To be booted out of one's own club just as you were getting ready to leave. Insufferable! And the insufferable Sears had planned it that way.

How retaliate in kind? Chance saw his opening. While writing the check that would cover his indebtedness to the club, he asked, "Is you father a Harvard man, Mr. Sears?"

"Yes. He will attend his fiftieth Class Reunion next June."

"Your mother enjoys good health, I trust?"

"Considering her years, she is quite active."

"That being the case, I shall add two dollars to the check I am now writing."

The chairman stepped right into it. "Why should you add two dollars?"

"Because that's the price of a marriage license in this state. Higgy, I want you to buy such a license for your parents."

The awfulness of the insult caused T. Higginson Sears to draw back in sheer fright. His gold-rimmed eyeglasses fell to the floor and lay there momentarily unretrieved.

"Oh, no," he moaned piteously, sinking back into a chair.

A tide of regret mounted in Chance. He picked up the chairman's glasses in token of his contrition.

"I'm truly sorry, Mr. Sears. I shouldn't have said a thing like that. Forgive me. I was overwrought."

God, thought Chance, how overwrought can a man get?

At the door, turning, he gazed pityingly at the man who had rolled away the stone that had sealed up Tomb 57A for a whole year.

"Goodbye, Mr. Sears," he said. "In case anyone should ask you, C. A. Woodhull doesn't live here any more. I must to the world again."

T. Higginson Sears made no reply. He couldn't. Because, you see, the thankless nature of his task and the insults borne in performing it had caused the chairman to faint.

Suitcase in hand, Chance surrendered the key to his room, stepped out into an evening of mild winter weather, felt like Hans freed of his grindstone. Although his future lay shrouded in doubt, he had at least regained the power of mobility.

A wonderful thing, mobility—if you know where you're going, if you've money to take you there, if arms are flung open with delight at your arrival. And all the other things—hot water, soap, towels, appetizing food, and a bed to sleep in when the time for sleeping comes—these are the normal expectations and rewards that mobility holds out to man.

None of these beckoned to Chance Woodhull now. For the first time in his life he had no bed of his own. Shelter! He must find it. Where? To the east, the city lay shrouded in darkness. But westward look, Broadway was bright! Bright with marquees bearing famous names—Healy, Claridge, Churchill (among others)—soon to be dimmed by the blight of Prohibition.

Crossing Broadway, he continued westward until he saw a signboard: HOTEL METROPOLE, ROOMS BY THE DAY OR WEEK. Chance entered. It had no foyer, elevator or bellboy. Behind a tiny desk in the corridor sat a pre-senile exhibit of the decay that would soon blight the ancient, no longer honorable race of vaudevillians. The night clerk at the Hotel Metropole had long ago exchanged the "boater" of the song-and-dance man for a standard green celluloid eye shade and steady work. He was so busy reliving his scrapbook past ("You should of caught me in Schenectady") that he barely glanced at the man who said, "I'd like the cheapest room you've got."

"One-twenty-five a night. Eight dollars a week. In advance."

So Push had come to Shove. From his wallet, Chance took his last twenty-dollar bill. "I'll try a three-day dose," he said.

"Playing a split week at the Palace—?"

"Split week? *Where?*" In his own voice, Chance heard echoes of Mr. Sears's puzzlement: *"O.Z. Who?"*

So late to learn; in wisdom still so young!

Chance's third-floor rear room was a composite of all single-occupancy chambers in a world of seventh-rate hotels. It smelled like a fish barrel that had been sluiced out with carbolic acid. An iron bedstead, once white, now swarmed with leprous scabs. A rickety washstand and a cracked basin stood beneath a mirror that had long ago lost its original silvering in the process of throwing back the reflections of too many anonymous transients. The only outstanding feature of the room was a religious calendar for the year 1917 bearing the gilt legend:

> *What is man that Thou art mindful of him*
> *or the son of man that Thou visitest him?*

Tough questions. Fortunately, Chance found no immediate need of answering them. Life lay all around him in vast chunks, waiting to be reappraised, seen anew, felt at closer quarters, experienced *ab initio*, listened to, and heard. With reviving curiosity, Chance wandered up, down and across Manhattan. Everything demanded attention—"Look at Me, See How Wonderful I Am." The cry was taken up by the el roaring overhead and splintered into fragments of ecstasy shining from unclaimed binoculars and signet rings in pawnshop windows. Chance saw men repairing docks on the waterfronts and marveled at those ingenious little chuffing bastards, the tugboats, snubbing ocean liners into their berths. Everything he saw, heard or touched became a partial answer to the cracked gilt questions on the religious calendar.

What puzzled Chance most was the *un*mindful attitude of those who stood to lose everything by the coming of prohibition. Café owners, bartenders, cabaret proprietors, headwaiters either knew something unknown to anyone else, or didn't know what everyone else knew—that the sale and possession of alcoholic liquors would become illegal as of midnight on Friday, January 16. The consensus took the form of a knowing headshake and a blithely contemptuous "Prohibition hit Broadway? That'll be the day!"

Only two things really bothered Chance. The first was a dwindling supply of cash; next, the seemingly endless unbroken shoals of bedbugs that infested the mattress, woodwork and straw matting of his room. These cunning little nippers were apparently part of the built-in equipment of being poor. The desk clerk assured Chance "You'll get used to them, mister. The exterminator's coming next week."

Neither the non-arrival of the exterminator nor the lack of ready money drove Chance, suitcase in hand, out of the Hotel Metropole, at 10:00 P.M. Friday, January 16, 1920. He became immediately aware of a febrile excitement, a noisy recklessness in the speech and manner of the people moving around him. Everyone was carrying a bottle of liquor; a stranger grasping a quart of whiskey hailed him. "Have a drink, Mac. Last time around."

"No, thanks."

Other men, in various stages of intoxication, were wambling from midstreet to sidewalk, waving whiskey bottles, breaking them against lampposts, or cracking them together over their heads as if to immerse themselves in some strange baptismal rite.

A mill-race tide of assorted human beings churning southward along Broadway caught Chance in its current. Plate-glass windows, unless braced by wooden cross-pieces or steel extension gates, were broken either by pressure of the tide or deliberately, by out-and-out looters. From every side-street, fresh eddies of ungartered citizens drove wedges into the main current, causing whirlpools that threatened to engulf even the mounted police who were discovering that the old formula "one horse can break up 2,000 men" had suddenly become obsolete.

At Forty-third Street, Chance witnessed a superb exhibition of horsemanship; a mounted cop brought his animal into the full rampant position. Chance knew that the rider was taking a calculated risk by exposing the vulnerable belly of his trained mount. One bullet, or a stiletto in the hand of a true revolutionist, would have brought the animal down. There were cries of "Cossack," "Cossack." As for the Cossack himself, a well-aimed bottle would have fractured his skull, but the revolutionary temper was lacking here. Standing in a doorway, Chance realized that the seeming riot was nothing more than a maudlin, unorganized, fruitless, bootless twelfth-hour protest of a few thousand people—a display of futility against a strategy, long planned, carefully timed and executed with masterly precision by that Generalissimo of the Dry Forces, Oliver C. Treadgood.

"Got a match, Mac?"

A one-armed man, no-faced, was asking Chance for the common charity of a light.

Making the automatic response, Chance dropped his suitcase, unbuttoned his Brooks Brothers jacket, produced an Ohio Blue Tip match and performed the full duty of a gentleman via the thumbnail method.

"Thanks, mister."

"Not at all." Chance felt himself being jostled.

"My wallet," he cried.

Too late. Gone. Lifted by professionals.

Where, on this *Walpurgisnacht* of screaming horror, should he report the loss? To the mounted policeman caracoling in a fresh attempt to keep the cross-walk clear? To Oliver Treadgood? To the bench of Dry witches engaged in stirring up a caldron of toil and trouble for the American people?

What did it matter? They had stolen more than a flat wallet. They had stolen the provenance of Chance Woodhull's subsistence. They had stolen the Water of Life and were spilling it in the gutter.

At Forty-second Street and Broadway, drunken recruits to an army without leaders milled in a counterclockwise circle of many rings. Chance extricated himself from the senseless reel and took refuge in the bar of the Knickerbocker Hotel. It was 11:45. The silvered steam tables, famous for *Hasenpfeffer,* goulash, salads and cold cuts (courtesy of the management with every glass of beer), had been gutted. The brass fittings of the long bar, once the standard of urbane elegance, were being ripped from their moorings by souvenir hunters. Men dragged away cuspidors that they might show their children and grandchildren these relics of an era forever passed. A full complement of bartenders was removing bottles from behind the bar, thrusting them into the hands of free-loaders who would not pay then or thereafter.

By the clock 11:50. In another ten minutes, the sale or possession of spirituous liquor would become a criminal offense. Fantastic. Not until he saw a bartender preparing to distribute a case of Old Landmark was Chance able to throw off the sense of unreality. He shouldered his way toward the bartender, waving his last dollar bill.

"Give me one of those."

"Sure thing, Jack. Not allowed to take money, though. The Knickerbocker isn't a package-goods store. It'll go down like the thing it was—a gentleman's bar."

With the glass talisman in his hand Chance drifted south and west looking for Branch No. 6 of the Green Light Hotel on Charles Street. Perley Gibbons had told him that his uncle was night manager there. "Just mention my name," Perley had said, "and Uncle Frank will put you up for the night."

Chance was eager to meet Uncle Frank. Doubtless, Uncle Frank would be happy to meet him too.

Now he was entering a region of Manhattan unfamiliar to him: a region of silent, deserted streets and long avenues lighted only by an occasional flickering lamp. Here the *Walpurgisnacht* had worn itself out. In unlighted rooms men and women were sleeping together, whether in joyousness or stale habitude, what difference did it make? At least they had a roof over their heads, a door to close, a mattress under them.

For every boy that's lonely
There's a girl who is lonely too,
For every heart that's aching,
There's a heart that's breaking too. . . .

Chance shook off the poignant sentimentality of the song and continued, his feet still treading the verge of nonexistence, southward and westward into a part of the city that had been swallowed up by warehouses.

He was beginning to be hungry. At 2:00 A.M. he saw the lights of a coffee pot, its white tiles beckoning. He crossed the street. Three men, two wearing leather caps and the other a green Fedora, were seated on stools at the lunch counter. Here were human beings, awake, apparently sober. With anticipation of gregarious pleasure ahead, Chance pushed open the door. He hung his tweed topcoat on a hook, removed his bowler, sat down on one of the stools and inspected the fly-blown menu over the gas range. The loose change in his pocket wouldn't take him far, even here. As for breaking the dollar bill, that would be dipping into capital. Mustn't dip.

"What'll it be, Mac?" Joe Doyle, the counterman, had never been very bright. He was an ex-con trying to go straight. His feet were tired and he needed a drink—oh, but bad. He couldn't have cared less about the gourmandizing about to take place.

"Think I'll have some corned-beef hash with a poached egg. Coffee, no milk. And a cruller."

"O'ny jelly doughnuts left, Mister."

"Make it a jelly doughnut, then."

The coffee was oily, rank, the drippings of yesterday's kettle. Chance was about to take a sip from the crockery mug when the counterman pointed to a sign—*Please Pay When Served.*

"Forty-five cents," said Joe Doyle.

"Thirty-five is all I've got." Chance was apologetic. "Take back the jelly doughnut."

"That'll still leave me a nickel short," Joe Doyle remonstrated feebly. "Say, Mister, am I gon'ta have trouble with you?"

The man wearing the green Fedora slid off his stool and approached Chance. "Never mind, Joe. I'll take care of this. Go ahead, Mister—eat up."

The man's teeth were excellent; his ungloved hand clean,

well manicured. His patent-leather shoes and the fur-collared coat of the impresario were all *en règle*. Definitely a type. Not Cambridge. Still, he had been kind.

"Thank you," said Chance.

The man's dark eyes were fascinated by the golden pig hanging from Chance's watch chain. Curiosity and contempt caused him to flip the Porcellian emblem.

"What kind of an outfit takes a pig for its trade-mark?"

"Small, very select." Chance flipped the snap brim of the man's Fedora. "What invisible hand and eye condemns you to wear that velveteen enormity?"

"Velveteen! This hat's a genuine Borsalino. Retails at forty dollars."

"Don't tell me that people deal in these things *wholesale*." Chance ingested two forkfuls of corned-beef hash. "Well, *non est disputandum*."

"I'm not looking for no disputes. Fosco Littorio—that's me; don't bother to shake hands. Fosco just listens, maybe learns something he didn't know. Being only a dago, there's a lot of things I don't understand about you pure-bred Anglo-Saxons."

"For instance?" Chance took a long tug at his coffee mug.

"For instance: you taking off your stiff hat before sitting down to eat in a joint like this. Everyone else wears a hat—me, Tomaso, Giuseppe wear hats. You take yours off. Why?"

"Well, you see," said Chance, "at Harvard they taught us that Christ is the unseen guest at every table. Now you wouldn't want to sit down with your hat on in Il Cristo's presence, would you?"

The novelty of the idea served as a temporary stopper. Chance packed away three or four solid mouthfuls before Fosco came off the ropes. "Seems you've got pretty close connections with our boy. Maybe that's a quart of sacramental whiskey in your overcoat pocket?"

"In a very real sense, it is."

"Mind if I look at it?" Fosco moved toward Chance's overcoat.

"I don't like the idea of being searched." Chance got off the stool, took the bottle of Old Landmark from his pocket and offered it in testimony of the truth.

The three men gazed at the bottle. They scrutinized it from cork to bottom before Fosco pronounced judgment.

"Say, this is a real high-class job. Nice label, revenue strips

—they'd fool anyone. Too bad. Don Falcone won't like the idea of the Golden Pig mob working our territory. How you feel about this, Tomaso?"

Tomaso made Pilatelike motions of washing hands. "God helpa Porcarinos."

"You think that way, Giuseppe?"

"I think pig should tell his boss to get lost."

"I haven't any boss," said Chance. "This happens to be a bottle of genuine Old Landmark whiskey."

"How you know?" asked Fosco.

"I made it. Read the fine print. I'm C. Woodhull."

Fosco read the fine print. "What happened to A.?"

"Died."

Littorio lifted his Borsalino in token of sympathy. "Some things I *do* understand. They get into the voice. It fails a little."

"Maybe so. Now, if you'll stop acting like a professional mummer, I'll dig deep into the Woodhull sock and cut myself a piece of raisin pie." Chance spread his last dollar bill on the counter.

"One piece raisin, please."

Fosco relayed the order to Joe Doyle and flipped a quarter to the counterman.

"Sorry, Fosco. I'll pay for my own piece of pie."

Tomaso and Giuseppe waited for their boss to take charge of the situation. Fosco didn't disappoint them.

"How you like making whiskey for nice little organization? Pick up hundred and fifty a week, easy?"

"Sorry, can't."

Fosco boosted the ante. "We give you two hundred and fifty a week. All you do is supervise, see. Nights, you take free chop at the girls."

"Sounds repulsive," said Chance.

"You call two-fifty a week, different girl every night—you call that repulsive?"

"No, no, don't misunderstand me. I've nothing against money or girls. Noble institutions. But you see, Fosco, I've made good whiskey all my life, and it's too late for me to make bad whiskey now." Chance finished his pie, waved aside a house toothpick offered by Littorio. "See you around."

Tomaso and Giuseppe blocked the doorway.

"Where you going?" asked Fosco.

"To the nearest branch of the Green Light Hotel. The

whimsey is on me. I want to turn myself in as the first violator of the Eighteenth Amendment."

Another kind of whimsey—constructive, entailing no dispute—in fact, winning a place quite near the central station of power—was on Fosco Littorio. He conveyed to Tomaso and Giuseppe the necessary minimum of his plan. "So we let him sleep in deep-freeze a couple hours. Give him time to digest rich food."

Something about the quaintness of Fosco's idea appealed to the henchman humor of Tomaso and Giuseppe. They laughed.

"Quite a walk to Precinct Six branch on Charles Street," said Fosco. "We'll drive you down. Tomaso drives all kinds car." Littorio opened the rear door for his guest of the evening. "After you."

Five minutes later the car pulled up in front of a green lamp shade. "There it is," said Fosco. "Precinct Six—Green Light Hotel. *Buona notte* . . . happy dreams."

"You, too," said Chance. A light snow was falling. "And thanks for the sleigh ride."

Desk Sergeant F. X. Tuohey stared in amazement at the personable citizen who apparently had something on his conscience; or, rather, in his hand.

"I've broken the Eighteenth Amendment," said Chance.

"Amendment to what, now?"

"The Constitution."

Twenty-five years of booking pickpockets, street-walkers, and such like had failed to widen or deepen Tuohey's knowledge of the Constitution. "State the means and manner of your breaking into same."

"I didn't break *into* anything, Sergeant," explained Chance. "But as of midnight, it became a felony to buy, sell or transport alcoholic beverages. Now, if you'll look at the label on this bottle, its alcoholic nature is clearly stated as one hundred and ten proof. *Res ipsa loquitur*. The thing speaks for itself. Having transported this quart of whiskey all the way from the Knickerbocker Hotel, I now have the honor of presenting myself as possibly the first person in the United States to break the Eighteenth Amendment."

" 'Tis a mutationable point at law," said the sergeant. "The question before me is 'Does the aforesaid Amendment apply to Precinct Six?"

"Precinct Six is part of the United States, is it not?"

"With the advice and consent of Tammany Hall, it is."

"Then I demand to be locked up until reasonable bail is posted, or my case brought before a Grand Jury."

"Before taking such steps, I must consult my superior officer, who at this time is in the arms of Morpherus with orders not to be disturbed."

Chance switched his argument. "Your nephew, Perley Gibbons, told me to look you up. The lack of hospitality hereabouts is disappointing."

"Perley! Why didn't you tell me Perley sent you? Ah, that Perley! Commixing with the nobility and gentry in the Harvard Club uptown, wherever it is. Sure, Mr. Woodhull, we'll put you in the *de loox* quarters reserved for visiting inspectors. For blotter purposes now, what's the charge?"

"Breaking the Eighteenth Amendment!"

"That bail you mentioned? Does a nominal amount seem reasonable?"

"Quite. Now, Sergeant, I'm very tired. If you'll be so kind."

"It will be necessary to confiscate the evidence."

"Correct. Confiscation rules the nation. *Pax vobiscum*, Sergeant."

"*Et cum spiritu* Tuohey." Old altar boy speaking.

Without removing his clothes, Chance Woodhull stretched himself on the iron cot reserved for visiting inspectors. He heard the key turn in the lock. The little hours began to climb out of night's coal sack. Tomorrow would be a new day—another day. A better day for a fresh attack upon life. He fell asleep and soon was dreaming a new kind of dream—a happy dream, unconnected with the past.

A dream about tomorrow.

The time was forenoon. Chance seemed to be standing on the sidewalk of the Curb Market, signaling to Perley Gibbons seated in a window overhead. "Buy one hundred shares Universal Hairpin at three (three cents, of course)."

Perley signaled back. "Order executed. . . . There will be a short wait."

Perley reappeared at window. "Universal Hairpin up a point. Advise sell."

"Wait till it reaches five," said Chance.

When Universal Hairpin hit five, Chance sold.

"Smart going," signaled Perley. Chance was preparing to collect his twenty dollars' profit when he felt himself being shaken by the official hand of Sergeant Tuohey.

"Some friends of yours are out here with bail money," said F. X. himself.

"Friends? Bail money?" Even in a world of going-to-sleepness such things hadn't existed. Chance began to understand when, through the coarse-meshed wires of the detention pen, he saw Fosco Littorio, a wad of goldbacks in his hand. Behind him stood Giuseppe and Tomaso, footmen of the line.

Littorio began to explain procedural matters to Tuohey. "Ordinarily, Sergeant, this man would be released on a bail-commissioner's signature. This time the bail commissioner's name is Cash." He thrust the roll of goldbacks at Tuohey. "Don't bother to count. No receipt necessary."

Tuohey was bringing his best legal brains to bear on the subject when Chance raised a point of personal privilege. "I'd rather not go with these men, Sergeant."

"But they've just bailed you out. 'Tis the equilavent of a writ of *hav' ye his corpus.*"

"I don't want them to have my corpus," said Chance.

Littorio displayed the edges of his fine teeth. He was not smiling. "Judge," he said, lifting the problem to a higher sphere, "got to see you private. Like in chambers."

"Request granted." Tuohey, a latter-day Daniel, arose. "This way, Counselor."

In chambers (a euphemism for the men's room) Littorio laid his case on the line. "Don Massimo order me on telephone, 'Bring this man to Clubhouse *immediatemente* or elsa.'" Fosco drew the edge of a not-so-imaginary razor across his throat. "You know what Massimo means when he say 'Or elsa'?"

As one subaltern to another Tuohey nodded sympathetically. "The monstrous crooelty of your departmental chief is well known to our organization. Ever sincet I started making me rounds, we've been coming to grips with Falcone about one little thing or another. Rest aisy, young man. In this instance the full weight of the judiciousary in on the side of youth." He extended a meaty paw. "In behalf of the Pension Committee for Retiring Desk Sergeants, I accept your additional contribution."

Returning to his desk, Tuohey rendered judgment: "Immedjacy being nineteen points of the law, the prisoner is hereby released, and his name ex-sponged from the blotter. Tricks we have in every trade," he added, holding up a bottle of ink remover. "As of this moment, all that remains is something that never happened."

Tuohey noted the official time of judgment: 4:29 A.M.

The previous night's suggestion of snow had carpeted West Twenty-second Street with seamless curb-to-curb covering. Chance was bundled into a black automobile by his bailors. "Handle him gently, boys," said Fosco. "Let's not be nasty to Harvard."

"Ex-Harvard," corrected Chance.

"*A La Pompa!*" Fosco commanded the driver. To Chance he said, "I hope you don't mind being blindfolded for two or three minutes. My handkerchief is clean."

"I prefer my own. Use it as you wish."

Blindfolded, he heard Littorio whispering, "Act like a man with *coglioni* and it will go better."

A minute later Fosco was making cabalistic knocks at a door. It opened on a vast underground chamber lighted by unshaded light bulbs suspended on wires from the ceiling. The ceiling of the chamber was a waterfront edge of the complex tapestry that is Manhattan; overhead, Chance saw water and gas mains, electric conduits, rusted iron valve wheels. On the walls were clock-faced gauges of corroded brass, their hands frozen at zero; fuse boxes, transformers, switches oxidized to cuprous green. Ancient steam boilers, their black doors sagging on broken hinges, were connected to sewage pumps. Sometime, long ago, this array of machinery, dials, switches, pipes, pumps and boilers had been serviceable to the city. At present it was the temporary headquarters of the Unione Sicilione, blood descendants of the Carbonari. Soon one would begin to hear them described as Mafia or, more simply, the Combine. A standing committee of twenty members (there seemed to be only one chair) was grouped behind the seated figure of Don Massimo Falcone.

Littorio advanced respectfully. "*Per favore,* Don Falcone. This is the man."

Massimo Falcone was the historic link between an older padrone system that exploited immigrant boys and a newer race of baronial gangsters yet to be spawned by Prohibition. As a youth, Massimo had fled from his native Sicily. He too had served his apprenticeship under a cruel master, as a street urchin, a *ragazzo*—bootblack, newsboy and orange seller. On bad days he was whipped by his brutal master and locked supperless together with a dozen other youths in an unfurnished attic on Mott Street. At seventeen, Massimo revolted, formed his own organization, "The Green Ones," and had climbed the rungs leading to the top: procurer, professional killer, dope peddler, always pushing upward until at fifty-five he held the position of "Don"—local leader in the Unione Sicilione.

Possessed of the peculiarly Sicilian gift of *combinazione*—that is, arranging, compromising, lubricating the disciplinary gears within his own organization (buying police protection the while) Don Massimo ran a really taut ship in lower Manhattan. The password was *Omertà*—translatable as loyalty, silence and "Donta squawk." With Don it was *Omertà*-up, *Omertà*-down. Canfields and Corbetts had come and gone; Falcone intended to stay.

His operations, wholesale, were carried on through a closely checked cadre of intermediaries. He dealt largely in heroin, girls, money (six dollars for five—pay up on Saturday or lose your teeth) and other oddments of crime. Making an inventory of his assets on January 1, 1920, Massimo could point to the small but solid Banco Palermo; a travel agency (used chiefly as a gate for illegal entry into the United States); and seventeen parcels of real estate on which stood high-class, medium-class, and definitely low-class houses of prostitution.

By a not-unexpected fall of the cards, Don Massimo was prepared to take over the making and distribution of whiskey on the West Side of Manhattan. He had already purchased several tons of corn sugar; stored it in bins in an abandoned pumping house on the North River that was now serving as his temporary headquarters. Bottles, labels, counterfeit revenue strips and, more important than these, outlets for the sale of whiskey (or a reasonable facsimile thereof) had been assembled and arranged. The only missing cog in the Falcone machine was a practical whiskey-maker—someone who knew how to make the stuff. Well, Fosco Littorio, one of Don Massimo's principal lieutenants, had unexpectedly discovered the missing cog. Barely an hour before, Fosco had phoned Massimo to inform him of the discovery. Speed being of the essence, Massimo went into action; at 3:30 A.M. he issued a general order to the top members of his division—the *lupinari*, he liked to call them. The pack had been called and all responded. Now they stood behind their chief—serviceable jackals, obedient, docile triggermen disciplined to his command. They had left their warm beds shared with prime-chop pieces of female property portioned out to them by the giver of all bounty, Don Massimo Falcone. A hard Master, but he paid off.

Such was the man who now addressed Chance Woodhull. "You know how makea whiskey?"

Chance nodded.

To test his man, Massimo pulled a coil of copper tubing from beneath his desk. "How you calla this?"

"That's a 'worm,' " said Chance.

Massimo had heard enough. "Unsheet the corpse," he said.

Eager hands pulled aside a tarpaulin disclosing several pieces of what had been a legitimate still. Chance recognized each piece; dephlegmator, doubler, bubble box and the belly of the still itself—a three-hundred-gallon kettle copper-jacketed for distillation by steam.

The broken still was more than a symbol of the whiskey-making industry. As it lay in meaningless confusion on the floor, it reminded Chance very much of his own life. Well, no time for melancholy ponderings now.

Falcone was asking a question. "You know how put this thing together?"

"It's one of the things I do know."

"Begin. *Svelto*. We pay you two hundred dollars a week for nicea work."

"Sorry," said Chance. "I've made good whiskey all my life and don't propose to make bad whiskey now."

Falcone gazed at his lieutenants. "Whatta he say?"

Knowing what lay ahead, Littorio conveyed Chance's meaning to Don Massimo.

"So he thinka like that, eh? Soon we change his mind. Bring out Il Rassori."

In making Il Rassori, nature had dug deep into its repertory of outrageousness. As the fourteenth child of a tubercular mother, Rafaello Ammuchi had entered this world like everyone else, with a spine and shinbones of half-jellied gristle. In order to live at all he had been forced to carry a mountain of calcium on his spine. In short, Il Rassori was a hunchback. A bandy-legged hunchback. Acromegalic, too, which is to say that his facial bones had become enlarged by the outpouring of calcium and had molded his features into leonine heaviness.

This human gargoyle had deliberately chosen to emphasize his grotesque appearance by apparel loud in color and odd as to cut. He was wearing a banana-yellow suit with an extremely long skirt that reached down nearly to the cuff of his peg-topped trousers. His shoes had curved-in toes and built-up heels. Crab-wise, he sidled toward Chance and pulled a leather razor case from the pocket of his long coat. In performing the role assigned to him, Il Rassori enjoyed heightening the preliminaries by gestures and comments, droll, sadistic, perverted and self-abasingly comical.

Chance stood with both hands on his hips, feet together, left knee slightly bent; his posture, an extension of his inner state of mind, conveyed exactly what he felt. And what he felt was this: I despise these proceedings. But let's get on with the business.

Il Rassori opened the case to display its contents: three razors, heavy, heavier, heaviest.

"You like-a close shave, medium close—how you like? Tell Il Rassori."

"I like to shave myself."

"This is union shop." Il Rassori turned his grotesque head toward the silent men grouped around their leader. "Unione Sicilione."

Falcone tossed his man a small coin of laughter. The high-ceilinged chamber magnified the Don's *ha-ha-ha,* tossed it about from wall to wall, re-echoed it from behind every black boiler and dismantled pump.

"*Ha-Ha-Ha-Ha-Ha.*"

All hope abandon when cruel men laugh, thought Chance.

"You know the name of this razor?" asked Rassori. "She is my sweetheart, Violetta. She make everything smell-a sweet." He murmured some endearing syllables, then let Violetta's blade leap forth from its handle. "*Concava e bellissima. La Donna Cacare*—you understand Italian?"

"A little. You just called your Violetta a concave beauty, a lady of something-or-other I'd rather not mention."

"When the customer is intelligent, things go better." Il Rassori drew a ball of twine from his pocket, "*Primo,* we tie up pantsa cuff on right leg, so. Next, same with lefta leg. This save-a the carpet," he explained. (General laughter.)

The carpet-saving preparations completed, Rassori turned

jocose. *"Cognosci la storia dell'uomo che faceva il domatori di leoni?"*

"I know the story." Chance thought of Johnno Normile telling that sure-fire laugh-maker about the man who aspired to be a lion tamer.

"You like-a be lion tamer?"

"The thought never crossed my mind."

"Violetta, she no work on the mind. Go mucha lower." The hunchback shot out a long arm, demonstrated Violetta's approach by severing the knot of Chance's necktie. In rapid succession Violetta flicked the buttons off Chance's sack suit. Il Rassori walked behind Chance; he sniffed clinically. *"Non sento niente."* Like a man reproaching his sweetheart not for infidelity but for lack of technical skill, he spoke to Violetta.

"You no mak-a sweet smell tonight. I put you back in box and bring out Donna Duchessa."

The Duchessa, with a heavier, longer blade, demonstrated her virtuosity by cutting Chance Woodhull's leather belt just behind the buckle. His trousers fell down.

Il Rassori laid the cutting corner of his blade against Chance's navel. "Now you mak-a whiskey?"

"No," said Chance.

Littorio shook his head in puzzlement. "What kind of grudge you got against the word *yes?*"

"*Yes* isn't a word, Fosco. It's the sum of a man's affirmation and consent. I can't say *yes* until I *feel* yes. Let this pitiful creature cut the tripes out of me, and my answer to his proposal will still be *no.*"

"Talka-talka," said Il Rassori. *"Vado un po piu basso.* We go still lower."

With the Duchessa at his scrotum, Chance's autonomic nervous system gave way. His anal sphincter, the final guardian and guarantor of civilized relationship, lost its normal tension.

It was there all right! Plenty of it.

"Now you mak-a whiskey?" The crouching hunchback gazed up at his victim.

"I'd rather be a lion tamer."

"Then putta your hand in place like story says."

The invitation, repulsive under any circumstance, struck Chance just below the water line of training and taboo. The only weapon of retaliation that could undercut the bestiality of his tormentors was there all right.

Plenty of it. His autonomic nervous system had failed temporarily. Thank God his motor apparatus was still working.

Chance thrust his hand down inside his shorts, scooped up a handful of fear-made-manifest, and slapped it into the eyes of Rassori.

The stinging drench—malodorous, semi-solid—plastered the hunchback's face, filled the concavities of his eyes, the orifices of his nose and mouth.

The Duchessa clattered to the floor.

Chance stepped on it and slugged Il Rassori with a second handful. "You mangy bastard! Whoever called you a lion?"

Laughter, coarse and barbaric, climbed from Falcone's belly, gained volume in his barrelly chest. "A hunchback lion!" he roared. The pipes and conduits overhead took up the echoes, bounced them back at the group of dark-featured men. They came in on cue. When Don Falcone took snuff, they all sneezed in unison. When Don Falcone laughed, they laughed too.

Ha-Ha-Ha-Ha-Ha-Ha.

Things ceased to be funny when Chance picked up Donna Duchessa. Six snub-nosed .45s went on target awaiting Falcone's nod to kill. Fosco Littorio interposed his body between the black weapons and Chance Woodhull.

Littorio bowed deferentially to Falcone. "*Per piacere,* Don, I think I can do business with this man. The sympathy between us will be more effective than razors or bullets."

Massimo Falcone knew how and when to delegate authority. "Make the business, then. There is no time to lose. The market is waiting." Speaking in Italian, he said, "Pay him his price. But make him understand also the meaning of *Omertà.* I go now for sleep." He beckoned to his followers. "Come, *lupinari.*"

The wolves followed their leader. At a distance behind them, shunned and discredited, limped the pitiful, befouled figure of Il Rassori.

"What do they teach you fellows at Harvard?" Littorio asked admiringly as he hosed Chance down with water—cold as the water of purification must always be.

"Nothing transferable." Chance opened his suitcase, pulled out a Harvard Club bath towel and dried himself. "Since my best suit of clothing is ruined, I shall be doubly charming in my second best."

Fully dressed, invigorated by the cold water, Chance listened to Littorio's proposition.

"Show me how to put this still together," said Fosco. "Instruct me in its use, and this thousand-dollar bill is yours."

Chance shook his head. "I've already said 'no' to Don Falcone and his barber friend. Why should I change my mind now?"

"Because—I stood between you and the *lupinari*. Because I promised my leader to make the business with you." Fosco added a third argument. "Because if I no make the business with you, people will ask 'What became of that *giovanotto* name of Littorio? He seemed to be going someplace.' Then he has big funeral. All his brains, ambition, good looks—all the happiness he bring to women—all the joy women give him back ten times over—so many *fiaschi di vino*—so many Borsalino hats—millions of dollars and good judgment spending money here, there—all broken pieces like a penny clay pipe that fell on sidewalk. The broken pieces of Fosco Littorio never get put together again if Chance Woodhull shakes his head 'no.' "

Littorio widened the angle of appeal. "When Caesars sat in the Coliseum, they spared a brave gladiator's life by holding up one thumb. Now you hold up one thumb for me, Chance?"

"After the trick you played on me last night—letting my food get way down before you bailed me out?"

"It turned out to be a pretty good trick."

"No credit to you, Fosco."

"No? Why did I tell you to act like a man with *coglioni*?" His finger was at Chance's breastbone. "Because I saw you had what it takes to stay always out in front. Littorio loads the dice. Woodhull still wins." He made a thumbs-down gesture. "Fosco goes down drain."

"Let's not get sentimental, Fosco. You say that your whole future—your life—depends on my putting this still together for you—but you offer me only one thousand dollars. Ante up, nice Italian boy. Mention a few more figures."

"Five thousand?"

Chance held up fingers of both hands. "Ten."

Fosco's wonderful teeth gleamed. "Now I understand what the Golden Pig means." He started counting out goldbacks of high denominations. His smile faded at the eight-thousand, one-hundred-dollar mark—"All the cash I have."

"Your credit's good with me, Fosco. Mail the rest of the money to this address." Chance scribbled on a piece of paper

(Perley Gibbons, c/o Harvard University Club, 27 West 44th St.). "Let's get going now."

"How long will it take?" asked Fosco.

"With the help of a steamfitter and his tool kit, I can assemble your still in three hours."

"I'm a steamfitter—that is, I used to be."

Chance looked at his watch. "I've a breakfast date at ten. That gives us three hours. What do you plan to cook?"

"Straight corn sugar. We've got tons of it."

"Good. It cuts fermentation time down to a minimum. But you need big tanks to hold the 'wash,' as it's called."

Littorio pulled a tarpaulin off seventeen bathtubs. "The girls will have to take showers for awhile," he said, laughing.

"Keep sex hygiene out of this, Fosco. Tell your lumpers to pour corn sugar up to the halfway mark in three of these tubs. Send out for yeast cakes: about a hundred of them. Don't tell me the stores aren't open. You're a big Mafiosa; just open the stores."

Fosco opened the door and bawled an order to his personal retainer: "Tomaso! Get hundred yeast cakes. *Prestissimo!*"

Chance, Fosco and Giuseppe dumped the required amount of corn sugar into three of the enameled bathtubs.

"What we need next is warm water," said Chance.

"Metropolitan Steam Company at your service!" Fosco screwed a length of rubber hose onto a steampipe, turned the valve and directed a stream of warm water into the tubs half filled with corn sugar.

"Take notes as we go along," said Chance. "Half tub corn sugar, half tub water, scalding. Add twelve yeast cakes, after previously stirring them in warm water. That's fermentation— *à la mode.*"

Assembling the still was a simple task. Chance explained each step of the process, drew diagrams, and answered Fosco's questions.

"What does the worm do?" asked Littorio, picking up the coil of copper tubing.

"It condenses the gases rising from the still, transforms them into droplets of liquid—and would you believe it, Fosco, that liquid is ethyl alcohol, the very stuff you're looking for. Add ten per cent of genuine whiskey and you'll be in business."

With an hour to go, Chance directed his crew to transfer

the fermenting corn sugar into the copper-bottomed still. "Live steam, *presto!*" he shouted.

Live steam under high pressure entered the copper jacketing around the body of the still.

"In twenty minutes you'll be getting a nice flow of one-hundred-and-eighty-proof alcohol," said Chance. "I prefer not to be on hand when it happens."

"*Capisco.* Can I drop you someplace?"

"Herald Square. The understanding is that you're not to follow or bother me thereafter."

"*Omertà,* Chance."

"*Omertà,* and as a token of my regard, Fosco, please accept this gold pig."

In his three-room suite on the eighth floor of the Waldorf-Astoria, Mr. Chance Woodhull was enjoying a hearty but rather late breakfast. Working on a third cup of coffee, he scanned the headlines of the *World,* noting, among other things, that the Eighteenth Amendment had gone into effect as of midnight, January 16.

Today being January 17, it might be expected that Oliver C. Treadgood would be making some kind of statement about the THING HE HAD DONE. Sure enough, here was a first-page photograph of Oom Treadgood himself, shaking hands with Congressional leaders on the Capitol steps. Treadgood had summoned the working press before making his historic announcement:

John Barleycorn is dead [the statement began]. No right-thinking citizen in this great land of ours laments his passing. Crime will cease, employment soar. Jails and poor-houses will be empty. Sobriety enthroned in the heart of every loyal American has now found its place in our Constitution. Huge sums formerly spent on alcoholic beverages will pour into the manufacture and purchase of stout shoes, mortgage-free homes equipped with lightning rods, bathrooms, running water and glass bookcases.

My fellow citizens, I greet you at the threshold of a new moral and economic millennium. Farewell to the saloon! Hail Law Enforcement!"

"Hail weemsterism," said Chance to no one in particular.

Outside, a parade of returning soldiers was marching up Fifth Avenue. No one was watching them. The Armistice rocket that had lighted the sky with a golden hope fourteen months ago had already come down a dead stick. Marching, the soldiers sang (only God knows why):

> *Mademoiselle from Armentières, parlez-vous . . .*
> *Hinky-dinky parlez-vous*

The old hinky-dink, thought Chance.

Wherever one looked, wherever one listened, hinky-dink blared and hinky-dink glistened. The weemsters were busy at their work, whether as chairmen of House committees, counsel for the Anti-Saloon League, desk sergeants, publishers of the daily papers—all engaged in a conspiracy to conceal things as they were, or to misrepresent them as they were not.

Personally, Mr. Chance Woodhull didn't intend to be imposed upon hereafter by weemsters of any size or shape.

Odd, the calculus of improbability that had brought him to this richly furnished suite. To get here he had lain for more than a year gazing at a blank ceiling, deafening his ears to echoes of a dead past. He had outstared the gray wall of loneliness; he had passed through the City of Dreadful Night.

He had suffered a catharsis of terror. He had utilized the excrement of his own body to overcome his tormentors. He had emerged from the shadow of Death—yes, and all the little deaths of convention, hypocrisy, pudor, regret and submission. He had established his authority over Life. He would never again be afraid of anything or anyone. He had regained the power to love.

Love? Love whom?

I'm not a raincoat today, Daddy. I'm an umbrella.

Chance Woodhull picked up the telephone. "Give me Long Distance, please."

"This is Long Distance."

"Operator, I wish to speak to Quin Woodhull. The number is Landmark, Indiana, 197."

"There may be a delay, sir. Shall I call you back?"

"No," said Chance. "I'll hold on."

ABOUT THE AUTHOR

Born in Boston in 1898 and graduated from Columbia College in 1923 after wartime naval service, Henry Morton Robinson began his writing career as a poet and regarded himself as a practicing member of this high-license fellowship. A collection, entitled The Enchanted Grindstone and Other Poems, *was published by Simon and Schuster in 1952.*

But to the reading public of many lands, Mr. Robinson was best known as a novelist. The Perfect Round *(1946),* The Great Snow *(1947) and* The Cardinal *(1950) have been translated into many tongues, and the last of these headed the best-seller list for well over a year. New editions are still appearing in various countries, including the U.S.A.*

As a critic, Mr. Robinson was best known for A Skeleton Key to Finnegan's Wake, *which he wrote with Joseph Campbell in 1944.*

Wherever he lived, the most important piece of furniture was the writing desk, from which he was never long separated. Yet his life was far from sedentary. He prided himself on his woodsmanship, on his handling of small craft, and on the fact that, at sixty-two, he could still break eighty-nine out of a hundred clay pigeons.

Mr. Robinson died in New York on January 13th, 1961.

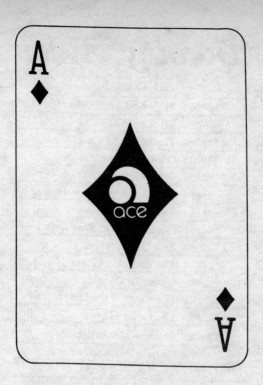

There are a lot more
where this one came from!

The Novels of

Dorothy Eden

$1.75 each

Available wherever paperbacks are sold or use this coupon.

ace books, (Dept. MM) Box 576, Times Square Station
New York, N.Y. 10036

Please send me titles checked above.

$. . . . . Add 35c handling fee per copy.

. . . .

. . . .

. . . . State. . . . . Zip. . . . .

5H